LAKE EFFECT

A 1986 GREAT LAKES STORY

McKees Sons docked at Lafarge Stone in
Marblehead, Ohio June 2011

DARLENE AND LOGAN POLLOCK

Trafford rev. 03/062014

 www.trafford.com

North America & international
toll-free: 1 888 232 4444 (USA & Canada)
fax: 812 355 4082

Dedicated to the men and women who work on
the Great Lakes-past, present, and future.

CONTENTS

S.S. GENTRY CREW ROSTER

William Kompsii-Captain/Master

Deck Officers:
*Dave(David) McCracken-First Mate
Andy(Andrew) Botzum-Third Officer

Wheelsmen:
Pete(Peter)Hall
Don MacDonough
Mike Ely-Wheelsman/Conveyorman

Deck Hand Gang:
Emerson Munson-Bosun
*Nick (Nicolette) Strickland/first person narrator-deckhand training for Wheelsman
Jim(James) Dixon-deckhand(injured)
Smitty(Jonathan Smith)-deckhand
Ron Karan-replacement deckhand
Hal(Harold Ostrander)-deckhand
Ed(Edward) Stephenson-deckhand
Al(Allen) Saunderson-deckhand

Engineers/Aft Section Gang:

Greg(Gregory) Brady-Chief Engineer
Hank Andersen-Second Engineer
Fred Westfall-Third Engineer
Brad(Bradley) O'Connel-Engine Wiper
Joe(Joseph) Jenkins-Oiler

Buster(Albert) Jones-Oiler
Kenny Fern-Machinist
Billy(Kid)Curtis-Apprentice

Unloading Boom/Conveyor Department:

DJ(Duane Jackson)-Gateman/Engine Wiper
Gary Tycon-Gateman/Oiler

Carl Bromley-Electrician's Mate
Mark(Marcus Cauley)-Radar/Radio Technician

Galley Department:

John Shaughnessy-Steward
Louie Franz-Second Cook
Earl Franklin-Porter: training as a deckhand

***The story characters are fictional and do not
represent anyone living, or dead.***

SECTION 1

THE DOWNBOUND RUN

JUMPING SHIP-AUGUST 1986

I t was a hot day in Detroit. It was humid as hell and you could sweat while standing still. The clouds that covered the sky earlier this morning, had moved off, leaving the city unprotected from the sun. I was sitting in a riverside cafe with my longtime friend and shipmate, Earl Franklin. We had just received word from the union hall that the steamship Gentry would be coming through, upbound, at around eight o'clock in the evening. I had spent the four previous shipping seasons on the Canadian MV Giovanni while Earl had been a veteran of many years on the Cliffs line. At the beginning of this season, we both had signed on to the grain carrier Mariner Enterprise for several months, then transferred to the grain carrier Spirit Independent. We both had had enough working for this shipping line and were about at our wits end. I got a tip from a secret admirer, who worked for a shipping line of Ore carriers, that there were openings on the Steamship Gentry. We were to board via the ladder, from the small mail boat, John Westcott. Thus, we were hanging around this cafe next to the Westcott dock on this miserably hot evening.

"Are you sure this ship is coming? They said that they hadn't heard from her," Earl said.

"Don't worry, old buddy, it's coming," I said.

"Nick, are you sure that you can trust this secret admirer of yours?" Earl asked.

"Don't worry guy. It sounds like most of the crew are old friends from the Cliffs line," I said.

"That's what you said back in April—don't worry," Earl said.

"How could I know that they were a bunch of sexist bastards that didn't want a woman on the boat," I said.

"I think half of them were queer anyways," Earl said.

"Shit for brains," I shot back.

3

"Such language from a nice young lady," he said.

"I'm a sailor first. If this deal goes belly-up, we'll go over to the Canadian side."

"You seem awful confident," Earl observed.

"I heard that this Captain Kompsii is a Finn from Fairport. You can always trust a Finn if they trust you," I said.

I looked out the window and saw the Westcott pull away from the dock and pass out of sight under the Ambassador Bridge. The Westcott is a floating mail truck that delivers to lakers and salties alike, as they travel on the river past Detroit. When the Westcott came back into view, it was heading upbound. It pulled in next to a freighter which dropped a red bucket to receive the mail.

"What boat is that?" Earl asked anxiously.

"I don't know, but it isn't the Gentry. It's a cabin aft freighter," I said.

"Let's go see what we can find out," Earl suggested.

"Okay, one hot cramped room is as good as another." I grabbed my seabag and my travel case as I stood up.

"Where's your toolbox?" Earl asked.

"I have it in storage in Duluth," I answered. Earl grabbed his carpet bag and a bundle of clothes. I left a tip and we headed toward the door. When we got outside, the air felt hot on my face. I was glad that it was a short walk to the little post office next to the dock. When we entered through the landward door, it took my eyes a minute to adjust to the dimly lit interior. I saw stacks of packages bearing the names of vessels they came from or were headed to. I looked at the blackboard on the wall, which had the name of boats that were due for deliveries. The fellow at the desk was talking on the radio, so I waited for him to finish. He set the radio receiver down and looked at me.

"We're supposed to catch the steamship Gentry from the Westcott," I informed him.

"Gentry? I haven't heard from her. When did they tell you?" he asked.

"Eight o'clock," I replied.

"You got awhile yet. Have a seat over there," he said. I nodded and turned toward Earl.

"Let's have a seat," I said.

We sat down on an old couch that looked like it should have been thrown out years ago. Through the window, I saw the Westcott dock and two men began to unload some boxes. Then they came in and grabbed some boxes that the guy behind the desk told them to take. Within ten minutes, they were back out in the river. I did not envy them their job on a day like today. After nearly an hour of listening to the radio and watching the Westcott, the guy behind the desk told us to go out and board the Westcott when it comes in. In a few minutes the Westcott does come in and tie up. Earl and I grab our stuff and head out the dockside door. The deckhand tells us to get onboard as he heads toward the post office, carrying a sack of mail. The Captain tells us to come inside the cabin until we are told to board the Gentry. As we pull away from the dock, I notice that the sun has nearly set. I looked to the portside and see that there is a large vessel heading north. The Westcott heads south, then abruptly turns and comes right up to the Gentry's starboard side ladder. A red bucket is lowered, then a rope was thrown down. The rope is tied to a large sack by the deckhand. After the sack was pulled up, we are told to go out on deck and get up the boarding ladder. I lead the way. I set my seabag on the ladder and put my travel case on my shoulder. Then I grabbed onto the ladder and stepped up onto the Westcotts bulwark and onto the ladder. I grabbed my seabag and headed up the ladder. After taking several steps, I turned and looked at Earl, who was doing what I just did. I continued up the ladder and throw my seabag over the railing and swing one leg over and push off, landing neatly on the deck. I looked up and saw a man about fifty years old looking at me.

"I'm Emerson Munson, the Bosun," he said, holding out his hand.

"I'm Nick Strickland," I said, shaking his hand. Earl landed on the deck, feet first and also shook hands with the Bosun.

"The Captain would like to see you in the wheelhouse, follow me," he said.

Three Months Later . . .

CHAPTER 1

Foul Weather Ahead

After five years, I had found it easier to sleep in my clothes instead of trying to find them in the dark. The ship, SS Gentry by name, was rolling somewhat. That was not unusual in the month of November. Pulling my parka from its hook on the wall, I opened the door to my quarters while putting it on. As I started walking down the passageway, I looked up and caught the icy stare of the first mate. He raised his left hand above his head, without looking and threw the switch. "AUGH-UGH". For the last three months, I resented the fact that the watchbell was right above my door. Needless to say, my groggy head did not need it. The first mate's icy stare changed into an ornery grin.

"Better zip up your coat. There's a breeze out there on the deck," he stated and he turned and headed for the wheelhouse. By this time the watch change was in full progress, even though the voices of crewmen and doors banging in hatchways could barely be heard over the ship's whistle and the sound of the ship in heavy weather. Walking a tilting passageway, I made my way down the steps and to the door on the after side of the forward deckhouse. Opening the door, I was greeted with a cold slap on the face by the wind and freezing spray from the lake. The wind was coming in gusts and when the ship rolled into a wave, water came up onto the spar deck. As a deckhand, it was my job to tie down the canvasses and to secure the rigging lines which had come loose during the storm. I immediately turned to the left and headed for the Crews hall, which was under the steps on the starboard side. Captain Kompsii likes everyone to be on watch within one minute of the bell. As I opened the door, the spray hit me again.

"Leave that stuff out side," Hal wisecracked. I entered and closed the door.

"So, they have me working with you now," Al said while handing me the clipboard.

"That's what the mate told me," I said, taking the clipboard.

"Why don't you tell these whining candy asses to make up their mind," Al said jokingly.

"Yes, certainly," I said softly as I looked at the clipboard. There was nothing new on there, so I signed it and handed it to Hal.

"We strung a safety line so you guys won't get washed overboard," Smitty said.

"I'll remember you in my will," Al wisecracked. The Bosun entered the Crews hall from the passageway door.

"Al, you report to the Chief. He's got some work for you, forward. Nick, I've got some things for you to do, aft," he said and he opened the door and stepped out onto the deck. I followed him out the door and we headed aft. The Bosun did not say anything as we headed aft. He is not the type of guy to say anything unless it is about the job at hand. He showed me some waste rags and other things that needed to go into drums. Then he told me to pull out the cable on the towing winch and oil it. Then fasten the canvas cover over the winch when I was done, then he left. The winch cable was really a two man job, especially in weather like this. I decided to tackle the waste drums first. I moved two empty drums to the fantail and began taking the tops off. The ship rolled and one of tops slid off the deck and into the lake. That's great, I thought, I'll have to go to the engine room and get another one. I put the drums inside the door and headed for the engine room. When I got there, the Bosun was talking to the Chief.

"I lost a lid overboard," I said when they looked at me.

"Oh, jeesh. We'll catch hell for that," the Bosun said.

"No problem, we have one over here," The Chief said. He walked over to a parts cabinet and pulled a drum top from behind the cabinet and handed it to me.

"I'll have to check with the Mate and see if we have to report this," the Bosun said, adding—"For god's sake, don't lose anything else overboard."

"Yes sir, I'll try not to," I said, and I turned and left. That's great, some f-king asshole is gonna' give me some shit about this, I was thinking as I went back to the fantail. I decided to leave the drums in the passageway while I filled them with the waste. I went to the engineers storage room and picked up some boxes with empty glass jars and bottles and set them on the two wheeled cart. I went out the door and ran into Pete and Joe in the passageway.

"Nice jugs," Joe wisecracked as they stepped aside. I gave them a dirty look as I passed them. 'The Village Idiots', I thought as I continued on my way. I finished filling the waste drums and put them in the firehose room. I pulled the cable forward, off of the after towing winch and left it in a big coil on the deck. Then went to the engine room to get a bucket of oil. When I came back, Al and the Bosun were there, looking at the cable.

"Al will help you with this. I want it done before the end of the watch," the Bosun said, then he left.

"Okay, this is a two man job anyway," I said as I set the bucket down and put on the heavy rubber gloves.

"I'll paint while you crank, guy."

"Sure," Al said, adding—"Watch your little pinkies."

"Good idea. I wouldn't want to break any finger nails," I said jokingly as I started applying the heavy oil with a wall paper brush. It took us about an hour to get the cable oiled and reeled back onto the winch. We found the canvas cover and got it over the winch and tied it down securely. We had about a half hour before watch change. I took the oil bucket back to the engine room. I went forward to write down what we did on the clipboard. When I got to the Crews hall, Earl was there.

"What's going on, guy?" I asked.

"Oh, I was just cleaning the night kitchen. Now I'm trying to hide. How was your morning?" he asked.

"I've had better. I think this roll is getting worse," I said. Al came in and told me that the Bosun wanted us to check the navigational lights again.

"Okay, see you later, Earl," I said as I went out the door after Al. He took the port side while I took the starboard side. I knew that we were gonna' get wet out on deck. The lights seemed okay on the starboard side. I met Al on the fantail. He said that two lights were out on the port side, so we went to the electricians cabinet and got two light bulbs. Al changed the light that was out, aft, while I changed the light forward, port side, next to the wheelhouse. I glanced in the wheelhouse and saw that the Mate was looking in my direction. Before I left, I looked in the window again and saw the Mate talking with Andy, the third officer. As I started down the portside steps, the ship was rolling to the starboard, making the steps less of an angle than usual. I hurried down the steps before the ship could roll the other way. When I got to the bottom of the steps, I was drenched by ice cold spray. I said a few words not normally heard in church, then ran to the door of the Crews hall. Al opened the door when I got there.

"I thought that one was gonna' get you for sure," he said as I ran through the door. Dixon tried to hand me clipboard, but I was so thoroughly soaked that I had to take my coat off first.

"You're suppose to leave the lake outside," Ed wisecracked.

"It ain't getting any better, guys." I took off my parka and hung it on one of the wooden pegs. My shirt and thermal underwear were also soaked and I was chilled to the bone. I signed the clipboard and handed it back to Dixon. This really sucks, I thought as I took my cold, soaked and thoroughly disgusted self back to my quarters. After changing, I shook out my wet clothes and hung them on the coat hooks on the bulkhead. The Captain had put me in the guest quarters on the starboard side. My quarters were warm and dry, unlike my quarters on the Spirit Independent. I heard someone walking past my door, so I looked that way. I noticed an envelope laying by my door. 'Son of a bitch' I thought as I went over and picked it up. Angrily, I tore it open and saw that it was just a notice of watch change instead of a notice of demerit. I was now to work the four to eight watches. Normally, I had worked the eight to twelve watches until earlier this evening. Relieved, I threw it in the waste basket and decided to go see about some late supper. It's going to take a couple days to get accustomed to the four to eight, I thought as I left my quarters and headed toward the Crews hall to get my parka. Nobody was there when I got there. I took my parka down from the peg. It felt a little damp on the inside but I put it on anyway and headed out the door. Crossing the deck, which was rolling as bad as it was earlier, I made my way to the after deckhouse, where the galley and mess were located. I was feeling in a better mood than I was earlier.

Upon entering the galley, I grabbed a tray and began surveying the supper menu.

A voice behind me said, "It looks like it's gonna' be Goulash again." Turning around, my eyes met the eyes of the first mate. I smiled.

"Perish the thought," I said and I turned back toward the steward, who was waiting impatiently for me to make a request.

"A bowl of Chili and a grilled cheese, please," I requested.

As the steward was ladling out the chili, the first mate said, "A good choice, John. I'll have the same."

"Yes Sir" the cook replied as he handed me a bowl, half filled with chili.

"The grilled cheese will take a minute." he said.

"Okay, I'll be back." I said, then I turned and headed for the crews mess. Rank does have its privilege, even in the merchant service, I thought. The Steward must have got his "sucking up" to superiors routine from when he was in the Navy. I looked down at my half bowl of chili. Getting up to retrieve my grilled cheese, I suddenly stopped when I heard a voice behind me. "We brought the rest of your dinner. May I join you?" the Mate asked.

"Yes, of course," I said, sitting back down. The Steward sat down the sandwich and the coffee and headed back to the galley. The mate pulled out a chair and sat down.

"I heard you had some trouble staying dry this evening," he said.

"It wasn't one of my better days," I replied.

"I don't like making that watch change, either. I don't like flying on jets for that reason." He should try flying to the Soviet Union, I thought.

"It's just something you got to adjust to," I said. The mate was quiet while we ate our chili. I could not help but wonder why he was talking to me like this. For the past three months, the man had barely said anything to me, other than an occassional 'hello'. I was taken by surprise when he asked me how my grandmother was doing. I had heard that he lived in Marblehead. It suddenly occurred to me that my childhood friend, Tommy McCracken, was his son. That he had indeed known my grandmother. They were almost neighbors. I remembered my grandmother had told me that his wife had died of Leukemia.

"Should I repeat the question?" he asked.

"My grandmother died, almost a year ago."

"I'm sorry, I hadn't heard," he said. We ate in silence for a few minutes.

"It's kinda' rough to be cooking," I said as the ship took a nasty roll to the starboard.

"Last year, John forgot to secure the roll bars on the stove. A pot of stew and a pot of spaghetti went on the floor during a storm. We had fig newtons and coffee for supper. We we're'nt too happy with him for that screwup," he said.

"I lost a drum top overboard, this evening," I said.

"Yes, the bosun told me about it. Since there was no hazardous material involved, we don't have to report it," he said. I nodded my approval of his decision, because my mouth was full of sandwich.

"What about you? Did you ever do anything stupid during your sailing career?" I inquired of the Mate.

He smiled and said, "Nothing that would put the ship or crew in danger, but I have made my share of mistakes. The only thing I can say is that life is like that. You have to take the good with the bad." I could not have agreed more, but it seemed to me that he was trying to hide something. I was thinking about what else I knew about him, while we ate in silence for a few minutes.

"I have to go forward," he said as he got up from his chair. I saw him looking down at me.

"I see you didn't get married," he said as he looked me in the eye.

"You haven't found the right man yet," he said softly. He winked and turned and left. I had been thinking that I would remain single the rest of my life, so I did not think twice about his statement. However, I could not stop thinking about my grandmother and realized how much I really did miss her. For a moment, I wanted to cry. I got up from the table and headed back to the galley. When I got there, I was surprised that nobody else was there to get a late snack. There was a tray of double chocolate cookies on the counter. I grabbed two and left before John saw me. When I got out on deck, it was raining and blowing right in my face. I reached to grab the safety line and dropped a cookie on the deck. A low flying gull landed right next to me and grabbed the cookie and was airborne again. I took the other cookie, which I had been holding in my mouth, and hurled it at him. "You hungry, son of a bitch?!" I shouted. Jim Dixon, the deckhand on watch, came up behind me.

Laughing, he said, "Nick, don't let that bird get to you. You know that low flying birds are a common occurrence here."

"I really wanted those cookies and I hate those fricking birds!"

"By the way, it looks like that sucker was trying to drop a load on you," Dixon said, laughing.

"Ha, Ha, very funny," I remarked, adding—"You know that we are required to wear hard hats when on deck. Leave it in the crew's hall. I'll pick it up later," I said, handing him my hard hat. Apparently he did not think that there was anything funny about that. He put the hardhat on and shook his head. He continued to go about his job, sounding the tanks.

When I reached my quarters, I took off my parka and hung it on the hook. I went into the bathroom, to the sink. I turned on the water and looked at my hair in the mirror and found nothing in my hair. Happy that I did not have to wash my hair, I washed my face and brushed my hair. Still feeling tired, I decided to lie down in my bunk. It was not long before I was sound asleep.

I dreamed that it was summer. A playmate and I were in a tree house. We were playing a game about pirates. He said that he had captured me and said I was supposed to walk the plank. I broke loose and jumped out of the tree house. Looking up at the boy, I was boasting—"Ha, Ha, you can't catch me." I ran away from the tree house. The scene changed. I was swinging on a rope swing, then a voice called out, "Nicolette, time for dinner, hurry child." It was a warm and gentle voice, but very distant. I jumped from the swing and ran toward a small cottage, but found myself on the beach, instead. I continued to run down the beach until I came to a wooden stairway. I climbed the stairs and kept climbing, but I never seemed to reach the top. Frustrated, I called out "I'm coming . . ."

A loud banging noise, like metal hitting metal and a rattling sound, jarred me from sleep. Even before I could open my eyes, my first thought was that we had hit another vessel. Jumping up out of bed and brushing the hair out of my eyes, I looked out the port hole. The collision alarm was blaring. Through the rain and the fog, I could see what looked like the conveyor boom, hanging over the side of the ship. Unsure of what to make of the situation, I grabbed my parka and life jacket and headed out the door.

Just then, I heard the Bosun shout—"Strickland, grab your tool belt and come on!"

Apparently, the unloading boom had come loose and become stuck off the side of the ship. An electrical failure was causing the conveyor to jettison the taconite cargo into the lake. Before coming to the Gentry, I had worked as a conveyorman on a Canadian vessel with an unloading boom, so I had a good understanding of its operation. First we need to cut the power supply to the conveyor belt, I thought as I reached the bottom of the steps. The switch box room was to the right, at the bottom of the steps. It contained the switch boxes for the entire forward end of the ship. I opened the door and quickly surveyed the switch boxes on the bulkhead. The damn electrician had neglected to label the switch boxes. I pulled down the handle on the main box for the conveyor. I heard the conveyor come to a stop. I ran down the passageway, to the Crews hall and grabbed my tool belt off the wall, then headed for the afterside door. When I opened the door, the Mate was there.

"Nice going, but you managed to shutdown all the operating systems for the conveyor. Third one down, left hand side," he said as he pushed past me. I went out on deck to look at the conveyor. The conveyor was still stuck over the side, but had ceased to unload taconite pellets. The Bosun informed me that the boom had knocked down the deckhand on watch, causing a head injury. He was being attended to and fortunate that he had not been knocked overboard. I got down on my hands and knees and using my flashlight, looked at the pivot of the conveyor.

"The boom is jammed. The main gears of the drivers are in place, good. The idler gear for the traverse mechanism is bent at the arm. We can disengage the idler gear for the time being and bring the boom back on board," I stated. Before I could get up to get a wrench, someone handed me the big aluminum stilson wrench. I put the wrench onto the big nut at the end of the idler gear arm and pulled hard on it. It came loose and after a few turns, I was able to unscrew it by hand. I hit upward on the arm and it came off the square end of the shaft. I grabbed it and dragged it out from under the conveyor.

"We should be ready now," I said as I stood up and backed away from the boom. The warning came over the loud speaker to clear the deck. After a minute, I heard the customary banging sound and then the rattling as the boom was raised and brought back on board. Once on board, we needed to determine why it broke loose in the first place. Upon arriving at the forward stanchion, I was told that someone on deckwatch had apparently forgot to check the boom, to see that it remained locked down.

"HORSE CRAP!" I shouted in disbelief as I turned around to see the Bosun staring at me.

"I checked those shackles before I came off watch and the bolts were tight." Just then, I noticed Earl standing at my side with what must have been three hundred pounds of half inch chain on his shoulders. Grabbing one end of the chain, I began to wrap it around the boom and the stanchion. Bolting the chain through the links. I repeated the procedure for the other side, while Earl passed me the chain. I was determined to have a look at those shackles before anyone else could get their hands on them.

After securing the boom, I climbed up the stanchion and got onto the boom. I side-stepped my way along the frame, almost to the end of the conveyor, where the outboard shackle was still attached. Evidently, the inboard shackle had fallen into the lake. Using my stilson wrench, I loosened the two one inch bolts, with some difficulty. The shackle was cocked and binding on the I-beam. I called to Earl to bring my three pound hammer from my tool box. I saw the Bosun hand him a hammer and he ran back and handed it up to me. Steadying myself, I directed a blow onto the right side of the shackle. Much to my surprise, the shackle broke into two pieces, which went spinning down to the deck before I could call out a warning to Earl below. The pieces struck the deck, making a hell of a racket. This caught the attention of the Bosun and the other men on deck, who came running to see what happened.

"What happened?" asked the second engineer, who had been welding on the railing.

"Nick hit the shackle with a hammer and it broke into two pieces and fell down," Earl replied.

"Are you sure it was broken before it hit the deck?" the Bosun asked.

"It doesn't matter," the second engineer said, adding

"That steel should never break like that. King Kong shouldn't be able to do that."

"I never saw anything like that before," the Bosun said.

"I have," I said. "It's called nil-ductility temperature failure," I added as I climbed down from the boom. "Some steel is defective because of a mistake made at the steel mill. Usually there wasn't enough manganese or too much sulphur. Below a certain temperature, the steel gets real brittle, like glass," I continued to explain.

"Nil-ductility failure is possible at this temperature," the second engineer said as he was examining the broken shackle. "Or it could be a crystallinity defect of some sort. I'll take it back to the Chief and have him examine it."

"What's wrong Hank?" asked the mate.

"Nick broke the shackle. We're trying to figure out why."

"Well Nick isn't Godzilla, Hank. What do you make of it?"

"Nick thinks it's nil-ductility failure. Are you familiar with that, Sir?"

"Yes, I remember hearing about it happening on Liberty ships made during the Second World War. Something about not enough manganese in the steel, wasn't it?" the Mate asked.

"Yes sir, but the problem might be crystallization. The Chief will know for sure when he examines it," replied Hank.

"Very good Hank. Also, I want you and Nick to make out a report on this before you go off watch. I want every detail. Is that clear, Nick?"

"Yes sir," I replied. The First Mate was not being bossy. Whenever there was a deviation from standard routine and procedures, he made sure that everyone knew what was expected of them. Having my name on an engineering report was certainly a deviation from my usual job.

I helped Hank carry the broken shackle to the machine shop. The machinist was sitting on a steel drum, eating doughnuts and drinking coffee. Not that he needed it, because he weighed at least three hundred and fifty pounds.

"Where's the Chief, Ken?" Hank asked.

"He's forward, with the electrician, looking at the conveyor." His reply coming through a doughnut he had shoved in his mouth.

"Well, he'll be back shortly. I'm sure the Mate has told him by now. We might as well get us some coffee. We got to keep you awake until the Chief gets done with you. I know it isn't your usual watch, anyway." Hank went to the large thermos and poured me a cup of coffee. I sat down on the machinist's bench and started thinking about the Chief. He always seemed annoyed. He always seemed ready to scream at somebody, but I never heard him raise his voice at anybody. I heard that he was a workaholic and a top notch administrator. God help any screwups in his department. Meanwhile, the machinist continued to munch away contentedly on his third dozen of doughnuts like some milk cow. When

The Chief entered, I rose from the bench. He motioned for me to sit down and then he started on the machinist.

"Don't get up on my account, Doinker, and try to stay amidships. We don't need the boat to turn turtle. I got enough problems as it is."

The machinist barely moved his head and grunted in acknowledgement of the Chief's wisecrack.

The Chief examined the shackle pieces and stated, "This shackle should bend like a pretzel without breaking and I don't see any fatigue cracking anywhere. 7036 steel shouldn't behave like this. You must be wonder woman or your 'brittle failure' theory is right. I'll heat this up and try hitting it. Then I'll cool it down and try the same thing. I'll be sure to include your name in my report. You should go forward now and get some sleep." As I walked toward the door, he said—"By the way, that was good work on the traverse gearing."

"Is it working now?" I asked.

"No, we have more problems than you can believe. See you later," he said as he turned to leave.

I went back to my quarters and looked at the clock. I had just over four hours to sleep before my morning watch. It seemed like I had hardly closed my eyes, when the watch bell woke me again. As I slipped on my parka, I noticed that the ship rolled gently. We must have outran the storm, I thought as I walked out the door. I met Don, one of the wheelsmen, in the passageway.

"It's smooth sailing for a while, lass. Of course, the Captain is in a bit of a snit. I don't know why, he's leaving. It's the rest of us who won't get our raises for the next five years. We're picking up the little British bastard and his pig faced friend at the lock, this afternoon."

"Say what?" I asked.

"The Maritime Operations Manager, Dick O'Blake, and the Ship Surveyor, Kenny Ring. Real birds, them." In spite of his words, his happy tone and smile never left him. I guess that's why the other guys called him 'smiley'. When I came out on deck, I was greeted by the Bosun.

"Have you seen Earl?" he asked.

"No," I said, "He might be aft, checking on Dixon. Is there a problem?"

"No, I'm just checking," he replied. As I checked rigging and lights, I noticed what a beautiful night it was. The water was calm, the sky

17

was clear and the stars and moon seemed close enough to reach out and grab. A perfect summer night, I thought as I stared at the silver wake of the ship, except it is mid November and it is almost freezing. Halfway through the watch, Al came and told me that the Captain wanted to see me in the wheelhouse.

I walked around to the front of the wheelhouse and entered by the watch door. The red lights were on, making everything red.

"Excuse me, young lady. This is the employees entrance. Visitors use the back door, please."

"Very funny, Pete. There is always a comedian on board or a crazy Nam vet. You fill both positions, aren't we lucky," I shot back.

"At your service, madamoiselle," he bowed.

"Where's the Captain?" I asked.

"Him, the Mate and the Chief have been in the Observation room for the last half hour. I don't know, it sounds like a gang bang to me," he said as he trailed off into 'can't get no satisfaction'. The third Officer, looking tired, came through the door. "The Captain will see you now, Miss Strickland," he said and I saw him head the other way.

I went down the steps and entered the observation room.

The Captain said, "Please sit down, Miss Strickland." I always liked the Captain. His name is William Kompsii. He has pretty blue eyes, like a child, but he squinted most of the time. He was honest and fair and he could spot a bull-shitter from a mile off. And he didn't like that type around him.

"I've seen the report by you, the Chief and the second engineer. It looks like the nil-ductility theory was right. Of course, the company will want to test the shackle on shore. A lock was never installed on the traverse mechanism of the boom. That keeps the boom from traversing when it's in the down position. So when the shackle failed, there was no lock to keep it from going overboard. Also, there is a limit switch that stops the conveyor when the boom is swung on board. There is an indicator light that comes on when the limit switch is activated, to remind the operator to shut off the power to the conveyor. The light is there, but it was never hooked up. So everytime the conveyor was swung overboard, the limit switch would turn the power on if no one shut it off manually. Fortunately, the cargo doors were closed, so only about fifty tons of pellets on the loop belt were lost. Naturally, I sent a Fax of the incident and reported Mister Dixon's condition to the company. We are going to put him off when we get to Sault Ste. Marie. We will also pick up the Maritime Operations Manager and the Ships Surveyor at that time. When the ship is rounding the headland and going through the lock, I would like you to be in the wheelhouse, observing. The Mate will arrange for someone else to take your watch on deck. Do you have anything to say, Miss Strickland?"

"No sir, nothing at this time," I replied.

"Very well then, Mister McCracken would like to see you when we're done in here. Would you like to wait in the Wheelhouse?"

"Yes sir," I replied as I started to get up.

"One more thing, Miss Strickland. I want to tell you that you're doing a good job."

"Thank you, sir." I replied and I turned and walked out the door.

In the wheelhouse, the red lights were still on and the wheelsman was still droning on with his silly singing.

"That was quick!" Pete exclaimed.

"Quick for what?" I questioned.

"Quick for three men and one woman to do their business. Or didn't they know you were a woman?"

"Pete, where did you lose your brain at?" I asked calmly, not getting riled at his type.

"In defense of my country, Doll face," he replied in a pathetic Bogart voice.

"Believe me, Pete. No country is worth that much!" I exclaimed as the first mate came into the Wheelhouse.

"I believe this is yours, isn't it, Miss Strickland?" asked the Mate as he held up an old style metal hardhat, considerably mangled.

"Yes sir," I replied.

"Dixon was wearing it. I'll have to ask why," he said.

"I lent it to him after I went off watch, earlier," I answered.

"That's what he told me too. I don't think there's a policy about trading hardhats. Personally, I believe that Dixon would have been a lot worse off if he hadn't been wearing the old type metal helmet. The plastic ones are not nearly as strong."

"How is Dixon doing?" I asked.

"No one can really tell for sure. The Captain is the only one that has any medical knowledge at all. He thinks that he has a concussion for sure and probably compression fractures in the neck vertebrae, but only X-rays can show that," the Mate replied, adding—"Since he seems to be in stable condition, the Coast Guard has agreed to let us put him off before we lock through."

"That's good, I like Dixon. He's always ready to help out other people," I said.

"I wish he could help us now. I don't know how so many errors could have been made. The dockyard certificate states that the indicator light was hooked up. Also, there is no mention of the lock on the conveyor, but the parts list has it. The Dockyard workers and the Commission Inspector missed it. The Chief didn't know about it because you have to be familiar with the gear to know it's supposed to be there," explained the Mate as he looked through the papers on his clipboard.

"I thought the company used reputable shipyards to do re-fit work," I said.

"We always used the Lorain yards, but this time our Mister O'Blake found a lower bid with a French-Canadian outfit. The big problem is that the Canadian outfit went out on strike about the time the work was to be completed, so someone apparently forgot to do their job."

"O'Blake will have to accept the facts of the matter, won't he?" I asked.

"I don't trust his type," the Mate replied, adding—"He's never been on a boat. He's got Oxford business school on the brain, and he's a damn Brit. He'll write his report any way he feels like. Well, I have to go aft. You can get a cup of coffee and finish your watch," the Mate said and he turned and headed through the door. As I poured the coffee, the wheelsman began his usual crap.

"That's always the way it starts, Ms. Strickland."

"What in the hell are you talking about!" I snapped.

"First you're sharing hardhats, then the next thing you know, you're taking warm showers together," Pete wisecracked.

"Why don't you take a cold shower, jerk!" I exclaimed, then I turned and walked through the wheelhouse door.

From the bow of the ship, I could see the sun begin to rise. Orange and red streaks coming through the violet murk. If this weather holds, I should get enough sleep, I thought to myself. The temperature had been going up as we crossed Superior, but that is not unusual on a downbound run into the lower lakes. Still, in the month of November you can never tell what is going to happen. I found Al at the fantail. He smiled as he handed me my binoculars.

"Thanks," I said.

Putting his binoculars to his eyes, he looked astern and said, "We have company." I looked astern with my binoculars but it took a minute before I could see the faint lights and an outline of a wheelhouse.

"Damn Al, you've got eyes like a hawk to spot that ship. It must be fifteen miles away."

"A little more than that,I think. She came out of the Canadian side and has been following us for half an hour. She's doing a bit more than us, maybe a knot. It'll be well into the afternoon before she's close."

"Maybe they're trying to race us to the lock," I said.

"It won't do him no good. The Captain is flying the flag for an injured man on board. She'll have to keep behind us until we get Dixon off."

"Maybe it's a Canadian cement carrier," I suggested.

"No, I don't think so. I believe she's one of the thousand footers," Al stated as he continued to look through his binoculars.

"I'm gonna' check the port side, Al. How long till the watch change?" I asked.

Looking at his watch, he said, "half an hour."

"Okay, I'll catch you later," I said as I headed for the port side.

I checked the boom first. The lake was calm enough that it wasn't creaking against the chains. I noticed that even more chains had been added to the ones I put there. Someone's being over careful, I thought. The hatch crane had been moved aft. Not unusual, the engineering department had been checking it. I made sure that it had been locked down. It was. I changed a light bulb on one of the deck lights, portside, and walked forward to the deckhouse. I paused to watch the sun rise, starboard of the bow. The orange and yellow light pushing back the darkness in the southeast horizon, while the sun itself was still concealed by clouds. How romantic, I thought, too bad this isn't a cruise ship. I heard a noise behind me, and turned to see the third engineer walking forward with a coffee pot.

"They ran out of Coffee forward, Fred?"

"No, I was just fixing the cord and I want to get it back to the wheelhouse or the gang up there will have the porter running his legs off," the third Engineer replied.

"A pretty sunrise this morning, isn't it?" he added.

"Yeah, too bad it's so cold," I said and I turned and headed toward the crews hall to write on the clipboard. A few minutes later the watch bell rang. I filled in the watch report and handed it to Ed, who was relieving me.

"Okay, I'm supposed to pull watch for you from six to eight PM."

"Great, you'll get some overtime after all. See you later then," I replied.

I went back to my quarters, showered and changed my clothes. I laid down on my bunk and thought about things. I thought about my grandmother and the little cemetery in Marblehead where she is buried. The little white cottage overlooking the lake. I dreamed that I was playing in a treehouse. It was a warm summer day. Grandmother called to me. She took me by the hand and we walked. I asked her where we were going. She said that we were going to see the ships. The ship was gigantic. It seemed to take up half the bay. It was so pretty, painted green and white. It was the Cliffs Victory. A big man picked me up and carried me up the ladder. Up, up we climbed. It seemed that we climbed the stairs for hours. Finally, he sat me down in a big black chair in the Wheelhouse. The room was filled with all sorts of instruments, valve wheels, levers, dials and switches. All shining in brass, stainless steel and porcelain. Another big man, the Captain, wearing a white hat, came in. He said 'Hi',as he pinched my cheeks. He said that I could drive the ship. I was so excited. I saw the big conveyors come. They started dumping ore into the hatches. Grandma and I were standing on the dock. The conveyors kept going, the sound was deafening.

I said, "Grandma, make them stop!" but she couldn't hear me.

The Victory began to sink, down and down. I saw the wheelhouse go under, the captain was still in there. The flag flew proudly until it too, sank into the bay. I woke with a start. Checking the time, I had barely slept an hour. I took a Unisome. That would knock me out for four hours at least. When I got up to get some water, I saw the Mate and the Bosun talking in the passageway. Returning to my bunk, I was asleep before my head hit the pillow.

When I awoke, it was one thirty in the afternoon. My watch was at four, so I had a while before I had to start. I donned my parka and headed aft to the galley. I could barely see the headland of Whitefish Bay on the starboard side. I knew that there was a lighthouse painted in red and white, helical stripes, like a barber's pole. White cottages dotted the shoreline. The air was clear and the sun was bright, giving the illusion of things looking closer than they really are. I looked astern to see if the other ship was there. It was. Even without my Binoculars, I could see that it was one of the super lakers. A Canadian ore carrier, slowly gaining on us. Its thousand foot hull could barely fit in the lock. Fully loaded, it would draft twenty eight feet. Its deck was flat, only hatchways protruded forward of the deckhouse astern. That class was driven by two-eight thousand horsepower diesel engines, turning two propeller shafts with variable pitch propellers. A two hundred and fifty foot conveyor was the only machinery above deck. It reminded me of my former ship, the Canadian MV Giovanni. I decided to see if Dixon could have visitors.

Dixon was above deck, in the spare Chief's quarters. Buster, the oiler on watch, told me that he was conscious and receiving visitors. I knocked lightly on the door, and a voice said: "Come in". When I opened the door, I saw Dixon lying on a bunk while Earl was apparently examining him.

"Hi, Nick," he said as he waved his hand weakly.

"Now, you lie still and don't you dare turn your head, is that clear?"

"Okay, Earl," he replied smiling.

"Well, Nick, I got conked on the noggin. I haven't been hit so hard since that bar fight in Detroit. Good thing I was wearing your hard hat," he said.

"Yeah, the mate showed it to me, it looked pretty bad," I replied.

"Well, you know how it is. Some people you just can't trust lending them anything," he joked.

"In a couple of hours, you'll be off this boat anyway, and in the hospital where you can recover," I said.

"I don't think that no doctor can take care of me like Earl has," he replied.

"I'm sorry Nick, but Dixon should rest for awhile," said Earl.

"Okay, partner," I said as I reached down and grabbed Dixon's hand, "See you later," then I turned and left.

23

I went to the galley to get some chow, since they were still serving lunch. I told John, the steward, to get me a hamburger and some French fries.

"I thought that you didn't like our hamburgers Nick," he said.

"I'm assuming that you've learned to cook hamburgers since the last time I bawled you out," I replied.

"One hamburger burned to carbon," announced the steward jokingly into his microphone.

"You might as well go sit down, it'll take a few minutes," he added. I went to the crew's mess. I saw the second engineer reading a book, so I decided to bother him.

"What's up Hank," I asked as I sat down.

"Oh, I'm reading the manual for the chief engineer's test," he replied as he sat the book down flat on the table.

"Those look like some pretty nasty turbines there. All those equations for that one turbine?" I asked as I glanced over both pages at once.

"Well, there's a lot more than that. As you know, there are reaction and impulse turbines. The test covers both types, so we have to study them. Only the most frequently used equations will be on the test. Further back, nil-ductility is covered, but you already know about that," Hank replied.

The steward brought my hamburger and French fries over.

'Here you go, Miss Particular."

"Thank you sir," I replied as I cut the sandwich in half to see if it was cooked to my culinary preference.

"I have to be getting back to my quarters. The Chief is helping me study. I'll see you later, when they take Dixon out," Hank said as he got up to leave.

"Okay," I replied.

Just about the time I was finished with my lunch, Earl came in. I motioned for him to join me.

"You came to get something for Dixon?" I asked as I got up to put the plate in the bin set out for the dirty dishes.

"No, he can only take chicken broth and liquid vitamins. He can't eat nothing else because he can't raise his head. I'm worried about complications. He seems to be getting constipated," Earl replied.

"All that training you got as a Medical Corpsman is being put to good use," I stated.

"I was a Medical Corpsman in the Navy, but this is a little different than my time in Nam with the Marines," Earl replied.

"I know that that was a bummer," I said.

"No, not really. No one's gonna' fire you for kicking the shit out of some asshole in a war. When you got to drag somebody's shot-up ass to safety, the other grunts start learning respect for you. I made a lot of friends in Nam. I never had to buy myself a drink after the first couple of weeks."

"I'll buy you a drink for this, old buddy. You're the first guy I've met who talks that way about the war. Most guys start crying in their beer, like the war has messed them up forever, or something," I said.

"A lot of guys did get messed up, blinded, burned, arms and legs blown off. There's a lot of cry babies though. Always saying things like, 'what in the hell are we fighting for'. Like knowing what you're fighting for is gonna' keep you from getting your fool head shot off. Most of them types used drugs. Probably before they ever got to Nam. I never let them get to me. It was after I got home, that I found out about my uncle dying in a mining accident and my brothers trying to turn my father against me because they were trying to get the farm. They were gonna' take all the money and leave me hanging. I had some problems when I came back, but I straightened things out."

"That's good," I said, adding—"Hey, you want to play cards in the Rec room. How about Five Card?" I asked getting up from the table.

"That's my game!" replied Earl as we headed for the recreation room. There were only two people in the room. One was an Oiler, named Joe. The other was a twenty year old apprentice. A curly, red haired kid, named Billy, but everybody called him "The Kid". Neither seemed to notice us come into the room. As we sat down, I heard them spout the usual male bull crap.

". . . That's Bull Shit," said the Kid.

"No shit, man," said Joe. "The Wheelsman said he saw it himself. The woman went into the Observation Room with the First Mate, the Captain, and the Chief. For fifteen minutes, they were banging in there, then out she comes looking fresh as daisies. Gets a cup of coffee. Puts her legs up on the railing and spreads them. Basking in the glow of the red lights, if you know what I mean. Then five minutes later, in comes the Mate, out of breath and clothes all wrinkled."

"Wow! exclaimed the Kid, "She didn't even let them take their clothes off!"

"I can't wait until she starts servicing the after end of the ship," Joe said.

"Excuse me, Nick," said Earl as he got up and headed for Joe and Billy's table. When he got to the table, I couldn't hear what he was saying to them.

I heard Joe say: "Who asked you, Hick!"

I never saw Earl move so fast. With one hand he picked Joe up by the neck and slammed his head into the bulk head. The Kid tried to grab him. He turned and kicked him so hard in the stomach that I heard bones crack. The Kid doubled up and fell over. Then he turned back to Joe and punched him real hard in the stomach. I swore his eyes popped out. Then he kneed him in the crotch and let him fall to the deck. Earl returned to our table.

"They said they're sorry, Nick."

"I bet they are now. Look Earl, you shouldn't be making enemies on this ship. I usually just take this kind of crap to the Captain or the Mate."

As if by magic, through the door came the Mate. He paused momentarily, looking at the men on the floor then at us. Striding over to the Kid.

"What's going on here?!" he demanded. The Kid was in a fetal position. Although not conducive to good speech, managed to blurt out a weak "Earl".

"Earl, what do you know about this?!" demanded the Mate.

"Why Sir, Earl has been with me since we came in," I said as innocently as possible.

"Alright, Miss Strickland. I didn't ask you, and that's not what I asked. Suppose you tell me what you saw and heard," demanded the Mate.

"I didn't see anything, but I heard something about 'Gilligan' coming from that direction, Sir," I replied.

"Very well, Miss Strickland, that will be enough!" the Mate said.

"Now, listen up! The biggest prick on the lakes is coming aboard in two hours. You wags pick yourselves up and stay in your quarters until your watch. I don't want no screw ups and don't mention this to anyone.

Is that clear?" "Yes, Sir," we replied. As Earl and I left the room, the Kid and Joe were picking themselves up from the deck.

"I got to say, Earl, you really know how to hurt a guy," I cracked, "And you don't even leave any bruises."

"I'm gonna' check on Dixon. I'll see you later," said Earl, not nearly as amused as I was. I headed forward since my watch would be starting in a couple hours. I went to my quarters and wrote a couple letters then I read for a while. The Bosun came by and told me to work the whole watch in the Wheelhouse. I changed my clothes and put my hair in a ponytail. On my way to the Wheelhouse, I met Don the Wheelsman.

"Good afternoon, Lass," he greeted me.

"Hello, Don," I said, "Are you at the wheel?"

"No, Pete will be steering, I'll be at the Motor Controls," he said.

"I'm supposed to be observing in the Wheelhouse on the four to eight watch," I said.

"I'm doubting you'll learn much from Pete. He don't say much when there are officers about. We just received word to tie up at the space closest to the lock. That will mean that we get to enter the lock first, right after we send Dixon ashore."

When we entered the wheelhouse, Michael, the wheelsman on first watch, was talking to the Mate.

"You're a little early today," Michael said.

"I thought I'd show Nick a few of the tricks before Pete got here," stated Don.

"Very well, Mister MacDonough. You may take the wheel now if you like," the Mate stated as he continued on with his navigational calculations. His eyes were firmly focused on the charts before him. Michael turned the wheel over to Don and went over to get a cup of coffee.

"Most of the time, Lass, there isn't any trick to steering a ship like this. The auto compass is right in front of you. The red pointer shows what heading you're on. Right now we're on the heading of 0-9-3, that's almost due east. In open water, all you got to watch for is holding your course and watching out for other ships. On auto, the compass will steer the ship for you. Just pull this lever, like this," Don said, as he indicated how to engage the auto pilot.

"Now," he continued, "this is the light switch. Push it to turn on. Twist to dim it. Those switches over there are the running lights. They go ON at night. They are different colors on the port than on the starboard, so other ships know what side they're on. Since we're entering a narrow waterway, we'll keep the auto pilot off. Normally, you would start looking for navigational buoys. See the flashing red light on the water. That indicates that we should keep that buoy to starboard in order to stay in the main shipping lane," Don explained.

Looking ahead from this high up, it looked like the Lake was coming to an end. Which in fact, it was. I could see the ship ahead to starboard, stopped. A ship to the port, heading toward us. Just having locked through. Pete came through the door and nodded in the direction of the Mate, who was sitting in the Captains' chair. Pete took the wheel and Don went over to the lever and the drum type Chadburn Motor Control.

"Hall on station at the wheel," said Pete.

"Very Well, Mister Hall," said the Mate.

"MacDonough on station at the motor," said Don.

"Very Well, Mister MacDonough," answered the Mate. I had not realized that announcing yourself was part of the watch change. I saw a flashing green light dead ahead of us. I figured we would turn slightly starboard to keep that light on our port side, but I did not want to ask because the Mate might be wanting to give an order.

It looked like the Mate was intending to run down the green light, when I heard him say: "Mister hall, steady as she goes, bring her around to one-two-three."

"Steady as she goes, one-two-three, yes sir," Pete replied in a professional tone.

"Mister MacDonough, change the speed to ahead one-third," the Mate ordered.

"Ahead one-third, yes sir," Don replied.

The ship began to swing starboard. For the first time, I could see the bridge and the locks ahead. The upbound ship passed us on the port side. A grain boat looking trim and smart. Still picking up speed. On the starboard side was a smallish ship, probably about five thousand tons. A coal carrier by appearance. Dirty black smoke coming from her stack. As we passed her, the Mate blew the whistle. Ahead of the coal carrier was another ore carrier. One of the smaller type super-lakers. She was almost stopped. As we started to pass her, the Mate said,

"Mister MacDonough, change speed to back one-third."

"Back one-third, yes Sir," he replied as he pulled the lever back on the drum and rang the bell. I could feel the ship start to slow.

Over the speaker came the message: "Station One, standing by at one-three, over."

The Mate picked up the phone and replied, "Roger Station One. W-B six two one three out," and put down the phone.

"Mister MacDonough, change speed back to slow," the Mate said.

"Back slow, yes Sir," Don replied as he moved the lever forward somewhat.

I saw an ambulance pull up to the edge of the sea wall, still over five hundred yards away. The sea wall was curved slightly. Our present course would bring us along side, right where the ambulance was stopped. The ship was going only a couple of knots, but it showed no signs of slowing any further. At a distance of two hundred yards, the Mate ordered the speed changed back twenty RPM. The ship appeared to be barely moving as the Wheelhouse passed the ambulance.

When the ship stopped completely, the Mate said "Mister MacDonough. all stop."

"All stop, yes Sir," Don replied pushing the lever to the Middle position.

I knew the Captain was out on deck giving orders for the gangway. I could see the short gangway being rigged on the starboard side. I would be doing that if I wasn't in the wheelhouse. I saw the deck gang bring out Dixon on a stretcher. The guys were shaking his hand. He waved as they carried him down the gangway. The ambulance attendants put him on their own stretcher and then placed him in the back of the ambulance. They climbed in and closed the door. In a few seconds, the ambulance was gone from sight. After the ambulance left, a taxi pulled up where it had been. Two men got out of the taxi. One was short, chubby and sour looking, with a cheap brown suit. The other man was of average height, round spectacles and skinny with droopy shoulders. In fact, everything about him seemed to droop. Behind the taxi came a white car. A man in a coast guard uniform got out. I recognized him as the Commander for the district. The Commander joined the two men at the seawall. I saw the Captain go down the gangway and head their direction.

Over the speaker, I heard a voice, "Mister McCracken please see the Captain at he starboard side gangway." The Mate got up and left the Wheelhouse.

"Looks like your darling's in some trouble now, Nick" Pete said in a smart aleck voice.

"Why don't you fuck off, Pete!" I snapped.

"Now, don't be so hard on the man, Lassie," Don said as he continued with a smirk on his face.

"He's had a rough childhood. When he was an altar boy he got kicked out of the church for molesting a priest."

Pete turned red at the remark, but he didn't seem to have anything more to say.

Turning my attention to the dock. It appeared that the short man was arguing with the District Commander about something. I was wondering how long he was planning to go on, when the Mate had joined them. The Captain handed the Mate a couple brief cases. The Mate took them and headed back to the gangway. The Coast Guard Commander ceased arguing with the short man. He said something to the Captain, saluted and headed back to his car. The two men followed the Captain to the gangway. As soon as they were on board, the deck gang un-rigged the gangway and replaced the railing.

The First Mate came through the door of the Wheelhouse still carrying the brief cases. He sat them down beside the chart table.

"Prepare to get underway," he ordered.

"Mister Hall, five degrees port rudder."

"Five degrees port rudder, yes Sir," Pete replied as he turned the wheel.

"Mister MacDonough, back one-third."

"Back one-third, yes Sir," Don replied as he pulled the lever back on the drum.

The ship vibrated as it began pulling away from the wall, stern first. When the ship had backed up about three hundred yards, the Mate ordered, "Mister MacDonough, ahead slow."

"Ahead slow, yes Sir."

"Mister Hall, rudder to hard port."

"Hard port, yes Sir," Pete replied as I saw him turn the wheel a couple of times to the left. The ship slowly began to move forward and the bow began to swing to port, heading for the gates of the big lock. When the bow was in line with the lock, the Mate ordered the Rudder amidships. Then he ordered "back slow" for the motors. The ship was barely moving as the bow entered the lock gates. the lock was big. It seemed big enough to hold two ships our size. The ship slowed to a stop, still two hundred fifty feet away from the lock gates.

"All stop, Mister MacDonough," the Mate ordered.

"All stop, Sir" Don replied as he pushed the handle up. The Mate had us stopped right in the middle of the lock. No sloppy seamanship here, I thought. I looked ahead, to the port side and saw a ship waiting to enter the lock over there. It was a Super laker. Something was familiar about it. I watched as the deck gang scrambled over the starboard side to secure the mooring cables to the bollards on the wall. I realized that it was my former ship, the Giovanni.

I leaned forward to get a better look, when the Mate asked, "Is there something interesting to port, Miss Strickland?"

"I was trying to catch the name of that ship waiting to lock through upbound, sir" I replied.

"It's a Canadian ore carrier, the Giovanni. I heard her code before we came into the lock," the Mate answered.

"Thank you, Sir."

I could see the deck watch, but it was too far away to make out anybody. The Mate blew the whistle once. The Giovanni blew her whistle. Our ship began to descend. In a few minutes, the ship had lowered twenty feet. I saw a small Coast Guard craft ahead of us on our port side. I had not realized that another boat was in the lock with us. The massive down bound gates swung opened slowly. The Coast Guard boat proceeded through the gates before they were fully opened. Once clear of the lock, the boat accelerated and headed into the channel. After the Mate got word that the lines were in, and the men back on board, he turned to Don.

"Ahead slow, Mister MacDonough," the Mate said.

"Ahead slow, yes Sir" Don replied.

"Steady as she goes, Mister Hall," the Mate stated.

"Steady as she goes, yes Sir" Pete said. The ship slowly moved through the gates.

Once out of the lock, the Mate ordered: "Mister Hall, at the range lights, change heading to one-six-two." "One-six-two, yes sir," Pete replied.

"Mister MacDonough, ahead one half," the Mate ordered.

"Ahead one half, yes sir," Don replied, pushing the lever forward on the drum.

Once again the ship vibrated as it picked up speed.

"Our guests will be here shortly, so look smart," the Mate said. I put my binoculars to my eyes, pretending like I was looking for something. The waterway opened up considerably. Another ship was approaching on our port side. Small boats were numerous. Most were staying near the shore. It was calm and cold, a good day for sailing. I heard the Captain summon Earl on the speaker.

"That looks very professional, Miss Strickland," the Mate said. I turned and saw him writing in the log book.

"In clear weather like this, the Officer and the Wheelsman usually are sufficient to keep a look out forward. In a fog or storms, we sometimes need an extra lookout up here. Over here is a short range Surface Detection radar called the SD set. It has a range of about twenty five miles. Its minimum range is about four hundred yards. It can't show anything within four hundred yards. In conditions of low visibility, we like to use the horn and the whistle a lot. Running into other ships is dumb seamanship," the Mate finished.

I looked at the tube of the radar set. A white line turned around the center. The land showed up as light green as did the ships, the water was dark green.

"The white line is called the PPI, or the Position Plan Indicator. It is set so that when it is straight up, the radar is looking forward. The frame is marked in degrees to give a relative bearing. If you toggle this switch when the PPI is on a ship. It will give you the range in meters," the Mate explained as he demonstrated how the range finder worked. As I was watching the radar screen, the Captain and the visitors came in the back door.

Company Ridership

The Captain introduced the short man as Dick O'Blake, and the other as Kenny Ring. As they went around shaking hands, the Captain said our names.

When the Captain said "Nickolette Strickland", Mister O'Blake asked if he knew me from somewhere.

"I don't think so, sir," I said. I had seen him a couple of times in a restaurant in Cleveland, called the *Top of the Town*, but I did not want him to know.

Shaking hands with Mister Ring was like wringing a wet rag, but he had the good sense not to say anything. The atmosphere in the Wheelhouse got considerably colder with those two around, that was for sure.

"Mister O'Blake will be quartered in the upper level, first midships stateroom. Mister Ring will be quartered aft, in the spare Chief's quarters," the Captain said.

That's great, I thought, the son-of-a-bitch is right next door to me. I can see why the Captain was summoning Earl. I'm surprised that O'Blake doesn't want his quarters painted before he moves in. Mister O'Blake asked about the brief cases. The Mate told him that they were under the chart table. Mister O'Blake reached under the chart table and pulled out the two brief cases.

"Can someone show me to my quarters, now?", his question sounding more like an order.

"Yes, of course. The porter will take your things and show you the way," the Captain said.

I had not noticed that Earl had entered the wheelhouse. He came forward and took the brief cases from Mister O'Blake.

"This way, sir," Earl said as he left by the back door. Mister O'Blake followed him.

"Miss Strickland, would you like to show Mister Ring to his quarters," the Captain said.

"Yes, Sir," I replied.

"There's no need for that Captain. I'm quite familiar with vessels such as this. I would like to see you in my quarters as soon as possible," Mister Ring said.

"Of course, I'll be there shortly," the Captain replied.

"Then I will see you later. Good Afternoon Ladies and Gentlemen," Mister Ring said, then he turned and went out the rear door.

"Mister McCracken, have you finished the entries in the log book?" the Captain asked.

"Yes, Sir," replied the Mate.

"Let me see the log book. I have a few things to add," said the Captain.

"Very good, Sir," the Mate replied as he handed him the log book. The Captain took the log book and began writing for a few minutes. After he had initialed and dated the last entry, he handed the log book to the Mate and got up to leave.

"Mister McCracken, are we returning to normal watch rotation on the next watch?" the Captain asked.

"Yes Sir, we have arranged for the deckwatch gang to fill in for Dixon," the Mate replied.

"Very good," the Captain said and he turned and left by the rear door.

It was past six o'clock, and starting to get dark in the east. I wondered if the Super-laker was behind us. I looked out the rear facing window, but I could not see anything. It was getting foggy astern, so visibility was not that good. I checked the SD set. There was a ship behind us about five miles, but I could not tell which one.

After watching the radar screen for a few minutes, the Mate asked— "Is there something on the radar screen, Miss Strickland?"

"I was wondering, there seems to be a ship behind us, about five miles," I replied, adding—"I think it's the smaller ship."

"No, it appears to be the big ship," the Mate replied.

"The blip doesn't appear to be that big, Sir" I said.

"Sometimes, all the echo you get is from the superstructure. Making the ship appear smaller than it really is. In a few minutes, it will probably straighten itself out. It's the blips ahead, we have to worry about. There is a ferry boat from the American side and other small craft out there," the Mate said. The small boats seemed to be heading to shore with the growing darkness. A few of the larger, private craft were at anchor, their small lights blinking. From the port side, I could see the green and white lights of a larger boat, maybe one hundred and fifty feet long. The Mate blew the whistle.

"That ferry's heading back to the American side, loaded with cars and passengers. It looks like we're on a collision course," the Mate said. We continued on our course, and the ferry continued on its course across our bow. The Mate's eyes remained fixed on the ferry. He reached up and blew the whistle when the ferry was six hundred yards away.

"Mister Hall, five degrees port rudder," the Mate ordered.

"Five degrees port rudder, yes sir," Pete replied as he turned the wheel to port. The bow began to swing to port. First pointing right at the ferry, then astern of her. We passed about fifty yards astern of the ferry. I could see people at the stern looking at us as we passed.

"Rudder amidship, Mister Hall," the Mate ordered.

"Rudder admidship, yes Sir," Pete said. After we got clear of the ferry, the Mate ordered a return to course one-one-two. The Mate turned on the red(night vision) lights.

"Keep a sharp look out forward!" the Mate ordered.

"Yes, Sir" we all replied in unison.

The Mate began writing in the log book. He did not look happy. Up ahead I could see small lights, mostly to the starboard. In this part of the lake, there are many islands. One has to be looking out for small craft all the time. Off to the starboard was a navigational buoy. Its flashing red light telling us that we were in the right place.

"With the red lights on in the Wheelhouse, it's hard to tell a red flashing light from a white flashing light," said the Mate, "Also, the red lines on the charts are hard to see. On the SD set you can see that there are islands ahead. We'll make a turn starboard in a few minutes and keep the islands on our port side. There will be a green flashing buoy on the port side that will mark the turning point," the Mate finished.

On the SD set another boat appeared to be coming up on us quickly from astern. I could see the two large blips of the freighters we passed at the lock. This vessel had passed them, and was coming up on us rapidly.

"That appears to be a Coast Guard cutter," the Mate remarked. Looking aft, I could see the lights approaching us, bobbing up and down. They were feeling the waves much more than we were. In the last few minutes the St Mary's river had changed. The waves were not that big, but they were choppy. A kind of betwixt and between condition that you could not even feel on a big ship, like the Gentry, but was much more noticeable on smaller boats. Looking astern again, I could see the blue and red flashing light.

"Five degrees rudder to port, Mr. Hall."

"Five degrees rudder to port, yes Sir," Pete replied. The ship eased over to port, allowing plenty of room for the Coast Guard cutter to pass. In a few minutes the Coast Guard cutter was up to our stern, off our starboard side. The Gentry was doing twelve knots. The Coast Guard cutter was doing twice that. Throwing up a bow wave and spray continually. As it passed us, I noticed it was rolling somewhat. Men were running fore and aft and a loud speaker was sounding. The Mate blew the whistle.

"Probably some kind of trouble up ahead," Don said. The Mate tuned the radio into the Coast Guard frequency. In a few minutes came a report that a barge had ran down a pleasure craft anchored at one of the islands up ahead. One small Coast Guard boat was there, but the pleasure craft had gone down immediately. More Coast Guard craft were coming in to look for survivors in the darkness.

"How long do you think a person in a life jacket could survive in this water, Mister McCracken?" Don asked.

"Ten or Fifteen minutes for most people. A real strong man might live half an hour," the Mate replied.

"Miss Strickland, a green buoy is coming up almost dead ahead."

"Yes, Sir. I can see it now," I replied.

"After we make the turn starboard, there will be a red buoy on the starboard. Then we will be on the right course for the main shipping lane, which incidentally is One-four-zero on the auto compass. Is that clear?" the Mate asked.

"Yes, Sir," I replied. When the flashing green light was about four hundred yards away, the Mate said-

"Mr. hall, steady as she goes, come around to one-four-zero."

"Steady as she goes to one-four-zero, yes Sir," Pete replied as he began turning the wheel slowly to the right.

When the ship stopped turning, I could see that we would pass the flashing buoy on our starboard side with plenty of room to spare. After a few minutes, I noticed that the wind had changed direction. It was coming from the southwest, our starboard side. The sky had become cloudy, no stars could be seen. This only added to the darkness up ahead. Not good for the Coast Guard, I thought. According to the chart, the island where the accident occurred was still several hours ahead. Our present course should take us well to the starboard of the area. The watch would be over in a few minutes. I said a silent prayer for those poor people.

I scanned the water ahead of us with my binoculars. Nothing but blackness. Not even a sea bird. Only an occasional white cap to break the choppy dark surface. The third officer and Mike, the Conveyorman, filling in as a wheelsman, came into the wheelhouse.

"Good evening, Andy," the Mate greeted the third officer as he handed him the log book.

"I heard you had an exciting evening," the third officer said to the Mate as he started to read the log book.

After the third officer signed it, the Mate said, "We've been receiving reports continually about the accident, but I haven't heard if there's any problem with traffic. I didn't want to bother the Coast Guard Station."

"I wouldn't bother them either," the third officer stated. "They would probably send a general message if there are any traffic problems,"

The third officer, Andy Botzum, was a nice guy and the youngest officer on the ship. He seemed likeable. He was the only officer on the ship who had any experience on ocean ships. He attended the Merchant Academy after high school. After a few years on the ocean, he came to the lakes. The other guys would kid him about getting sea sick on the ocean.

"I got Hal with night binoculars on lookout forward," the third officer said.

"Very well." the Mate replied as he reached down and opened a drawer under the chart table. He handed two manuals to me.

"You can study these manuals when you're off watch. One covers everything in the wheelhouse and the other covers the wheelsmans' duties," the Mate said.

"Thank you, sir," I replied taking the manuals. After being relieved at the wheelhouse watch, I headed down to my quarters to drop off the manuals. When I go to my quarters, I sat down on the bunk and briefly looked through the manuals. Everything seemed to be included in the manuals-buoys, signaling, charts, 'rules of the road', etc. This is going to take a while to learn, I thought. I decided to go to the galley and get something to eat before I went to bed. As I was walking aft, I met Ed the deckhand on watch.

"How's it going, Ed?" I asked.

"Not so great," Ed replied, "That slimey limey expects everyone to be standing at attention, polishing a valve or something. Too bad there aren't any sharks, gators, or poisonous water snakes in this lake."

"Well, the weather is supposed to get worse. Maybe that will keep him off the deck," I replied as I went on my way. I entered the after deckhouse and went down to the galley. I noticed that there was a lot of noise coming from the back of the galley.

"What will it be?" the steward asked. Looking over the menu, I told him that I would have the lasagna.

"What's the noise in back, Louie?" I asked.

"The Chief has the machinist and 'The Kid' working on the metal cabinets. They're beating the sheet metal with hammers. It's really annoying me," he replied as he dished up the Lasagna. He included the garlic bread and coffee without being told. I've got him trained, I thought.

"Thanks, Louie," I said and I headed to the crews mess. When I got to the crews mess, the second engineer, Hank, called me over to his table. Mister Ring was with him.

"Nick, this is Mister Ring, the ship surveyor," Hank said.

"I know, we met in the wheelhouse," I replied.

"Please, just call me Kenny," he said.

"Kenny is very interested in the nil-ductility temperature failure of the shackle," Hank said.

"Yes, I've never actually seen nil-ductility failure. I am surprised to see it at this high a temperature," the surveyor said.

"At any rate we'll be tied up in Cleveland for at least four days. The Coast Guard won't clear us to leave port until the repairs have been made and the lock installed. The Maritime Commission Inspector will have to come down from Detroit. That will involve a lot of time and paper work," Hank said.

"I think we might be able to get the repairs done in a day and wait for the certification when the ship gets back to Duluth," Mister Ring said.

"I doubt it," Hank said. "I don't think the Coast Guard will let us clear port until we're re-certified. Especially since there was an accident involving a serious injury to a crewman."

Mister Ring did not seem happy with what Hank had to say. He seem to droop even more then he had before. He excused himself by saying that he had work to do.

"Well, Hank you certainly know how to get on his good side," I wisecracked.

"If it were up to him and O'Blake, they would have everything fixed before we got into port. The Company and the Maritime Commission have agreed that no work is to be done until after the ship off loads in Cleveland. There will be a lot of VIPs on the dock when we get there. This could mean fines to shipyards, lawsuits, unhappy insurance companies, the whole deal. Four days might turn out to be conservative," Hank said.

"Well, I need a holiday anyways," I said.

"You might get one, I won't. The Captain and the Chief will have to stay on the ship. The Chief won't let me go if he can't," Hank said. I saw Earl come up behind Hank.

"May I join you?" he asked.

"Of course, Earl, have a seat," I said.

"Well, our guests decided to let you have a minutes peace afterall," Hank remarked.

"They decided to irritate the Captain for a while, so I let them get back to their fun," Earl said as he pulled out a chair and sat down at the table.

"Have you heard anything about Dixon yet?" Hank asked.

"No, the Coast Guard has the airways pretty well tied up after the accident up ahead, so I didn't want to try to break through. I'll give it a try later," Earl said.

"Aren't you going to get something to eat, Earl?" I asked.

"No, I ate already," Earl replied.

"I'm suppose to be on watch with you, four to eight A.M.," he added.

"I got to be going. Gotta' get some sleep," Hank said excusing himself.

"Catch you later, Hank," I said.

"Do you want to finish that card game?" I asked Earl.

"No, I better get some sleep. I've got a lot of things to do later," Earl replied.

"Who's going to take over your porter duties while you're on watch with me?" I asked.

"The Kid has no time in the union so they bumped him down to doing porter duties. Buster, the other new Oiler, will be doing deck watch for Dixon," Earl replied. I heard the Bosun summon Earl over the intercom.

"I'll catch you later, Nick," Earl said and he got up and left.

After finishing my lasagna, I went forward to my quarters. When I went through the door of the quarter deck, I saw the Bosun and Mister O'Blake in the passageway. When I got to the door of my quarters, the Bosun walked away and Mister O'Blake turned toward me.

"Good Evening, Miss—err I can't remember your name."

"Strickland, Nick Strickland," I replied.

"Yes, Miss Strickland. I've been wondering—you seem to know a lot about what goes on here. Have you noticed anything unusual going on lately?" He asked, adding, "This is only between you and me, of course."

"I'd say that the unloading boom going overboard and a man getting hurt is unusual for this ship," I said. "If you'll excuse me, I have to get some sleep."

I entered my quarters. I laid down on my bunk, and I looked at the wheelhouse manual. The first section was about radar plotting and Direction of Relative Motion Rules, or DRM. DRM rules for course change and speed change. I was thinking about the incident with the ferry earlier. I can never understand why a ship that has the whole lake to navigate on would choose a course that will take it on a collision course with us. I fell asleep. I dreamed of an old boy friend. Bill was laughing at me. I told him to get lost. He got in his car and drove off. I was onboard my old ship, the Giovanni. Bill came on the ship and tried to take me away. I punched him and he fell down. I told him I would really hurt him if he didn't go away. Then I dreamed about the secret admirer. The man that had been sending me letters for the last six months. I could never see him. Always a dark figure writing me letters, but never revealing himself. Sometimes I thought it was so high schoolish. At other times, I thought he might be some kind of stalker. Then I dreamed about being in Marblehead. My grandmother was lying on a funeral ship, sailing away into the lake. I kept calling for them to come back, so I could say "Good Bye" but they kept sailing on until they were out of sight.

I woke up to the alarm, it was three A.M. I turned on the light, and looked at the manuals. Basic radar plotting, how interesting, I thought. Putting the manual down, I went to get a cup of coffee in the night kitchen, forward. There was no one moving in the forward deck house, except the Captain and the men on duty. I got a cup of coffee and went back to my quarters. I picked up the manual and read until the bell for watch change sounded.

I went out on deck and looked around for Earl. I walked aft checking the cables and lines. I looked forward and saw one of the lights on the mast was out. When I got to the after deckhouse, I found the electrician and got a light bulb for the mast light. I met Earl on my way forward.

"Come on, Earl, let's change a light bulb," I said. Stopping at the jobox in the Crews hall, I got a safety belt and a short rope.

"I'll climb up the mast and change the bulb. Then I'll throw down the old bulb and you catch it," I said.

"Gotcha, Nick.", Earl said.

Putting the safety belt around the mast, I then attached it to my waist. I checked my tool belt and put on my gloves. I grabbed the rungs and began to climb the mast. I noticed that the lights were on over the chart room table. As I climbed higher, the wind seemed to be blowing harder. It must be the slipstream of the forward deckhouse moving through the air, I thought. When I reached the light, I tied one end of the short rope to the globe housing. I wrapped the rope around the mast so the housing could hang there when I took it off. I took a large screwdriver and removed the screws that held the globe housing. I lifted it off the base, and allowed it to hang against the mast. I unscrewed the bulb and tossed it down to Earl. To my surprise, I noticed the Mate was standing next to Earl. It's a good thing Earl caught that bulb, I thought. I screwed in the new bulb and replaced the globe housing. After finishing, I started to climb down the rungs.

"Miss Strickland!", the Mate called.

"Yes, Sir.", I replied.

"I want to see you in the Wheelhouse when you're finished."

"Very well, Sir" I replied.

When I got down to the deck, I unfastened the safety belt and put it back in the equipment box.

"Well, I better go see what the Mate wants," I said.

"You want me to come with you?" Earl asked.

"No, I better go alone. You take the deck watch until I get back," I replied. I went up the steel stairway and knocked on the rear door of the Wheelhouse.

"Enter," the Mate said.

"You wanted to see me, Sir?" I asked.

"Yes, Miss Strickland. We usually have two people climb the mast. A deckhand is usually accompanied by an electrician for that task," the Mate stated.

"I'm aware of the usual procedure, Sir. I checked with the electrician, he was not available. Also, the regulations state that one person can go up the mast alone, provided that there is someone on the deck to assist them. I don't know if you are aware of it, but I am a certified rigger, Sir.", I said.

"I'm aware of your certification, Miss Strickland. And I know about the regulations. I don't know if tossing light bulbs around is permissible. Otherwise, I just want to be sure that you understand the procedures on this ship," the Mate said.

"Yes, Sir.", I replied.

"Very well, you may go now.", he said.

I turned and left the Wheelhouse. When I got back to the spar deck, Earl remarked: "You and 'Gilligan' looked real cozy up there in the chart room."

"That's real pathetic, Earl." I shot back jokingly.

"Some guys say that they know that McCracken and you have something going on," Earl said, smiling deviously.

"Well, McCracken and I don't know anything about it," I said surprised.

"You know how the guys gossip. You can't pay any attention to what is said.", I added.

"I didn't think so," Earl said.

As we made our way aft, I pointed out to Earl that three lights were out at the railing.

"We'll go and get some bulbs from the electrician and change them in a few minutes," I said.

"I thought you would like to know, the Captain made a ship to shore call to the hospital and talked to Dixon for a few minutes," Earl said.

"How's he doing?" I asked.

"They haven't told him anything yet for sure. I guess he's the same as he was," Earl replied.

"I hope everything works out okay," I said.

"I wonder how things worked out in that accident in the islands? I was asleep when we passed that area," I added.

"I heard that one man was pulled up immediately after the collision. The Coast Guard thinks that everyone else went down. No more bodies have been found," Earl replied.

We entered the after deckhouse and went to the electrician's shop. I saw the electrician with Mister O'Blake and Mister Ring. Mister O'Blake turned around and his face fell apart in a look that said-'What the hell are you doing here'.

"Excuse me, Carl. Do you have any of those slim light bulbs for the railing lights?" I asked.

"I think so. I'll have to unlock the safety cabinet. Excuse me, Gentlemen," Carl said.

Earl and I followed Carl down the steps and through the door to the after equipment locker.

"Don't you have those bulbs in the shop cabinet?", I asked.

"Yes," Carl replied, "but I wanted to get away from those two jokers. They really aggravate me."

"I know what you mean. They were questioning me earlier. I told them that the only unusual thing on this ship was them," I said.

"I bet they liked that real well," Carl replied.

"I don't think that they will be asking me anything again," I said.

"Here's your bulbs, Nick.", Carl said, handing me three light bulbs.

"Thank you, Carl.", I said, taking them.

"I'll see you later."

Earl and I went back the way we came but we didn't see O'Blake or Ring anywhere.

"Our guests seem to come and go as the spirit moves them," I said to Earl.

"As the spirits move them, more likely," Earl said.

"How do you mean, Earl?" I asked.

"When I was cleaning his quarters, I accidently opened his suitcase and found a couple bottles of Gin and Vermouth," Earl confided.

"It sounds like he likes a Martini night cap before going to bed," I said. "Rules are rules. No one is suppose to have booze on this ship. It's not a cruise ship for God's sake," Earl said, sounding a little irritated.

"Have you told anybody else, yet?" I asked.

"Not yet. I was thinking of slipping an anonymous note to the Captain," Earl replied.

"Yeah, let the Captain handle it," I said.

We were at the burned out light, so I took my screwdriver and removed the screws that held the guard and the glass cover. I unscrewed the light bulb and put another one in. I put the glass cover and the guard over the bulb, then tightened down the four screws.

"Well, there's that one. Do you want to do the other two?" I asked, holding the screw driver out to Earl.

"I guess so," Earl said, taking the screw driver and heading over to the port side where the other burned out lights were located. Earl changed the first light, then the second one, without a hitch.

"Very good, Earl. Of course, it's a little more difficult when the waves are coming over the deck," I said as Earl handed me my screw driver. "Let's check the hatch covers."

I explained to Earl about the regulations for hatch covers as we walked around checking the clamps.

"If the hatches are wood, the wood must be at least two and three eighths inches thick. The hatches must be covered with two layers of number six canvas. Since our hatches are steel, you will probably never need to know that, except for the test. These hatches are held by the clamps as you can see. A single piece of half inch boiler plate with channel iron welded to the bottom side."

I was interrupted by the sound of the bell for the watch change.

"Well, that's it for now," I said, adding—"Let's go forward and sign the clip board, then head aft and get some breakfast."

"Okay," replied Earl.

We walked forward to the deckhouse and I handed the clipboard to Earl. I let him make the notations for the work done on the watch. Earl handed the clipboard to Ed, he looked at it for a minute and signed it.

"Okay, folks I'll take it from here."

"Catch you later, Ed" I said and headed for after deck house with Earl.

"I heard the weather's not going to be too bad for a few days, Nick.", Earl said.

"It's hard to tell, Earl. A storm can kick up in a 'New York' minute," I replied.

"I'm sure the television will be on. Maybe we can catch the early news," Earl said.

"I want to get some breakfast first," I replied.

We entered the after deckhouse and went down to the galley. John, the steward was on duty.

"Well, Miss Particular, the special this morning is ham and eggs," he said. "Very funny, John. Don't you have anything kosher this morning?"

"Steak and eggs for Miss Particular," John answered.

"That sounds good, John.", I said. The steward put the food on my tray, then turned to Earl.

"What can I do for you, partner?"

"I'll have the ham and eggs," Earl replied.

"Coming right up," the Steward replied. As he put the food on Earl's tray, he remarked, "You know if I wanted to put up with a difficult woman, I could have stayed at home this season."

I ignored the remark and headed for the crew's mess. I sat down and Earl sat down. He passed me the butter for my toast.

"Well, what are you going to do when the season ends?" I asked Earl.

"Probably get drunk," he replied.

"Everybody gets drunk at the party," I said, "I mean when you get home?"

"Oh, I've gotta' turn the little farm into a paying business. Gotta' plant some corn and get some milking cows," Earl answered.

"That sounds interesting," I replied.

"Are you going back to Alliance?", Earl asked.

"I'll be back there alot. I'll arrange to take my last two courses as individual study. I moved into my Grandmother's house in Sandusky. I'll spend most of the winter there," I replied.

"Is that a big house in Sandusky?" Earl asked.

"Actually, it's not really in Sandusky, it's in Marblehead. It's a small two story cottage. They call them three-quarter cape cods."

"That sounds cozy," Earl replied.

"Yes, Grandmother kept the house in very good shape and all her furniture is still there. I left everything as she had it," I explained.

"The Mate lives in Sandusky somewhere, doesn't he?" Earl asked.

"I heard him say that he does, but I am not sure where," I replied, hiding the fact that I had known the Mate's son when I was a child.

"When we get done down here, let's watch the TV. Maybe we can catch the Football scores," Earl suggested.

"That sounds good, Earl. Maybe my alma mater, Mount Union, played this weekend. They've been undefeated so far," I said.

"My brother Joe is a janitor at Mount Union. Did you know him?", Earl asked.

"No, there were so many in the four years I was there. I really didn't know that many of the maintenance staff."

When we finished our breakfast, we headed for the television in the recreation room. There were four guys at the TV, Pete, The Kid, the Oiler, and the Electrician, Carl.

"Hey guys, can we watch the sports segment?", I asked.

"Well, I don't know Nick. We were just getting into the cartoons, when you so rudely interrupted us," Pete wisecracked.

"Well, put your intellect on hold for a few minutes, until we catch the football scores." I shot back as Carl changed the channel. The guys whistled and booed as the professional scores were shown.

"Hey, Nick what team did you want?" the Oiler asked.

"Mount Union," I replied.

"The college scores are coming up," Carl said.

"Why do you like, Mount Union?" the Kid asked.

"That's the school I went to," I replied.

"My son goes to Baldwin-Wallace," Pete said.

"He does not, he flunked out?", the Oiler retorted. When the scores came up, Mount Union had narrowly lost to Baldwin-Wallace. Pete and The Kid began to laugh.

"Ha, ha, loser, loser" Pete chortled.

"Settle down, Pete. I don't want to have to hurt you," I jokingly shot back. "Well that's not true. I would like to hurt you, but my religion forbids it." I continued.

"Yeah, the church of latter day losers, no doubt," Pete wisecracked.

"Come on Earl, let's let Pete get back to his cartoons," I said as I got up and turned to leave.

"Mount Union losing to Baldwin-Wallace, what a bummer.", I said when we got back out on deck.

"When Mount Union loses to a school like B-W, it's just a mistake," Earl replied.

"You want to go to the Observation Room and play some cards?" Earl asked.

"Do you think the Officers would mind?" I asked.

"No, I read up there all the time. The only time the Officers sleep up there is in stormy weather. As long as we keep quiet, no one will say anything.", Earl replied.

We played Gin Rummy for a half an hour. Only the Chief and the First Mate came in to get coffee while we were there. As they passed our table, the Mate stopped and turned to me.

"Miss Strickland, we'll be getting mail delivery from the Westcott on your next watch. I have some papers and payroll forms in the lock box that have to be sent out.", the Mate said.

"Yes Sir, I'll be sure the box goes in the bag," I replied.

"Very good, Miss Strickland," the Mate said and he turned and walked out with the Chief.

"Well, another thing for us to do, Earl" I said trying to act like I wasn't excited.

"Are you expecting anything in the mail, Earl?" I asked. Suddenly realizing that I was prying when I saw the look on his face.

"No, I never get anything except bad news. Usually I hope that I won't get any mail," Earl replied.

"Well, I'm gonna hit the sack," I said.

"Okay, see you later," Earl said.

I took the short cut to my quarters. Fortunately I did not see Mister O'Blake. He must be a late riser, I thought. When I got to my quarters, I put the letter to my secret admirer in a little blue envelope and put a stamp on it. I addressed it to the post office box number in Detroit, that the mysterious letter writer had given me. I also had another letter to a lawyer in Sandusky. My grandmother's lawyer. In the letter, I instructed him to pay the taxes with the checks I had left him. I put the letters back in my travel case and laid down on my bunk. I started thinking about Mount Union College. Remembering how pretty it looked in the spring and summertime. All I have now is coffee cups and sweat shirts to remind me of those days. Just boring stories that no body wants to hear. I fell asleep and dreamed. I was riding my Harley Sportster down in Daytona Beach during Bike Week. There were millions of motorcycles there. I was riding on the beach, the wind in my hair, the salt spray in my face. The beach seemed to go on for ever, I wondered when it would end . . .

I woke up and looked at the clock, it was twelve thirty P.M. I read the manual for a little while, then I fell back to sleep. The alarm woke me at three o'clock. I got dressed and headed aft to get some dinner. On the way aft I ran into Smitty, the first watch deckhand.

"What say.", Smitty called out.

"Keeping out of mischief," I replied.

Smitty came over to where I was.

"I heard that Dixon was up and walking around today. He's wearing some kind of neck brace, but the doctors think that he'll be okay next season."

"That's good, I'm glad to hear that," I said relieved.

"There's more. The doctor said that if Earl hadn't taken care of him and immobilized his neck, he could have been a lot worse. Of course, there'll be the usual Workmens Compensation hassle but I think 'ol Dixon is gonna' make out okay.", Smitty finished.

"Great, that's good news," I said, adding—"I'd like to work with him next season."

"Catch you later," Smitty said and headed forward. I entered the deckhouse and went down to the galley.

Louie the Steward greeted me.

"What'll it be today, Nick?"

"Are those Stuffed Peppers any good?" I asked.

"Of course, they're good, I made them. I always make good Stuffed Peppers. John has me make them because I do the best. The best on the Lakes.", Louie replied.

"Okay, stop with the commercial. I'll take one, some French Bread, and some coffee, too.", I said.

"That British Dude was in here running his mouth. I can't cook British style. Hell, I didn't know 'freakin' British' was two words until I was in high school," Louie stated in a half serious tone as he put the food on the plate.

"Yeah, I know what you mean. The next time he asks me anything, I'm going to tell him to ask the Captain. I'm not the damn 'answer man'. I'll catch you later, Louie.", I said as I headed for the crew's mess.

I did not see anyone in there, except for the Third Officer Andy. I went over to his table.

"May I sit here?" I asked.

"Sure," Andy replied. I sat down and began to eat.

"How are things going, Nick?" Andy asked.

"Not too bad. I can't complain. Will you tell your driver to take it easy through the 'speed bumps'."

"Yes, the waves are getting worse but we'll be in the Saint Clair soon." he replied.

"What are you doing up at this hour?" I asked.

"I was studying for the First mate's test. I was thinking about taking the exams over the winter.", he replied.

"You and the Mate are like 'sharks smelling blood' since the Captain's retiring.", I joked.

"I don't know about that 'Miss Wheelsman'. Maybe we could ask Mister McCracken. He said that he would be joining me-or rather us.", Andy countered.

"I better keep my 'big mouth' closed or I'll be a wheelsman for the garbage barge." I said adding—"Where are you taking the test?"

"I think I'll take it in Detroit. I live in Toledo, so it won't be far for me to drive."

"I'll bet your wife isn't going to like you being away for a week. Since you're gone nine months as it is anyway.", I said.

"Yes, Eileen and the Girls won't like it one bit, I'm sure," Andy replied. "How old are your girls now?" I asked.

"Three and almost five, now," Andy answered. "I got a picture of them that Eileen had sent me," he said as he took out his wallet, and removed the pictures without even looking down. He's done that a lot, I thought. He showed me a picture of two little girls in white dresses. They looked so happy in the picture. As I looked at it, I got a strange feeling in my stomach. I wished that I had had a sister to play with when I was young. I handed the picture back to him before my emotions could take a hold of me.

"It looks like you've got a very nice family there, Andy.", I said.

"Yes, they're my pride and joy," he replied.

"Do you have a family, Nick?" he asked.

One friend is as good as a thousand enemies, I thought.

"No, I had a Grandmother in Marblehead. She died last year.", I said.

"I'm sorry to hear that. Was she on your mother or father's side?"

"My father's mother. She raised me most of the time as I was growing up. I understand that my parents are still alive, but their whereabouts are unknown to me," I replied. A stock answer I had used several times, like an actor saying a line without emotion or feeling.

"My mother's still alive, but my father died last year. He was in the Navy. He was from Lorain. He knew Admiral King's family. He wanted me in the Navy, but I wanted the Merchant Marine. He didn't hold that against me. He did every thing for me. Got me in the Academy. A good berth on a ship, and he got me into this outfit. He died while I was away. I guess I never did anything for him," Andy said.

I saw the Mate and Mister O'Blake come our way. I looked at them and Andy looked that way.

"Please join us, Gentlemen," Andy said as we stood up.

"I hope I'm not interrupting you," Mister O'Blake said.

"Not at all, sir." Andy replied.

I noticed that O'Blake seems to be testing the Mate's patience as well.

"I have to be going, Gentlemen," I said as I picked up my plate.

"Oh, by the way Miss Strickland. I'd like to see you in my quarters concerning something we talked about earlier." Mister O'Blake said.

"I'm sorry, sir. It is not permissible for me to be in anyone's quarters on this ship. It would be more appropriate to direct any questions concerning the ship's operations to the Captain or the Deck Officers." I stated politely as I sat the plate in the bin.

"Good Day, Gentlemen," I said and I turned and left.

When I got out on deck, I looked around for Earl but I did not see him. I headed forward to check the clipboard, since the first watch was nearly over. I could see land forward of us. We would be out of the lake and in Saint Clair River, when we passed under the Blue water bridge. No waves there, thank goodness. The ship was starting to roll a little bit in the choppy sea. I entered the forward deckhouse and saw Smitty. He handed me the clip board and I looked at it and signed it.

"Just the repair of the starboard railing cable?" I asked.

"Yes," Smitty replied.

"Have you seen Earl?", I asked.

"No, I haven't seen him since the beginning of the watch."

"Okay, I got it now. We'll see you later, Smitty."

"Okay," Smitty said, and he headed aft.

I went to my quarters and got my letters and stuck them in the big pockets of my parka. I went out on deck and looked around for Earl again, but he was not around anywhere. I made my way aft checking the lights, cables, and hatches. Everything was shipshape. When I got to the after deckhouse, I ran into the Mate.

"I want you to check the port side davits. The cables look rusty. Inspect them. If they don't need replaced, then oil them and grease the fittings. I'm going forward to collect the mail," the Mate stated.

"Sir, I have some mail that has to go out," I said pulling the two letters from the pocket of my coat.

"Very well," said the Mate, looking at the letters.

"I'll see that these get to where they're going."

"Thank you, Sir," I said. I went to the port side davits and checked the cables. The cables were in good shape. There was only a few rusty places on them. I went to the Machinist to get an oil can, grease gun and rags. I asked the Machinist if he has seen Earl. He had not. I went back to the davits. Taking the grease gun, I greased all the fittings and sheaves. Then took a rag and oil can, and oiled the cables. I dropped a rag and the wind blew it into the lake. I hope that rag doesn't have the ship's name on it, I thought. When I finished, I put the grease gun and oil can in the machine shop. I put the oily rags in the waste drum. When I went back out on deck, I heard a slight rattling sound coming from the roof of the aft deckhouse. I thought that one of the little cables that hold the pole for the weather instruments, may be loose, so I climbed the ladder and walked around checking the cables. They seemed tight.

I saw that the ship was entering the Saint Clair River, so I decided to get back on deck. As I climbed down the ladder backwards, I bumped into someone. Turning around abruptly, I saw Earl standing behind me.

His presence took me by surprise, and without thinking I blurted out: "WHERE IN THE HELL WERE YOU? YOU KNOW WHEN THIS WATCH STARTS, AND WHERE YOU'RE SUPPOSE TO BE!"

Earl looked at me perplexed, and stated as he backed away.

"I'm sorry, Nick. I over slept. The Kid messed things up and I had to put everything right before I went to bed."

I let my anger get the best of me. After all I had no right to reprimand Earl just because I was training him as a deckhand. Earl is technically the ship's porter, but after ten years of service it was time for a change.

"I'm sorry, Earl. I had no right to give you hell. I was able to handle it anyway."

Earl poured coffee from his thermos and handed it to me.

"Here, your apology is accepted. I'll try harder next time," he said as he sat down beside me.

"Earl, you are doing a good job. Let's not blow it by missing assigned watches. As we both know, the Captain and the First Mate are in no mood for screw ups," I remarked as I got up to take out a cigarette.

"The First Mate thinks that I sabotaged the unloading boom. He's screwed me out of chances for promotions. The man hates my guts and vows to have me fired one way or another," Earl stated as he was kicking taconite pellets about.

"Nonsense, you're just being paranoid. Come on, we better get to work before we both find both of our rear ends terminated," I said.

As we made our way forward, I explained to Earl about the things that were on the test. When we had almost reached the forward deckhouse, the beeper on my radio went off. I pulled the radio from my belt. Pushing the receiver button, I answered "Yes".

"Westcott's due, port side. ETA about thirty minutes!" responded a voice.

"Copy that, over." I replied, then hooked the radio back on my belt.

"Come on, Earl it's mail call," I remarked as we headed for the crew's hall to get the out going mail.

The J. W. Westcott II serves the Great Lakes freighters as mail carrier. It not only delivers the mail, but also personal messages and packages. I was anticipating a letter from a 'Secret Admirer'. For the last six months, we have been corresponding. He had informed me about the deckhand position on the S.S. Gentry, which I had applied for and accepted with reservation. He's the only man who understands my desire to stay in the merchant service. He was a man I wanted to know more about.

I instructed Earl to go to the mail room to get the out going mail. Informing him that if it does not go out on this run, we might not get our pay checks on time. I was impressed with Earl's enthusiasm when pay checks were mentioned. He quickly returned with a large canvas bag slung over his shoulders. He sat the bag down next to the railing. Meanwhile, I was scanning the area to see if we could see the boat.

"You have to be sure that this is tied tight and that you have enough line for about a thirty foot drop. We don't want to drop this in the river. It might piss off a lot of people," I explained as I tied the rope. Earl watched intently, then he made sure that the rope was secure. "There it's ready," he stated as he brushed his hands on his overalls.

"No, it's not. We need the pay roll slips and Dixon's Workmen Compensation forms. They are in a metal lock box stamped with the company's name and address. The First Mate keeps the box on his desk. You'll need to go to his quarters to retrieve it. We need to hurry, because if those forms don't go this trip then there might be problems," I explained as I watched for the Westcott through my binoculars.

Earl reached for his belt, pulling off a set of keys. Thumbing the keys nervously until he found the one he needed.

Handing the key to me, he said: "I won't go in there!" Taking the keys from him and not waiting for an explanation, I headed to portside door and down the passageway to the Mate's quarters. Inserting the key into the lock, I unlocked the door and pushed it open. The light was already on. Quickly surveying the room, I did not see the lock box in plain sight, anywhere. I looked in the passageway, to see if anybody was out there who could get the Mate, but I saw no one. I went back to the Mate's quarters to look around. The drawers of the wooden desk were too small to hold the box. I noticed a small sea chest under the Mate's bunk. I got down and grabbed the chest by its' handle and started to pull it from under the bunk.

"An unusual position to find you in, Miss Strickland!" the Mate exclaimed.

Startled and jumping up, I said nervously, "I was looking for the lock box."

The Mate responded, "I sent it down with the Bosun already. The guys would really like to hear that you were down on your hands and knees in my quarters. Since it's my quarters, we better not let this get out, Miss Strickland."

"Yes, Sir. You don't have to be so condescending, Sir. It is innocent enough as it is," I remarked as I turned and walked out the door. When I got back to Earl, he was re-tying the sack.

"You got the lock box shipshape, Earl?"

"Yes, Sir", he said jokingly as we both chuckled at his reply.

"Okay, fasten the line. The Westcott will be here any minute," I said as I took my binoculars and put them to my eyes.

"What's the problem with you going into the Mate's quarters? You're granted access to everyone's quarters, but mine." I asked as I continued to survey our surroundings with the binoculars.

Earl stopped shuffling his feet. "I worked on the Vic . . . I mean as a crew member on the Victory," Earl stated as he continued to look down, placing his hands in the pockets of his coveralls. "They hired me because I was exceptionally strong, not for my brains. I got the job because of who I knew, not for what I was capable of!" Earl did not remove his eyes from the deck.

"What is your problem with our First Mate? In other words, Why do you think that he is 'out to get you'?" I questioned as I lit a cigarette and sat down on a cargo hatch.

"The Mate of the Victory accused me of taking the lock box. As you know, I would not take anything that was not mine. But since I was, in his words, a 'stupid hillbilly hick'. And because I came from a farming family 'from down in the sticks'. He believed that I was the one responsible for taking it. There was a confrontation. I hit him and knocked him out. As a result, he had me fired and vowed to have me 'black balled' from the merchant service." By this time, Earl was shaking. It looked like to me that he was ready to cry.

"You're here now," I said as I got up to check for the Westcott.

"After they let me go, it was found out that the Third Officer, McCracken, was at fault. He had mis-placed the lock box. The Captain found it under a pile of charts. To cover his own ass, he wrote a recommendation," Earl said in a pitiful tone.

"I think that there's more to it than that, Earl. I don't want to pry. I don't think that he's holding any grudges, so why should you. It sounds like to me, that you have a low opinion about yourself. Come on, Dude, get a grip," I said as I searched for the Westcott with binoculars.

The Saint Clair is a very wide river. Up ahead, I looked for a small boat. It would not be easy to see in traffic. Astern of the nearest ship, I spotted her. A forty-five foot pilot boat with a white wheelhouse. She came across our bow to our port side and turned on a parallel course. The Gentry maintained the river speed as the Westcott pulled along side and bumped us. I handed the line to Earl and picked up the sack and threw it so that it swung down on the deck of the Westcott. My estimation of the rope length was perfect, causing the sack to drop right at the feet of the crewman. He untied the sack and quickly tied the rope to another sack.

"Haul away, Earl" I said, and Earl quickly pulled the sack up to our deck. I untied the rope and made a small coil of the last twenty feet and threw it back down to the Westcott.

"Somebody has some laundry," I said as the crewman on the Westcott secured the rope to a large bundle.

The crewman waved, and I told Earl to haul away. When we got the bundle on deck, the Westcott blew its whistle and backed away as the Gentry blew her whistle.

"Let's carry this stuff to the crew's hall," I said to Earl.

Earl grabbed the bundle and I grabbed the mail bag, we headed for the Crew's hall. The Bosun was waiting in there. He told us to put the mail on the big table. It was his job to distribute the mail to the crew.

"It looks like somebody's got some laundry," I said.

"Several people, in fact," the Bosun remarked looking at the tags.

"Don't steal my fruitcake," Earl wisecracked.

The Bosun gave him a dirty look. It was a joke on the ship that the Bosun stole the fruitcakes. It originated from an incident twenty years ago when a Bosun mistakenly took someone's fruitcake. We turned to leave, I said, "let's check forward, Earl."

We came out on the quarter deck and walked around the bow, checking the cables and the bulwark fittings. Standing at the bow and looking forward, I looked at Detroit in the darkness.

"We'll be out of Detroit soon."

"Too bad, I know a lot of good places in Detroit," Earl replied. I took off my hard hat and shook my head in a very cool wind. Allowing my hair to hang down, I put my hat back on.

"There's nothing for me in Detroit," I said adding," I can't wait to get back to Sandusky, though."

I looked up at the Wheelhouse, and I saw the Mate's face in the window.

"Well, we better be making our rounds, before your 'buddy' McCracken blows his gaskets," I said.

"He ain't my buddy. I don't have many friends on this ship. You're about the only one that doesn't put me down and accepts me for who I am," Earl said.

"There's nothing wrong with where you came from or who you are, Earl. I've learned that my biggest enemy in life is myself. I had to face up to that fact, and make things happen for myself," I said. As we headed aft, I saw Mister O'Blake and Mister Ring heading forward.

"They're probably going to check if they got any mail," I said half jokingly.

"Did you notice any booze bottles in the bundle, Earl?"

We went aft and I showed Earl where I had greased the davits and oiled the cables. We checked the canvases on the life boats and the equipment.

"On watch, a deckhand should have a flare gun, or a flashlight. You will have need of those if you fall overboard. If Dixon had gone overboard, he probably would have been a 'goner'. As injured as he was, he wouldn't have been able to use his flare gun. A man would not live very long in freezing water as it is," I explained. "Fortunately, we are not required to go out on deck when the waves are really bad. We can sit in the forward and aft deckhouse and watch out for other ships, rocks and the like."

"I always use the catwalk under the cargo holds to go fore and aft when the waves are bad," Earl said.

"I try not to go down there if I can help it. Sometimes there are rats down there," I stated.

I looked at my watch, it was nearly eight o'clock.

"Let's go forward. You can fill in the clipboard Earl," I said as we began to walk forward.

A cold sleet began. The wind was blowing it right in our faces.

"We managed to stay relatively dry, now we get it in the end," I complained.

"At least there aren't any thirty foot waves," Earl said. When we got to the forward deckhouse, I handed the clip board to Earl. He filled in the work done on the watch, and we waited for Ed. The watch bell sounded and a minute later Ed greeted us.

"Good Evening, People."

"Hi, Ed" I replied. Ed looked at the clipboard.

"Are you keeping Earl out of trouble?" Ed asked jokingly.

"It's a tough job, but somebody's got to do it," I replied with a smile.

"Okay, everything looks good, we'll see you guys later," Ed said and left.

"Well, Earl let's go up and collect our mail," I said.

We went up to the observation room. Half the crew was in there and everybody was talking.

"Hey, Nick where's my mail!" Pete shouted.

"I threw it in the river," I shot back.

"He didn't get any mail. Nobody loves him." John, the Steward said.

"This ship is the only place where the bill collectors and 'loan sharks' can't get to him," Buster, the Oiler said.

"You guys pipe down for a minute, and I'll get your mail!" the Bosun shouted. The room became quiet.

"Nick, here's your mail," the Bosun said.

"Ladies before Gentlemen," Pete sneered.

"Brains before ugly," I shot back as the Bosun handed me three envelopes and a magazine.

"Hey Nick, Joe wants to see your 'Play Girl' when you're done with it," Mark the other Electrician shouted.

"Earl, I'll wait until you get your mail, and we'll go aft to get some coffee." In a few minutes, the Bosun called out "Earl Franklin". Earl pushed his way through the crowd silently and took the single envelope.

"Well, let's get going, Nick," Earl said when he came back.

"Let's go down to my quarters so I can drop these off," I suggested.

"Whatever you say," Earl replied as we headed out the door.

I looked at the envelopes and saw that one was from Grandmother's lawyer. One from a former ship mate on the Giovanni, and the last one was from my 'secret admirer'. I put the letters and the motorcycle magazine in my travel case.

"What did you get, Earl?" I said as I closed the door behind me.

"I just got a letter from a lawyer," Earl said.

I decided to drop the subject, though curiosity had me wondering if it concerned the farm trouble that Earl had spoke of earlier in the season.

As we headed aft, I saw the Captain and our guests walking forward.

"Those guys seem to be really bugging the Captain," I said.

"Yeah, maybe our guests want to stop off in Detroit and get some booze. I noticed that he was getting low," Earl remarked.

"You should show the Captain your 'Ratwalk'. I'm sure that our guests wouldn't be interested in going down there," I said in a semi-serious tone. As we entered the deckhouse, we ran into the Chief.

"Hey, Chief what's going on?" I asked.

"The 'Little Brit' is calling another meeting. We have a meeting at least twice a day," the Chief replied adding,

"Whenever the obnoxious little twit doesn't get his way, he calls another meeting."

"Maybe he's trying to wear you down," I suggested.

"The only thing he's wearing down is the Captain's patience," the Chief replied.

"He's already told him that we've had enough meetings and that we have other duties to attend to."

"Just out of curiosity, who's going to be at the meeting?" I asked.

"O'Blake, Ring, the Captain, First Mate, Third Officer, and myself," the Chief replied.

"I hate to say this Chief, but it's better you than me," I said.

"I'll see that you get invited to the next one," he remarked as he went through the door.

We went down to the galley, got a cup of coffee and a doughnut and went to the recreation room. We saw Don, the wheelsman and decided to join him.

"Hi, Don" I said.

"Hello Lass, why don't you two join me," Don said.

We sat down and started playing cards with Don.

"Well, what's on the top these days?" he asked.

"Your British friend and his lackey seem to be bugging the hell out of the officers on this ship," I remarked.

"Ach so, the little dickens is up to it again is he," Don replied.

"Can't he see that the Captain is not a man to be intimidated like that?" I asked.

"He can't help it, he's a Brit. It's bred into them to think that they are the 'masters of the whole bloody world'. They have a special breed of short, fat, obnoxious twit that they send abroad to muck up the rest of the world. They've been doing it to Ireland for years. Always the same type," Don replied.

"You think that it's a deliberate plan, then," I said laughingly.

"Sure, you're Jewish. You know how the British voted for a U.N. resolution to establish a Jewish state in Palestine. Then they did everything they could to subvert and destroy the establishment of Isreal. Kept the Jews out, armed the Arabs. They've been doing the same thing in Ireland for centuries. Always promising to leave, and always staying on. The army in Ireland should drive the bastards out of Northern Ireland for good. Unfortunately, we Irish are peace-loving people. Much the pity," Don said.

"Louie said that he didn't know that 'damn british' was two words until he was in high school," I said.

"I don't know it yet," Don replied.

"At any rate, we'll be rid of our guest in another day. What do you have for cards, Earl?" I asked.

"Full boat, Jacks and Sixes," Earl replied.

"That beats me," I said throwing my cards in the middle of the table.

"I'm out, too. I have to be going people. See you soon," Don said as he got up, then he left.

"You want to play another hand, Earl?" I asked.

"No, I better get some sleep. I'll see you on the next watch," Earl said.

"I'll walk forward with you," I said.

As we walked forward, we could see the lights of America on the starboard side and the lights of Canada on the port side.

"It looks pretty in the dark, doesn't it?" I asked.

"Yeah, too bad we ain't stopping," Earl replied.

"If we stop now, most of you guys would be 'lit' all the way to Cleveland," I said smiling.

"Yeah, life is great when you can't feel no pain," Earl replied.

"I'm going up to my quarters, Earl. Catch you later," I said.

As I was walking down the passageway to my quarters, I saw Mister O'Blake coming the other way, not looking happy. That wasn't a very long meeting, I thought. Fortunately, he did not even try to talk to me, so I entered my quarters undisturbed.

I opened my travel case, removed the letters, and laid down on my bunk. I decided to read the letter from my 'secret admirer' first. I opened the envelope, removed the letter and read:

Dearest Nick,

I was so excited when I received your last letter. You don't know how much it means when you write me. I am absolutely serious when I say that I am in love with you. I don't mind it at all when you ask me about my love for you.

For a few months, I thought it might be just an infatuation, but I am sure now that it is really love. I have a picture of you that I took when you weren't aware of it. I'm sorry that I did that, but I didn't want you to know. I know that you've been hurt by men before and I wouldn't hurt you for the world.

I have a house near the water. I am not married. I have a son about your age, but I haven't seen him in awhile. I have no problem with your religion. I am Catholic, but I usually don't go to church. I just got out of the habit, being on the Lakes nine months a year. I was happy to hear that you didn't think that the differences in our ages would be a problem. I hope that someday soon, I can tell you who I am. You're a very intelligent person, so I'm afraid that you may find out before I'm ready.

I'm glad you got a position on the Gentry. That's a good ship. I know the Captain and some of the crew. Just behave yourself and you won't have any problems. I know that you'll behave yourself, you always do. I know I sound silly. I get all mixed up in my head when I think about you. I have to look at your picture and I feel happy again. I have to be going. Our ship is about ready to leave Duluth. Take care of yourself. I'll write you again soon.

With Love,
Your Admirer.

I read the letter three times. I was impressed with his straight forward, honest way of writing. I was convinced of his sincerity. A bull shitter can not sound sincere. They can try, but you can see through it every time. This guy will be here for the long haul, I was sure of that. Next, I read the letter from my lawyer. He reminded me again, that the taxes on Grandmother's house were due in January. He requested to see me in that month. I put that letter away and opened the letter from my former shipmate and good friend, Lukesia. I was happy to read about her good news as well. I was not surprised to find out that Luke' and Dante were planning to be married.

Although she had swore that no man was good enough to give up her job for. I had seen it coming for a long time. Lukesia had always talked about how 'fine' she thought Dante was. He would seem be in a daze whenever she was present. Both are very intelligent, educated, and have a lot of love for each other. Lukesia's father was an African immigrant from Kenya. But she, like her fiance Dante, is Canadian-born. Both Dante's father and grandfather had worked on the Great Lakes merchant service.

That Lukesia, always good for a laugh, I thought as I put the letters away. I laid down on my bunk, closed my eyes and thought about the old times on the Giovanni. Luke and I were the only women on the ship and we had to stick up for ourselves. The guys were always trying to get in our pants. I drifted off to sleep, and dreamed:

> I was a little girl. It was summer. I had been left at my Grandmother's cottage by my parents. My parents were alcoholics, all they did was fight. When they got tired of fighting each other they would turn on me. It seemed that they fought with each other every day. My father would throw things and my mother would throw things at him. When hardly anything remained of the furniture, they would throw beer and whisky bottles. I was glad to be at Grandmother's cottage. It was so quiet up there and I did not have to cower in the attic. I was swinging on the swings in the little park. Tommy McCracken came over and sat on the swing next to me. He wanted to play pirates. We got off the swings and ran down to the beach, picking up sticks to use as sailor cutlasses. We ran up to the big tree in Grandmother's front yard. There was a rope ladder that went up to the tree house. We climbed up to the tree house and started to play pirates. Tommy was trying to hold me at sword point and make me walk the plank. I jumped out of the tree house and started to run. I heard Tommy scream. I turned around and saw him lying on his back, hollering. My Grandmother came and picked Tommy up and carried him home. I was sitting on Grandmother's front porch, crying because Tommy broke his arm.

> I woke up. I went to the small bathroom, washed my face and got a drink of water. I went back to bed and slept until the alarm clock rang at three-thirty A.M.

CHAPTER 2

More foul Weather Ahead

I could hear the rain against the steel superstructure of the deck house. The ship was rolling somewhat, not real bad, but a definite roll. The ship has passed through the Detroit River and had entered Lake Erie. A stormy Lake Erie is as miserable as any lake can get. As I put on my parka, I decided to forget the rain gear, and go aft via the 'ratwalk' below deck. As I left my quarters, I ran into the Bosun in the passageway.

"Have you seen Franklin, Nick?" He asked.

"No, I haven't seen him. The watch doesn't start for another twenty minutes. Earl usually doesn't start early," I said.

"I'm aware of that, Miss Strickland. I was looking for him in regard to another matter," the Bosun replied as he turned and walked down the passageway. Earl's quarters were located aft, so I decided to stop by his quarters when I got back there.

I went down the ladder into the cargo gate area. Carl was checking the unloading boom's electrical system. He looked up and smiled at me.

"What brings you down here?" he asked.

"It's coming down in buckets. I figured I'd take the tunnel aft," I said as I walked past him.

I entered the long narrow passage. I flipped a swith which turned on the passageway lights. Great, I thought, there's not even enough light to see where I'm going. I found myself regretting that I chose to take this route. As I quickly made my way aft through a tilting passageway, I could hear the sound of the waves hitting the side of the ship and the sound of taconite pellets shifting in the cargo holds. I thought about the tale of Huckleberry Finn being lost in Injun' Joe's cave. A lake rat suddenly fell from a pipe over head. Startled, I lashed out with my foot and kicked the darn thing out of my way. I was getting ready to stomp on it when I noticed that the rat was already dead. The rat had hit the hull plates and apparently broke its neck. How freakin' gross, I thought to myself as I continued down through the passageway. The sound of water running through the pipes and a humming noise became even louder as I was approaching the after end of number five cargo hold. I climbed the ladder that led to the next level. I reached the water tight door and started to turn the lever. I discovered that the door was locked. I would have to go back down the ladder and crawl under the belt and try the door on the starboard side. To hell with it, I thought, as I turned to go the way I came. Just then, someone opened the door. I walked through, only to find myself in the Boiler room.

"Well, well, it's Miss Shackles and Chains coming out of the dungeon," remarked the Second Engineer as he went back to watching the dials.

"I thought you guys were gonna' do something about the rat problem."

"There's just a few. We consider them to be pets." Brad said, adding—"Joe names them."

"Well, I just killed one, so he can grieve for it." I said, smiling.

It was common knowledge amongst the crew, that I usually avoid the 'ratwalk' that runs along the length of the cargo bay area, unless I really have to use it.

"You know where the equipment supply room is. Please, don't forget to sign out what you take from there," stated the Second Engineer as he was surveying his instruments.

"I am not here for supplies. I'm checking to see if Earl is in his quarters," I replied.

"Oh, you make house calls," the Oiler, Joe wisecracked.

"Think again, Joe! The Bosun is looking for him. I thought I'd check to see if he was back here," I retorted.

"He came through about twenty minutes ago. He went through that door," the Engineer stated as he pointed to the doorway on the other side of the boilers.

"Thank you," I stated as I started to head toward the doorway.

"Nick, we're only joking with you," remarked the Engineer.

"I know that," I called back as I went through the doorway.

I ascended the steps, which took me up to the next level of the deckhouse. I asked 'The Kid' in the welding shop, if he had seen Earl. He hadn't. I went out the starboard side of the deckhouse. I looked to my right and saw something moving by the life boat. I started to walk that way, when I heard Earl's voice.

"Is that you, Nick?"

"Yeah, it's me," I replied, "What are you doing out here in the rain?"

"I was just getting some fresh air," Earl replied.

"This is a hell of a place to get fresh air!" I exclaimed, noticing that he looked like he was trying to hide something.

"The other guys were bugging me, I wanted to be alone," he said looking down at the deck.

Figuring it best to drop the subject, I said, "Okay, the watch starts in five minutes, you know the place." I turned and headed back toward the after deckhouse to get a rain coat. While I was in the deckhouse, I heard someone on the loud speaker, but I could not make out what was being said because of the static. The rain must be causing a short out, I thought as I left by the forward door and headed forward. I ran into Ed at the door of the Crew's hall.

"Did somebody report that the intercom is all static in the after deckhouse?" I asked him.

"As far as I know, it was working fine," he replied.

"You better call up to the Wheelhouse and report it," he added.

I picked up the white phone and pressed the button that would ring the phone in the Wheelhouse. A voice came over the telephone.

"Wheelhouse, McCracken."

"Strickland here. There seems to be a problem with the intercom in the after deckhouse," I said.

"What seems to be the problem?" asked the Mate.

"A message came through, broken up by static. I could not make it out," I replied.

"How long ago was this?" he asked.

"I just came from there, so it was only a couple of minutes ago," I replied.

"The intercom wasn't used up here. Very well Ms. Strickland. I'll check it out, over," and the Mate hung up the phone.

I hung up the phone and Ed handed me the clipboard. Since Earl wasn't here yet, I signed the clipboard and allowed Ed to leave. I looked aft to see if Earl was coming, but I did not see anyone. I heard the door open behind me and I turned and saw Earl.

"You must have come from below deck," I said.

"Yeah, we'll be out in the rain enough as it is," Earl replied.

I opened the door to the spar deck and stepped out into the rain and wind. The wind was blowing hard, but it was not as cold as it had been in the upper lakes. My Grandmother would call the week of warmer weather in November, the 'Indian Summer'. I had read in the weather report, that a series of thunderstorms was heading through this area. That would be the end of 'Indian Summer', I thought.

We walked down the port side, checking the lights and the cables. I saw lightning flash off the port quarter.

"It looks like we're getting a little electricity, Earl," I said.

I saw Earl nod his head. I laughed to myself. Earl had the old style hat, called a Sou-wester, tied down so tight around his face, that it looked like a Quaker bonnet. The wind started to gust something fierce from the starboard side and the rain started to come down in buckets. More correctly, like a fire hose, since it was blowing straight sideways. For five minutes we hung onto the storm ropes that had been rigged out in Lake Superior.

"Not quite a luxury cruise," I shouted above the wind and the thunder.

"No, it sure ain't," replied Earl, who seemed to have a hard time staying on his feet.

"Let's try to get aft," I shouted. Slowly we made our way aft, taking care, lest we get thrown off our feet by the wind and the rolling of the ship. When we reached the after deckhouse, someone opened the port side door, and we ran in.

"Well, you folks been singing in the rain," Hank remarked.

"Singing the blues," I shot back.

"Well, get dried for a few minutes. I'll need Earl back here and you can take Mister O'Blake forward," Hank said.

"Good! I'll take him below deck," I exclaimed.

"No can do, Com padre. The big bosses don't travel via the bilges. They're afraid of the rats. It's gonna' be a 'romantic stroll' on the main deck," Hank replied. "That's just charming," I remarked while rolling my eyes and hoping that Hank did not see me do it.

"He'll be up here in a few minutes. Try not to let him go overboard," Hank winked and he left with Earl.

I was wondering if O'Blake was suffering from insomnia or if he was just upset because of the storm. Maybe since the waves were following us, he felt safer in the bow. I heard a noise. I turned and saw O'Blake struggling with his equipment. I helped him with his rain gear.

"It looks like you may be needing this," I said as I handed him a rain hat.

"Tie it on tight," I added.

"I can't see how the blasted thing goes on," He replied, not trying to hide his irritation.

I tied it on for him.

"Just hang on to the rope and always walk up hill with the roll of the ship," I said.

I opened the door and stepped out into the storm. I saw O'Blake hesitate, then he followed me as I started walking forward. Lightning flashed real close by, and O'Blake jumped.

"Keep your feet firmly on the deck or you'll slip," I shouted into the wind.

O'Blake nodded and shouted back, "Will the lightning hurt us if it hits us?"

"I don't know, I've never been hit by lightning. Have you?" I shouted, shaking my head in disbelief.

He looked at me with a dumb look on his face and said nothing. When we were about one hundred feet from the forward deckhouse, O'Blake grabbed me by the arm so hard that he almost caused me to loose my balance.

"WHAT?" I shouted.

"Look!" he said.

I looked up at the Mast, where he was pointing. What appeared to be several luminous balls, moved crazily on the arm of the Mast.

"Yep, strange to see it this late in the year," I shouted over the howling wind.

"What is it?" O'Blake shouted.

"Saint Elmo's Fire," I replied.

"Are we in trouble?" he shouted.

"No, it's just static discharge caused by the lightning. It's suppose to be good luck," I shouted back.

He looked at me, incredulous.

"Let's go," I shouted and ran for the sheltered location under the stairs to the quarter deck.

When we got to the cubby hole under the stairs, I pulled my hood back and turned to Mister O'Blake and said, "Well, that was fun." O'Blake just stared at me.

When the ship rolled to the starboard, we ran to the rear door of the Crews hall and quickly entered. Inside the crews hall, I saw Hank and Earl checking the wiring where it passed through the bulkhead.

Hank turned to me and said, "What's up guys?"

"We caught some Saint Elmo's Fire," I replied.

"That's strange, the Mast should be well grounded. That must be playing hell with the SD. I'll inform the Mate." Hank headed for the white telephone on the wall. I saw O'Blake walk through the forward door without saying a word to anybody.

"I'm glad to be rid of him," I said, only loud enough for Earl to hear.

"Yeah, he's a real pain and he doesn't know when to quit," Earl replied.

Hank came back and said, "The Mate said that there was interference for a minute but the SD set is working okay now."

I waited as Hank and Earl continued to check the wiring.

"The wiring to the intercom runs under the deck plates enclosed in conduits. At the after deckhouse, it branches off. Below the deck, the intercom is working okay. I think that the trouble might be aft, above the deck," Hank said as he put his test equipment in his box.

He went over to the white telephone and talked to the Mate for a few minutes.

"This job might take a while, Earl," I said.

"Yeah, I hope we can stay out of the rain while we find the problem," Earl replied.

"Nick, Dave wants to know if everything is secure out on deck?" Hank asked.

"Everything is shipshape," I replied loud enough for the Mate to hear me.

"Sounds like more problems," Earl said. In a minute, Hank returned.

"Nick, Mister McCracken wants you to station yourself in the wheelhouse. Earl is going to assist me with the intercom repairs."

"Very well, Hank. I'll see you when the watch is over, Earl," I said and I headed for the Wheelhouse.

The Mate thought it was bad enough to call off the watch out on the deck.

When I entered the wheelhouse, the red lights were on. Lightning flashes would light up the wheelhouse to a glaring pink color.

"Strickland on watch," I announced. The Mate acknowledged and handed me a pair of night binoculars.

"We had to go to anchor for three hours at Grosse Isle, so we're coming up on the Erie Islands now. Keep a lookout forward and to the starboard," he ordered.

"Very well, Sir," I replied.

I put the binoculars to my eyes and searched the horizon for other boats in the storm. The Mate was keeping his eyes on the radar set.

"Pelee Island is on our port side. In about a half an hour, we'll pass Marblehead on our starboard side," the Mate said. After looking for a few minutes, I saw a light off our bow, to the starboard.

"Lights, broad on the starboard bow," I reported.

"Yes, I've been watching her. A smaller ship. Probably out of Sandusky. Heading this way," the Mate replied. I saw a flashing red light slightly starboard of the bow.

"Navigational buoy ahead," I reported.

"We're right on course," the Mate said. As I looked to the starboard, the lighning flashed several times in rapid succession. Taking the same crooked path in the sky. In the light, I could make out a ship. A small vessel of five or six thousand tons. An older vessel with a small island and only a stack aft. They seemed to be having a hard time of it, pitching like a roller coaster. Its present course should take it well astern of us. I looked over and saw the Mate marking a line on the clear plastic film used for plotting a ship's course on the radar set.

He looked up at me and said, "She should pass astern of us with lots of clearance. Have you seen her yet?"

"Yes, a smaller vessel with only a stack aft," I replied.

"The smaller ships come into Sandusky and load coal or limestone. She might be upbound with coal to Minnesota. Must be having a rough time of it with this weather," he replied.

"It could be worse," I said. "I've seen thirty feet waves in Lake Erie. You know where the baseball field is in Township Park?" he asked. I nodded an affirmative.

"That's eighteen feet above the lake. I've seen the waves breaking on the baseball field. These ten feet waves seem like babies compared to that," the Mate said. As we passed by the buoy on our starboard side, the Mate ordered a course change of 0-8-0.

"This storm is slowing us down a bit, but the worst should be past by watch change," the Mate said.

"Good, I'd like to get some sleep," I said, suddenly realizing how dumb I was sounding.

"I wonder if our Mister O'Blake is getting much sleep," the Mate stated rather than questioned.

I continued to look with the binoculars and did not offer a reply. I could not see anything but rain, lightning and waves. The waves seemed to beat angrily against the side of the ship, the spray hitting the windows of the Wheelhouse. I kept looking starboard to where I thought Marblehead should be, but I did not see any lights.

"If we're lucky, we may be able to see the Marblehead Light," the Mate said.

Still holding the binoculars to my eyes, I said, "I don't see anything yet."

I thought about when I was a little child. The light of the lighthouse would shine through my window and light up a small square spot on my wall. It seemed so comforting to have the light. You could always depend on it. The ship rolled again, ending my daydream.

"There should be a ship coming up on our port side," the Mate said. I looked but I could not see anything in the darkness.

"It's on a parallel course."

I looked over at the Mate, he was calculating the ship's course and speed.

"It should be passing us in about ten minutes," the Mate said.

I looked over to the starboard side. Broad off the bow, I saw a green light flash, then again a few seconds later.

"A lighthouse broad on the starboard bow," I reported.

"That will be the Marblehead Light," the Mate replied, looking at the radar plot.

"The islands will be on our starboard side."

I saw a small red light blinking quickly off our starboard side then it seem to vanish.

"Blinking red light off our starboard," I reported.

"That's probably the warning buoy for the reefs around Bass Island," the Mate replied.

For a minute, I thought about the time my grandmother walked me across the ice to Johnson's Island. There were not many people back in those days. We looked around the ruins of the prison camp from the Civil War. A lot of Confederate officers died there and were buried in the adjoining cemetery. The lightning flashed and I could see all three islands at once. The large gray shape of Kelley's Island, to the right of the smaller and darker outlines of Bass and Sugar Islands.

"The islands are coming up on the starboard," I reported.

"Very well, Ms. Strickland. You should be able to see the other ship coming up on our port side," the Mate replied.

I looked at the port side for a minute, but could not see anything. The Mate began blowing the horn at regular intervals. He must be getting nervous, I thought.

"Mister Hall stand by on helm," the Mate ordered.

"Standing by, Sir," Pete said.

"She'll be within minimum radar range in one minute," the Mate said, keeping his eyes fixed on the rain splattered window right in front of him.

I realized that I was looking too far to the left, the other vessel would pass much closer to us. The Mate hit the horn again, and turned on the search light. He could control it remotely from the wheelhouse. I could see the white flash of the search light cut through the rain and the darkness and reflect off the wheelhouse of the other vessel. It was almost bows on to us and would pass less than two hundred yards to our port side. The Mate did a good job holding the search light onto the deckhouse of a vessel pitching up and down in the waves, while our ship was also pitching and rolling. The Mate blew the fog horn again, and this time I could hear the horn of the other vessel. It was another six hundred footer. Much the same as our ship and making about the same speed.

As it passed by our port side, the Mate remarked: "What do they think this is, a romantic cruise through the islands."

"I'll bet that woke them up," Pete said.

I saw the Mate writing in the log book. I looked to the starboard and saw Kelley's Island off to our starboard side. After we pass the island, I should be able to see the Marblehead Light, I thought.

A few minutes after passing the islands, the rain diminished suddenly to a drizzle, although the wind kept blowing steady. I could see the Marblehead Light, obscured occasionally by low scudding clouds. It should be getting light soon, I thought. Doubtless, daylight would be delayed by the heavy cloud cover. The Mate reported that the radar was clear of ships forward, but I still had to keep a lookout forward until the end of the watch. Finally, daylight came to the eastern sky and the watch bell rang. The Third Officer came into the Wheelhouse and informed the Mate that the captain wanted to see him. Mike, the third watch wheelsman, came and relieved Pete. I went down to the Crews hall. I filled in the watch report on the clip board and gave it to Smitty. I put on a raincoat over my parka and headed aft. When I got to the galley, John had breakfast ready. I got a cup of coffee and some eggs over easy with toast and headed into the Crew's mess. I saw Earl sitting by himself, so I went over and sat down at his table.

"Well, buddy how was your watch?" I asked.

"Okay, I guess," Earl replied.

"Hank gave you a lesson in electronics?" I asked.

"He said, he found the problem. I don't know what it was," Earl replied, looking like he was a thousand miles away.

"I didn't have much fun in the Wheelhouse either," I said.

Moving my chair so that the motion of the ship didn't upset my breakfast too much.

"I was thinking, everybody says that we're gonna' have a few days off when we get to Cleveland. Do you want me to drive down to Alliance with you?" I asked.

"No, thanks anyway. I don't think I'll go home 'till the end of the season," Earl replied.

"Okay," I said.

"I gotta be going, but there's something I want to show you."

He pulled a small blue envelope from the hip pocket of his Dungarees and handed it to me. I instantly recognized it as the letter I sent to my secret admirer. It was supposed to go out on the Westcott, but it apparently never got there. I checked the envelope again and I recognized a correction I made in the address when I wrote it. My face felt hot and the hair stood up on the back of my neck.

"Son-of-a-bitch!", I exclaimed. "Where did you get this, Earl?" I asked, suddenly realizing that I was using an angry tone.

"I found it in the waste drum in the machine shop. I thought I recognized it as the one you had in your hand." Earl hesitated. "I'll catch you later, Nick," he added, then got up and left.

I was fit to be tied. I put the envelope in the pocket of my parka, and finished my breakfast.

I decided to go right to the Captain with this problem. I just hoped he would not see how incensed I was that someone had took my mail and read it. I walked forward to the deckhouse and saw the Bosun coming out of the Crews hall.

"Sir, I would like to talk to the Captain, privately," I said.

"Is there something I can help you with Nick? Is there some trouble with one of the crewmen?" he asked.

"Perhaps, I don't know for sure. I don't think that it's a union matter though," I replied.

"Very well, I'll see if he can see you. Why don't you wait here," he replied, then he turned and went up the passageway.

I felt nervously, for the envelope in my pocket. Suddenly it seemed silly to talk to the Captain. I started worrying about how I was going to say it. I started to get nervous when the Bosun came back.

"The Captain will see you now, Miss Strickland. He's in his quarters."

I walked past the Radio Room and went up the steps to the starboard side quarters. I knocked on the door of the Captain's quarters.

"One moment, Miss Strickland," I heard the Captain say. I was surprised to hear the voice of someone else in his quarters.

I heard the Captain say in a gruff voice, "I don't care what you tell the owners, Mister O'Blake. Right now, you will leave my quarters. Is that understood?!"

A moment later, O'Blake opened the door, looked at me and headed the other way.

"Come in, Miss Strickland."

"I'm sorry, Sir. I had a complaint." I hesitated.

"Well, Miss Strickland this seeems to be the day for it," the Captain replied in a very pleasant tone.

This guy can turn it on and off like a faucet, I thought as I dug into my coat pocket and pulled out the envelope.

"Earl found this in the waste drum. It was suppose to have gone out in the Westcott mail. Somebody took it and removed the letter," I said as I handed the blue envelope to the Captain.

The Captain looked at it for a moment and said, "Do you mind if I ask you a question about this letter, Miss Strickland?"

"Go ahead," I replied.

"Can you tell me who this letter was going to?" he asked.

"I don't really know for sure. Some guy I've been corresponding with. He doesn't want me to know who he is. A kinda' secret admirer, I guess you could say," I replied.

The Captain thought for a moment and said, "Another possibility occurs to me, Ms Strickland. Your secret friend could be on this boat."

I was taken completely by surprise by what he said.

"I never considered that possibility, Sir", I replied, wanting to say more, but just couldn't think of what to say.

"Well, Ms. Strickland. There are twenty-seven lonely men on this ship. I'm excluding myself of course. There are ten or eleven that aren't married, so it is a definite possibility," the Captain said, adding-"Would you like me to check into it?"

"No, I think that I will let it go for now. Thank you, Sir," I said.

"Very well, Miss Strickland," he replied. I turned and left.

I went down to my quarters, laid down on my bunk and thought for a minute. I sat up, reached under my bunk and pulled out my travel case. I opened it and took out the last letter from my secret admirer and checked the post mark. It was post marked in Duluth, the same day that we left. There were three or four other ships ready to leave that same afternoon, so it could have been a crewman on one of those. There was a mail call for us when the mail truck came to the pier. I remember that the Third Officer, the Chief, and most of the crew not on watch, including myself, went down and gave mail to the mail man. Of course, someone could have given a letter to one of the guys that went on mail call. Great work, 'Nancy Drew'! You've narrowed it down to everybody, I thought. Not willing to let this one go that easily, I took out the last letter from my secret friend and read it again. He knew a lot about the Gentry and he is somewhat older than me. But something kept sticking me like a thumb in the eye, every time I read the letter. Then it occurred to me—"I know that you've been hurt by men before". That was the line that was giving it away. My problems with the ex-boyfriend, Bill, happened when I lived in Alliance. That was five years ago. No one on this ship, except Earl, could have known about my problems with Bill. The Captain knew that I drank for about six months after the breakup with Bill. I told him because I had told the Captain of the Giovanni. Captain Kompsii liked to interview the new crewmen and he did not pull any punches when it came to questions and answers. Like he told me—"You don't have to look back, just look ahead." I was sure that the Captain would not be gossiping about me to the officers and crew. I never knew Earl to gossip either. Most of the time, he was trying to avoid talking about anything to most of the crew and officers. Of course, when he was ashore and drunk he might be wagging his tongue, but I never heard anybody mention anything about me coming from Earl. The other guys would talk about me, I was sure about that, but it is always the same old male B.S. They do not know anything about my life in Alliance.

I thought about mailing the last letter. I gave my mail to the Mate when he was going forward. I thought the Mate could have put the letter in the mail bag or he could have given it to the Bosun or anyone else with a key to the mail bag. There were at least six people with a key to the mail bag and someone else could have secretly made a key without anyone knowing about it. I was thinking about asking him what he did with the letter, but I decided against it for the same reason I told Captain Kompsii not to investigate. Because the less anybody else knew about it, the better it would be for me. There was no use in letting the whole ship know about it. I put the letter and the envelope away and read the motorcycle magazine until I went to sleep.

I slept restlessly because of the rolling of the ship and the possibility that my secret admirer was on board. I got up at twelve thirty P.M. to get some water. I heard Mister O'Blake banging around next door. That guy is a total jerk, I thought. I laid down again for a short nap. I woke up to the alarm at one thirty. I noticed that the ship wasn't pitching and rolling as bad as it had been. I estimated from the motion of the ship, that the waves were about six feet. I slipped on my boots, put on my parka and walked to the door. I heard the sound of someone moving outside. I wondered who it could be. I opened the door and saw the Mate standing in the passageway, looking lost.

"Good afternoon, Mister McCracken," I said.

"Good Afternoon," he replied.

"I'm heading aft. Are you going that way?" I asked.

"Yes, I can go that way," he said in a low voice.

I was feeling good. I had not realized that I was betraying my enthusiasm at the prospect of a shore leave by the way I was smiling and talking.

When we got down to the spar deck, I asked, "Were you checking on our Mister O'Blake?"

"Something like that," he replied still keeping a low tone.

"I heard him banging around in there this morning. It sounded like wrestlemania in there!" I exclaimed, noticing that the Mate was looking surprised.

"I think he had another run-in with the Captain," he replied, smiling slightly.

"I heard that he was a 'fair-haired boy' to the owners. the Captain doesn't lack for pluck taking him on," I said.

"I'll tell you a little secret, Nick," he hesitated.

"The Captain's wife and her brother are five percent owners of the Company. The Captain isn't going to do anything that O'Blake is trying to push on him," he explained.

"Doesn't he know that there's a union to deal with. Along with all the other authorities?" I asked.

"He gets the craziest ideas. He said that the Mast was on fire. And now he wants tornado drills because of the water spouts that were sighted last spring," the Mate replied.

He held the door for me and we entered the aft deckhouse and headed into the galley. We stood by the counter for a minute, until John, the Steward came out.

"What's the deal today, John?" I asked.

"We can expect the usual half hour of whining from you," he replied, half seriously.

"Not today, 'burger flipper'. Give me the mushroom pizza and a milkshake. I ain't got time for chatter," I wisecracked.

"What will it be for you, Sir?" John asked the Mate.

"I'll have the pepperoni pizza, salad and a cup of coffee," the Mate replied.

John turned and headed for the far shelf to get the large bowls for the salad.

"What's the ETA in C Town . . . er, Cleveland?" I asked.

"We should be passing the breakwall just before three o'clock. The Captain has already informed the port authorities of our intentions to unload. Everything should be ready for us when we get in."

John returned with the Mate's salad and my milkshake. He put them on the trays with the pizza and handed it to us.

"Nick, you can complain about someone else's cooking for a few days," the Steward said jokingly.

"My stomach can use the break," I shot back jokingly, in return.

We made our way into the Crew's mess and sat down with the Third Officer.

"Hi, Andy. What's up?" I said as we sat down.

"I'm just sitting here, looking forward to my shore leave," Andy replied.

"Is that all?", I questioned.

"Well, I'm also looking forward to getting shed of our guests as well," Andy said, smiling deviously.

"He's suppose to be the Maritime Operations Manager. Have you increased his maritime operations knowledge?" I asked mildly sarcastic.

"Are you asking my opinion?" Andy asked.

"Sure," I replied.

"He didn't know squat when he came on board, and now he knows diddly squat," Andy replied with a grin.

"It sounds like he's lost ground, if anything!" I exclaimed, adding— "How about his friend, Mister Ring?"

"If, we're talking ignorance, that's off the scale. What do you think, Dave?" Andy asked.

"Off the record, of course. I think that he's more interested in pleasing Mister O'Blake than in tending to technical matters," the Mate replied.

"He's sounding like a politician. What do you think, Nick?" Andy wisecracked.

"I don't know. It sounds like a pretty fair assessment of Mister Ring to me. Of course, I don't know him like you guys do," I replied, trying to sound perfectly non-chalant.

"Believe me, Nick, the way I've heard Dave talk about those two clowns. I assure you that he's playing the 'Officer and Gentleman' routine to the hilt," Andy replied.

"OK, I don't pretend to love the S.O.B. I was just trying to be gracious," the Mate replied.

"I'd better be leaving, before I drown in this BS," Andy said, adding—"Hey Nick, Dave has to buy all the beer for us at Captain Jacks."

"Thanks Andy, I'll be sure to be there." Andy got up and walked through the door.

For a few minutes we ate in silence, struggling with pizza.

"I don't know of any way to eat pizza gracefully," the Mate said before taking a bite of pizza.

"Yeah, it's pretty hard to do. It's a good thing that the ship isn't rolling any more than it is," I replied.

"That reminds me of when I was a kid. I saw the old Charlie Chaplin silent movie about those immigrants trying to eat soup. The bowl would slide from one side of the table to the other. That part reminded me of some storms we've been in," the Mate said.

"Yeah, that film was funny. It reminds of the time my Grandmother and I were on the Kelley Island Ferry during a storm. It was loaded down with cars. Only about a foot of freeboard. The waves were coming over the bulwarks. It was rolling like crazy. I never saw anything like that," I said.

"I remember your grandmother talking about that ferry trip," the Mate replied.

"I didn't know that you knew my grandmother that well," I replied, surprised.

"Actually, I didn't know her that well. I think I heard the story through someone else. Probably the Mayor's wife. She would talk about your grandmother sometimes," the Mate said.

"Yes, I recall that the Mayor's wife would visit with my grandmother frequently when she was living in Marblehead.

"Well, I gotta' go. I'll have to start early and find Earl."

"One more thing, Nick. I was thinking that since we are both headed to Marblehead. I was planning on renting a car. You could ride up with me if you like."

"We'll see. They may want you to stay on the ship for awhile. If you can arrange to get off the ship soon enough, I may be able to do that. Catch me later," I said and I turned and walked out of the galley.

—

CHAPTER 3

Off-Loading in Cleveland!

As I left the after deckhouse, I saw the Chief and Mister Ring walking quickly aft, on the port side. I waved to the Chief and he waved back. I was looking for Earl on deck, as I was walking forward, but I did not see him anywhere. When I got to the Crew's hall, I saw Smitty lounging around.

"Have you seen Earl yet?" I asked.

"No, I haven't seen him all watch," Smitty replied.

"Alright, I'm going to run down to my quarters," I said and headed out the door.

I decided to check the cargo belt area at the forward end of the rat walk. I went down the two stairs and entered the door to the cargo bay area. When I turned on the light, I saw Earl lying on the belt.

He rolled over and said, "Hi, Nick. Is it that time again?"

"About an hour. But they could be calling us anytime now, old buddy," I said.

"Okay, let's go," he said, rolling off the belt and landing on his feet.

I decided to skip going back to my quarters, so Earl and I headed back to the Crew's hall.

"What in Sam Hill were you doing on the belt?" I asked.

"It was too noisy in my quarters, so I decided to sleep there," Earl replied.

"It's kind'a cold and damp down there, don't you think? What if the belt started with you on it?" I asked.

"The cold doesn't bother me. The Gateman has to come down there before the conveyor can be started," he replied.

"I wouldn't count on the conveyor not starting. Remember it was running when Dixon got hurt," I pointed out.

"Yeah, I never thought of that," Earl replied. As we ascended the stairs to the main deck, we ran into the Gateman, the Electrician, Carl and Mister Ring.

"Hi, guys," I said.

As we passed, Carl replied, "Hi, Nick, Earl."

"I wonder what they are up to," Earl said when we got to the top of the stairs.

"I think our guests are trying to Poo-hoo this conveyor business. Mister O'Blake probably wants the conveyor belt checked again before we off-load," I replied.

We reached the top of the stairs and turned left and headed down the passageway. We ran into the Bosun in the night kitchen.

"We'll be in Cleveland, about three o'clock. I don't know where we'll be unloading, but prepare to rig out the short gangway on the starboard side. I'll let you know if there are any berthing instructions, when I get them."

"Very well, Sir," I replied.

"Earl will be needed for porter duties. Earl you are to report to the Captain."

"Yes, Sir," Earl replied.

"Well, Earl, I'll catch you later," I said.

"Okay, Nick," Earl replied, and he went up the steps to the Wheelhouse.

It was only two in the afternoon. Since the Bosun had given me something to do, I had to start working. I went to the Crew's hall and signed the clipboard. I went out on deck, but I did not see Al. I went over to the gangway, which was collapsed and secured to the deck. I checked the bolts and the cables that held it when it was rigged out. Everything was shipshape, so I walked over to the conveyor. The Mate and the Chief were supervising the work as Ed and Al removed some of the chains that held the conveyor boom. I helped Al carry the chains forward, into the chain locker.

"How many chains are staying on?" I asked.

"Three chains will stay on until we are ready to unload. That is the minimum that is required to hold it secure, according to the Chief," Al replied as we stowed the chains on hooks in the locker.

80

When we got back out on deck, I looked aft, to the side and could see the steel mills and ship yards in Lorain, far astern. The sun was shining through the broken cloud cover. The wind was blowing, but it was not as cold as I expected. I could see the waves hitting on the break wall, throwing up spray. Looking forward, I could barely see the city of Cleveland. the taller building looked like dark fingers pointing to the sky. As we walked back to the conveyor, we passed Mike, the Wheelsman.

"It looks like we got the honor of handling the boom," Mike said.

"Duck Soup!" Al replied.

"Yeah, if the damn thing works like it's suppose to," Mike shot back as he ascended the steps to the deckhouse.

"Everybody seems to be in a tense mood today," Al noted.

"Yeah, I'm not though. I am happy to be going home for a couple of days," I replied.

When we got back to the conveyor, the Mate was talking to the Bosun.

The Mate turned to Al and I, "We don't know yet when we'll be off-loading. Nick, you can stand by the after line and Al, you handle the forward line."

"Yes, Sir." We both replied, then the Mate headed aft.

"I'm gonna' head aft, Al and check the mooring lines," I said.

"Yeah, that's a good idea. I think I'll do the same. See you later," Al said, and we headed in opposite directions.

I passed the Chief and Mister Ring. They were talking to the Mate. When I got to the aft deckhouse, I saw Earl coming out of the side door carrying two duffel bags.

"I see you're hard at work," I said.

"Yup, these jokers don't do anything. They wait until they are hopelessly behind, then they go crying to the Captain and he makes me do it," Earl complained, although not sounding too unhappy.

"I'll catch you later, buddy," I replied, adding—"I gotta' check the mooring lines."

The mooring lines were contained in tubs on the starboard and port sides, by the railing. I unscrewed the large wing nuts and pulled back the top of the tub. The lines were one and half inch thick Manila ropes with a heaving line and a weight tied to the end. The rope was neatly coiled, Flemish style, in the tub. I secured the top in open position. I went over to the port side, checked the mooring line in the same way, except I closed the lid and secured it with the wing nuts. I was sure that we would be tying up and unloading on the starboard side. A few minutes later, the Bosun came aft and told me that we may need the mooring cables for berthing. The Gentry could be pulled into berth by cables powered by steam driven draw works. Sailors call these, mooring winches. There is one forward and one aft of the hatches, on the spar deck. The Super Lakers have propellers, called side thrusters, on the port and starboard side. These move the vessel sideways without the aid of tugs.

I checked the cable on the mooring winch, aft. A few minutes later, the Chief and Mister O'Blake came aft. The Chief explained the operation of the winch to Mister O'Blake, although he seemed not at all interested in it. Mister O'Blake left and I went over to the Chief.

"Hi, Chief, what's up?" I asked.

"I'm still giving our guests the twenty five cent tour of the ship," he said.

"Well, you tried, but some people never learn," I said.

"That seems to be the case here," The Chief replied, adding—"I have to go forward to check the conveyor again. I'll see you later, Nick."

"See yah, Chief," I replied.

I stood by the railing alone and smoked a cigarette. Slowly the City of Cleveland grew closer. We passed Bay Village, Lakewood, and Edgewater Park. As we approached the break wall, I could see the familiar lighthouse. The loud speaker blared, and I could hear somebody shouting instructions. The Bosun ran back to where I was standing and told me that the cargo was to be unloaded into lighters. They were rafted inside the breakwall and had tugs standing by. That's interesting, I thought. This would be the first time we ever unloaded into barges. That goes to show how much more versatile we were with the unloading boom. The barges were not much more than rectangular steel boxes. The larger ones had hatch covers and could hold five thousand tons of taconite. They would be pushed up the Cuyahoga River by tugs. Probably to the steel mills in the Flats. Somebody must have been interested in getting a load of Taconite before things froze up and nobody could get any more pellets through Lake Superior. Probably getting a good price for a ton of pellets this late in the season.

The ship turned to the starboard and went through the gap in the break wall. Past the light house and turned to the port as soon as we cleared the piers. A Coast Guard cutter maneuvered to get out of our path. Slowing down, the ship made another port turn. We straightened out, heading east, parallel to the breakwall and stopped next to the line of barges anchored inside the breakwall. A tug pushed a barge along our starboard side. The Mate stood at the railing and waved flags at the Tug Captain, to direct him in placing the barge where our conveyor boom could reach it. When the tug stopped, the Bosun came over the loud speaker, giving an order to throw over the mooring lines to the barge. I picked up the heaving weight, and made several large coils of rope in my left hand. I drew back with my right hand and threw the weighted end toward to the closest end of the barge. The end of the rope hit the deck of the barge and slid a few feet before coming to a stop. A crewman on the barge, grabbed the heaving line and pulled the mooring line out of the tub. When he had the end of mooring line, he secured it to a cleat on the deck. I secured the rope to the cleat on our deck, after pulling it tight. I heard the sound of chains falling on the deck. I heard the loud rattling noise of the gears engaging as I looked forward from the after deckhouse. With the gears engaged, the boom of the two hundred foot conveyor began to raise slowly. When the boom was about fifteen feet up, it stopped rising. I heard a loud humming noise as the boom swung over to the starboard side. It swung until the end came over the after hold of the barge. The Bosun came out of the forward deckhouse and waved to the conveyorman. The belt screeched when it began to run. As it ran up to full speed, it made a roar like a freight train and just as loud. Below deck, I heard several metallic clangs as the cargo gates opened. The belt slowed down somewhat as it took on the weight of Taconite pellets from the cargo hold. The gray pellets began pouring off the end of the belt and falling into the barge, making even more noise than before. The First Mate waved for me to come forward. I crossed over to the port side to avoid walking under the conveyor. I climbed the ladder to the quarter deck where the Mate was waiting. He motioned for me to enter the Observation Room, so I followed him through the rear door.

He handed me a pair of ear protectors, and asked, "Can you relieve Mike on the conveyor at five o'clock?"

"Yes, that won't be any problem." I replied.

"Very good, Ms. Strickland. Also it would be good if you wore the ear protectors while out on deck. There are a lot of people coming to observe the unloading. The Company thinks it would be a good idea if everyone on deck wore those," the Mate said.

"There's just one problem. In a little while, the barge will need to be shifted. I won't be able to hear the communications when that happens, Sir," I replied.

"I'll have the Bosun get you a set with a radio," the Mate said. Just then the Captain, Mister Ring, and Mister O'Blake came into the Observation Room. The Captain told Mister O'Blake that nothing had been resolved with the unloading conveyor.

Mister O'Blake said, "I told you Captain, there's nothing wrong with that conveyor!"

As if by magic, the conveyor chose that moment to screech to a stop. We all left by the back door to check what the problem was. I heard Mike tell the Bosun over the radio that the conveyor lost power. I followed the Mate down the steps. I heard shouting and saw the Chief and the Electrician running across the deck. The Captain told the Mate to stay on deck, then he disappeared through the doorway. The Mate told me that I could return to my station aft. I walked aft, crossing over to the starboard side, after I passed the conveyor. I met the Bosun and the Gateman. I told the Bosun that I needed ear protectors with a radio built in. He nodded in acknowledgement. When I got to my station aft, I ran into the Engine Wiper, Gary.

"Hi, Nick. What's up?" he said.

"Something stopped the conveyor. So everybody's running around up there, trying to find out why," I replied.

"Situation normal, all fouled up," he said.

"Our Mr. O'Blake seems to think so. He keeps insisting that the only thing wrong on this ship is the crew and officers," I said. Gary flicked his cigarette overboard in such a relaxed fashion. He seemed to do everything in a graceful way. He had a body of a male model and a rugged good looking face. Surprisingly, he did not seem to flaunt it. He was not married, but I was sure he did not have any trouble getting a date ashore.

"I should quit these damn cigarettes." he said,adding—"Do you smoke?"

"On occasion, I do smoke. Mostly out of boredom," I said.

"I don't think I ever saw Mister O'Blake. I've heard the other guys talk about him. The other guy, Ring, walked through a couple of times," he said.

"You gotta' be kidding. He's been all over this ship since he came on board," I said.

"He doesn't come down to the weight room," Gary replied.

"Yeah, he doesn't seem to be the type to hang around the weight room," I said.

Remembering that this is only the second time I had seen Gary since the ship left Duluth.

"If we ever get this ore unloaded, we can go ashore," Gary said.

"Are you going home on your leave?" I asked.

"No, I moved to Florida last spring, so there won't be time to go home. I'm gonna' hang out with some of the guys for a couple of days. We're gonna' start at the Wheel & Anchor in the Flats," he said.

"It's gonna' be well past dark before we get this load off, but I'm sure there'll be plenty of beer left," I said.

"Are you going with us?" Gary asked.

"I may. I was thinking about getting something to eat at Captain Jacks," I replied.

"They got food at the Wheel & Anchor. I don't know if you'd want to eat it though. I'd better get below again. I'll see you later, Nick."

He turned and walked through the starboard door of the after deckhouse. I thought it was strange for him to talk to me that much. I began to wonder if he was the secret admirer. I had to dismiss the idea after a few minutes, because the secret admirer is somewhat older than me. Gary is younger than me. I looked around, I could see Captain Jacks easily from this vantage point. Astern of us on the starboard side, was the repair dock. That's where we would be going after we unload. I looked forward and saw Mike walking up the boom to his station at the end of it. Over the radio, the Mate asked me if everything was shipshape. I took the radio off my belt and told him that it was. He said that the Bosun would be coming back with my ear protectors, shortly. A minute later, the order came over the loud speaker to start the conveyor.

The conveyor screeched as it ran up to full speed and resumed its usual roar as the taconite pellets poured into the barge. After fifteen minutes, orders came over the radio to release the lines fore and aft. I unwrapped the rope from the cleat and held it so it would not fall in the lake. I reported over the radio that the line was slack. The tug pushed the barge slowly ahead about fifty feet before coming to a complete stop. The order came over the radio to secure the lines. I wrapped the rope around the cleat. In a few minutes, the Bosun came aft with walkie-talkie ear protectors. We called them 'Mickey Mouse' headsets. With the 'Mickey Mouse' headsets, it was possible to have both hands free all the time. Three more times, I had handled the rope as the barge was moved forward. When the barge was filled with pellets, the conveyor stopped. The crewman unwrapped the mooring line from the cleat. I pulled it in, coiling the rope on the deck. Al came aft to handle the mooring line and the Bosun told me to come to the conveyor.

When I got forward, I climbed the ladder. A scary thing. The rungs were welded to the pivot side and don't offer very good footing. When I got to the top, I walked out on the catwalk, to the end of the boom. At the end of the boom was a pedestal with four levers to control the up and the down, and the swing of the boom. Down below me another barge was being pushed into place by a tug. I could see the other barge, low in the water, being pushed to the mouth of the Cuyahoga River. When the forward hold of the barge was under the end of the boom, the lines were heaved over to the barge and secured. The order came to start the conveyor. The vibration and the noise level increased as the belt picked up speed. At full speed it was like standing by a train going fast. The taconite covered the belt all the way across. Down below, the cargo doors were opened as far as they dared, trying to get the cargo off as fast as possible. Although the belt was laboring, there was no stoppage. I had to slowly swing the boom aft as the barge filled forward. When I could swing the boom no further, with out going over the side of the barge, I called for the conveyor to stop. The barge was shifted forward and the belt started again. The same routine was repeated over and over again for the next two hours and the next two barges. Finally, there were no more Taconite pellets in the hold and the belt screeched to a stop. The ships whistle blew as the lines were untied and taken in. The tug blew smoke as it pushed the barge away from the ship. The lights were turned off since they were no longer needed to illuminate the barge. I walked back on the catwalk and climbed down the ladder. I walked over to the port side to stay clear of the unloading conveyor as it was being swung back on board. The

Bosun told me that Al and Ed would chain the unloading conveyor and to take a rest. After the Bosun left, Earl came by.

"Well, how's the conveyorman doing?" he asked smiling.

"My head is spinning and my guts are in disorder," I replied, trying to sound as if I was joking.

"My mother use to say that that kind of thing made dead babies," Earl said from out of left field.

"You say the damndest things, Earl," I remarked, adding-

"Let's go aft." As we started aft, the ship began to move forward.

"I heard the Captain say we're going to the repair dock, instead of the company dock," Earl said. As we walked past the guys chaining the boom, we met Hank.

"What's the deal up there, Hank?" I asked.

"O'Blake is having fits again, about the conveyor shutdown during the off-load. We found the problem. A breaker on the generator was corroded. It heated up and cut out after awhile at full power. The damn thing was hot as hell. It's a wonder it didn't burn," Hank replied.

"So what now, another meeting?" I asked.

"No, we just have to get all the reports and defective parts together, then we can go ashore," he said.

"That's good, Hank. Catch you later," I said.

"See you later, Nick," he replied. We turned and continued aft.

"It's past eight, Earl. I wonder if the Wheel & Anchor still has any beer left," I said jokingly.

"Yeah, it's only Thursday. They never run out except on Friday, before the beer deliveries," he said.

As we were about to enter the deckhouse, I noticed that the ship was making a turn to port.

"It won't be long now, Earl. We better get some coffee, then head forward," I said. When we got to the galley, Louie was on duty.

"Hi, guys. What's happening topside?" Louie asked.

"We're heading into the repair dock by the old Whisky Island station," I replied.

"Good, we'll be able to get off soon. After we get done at the Wheel & Anchor, I'm going to Detroit," Louie said.

"You guys won't be done at the Wheel & Anchor until this ship is ready to leave," I wisecracked as I took a coffee cup off the rack.

As Louie poured the coffee, I told Earl, "We better take the 'ratwalk'. Otherwise, somebody's going to commandeer you for some little bullshit chore."

After Louie finished with the coffee, we headed for the crew's mess. About ten guys were in the dining area. All seemingly happy at the prospect of a shore leave.

When we sat down, I asked, "Where are you going to be staying, since you're not going home?"

"I'll find a place to flop with the other guys," Earl Replied.

"How are you getting home?"

"I may rent a car or ride up with the Mate. If he can get away from the ship," I replied.

"I'd walk to Sandusky before I rode with that son-of-a-bitch!" Earl said, with a dark look.

"I'm gonna' have to straighten both you guys out. You and him both are gonna' have to let the past lie and forget about it. No good will ever come from a vendetta. Otherwise, there could be more trouble. I like you, Earl. I personally don't have anything against either of you. There is no good reason to carry a grudge now!" I exclaimed, hoping that Earl would cease with his grudge toward the Mate.

"Okay, Nick. If you think it's for the best, I'll forget about it," Earl replied.

"Good!" I stated, though I did not believe Earl could put it aside that easily.

After we finished our coffee, we made our way to the 'ratwalk'. We passed through the boiler room on the starboard side. Everyone was cleaning and securing equipment. We walked through the doorway to the cargo area. The door was already opened.

"We may not be alone down here," I said. As we walked forward, I could hear the sound of water sloshing around below the deck plates, even though the ship was not rolling or pitching. When we got forward, we ran into the Gateman, the Chief, the Mate and Mister O'Blake.

I said, "Hi, Guys," as we passed.

We went up two flights of steps and came out in the passageway on the main deck.

"I'm going to my quarters. I'll catch you later, Earl," I said.

88

I went down the passageway and up the steps to my quarters. When I got to my quarters, I went over to the little metal closet and looked at my clothes. After thinking for a few seconds, I decided to wear my duck suit, and pack my leather jacket and casual outfit in my nylon gym bag. I would not need anything else, until I got back to Marblehead.

Next door, I heard Mister O'Blake bang around again. A few minutes later, I heard a voice over the intercom, summoning Earl to the Observation room. Poor Earl, I thought, he's gonna' be happy to leave this ship for awhile. I felt a shivering under my feet. Even from way up here, one could feel the propellors reversing, when there is no cargo in the hold to dampen the vibration. I decided to go out on the deck to watch the ship dock. As I walked down the passageway, I passed Earl and the Bosun. I knew that they were going to get Mister O'Blake's luggage. When I got out on deck it, was completely dark out on the lake. Looking forward, I could see the long pier with all the cranes. The lights made the cranes look like some kind of Christmas light display. The harbor and city looked strangely beautiful lit up in the dark. I heard a voice over the loud speaker giving the order to stand by the lines.

Al and Ed were already at the mooring lines forward and aft. I saw the Bosun and DJ head over to the starboard side, where the short gangway was secured. More men were starting to come out on the deck now. I looked up and behind me and saw Mike, the Wheelsman and the Mate standing at the railing by the chart room. Don, the Wheelsman, came out of the forward deckhouse and came over to me.

"T'is a lovely sight Lass. Especially when you're going ashore."

"Yes, it is. Who's driving the ship?" I asked.

"The Captain is docking her and Andy is at the Motor. Pete is at the Wheel and our land birds are observing," he replied.

"Not enough room up there for you?" I asked jokingly.

"Too much hot air. I like a little peace and fresh air," Don replied.

"You won't get much of that at the Wheel & Anchor," I said.

"I won't be going there, Lass. My Ellen's coming in a car to pick me up. She should be just about here when we tie up," Don replied.

"That's good. I am glad to see that there's still some repectability among this crew," I said. An order came over the loudspeaker to stand by to rig out the gangway.

"Erie's about one hundred miles by freeway. You should be there well before midnight," I said, as we watched the Bosun and DJ swing the gangway over the side by its little cranes.

The pier was just crawling by now. Green and amber lights indicated the tie-up points. In less than half a minute, the ship was completely stopped. The order came over the loudspeaker to throw over the mooring lines.

Shore Leave

I heard Ed and Al report over the radio that the mooring lines were secure. The order came over the loudspeaker to lower the gangway on the starboard side. The Bosun pushed the lever and the gangway lowered on the cables. I heard voices behind me. I turned and saw Mister O'Blake and Mister Ring coming down the steps from the Wheelhouse. Behind them was the Captain and behind him, Earl and the Kid carrying O'Blake's luggage. This amounted to several large suitcases and a sea bag.

"It's a wonder he doesn't have a steamer trunk," I commented.

"Farewell to the little darling. Parting is such sweet sorrow," Don remarked.

The Bosun preceded them down the gangway, while Earl and the Kid brought up the rear. A white van and several black Lincolns pulled up next to the ship.

"How nice, door to door pimp-mobile service," I said.

"Now, now Lass it's all strictly legal." Don replied.

"Generally passenger vehicles aren't allowed on the repair dock. VIPs have to ride those three-wheeled sidewalk trucks," I said.

"It's a cold night. We wouldn't want the little darling to catch his death of a cold, would we?" Don asked.

As we were talking, six men in peacoats got out of the van and headed for the gangway. They waited until our party got clear, then they came up the gangway.

"Good, the relief watch is here. We'll be able to go soon," I said.

They passed us and headed up the steps to the Wheelhouse. From one of the cars, came several men in business suits. I could not see who they were because the lights were not on them. They shook hands with the Captain, then with Mister O'Blake and Mister Ring. They talked for a few seconds, then one of them motioned toward the cars. They all got into the cars, except the Captain. Earl and the Kid put the luggage in the trunk of the first and second cars and the drivers closed the lid. In a few seconds, the cars pulled away leaving the van only. The Captain passed by us and headed up the steps to the Wheelhouse.

"It won't be long now. We'll be safe and warm in our own beds tonight. That reminds me, I've got some things to do in my quarters. I'll see you later, Don," I said as I turned and walked to the forward deckhouse.

When I got to my quarters, I laid down on my bunk. I tried to clear my mind, while I was waiting for the call for shore leave. In about twenty minutes, I heard a voice on the loudspeaker,informing everyone not currently on watch to report to the Observation room for shore leave assignment. I decided to take my nylon bag with me. I hung my parka in the closet and put on my leather jacket. I grabbed my bag and headed for the Observation room. Most of the crew were already there, when I got there. The board had the names of everybody and the date they are due back. The Mate announced that everybody was due back on board by twelve noon on the return date. Then he told the Bosun to dismiss the shore leave party. Technically, the Bosun was suppose to stand by the gangway to make sure that only those on shore leave left the ship. He apparently felt that this was not necessary. As I left the Observation room,I heard someone call my name. I turned and saw the Mate so I went back inside.

"Miss Strickland, I'll be a little late getting off the ship tonight. I'm planning on going to Captain Jacks when I get off," he stated.

"Do you know when you'll be getting off?" I asked.

"It will be ten thirty at least. I'll try to be at Captain Jacks by eleven," he replied.

"Okay, I should be there by then," I said.

I turned and left. I walked down the gangway with Carl and Louie. Carl carried my bag.

"Where's Earl?" I asked.

"Are you kidding?" Carl replied. "Earl was down the gangway as soon as leave was posted."

"You should talk," Louie said. "It would have been a dead heat with you and Earl if we hadn't held you back."

"I remember when I was in the Navy," Carl began, "They gave us shore leave about six in the evening and we all went out and got plastered. Then at midnight, they wanted us back out on sub patrols. The shore patrol was rounding everybody up. The officer of the deck was plastered as hell. He was saluting everything that moved. The gangway slanted down to the ship because the pier was higher than the deck. Everybody was tripping and falling as they came on board. It was funny as hell."

"I've seen enough of the crew here and on the Giovanni have trouble with the gangway," I said.

There was about five hundred feet of pier to walk before we came to the street. Before we got there, I could see taxis waiting to pick up sailors. When we got up to the street, a cab pulled up to us. Carl opened the door and motioned for me to get in.

"I think I'll take a little ride around first. You guys go ahead," I said.

"You take this one then, we'll take the next one," Carl offered.

I got into the cab and Carl handed me my bag.

"Don't be too long. We'll be saving a seat for you," Carl added.

"I shouldn't be. See you guys later," I said. Carl closed the door.

.

I told the driver to take me to the old iron loading pier. The driver was a black man, about forty years old.

As he pulled away from the pier, he asked—"What do yah want to go over there for? That old wooden pier is all fallen in."

"Just to say good bye to an old friend," I replied.

"Ain't nobody there but rats. The winos only hang around there when it's warm," He said.

It started drizzling and he turned on the wipers.

"I don't see many women sailors here," he added.

"There's a few. More on the Canadian side I think," I replied.

"That don't seem like hardly a fit job for a woman, on that ship with all those men," he said.

"We've got a union and a Captain that will kill any man that touches a woman on his ship," I replied.

In a few minutes, we were at the old pier. I told the driver to wait while I went for a walk. When I got out, the cold drizzle hit me in the face, stinging my skin. This is gonna' be a short walk, I thought. Even though there were lights all around, the pier itself was dark and eerie. The sound of traffic on the shoreway seemed to fade as I walked out on the pier. I could hear the water sloshing around the wooden pilings. I walked along the railroad tracks.

When I was a child, my Grandmother would bring me down here to watch the ships while they were loading and unloading. A small diesel locomotive would push the rail cars out onto the pier. The overhead conveyor would take the ore from the bridge unloaders and move it to the gates. The gates would open and the ore would pour into the cars until they were full. Then the little engine would push them back up to the pier and get more cars. Sometimes the rail cars would be loaded with coal from West Virginia or Pennsylvania. Steel funnels were positioned between the rail ties. The doors on the bottom of the rail cars would be opened and the coal would pour down through the funnels and into the chutes which were positioned over the opened cargo hatches of the ships below.

After a few minutes, I went back to the cab. When I got in the cab, the driver asked me where I was going. I told him to take me to the Wheel & Anchor in the Flats. He said he knew the place. After a minute the driver began to talk.

"Yah know, when I was young, I use to drive a steel truck from Akron to Cleveland, sometimes to Detroit. I remember when ships used to load at that old pier. Something always going on there. You must remember that too," he said.

"Yes, I do," I replied.

"Did you know somebody that worked down there?" he asked.

"Yeah, something like that," I replied.

"Yeah, I figured that. Nobody hardly goes down there anymore. Not respectable folks anyways. Last year a college girl went down there and jumped off and drowned herself. I think the city is gonna' tear it down soon," he said, adding—"Are you meeting those other fellas up there at the bar?"

"Yes, I'm sure that just about the whole crew will be there by now," I replied.

"Good," the driver said, "The Flats ain't no place for a woman to be alone this late at night."

In a few minutes the cab pulled up in front of the Wheel & Anchor. The driver turned the car off, got out and opened the door for me. I got out and got my bag.

"What's the fare?" I asked.

"The other guy at the dock paid me already," he replied.

"You want me to take you to the door?"

"No, thank you for asking," I replied.

"Okay, good night then," he said.

"Good night," I said, and he drove off.

The Wheel & Anchor was an old place. For years it had been a hang out for sailors. It has had its ups and downs. Unfortunately it has gone too far up in recent years. A section of the Flats have been rennovated and became a Yuppie neighborhood. The Wheel & Anchor was being taken over by the Yuppie-types. Pictures of lake freighters, recent and old, still hung on the walls, but much of the sailing paraphenalia that decorated the place was gone. It had the run of the mill look of an ordinary bar. When I entered, I found the darkness and loud music quite objectionable. I ran into Buster, Gary, and Brad.

"Hi, guys," I said loudly to be heard over the music.

"Have a beer, Nick. Smitty's buying this round," Gary said.

"Thanks, Gary," I said as Brad moved over one stool and I sat down at the bar. Buster slid a glass of beer down to me.

"Quite a place here, don't you think, Nick?" Gary asked.

"We could do without the music," I remarked.

"Okay, I'll handle it," Gary said and he motioned for the bartender.

"What'll it be?" the bartender asked.

"I want you to turn the music down, Jack," Gary said.

"Sorry Buddy," the bartender replied, "I can't do anything about it."

"Well I can!" Gary said as he stood up and launched his beer glass into the juke box. Although the glass went through the front of the juke box, it kept on playing.

"THAT DOES IT CLOWN. YOU'RE OUT OF HERE!" the bartender shouted.

All the crew at the bar stood up.

Pete said, "You're gonna' have to throw all of us out of here and we're gonna' make it worth your trouble if you try it."

"You guys are gonna' pay for the damages," the bartender said.

"No problem Mac," Pete replied, and everybody sat down again. The bartender went over to the juke box and unplugged it.

"All we need is a little cooperation and everything will be fine here," DJ said.

On the other side of the bar, a balding man in a business suit began to complain that the Kid got a hair in his cocktail.

Joe got in his face and said, "Why don't you take the hair out of your glass and wear it then?"

All the crew members laughed at the wisecrack. On the other side of the bar were two men about thirty years old, both wearing three-piece business suits. After a few minutes, one of them came over and stood behind me.

"Excuse me," he said, "Haven't I seen you here before?"

"That could be," I replied.

"Do you come here often?" he asked.

Here it comes, I thought, God's gift to women is gonna' try to pick me up.

"Whenever our ship comes in," I replied.

"Oh, you're sailor!" he exclaimed. "How interesting, I never met a woman sailor before. I'm an attorney myself. My name is Tom."

He held out his hand but I ignored it and didn't bother to tell him my name.

"Can I buy you a drink?" he asked.

"I think there's enough guys here already that want to buy me a drink," I replied.

"I know a nice nightclub we can go to. I'll buy you a drink there," he said.

"I don't think so," I replied.

"Come on Baby, I just want to show you a good time," he said, putting his hand on my shoulder.

"Take your grubby hands off me," I snapped, "or you'll regret it!"

"No woman ever regrets it with me," he said.

I grabbed my beer glass and spun around and struck him on the side of the head with it. He fell to the floor, unconscious. The bartender ran over to see what the commotion was all about. Louie told him that the guy slipped in a puddle of beer.

"BULL SHIT!" the bartender replied.

"It sounds like a law suit to me, and this guy's a lawyer. Too bad guy," Louie said.

"I'll have to call the police!" the bartender exclaimed.

"Good, a police report, this sucker will own the place before you're through," Louie said.

The bartender hesitated for a few seconds. By this time, his friend from the other side of the bar had come over. He and the bartender lifted the prostrated man to his feet. The man came to and started swinging with his fists. His friend and the bartender had to restrain him. They sat him down at the nearest table and he held onto his head. His friend came back to where I was.

"I'm sorry about the way Tom acted."

"That's okay, I think he learned," I stated.

I liked his friend. He was about six feet two inches tall, good looking and acted very much like a gentleman. He gave me a business card and told me that if I ever needed an attorney, to give him a call. As he handed me the card, I noticed he was wearing a wedding ring. Too bad, I thought. I thanked him politely. The bartender interrupted us. He told the attorney to tell the police that somebody cold cocked his friend outside with a bottle. The attorney said not to worry, this kind of thing has happened before. Then he and the bartender helped his friend out the door.

"Good work, you threw the first punch of the night, now you don't have to buy the drinks," Mike said.

"Yeah Nick, you showed him the hard way to get a piece of ass," remarked Pete.

"You're just jealous because you won't be getting any either, Petey," I shot back.

"By the way, where's Earl?" I asked no one in particular.

"He's at a table somewhere back in that corner," replied Buster, pointing to the back of the room. I got up and headed diagonally across the room. I figured that Earl would be as far back in the corner as he could get. Most of the tables were occupied by other people. I found Earl, Kenny and Carl at a table by the wall.

"Hi, guys. What's up?" I asked.

"Sit down here, Nick," Carl replied, "We're just waiting for you to cold-cock another masher with a beer glass."

"Some guys just ask for it," I said, adding—"How are you doing, Earl?"

"I'-mmmm not sure," Earl replied the best he could in his thoroughly plastered condition.

"You won't get much from him," Kenny stated.

"He's three sheets to the wind already." Then he flicked a half dollar off the table, onto the floor.

"What are you doing that for?" I asked.

"Doing what?" Kenny asked in return.

"He does that all the time, Nick. The barmaids are always looking for change on the floor. He throws change on the floor so he can watch the barmaids as they bend over to pick it up. His idea of a cheap thrill," Carl answered.

"Save his change and go down to Prospect Avenue!" Earl blurted out.

"Well, well, Earl's back from the dead," Kenny remarked as he flicked another coin onto the floor.

"Earl, I'm going to Captain Jacks. Do you want to come with me?" I asked.

"So you can be with your lover!" Earl blurted out, even louder than before.

"Look Earl, I don't take that kind of shit from any man, drunk or sober!" I shouted back.

"Well, don't go away mad, just go away, you damn dyke bitch!" Earl spit out.

I saw red. Before I knew what I was doing, I had vaulted over the table and landed on Earl, knocking him and the chair to the floor.

"You better take that back, Franklin, while you still got breath in your body!" I shouted.

Earl was too drunk to put up much of a fight. I took my foot off his throat and stepped back. Someone tried to grab me from behind. I spun around ready to crotch kick him, but it was only the bartender.

"Young Lady, this is the second fight you've been in within the last fifteen minutes. I'm afraid you'll have to leave!"

Pete got in the bartender's face.

"Listen booze slinger, this is an argument between crewmen and nobody has any business butting in. So unless you want to really get hurt, you better leave her alone!"

"Don't bother, Pete. I'm leaving anyway," I said.

I said good-bye to Kenny, Carl and the other guys as I passed them at the bar. Gary said he would wait outside with me until I got a cab. When we got outside, the cold drizzle had got worse.

"Oh well, I guess I balled things up pretty good," I remarked.

"Are you kidding? I haven't seen this much action in months. I wish you weren't leaving," Gary stated.

"Yeah, maybe I can get into a fight with the rest of the crew," I said, sarcastically.

"Everybody gets pissed off at Earl. Especially when he's drunk. When he gets sober, he'll beg you to forgive him," Gary said.

"I hope so," I said quietly.

A taxi pulled up and let a couple out. Gary ran out and talked to the driver, then he waved to me. I ran out and got into the cab while Gary held the door open for me.

"This guy can speak some English. I think you'll have no problem," Gary said as he handed me my bag.

I saw him hand the driver some money. The driver could speak English okay, but I soon discovered that he had no knowledge of the city of Cleveland. After showing him where I wanted to go on his map fives times, I finally let him drive while I told him which way to turn when we got to the right street. It was shortly after eleven P.M. when we pulled up to the Ninth Street pier.

"Is the fare covered?" I asked.

"Say again Miss?" the driver replied.

"Did Gary give you enough money?" I asked.

"Yes, Miss. Thank you." he said. I grabbed my bag and stepped out of the cab and closed the door.

It was a short walk down to the pier to Captain Jacks. When I got there, the host opened the door for me.

"Would you like me to check your coat and your bag, Miss?" he asked.

"Yes," I replied as I handed him my bag. I took off my coat and handed it to him also. He left and returned in a minute.

"Table for one or are you expecting another party?" he asked.

"Has David McCracken, First Mate from the Gentry, arrived yet?" I asked.

"Yes, he has," the host replied. "Are you Miss Strickland?"

"I am," I replied.

"Right this way, Miss Strickland." When we got to the table, I saw the Mate reading the newspaper.

"Your party has arrived, Sir," the host announced. The Mate stood up and put the newspaper down.

"You're right on time, Miss Strickland," he said.

"I thought that it was fashionable to be late," I replied.

"Not on our ship," the Mate shot back, then we sat down.

"The waiter will be right down. Would you like a drink first?" the host asked.

"I'll have a Chianti," I replied.

"I'll have a Rye Whiskey," the Mate replied.

"Very good," the host said and he left.

"Did you make it to the Wheel & Anchor, Miss Strickland?" the Mate asked.

"Yes, I was up there for awhile but it was getting too rowdy. Let's drop this Miss Strickland stuff when we're not on the ship. You can call me Nick."

"That sounds fair enough. You can call me David," the Mate replied.

"I thought we'd get something to eat then rent a car and drive home tonight. Is that okay with you?"

"Yes, but you may have to do the driving. I don't know if I can last more then a couple of hours," I said.

"No problem, I got plenty of rest," the Mate said.

"Have you been waiting here long?" I asked.

"I got off the ship around ten thirty. I stopped off at another place before I came here," he said.

"What a coincidence, I went sight seeing too!" I exclaimed.

"Is that right? Where did you go?" the Mate asked.

"The old wooden loading pier at Whiskey Island," I replied.

"Oh yes, that brings back a lot of memories. We docked there many times when I used to work for the former Cliffs line," the Mate said.

"Yeah, it was very sad to see that old line pass away so suddenly," I replied.

I started to feel hotness on the back on my neck.

"You were the third officer on the Victory, weren't you?" I asked, not realizing that my voice was clipped.

"Yes, the year my wife got sick, in nineteen eighty-three," he replied.

99

"Earl was on the Victory at that time, wasn't he?" I stated rather than asked.

"Yes, he was," the Mate replied.

"He says he got fired because of a screw up by you," I snapped.

"Earl got fired because he lost his cool and punched the crap out of the first mate. He had been drinking as well," he replied.

"It's my understanding that if you hadn't been drinking and misplaced the lock box, then the confrontation between the mate and Earl would not have happened," I said.

"That could be. It didn't make much of a difference anyway. The Maritime Operations Division was discontinued that year and we all were basically out of a job," the Mate replied.

"You think it doesn't make a difference! It's called responsibility. If you screw up and it causes trouble for someone else, even indirectly, you should be a man and take the responsibility. All the responsibility. That's called constancy to your fellow man!" I exclaimed.

"You didn't get the whole story!" the Mate exclaimed. "I went to the Captain and explained everything. I made sure that the Captain got him another job. I've been babysitting him for the last three years. Sure, I screwed up, started drinking. It hurts to lose someone you love. I didn't think I'd have to explain that to you Miss Strick . . ." The Mate suddenly stopped talking when I jumped up in anger.

"You . . . You!" I wanted to say son-of-a-bitch, asshole-anything, but the realization swept over me like a Lake Superior wave. "You're Him!" The Mate looked down at the table. "You're the mystery man," I choked out.

I fell back into the chair. I could not believe it. I was speechless, my whole body went numb. I tried to talk, but I could not say anything. Fortunately, the Mate began to talk.

"I figured you'd find out soon enough. The Captain knew about it. He's been after me to tell you. He really doesn't like secret romances going on aboard his ship," he said rather contritely.

"I'm sorry, I didn't know!" My eyes filled with tears. "I'm so ashamed of the way I acted," I sobbed.

The Mate handed me a handkerchief.

"That's okay, Nick. I beat myself up a lot worse than that for not taking out the trash."

I started to laugh and cry at the same time. The waiter returned with the drinks.

"Is there something wrong, young lady?" he asked.

"Just a death in her pet dog's immediate family," the Mate replied.

"I see," the waiter said. "Are you sure you need these drinks?" he added, sarcastically.

"We'll be ready to order in a minute," the Mate replied.

"Very good, Sir," the waiter replied and he left.

"Well, you steered him like a ship," I said after regaining my composure.

"I'm sure he's back in the kitchen telling everyone that we've been at sea too long," the Mate said.

"He's probably glad that he's not serving drinks at the Wheel & Anchor," I said.

The waiter returned.

"You go first," I said.

"Are you ready to order?" he said.

"Yes," the Mate said, "I'll have the buttered Halibut, Rice Pilaf and fried mushrooms with gravy. For dessert, I'll have the Strawberry Shortcake."

"Very good, sir and you, Miss."

"I'll have the Seafood Platter with extra lemon juice. For dessert, I'll also have the Strawberry Shortcake, please," I said.

"Very good, Miss," the waiter said, then he turned and left.

"I always come here. This place has the best seafood in Cleveland," the Mate said.

"I was here a few years ago, with my grandmother, on her birthday," I said.

"Is that right?" the Mate said, adding—"I remember seeing her at the 'Clansman', in Marblehead, quite a few times."

"Yes. She loved to go there because it had that Highland decor and the people would speak Gaelic to you at your request." I thought for a few seconds. "How did you know all that stuff about me?" I asked.

"Through several people actually. Anything in particular you want to ask about?"

"Yes. How did you know about my boyfriend Bill, our break up and the drinking I did for six months?" I asked.

The Mate hesitated, then he looked me in the eye.

"Through your father orginally," he said.

"I didn't know that you knew my father," I said.

"When my wife died, I hit the booze pretty hard. I talked to your father several times in the bars around Marblehead," the Mate replied.

"That figures. The only time my father would visit his mother is when he was mooching money. He couldn't go anywhere without stopping at a bar before and after. He'd bad mouth everybody, inluding his mother, when he was drunk. And most of the time, he tried to stay drunk," I said.

"Yes, he had a very abusive mouth as I recall," the Mate interjected.

"I don't understand how you got anything that made any sense out of him," I said.

"Well, I sifted through all the abusive language and managed to ascertain that you had attended and worked at Mount Union College and had supported a guy named Bill. But you found out that this guy was taking advantage of you and playing you for a sucker until you couldn't take it anymore. So you kicked him out. Is that about right?" the Mate asked.

"I let this guy live with me. I paid all of his expenses for a year. All the son-of-a-bitch had to do was to stay faithful to me, but he couldn't even do that. I finally got tired of him messing with my head and kicked him out. I gave him all his stuff, but he kept coming back when I wasn't home and ripping off my stuff. I got pissed off about that. I caught him in a parking lot with a teenage girl and I whipped his ass real good. Put him in the hospital. I went home and got drunk and kept drinking for six months. When I got off work, I'd get plastered until I fell asleep. My grandmother took me with her to Marblehead to get me away from Alliance and the booze. I met the Captain of the Giovanni, got in the union and you know the rest."

"You must have been the little girl that would play with my son Tommy, in the summertime," the Mate said.

I hesitated for a minute, I drank down the rest of my wine.

"There's something I have to tell you. I am the one responsible for your son breaking his arm. I jumped out of the tree house. He tried it, apparently didn't land right. I heard him scream and I saw him hold his arm. My grandmother went over to your house and got his mother. That's what happened," I explained.

"Really? I didn't know that was you. Of course I was away at the time. When I saw him, the cast was already off. Don't worry about that, you were just kids. Some children are more accident prone than others," the Mate said.

"I never got to tell him that I was sorry. I wish I could have seen him and told him," I said.

"Tommy comes by once in awhile. You will probably see him this winter," the Mate said.

"What's he doing now?" I asked.

"He graduated from business school and he's working for an automobile company in Dearborn. I wanted to get him in the Merchant Academy, but he wouldn't do it. He was afraid of ships and water. We grew apart. I guess Emma, his mother, was the only thing keeping us together. When she died, he blamed me. I guess he needed someone to blame. We still talk, but not as father and son. More like occasional business associates."

"Well, don't worry, I'm sure that eventually you two will become closer. Frequently children will identify more with their parents as they get older. Especially, when they have children of their own. Of course, I could never associate with my parents again," I said.

"Not to broach the subject again, but I've heard that your father has been hanging around Marblehead recently," the Mate said.

"Old habits are hard to break. Him and my mother lost their house through foreclosure. His odd jobs weren't earning him squat and he drank up most of that. They lived in eleven different places in the last two years. Yeah, he can come to Marblehead, but he won't find any money there. Not this time."

"It sounds like there's no chance for a reconciliation, then?" the Mate asked.

"In their freakin' dreams maybe," I shot back. "You can't believe the mental abuse I had to take during my childhood. When I brought home a report card with straight A's and showed it to my parents, they said—'You're only looking for attention. Throw it in the waste basket.' You'd think any parent would be proud of straight A's, not my parents! They always treated me like dirt and hated me for any positive accomplishments." I decided to drop this harangue out of disgust.

"It looks like the waiter's coming with our food," the Mate said.

I looked behind me and saw the waiter pushing a cart. When he got to our table, he turned the cart around.

"Let's see, you wanted the seafood platter," he said as he sat the platter in front of me. And you wanted the Halibut with rice and mushrooms." And he sat the plate in front of the Mate. "I'll be back later with your dessert. Is there anything else I can get for you?" he asked.

"No, this will be fine. Thank you," we said and the waiter left.

I said a short grace silently and began eating. After a few minutes, I said, "This French Fried Shirmp is great! Much better than what John makes. But don't tell him I said that."

"John takes a lot of pride in his work," the Mate said.

"I know," I said, "but you should have seen him at the Wheel & Anchor. He was so plastered, I thought he was going to fall off the bar stool. He was singing something about the 'Brady Bunch'. It was funny as hell."

"It wouldn't be so funny if the Chief finds out," the Mate remarked.

"How's that?" I asked.

"The Chief's name is Gregory Brady. He doesn't like to be ridiculed about it. That song is very derogatory," the Mate replied.

"I didn't get the words, just the chorus," I said.

"It starts out-'Here's a story about a fag named Brady, who was busy with three boys in the engine room . . . then, it gets worse," he explained.

"Wow! I can understand why that would make him mad," I said.

"Those guys will be all sung out by the time they get back, anyway," the Mate said, adding—"If you don't mind my asking, do you have any special plans for shore leave?"

"I thought I'd hang around home the first day, then go to the synagogue service in the evening. On Saturday, I thought I'd do some winter shopping in the evening. On sunday, I was going to work on my motorcycle or maybe go to the movies," I replied.

"You can't do anything on Saturday?" the Mate asked.

"No, I shouldn't. It's the Shabbat. Since I'm not on the ship, I should observe the Shabbat," I said.

"I've never been to a synagogue service," the Mate said.

"Oh, it's a blast. Do you want to come to the service?" I asked.

"Yes, I think that I would like that," the Mate replied.

"You don't have to wear a kaftan, just wear your good suit. The service lasts a couple of hours with the Oneg Shabbat," I said adding—"It starts at eight o'clock."

"Why don't I take you? Also I was thinking of taking you to lunch tomorrow, if you like. I don't know when I'll be called back to the ship. I may not get all my three days," the Mate said.

"Okay, I can spend some time with you tomorrow, if I can get out of bed," I said.

"Great, I'll pick you up then," the Mate suggested.

"It might be better if I walk over to your house when I'm ready," I said.

"That will be fine," the Mate agreed, adding—"I'm ready for dessert. How about you?"

"I don't know what I'll do with it. I really pigged out on this seafood platter," I replied.

The Mate whistled for the waiter. The Waiter came over.

"Ready for dessert, Sir?" he asked.

"Yes," the Mate replied.

The waiter returned in a minute with the dessert cart. "Here you go, sir, and here you go young lady," he said as he placed the dessert on the table.

"John would kill me if he knew what I was thinking, Dave," I said.

"What's that, Nick?" the Mate asked.

"That he should take cooking lessons here," I replied.

"I think John cooks well enough. However, he can't get the fresh food like they get here," the Mate said.

"Yes, I'm sure he can't and I'll bet he doesn't get near a stove when he's at home," I said.

"I don't usually take a cruise when I'm off for the winter," the Mate said.

"I don't know, a cruise sounds like it might be nice," I said, adding—"I think it might be difficult for you to stay out of the wheelhouse."

"Old habits are hard to break, as you say," the Mate said. After we finished our dessert, the Mate called the waiter over and handed him the check and some money and asked him to call a cab for us.

"You know, it's strange how life doesn't gently push you along. Instead, it hits you with hammer blows that leave you struggling to regain control of your life," I said.

"Yes, sometimes that seems to be the case." the Mate agreed.

"I never dreamed I would meet my secret admirer under these circumstances," I said, adding—"I'm sorry for what I said. I shouldn't have been so hot headed."

"I like you because you're that way. If I'm screwing up, I like someone to tell me," the Mate replied.

In a few minutes the waiter told us the cab was here. When we got to the door, the Host helped me with my coat and gave me my bag.

When we got outside, a cold sleet hit us in the face. We ran to the cab.

"Where to?" the driver asked when we got in the cab.

"Terminal Tower, lower level," the Mate replied.

It was a short ride to the Terminal Tower, the traffic was very light. The Mate paid the driver and we walked to the car rental agency. The car was ready when we got there. The Mate had called ahead. All he had to do was show his credit card. We walked out to the car, a red '86 Cavalier. The Mate held the door for me and I got in. I put my bag on the back seat. We came out on Public square and turned east when we got to Superior avenue.

"Taking the scenic route," I asked.

"The Detroit-Superior bridge is closed for repairs," the Mate said, adding—"I think this will be the fastest way."

"Too bad, I like the view from the bridge," I said.

We turned south at Ninth Street. Past Carnegie, we made a right and got on Rt.90 west.

"So much for the scenery. All we see now is freeway," I said as I reclined the seat.

"I didn't think the scenery was that great," the Mate said.

"At night the bridges have their lights on. It looks real pretty on a clear night from the Detroit-Superior bridge," I said, adding—"I think I'll take a nap. Wake me up when we get to Marblehead."

"Okay, pleasant dreams," the Mate replied.

I closed my eyes. The hum of the wheels on the road was singing me to sleep. I thought about my old Cutlass. How many times I slept in that car, sitting up and woke up with a neck or backache because it didn't have reclining seats. My head slipped sideways until it rested against something. I drifted into sleep. It seemed like only a few minutes, then the Mate was gently shaking me awake. I opened my eyes and saw the Mates arm. I realized that I had been sleeping with my head on his shoulder. I sat up.

"Are we there?" I asked.

"In a few minutes," the Mate replied. "Will your house be warm enough?"

"I informed my neighbors that I'll be coming home, so they'll have the heat on for me," I said.

"My neighbors watch the house when I'm gone, too," the Mate said.

He turned the car onto the one lane gravel road that led to my Grandmother's cottage. It was a little over a year ago, when I drove up this road to bury my Grandmother. I had survived a whole season with my Grandmother gone. It still seemed strange. I always expected that my Grandmother would still, somehow, be there when I got home.

CHAPTER 4

Marblehead

The Mate pulled up next to my house. I opened the door and got out. the Mate got out and handed me my bag.

"I can get the door for you," he said.

"You don't have to do that," I said.

"That's what my wife used to say."

"She did?" I asked.

"No, she would say-'I open my own doors nine months of the year, I can do it now'," the Mate said.

I opened the front door and turned on the lights.

"I'll turn the heat up," the Mate said.

"Would you check upstairs to make sure no bats have come in?" I asked.

"Sure," he said and he headed up the stairs.

After a couple minute he came down the stairs.

"Everything looks good up there," he said.

"Thank you, David," I said.

"I'll see you tomorrow then," he said.

"Okay, as soon as I get out of bed. Good night, Dave," I said.

"Good night, Nick," he said and he went out the door.

I locked the front door and went into the downstairs bedroom. My grandmother's bedroom. Everything was just as I left it. I sat my bag on the bed and went to my large dresser. I opened the top drawer and I took out my jewelry box and sat it on top of the dresser. I took out my grandfather's Smith & Wesson Model 1917 from the first World War. I pressed the cylinder latch and swung the cylinder out to make sure it was loaded. I closed the cylinder and put the revolver back in the drawer. My Grandmother had always kept the pistol in the drawer since Grandfather died. I opened the jewelry box and looked at its' contents. I had a diamond tennis bracelet, three gold chains, Grandmother's one carat diamond wedding ring, diamond earrings, pearl earrings, and gold hoop earrings. After verifying that everything was there, I closed the lid and put the jewelry box back in the top drawer. I closed the drawer and went back to my bed. I took off my clothes and put a night gown on. I pulled the blanket back and turned off the light and got into bed. It took me a few minutes to go to sleep.

I dreamed that I was in a thirteen foot boat out in the bay. After a few minutes, the Mate was in the boat with me. He smiled and said that I was a good steersman. We sailed along into the sunset. When it got dark, I couldn't see where I was going. The Mate had disappeared. I called out Dave, Dave . . . I woke up. I looked around in panic, I did not know where I was. Then I remembered that I was back home. I looked at the clock, it was almost five o'clock in the morning. I got up and got some water. When I laid back down, I was asleep almost instantly. I was woke up by a car horn. I got up and looked out the window. The car was at my neighbor's house. I took a quick shower and got dressed. I remembered that the Mate wanted to take me out for breakfast, so I put on my good coat. I put my wallet in my coat pocket and headed out the front door, locking it behind me.

The Mate's house was on the other side of the gully, less than a quarter mile away. I walked down the hill to the path that led through a small wooded area. There was a stream with a log across it. I walked across the log and continued up the other side of the gully until I came to the road. I was at the Mate's house. I knocked on the door, then I heard him calling out to me. In a minute, he opened the door, wearing only his trousers and a tee-shirt.

"Good morning, Dave," I said.

"Good morning, Nick," he said, adding—"I was just getting ready. I have to call the Chief. Sit down and make yourself comfortable."

I sat down and the Mate dialed the phone.

"Hello, Greg.—No, I haven't talked to the Captain yet.—I understand. I'll get back to you later on that. The Bosun has the paper work."

He was silent for a minute.

"Yes, she's here. Is that right? I hadn't heard about that. No, it's all quiet, no problems—okay. I'll get back to you. Bye-bye." He hung up the phone.

"The Chief said there was some crazed, mad woman raising havoc at the Wheel & Anchor last night," the Mate said.

"She must have got there after I left," I said, innocently.

"She left the same time you did, is what I heard." the Mate said, adding—"Did you hit an attorney over the head with a beer bottle?"

"It was a beer glass. I told him to take his grubby hands off me and he wouldn't so I cold-cocked him," I replied.

"I'm not gonna' bother to ask you what happened with Earl," the Mate said.

"He called you my lover and called me a Dyke bitch. So I knocked him down and stomped him a little bit," I said.

"I should wonder what phrase pissed you off," the Mate said with a grin.

"Anyways, the Chief said I should fear for my life with you here."

"I don't think you need to worry. I'm in a better mood this morning," I said.

"I noticed," he agreed. "By the way, how did you get the better of Earl?"

"He was too drunk to put up much of a fight," I said.

"Earl can usually put up a pretty good fight, even when he's drunk," the Mate said, adding—"I was thinking about the Ship's Bell. What do you think?"

"That sounds great, I'm hungry as heck," I replied. The Mate went into the other room. In a few minutes, he emerged fully dressed, with his peacoat on.

"Are you ready?" he asked.

"Sure am," I replied. The Mate held the front door for me.

"We'll take the van, Nick," the Mate said.

"Right-Oh," I acknowledged. I walked over to the right side of a gray and black Plymouth van.

"I'll get that for you," the Mate said.

He unlocked the door and opened it for me. I got in and he closed the door. The Mate got in and started the van.

"That worked like a charm," I remarked.

"I started it last night. My neighbor will start it occasionally when I'm not here," he said.

"I haven't tried to start my truck yet," I said.

The Mate backed his van out of the drive way and headed down Bay Shore Road.

The diner was a mile and a half down the road. It was not raining but the sky was gray. Most of the trees had lost their leaves. Starlings and sparrows were the only birds in the air, besides the sea gulls. The lake was surprising calm, although the water looked gray and unfriendly.

"The real estate doesn't look much better than the lake this morning," I commented.

"A typical gray November day," the Mate said.

We passed by the marina. Most of the boats were pulled out for the winter. Next to the marina was the Ship's Bell. A one story structure that was in need of a paint job. The weathered look gave it the appearance of a veteran of many years on the lake. In fact, it was a favorite hang out for sailors from all the lines, when they were in Sandusky. We got out of the van.

"I hope the pancakes are as good as they use to be," I said.

"I think that I'll have the pancakes too," the Mate said as he held the door open for me.

We went in and sat at a table by the front window. A minute later, the waitress came over.

"Good morning folks," the waitress said, adding—"What will you have this morning?"

"I'll have the bluebery pancakes. Please bring exra butter and syrup," I requested politely.

"I'll have the same and please bring us a little pitcher of orange juice and a pot of coffee."

"Very good, sir," the waitress replied and left.

"So besides me, what else was the Chief talking about?" I asked.

"The shorebirds are cleaning the holds. We'll make another trip up to Duluth with coal, either from Sandusky or Lorain. The parts are expected today. The inspection and recertification should be completed by Monday," the Mate replied.

"They can do it that fast?" I asked.

"Yes, there's an inspector there right now. He'll stay the entire weekend while the work's in progress," he answered.

"I can't believe that everyone is so enthusiastic about working the weekend," I said.

"George Succodich, the shipyard manager, is pushing the project. Believe me, the paper work and the regulations are more work than the actual repairs. I'll have to work on the report to the Coast Guard this weekend," the Mate replied.

"Tomorrow would be a good time to do that while I'm observing the Shabbat," I said.

"I was wondering what we could do today?" the Mate asked.

"I was thinking about doing some shopping for clothes, or at least look around. Then go to the cemetery to see my Grandmother's grave," I replied.

"That sounds good. Emma's grave is nearby, so we can see it too," the Mate said.

"I wish it was summertime. My Grandmother would sit with me on the grassy bank and read to me or teach me Russian when I was a kid," I said.

"Your Grandmother spoke Russian?" the Mate asked.

"Oh yes, she was from Russia originally. She came to America in 1912, when she was seven years old. Her parents were killed in a pogrom, so her older brother took the other children and fled to Germany, and eventually to England and America," I said.

"I remember she was married to a Scottish man named Eichann. He died about six or seven years ago, wasn't it?" the Mate asked.

"Yes she was, but he was her second husband. Her first husband was Simon Strickland. He worked for a rubber company in Akron. He was smart as a whip and I remember him as a very nice man when I was a child. He died of cancer when I was eight years old," I said.

"Wasn't he a tall man, about six feet four inches, light brown hair and thin?" the Mate asked.

"Yes, that sounds like him," I replied.

"I saw him a couple of times. He seemed like a pretty decent fellow," the Mate said, adding—"Of course, most of the time during the summer, I was on the Lakes, so I didn't know him that well."

"I had great times here when I was a child. Unfortunately, I had to spend the winter in Akron with my idiotic parents. When they were tired of having me around, they sent me to live with my grandmother in Alliance. During the summer, she would stay in Marblehead. She devoted most of her time off from teaching college, to doing research and taking care of me. Well enough about me. Give me some background, David, please."

"It sounds like you're writing a book," the Mate said jokingly. "I was born in Grand River, in Lake County, in 1942. My father was a dock master at the Stone and Coal Dock in Fairport. I grew up next to the lake and always wanted to work on a freighter. During the Second World War, the guys on the lakes were exempt from the draft, so my father didn't have to fight. He stayed home and made babies, my brother and I. When I was eighteen, I went to the Merchant Academy for a year, then my father got me a berth on a freighter that came into Fairport regularly. We carried every thing, steel, machinery, lumber, grain, limestone, coal, just about any thing. A couple years at that, I took some tests and got a berth on an ore carrier and been doing this ever since."

"Do your parents still live in Grand River?" I asked.

"No, my father died, my mother had to move when the Corps of Engineers were planning on expanding the harbor. Unfortunately, the project was not carried through. The land was sold to a developer. The developer put expensive houses there. The river flooded in the springtime. The water and ice severely damaged the houses, and the people had to move out," the Mate said.

"I bet you weren't too happy about that." I said.

"It was one of those Idyllic little places. One lane dirt roads, little cottages, everybody was friendly. Somebody always has to come along and ruin something like that," the Mate replied.

"It sounds like Marblehead," I remarked.

"I bought the house in Marblehead because it reminded me of Grand River," the Mate said.

The waitress came with the pancakes. She sat the platter in the middle of the table, then she sat down the coffee pot and the orange juice.

"Let me know if you need anything else," she said, then she left.

"These pancakes sure are big," I said as I pulled two off the platter onto my plate.

"I love the smell of pancakes in the morning," the Mate said as he dished up his helping of pancakes.

"Grandmother did not make pancakes, because they made her sick. She always had eggs and toast or steak and eggs on the weekend," I said, looking out the window.

I could see a ship in the bay. A small ship that looked like the one at the lock. In fact it might have been one at the lock.

"That ship looks like the one we saw at the lock," I said.

The Mate looked out the window.

"Yes, it does. A five thousand ton coal carrier. The old type with coal fired boilers and triple expansion engines. There's not many like that anymore," the Mate said.

I watched the ship as it crossed the bay to the coal docks on the other side. It looked so small. Black smoke came from the stack as it manouvered its way under the coal chutes.

"That little ship doesn't lack for turning ability," I said.

"Yes, those smaller hulls are more manouverable. It's the triple expansion engines that are impressive. They can change speed and reverse very quickly. Also the torque is excellent at any speed. No need for reduction gearing like our turbines need," explained the Mate.

He must not have known that I worked on the Spirit Independent.

"The engine room of the Giovanni was so noisy when those big diesels were running. The turbines are much less noisy," I said.

"Those old steam engines are somewhat noisier than turbines," the Mate said.

We ate in silence a few minutes before I spoke again.

"I'm really making a pig of myself with these pancakes," I said when I realized that I was on my second, while the Mate was on his first.

"I like to take my time eating. On the ship we always have to worry about getting interrupted in the mess hall. That's not good, it can give you ulcers," the Mate said.

"I wouldn't say that around John. If anybody gets ulcers on the Gentry, he takes it personally," I said jokingly.

I looked up at the Mate, he was staring at me. When our eyes met, he looked down again. We're playing an adolescent game here, I thought.

He's afraid to show that he's sweet on me, even though he's not afraid to say it. Still as embarassed as a school boy.

"I'm looking forward to getting out today. I hope I don't drive you crazy," I said.

"I don't think that there's any chance of that," the Mate replied.

"Did your wife ever irritate you when she took you shopping . . . uh, if you don't mind me asking?" I asked.

"I don't mind you asking," the Mate replied, then he continued— "Emma was a sensible woman. She would never do anything to annoy me. She was always aware of the kind of mood I was in."

"She must have been a very perceptive person. I must admit that I am not very good at that. I have to ask sometimes," I said.

"It doesn't matter, you can ask me anytime," the Mate said.

"Well, try to be patient with me," I said, and the Mate smiled.

"If you don't mind my saying so, a smile is an emotional outburst for you," I said as I poured a glass of orange juice.

"I'll try to control myself in the future," the Mate replied with a wink.

"Oh no, that officer and gentlemen routine is okay on the ship, but if I'm ever going to know you, you have to be yourself, okay?" I said.

"Okay, I think I can survive that," the Mate replied, smiling slightly.

"Well, we have to do some shopping, go to the cemetery and the synagogue. Not necessarily in that order. Is there anything else you can think of?" I asked.

"Maybe see a couple of friends, if we have time," the Mate suggested.

"That sounds good," I said, adding—"Maybe we'll run into some old friends."

Friends Old and New

I heard the bell, over the door, ring. I saw a large man in a peacoat enter. I saw the cook start walking quickly in his direction. The Mate turned around and stood up and waved in his direction. He turned and headed in our direction. When he got to our table, I stood up.

"Nicolette Strickland, this is Stephen Monk. Stephen this is Nick," the Mate said.

I held out my hand. His hand was big, hard and calloused, but his grip was proper.

"Join us please," the Mate invited.

"I wouldn't be interrupting you two, would I?" he asked.

"Not at all," the Mate replied. "We were just talking about the old days of coal burners and triple expansion engines."

Mister Monk took off his coat and hung it on the back of the chair. He was wearing a heavy denim shirt, but it had no sleeves and was unbuttoned except for the bottom three buttons. He had a big chest and arms that looked slightly flabby. Not unusual for his age, which I estimated at forty-five to fifty years.

"Nick, Stephen and I go back a lot of years," the Mate said.

"Let me guess, in the engineering department," I guessed.

"That's very perceptive of you, young lady," Mister Monk replied.

"Nick is on our deckhand gang, Steve. She's been on the lakes five years now," the Mate said.

"I never served on a boat with any women. I don't think our old Skippers would allow it," Mister Monk said.

"Nick pulls her load for sure. I think most of the guys behave better than usual, because Nick and Captain Kompsii don't take any guff," the Mate said, adding—"Please, help yourself to some chow, Steve."

"Thanks, Mate," Mister Monk said as he took the three remaining pancakes. "I have to watch my step these days. Most of the places around here won't allow me in," Stephen said.

"Have you been fighting?" the Mate asked.

"Yeah, I lost a berth on a cement carrier about a month ago. Two 'wharf rats' jumped me at the Last Stop. One hit me with a cue stick. The other tried to stick me with a knife. I laid them both out pretty good. Went to jail for a week before they decided to drop the charges, after they recovered enough," Mister Monk said.

"I'm not surprised," the Mate said. "Stephen is one of the few men that didn't back down from Earl . . . er, uh men or women, I should say."

"Yeah, Earl Franklin and I have had some good times together. The damn police and judges are too damn mamby-pamby these days. You'd think they never heard of a fight," Mister Monk remarked.

"So what have you been doing lately?" the Mate asked.

"I've been working in the coal yard until I can get another berth," he replied and went on eating his pancakes.

I got the idea that he wanted to talk to the Mate in private, so I figured I'd excuse myself.

"Can you gentlemen excuse me for a few minutes?"

"Sure, Nick," the Mate replied.

I got up and headed for the ladies' room. I decided to take my time so Mister Monk and the Mate could discuss their business. I waited ten minutes, then I returned. I saw Mister Monk and the Mate still talking, although they stopped talking when they saw me coming toward them.

"It looks like we may get some rain," I said as I sat down.

"I don't think so," Mister Monk stated, adding—"Just a few dark clouds."

"Well Steve you always did have a good weather eye. We'll take your word for it," the Mate said.

The waitress came to the table and asked if we wanted any thing else. The Mate said "No" and she handed him the check.

"One moment, please," the Mate said as he removed a twenty dollar bill from his wallet, then handed it to the waitress. "Keep the change, young lady," the Mate said.

"Thank you, sir," the waitress said and she left.

"David, is Steve gonna' be able to join us?" I asked.

"No, I'm afraid not Miss Strickland. I've got to be getting back to the coal yard."

"Well, maybe we'll be seeing you again before we leave," I said.

"I am looking forward to that, young lady," Mister Monk said.

The three of us headed for the door. The waitress handed the Mate and I, our coats, Monk already had his.

"Thank you," the Mate said and Mister Monk doffed his cap. Once outside, Mister Monk said "Good-Bye" and headed across the parking lot.

The Mate and I went back to his van. He held the door for me and I got in. He got in and started the engine.

"You were very gracious to Steve. I appreciate that."

"Not at all. I was treating him like any other sailor," I said.

"Some of the so called Gentle ladies I've known, would have scoffed at a guy like Steve," The Mate said.

"Any friend of yours is a friend of mine until I have reason to think otherwise," I stated.

"Steve is a good friend alright. He has saved my life and my job, on more than one occasion, when I was younger," the Mate said, adding— "Do you want to go to the cemetery first?"

"That will be fine," I said.

The Mate backed up the van then put it into drive and headed out onto Bayshore Road. We turned off of Bayshore and on to the little dirt road where the cemetery is. Puddles had formed in the potholes. The road looked awful. I remembered when I was younger and my Grandmother walked with me down the road to see my Grandfather's grave. I remember the dust on the road and the smell of weeds that lined the side of the road. In less than a minute, we were at the little parking area by the cemetery gate. The only other vehicle there was an old, beat up, white pickup truck. We got out and walked through the gate.

"Emma's grave is closest. Do you want to see that first?" the Mate asked.

"That'll be fine," I replied as we started walking down the lane through the cemetery. The wind had been blowing fairly steady, now it began blowing gusts. It was only about one hundred and fifty feet to the grave of the Mate's wife. We walked in silence. The monument was white marble, about four feet long and three feet high. The top sloped like a roof. Columns were carved in relief at the corners. Besides her name and dates of birth and death, there was an epitaph—"An inspiration to those who knew her. A light in their hearts."

"That's a nice thought," I said.

The Mate did not say anything for a few minutes.

"Emma knew she had Leukemia, shortly after the season started. She wouldn't tell me. She wouldn't let Tommy tell me. There was no chance for a bone marrow transplant. The Chemotherapy wasn't doing any good. When I got home in October, I was so angry that she hadn't told me but I couldn't yell at her. 'There's no use in you suffering for the last six months,' she told me. In February of '84, she died. The winter was very cold. The men had to use picks to dig the grave. A numbness crept into me, standing here by the hole. I couldn't cry, couldn't holler or pray or even speak. This is the first time since that day that I've been able to talk about what happened," the Mate said weakly.

I put my hand on his shoulder. After a few minutes of silence, he said, "Let's go see your Grandmother."

Grandmother's grave was in the back, overlooking the lake. As we approached the area, I saw a man dressed in an overcoat and a woman dressed in a brown coat, hurry away at a right angle to us. They kept their faces turned away from us.

"That's odd," I said.

"What's that?" the Mate asked.

"Oh, nothing," I replied as I watched the couple retreat into the distance.

For a moment, I thought I had recognized them. Grandmother's headstone was about two and a half feet long and about two feet high. It was gray granite with a slightly arched top. It had a Star of David. The inscription was in Hebrew and English. I translated for the Mate, explaining that her name was written as her real name in Russian. Loving wife of Simon Strickland, and Zikronah-Leberachah.

"That means—*May their memory be for a blessing*, I explained.

"That's nice. It's a good way to feel about the death of a loved one," the Mate replied.

I recited the Mourners Kaddish, then placed a small rock on the headstone. Then the Mate placed a rock next to it.

"Grandmother would like that," I said, smiling.

The Mate smiled too. The evergreen bushes on both sides were doing well, I noted. We turned and walked back to the van.

"This is the first time I've been back here since that day," the Mate said.

"I like coming here. I like to look at the grave stones and think about what kind of people they were. When I die, I hope that someone comes by to look at my gravestone as well," I said.

"Don't think about that kind of thing. Live life for today," the Mate said as we got into his van.

"Where to now, David?" I asked.

"Let's go to the Mall," he replied.

"Sounds good," I agreed.

We headed down the peninsula and crossed the Route Two bridge to the Sandusky side. In ten minutes, we were at the Sandusky Mall. We parked the van by a large department store and went in on the first floor.

"They have some nice charms here," I remarked as we passed by one of the jewelry counters.

"Yes, they do," the Mate agreed.

We headed back to the women's coats. They had an equisite selection of leather coats. I noticed the display touting the 'nautical look'.

"Those petite, little women don't look like they could stand a deck watch," I remarked.

"You don't think so?" the Mate asked.

"Yeah, right," I replied. "At the first little squall, they'd run screaming to their bunks. Look at that outfit, tied up above her waist. She looks like she's ready to clean the firebox," I said sarcastically.

"Unfortunately, the crew would be ready to clean her firebox," the Mate thought out loud.

"David, I'm shocked," I said in mock seriousness.

"I'm sorry. I didn't mean to be crude," he apologized.

"I know what you meant, you devil," I shot back jokingly. A sales lady appeared.

"Can I help you?" she asked.

"Yes, I want to try on a couple of these coats," I replied.

"The leather Trench coat or the Australian Duster?" she asked.

"I think I'll try both," I replied.

"Very good, I think your size is over here," she said.

"I'll be back in a few minutes," the Mate said.

"Okay," I said.

I picked out a brown and a green Duster and a tan Trench coat. I tried on all three and looked in the mirror, but I couldn't make up my mind. I saw a reddish-brown maxi and decided to try it on. I put on the maxi and was adjusting the belt when I saw the Mate.

"David, I just can't make up my mind."

"Is it for shipboard use?" he asked.

"Of course not. I'll use my peacoat for shipboard use," I replied.

"Are you going on a cruise?" the sales lady asked.

"No, we work on a ship," I replied.

"Oh, how interesting. Have you seen our nautical collection?" she asked.

"We don't work on the 'Love Boat'. We work on an ore carrier," I replied.

"Oh my goodness!" the sales lady exclaimed.

"Walk up and down the aisle," the Mate suggested.

I walked to the escalator stairs and back to the sales counter, passing the Mate then coming back.

"What do you think, Dave?" I asked.

"You look great!" he replied.

"I think I'll take this one," I told the sales Lady.

"That's a beautiful coat," she said as I handed it to her.

We went over to the cash register. As the sales lady rang up the coat, I took out my credit card and handed it to her. The sales lady put the coat in a bag and handed me the slip. I signed it and gave it back to her. She put the receipt in the bag and handed the bag to me.

"Thank You, have a nice day," she said.

"You too,bye-bye," I said, and we turned and left.

As we were walking back to the entrance, I asked, "Did you see anything you liked?"

"Yes, in fact I did." the Mate replied.

"Why didn't you buy it?" I asked.

"I did" the Mate replied, adding—"I bought it for you."

"What!" I exclaimed.

The Mate pulled a small black jewelry case from his pocket.

"Oh David, what is it?" I nearly shouted.

"Just a little gift, I want you to have. But I don't want you to feel that it obligates you to make any kind of commitment to me. Okay?"

"Okay, David," I replied, trying to control myself.

He handed me the black box. I opened it and saw a gold charm. It was an anchor with a small ship's wheel on the shank. It was about an inch and a half high. It looked similar to the logo at the 'Wheel & Anchor' bar.

"Oh David, it's beautiful," I said.

"I'm glad you like it," he said.

"I love it," I declared.

Before I knew it, I put my arms around his neck and kissed him. I pulled the charm, with its chain, from the box and handed it to the Mate.

"Would you put it on for me?" I asked as I pulled my hair up off my neck.

The Mate put the chain around my neck and fastened it in back. I looked at it for a minute.

"It looks lovely on you," the Mate said.

"Let's go for a walk in the mall," I suggested.

"Alright," the Mate replied.

"I've been looking for a new quilt for my bed. I wonder if they have them here."

In the main aisle, there was an art show. An artist who was famous for painting scenes on Lake Erie, was showing his work. After looking at his paintings for a long time, I picked out one of the Marblehead light. The Mate insisted on paying for it.

"I think I'll hang this one in the bedroom," I said.

"A small picture like that is better in a stairway or hallway," the Mate suggested.

"I think you're right," I replied. "I'll hang it on the wall going up the stairway."

Further down the aisle, we came to a shop selling decorative plates. I bought the Mate a plate showing indians hunting in the winter. After that we just walked around the mall for a while. We stopped at a juice stand and got an orange julius.

"I think I'll call home to see if there are any messages," I said.

"Okay" he said.

I went to the public phone and dialed the number for my answering machine. The only message was from an old shipmate on the Giovanni, named Guiddo. His voice was weak. He wanted to know if I could stop by his place. I hung up the phone and returned to where the Mate was.

"You look worried, Nick," the Mate said.

"An old shipmate called. He doesn't sound too good. He wants me to see him sometime soon," I said.

"Where does he live?" he asked.

"In Toledo. I was thinking of going to see him tomorrow. It's Okay to visit sick people on the shabbat," I replied.

"Would you like me to come with you?" the Mate asked.

"I think Guiddo would like that. I think he's lonely," I replied, adding—"Do you mind if we stop at the grocery store before we go home?"

"Not at all. I have to get a few things myself," he replied.

After we stopped at the grocery store, the Mate took me home. I put the groceries away, then I went in the garage and started up the truck. I found the gas can and put some gas in the Sportster. I connected the battery then I kicked it over with the kickstarter a couple of times. I hit the electric starter and it started right up. I opened the garage door and I rode the Sportster down the driveway to the end of the road and back. I parked the bike in the garage and closed the door. I read the mail, then I made out some bills. I picked out some clothes for the Synagogue. I put some chicken in the oven to bake, then I read part of the manual that the Mate had given me. Later in the afternoon, I visited my neighbors, Chuck and Betty. The ones that watch my house for me. They are a nice old couple, about seventy years old. We talked for a while. As usual, they still refused to take any money for taking care of my house. When I returned home, it was seven o'clock in the evening. I started getting ready for the synagogue service. I put on my mid-length blue dress. I put the wheel and anchor charm inside my dress and put on the silver 'star of David' necklace. I put on my blue flats, brushed my hair and put on my blue dress hat. The Mate arrived at seven thirty sharp. He was dressed in a dark blue jacket and a striped tie. I hardly recognized him.

"My, you look handsome," I greeted him.

"Thank you. You look great too," he said.

"I'm wearing the charm under my dress. I hope you don't mind?" I asked.

"Not at all. The Star of David looks very nice," the Mate replied.

I grabbed my purse and put my coat on. "Let's roll."

The synagogue was on the Sandusky side. Enroute, the Mate said, "I've never been to a synagogue service."

"It's a reform service. It's not much different from a Catholic high mass in Latin. Stand up and sing. Sit down and pray. Just do what I do," I said, adding—"Turn on the light. I have something for you."

The Mate turned on the dome light and I pulled out my Grandfather's Yarmulke.

"What's that?" the Mate asked.

"A Yarmulke. My Grandmother made it for my Grandfather. I'd like you to wear it," I said.

"Is this really necessary?" he asked.

"They used to request that all males wear one. Now a lot of guys don't," I said.

I placed the yarmulke on his head. His reddish brown hair seemed to go well with the black and gold of the Yarmulke.

"There, That looks great," I said.

"I bet I look silly," the Mate said.

"On the contrary, you look . . ."

"Look like what?" the Mate asked.

"Look like you're going to a wedding," I replied, turning away embarassed.

I wanted to embrace him and hold him forever. I directed the Mate to the parking lot of the synagogue. A policeman stopped traffic while we crossed the street.

"In the old days, the men sat in the sanctuary and the women sat in the balconies," I said as we approached the front entrance. We met Mrs. Kosh at the entrance.

"Shabbat Shalom," I greeted her.

"Shabbat Shalom," she replied looking surprised. "I thought we lost you."

"Not at all. The life of a sailor requires me to be away nine months of the year. I'd like you to meet David McCracken. David, this is Kathy Kosh."

After the introduction, I told her that David was the first mate on my ship.

"Oh, how nice. I have to see the Rabbi's wife. Catch you later at the Oneg Shabbat down stairs, bye-bye," she said and left.

In fifteen minutes, I had to repeat the introduction about one hundred times. When the ushers opened the doors to the sanctuary, I was glad for the half minute of respite.

"They love you. I'm thinking of hanging a sign around your neck with your name and personal information on it. My mouth is getting tired," I said as we made our way towards the front.

It was the usual Shabbat service. Cantor Shapiro was celebrating his sixty fifth birthday. He said he had no plans for retirement. The synagogue was everything to the Cantor. After the service, we went down to the Oneg. I introduced the Mate to another one hundred people, before the Rabbi came over. I introduced him to Mr. McCracken, then told him he was the Mate on the Gentry.

"How nice," the Rabbi said. "Are you two in love?" he asked.

"Oh Rabbi, you say the darnest things. I wanted to talk to you about a donation in the memory of my grandmother. Is there any room on the Etz Hayyim?" I asked.

"No, the Etz Hayyim is full. But we have the big Star of David at the bottom of the stairs. See Mrs. Barger, she'll arrange it for you. I wanted to talk to you about a Yahrzeit service."

"Okay. I'll see you about it when I come back in a couple of weeks," I said.

"Very good. It's nice seeing you again. And it was nice meeting you, Mr. McCracken," the Rabbi said as he shook hands with the Mate.

We went up the stairs and went to the secretary's office. I talked to Mrs. Bargar about a place on the Star of David for my Grandmother's memory. We worked out the wording and I paid the two hundred dollar donation. We went to the coat room, got our coats and left. When we got to the Mate's van, he gave me that goofy grin.

"Okay, what's wrong with you?" I asked.

"That's just like the Catholic church. You have to make a donation to get your name on the wall," the Mate replied.

"Such a cynic. Now, let's not have anymore of this on the shabbat," I said in mock seriousness.

"You seemed taken aback by the Rabbi's question," the Mate said after a few minutes.

"It came out of left field, wouldn't you say?" I asked.

"The Rabbi probably has had a lot of young women introduce him to some guy, then they end up getting married. Or maybe he mistook your enthusiasm for seeing your old friends again for something else," the Mate answered.

I was silent for a moment. "I'm very happy that you came with me."

"I'm happy that I came. The people seem to be very nice there," the Mate said, adding—"Who was that guy with the beard that talked to you?"

"Rueben Schwarz. I've known him since I was a kid," I said.

"He looks to be interested in you," the Mate observed.

"I never liked him that much. Square as a bear. He's some kind of lawyer, he says. I never liked him because he's shorter than me," I said.

"I'd say that's mean except that's one less rival to worry about," the Mate said.

"You don't have anything to worry about, David. You look so handsome with the Yarmulke, I only have eyes for you."

When we got to my house, David walked me to the door.

"I'd like to leave at eight in the morning. Can you be here by then?" I asked.

"Sure," the Mate replied as I opened the door.

"Okay, I will see you then," I said as I reached up and took the yarmulke off his head.

He bent his head forward and I kissed him. I went inside and watched him as he left. I went to bed. It seemed that I had just closed my eyes when the alarm rang. I got up and got dressed. I ate a cold roast beef sandwich, then I looked through my old pictures of the Giovanni crew. I heard the Mate pull into the driveway just before eight o'clock. I locked the front door and walked out to the van.

"Good morning, David," I said.

"Good morning, Nick. Sleep well?" he asked.

"Out like a light," I replied. "Can I recline the seat?"

"Sure, I'll let you know when we get to Dorr Street," the Mate replied.

Toledo was not that far away, but I was dead to the world when the Mate awoke me.

"We're here, Nick," he said.

"Okay, make a left," I replied as I sat up.

About a mile south was Guiddo's house. I knocked on the door, after a minute I heard a weak voice then the door opened. There was Guiddo, standing with a cane, looking pale and sick.

"Come in, Nick. I see you brought a friend," Guiddo said, trying to sound cheerful although his voice was weak.

"Guiddo, do you know David McCracken?" I asked.

"By reputation, of course," Guiddo replied, shaking his hand.

"This is Guiddo Scarapitti, our cook on the Giovanni and the best cook on the Lakes," I said.

"That's quite a recommendation from Nick," the Mate said.

"Nick isn't hard to please. Not like some guys I cooked for," Guiddo remarked.

"Please, sit," he invited as he tried to settle himself in a Windsor chair. "It was that damn stroke. Blood pressure was high. My whole right leg has no feeling anymore. I was forced to retire from the line."

"Are you recovering okay, otherwise, Guiddo?" I asked.

"The doctors say I ain't gonna' get any better than this. They say I can't ride my Harley. No women, no wine, no more ships."

"I always told you the wine and women were gonna' get you into trouble," I said jokingly.

"An old Sicilian is better off dead than doing without those," Guiddo said, adding—"This nurse they sent me isn't much company. The only thing she says is, 'NO VISITORS', TAKE YOUR PILLS, REST. She drives me crazy."

"Your old ship mates come by don't they?" I asked.

"Yeah, I suppose they will, but they're out now," he replied. "Nick, I can't ride that Dyna-glide anymore. I want you to take it with you," he said.

"I can't take it, that bike means the world to you," I said.

"It would mean the world to me if you took it with you. You always been a good girl, Nick. I wanted to do something for you. You always kept an old man company," he said.

"Okay, I'll take it, but I'm just keeping it for you until you can ride it again."

"I know you'll take care of it. I'm going to give you some other things too."

"That's ridiculous, Guiddo," I said trying to sound angry.

"Listen Nick, you know how the guy's would say I'm in the Mafia. That's not true. I was never in the mob. My father was honest, he wouldn't have nothing to do with those bums. My uncle was in prostitution, gambling, everything, in New York. I got two younger brothers left, they both followed my uncle. They ain't no good. I told them I'll do the state a favor if they ever came around here. When I die, they'll come to the funeral. They're going to figure on an inheritance. I got my father's money, which pissed them off. I put all the assets into the sailor's relief fund, except for a small trust fund. I told the lawyer to transfer the funds to you when I die."

"I can't take your money, Guiddo. I really can't," I said.

"Now, there's no turning back, Nick. You take the money and finish school, or do what ever you want. Mister McCracken is a good man, you take care of him. You've always been a good girl."

"Enough of this foolish talk. I came here to talk about the old days on the Giovanni," I said, acting angry to keep from crying.

"Okay Nick," Guiddo said, continuing—"I'll tell you about the first time I met your friend. I was on the steamship McGonagle. We was tied up next to the Edward B. Greene in Conneaut, waiting to unload. That was about 1962, I guess. Anyway, some of the guys went ashore and a fight started with some guys from the Greene. Well the fight moved out to the dock and McCracken here, comes down hollering and Lefty Llewellyn hits him right in the jaw. So he starts stumbling backward and I grabbed him by the arm as he was falling off the pier."

"I never knew who that was, but I remember you saying-'This ain't no place for a cub," the Mate said.

"Yeah, we really paid for that one. The mate was named Darling. He made sure that he beat all of our asses for that," Guiddo said.

"Yes, I remember Darling," the Mate said, adding—"If there ever was a man with the wrong name, it was him. It took Steve Monk, Pete Bowers and Harry Hill, all three of them to take him down. This guy was big, Nick. His arms were like tree trunks. It seemed that guys could hit on him all day and not hurt him."

"I remember those guys," Guiddo said.

It seemed they knew just about every sailor on both sides of the border. They talked for hours. I made some lunch, then we talked some more about the Giovanni. We went out to the garage and Guiddo handed me the title to the motorcycle. We pushed the motorcycle onto the trailer and secured it. Then we hitched the trailer to the Mate's van.

"We'll get all this work done before that pain of a nurse comes," Guiddo said, smiling.

About two o'clock, the nurse came. She was bossy as hell. Guiddo was getting angry with her and told her off in no uncertain terms. I told Guiddo that we had to be going because the Mate had reports to do. We promised that we would see him again at the end of the season. I kissed him on the cheek and told him to behave himself, then we left.

As we were driving home, the Mate seemed quieter than usual.

"Something on your mind?" I asked. The Mate looked at me.

"Was there something between you and Guiddo?" he asked.

"You mean something like an affair?" I asked, adding—"What makes you ask that?"

"He treats you like an old girlfriend," the Mate replied.

"It was three days in September, last year. It was warm and I came over on my Sportster and we rode for awhile. Then we did some wine tasting. I got a little 'lit'. I wasn't intending to have an affair. He kissed me on the neck, then he carried me to his bed. For three days we had a fun time. Guiddo was a perfect gentleman, he never told anyone else."

"I can see that," the Mate said. "See what?" I asked.

"A whore demands payment. She lets you know before you get started. A nice girl doesn't ask for anything. A decent man will want to give her things because she makes him happy. Any man with any brains knows long before he gets a woman into bed, what kind of woman he has."

"I wish I could believe that. I had three boyfriends in College. One was a professor," I said.

"A professor. That sounds classy," the Mate remarked.

"He was a capital jerk," I shot back.

"After getting a piece of ass, he started showing his true self. He would holler at me for hours over some stupid thing. Always accusing me of looking at other guys. Totally irrational. I told him to get lost, but he kept calling me for months. I'm not ashamed of my dating activities. I'm not going to tolerate no jerk either. Guiddo was the best guy I ever knew like that. He offered to marry me and take care of me, but not own me. I guess I let him down," I said.

"How's that?" the Mate asked.

"I don't want to be in my twenties and changing my husband's diaper. I know that sounds crappy, but I just could not stand it," I said.

"Do you want to hear about my love affairs?" the Mate asked.

"If you want to tell me," I replied.

"The last one was with Mrs. Kefauver," he said.

"Pfft, that's a laugh . . . I'm sorry," I said.

"It was really disgusting. She couldn't wait to get it over with. She wanted me to marry her before we had sex. I figured I'd better not. We were totally incompatible," he said.

"You think women are like shoes. You have to try them on before you buy them," I wisecracked.

"Not at all. I married Emma before we had sex," he replied, adding—"Then of course, there was Mrs. Kinsey. She would scream when she saw a spider in the house."

I started to laugh.

"What's so funny?" the Mate asked.

"I was wondering if she screamed when she saw your . . . er uh Manhood?" I asked.

"She had a way around that. She insisted that it be totally dark when we undressed," he replied.

"Good, she might have fainted," I wisecracked.

"I guess I haven't had much luck," the Mate said.

"You never know," I replied.

"I'm sorry for bringing up the subject of affairs," the Mate said.

"It's okay, you can't help but feel the way you do. It's the maleness in you, I understand. You have to understand that there's no other man in my life right now, so don't worry about it," I said.

He smiled at me and I got that feeling again, so I turned away.

When we got to my house, the Mate helped me unload the Dynaglide and push it into the garage. I looked at the title. Guiddo had already signed it over to me. Also, he had put in some money to pay the tax and title fee. I looked in the tool box under the seat and found the key. On the key ring was a large, gold man's ring. It looked very old. It had a large, square diamond set in it.

"What's that?" the Mate asked.

"That's Guiddo's father's ring. He must have forgot it was on the keyring. I'll call him and tell him about it," I said.

We went into the house and I put on some coffee, then I dialled Guiddo's number. The nurse answered the phone.

"Hello, this is Nick Strickland. I was just there. I need to talk to Guiddo," I said.

"I'll see if he's awake," she answered.

After a minute, Guiddo came to the phone.

"Hello Nick," he said.

"Hello Guiddo. Look, I found your father's ring with the motorcycle key. I'll bring it over tomorrow. I wanted to be sure you'll be home."

"No, I want you to keep that ring, most of all. My Grandfather killed a mafia chief back in Sicily and took it from him. That's a big status symbol to have a ring like that. I don't want those no good brothers of mine to get it."

"But it's a family heirloom. Surely there's someone in your family who should have it."

"No, I'd rather throw it in the lake first. Listen, that was my father's orders to me. You keep it or give it to your friend or destroy it. Don't let my brothers know you got it. No matter what they say," Guiddo said.

"Okay, I'll keep it for you," I replied.

"Good, I know I can trust you Nick," Guiddo said, adding—"I got to be going. This nurse is bugging me again."

"Okay Guiddo. I'll see you in a couple weeks."

"Sure, and bring some more of your friends," he said.

"Okay Guiddo, bye-bye." I hung up the phone.

The Mate handed me a cup of coffee.

"Guiddo said to keep it, give it to you, or destroy it. Don't let his brothers know I got it. It's a big thing with the Mafia to have a ring like that. He told me when he was in Sicily, during World War Two. He wore that ring and the people would treat him real good," I said.

"We'll put it somewhere safe," the Mate said.

"I'll put it in my Grandmother's safety deposit box." I sat next to the Mate on the couch.

"I've got to get back to the ship tomorrow. I'll have to leave early in the morning. I wish I could spend more time with you," the Mate said.

"Well, you have to do your reports," I said, adding—"You wouldn't want to disappoint Captain Kompsii. One more trip to Duluth and then we can pick up where we left off, hopefully."

The word 'hopefully' brought a surprised look from the Mate.

"I'll be honest with you David. There is a lot I have to think about and a lot we have to talk about."

"I realize that," he said. We stood up.

"I know you've got to leave," I said, then I embraced him and kissed him as hard as I could.

I did not want to let go. He kissed me on the neck.

"We better not David, or we wouldn't be able to stop. The Captain and the Company would not like that at all." We relaxed our embrace.

"I'll see you Monday," I said.

"Bye-bye, Nick." He smiled and then he walked out to his van and drove away.

I went to my study area, which is actually part of grandmother's bedroom. I sat at my Grandfather's desk and tried to read the Talmud. It took a long time to get David and Guiddo off my mind. I read until dark, then I lit the Havdalah candle and recited the Kiddish to mark the end of the Sabbat.

I read the newspaper, while I cooked supper. After supper, I went to the garage and looked at the Dyna-glide. It was a pretty bike for sure. It had a dark blue gas tank and on both sides, there was painted, the head of a young woman with her long black hair blowing in the wind. The name Bella Signora, was Italian for Lovely Lady. The battery and gas were okay. The oil was up so I decided to give it a few kicks to check the compression. I was surprised when it started because my hand was off the throttle. I gave it a little throttle and it roared. The megaphone silencers made it sound like a freight train. It would be a shame to waste all that power, so I took it out on the road. I do not usually ride without a helmet. The cold air on my face, was uncomfortable, but the ride was fun. The big Evo had twin mikuni carbs, it could do 110 M.P.H easy. I made it a short ride, so as not to irritate my neighbors too much. After the motorcycle ride, I got dressed for bed and read the Wheelsman Manual. After about an hour, I fell asleep. I dreamed of my grandmother. She was telling me about her childhood in Russia. I dreamed about the storms I had seen. The storm in my dream was so strong that it blew the lighthouse down. Ships were grounded all up and down the beach.

I woke up at seven o'clock. I had forgotten to turn off the alarm. I got dressed and drove to the diner to get some breakfast. Then I drove to the bus station to buy a ticket for tomorrow morning. I drove to the hardware store and bought some things for the house. Then I drove around for a while. When I got home, I saw a white pickup truck, the same one I saw at the cemetery, parked in my driveway. I realized that it was my mother and father. I got out of my truck and walked around the house. I saw them in the back yard. They turned and looked at me with a disgusted look.

"I don't remember asking you to visit," I snapped.

"Who do you think you are, talking to us like that?" my father sneered. Obviously, he had been drinking.

"Well, I ain't your little girl to kick around," I shot back, gripping my teeth.

"What the fuck are you doing here anyways!?" my father shouted.

"This is my house remember!" I snapped.

"It was my mother's house! It belongs to me!" he sneered.

"You got a copy of the will, Bozo. Now leave!" I said pointing the way.

"You Whore!" my father shouted as he tried to push me.

I kicked him in the crotch and he doubled up. I punched him in the face, when he tried to trip me.

"I'm going to call the police and have you ejected," I said, trying to keep my composure as I walked to the house.

What I did, was get a baseball bat. When I looked out the window, they were getting into their truck.

"Come back here and I'll have you arrested!" I shouted. I heard my father cussing at me, then they left. I went outside to check to see if they had messed with anything.

After the run in with my parents, I went to Grandmother's room and started looking through old pictures. She had a few pictures of her family, when they lived in Russia. They looked so strange. The men wore heavy black coats, and the women wore dresses with puffy sleeves. They neither smiled nor frowned. Even the children had blank expressions. It was a large family, two parents and five children. Only three children had lived long enough to produce families. The rest had died in Pogroms or prison. I made a mental note to look for the addresses of her nephews and nieces. Grandmother was a beautiful woman when she was a teenager. Even with primitive state of photography in the 1920s, she looked like a super model. It's strange, I thought, how different she looked from the little girl in Russia. From any of the people in Russia. There were a lot of people I did not know in the pictures. My grandmother had told me who they were when I was younger. Fortunately, she had the names written in Cyrillic letters. My grandfather was a handsome man and like my grandmother. A light seemed to be shining in his face, always. The pictures of my father were different. Although he was not bad looking, a darkness like a shadow, always seemed to be on his face. Like my great uncle, an incarnate evil.

It took a couple of hours to look through all the pictures. I looked through some of her writings, theses, histories, etc. She also had some professional journals, which contained research papers that she had written. Most of them were about Russian History before, during and after the Menshevik-Bolshevik Revolution. I had always found her writing extraordinary. Because her second husband was from Scotland, she took an interest in Scottish history also. I remembered when she had dictated a fifteen hundred word report to me in high school. Fifteen hundred words came out without a break, much faster than I could write. She had also received letters from universities and organizations around the world. Most were in admiration of her work, except for the ones from the Soviet and British governments.

In the evening, I took a walk around the area where I had played as a child. A few boards remained up in the tree where our tree house had been. I climbed one of our favorite climbing trees. I thought about Tommy, the Mate's son. I wondered what he would think about his father having an affair with his childhood playmate. When I thought about things like that, I became so confused. The conflicts seemed endless. The affairs were simple, although hardly satisfying most of the time. I did not have answers to any of the the questions and conflicts. I walked on the rocks, trying not to think about the Mate or anything else. The lake looked gray and angry beating relentlessly on the shore. I started thinking about my grandmother. She always believed that I should give up the Maritime life and go back to school. She never tried to persuade me into doing something that I did not want to do. I could hear her gentle voice in my mind, telling me that when I time came, I would know what I should do. I was close to the Marina Del Isle, so I had dinner there.

When I got home, there was a phone call from David on the answering machine. He had called at seven P.M., and said he would call back every hour. I sat by the phone and read the motorcycle magazine. I had trouble keeping my mind from wondering to the clock. At eight o'clock, the phone rang. I picked it up.

"Hello, Nick. I just wanted to call you to see if things are okay."

"I had a little trouble this morning. My parents came over while I was out. I had to punch out my father, then they left."

"Did you call the police?" David asked.

"No, I don't think they'll be back. I'll tell my neighbors to call the police, if they come back while I'm gone," I said.

Dave was silent for a minute.

"You're being awful quiet," I said.

"I wanted to tell you that I missed you very much," he said.

"I've been thinking about things . . . about us," I said.

"You have?" the Mate asked, acting surprised.

"I couldn't think about anything else. Listen, some things are troubling me, Tommy . . ." I hesitated.

"Funny you should mention Tommy, he called me last night," Dave said.

"How's he doing? Did you say anything about us?" I asked.

"He's doing fine. I tried to explain about us. He wished good luck to both of us and said he hoped things would work out," Dave replied.

"That's sweet. Were you embarrassed explaining the situation to him?" I asked.

"In fact, I felt the same way I did when I told my father about Emma," he said.

"Well, it doesn't sound like Tommy is gonna' be a problem. But there's still a lot of other things, children, the house, our careers. There must be a thousand issue to work out," I said.

"As for children, I'll leave that up to you, whatever you want. I agree that we'll have to make a decision on some things, but that's normal anytime marriage is considered," Dave said.

"There's another thing, especially since I saw Guiddo. I really don't want to have to bury my husband," I said. David was silent for a minute.

"I never thought I'd have to bury Emma. We never thought about dying, we thought about living. My mother always told me that love is about living, not dying. Which reminds me, not to change the subject, but I would like you to meet my mother sometime, soon."

"Okay, when the season is over, we'll go see her," I said.

"Good. Now I don't want you to worry so much, Nick."

"Okay David, I feel better when I talk to you," I said.

"Good. I'll see you tomorrow then, sweet dreams," he said.

"Okay Dave, Bye-bye," I replied.

After talking with David, I went over to my neighbor's house. I told them about the confrontation with my parents. They said that they would call the police, if they saw anybody over there. I returned home and turned in early because I had to catch the bus at six o'clock in the morning. I read until I fell asleep. I was awaken several times during the night by the sound of the wind and the rain on the windows.

CHAPTER **5**

Back On Board

At five o'clock, I woke with the alarm. I packed my stuff, ate a quick breakfast and called for a cab. I secured everything in the house. When the cab arrived, I waved at him, then I turned the lights off, locked the door and closed it. I walked out to the cab in the freezing rain. The ride to the bus station did not take that long. Although the rain was bad, the traffic was sparse at five thirty in the morning. At the bus station, I sat at one of those little coin operated TVs and watched "Farmfare", the latest news in agriculture. At six oh five, the loud speaker announced that the bus to Cleveland was now loading. I grabbed my travel bag and headed for the door. I stopped under the overhang and handed my ticket to the driver, then ran out to the bus. The seat behind me was empty, so I reclined my seat and closed my eyes. I woke up in Lorain, when a man bumped me with his brief case. It was still dark and now it was snowing a bit. The man who bumped me, apologized. He told me his name. He said that he was in charge of Cost and Accounting for a Cleveland Company. He rode the bus often to save the expense of parking downtown. I told him, I was a sailor on an ore ship and that we were making our last trip to Duluth. He said he found it amazing that I worked on a cargo ship. He thought I was a college student.

When the bus arrived at the station, the snow had stopped. I walked down Ninth Street to the submarine that was docked just east of there. After looking at the submarine, I walked up to the Bond Court Market and got something to eat. I walked past the Soldiers and Sailor's Monument and caught a cab down to the harbor. I walked past a ship which was from Poland. The crew were not allowed to leave their ship. A few guys stood at the railing and waved at me. I waved in return. Our ship was tied up at the end of the repair dock. I walked up the gangway and headed toward my quarters. I heard someone shouting from the Pilot deck. I looked up, but could not make out who it was. As I walked down the passage, I heard somebody behind me. I turned and saw a security guard.

"Young lady, only employees of the Company are allowed on this ship," he said.

Don't that beat all, him calling me a young lady, when he's barely twenty years old, I thought.

"Young man(though I was thinking, punk)I am a member of this ship's crew," I replied with a calm voice.

"I wasn't told about any woman being on this ship. You'll have to come with me!" he demanded.

"Well, I wasn't told about any security guard being on this ship and I only take orders from the officers on this ship Mac! Understand? Now I'm gonna' be in here," I said, indicating my quarters. "If you have any problems with that, then go find somebody who knows what in hell they are doing," I said, trying not to raise my voice.

"I can't let you do that," he said in a cocky tone.

"Get bent, Dude!" I said and I entered my quarters, closing the door behind me.

I heard a radio outside and I laughed to myself. That asshole does not know when to quit, I thought. A few minutes later, I heard a knock on the door.

"Nick," the Bosun called.

I opened the door. The Bosun, the security guard and another guy were standing there.

"Yes, Sir," I said.

"I'm sorry, Nick, but there seems to be some misunderstanding here. Mister Leach says you failed to identify yourself when he talked to you," the Bosun said.

"I told him that I was a member of the ship's crew," I said.

"Did you tell him your name?" he asked.

"He didn't ask," I replied, adding—"He told me to go with him. I told him that I follow orders from the ships' officers only. If this is an inquest, I would like the Captain or the Mate present, in accordance with the maritime rules in chapter six."

"No, this is not an inquiry. Nothing is being said for the record. I'm just trying to clear up a misunderstanding here," the Bosun said.

"As I understand the maritime rules, the problem is that those rules weren't followed," I said.

"I know Nick. These guys aren't my idea," he said.

"Perhaps, you should take this up with the Captain, Dave or Andy, before this gets out of hand," I suggested.

"I'll talk to them later. They're in a meeting as we speak," he said.

"Good. I hope there isn't going to be more problems," I said.

"Yeah, there's a muster at twelve in the Observation room," the Bosun said.

"Okay, I'll see you then," I replied.

I unpacked my things, then laid on my bunk and thought about what I could do for two hours. Those security guards were a pain. They must have been O'Blake's idea. That was really sticking his neck out. Everybody has to follow the rules, even that pathetic limey bastard, I thought. I put my peacoat on and headed aft. I ran into Fred, the Third Engineer on deck.

"Hi, Nick. I heard there was some trouble."

"You mean at the Wheel & Anchor?" I asked.

"No, a little while ago, with the guards," he said.

"They're real pathetic idiots. It's a wonder there hasn't been more trouble," I said.

"I'm looking for more trouble. There will be grievances written, that's for sure. O'Blake put them on board without asking anybody, while the Captain was away. He thinks the crew is trying to sabotage the ship. When the Captain gets here, He'll be screaming."

"Maybe we better hide," I suggested.

"I have to see the Bosun. I'll catch you later, Nick," he said and he walked forward.

I decided to go to the recreation room to see if anyone was there. When I entered the rec room, only Kenny and Buster were there.

"Hey come over and join us Nick," Buster said. He stood up and started punching at the air like a boxer.

"What's matter with you?" I asked.

"I'm just getting warmed up," he said.

"Do you really think that's necessary?" I asked.

"I heard you've been fighting all weekend," Buster replied.

"That's ridiculous," I said.

"We heard the security guard over the radio, saying that there was a belligerent woman forward. We knew right away who it was."

"That's another asshole I should have cold cocked," I said.

"Things got really dull after you left the bar. Everybody cleared out except for us," Buster said.

"Have you guys seen Earl?" I asked.

"He should be along, about noon. With a hell of a hang over, I'll bet," Kenny said.

"Is he alright?" I asked.

"Yeah, he's really worried that you won't like him anymore because of what he said."

"He was too plastered to realize what he was saying. I should have looked out for him like you guys do, instead of getting angry and hitting him," I said.

"He'll be glad to hear that you're not angry. I've got to make a few phone calls. I'll catch you later, Nick," Buster said, and he left.

"Did Earl stay with you over the weekend?" I asked Kenny.

"Yeah, we stayed at Motel Six when we weren't at the bars," Kenny replied.

"Good, I'm happy to hear that," I said.

A voice came over the loud speaker.

"I got to be going. I'll see you later, Nick," Kenny said.

"Okay," I said.

There was nobody aft, so I decided to go forward. As I left the after deckhouse, I met the Bosun.

"Mister McCracken would like to see you in the Wheelhouse," he said.

"Okay, enroute," I replied. As I walked forward, I saw Don, Pete and Al coming up the gangway.

"Hi, guys," I said, waving. They waved.

"You have a good vacation Lass?" Don asked.

"It was a tough fight, but clean living prevailed. Watch out for the private security jerks," I said.

"What in the hell are they doing on board this ship?" Pete asked.

"O'Blake's 'bright idea' apparently. See you later," I said.

I climbed the stairs to the quarter deck and then up to the Texas deck. The security guard gave me a dirty look. He was in my way, so I said, "Excuse me."

He stepped aside, still giving me a dark look. I figured I would bang the door, hard, into the son of a bitch, on my way out, if he was still there. I passed the chart table on my way into the Wheelhouse.

The Mate was sitting in the commander's chair. He was writing something on the clipboard.

"You wanted to see me, Sir," I asked.

"Yes, the Captain said to put you on the wheel, outbound. Do you feel up to it?" he asked.

"I think so, Sir," I replied.

"It's really a breeze. We'll back straight out, then we'll have a lot of water," he said, adding—"I heard there was some problem with one of the security guards."

"Yes, I told him I was a member of the crew, but he didn't believe me. I think he's some kind of sexist bastard," I replied.

"When the Captain gets here, he'll throw them off the ship," he said.

"When is the Captain due back?" I asked.

"That's hard to say. Except for the paperwork, the recertification is completed," he said, adding—"Did you have a nice trip?"

"Yes, it was okay," I replied.

"Good, I wanted to inform you that the rumors are getting really ripe," he said.

"I can handle it. I've already heard some of it. They'll get the story straight soon enough, I think."

We talked for a few minutes, then the Bosun came over the loudspeaker, requesting the Mate on deck aft.

"Sounds like trouble," the Mate said as he headed out the door.

I decided to follow a little distance behind. When I got aft, a small crowd had already formed by the starboard life boat. Don, Al, Pete, Buster and Earl, claimed that the guy slipped and fell, hitting the side of his head. The security guard claimed that Earl had hit him. The Mate had him taken forward to the Observation room and told the other guard to watch him. The Mate said the muster would be postponed until the Captain arrived. I ran into Earl as we were walking forward.

"Hi buddy," I said.

"Hi Nick," he replied, not looking directly at me.

"I heard you were a bad boy," I said.

"We had stashed a little beer in the life boat and were moving it to a safer place, when 'Captain America' interrupted us," he said.

"He's got a sore head now. You should have hit the other bastard too. He's the one that was hassling me," I said, adding—"How was your shore leave?"

"Fine, I think. I can't remember most of it. How was yours?" he asked, turning away.

"Fine," I said, then continued, "I know there's gonna' be a lot of talk, but I know that I can trust you. Thursday night he took me straight home. Friday, we went shopping and to the Synagogue. Saturday, we went to see an old friend in Toledo. Then I studied Talmud the rest of the day. Sunday, I was by myself the whole day. I found out that McCracken was the guy sending me letters. He cares for me very much. I like him too, but we didn't do anything."

"Okay Nick. I Believe you," he said.

"Also, I don't see any reason why this should effect our friendship," I stated.

"Okay Nick, and I'm sorry about what I said at the Wheel & Anchor. I didn't mean it," Earl replied.

"That's okay Earl. I know you didn't," I replied, adding—"We ran into an old friend of yours, one Stephen Monk."

"Oh, yeah! I haven't seen him in probably six years. How's he doing?"

"Okay, but he lost his job on the cement carrier, so he was working in a coal yard," I replied.

"Yeah, old Steve could never resist a fight, that's for sure," he said.

I heard a car horn, then saw the Captain coming up the gangway.

"I'd better get going, the Captain wants me in the wheelhouse. I'll see you later," I said.

"Okay, Nick," Earl said.

The Bosum met the Captain on deck, then they headed for the Observation room. As I was climbing the steps, I saw the Mate and the Bosun escorting the security guards toward the gangway. I figured the

Captain would be in the Wheelhouse real quick, so I hurried up the steps. The Captain came into the Wheelhouse about one minute after I got there. I was looking at the plot board.

"Good Afternoon, Miss Strickland," he said.

"Good Afternoon, Captain Kompsii," I replied.

The Captain looked in the log book then looked at the clipboard for a minute. He picked up the microphone and summoned the Mate and the Bosun.

"Are you ready to take her out this afternoon, Miss Strickland?" the Captain asked.

"Yes, Sir," I replied, trying to sound confident and not cocky.

"Good. We'll be going to Lorain and loading 14,000 tons of coal, then head straight to Duluth."

After a minute, the Mate and the Bosun came into the Wheelhouse.

"We're waiting for a telephone call from the Maritime Commission to confirm the approval of the Coast Guard. Is everyone accounted for, Mr. Munson?" the Captain asked.

"Yes sir," the Bosun replied.

"Dave, call a muster in the Observation room immediately."

"Yes sir," the Mate replied. He picked up the microphone. "All hands, all hands, muster in the Observation room. That is, Muster in the observation room, out."

After the Captain and Bosun left, I turned and headed for the door. The Mate held the door for me.

"Another boring meeting," I said in a low voice as I passed by him.

In a few minutes, everybody was in the Observation room. The Bosun passed out the watch assignments to the crew. Then he passed out some letters from the company to a few of the crew. I got two. After the Bosun finished, the Captain announced that we were going to Lorain for a load of coal, then to Duluth. He said that this would be his last trip with us and he hoped it would be smooth sailing. He said that we would be underway as soon as he got a phone call from the Coast Guard, granting us clearance. After the Captain finished, The Chief summarized the repairs and some engineering changes made to the conveyor. Then the Mate talked about some additional administrative matters and the watch rotation. There were no questions, so everyone was dismissed.

I walked up the steps to the wheelhouse. The Mate was behind me, and Mike, who would normally be at the wheel, was behind him. When we got to the wheelhouse, a cold sleet was falling, hitting the glass and making a rattling sound. I took a seat in the perch, a heavy oak chair behind the wheel. In front of me was the gyrocompass. To the left, a binnacle, a magnetic compass in a heavy brass casing. To the right is the chadburn. A drum with a lever used to send motor signals to the engine room. To my left is the Captain's chair. In front of that is the radar scope, Loran instrument, RPM and rudder indicator, depth reader, search light, whistle, horn, two radios, a fan, clipboard and a thousand other gadgets. An endless array of stainless steel, brass and porcelain levers and switches. Behind me is a wooden cabinet containing binoculars and other gear. On top of that is a coffee pot. At the back wall is a table with charts. On the wall is the Captain's and officers' licenses and the shipyard certificates.

Since it looked like it was going to be a couple of minutes until we had to do anything. I asked for and received permission to read my letters. The first letter was a notification that I would get a pay raise next year. The other letter was a notification that my bid had been received for the wheelsman's position. In the lake service, the union operated almost the same as other unions on land. With a few exceptions, seniority, bidding on a particular job and also bumping rights were prevalent. Service on Canadian boats was recognized. Sometimes, strangers from other ships, displaced crewmen and upset people. In fact, I was a stranger from another ship. Some transfers were inevitable, but being accepted by the crew could be problematic.

After a few minutes, the Captain came over the loud speaker, giving the order for the Chief to disconnect the telephone lines to shore. A guy from the relief watch came into the wheelhouse and signed something on the clipboard, then left. I knew the Captain would be in the wheelhouse soon. The Captain must always be in the wheelhouse when the ship is in maneuvering waters. Such as coming into or leaving port, navigating through channels, rivers and locks, as a rule. I heard the Bosun on my radio, give the order to take in all the lines except the bow line. After that, I could hear the Chief talk to the first engineer. The Gentry was built in the late forties before the days of computer control. The Captain will give orders to the engineer on watch via a radio-telephone or chadburn. Engine speed and direction have to be changed with as little delay as possible. The engineer has to be alert and ready.

The Captain came up the steps and entered the wheelhouse. He handed the clipboard to the Mate and told him to file the documents. He informed us that there will be some ridership, a Coast Guard officer to check out some ship board procedures. I figured there will be a lifeboat, fire or a collision drill. There usually is when a Coast Guard officer comes on board for ridership. The Chief called the Captain, informing him that everything was ready and steam was up. In a few minutes, the Captain told the Mate to standby the starboard gangway. A minute later, the Bosun reported a Coast Guard car on the pier. The Mate was to meet the Coast Guard officer and escort him to the wheelhouse. A matter of protocol. The Captain always followed standard protocol. I heard the Bosun on the radio giving the orders to secure the starboard gangway.

The Mate came into wheelhouse with an officer. He introduced him to the Captain as Commander Seacrist. The commander shook hands with the Captain after saluting. It was obvious that they had met before.

"Anytime you're ready, Bill," the Commander said.

The Captain picked up the radio: "W-B-6-2-1-3 to station 1-3."

"Station 1-3." a voice responded over the radio.

"Intending to depart pier 3-6, ASAP, over," the Captain stated.

"We don't have any traffic that way. You're clear to depart."

"Roger, W-B-6-2-1-3, out," the Captain said.

"Station 1-3, out," a voice answered.

The Captain got on the intercom, "Take in the bow line."

"Bow line in, all lines on board," the Bosun reported over the loudspeaker.

"Ready on deck," the Captain called out.

"Strickland at the wheel," I answered.

"Very well, Miss Strickland," the Captain acknowledged.

"Mr. MacDonough at the motor," Don called out.

"Very well, Mr. MacDonough," the Captain acknowledged, adding—"Rudder amidship, Miss Strickland."

"Rudder amidship, Sir," I replied.

"Back slow, Mr. MacDonough."

"Back slow, aye," Don replied as he moved the lever on the drum. In a few seconds, we could feel the slight vibration as the propeller began to turn. The ship began to move backward slowly. It did not take long to clear the pier, since we had been tied up near the end of the pier. We continued to back straight for about two hundred yards, then the Captain gave the order for five degree starboard rudder. I acknowledged the order and began turning the wheel to the right.

"Steady as she goes, Miss Strickland," the Captain ordered.

"Steady as she goes, sir," I replied. The stern began to pull to the left. In a minute, we had turned ninety degrees.

"Rudder amidships," the Captain ordered.

"Rudder amidships, sir," I replied, turning the wheel counter clockwise and watching the rudder indicator.

When the rudder was amidships, the Captain ordered "All Stop".

Don pushed the lever up on the drum, and replied, "All stop, sir."

The Captain picked up the microphone, "Deckwatch to launch the starboard life boat," he said, then he switched on the alarm horn.

The Coast Guard Commander was not in the Wheelhouse anymore. He must have left when I was steering. Doubtless he was aft, observing the lifeboat launching. I could not see very well from where I was. I saw a couple of guys run aft. The life boat was suspended on davits, the lines that kept it from swinging would be released. Only two hooks held the life boat, one on either end. The davits could slide outboard to the edge of the deck on rails, then the boat could be lowered with block and tackle. The boat had to be lowered evenly, that is kept relatively horizontal, or the boat could turn over and things would be in a hell of a mess. Five or six men could launch a boat in less than a minute if everything goes right. Even in calm water, life boat launchings do not always go according to plan. In a rough sea, it is nearly impossible to launch a boat successfully. It was quiet in the wheelhouse, until we heard the Chief on the radio saying that it took two minutes and six seconds to launch the lifeboat in the water. I was thinking that the Chief would have them heaving their back sides off getting the boat back on board. I saw a group heading forward being led by the Commander. The mate came into the wheelhouse and told the Captain that the Commander wanted me to participate in the life raft drill.

"Very well, Miss Strickland, go with Mr. McCracken," the Captain said.

"Yes, sir," I replied.

I followed the mate down to the main deck, forward. The Commander asked me if I was familiar with the raft gear. I told him that I was.

"Would you like to demonstrate how to inflate a raft overboard and how to get into one?" the Commander asked.

"Very well," I replied. I removed the raft from its fiberglass box and hooked the hook through its eye. The raft is heavy, all folded up into a square. I set it on the bulwark and pulled the ring that released the compressed air. When I heard it the pop, I threw it overboard. In a few seconds, the raft was completely inflated. I put on the life jacket and fastened a hemp rope to an eye on the bulwark. I passed the rope under my arm and around my leg like a mountain climber. I was glad that I had done this kind of thing before in college. I stepped onto the box and then to the bulwark. I pulled the rope tight then I began to rapell down the side of the ship. Unfortunately, the sleet started at this time and the side of the ship already had a glaze of ice, so I had to descend somewhat gingerly. When I got four feet away from the water, I pushed away from the ship as hard as I could and slid down the rope into the raft. I went down on my knees in the raft, to keep from falling over. I looked up and saw half the crew looking down at me. A rope ladder was thrown over the side.

"Tie the rope to yourself, then climb up the ladder," the Commander said.

I tied the rope to my belt and leaned over and grabbed the rope ladder. A rope ladder lies flat against the side of a ship like the Gentry. You have to use your hands and feet to pull the ladder away from the side of the ship every time you take a step up. I was making good progress up the ladder. When I got as high as the bulwark, I went to heave myself over the side, but I slipped and started to fall sideways over the bulwark. The Mate grabbed me by the waist and sat me down on my feet. A few snickers came from the crew.

"That was very good, young lady. I'm assuming that every man of this crew can perform this procedure with equal acumen." Then the Commander left.

I started untying the rope from my belt. I heard the Chief tell Al and Ed to haul the raft aboard and to pull up the ladder. I unfastened the rope from the bulwark.

"I'll get the rope, Nick," the Chief said.

"Okay, Chief," I said.

"That was a good demonstration of life raft launching," the Chief said.

"Thank you," I replied, adding—"I hope the Coast Guard is happy."

"I think he was impressed. I don't think I could have done as good," he said.

"You'll never have to. This is a good, strong ship, it will always bring us home safe," I replied adding—"How did the lifeboat drill go?"

"A lot slower than I would have liked, but they got the boat into the water properly," the Chief replied.

"Good. I better get back to the wheelhouse. See you later, Chief," I said.

"See ya' later, Nick," he said. I headed up the stairs to the Pilot deck.

When I got to the wheelhouse, the Captain and the Mate were talking to the commander. The Mate looked my way, then handed me a clipboard.

"The Commander would like you to sign at the bottom, Nick," he said.

I took the clipboard and looked at the bottom. There were six names there. The guys that launched the lifeboat. I signed my name and handed the clipboard to the Mate. I looked at the Captain.

He was smiling as he said, "Dave, do you think you could take the conn after we clear the breakwall?"

"Yes Captain," the Mate replied.

"Very well," the Captain said. "Mr. MacDonough, ahead one-half."

"Ahead one-half, Aye," Don replied, as he pushed the lever forward on the drum.

"Miss Strickland, steady as she goes, come around to 080."

"Steady as she goes to 080, Aye," I replied, and I turned the wheel slowly to the left until the red needle was on 080.

The sleet was getting worse. The wipers were going full speed. Up ahead, through the mist, I could see the lights of another ship. Apparently headed for the Cuyahoga River. Ahead to the port side, I could see the lighthouse that marked the entrance to the breakwall. It took about ten minutes to reach the gap in the breakwall. At the Captain's command, I turned the ship almost straight north, and we headed into the open lake.

SECTION 2

THE UPBOUND RUN

ON-LOADING—"COLLISION BEND" MANEUVERS

The wind had whipped the water into whitecaps. Six foot waves beat against the ship in rapid succession. Since the ship was empty, we could feel the waves more than usual. The Captain ordered a course change to 270 and the speed changed to standard speed, then he left with the Commander. The weather continued to worsen by the minute, the Mate ordered the deckwatch to look out fore and aft.

"There's two ships ahead of us and a smaller one, probably a coast guard cutter. Over here is a dredge barge operated by the Corps of Engineers. They're working at the Lorain harbor entrance."

"It must be alot calmer over there," Don remarked.

"They're working in the lee of the breakwall, over there. We'll come in on the leeward side too, but will have plenty of room," the Mate said.

It took a little over two hours to get to Lorain. The weather had not improved any during the trip. We passed the Corps of Engineers' dredger as we went to the leeward of the breakwall. When we entered the harbor proper, the Captain and the Commander came into the Wheelhouse.

"I'll take over the conn now, Dave," the Captain said.

"Very good," the Mate said.

"Miss Strickland, steady as she goes, port rudder, come around to 1-7-0." the Captain said.

"Port rudder, come around to 1-7-0, steady as she goes, yes sir," I replied, as I turned the wheel to the left.

The bow swung to the left, until we were heading nearly south. Ahead and to the starboard side were the coal and limestone docks. The huge heaps of black and gray marking their location. The Captain picked up the microphone.

"W-B 6-2-1-3, clear for station 1-2, over."

In a moment came a reply.

"Station 1-2, go ahead W-B 6-2-1-3."

"Requesting clearance for dock 42-U, over," the Captain said.

"Copy, you have clearance for 42-U. They're tight on 12 and 16, three bottoms waiting, over."

"Copy 1-2, we'll stay clear of that area, W-B 6-2-1-3, over."

"Copy, Station 1-2, out." The Captain put down the microphone.

There were three ships waiting to unload at the large pier that was further upriver. Every time a freighter came in, the bridges had to be raised. That would tie up traffic for half an hour at least. We would be going to the older pier at the mouth of the river. Coal dumpers were there to load six hundred footers like us. Fortunately, there were no other ships at that pier, so we would not have to wait to load. Our present course would take us right to it.

"Mister MacDonough back one third," the Captain ordered.

"Back one third,aye sir," Don replied as he pulled the lever back on the drum.

The ship slowed a lot better without a load and manouvered better too. When the bow was about two hundred feet away from the pier, the Captain ordered back slow for the propeller.

The ship would come to a stop under the coal chutes. The Captain gave the order to have the hatch covers opened and to stand by the mooring lines. In a minute, the ship had come to a stop at the pier. The deck gang threw the bow and stern lines over to the pier. The Captain gave the order to rig out the gangway. The Captain told the Mate that he was going ashore with the Commander and told him to take over, then the Captain left the Wheelhouse with the Commander. The Mate got on the radio to the Chief for a progress report. The Chief said that the hatches were coming off okay, but there was a problem with the gangway. The Mate hung up the microphone and left the Wheelhouse quickly.

"The Captain's gonna' be pissed-oled if those guys don't get the gangway rigged out," I remarked.

"Just a wee-bit of a problem, Lass. The Chief will have it put to right straight off," Don said.

From the rear window, I could see the Mate walking across the deck. A minute later he walked over to the hatch crane. I saw him wave to somebody on shore, then he talked to somebody on the radio for a minute. Then he headed forward again. In a few minutes, he came to the Wheelhouse and started writing on the clipboard.

"The problem with the gangway was minor, just a kinked cable that jammed in the sheave. It was cleared and rigged out by the time the Captain got there. It's going to take another ten minutes to get the hatches off, then we'll start loading."

"Was that an old friend of yours at the coal chutes?" Don asked.

"A friend of my father's, named Don Barry," the Mate replied.

On the intercom, we heard the Bosun reporting the hatch covers being removed. The Gentry can take a full hold of coal, so it would be necessary to remove every hatch cover. There are sixteen hatch covers. Each one has fifty-six clamps that must be loosened. The deck watch gang were loosening the clamps, the Gate man and Bosun were operating the hatch crane. The wind and the sleet were not making the job any easier.

Earl entered the Wheelhouse.

"Excuse me, Sir. The Captain said to see you about some cleaning supplies," Earl said.

"Yes, there's some soap and cleaning solvent on the dock by the gangway. Is there anyone down on the deck to help you?" the Mate asked.

"I think everyone is occupied with the hatches," Earl replied.

"Very well. Nick, can you give Earl a hand with the supplies?"

"Yes, Sir," I replied getting up from the swivel chair.

"It will be well into the next watch before we are loaded. They'll probably need you to help with the hatch covers," the Mate said.

"No problem, Sir," I replied, then I turned and left with Earl.

"All this over time is gonna' kill us, Earl," I said jokingly, as we descended the stairs. We stopped at the forward storage room and grabbed the four wheel cart. When we got out on deck, I was glad that I had my parka, the wind and sleet were getting worse. We walked over to the gangway and left the cart. On the dock was a pile of boxes. We walked down the gangway and over to the boxes.

"We'll take them up on deck first, then we'll take them aft on the cart," Earl said.

"That sounds like a plan," I said as I grabbed a box and headed up the gangway. In a few minutes we were almost done. Earl grabbed the last box.

I was headed up the gangway, when I heard someone holler my name. When I turned around, I saw a guy I knew, Jeff. He was a geology major at Mount Union.

"Hey Jeff, long time no see. What have you been up to?"

"I've been working for the Corps of Engineers. We're dredging now," he said.

"You got tired of well logging?" I asked.

"No, that deal dried up last year when the price of crude oil dropped through the floor. So I've been doing this deal. The salary isn't that great, but there isn't anything else."

"How's Dolly doing?" I asked.

"Great, we got two kids now, so she's pretty busy," he replied.

"You don't say, well give that poor woman a break for a while. How's the Gunman doing?" I asked.

"He got laid off when I did. He's working for a Chemical Company in Akron now. He's got four kids."

"Four kids? Oh my!" I exclaimed.

"Do you still live in Cleveland?" I asked.

"No, I live in Euclid," he replied, adding—"I'll give you my address."

He pulled a card out of his pocket and wrote on the back. I looked at the card.

"Great, the season will be over in a week or so, I'll give you a call."

"Good, I'll catch you later Nick."

"Bye-bye, Jeff," I said, and he turned and left.

Earl had the cart loaded and was waiting for me, when I got on deck.

"Got it all loaded? Great, let's head aft," I said.

"That guy a friend of yours?" Earl asked.

"Yeah, a geology major from school," I replied as we headed aft, Earl pushing the cart.

When we reached the aft deckhouse, the order came over the loudspeaker to clear the deck. The boom had already been raised and swung over to the starboard side. After a minute, the coal chutes were lowered and coal began pouring into the hold. The coal dust was coming out of the open hatchways. Fortunately, the wind was blowing most of it over the side and into the river.

"The ship's gonna' be dirty as heck," I said, as we headed toward the dumbwaiter, for the laundry room, in the passageway.

154

Earl went down to the laundry room, as I loaded the dumbwaiter. When it was loaded, I shut the door and hit the down button. When I got down to the laundry room, Earl had most of the stuff on the shelf already.

"It looks like we'll be taking the 'ratwalk' forward," I said.

"Yeah, it shouldn't be too dusty up there. I got some more things I got to do up there anyways," Earl said as he closed the sliding door and latched it.

"Oh, shoot!" I exclaimed. "I left the cart by the dumbwaiter."

"That's okay, it ain't going anywhere," Earl replied. We headed forward, through the boiler room, and opened the door to the 'ratwalk'. I heard a whining noise as we entered the below deck passageway.

"They're pumping ballast," I said.

We could hear the coal rattling against the steel plates of the hold.

"We must be taking on a hundred tons a minute," I said, adding— "We should be loaded in less than three hours."

"Yeah, they'll need at least two coal trains so we can load directly from rail cars," Earl explained.

When we got forward, I left Earl in the Crew's hall and went to my quarters to get my tool belt.

In a few minutes, I was back in the Wheelhouse. The Mate was talking to the Bosun over the radio. I watched as the rail cars were being emptied into the chutes. The hydraulic arms would grab a rail car, like a child picking up a toy, and dump it directly in the hopper. Rail cars could be emptied faster than they could be pushed into place with this machinery. The Mate turned toward me.

"We should be loaded in a little more than two hours," he said.

"Is there enough coal?" I asked.

"There should be as long as they keep unloading rail cars," he replied.

"That's a dirty, miserable job, especially in this weather. Your friend, Steve, is probably not having a good time," I commented.

"Yes, unfortunately, he's having a hell of a time finding another berth," he said.

"Is he having a hard time adjusting to his job at the coal yard?" I asked.

"There isn't many places where a man with an eighth grade education is going to get a job making fifty thousand dollars a year. That's what he's accustomed to earning," the Mate replied.

The voice of the Bosun came over the load speaker. The Mate picked up the microphone and began to conversing with the Bosun and the Chief about the way the ship was being loaded. The Bosun had some questions about the trim. I looked at the pile of coal. A long black ridge stretching inland. Next to the coal was taconite. Forty or fifty piles merged into one another. It was odd how the lights of the dockyard, brought out the different shades on the peaks. Like a surrealistic mountain scene painted by some demented artist.

I heard the Mate talking—"I don't feel like shifting our fuel oil around, so we'll slow up loading the after three holds until we get our ballast all pumped," he said, adding—"You look to be a million miles away."

"I was just thinking about some of the problems of loading," I said.

"You may be working a double," the Mate said.

"I don't mind, I got plenty of rest," I replied.

"Too bad you can't take her out. Mike will be at the wheel," he said.

"This ship steers like a row boat compared to the Giovanni. It took ten miles to slow her to a stop," I said.

"Yes, the new thousand footers don't have enough propellers, rudders, or engines for that matter. To save money in building them, they gave them just enough power to push them along. We had an old destroyer at the Academy that could turn ten times shorter than this ship and stop shorter than you can believe. You could broad side it to a stop in nothing flat," the Mate said.

"Did they have turbines?" I asked.

"No, they had uniflow engines, twin screws and rudders, plenty big enough. The engine crew could change speed and reverse quickly enough, but they had to stay awake down there," he replied.

"The diesels on the Giovanni did not require much attention, except on start up. Once in awhile the crankcase had to be checked to make sure no cooling fluid was in there. The control of the engine speed and the gearing was automatic, controlled by a bridge computer. The engineering guys would walk around with their tool box, trying to look busy. The only time they were busy is when something needed repaired," I said.

"I served on a packet freighter out of Fairport. The old wishbone fleet. We had diesel engines on that one, but they seemed to require a lot of work. The Chief had to heat the engines with a torch to get them turning over. We used to carry logs on the deck, piled so high, it looked like a floating wood pile. We carried automobiles, rail cars, airplanes, right out on deck. Fresh water won't bother that stuff like salt water. Getting loaded and unloaded was a pain, sometimes," the Mate said.

"I knew some guys on the Canadian side that served on those ships in those days. They called them short ships because they could fit into the locks of the Welland Canal. The Liberty ships couldn't get into the lakes that way, but they could get out to Quebec and load the ships there," I said.

"Yes, after they got through the Welland locks and Lake Ontario, they had to thread their way through the narrows in the St. Lawrence river," he said.

"The Victory was a liberty ship, wasn't she?" I asked.

"Yes, she was converted and lengthened in New Orleans in 1950. Tugs took her up the Mississippi, then to the Chicago River and into Lake Michigan." he said.

"Weren't you afraid that the old liberty ship would crack in half?" I asked.

"Originally the Marine engineers said the method of construction was at fault because the sections were welded inland and moved to the shipyard for assembly. Of course, the real reason was the bad steel that was used in the hull plating. When they lengthened her at the building yard, a lot of the original plating was replaced when the new midsection was welded in," he said.

"Loading and unloading must have been a real pain with that after cargo hold astern of the Midship deckhouse like that," I said.

"Yes, she was built for salt water sailing. I've heard that she's back there again, trading between Taiwan and the Phillipines," he said.

"I remember when I was young, Tommy and I were playing by the shore in the summertime. We saw the Victory coming into Sandusky. Tommy got real excited and started shouting 'That's my dad's ship!' then he ran home. Later, we went down to the dock to see the ship," I said.

"Was that the time I smacked both of you because you were trying to push each other off the dock?" the Mate asked.

"Yes. When I went home, I didn't say anything to my Grandmother. I thought you were going to call her and she would smack me again," I said.

"I was plenty mad, that was very dangerous," the Mate said, before being interrupted by the Chief on the loud speaker.

He picked up the receiver, "Yes Chief . . . Very well, switch from number two to number four pump . . . Okay, let me know when, out." then he put the receiver down and wrote something on the clipboard.

"I thought I noticed a list," I said jokingly.

"Not yet, but the port side is filling faster than the starboard," he said, as he continued writing notes on the clipboard.

John, the Steward, came into the Wheelhouse.

"Yes, John," the Mate said.

"Sir, there is a problem. The supply delivery didn't have the Baker's Chocolate, I ordered. It's right here on the order invoice!" John exclaimed, brandishing the paper, adding—"I guess those idiots can't read."

"Yes, that must be. I'm sure there's some Baker's Chocolate somewhere in the city of Cleveland. We'll see if the Westcott can bring us out some when we get to Detroit," the Mate said.

"Alright, but I don't know how I'll manage until then," John replied and he turned and left.

"It looks like there'll be no chocolate doughnuts until we reach Detroit," the Mate said.

"The way these guys like chocolate doughnuts, we may have a mutiny before then," I said jokingly.

"The crew may drown him in his soup first. If he hadn't been so schlocked when he came on board, he might have noticed there was no chocolate. He could have got some before we left Cleveland," the Mate said.

"It's not all his fault, the chandler made the screw up," I said

"When you have a responsibility on a ship, you don't assume anything, you make sure. Those guys ashore, some of them only make minimum wage. Many of them don't care if the job gets done right or not," the Mate said.

"We're switching to both pumps now," the Chief said over the loud speaker.

"Very well Chief," the Mate acknowledged.

I pulled out Jeff's card and looked at it. I saw the Mate looking at me.

"I saw Jeff down on the dock when we were getting supplies. He's an old chum from Mount Union."

"Were you in the same classes?" the Mate asked.

"No, he was a geology major. He was a good friend, like a brother to me. He beat up a foreign student that was bothering me one time. One time a boy friend and I went to a sports banquet. Jeff gave me his ticket to check the number for him. His number came up for tickets to a Cavs game. My so-called boy friend was gonna' take the tickets and tell Jeff he didn't win. I got so pissed off, I broke up with him on the spot. I can't stand a low life like that, trying to screw over a friend of mine. Jeff should have beat the hell out of him for that," I said.

"Does your friend work around here?" he asked.

"He works for the Corps of Engineers in this district," I replied adding—"Of course, if Reagan and Congress don't resolve this budget fight,he might not be working at all."

"That won't effect us one way or the other," the Mate said.

"Yeah, I suppose Reagan has messed up this industry as much as he can already. Except the harbors and rivers will start silting up without the Corps of Engineers," I replied.

"I take it you don't think much of President Reagan," the Mate said.

"What's there to like? He's a pretty boy PR man for the rich people. He has screwed up this business. Took all the money that was going to education and gave it to the military. Ran up budget deficits like crazy. Oh sure, he can talk pretty, but his message really sucks. I can't believe that turkey got elected again!" I said.

"I guess a lot of people like him in spite of all of that," the Mate replied.

"Maybe in Lake County, a bastion of Republicanism. How about those steel workers in Cleveland? The rich bastards were going to take millions of dollars for themselves. Shut the plant down, then say there is no money for the pension fund. That idiot Reagan did nothing about it. Senator Metzenbaum put a stop to that nonsense. Made them keep the plant open or no more business from the government. How many ships did that save on the American side, I wonder?" I asked.

"Enough for sure and in a nick of time. The business is in a period of transition. I guess that can't be helped," the Mate said.

"Period of transition? That sounds like a tactful way of ripping the guts out of the shipping industry. Look at the Canadian side. They haven't lost hardly any of the ships or men like over here," I said, adding—"American Shipbuilding hasn't built a ship here for years. The owners are turning it into a marina. That's a disgrace, this ship was built here."

A call came for the Mate to pick up the phone so he did.

"Yes, I see. Have him hold until the loading is finished. The Captain will be coming on board then . . . okay. I have the charge numbers already . . . very well, good bye," then he hung up the phone.

"Well, we'll be getting another guy after all. Ronald Karan from Fairport. A Finn. Must be a friend of the Captain's," he said.

"Maybe he's from Grand River," I said jokingly.

"The name sounds familiar, but Fairport and Grand River are so small, it's easy to hear someone's name. I guess he's about forty and has been on the lakes for a while," the Mate said.

"Maybe you two can talk about the old days when you were growing up," I said.

"Yeah, maybe he knows the developer," the Mate said, adding—"I went to school with the sorry jackass."

"Just so he doesn't show up in Marblehead. There's enough condominiums already. The so-called developers, though they are really destroyers, have just about ruined the islands and peninsula already," I said.

"Yes, we have to start an anti-development movement in Marblehead," the Mate said.

We could hear some chatter on the radio. Another ship requesting permission to dock.

"It looks like we got some company and some trouble," the Mate said, adding—"If they block us, we'll have to go into the river and turn around by cable."

After a minute, we could see another ship coming through the weather. It was a newer type ore carrier with the wheelhouse astern like the superlakers but only six hundred and eighty feet long, all self unloaders. It's present course would take it to our dock after it made a turn.

160

"It looks like you're right, David. I think it's heading our way and it's gonna' dock before we're done," I said.

"That will make your job alot harder," the Mate said.

"Well, that's what we get paid the big money for," I replied.

"That's the spirit. You guys be careful out there," the Mate said.

Mike,the Wheelsman, came into the pilot house.

"About time for shift change," he said.

The Mate looked at the clock then pressed the toggle switch for the watch bell.

"Well, I'd better get down on deck. Catch you guys later," I said, then I turned and left. I stopped at my quarters and got my deck parka and hard hat, then I headed for the Crews hall. When I got there, I found that Al, Ed, Brad and Smitty were shooting craps.

"Good afternoon, Gentleman," I said.

"Gentlemen! Boy you're using that term loosely," Brad wisecracked.

"Well, I always heard you were a loose gentleman," Al shot back.

"He's got loaded dice for sure," Smitty said. "They just about got her loaded, Nick?" Al asked.

"Yeah, it shouldn't be long now. It looks like another ship may be docking behind us. We may have to go into the river and use the cables to turn," I said.

"That's great. In this weather, that'll be a lot of fun," Ed said.

"Mr. McCracken said to watch yourself out there. It may be slippery," I said.

"That's wonderful," Ed said, adding—"Did Mr. McCracken tell you anything we don't already know?"

"There's supposed to be a new guy coming on board for deckwatch. One Ronald Karan from Fairport, they say," I replied.

"I don't remember him," Ed said.

"I do," Al said. "He used to work on the Cliffs line a few years back. I didn't know he still worked on the lakes, though."

"The Mate says he may be a friend of the Captain's," I added.

"Maybe a friend of the Mate's," Brad said.

"Nah, I don't think so. He's got a friend, Stephen Monk, he's trying to get a berth for," I said.

"You know Monk?" Al asked.

"I met him in Marblehead. He said that he ended up in jail and his ship left without him. I think he was crying the blues to Mr. McCracken," I replied.

"Tough Break. Monk's a decent guy. He knows steam engines inside and out, for sure," Al said, adding—"What's he doing now?"

"He's working at the coal yard in Sandusky," I replied.

"It's your turn, Al. Are you in this game, Nick?" Brad asked.

"No, I'll pass," I said, then I grabbed my tool belt and hardhat and went into the Observation room to get a cup of coffee.

Hank, the Engineer, was sitting in there drinking a cup of coffee.

"Hi, Hank," I said.

"Hello, Nick. What's the good news?" he asked.

"I was wondering if you and the Chief have got this boat in good trim?" I asked.

"As good as it's going to get until we are fully loaded. I've got to man the winch forward until we get out of this mess," he complained.

"You've got the gravy job, old buddy. It's only gonna' be for ten minutes. The bridges will be raised by that time, I think," I said.

"Yeah, this weather is getting worse. That's not making it any easier for you guys," he said.

"It's getting dark. In a few minutes, it will be dark as midnight because of these clouds. That's what worries me the most. The light is never good enough down there for handling cables. I hope this new guy knows what he's doing," I said.

"Are we getting a new guy?" Hank asked.

"The Mate got a call on the radio, saying that a replacement for Dixon is standing by on shore. He's supposed to have a lot of time on the lakes."

"I hope so. Well, I got to see the Chief. I'll catch you later, Nick," Hank said, then left.

For fifteen minutes, I was alone in the observation room. The sound of the loading began to diminish. I looked out the window. I could see that the boat had been pulled ahead so that the chute was over number fifteen. It won't be long now, I thought. I went down to the jobox in the Crews hall and checked my air wrench to make sure it had plenty of oil. An air wrench can freeze up after a while in this kind of weather because the air is cold but still has a lot of himidity. The decompression of air within the wrench causes ice to form, which can stop it cold, so to speak. I put my hard hat on and waited. I saw the Bosun, Hank and the Gateman head forward to the hatch crane. In another fifteen minutes, the coal chutes were raised. The call came for the deckwatch to secure the hatch covers. I came out on deck as the hatch crane was starting to put on the number two hatch cover. I plugged the air hose into the compressed air quick disconnect and plugged it into my air wrench. Then I began to tighten the hatch clamps. I was glad that I was wearing my warm leather gloves. The wind was getting fierce. Brad began tightening the clamps on the other side. I could hear shouting and see people pass by. It was almost dark now. The deck lights were on, but there always seemed to be a shadow, so half the time I was working in the dark.

"We could always use more light here," I said, but the noise of the air wrenches kept Brad from hearing me.

I saw Al and someone else working on the number two hatch cover. The other guy was wearing an old style yellow bib overalls. Those were good foul weather gear but the modern waterproof Goretex gear were lighter and less bulky and had largely supplanted the older style rubberized cloth. I had finished my side when I looked up and saw Brad messing with his air wrench.

"Your wrench freeze up?" I asked.

"I think so," Brad said, adding—"I'll have to go and get another one."

I finished tightening the other side then I moved on to the number three hatch cover. The quick disconnect for the compressed air line at the number three hatch cover was covered with ice. I had to bang on it with the air wrench to knock off the ice. I started tightening one side, while Smitty came over and started working on the other side. Brad and the new guy began working on the number four hatch cover. We were making good time in spite of the darkness and bad weather. It took a little more than an hour to get the hatches secured. Meanwhile, the Bosun and the gateman had finished with the hatch crane and were washing down the deck with hoses. When we finished, the unloading conveyor was brought back on board and we attached the new shackles, which had cable stays. Finally, we adjourned to the Crew's hall to warm up. I went over to the coffee pot and the guys began talking.

"Where's the new guy?" Brad asked.

"He had to go topside to see the Captain. Probably to sign some paperwork or something," Smitty said.

"The Captain's on board?" Brad asked.

"You must be blind, boy. The Captain came on board about half an hour ago," Ed said.

"Well excuse me! I was working, I didn't have time for sightseeing," Brad said.

"You won't have much time to thaw out either. The Bosun told me that the Old Man wants to get going right away," Smitty said.

"This is a real f—king pain," Ed said.

After that, the Mate entered the room with the new guy.

"Ladies and gentleman, I would like you to meet Ronald Karan. He will be working deckwatch on the third watch."

We shook hands and introduced ourselves all around.

"I'm sure you've heard that we'll have to go into the river and turn with the cables. Al and Ed will stay on deck and handle the cables here. The rest of you will take the ladder off the port side and run the cables, until we get straightened out. Let's be careful out there. We don't want any OSHA recordable injuries. Nick, you and Al secure the port gangway. Smitty and Ron, standby the lines forward. Brad and Ed, standby the lines aft. Any questions?" Since there were none, The Mate added—"Very well, carry on," then he turned and left.

I put my hard hat on, zipped up my parka and put on my leather work gloves. Al was ready, so I went out the door.

"It looks like they used half the lake to wash down the deck," I said jokingly.

"Yeah, don't they know this stuff freezes," Al said. When we got to the portside gangway, I pressed the lever to raise it. When it raised all the way, we swung it inboard and collapsed it on deck and secured it with the wing bolts. When we got it secured, we heard the order to take in the lines bow and stern. I keyed my radio and reported the gangway secured. I heard the fore and aft report that the lines were in. The whistle blew twice for the departing signal. I always got a feeling of exhilaration when the ship set sail. Eventhough it was just a job and I had done it a thousand times, I still got that childlike feeling of adventure.

"Blast it all with that whistle," Al cursed.

"It's not that bad," I said.

I laughed to myself as I saw the snow begin to accumulate on Al.

"It's wet snow, it won't last."

"If they weren't so damn cheap, they would hire a tug or install bow thrusters," Al remarked.

"Well, we might be the last ship to ever be turned by cables. Think of it as a historical event," I said jokingly.

"They can save the distinction for somebody else," Al shot back as we headed toward the starboard side.

Since the ship was pretty close to the dock on the starboard side and we couldn't back up, the Captain had to pull straight ahead for a cables length before easing over to port. The Captain continued to sail up the middle of the river, then he brought the ship to a stop at the first turning basin The Bosun and Gateman lowered the long boarding ladder until the top was hooked over the railing and the bottom rested on the concrete.

"I hope this ship don't move," Brad said as he swung his leg onto the ladder.

"If it does, You'll be the first to know," the Bosun wisecracked.

When Brad got to the bottom, I got up on the ladder.

"Keep those guys in line, Nick," the Bosun said.

"Somebody's got to do it," I replied.

When I looked up, I saw the Mate coming our way. I stepped down the ladder, which was at less than a forty-five degree angle. When I got to the bottom, the concrete was covered with ice. I headed forward to join Brad. Al threw us a cable, then Ed threw another cable to us. The Mate told us to hook the loop in the end of the cable, over the yellow bollard. The bollards were color coded for identification years ago. After we had the cables hooked up, I could hear the hammering noise of the winch forward. The cables went taut immediately, then, almost imperceptively, the bow seemed to pull toward us. A minute later the Captain started the rudder hard over. The stern began to pull away from the wall as the bow inched forward and toward us. The Mate slacked off one of the cables, and told us over the bullhorn to move it to the next bollard. I lifted the loop, in the end of the cable, off the bollard and Ron helped me to run it to the next one. We slipped it over the bollard.

"F—k, F—k," Ron cursed.

"It's not all that bad, bud," I said.

"I've got a sliver in my hand," he said, removing his glove. The sliver had broken off. Fortunately, he was able to remove it from his hand without much ado.

"You gonna' be okay with that hand?" I asked.

"Oh yeah, no problem. It's not bleeding," he replied as he put his glove back on.

I waved to the people on deck as we stepped out of the way of the cable. The snow was getting worse by the minute. Brad and Smitty ran by with the other cable to the next bollard. After a couple minutes of pulling, our cable was slacked. The Mate told us to unhook it. When we did, the cable was pulled on board. Using the winch and the rudder, The Captain was able to straighten the ship in the turning basin

As the ship started to back, we ran around the turning basin and across the bridge,to the bollards on the river side. It was about three hundred and fifty yards to the river side bollards. The snow was falling like crazy and half the time we were running in the dark. We got to the river side before the Gentry did. Fortunately the railroad bridge was raised. Good news for us, we wouldn't have to stop the operation to wait for the bridge.

"I wish the Captain would get a move on. My hands are freezing off," Brad complained.

"I told you those cotton gloves weren't any good," I said.

I reached into the pocket of my parka and pulled out a new pair of leather gloves and handed them to him.

"These are nice and warm," Brad said.

The other guys snickered at his statement.

"Genuine Moose hide. I got them from the Giovanni," I said.

We heard the hail from the Mate. A few seconds later, a heaving line came flying through the air, landing next to us. Smitty and Ron grabbed it and started pulling out the mooring cable. The Captain was bringing the starboard side as close to the wall as possible to facilitate making the turn as well as to be in a position to pick us up. The stern was in the narrow channel, which prevented the Captain from using the rudder as much as he did coming in. Also, the cable was from the after towing winch. In fact, half of the ship had to be sticking out into the river before they could start pulling it around on the cable. The operation would be more difficult and slower than before. Too much strain could not be put on the cable or it would break, causing a tremendous pain in the neck for all of us. The Captain was blowing the whistle every thirty seconds to warn other ships of our presence in the river. The darkness and the snow storm were causing the Captain some anxiety. The cable went taut and we heard the characteristic hammering sound of the winch as it slowly pulled in the cable. Every foot the ship was pulled toward us, allowed the Captain to back a foot or two and give him a little room to use the ship's rudder. Trying to move a six hundred and forty feet long ship, loaded with fourteen thousand tons of coal, along a few feet at a time, is no mean feat for even the best of Captains. The Captain also had the current in the river to consider, which, no doubt, he was trying to use to his advantage. After ten minutes of pulling, the Mate ordered the cable moved to the next bollard. When the cable went slack, Brad and I ran it to the bollard and secured it. I informed the Mate over the radio and he acknowledged.

"It's getting G-d damn cold," Brad said, jumping up and down and slapping himself.

"It's a fine day. Not too hot, nice breeze," I wisecracked.

"Not exactly swimsuit weather," Smitty said.

"How's the hand?" I asked Ron.

"Fine, I can't feel a thing," Ron replied.

I looked toward the ship. Even through the snow and the darkness, I could see the stern swinging slowly toward us. The Captain must have gotten some room to use the ships rudder. The first time he only got about ten degrees of turn on the cable. This time, he was apparently able to bring the ship all the way through the turn.

"I think the Captain's got it this time," I said.

"Yeah, the old man can turn her in his bath tub," Smitty said.

"Yeah, as long as he don't have to be down here handling the cables," Brad sneered.

"Ah, quit griping," Smitty shot back, "You'll be safe and warm in your bunk in a few minutes. Maybe the Captain will have a teddy bear for you."

"Mr. Wiseguy," Brad remarked.

"I'll take a 'teddy bear' brewed in Pittsburgh," Ron said.

"That's Monongahela bilge water. It shouldn't even be called beer," Smitty said.

"Better than that Milwaukee horse piss you call beer," Ron shot back.

"If it didn't have a freakin' label on it, you guys wouldn't know where in the hell it came from," I said.

"Oh, a connesouier of beer. Tell us which beer do you drink or hit people over the head with," Brad asked jokingly.

"The Canadian beers are better on both counts," I replied.

"How do you figure?" Smitty asked.

"More alcohol, if you cut them, it cleans the wound better," I said, adding—"Of course, I don't know how it works on juke boxes."

"We were getting pretty loud without the juke box, most of the yuppie crowd left in disgust. Earl was cursing you pretty bad, then, not even a half an hour later, he starts the whiney, sniveling rant, 'I lost my friend. She's mad at me. She's gonna spend the weekend with the Mate'," Brad said.

I noticed that all the guys were staring at me, so I figured I'd have to say something sooner or later.

"I've already told Earl that he'll always be my friend. Earl also knows that the Mate lives one street over from me in Marblehead. That's why we decided to drive home together. No use renting two cars was there? I was thinking of driving down to Alliance with Earl, but since he wasn't going, I went home instead. On Friday, I went to the Mall and later to the synagogue. On Saturday, the Mate and I went to see an old friend named Guiddo Scarapitti, in Toledo. He had a stroke and was partially crippled. Saturday afternoon the Mate said that he had to work on paper work since he had to be back on the ship Sunday morning. I studied Talmud. Sunday, I was slumming. Any questions?" I asked.

"The guys didn't mean anything with that talk about you and the Mate being in love," Smitty said.

"Well if anybody asks you, tell them I said, I have no relationship with any man right now," I stated.

"Sure Nick. We don't believe those stories that Pete tells," Brad said, adding—"He never tells a story straight."

"Someday, somebody's gonna get the story straight for him," I replied.

We heard the order to stand by and wait for the ladder.

"Old Cappy's gonna' make it easy for us," Smitty said.

"Not easy enough," Brad said.

"What do you want, a f—cking elevator?" Smitty asked.

"I remember we used to have a joke about the ship's elevator on the Giovanni. The guys would drive the new kids crazy telling them to take the elevator," I said.

"How's that?" Ron asked.

"They would direct them to the Captain's quarters and tell them that was the elevator," I replied.

"Remember the 'spark watch'?" Smitty asked.

"What's the 'spark watch'?" I asked.

"The deck watch would tell the new guys to watch for sparks. If they saw one, go wake the Bosun. Those old coal burners always gave off a lot of sparks," Smitty replied.

"That's like the old gag about getting the keys for the Soo locks and giving them to the Bosun," I said.

"Yeah, that's probably the oldest gag on the lakes," Brad said.

We started walking along the riverside wall as the ship approached closer.

"Look at these damn bastards, they got their Christmas lights up already and it's two days before Thanksgiving!" Ron said.

"Yeah, it looks like a damn bar," Smitty said.

"What in the hell does that mean?" Brad asked.

"I grew up in a little Presbyterian town in Canada. In those days, nobody had holiday lights on the outside of their house. Only the bars had the outside lights," Smitty replied.

"Kinda' hard to have Christmas lights, if you don't have electricity," Brad said.

"Even after we had electricity, nobody had electric Christmas lights. We still lit candles and placed them in the windows and on the Christmas tree," Smitty replied.

"On the tree? That's crazy, the tree would catch fire in an instant," Brad said.

"My father always told my mother not to light the candles, but she did it anyway. There were many of time, when my father had to run out of the house, carrying a burning Christmas tree, beating it on the snow. It played hell with the glass bulbs, I tell yah. My father wasn't too happy about going outside, barefooted, in his night shirt. Winters were cold then," Smitty said.

"Ha, ha, that sounds like some of the crazy things my great aunt and uncle would do. I don't think that they ever agreed on anything," I said, adding—"Christmas was a real trip at their house."

"I thought you were Jewish," Smitty said suddenly.

"I am. My grandmother and my grandfather on my father's side were Jewish. On my mother's side, they were all Christian, if you could call it that. They sure didn't act like it. I still have a few of their old ornaments made for candles," I said.

"Didn't you feel left out, not having Christmas when the other kids were?"

"No, Christmas with my mothers' relatives was a real bummer, so I was happy to have Chanukah at my paternal grandmother's home. When my paternal grandfather died, my grandmother married a Scotsman named Eichann. He was a Christian. He had a bitch of a daughter. A materialistic, know-it-all, over bearing, epitome of an evil witch. I didn't like going over to her house for Christmas. Nothing anybody did was good enough for her. Nothing to miss there," I said.

"Don't hold back tell us what you really feel," Smitty said jokingly.

The ship whistle blew. We heard the Bosun give the order to put down the ladder. Al and Ed lowered the boarding ladder over the side.

"Express elevator to the penthouse suite," Ed called down.

"Ladies first," Smitty said.

"Thank you," I said, as I started to climb the ladder. The wind was blowing like all thunderation. I had to hang on tight while climbing the ladder. When I got over the railing, I swung off the ladder, landing lightly on the deck.

"Real nice form on the dismount, Nick," the Bosun said.

"She didn't need the Mate this time," Ed wisecracked.

"Brad's suffering from the cold. He may need help," I said.

We watched Brad come up the ladder. About half way up, his foot slipped on a rung, but he managed to hang on and recover his balance.

"I'm okay," he said as he climbed up the ladder again. When he got to the top, Ed grabbed him as he stepped off the ladder.

"I'm okay. Just a little stiff from the cold," he said, then he jumped down on the deck.

Ron and Smitty got up the ladder without incident. The Bosun told Al and Ed to bring up the ladder and to secure it. Then he informed the Captain via radio that everyone was back on board. The other guys went aft to get warmed up. I headed forward to my quarters to get some sleep. The Captain blew the whistle and the ship began to move down the river.

CHAPTER 6

Situation Normal, All Fouled Up!

Just after I got to my quarters, the watch bell rang. It was 8:00 PM, the end of my watch, normally. I noticed an envelope by the door, so I picked it up. I opened the envelope and found a notice from the union and a note from the Mate, asking me to join him in the mess aft. I decided to accept the Mate's invitation to join him aft. I zipped up my parka and headed aft.

When I got out on deck, I saw the ship was just leaving the river. In a few minutes we would be past the sheltering break wall and onto the stormy lake. I decided to get to where I was going before the ship had entered the lake proper. As I hurried aft on the starboard side, I noticed the wind was coming from the northeast, blowing fast and steady and the snow was continuing undiminished.

"Hi Nick," I heard Al say.

"Hi Al, mean night, huh?" I commented.

"Yeah, if you're going aft, your buddy is already there," he said.

"My buddy? You mean Earl?" I asked.

"No, the Mate," he replied.

"Oh good. There's an administrative matter I have to see him about," I lied, adding—"I'll catch you later, Al," then I continued aft.

When I entered the after deckhouse, I ran into the Chief, Fred and Kenny.

"Hi guys. How's it going?" I asked.

"Hi Nick," the Chief said, continuing, "It's hard to tell how it's going yet. We'll know in a couple of hours."

"Okay, see you later," I said and continued on my way. Something must be wrong. The Chief usually doesn't talk like that, I thought to myself.

When I entered the galley, John was on duty.

"Hello John," I said.

"Hi Nick, looking for some supper?" John asked.

"You got anything ready to go?" I asked.

"The only thing we have is Sloppy Joes and fried potatoes," he said.

"That sounds good, and some coffee too," I requested.

"Coming right up," John said.

"It looks like there's quite a crowd in there," I observed, when John returned.

"Yeah, some kind of trouble in engineering, I think," John replied.

"I wonder what it can be," I said, thinking out loud.

"I ain't got no idea. As long as it doesn't effect me, I'm not going to worry about it," he said as he handed the tray to me, then he turned and headed back to the galley.

Everyone was sitting at the long table, so I went over there and sat down at the only space, which was next to Carl.

"Hi guys what's up?" I asked.

"There's oil in the steam condensation line. The Chief is trying to track down the source of the contamination," the Mate replied, adding—"If there's oil in the boilers, we may have to be towed back to Cleveland."

"It may be a leaking bearing in the turbines. If that's the case, the condensation sump will have caught the oil so it would not get back to the boilers," Buster said.

"We got us a boiler expert here," Pete wisecracked.

"You better believe it, jar head. I have a third class stationary engineer's license." Buster shot back.

"I don't understand how oil could get in the boiler water in the first place?" Billy asked.

"The hydro-seal pumps are oil driven, if one of the seals go bad, then oil could leak through into the boiler water," the Mate said, adding—"The engineering guys are sampling the steam and water everywhere they can, to try to locate the source of the oil."

After a few minutes, a call came over the loudspeaker for the Mate to see the Chief in the number two boiler room.

Right after the Mate left, Earl came into the room with a cup of coffee.

"Hey Earl, there's a place over here," Carl called out. Earl came over and sat down on the other side of Carl.

"Yeah, sit right down there. Nick's been getting lonely since the Mate left," Pete wisecracked.

"You're a real pain in the ass, Hall!" Earl exclaimed.

"Weren't you with the 20th Division, Quarter Master Corps, in Tri Nang?" Ron asked.

"No, I was with the first Marines at the DMZ," Earl replied.

"Uh no . . . I was talking about Mr. Hall," Ron said.

"Well, how about it?" Brad asked.

"About what?" Pete shot back.

"Ron wants to know if you were in the 20th Division Quartermaster at Tri Nang," Brad repeated.

"Yeah, I was there for awhile," Pete said.

"I was with the Air Cavs up there, for a couple of weeks during the Tet Offensive," Ron said, adding—"I thought I recognized you from the PX."

"Yeah man, I find the green machine days a real bummer," Pete said as he got up. "See you guys later," he said, then he walked out.

"What's wrong with him? He usually don't mind talking about Vietnam," Smitty said, adding—"You knew him in Nam."

"Yes, we were moved to the Tri Nang area during the Tet Offensive because of heavy enemy activity in the area. Tri Nang was one of the major towns that hadn't been overrun in that region. I remember a couple days after our arrival, there was a rocket attack at night. Pete was on the second floor of this five story hooch. A rocket went down through all five floors and exploded on the first floor, causing a fire. Pete jumped out the second floor window and broke his leg. We carried him to the hospital and a doctor set his leg," Ron said.

"Pete, the war hero," Brad snorted.

"Yeah, he put himself in for the Purple Heart. I heard the doctor wouldn't sign the combat citation, so he got a Colonel, somewhere, to sign it," Ron said.

"I'm surprised he didn't get a Silver Star out of it," Brad said, and everybody laughed.

"I bet old Earl here, is a war hero," Billy said jokingly.

"Earl doesn't like to talk about Vietnam. He lost a lot of friends over there," I said.

"That's okay, Nick," Earl said, adding—"I have twenty two combat citations, including two Silver Stars and a bronze star."

"I had a friend I went to school with, named Mike Yates. He was at the rock pile during the Tet. Did you know him?" Ron asked.

"I'm sorry, I forgot most of the guys I knew. I didn't keep a diary or anything like a that," Earl said.

A call came over the loudspeaker for the personnel in the engineering department to report to the Chief.

"Well, party time is over. We'll probably be rowing this son-of-a-bitch to Duluth before the night is over," Buster said as he and the other guys got up to leave.

"I'm going forward to get some sleep," I said to Earl as I got up to leave, "You want to walk forward with me?"

"I wish I could. There's some extra laundry the Chief gave me to do back there. He wants it right away," Earl said.

"Okay buddy, I'll catch you later." I said, then I left the Crew's mess and headed forward.

Even before I got outside, I noticed the ship wasn't rolling or pitching like it should have been. Of course, the Captain is a sensible man. He's not going to take the ship out in any kind of weather, if he has a major problem with the boilers or turbines.

When I got outside, the wind was still blowing hard from the northeast and the snow was as bad as ever. I put my hood up and started forward. The deck was well lit. In fact, every light on the ship seemed to be on. The Captain had us hove to the shelter of the break wall. He did not want another ship colliding with us in the darkness and the storm. I heard a ship's whistle blow. I looked around on the starboard side, but did not see anything. I did not see anything on the port side either.

"She's almost off our bow, now," I heard someone say.

I looked behind me and saw someone in a yellow raingear, approaching. I knew it was the new guy, Ron Karan.

"It looked like the American Republic. she passed us a couple of minutes ago," he said.

"Yeah, I think we'll be here for awhile," I replied.

"Are you the only Nick on this ship?" he asked.

"Yes," I replied.

"Then this must be for you," he said, holding out a small cardboard box.

I hesitated for a second, I thought it was something from the Mate. I was taken aback by such indiscretion, then I realized that the Mate would not deliver anything to me via somebody he did not know.

"Who's this from?" I asked, as I reached out and took the little box.

"A guy named Joe Wesley, he was a fireman on the Anoka for years," Ron replied.

"Let's go to the Crew's Hall," I said, adding—"It's colder than hell out here."

On the way forward, I was trying to remember where I knew a Joe Wesley from. When we got to the Crew's hall, I opened the box, then I nearly dropped it in surprise. Inside the box was a fine rendition of a Pegasus, carved from a coal clinker. I carefully inspected the work of art, and it truly was a work of art in spite of the humble medium. I felt ashamed of myself for not recognizing the name. Guiddo and I went over to Joey's house last winter. He collected coal clinkers of the right shapes and carved things from them. A folk artist extraordinary, no doubt. He told me that when he raked the clinkers from the fire grates, he could see animals, birds and things like that in them. He had been carving objects from coal clinkers for at least thirty years. His artistry was famous on both sides of the border. Many an officer and crewman considered himself lucky to have an example of his work.

"It's the most beautiful thing I've ever seen. Joey has really out done himself this time," I said. I saw a card in the box, I picked it up and read it: 'To my friend Nicolette-A Wild Spirit-As Always, Joey.'

"That's a beautiful horse. Joe told me to give it to Nick on the Gentry. I naturally assumed you were a man," Ron said.

"Joey always told me that he would carve me a Pegasus. I never thought he could find a clinker the right shape," I said.

I placed it carefully back in the box.

"I need to get some shut eye. I'll catch you later and thank you very much," I said.

"Think nothing of it. I'll see you later," Ron said.

When I got to my quarters, I was really tired. I took off my parka and my boots, then I laid down on the bunk. I could hear the steam line banging on the other side of my quarters. Must be a water pocket somewhere, I thought. Then I heard the banging again. I realized that it was too rhythmic for water. Somebody was using a hammer aft and the noise was being carried all this way. The Chief must be giving those guys the devil, I thought then I drifted off to sleep.

A couple hours later, I was woke up by the sound of bells ringing, then I went back to sleep. I slept for a few hours more, then I was awaken by the rolling of the ship. I got up and went to the small bathroom across the passageway, to get a drink of water. I realized by the rolling and the noise that the ship was definitely underway. When I got back to my quarters, I checked the time, it was 12:30. I am going to get three hours of sleep if it kills me, I thought. I laid down and drifted off to sleep right away. It seemed like I had just fallen asleep, when I heard a knock on the door. If it is one of those pranksters, I'm going to kill them, I thought. I called out, then I looked at the clock-3:25am. It was time for me to get up anyways. I went to the door and opened it, the Bosun was there.

"I'm sorry Nick, the Captain wants a special meeting with those people coming on watch. Can you be in the Observation room in five minutes?" he asked.

"Okay, I'll be right up," I said. I put my tool belt over my shoulder and I headed for the observation room. On the way, I ran into Ron.

"You pulling a watch with me?" I asked.

"With Pete, I was told," he replied.

"That is strange, another watch change. It must be because of the trouble aft."

"Yeah, I guess," he replied, as we entered the observation room.

It looked like half of the crew was there. I grabbed a doughnut and a cup of coffee. The ship always chooses that moment to roll, when you're pouring coffee.

"Rough morning, huh Nick?" Mike asked.

"I've seen worse," I replied, as I wiped up the coffee spill.

"Well this one is going to get worse yet," he replied.

"Thanks for cheering me up," I said and he chuckled.

The Captain walked through with Andy and they headed up the steps towards the Wheelhouse.

"I wonder where the Old Man's heading? I thought he was going to give us a speech," I heard DJ say.

"Maybe you don't want to hear what he's got to say," Mark, the electrician commented.

Hank, the second engineer, came into the observation room and sat down beside me.

"Well, you got this ship going again. Good work, old buddy," I said.

"The work's not half over yet. The Chief had to swear on his wife's fidelity that we could proceed at nine knots safely. The Captain took some convincing. When it comes to this ship, the Captain doesn't like to take any chances . . ."

Hank was interrupted by the Chief coming into the observation room.

"Good morning ladies and gentlemen. We have a lot of work to do, so I'll try to be brief. Yesterday at 19:25 hours,the engineer on duty found a small amount of oil in the condensate line when he was sampling condensate water. A resampling confirmed this. The engineering department immediately began sampling the entire engine system to determine the point of ingress and to determine if any of the oil had entered the boilers. At approximately 21:00, we determined that the point of ingress was a seal in a bearing in the low pressure turbine. Fortunately, the condensation sump was able to retain all the oil, so none of it apparently got back to the boilers. To be safe, we've cleaned all the oil from the line and the sump. Also, we replaced the boiler water. The Captain has given us permission to continue on the high pressure turbine. This will allow us to steam at nine knots safely without overworking the turbine. Meanwhile, we will dismantle the low pressure turbine and repair it. The weather is far from ideal for doing this. However, when we get in the St. Clair river, the waves won't be bad, so we should be able to align the bearings properly at that time. The officers and wheelsmen will double-up for deckwatch duties to replace the following people-Nicolette Strickland, Harold Ostrander, Earl Franklin, Jonathan Smith and Ronald Karan. These people will report to the number two boiler room as soon as we adjourn. Any Questions?"

"Once again we have to save engineering's ass," I heard Hal say.

"What's that?" the Chief asked.

"I said-Let's make this a team effort from from first to last," Hal replied.

"That's the spirit," the Chief said. "If there are no questions, I'll see you all aft in five minutes.", then he left.

"Where's Earl?" I asked.

"I'll go find him," the Bosun said and he left.

I started walking aft with the other guys.

"You get plenty of sleep, there, Brad?" Smitty wisecracked.

"F—k no! I wasn't planning on having to do everyone's work for them," Brad snarled.

"Well guy, it'll be nice and warm back here. You won't even need your coat," Ron said.

"These guys are picking on me again, Nick," Brad complained.

"Sorry, old buddy. I didn't get my beauty sleep either," I said.

"The Chief can't stay awake forever. You can snooze when he does," Smitty said.

"Are you kidding! I've never seen that sucker sleep when things are alright. He sure in the hell ain't gonna' be sleeping until this turbine is on line," Brad replied.

"Don't worry Brad, we'll give you a break. We'll also show you a new place to sleep," Hank said.

When we got to the boiler room, the Chief gave us some high temperature gloves and nomex sleeve protectors. When we got to the engine room, we could see the engineering guys already working on the casing and the piping. The low pressure turbine was right next to the high pressure turbine, which, although it was insulated, was giving off a hell of a lot of heat and a loud whine. The Chief warned us that the bypass pipe was hot and it wasn't insulated. The reduction gearing on the low pressure side was disengaged from the propeller shaft coupling already. We had to unbolt the quill shaft from the reduction gearing, so the turbine could eventually be lifted out. When Earl showed up, the Chief had us rig four chain falls to the I-beams overhead. There were already two chain falls there, but it would take four chain hoists, just to raise the upper casing safely enough on a rolling ship. After rigging the chain hoists, we moved some equipment around and laid some timbers on the deck plating, for a bed to receive the upper casing when we got it off. The steam had to be shut off to the high pressure turbine for a few minutes, until a blank flange could be installed on the cross-over pipe to the low pressure turbine. That was a hell of a job. That pipe was at superheat temperature. I was surprised that they got it done in less than ten minutes. The Chief had to supervise the whole operation and reduce the superheat steam coming from the boilers.

After two hours, we were allowed to get a sandwich, two at a time, for fifteen minutes.

"I never thought I'd be happy to feel that cold wind again," I told Earl as we sat in the rec room.

"Yeah, it's usually hotter than that in there. They got the fantail door opened to the engine room stairs, but even that wind can't make it past all that heat down there," Earl said.

"When we get back down there, it should be about time to pull the casing," I said.

"Yeah, I suppose," Earl said.

"You're accustomed to working back here dude. Show some enthusiasm," I said.

"The guys are always saying things about me," Earl said.

"I didn't hear them say anything about you," I said.

"Oh, that stuff about being a war hero," he replied.

"I know you don't like talking about Vietnam, but I think the other guys were impressed with your citations," I said, adding—"We better get below again."

When we got to the engine room, the other guys had the tackles hooked to the casing.

"What do you think, Nick?" Buster asked.

"I think we should attach timbers for spreaders, so we don't bend the casing."

"I don't think the casing will bend, but spreaders are a good idea. Put them in, Fred," the Chief said.

"Very good, sir," Fred replied.

The Mate came in and he and the Chief left together.

"It looks like your darling, Nick," Billy wisecracked.

"He was a Son-of—a-bitch!" Ron said.

"Who?" Billy asked.

"Stan Darling, the old mate on the steamer Independent," Ron replied.

"What was wrong with him?" Billy asked.

"He was a Bully and a jerk. He tried to pick a fight with everybody. Nobody felt bad about beating his ass, even if it took ten men to do it," Smitty replied, as he was drilling the holes to secure the spreaders.

"He didn't like me because he was from Geneva. He wanted a Geneva boy on his ship. He started some crap with me in Ashtabula harbor. I broke four cue sticks on him and bounced a couple cue balls off his head. Then six other guys jumped him for good measure. We all ended up in jail. The Captain was pissed off. That was Darling's last trip on the Independent," Ron said.

"You hear that crap,Gary?" Buster asked.

"Yeah, same old stuff," Gary replied.

"You gonna' come with us at the end of the season," DJ asked.

"No, I'm catching the first bus to Florida," Gary replied.

"Mr. Big Bucks, he can't wait to get back to Florida," Brad wisecracked.

"How long have you lived in Florida?" I asked.

"I just moved there in January. My parents still live in Lake County."

"So what in the hell is wrong with Lake County?" Ron asked.

"I used to work in a chemical plant in Avon Lake. I wore out a new car in two years, commuting everyday. Here, I don't have to commute nowhere and I can live where ever I want. I'm into water sports now, so I'm staying in Florida," Gary replied.

"We got to get all you single guys married. I hate to see you so happy," Smitty said.

Kenny, the Machinist came into the engine room.

"Hi, Brad," he said in a feminine voice.

"Hi big guy, long time no see," Brad said, in an equally feminine voice.

"You faggots knock it off and help us with these!" Fred commanded, as Smitty handed him a spreader.

"Get us some half by six inch bolts and nuts and washer," Fred told Brad.

"Right away, Great Sahib," Brad wisecracked, as he headed for the parts cabinet.

"I hope we're getting engineering pay for doing this stuff," Ron said as he handed Fred another two by six.

"Don't worry, the Captain is gonna' give you guys overtime at engineering scale. Which I regret to inform you, isn't that much more than deck pay," Fred said.

"I can read a union pay scale as good as anybody else. So we better be getting assistant engineers' pay for this job, not the wipers' rate, or there's gonna' be mega grievances for sure," Smitty said.

"Yeah, yeah, take it up with the Mate," Fred replied, adding—"Give me a hand here guys."

We held up the two by sixes while Fred pushed the half inch bolts through the links of the chains and tightened the nuts.

"Nick, you and Earl man the hoists," Fred said, adding—"Let's take up some slack here."

Earl pulled the chain on the left side hoist, while I pulled the chain on the right side hoist. When the chains were pulled up tight, we switched to the front side of the turbine casing and repeated the same procedure.

"Okay, we'll leave it like this until the Chief gets back," Fred said.

"How much do you think this casing weighs?" Buster asked.

"We estimate between five and six tons, a mere pittance," Fred replied.

"These four hoists are two tons each, that ought to be enough," Buster said.

"One would probably do it. There's a safety factor of three for these hoists. There will be two men on every hoist, more than enough," Fred added.

"I hope this ship doesn't do any bad rolling or pitching while we're hoisting," Gary said.

"The spreaders should keep the weight pretty much even on all the hoists," Fred said, adding—"The Chief will inform the Wheelhouse when we're ready to hoist."

"Maybe the Old Man can take her into Sandusky Bay," DJ said.

"The Captain doesn't have room to maneuver in there. The astern turbines are in the low pressure turbine, so backing is out. I think the Captain will try to stay in the lee of the islands while we're hoisting. The waves shouldn't be as bad there," Fred said.

"Do we get a break after we pull this?" Billy asked.

"The turbine shaft has to be lifted and placed in its cradles, then that will be all for a couple of hours. Meanwhile, we'll be fixing the bearing seals, so we don't get a rest," Fred replied.

"Poor Baby! This turbine job is probably gonna' pay of his house," Kenny wisecracked.

"I bet it's costing the company enough," Smitty said.

"The company's got money enough," Buster remarked.

"If this coal doesn't get to Duluth, it will cost the company plenty," Fred said.

"I'm getting an AR-15 with my over-time money," Carl said.

"Oh, you're always getting an AR-15, an M-1 or some damn thing. All you ever do is look at that gun magazine," Buster said.

"I like to go hunting. What am I suppose to hunt with, my bare hands?"

"Will there be enough time to go deer hunting?" Ron asked.

"If it doesn't take us all winter to get to Duluth. The season starts Monday, after Thanksgiving and goes for eight days."

"You should go to Michigan, the season's longer and you can use your M-1," DJ said.

"Yeah, and I can pay half a years' salary to get a non-resident license," Carl said.

"Ohio deer are better, corn fed. Those scrawny things in Michigan eat tree bark all year," Ron said.

"Horse Crap! Michigan deer are the same as Ohio deer, except ours play football better," DJ said.

"Them's fighting words boy and for your information, your beloved coach is from Barberton, Ohio," Smitty said.

"At least he had the good sense to leave Ohio," Brad said.

"Gentlemen, let's have your attention!" the Chief called out as he entered the engine room. "In approximately two minutes we'll be ready to commence. Carl, Gary and Kenny will man the rope and pull the casing over after it is raised. Two men will be at each hoist. We'll have to bring it up straight and even, then lower it the same way. Any questions?" Since no one had any questions, he continued, "Very well then, assume your stations."

Earl and I went to the front right corner.

"I bet you didn't have to pull the engines on that Kanook MV of yours," Smitty remarked.

"We had to work on the engines sometimes. It had 8000 horse power, two cycle diesels. The screws were reversible so the engine only had to turn one way," I said.

"It sounds like a luxury liner," Ron remarked.

"It had a hundred and five foot beam and drafted twenty-eight feet. When it was loaded, it rode smoother than this ship does. It was a real chore to get into the locks though," I said.

"I've been on these steamers for twenty years, but this is the first time I've seen a turbine pulled," Smitty said.

"I worked for Ohio Power. We used to pull the turbines all the time and rebuild them," Buster said.

"Stand-by at the hoists!" the Chief ordered.

We took up the slack in the chains.

"Pull two feet of chain, on command. Ready? Heave!" We pulled out two feet of lift chain, the load was not as great as I thought. Fred and the Chief went around the casing loosening the gasket.

"Okay, keep it level, pull away," the Chief said.

We started pulling the chain continuously and the casing rose slowly and stayed level. Surprisingly, the ship was not rolling as much as I thought. In a minute, we had the casing well clear of the turbine.

"Okay lads, put your backs into it!" the Chief told Gary, Carl and Kenny.

They began to pull the casing over to the wooden bed we made for it as we walked along. When the casing was positioned over the wooden bed, we lowered it slowly until it came to a rest.

"We can leave it like that for now. It's not going anywhere," the Chief said, adding—"Get a couple of slings around the turbine shaft."

Fred had the slings ready to go. Two hoists were unhooked from the casing and slid over to the turbine. The hooks were slipped through the eyes of the sling. Ron, Smitty, Buster and Brad raised the turbine a couple of feet. Fred and the Chief slid the cradles under the shaft and they lowered it onto the cradles.

"Good Guys," the Chief said as he and Fred secured the shaft in the cradles. "It's going to take us about two hours here, then we'll call you. Be sure to listen for the call," the Chief said. As we were leaving the engine room, we ran into Mark, Hank and the Oiler Joe.

"Good luck, guys," DJ said.

"Stick around, we'll find some work for you," Mark remarked.

"No can do, I gotta' get some sleep," Buster said as he headed for his quarters.

"Are you going to your quarters?" Earl asked.

"No, I think I'll get some coffee and go to the lounge," I said.

"Can I join you?" Earl asked.

"Sure," I replied.

We stopped by the galley and poured a cup of coffee from the kettle.

"Well, how are our turbine technicians doing?" Louie asked.

"Coming along nicely, I think," I replied.

"You all want sandwiches or something?" Louie asked.

"No, not now. Maybe before we go back," I said.

We went to the Rec room and sat down by the television. In a few minutes, Ron, Smitty, DJ and the Kid came in and sat down.

"There goes the neighborhood," I remarked.

"Don't worry, Nick, we'll be good," Smitty said.

"You guys gonna' watch TV?" Ron asked.

"Yeah, go ahead," I said.

Billy turned on the TV.

"Maybe 'Gilligan's Island' will be on, or 'The Brady Bunch'," he said.

"Sorry, guy. We don't pander to the lunatic fringe on this ship," DJ wisecracked.

"Whatta' ya' mean? This is good, wholesome family entertainment!" Billy exclaimed.

"Yeah, until the Mate and the Chief find out," Smitty said.

"Well, if you guys would rather tell war stories, then go ahead," Billy said.

"Please guys, I think we heard them all, twenty times, already," I groaned in protest.

"Oh contrare, we got some new blood here and maybe Earl will honor us with a story or two. How about it, Earl?" Billy asked.

"I'll tell you some crap kid, it might save your life sometime," Ron said. "We were a couple of clicks outside a town called Plei Ku. We came to a village out in the jungle, nobody was moving. I just got to Nam. Me and five others straight out of the repo-depot in Okinawa. Anyway, we started walking down this road toward this little village. A jungle road ain't much to speak of, just a dirt path wide enough for a jeep. The first guy to enter the village was one of the replacements. Bang! He steps on a mine, and gets his leg blown off. The headman comes out shouting-'No VC here!'. The first sergeant beats him on the head with a rifle butt 'till his head breaks clean in half. They must have thought we were really stupid. They use their road all day and nobody steps on a mine, but the first American to come through steps on a mine. They knew where the mines were planted, or they had planted the mines themselves. We went into this other village, they sent their kids out to mob us and slow us down. I rifle-butted the first kid, knocked him senseless, the rest changed their mind and went away. We started rounding up all the villagers, when an ARVIN platoon helo'd in. Out comes this colonel, mister gold braid, named Kue. He says-'You search this village?' A really civil, friendly f-cker! 'What's this, a pot of rice for fifty people? A family only cooks for themselves,' he says, then he shoots the hell out of it. 'Look at this, a lot of young adults here, men and women. Most villages have few young adults, all away in the Army. Check identification cards, peasant cards are dirty and worn out, one can barely read them. VC cards are always clean and look new. Look at the children. Parents told by VC don't look at your children. The VC hold children like their own children. See how the children are always looking and pulling toward their real parents.' He gave orders to his men to get the VC. A young woman let go of a kid who ran to his real mother. She pulled a pistol, but she didn't get a chance to use it. She was cut down cold. So, Colonel Charming has the rest of the VC separated from the villagers. He asks one question, no answer from him, so he cuts his throat; next guy,same thing. He goes down the line, cutting throats. Kills twenty-five that way, all in a row. He gets a little kid, a villager, gives him candy, asks him where the weapons are hidden. The kid takes him right to the weapons, no problem. The sergeant asks, 'Why in the hell didn't you just ask the kid in the first place?' He says: 'The child might have talked, or maybe not. The VC would kill him for sure. This way the VC are dead and the weapons captured.' His men spread the bodies around like they died fighting. Told us we could have a body count, then he left with his men," Ron concluded his story.

"A real nice guy. I bet he's done that before," DJ said.

"I saw this Colonel again, interrogating prisoners in Da Nang. The prisoners would piss themselves and shake like frightened children, when this guy interrogated them," Ron added.

"I'll bet you were glad to be rid of that guy," Smitty said.

"Not really, I always felt safe around him. He taught me a lot of things that would save my ass later. Surprisingly, he recognized me later, after the Tet Offensive. I went to his house and he introduced me to his family. He thought the Americans were the most civilized people in the world, but the French were real barbarians."

"All right, that's a good enough story. How about you, Earl?" Billy said.

"Haven't you had enough of these war stories?" I exclaimed adding— "For god sakes, you should have joined up if you're so interested!"

"Come on, Earl, you said you have two Silver Stars, tell us how you got your first one," Billy cajoled him, ignoring me.

Earl hesitated for a few moments, then began—"It was during an attack on the DMZ, in May of '67. We had taken a lot of enemy fire and had a lot of casualties. The choppers came in and we started loading the medevacs as fast as we could. I was loading wounded men into the left side door of the Huey that had just landed. I looked through the Huey and saw a bunch of Dinks, NVA regulars, charging us from the right side. I pulled out a .45 and shot seven of them. I jumped through the helicopter and came out the right side. I used my KaBar to kill another, but I got it stuck in the Dink and I couldn't get it out. Two more came at me with their bayonets fixed. I got outta' the way of their bayonets, then I grabbed them both by their necks and banged their heads together until I had killed them, then I went back to loading wounded guys into the helicopter."

"Wow, weren't you scared while all of this is going on?" Billy asked.

"No, I was never scared in combat. I always had to much to do," Earl replied.

"I never heard of a medical Corpsman carrying a side arm," DJ said.

"I didn't, I took it off one of the wounded guys," Earl replied.

"Jeesh, you must have been one crazy son-of-a-bitch," DJ said. "I spent two years on an air craft carrier . Fusing bombs, putting them on airplanes. One time some bombs blew up, blowing holes in the flight deck, but I wasn't on board at the time. I guess about thirty guys got killed. No glory in an operational accident, I guess."

"Too bad you weren't on board, they could have blamed it on you," Smitty wisecracked.

"My old man told me those bombs were so dangerous. If you even touched the fuse, they would blow up," Billy said.

"We started fitting them with an anti-withdrawal device on the fuse, after the Dinks made a propaganda film showing a Dink pulling a fuse from one of our bombs that didn't explode. It was still possible to withdraw the fuse with the right equipment, but it was thought to be too risky. If a plane came back with bombs, we pushed them overboard, that was the regulation," DJ said.

"Gilligan's Island is looking better all the time," I remarked.

"You don't like our war stories, Nick?" Ron asked.

"I appreciate your service and your sacrifice for your country. Probably the second greatest thing you could do for humanity . . ."

"What do you mean, second greatest? I'm insulted!" DJ interrupted me.

"It's not a denigration, for sure. It's a good thing to fight and die for somebody else's rights overseas and you guys should be given every honor coming to you. However, I always believed that men who died in labor strikes in this country died for even a higher cause. Nietzsche said-'A man who doesn't know the cause he will die for, isn't fit to live.' If I could choose the cause I would die for, it would be for the working men and women in America," I said.

"It sounds like too much education," DJ said.

"My father was severely beaten by police during a railroad strike in the 1940s. Nick's right, where do all these guys who fought in these wars come from? From working men like us. My father went to France to fight for his country, then when he came home, he had to fight the government. Big f-cking deal war hero! There were more people in Canada that needed their ass shot than over in Germany," Smitty said.

"I should give your name to the Prime minister. Some kind of free thinking anarchist or something," DJ remarked.

At that time, the Mate entered carrying a cup of coffee.

"How's the work progressing?" Smitty asked.

"Fairly well. The bad seal has already been pulled and Kenny had the retaining ring already machined. They're putting the seal together now. It should take only about a half an hour more to install it, then you guys can go back to it," the Mate said, adding—"The Coast Guard says we'll have to anchor in the river until the turbine is operational."

"Uh Sir, there's some question about overtime," DJ broached the issue.

"Everybody that are not engineering personnel will get two times their usual rates," the Mate replied.

"Ahem, that doesn't sound fair," Billy said.

"I checked with the Bosun, that's what the union contract stipulates for non-emergency situations where non-classification personnel are required," the Mate stated.

"Well, it looks like we get the old screw-ola again!" Smitty said.

"I think we got us a lot of trouble-makers here, Mister McCracken," DJ said.

"Such as?" the Mate asked.

"Miss Strickland and Smitty here," DJ replied.

"I've known Nick and Smitty both, for twenty years. If there was anything wrong with them, I think I would know by now," the Mate replied, adding—"I'll need help with some insulation. Nick, do you and Earl want to give me a hand here?"

"No problem, let's go old buddy," I said.

We followed the Mate to the galley and put our coffee cups in the rack, then we headed below deck.

We went to the little store room in the steerage compartment and removed some rolls of fiberglass insulation.

"This will suffice for the rest of the trip. Before fitting out next year, the whole turbine will be insulated again," the Mate said.

When we entered the engine room, the Chief was supervising the alignment of the shaft bearings with a length of piano wire stretched tight.

"How's it going guys?" the Mate asked.

"This would be a lot easier with a laser sighter," Buster said.

"We don't have a laser leveler, goofy. We were sighting bearings like this for years before anybody had laser levelers," Hank said.

"Great, you got the insulation. We need the high temperature tape from the boiler room cabinets," the Chief said, adding—"And while you're in there, you might as well get a couple of rolls of that four inch fiberglass ribbon."

"Okay, Chief," the Mate replied, and we headed for the boiler room.

"It sounds like you guys were in to some deep ideological discussion back there," the Mate said.

"Yes, I had to start one to stop the guys from telling their war stories," I said.

"And what was the heated topic of debate this time?" the Mate asked.

"Whether it is nobler to die in labor struggles here, or die for somebody else's rights overseas," I answered.

"That is deep. I'm surprised those guys could handle it as well as they did," the Mate remarked.

"Well President Reagan has got them pumped full of crap, pretty well, so it's gonna' take awhile to straighten them out," I said.

"About anything in particular?" the Mate asked.

"About a lot of things. Number one-this country's about one inch away from a fascist dictatorship," I said.

"Hmmm, that's one I haven't heard before. How do you figure?" the Mate asked.

"For one thing, we're always hearing judges and politicians say they got a mandate for something. When somebody thinks they have a mandate, they think they are empowered to do anything they want, when they want. Dictators are always saying they have a mandate. In this country, we have Law. Even authority figures must follow the Law, but everybody seems to have forgotten that fact," I said.

"Yes, sometimes it seems so," the Mate said.

"Hell yes," I stated, adding—"Three-forths of the politicians and judges would like to install themselves in office permanently like some 'banana republic'."

"This sounds like a dangerous situation," the Mate replied, not really serious. "It is! Only the fact that since this country was founded, that the people are accustomed to ruling themselves in an orderly fashion, that we've become accustomed to having our civil rights. How many times in the last year have you heard someone say-people shouldn't have guns, voting is a privilege-not a right, the justice system should be changed. They always say that it is for the public's good, horse crap! I'm not willing to give up even one of my rights, not even one."

"What are you going to do when they come to take away your gun?" the Mate asked jokingly.

"Give it to them bullets first. I'd sure rather die in Marblehead than in Vietnam, or some damn place like that," I replied seriously.

The Mate looked at me with a surprised look.

"What's wrong? Is this the first time you've seen a wicked political activist?" I asked.

"No, you remind me of somebody," the Mate replied.

"Who? Tommy?" I asked.

"No, his mother," he replied.

"Really?" I asked.

"Yes, when I was eighteen. Right before we were married, Emma was giving me a similiar harangue. Emma was carrying on about how John

Kennedy had to be elected, or the country would go down the tubes for sure," he said.

"I never thought of Emma as a political activist," I said.

"Oh, Yeah! She hated President Eisenhower and Vice President Nixon with a passion. She was carrying on for hours about the Committee for Unamerican Affairs. How Charlie Chaplin was kicked out of the country without a trial, and anything else she could think of."

"Did you agree with her, or not?" I asked.

"I wanted to get married and start the honeymoon before I had to go back out. Politics was not the first thing on my mind," the Mate replied.

"Your appreciation of the political situation in those days was commendable," I said jokingly.

"I make it a rule not to discuss religion or politics with friends," the Mate said.

"The only thing that leaves is sex," I shot back.

"Perhaps Nietzsche was right about women and sex," the Mate said.

"Nietzsche was not right about everything. The syphillis was taking effect about that time. That messed up some of his thinking for sure," I replied.

"Contracting syphillis may have been the reason for his attitude toward women," the Mate said.

"I see I'm not going to win this discussion," I conceded.

"Quite the contrary, you've already won. Nietzsche's mother was a woman. Virtue doesn't spring from dirt, even in Nietzsche's case," the Mate replied.

"Your knowledge of philosophy is surprising," I said.

"I studied a little bit in school," the Mate said, as he handed me a roll of fiberglass ribbon.

"Your scope covers a little more than I was taught in high school," I said.

"Emma would lecture on the subject once in awhile," the Mate explained.

"Hmmm, that sounds interesting. Did she teach you anything else?" I asked.

"As a matter of fact, she taught me how to shoot a pistol without shooting my foot off," he replied.

"That's good, my grandmother and step-grandfather taught me how to shoot that old Model 1917. Maybe we can go shooting sometime soon," I said.

"That sounds good," the Mate said, adding—""We'd better get this stuff back to the Chief."

"I hope we don't delay too long. I hear the ice will be early this year," I said.

"Did you ever hear the story about the Captain who got stuck in the ice, and ordered the crew to spread salt around the ship to melt the ice?" the Mate asked, trying not to laugh.

"That sounds like the story about the Captain who had the cargo holds waxed so the taconite would slide out faster," I said with a smile.

"We have a similar story here. When I was young, we had a ship that carried coal and salt all over the lakes. Well, the Captain unloaded 6,000 tons of coal, then he got really worried because we only loaded 5,200 tons of salt. The Mate and the Bosun tried to explain to him that the salt was in long tons, but he never got it. He thought we were going to get hollered at when we got to Chicago," the Mate said.

"That guy wasn't too bright, I take it."

"He was one of those oldfashioned Captains that worked his way up through the ranks without having much of a formal education," the Mate replied.

"He must have started out in the days of sail," I remarked.

"Quite possibly. I remember in the nineteen fifties, there were a few of the fore and aft rigged schooners still sailing," the Mate replied as we entered the engine room.

"It looks like you guys are breaking records in here," the Mate said to the Chief.

"So far, we're been making good progress. Everything has gone right," the Chief replied.

"Of course, it always does in this department," the Mate said, adding—"We'll be in the river soon. The Captain is planning to anchor in the lee of Grosse Ille until the work is completed."

"Good, we can shut the steam off to the high pressure turbine also," the Chief replied. "I'll head back to the Wheelhouse, the Captain will be calling soon. I'll catch you later, Greg," the Mate said, then he left.

I noticed that Earl was helping Kenny pull the carbon seals on the turbine shaft, so I went over to help.

"Hi guys, need a hand here?" I asked.

"Yeah, you can explain to Earl how this 'oversize house fan' as he calls it, can propel this ship," Kenny said, exasperated.

"Well Earl, the steam pushes against these blades at 100 pounds per square inch. You can see this blade has about fifty square inches of area, so even a man like you couldn't hold back even one blade against that kind of pressure. Now it looks like we got about a couple hundred blades here, all working together, plus all those blades in the high pressure turbine. Both shafts go back to the double helical gears which cuts the rotation to one-twentieth of the turbine speed and it also increases the power by twenty times. Something like a transmission of a car. So we end up with a lot of power going to the propeller shaft," I said.

I heard the engine bell ring.

"They're going to ahead slow," Kenny said.

I saw the Chief close the throttle valve to the high pressure turbine, four or five turns.

"Maybe the turbine will be cooler this time. I hate crawling around on a hot son-of-a-bitch," Kenny remarked, adding—"Hey Nick, can you give Earl a hand here, he's taking all night."

"Sure no problem," I replied.

I began helping Earl put the carbon seals together. Carbon seals are rings of carbon that fit into grooves machined into the upper and lower casing. Although they have a chamfer on the outer edges to make assembly easier, the groove clearance is only about two thousandth of an inch and carbon seals don't bend, they break, so proper assembly is essential.

"One more week and we'll be back home, old buddy," I said

"Yeah, that will be nice," Earl said.

"Yes Sir, 'Vacation city'! Maybe I'll take a cruise. Spend a month laying in the sun while somebody feeds me shrimp and key lime pie," I said.

"Don't you get enough of ships and water already?" Earl asked.

"Maybe. I guess the Bahamas and most of the Caribbean have been ruined by the drug gangs. I hear Mexico is opening a new resort in Cancun that sounds real nice," I said.

"Yeah, for a few days, but I don't feel like paying that kind of money."

"Yeah, I know what you mean. I'd rather spend my vacation on Kelleys Island or Mackinac Island, than anywhere else. Unfortunately, I only got one week this summer," I said.

It took us about fifteen minutes to get the carbon seals assembled on the turbine shaft.

We heard the engine bell for all stop. The Chief closed the manual valve for the steam manifold. He opened the drain cocks for the turbine, then told Hank to reduce the boiler steam. In a few minutes, the turbine was ready to go into place.

"Don't you think this baby will need balanced," Buster wisecracked, and the Chief gave him a dirty look.

"Okay guys, nice and gentle now. Heave!" the Chief said. We pulled a couple of feet on the lift chain then stopped while the chief and Hank pulled the cradles out from under the shaft. We slowly lowered the shaft until the bearings and seals were about to enter into the recesses. The Chief called out for us to stop. The Chief, Buster,Hank and Fred positioned themselves on the casing so they could observe the bearings and seals as we lowered the turbine. They shifted the whole thing about a quarter of an inch by hand power, then the Chief told us to lower one chain link at a time. In a few minutes, we had the turbine lowered all the way and the slings removed. The raceways were removed from the upper casing then it was ready to be hoisted.

"Call the other guys," the Chief told me.

I keyed the intercom button.

"Turbine repair detail, report to the engine room," I said twice, then released the button.

While we waited for the other guys to assemble, the Chief had Hank and Kenny remove the blank flange from the high pressure turbine crossover pipe.

"We can't let any foreign material get into there or it's curtains for that turbine," The Chief said as they covered the opening with a Nomex cloth. When the other guys came in, the Chief had the new gaskets put on.

"Okay guys, straight up and over then straight down. It has to be done right the first time or all this time and work will be for nothing," the Chief stated. We hooked up the two hoists that had been holding the turbine. Then we took up the slack, while waiting for the Chief to give us the word.

"Hey, when do we eat here?" Smitty wisecracked to Fred.

"Eating and sleeping has become a longed for memory here," Fred replied.

"You'll get your eating and sleeping as soon as we get this casing on," the Chief said, as he walked around the turbine inspecting everything.

"Okay Lads, bring it up straight and even, Heave!" the Chief ordered. We began pulling the chain and slowly the casing raised up straight and even. The ship was not rolling as bad as it had been when we pulled the casing. When we got it high enough, Gary, Carl and Kenny pulled it over to the turbine.

"Okay, bring it down real slow," the Chief said. As we lowered it, Buster and Kenny took up position by the cross-over pipe to guide it to the high pressure turbine flange. Carl took Buster's place at the hoist. We lowered the casing while Fred and the Chief watched the gasket. When the casing got to the guide pins, the Chief and Fred pushed it over about an inch.

"How's it doing over there?" the Chief called out.

"Fine, now," Buster replied.

"Okay, lower about an inch then hold it." the Chief ordered. We lowered it and waited about a minute. "Okay guys, it's on the pins. Bring it down slow," the Chief said. We slowly pulled the unload chain, until, after a minute, the casing came to a stop. Buster and Kenny were already installing the bolts that joined the cross-over pipe. The Mate came into the engine room at this time.

"It figures, an officer shows up right after the work is done," Brad wisecracked.

"Okay wise guy, I got some work for you over here," the Chief snapped. "Get these chains unhooked and get this gear out of the way," the Chief ordered. We unhooked the chains and stowed them, then we secured the hoists overhead. The engineering guys worked like fiends to get the casing bolted down, while we bolted the quill shaft to the reduction gearing. It took an hour and a half to get the casing bolted down and the other equipment hooked up.

"Some insulation will be required on the cross-over pipe," the Chief said, adding—"The rest of the insulation can wait until the turbine is in service again."

I waited around until the turbine was ready to start up. The Chief closed the drain cocks, shut off the preheat steam and made sure the condenser water was going at full capacity. the Chief called the wheelhouse and informed the Captain that he was ready to start up.

The Mate discussed the situation with the Chief, then called the Captain. After a few minutes of talking to the Captain, the Chief ordered operational boiler pressure. The Chief opened the manual valve for ahead slow. The turbine shafts started turning immediately. The Chief watched the turbine instruments, the pressure, the temperature and RPM. After a few minutes, he opened the regulator and watched his instruments. The turbines were making their familiar whining sound. The Chief closed the manual valve to the high pressure turbine and opened the astern valve to the low pressure turbine. The low pressure turbine began to turn backwards.

"The Chief's got a reverse now. I think he's happy," I said to Earl.

"I hope so. I'd like to get some sleep." Earl replied.

After about ten minutes in reverse, the Captain requested forward again. The Chief closed the astern valve and opened the valve to the high pressure turbine. I checked my watch, it was 7:20 PM, tomorrow was Thanksgiving Day. The Mate thanked the turbine detail and asked Brad and Ron if they could take the eight to twelve watch. They said they could. Then he asked me if I could take the four to eight watch. I said I could.

"Good, by tomorrow the watch assignments will be back to normal," the Mate said.

"I'm going to my quarters, are you heading forward, Earl?" I asked.

"No, I got to get some shut-eye," Earl said, adding—"I'll catch you later Nick."

"Okay, old buddy." I said and I left the engine room.

I ran into Brad, Ron and the Mate again, when I stopped at the entrance passageway to get my parka.

"It looks to be a real nasty night," I said.

"Don't worry Nick, we'll walk you to your door," Brad said.

"Who said Chivalry was dead?" I asked, jokingly as we walked out into the night.

The wind had died to almost nothing, but the snow was falling like crazy. I could not see how anymore snow could be in the air, it was really zero-zero conditions.

"Are you still planning on meeting the Westcott?" I asked.

"That's the plan," the Mate replied.

"Good luck finding it guys," I said.

"We've been running through local squalls like this all day. It maybe better in Detroit," the Mate said.

"The traffic's worse, that's for sure," Brad said.

"We'll let the Westcott's skipper worry about that," the Mate replied.

"If I was him, I'd tell everybody to shove off then I'd go home," Ron said.

"Well, the snow is bad but it's in sheltered water. I'll be on deck with you guys. Andy will notify me when he spots her. As long as nobody falls overboard, we'll be okay," the Mate said.

When we got to the forward deckhouse, we parted company. The Mate went to the Wheelhouse, Brad and Ron to the Crews hall, and I went to my quarters. I wondered how they would be handling their watch. They did not get much sleep in the last twenty-four hours.

Tired, sweaty and grimy from turbine detail, I took a warm shower, changed my clothes, then laid down on my bunk and thought about Thanksgiving tomorrow. I began thinking about Thanksgiving dinner at Grandmother's house and how she would put so much work in preparing a Thanksgiving feast. My parents would always ruin the holiday ambience by acting like fools. I came to a conclusion that their only reason for living was to mess up their own lives and everybody else's life as well. As I drifted off to sleep, I could see her in my mind, she was showing me how to make a template for a Mariner's Compass quilt block. Then I went to sleep. After a while, I was awaken by the ship's whistle. I sat up, wondering if there was something wrong with the turbine again. Then I heard the loudspeaker faintly saying that the Westcott was along side. I wondered if I got any mail, then I laid back down and went to sleep. The alarm awoke me at three-thirty. I got up, got dressed, then went to the observation room to get some coffee and to check my mail.

There was no one in there and the mail bag had not been opened, so I assumed everyone had been too tired to tend to that duty. I would check my mail later. I took the ratwalk aft to get a sandwich before the watch change. When I got to the galley, Louie was on duty.

"Hi, Nick. What's up?"

"Well, I am. What do you have for sandwiches?" I asked.

"Roast beef and how about some French fries," he suggested.

"That sounds great," I said.

Louie brought the food right out.

"Did John get his baker's chocolate?" I asked.

"He got a twenty-five pound bucket from the Westcott delivery. That should be enough, the good stuff goes further," he replied.

"Good deal and in a nick of time," I said.

"You're not kidding, these guys start getting homicidal toward the galley if they don't get their chocolate treats at Thanksgiving," Louie said.

"Well, I'll catch you later," I said and I headed for the Crews mess.

The only one in there, was the Chief, so I went over and sat by him.

"I think you're slipping, old buddy," I said.

"How's that Nick?" he asked.

"All the guys in your department swear you don't eat or sleep on the water," I replied.

"I certainly haven't been able to do much of either on this trip," the Chief said.

"I think that it will be smooth sailing now, for your department at least," I said.

"Dave told me that on your motor vessel, you didn't have much work to do on the engines. Were you in the engineering department?" he asked.

"I was a QMED, something like an oiler. We did fueling, filter changes, ballasting, and engine maintenance," I explained.

"You did a good job in the engine room. I should have you back here," he said. "Perhaps, maybe one of these seasons," I replied.

"I don't think this ship has many seasons left," the Chief said, adding—"They're all going to the breaker yards."

"You'll have to get a job on one of those super-lakers," I said.

"There's three of them in Toledo, almost new, selling for half what they're worth. I have to see the Captain, I'll see you later," he said, as he got up to leave.

"Okay, Chief." I finished my sandwich and left.

I ran into Smitty on my way forward.

"Ed and I had been taking turns at the bow while we were in the river. Since it's opened out a little bit and this blasted snow is letting up, maybe you won't have to," he said.

"I guess the Captain can be a cruel task master sometimes," I remarked as I looked up and noticed that I could see the moon and a few stars.

"It looks to be clearing somewhat, maybe we'll have some sunshine," I remarked. When we got to the Crew's hall, I read the clipboard and signed it.

"You were taking tank soundings?" I asked.

"Yeah, the Bosun and the Chief want to check their instruments. They weren't happy with the readings they were getting while we were loading," he replied.

"Okay, I can take it from here," I said.

"Okay, see you at the feast," Smitty said then he left. I put my hood up and walked around the bow where I met Ed.

"How's it going guy?" I asked.

"It's been a real charmer out here in the wind," he replied.

"I'll check with the Mate to see if this is necessary," I said and I headed up the steps to the Wheelhouse. When I got to the Wheelhouse, the Mate and the Chief were discussing something with the Captain, so I turned to leave.

"Hold there a minute, Miss Strickland," the Mate said. After a few minutes, they finished talking and the Captain and the Chief left.

"Yes, Miss Strickland," he said.

"The previous watch had a lookout at the bow, do you wish to continue this practice?" I asked.

"No, the waterway is open here and the visibility is better. A bow lookout won't be necessary now," he stated.

"Very good, Sir," I said and I left.

When I got down on deck, Al was talking to Ed. They stopped and looked at me.

"A bow watch won't be necessary," I said.

"Good," Al agreed.

"We got a light coming up on the port side." "The Huron ship?" I asked.

"No. We passed that, this must be the Fort Gratiot Light," Ed said.

"I'll bet it's going to be rough," I said. "The Captain said he heard that a south wind blew the waves down flat," Ed said.

"That's what they always say. I was on a destroyer, then on these steamers for over twenty years. I never saw that happen," Al said. "I'll catch you folks at the Thanksgiving dinner," Ed said, then he left.

"I'm gonna' check out aft, then take some tank soundings," I said.

"Okay, Nick" Al said. As I headed aft, I could see lights of a town far astern. We won't be seeing any lights for more than a day, I thought. The smoke from the stack was heading straight for the bow which meant that the wind was coming from the south. I decided I would take the soundings on the way forward. I checked the life boats and the gear aft, then I started forward on the port side. There are four pipes that protrude through the deck on the port side and four on the starboard side. They go all the way through to the bottom plates.

I removed the stick and the chain from its box, then I lifted the spring loaded cap with the toe of my boot and held it with my foot. I lowered the stick on its chain until it touched the bottom. I pulled the stick up on the chain, it had a reading of ten inches. I repeated the procedure for the other seven pipes and got similar results. I stowed the stick and the chain in its box and recorded the results on the log for the watch. I went over to the phone and rang the Wheelhouse. When the Mate picked up the phone, I repeated the soundings to him. He asked me to come to the Wheelhouse.

When I got to the Wheelhouse, I noticed that no one was in there except the Mate. I could only see his face which was illuminated by the radar screen.

"You're in here by yourself?" I asked

"Yes, Mister Hall needed to get some sleep, we're on auto-pilot now," the Mate said.

Poor baby, needs to give his smart aleck mouth a rest, I thought.

"The nearest ship is ten miles away, so there's no problem right now."

"You shouldn't look at the radar screen too much, it's bad for your eyes," I said.

The Mate gave me a strange look.

"It's true. Those computer screens would hurt my eyes after about an hour and the CRT is worse than that. More microwaves in that sucker," I said.

"Is that right? I hadn't heard that," the Mate said.

"It's a proven fact and I wouldn't want you to hurt your eyes," I said.

"No, certainly not," the Mate said, smiling at me. "I have a surprise for you, later at the Thanksgiving dinner."

"A surprise for me? I can't wait. Well, I better get back down on deck, the other guys might start talking about me being up here alone with you," I said.

"Okay, I'll talk to you later," the Mate said, then I turned and left.

When I got back on deck, I ran into Al.

"I took the soundings and gave them to Mister McCracken," I said.

"He wanted them right away?" Al asked.

"No, he wanted to see me about something else, so I gave them to him while I was there," I said.

"Good. I'm glad that job's done. We're heading into the lake proper. It's going to get rough!" Al remarked.

"The wind is following us, maybe the waves won't be beating us too bad." I said, remembering the tales I have heard about the dreaded Three Sisters. Following waves capable of sending a ship to the bottom of the lake. During my five years on the lakes, I had only once seen thirty foot waves come over the deck during a severe storm. But one never knows about the Gales of November either, I thought.

"Let's check the railing cables now, while it's relatively calm," Al suggested.

"Okay, I'll check the port side and meet you on the fantail," I said.

"Sounds good," Al said.

I went to the port side and began checking the cables of the railing. When I got to the after deckhouse, I heard somebody laughing.

"Be careful, he's sensitive today," Buster wisecracked.

"F-ck off!" Billy shot back.

"It must be that time of month," Mark wisecracked.

"I'm gonna' have to kick all your asses," Billy declared. They were laughing as they walked out the door and headed forward. They did not see me. I walked around the fantail and waited for Al to show up. In a few minutes, Al came to the fantail.

"Everything okay on the starboard side?" I asked.

"The railing was okay. There were a few loose ropes on the lifeboat cover, so I tied them up again," Al replied.

"Good. I didn't find anything on the port side," I said. I was wondering why those guys were still messing with the life boat, when I was sure that the beer was gone by this time. We headed forward again on the port side.

"I expected the waves to be worse than this, maybe the wind did flatten the waves," I said.

"Yeah, could be. They're looking pretty flat and not moving very fast," Al replied.

"Not like your destroyer days," I observed.

"When the Captain ordered full speed and went into the waves, that old ship would go through the wave instead of over it. Half the time we were under water. We use to joke about being in the submarine service," Al recalled.

"Pretty rough on deck," I observed.

"Yeah, we had ropes to hang on to. When you saw a wave coming, you would flatten yourself against the superstructure and hang on tight. If your head or anything wasn't tight against the steel plates, the wave would bash it into the plates," he explained.

"Yeah, the guys on the Giovanni told me the same thing," I said, adding—"Maybe the waves will start from the south if this wind keeps up."

"Doubtless they will, but it's always better to be running with the waves. Just so it doesn't spoil our Thanksgiving feast," Al remarked.

"I hear you there!" I agreed.

When we were almost to the forward deckhouse, Al looked up.

"Who in the hell is that!?" he exclaimed.

"I saw Mark, Buster and Billy heading forward. They must be working on something up there. Maybe the radar," I said.

Over the radio we heard the Mate give the command for "Lookouts forward".

"Oh, joy!" Al groaned.

"This doesn't sound good, does it?" I remarked, as I started climbing steps two at a time. When we entered the Wheelhouse, the Mate was at the wheel.

"Would you like to take the wheel, Miss Strickland?" the Mate asked.

"Very well, Sir," I replied, and I took over the wheel.

"Hold it steady on zero-zero-zero true," he said.

"Zero-zero-zero, very good, Sir," I replied.

"The radar has to be shut down temporary while the ATR tube is being replaced. I'll take the lookout forward. Al, you take the lookout aft. Keep me posted continually on the positions of the ships aft."

"Yes, Sir," Al acknowledged.

"Very well, that will be all," the Mate said, and Al turned and left. The Mate wrote in the log book for a few minutes. There was a flurry of banging on the roof.

"It sounds like they're dancing the balaklava up there," I remarked.

"Yes, I remember about ten years ago, there was an ethnic festival in Marblehead. You and your grandmother were dancing the balaklava with the Ukrainian dancers," the Mate said.

"I didn't know you were there. My grandmother never could resist dancing the folk dances," I said.

"One time she and Eichann came over to our house and started teaching some dances to Emma. She had a blast."

"Really? She didn't tell me anything about that," I said.

"Oh yeah! Natalie was her favorite neighbor. She would discuss politics, religion and everything else with her," the Mate said.

"It's strange to hear you call her Natalie. I never heard that before. A lot of people called her Nadja at school. Nadalya was her real name, but she went by several names. It's an old Russian tradition to have several names," I said.

"Why's that?" the Mate asked.

"The only thing I can figure is that it's to keep the secret police confused," I said.

"How did you address her?" the Mate asked. "As Matuskhka, which means 'Little Mother'. It's commonly used to address a woman figure in authority. She wouldn't tolerate being called babushka, because it sounds like an uneducated peasant woman," I replied.

"Was your grandmother an Aristocrat?" the Mate asked.

"No, Jews were not allowed to be in the aristocracy or Boyar. Her grandfather was a well-to-do merchant. He had houses in St. Petersburg, Moscow, Kiev and Vilnius. That was the most prosperous area of Russia in those days. Her father had part of the business by the time she was born. The secret police started to spy on them, because some of the employees were involved in protests and other activities against the government. In 1912, her father and mother were arrested along with an older brother. The rest of the family thought it wise to flee Russia with what little money they had, until it was safe to return. Which never happened of course."

"Were they really involved with revolutionaries?" the Mate asked.

"When Grandmother went to the Soviet Union, ten years ago, to do research on her family. She found out that

Gregory Nikulin, the deputy to Yurovsky, was an employee of her father. Yurovsky was the commander who shot the Tsar's family. She didn't have time to do a complete search of records and naturally the police records are inaccessible," I replied.

"Her father and grandfather had revolutionaries in their employ. That was probably excuse enough to have them arrested. Especially since they were Jewish. Nobody needed a valid reason to start a Pogrom in those days," the Mate said.

"That's for sure. My great-great grandfather had several merchant ships he leased. My grandmother was told that the revolutionaries smuggled things into Russia via those ships. It's probably true, but the revolutionaries didn't keep records for obvious reasons," I said.

"I can't imagine sailing in Russian waters," the Mate said.

"There's a light ahead, to port," I reported.

"Yes, I see it," the Mate said.

"That can't be the Pointe Aux Barques Light, yet," I said.

"No, We're only half way there. It must be another ship's mast beacon," the Mate said.

The light continued to blink awhile, then it vanished. Al called up to the bridge, reporting that the two ships aft were holding their distance.

"That must have been a fishing boat from one of the little villages around here," the Mate said, adding—"It should be getting light in about an hour."

"Hopefully the waves won't be getting any worse," I remarked.

"The weather report from the Coast Guard says that the waves won't be getting any worse until this afternoon," the Mate replied.

"Good, we don't have to be eating our Thanksgiving dinners like the immigrants," I said, adding—"I wonder if the Bosun had sorted the mail yet."

"He should be sorting it about now," the Mate said.

"Good, I'm expecting a letter from my secret admirer," I said jokingly.

"What makes you think he'll write you?" the Mate said.

"Oh, he always sends me a letter in the Westcott mail. He's a pretty steady fellow to be sure," I said.

"In retrospect, that was rather juvenile, don't you think?" the Mate asked.

"Maybe, but it was cute just the same," I replied with a smile.

At that time, Buster, Mark and Billy entered the Wheelhouse.

"Dave, we've changed the ATR tube, you can try the set now," Mark said.

The Mate went over to the radar with Mark. Billy sat down in the chair by the chart table and began to take his shirt off.

"The Boss is here, you better jump up," Buster wisecracked.

"He won't jump up until watch change," Mark replied, adding— "Don't be taking your shirt off with a woman present, boy!"

"It's a wonder he can keep his pants on," Buster said.

"It's coming up now, Mark," the Mate said.

He looked at it for a minute.

"It seems to be off slightly. I'll try to align the PPI." The Mate twisted the knob slightly.

"I don't see how it could be off. It's the same damn tube that was there before," Mark said.

"It may have been weak, causing the image to lag somewhat. So someone advanced it to compensate for it," the Mate said.

They watched the radar screen for a minute.

"That looks good Mark, Thanks," the Mate said.

"Okay, wonder boy, get your clothes back on," Buster wisecracked.

"What time is it?" Billy asked while putting his shirt on.

"Almost seven o'clock," Mark replied.

"Good, the watch will be over in an hour," Billy said.

"Poor baby, are you tired?" Buster joked.

"I feel like I'm catching something, probably from Buster," Billy said as he headed out the door.

"You two been kissing again?" Mark wisecracked as he went through the door.

"Everything ship-shape now?" I asked.

"Yes, everything seems to be working okay," the Mate replied, adding—"You can go back down on deck, if you like."

"I don't know if I like it, but I better go. I'll see you at the feast," I said.

I engaged the auto pilot and went out the door.

When I got on deck, the wind was blowing from astern, crisp and cold. I put my hardhat on and headed aft to find Al. The ship was pitching and rolling hardly at all. When I got to the fantail, Al was looking aft with binoculars.

"The Mate called off the lookout aft," I said.

"Yes, I know. He called me on the radio a couple of minutes ago," Al replied.

"Something interesting back there?" I asked.

"There are two ships back there, you can barely see them," Al replied.

"I can't see any lights, even on the shore," I said.

"Yeah, we're pretty far from the shore now. There's a mist on the water, it would be hard to see land even if it was light," Al said.

"It should be light in less than an hour now," I said.

"Maybe we'll see the other ships later. Was there anything ahead of us?" Al asked.

"Just a few fishing boats, but they were heading in," I said.

"Hopefully the waves don't get any worse. I can't eat when it's rough," Al remarked.

"I'll think it will hold for awhile. There isn't any good place to pull into here," I said, adding—"I'm going to check everything again before we go off watch. I'll see you later."

"Okay Nick," Al said.

I walked forward, checking the railing lights. I stopped and checked the conveyor and hatch crane. When I got to the bow, I noticed the fire hose was becoming unwrapped. I rolled it onto the reel and secured the nozzle. I examined the other equipment forward, then I went to the rear of the forward deckhouse to check things there. I ran into the Bosun and Earl coming out of the crews hall.

"Hi guys. What's going on?" I asked.

"Just tending to some business," the Bosun replied.

"Have you got the mail sorted yet?" I asked.

"Yes, I finished that. I think you got something," the Bosun said.

"Great. I'll see you guys later," I said, and they proceeded aft.

I was checking the lights on the starboard side, when I heard the watch bell. When I got to the Crew's hall, Hal and Ron were looking at the clipboard.

"Nothing to report guys, everything is ship-shape."

Hal handed me the clipboard, I signed it and handed it back to him. "Okay, we'll take it from here Nick."

"Catch you guys later," I said then I went through the door to the Observation room.

I checked the mail box and found two letters. One from my grandmother's lawyer, the other one had no return address on it which I thought was very odd. I went to my quarters and sat down on my bunk and opened the letter from my grandmother's lawyer. He informed me that he had a visit from my mother and father. They claimed that they had an attorney and were going to contest my grandmother's will. None of this was very alarming to me or to my lawyer apparently. I put the letter in my travel case and opened the other letter and started to read it:

To: Nicolette Strickland

From: Thomas L. McCracken

My father informed me, on November 20th of his relationship with you. I take no joy in this revelation. I wish you to know that I have no significant relationship with my father. You can not now, or will ever be able to replace my mother. My father's happiness is irrelevant to me now. I have very little communication with him and expect none from you. The End.

I was in shock when I read the letter. No hello or good-bye, just go to hell in plain English. I thought maybe Tommy had not forgave me for the time he broke his arm. I could not think of any other reason for Tommy to write me such a letter. For a minute I felt like crying. I decided to find the Mate and show him the letter. I stuck the letter in my pocket and headed down the passageway. I saw the Mate coming down the steps with the Chief.

"Hello, Gentlemen. Please, give me your opinion on this when you get a chance, will you Sir?" I asked politely as I handed the letter to the Mate.

"Very well, Miss Strickland. I'll get to it in a few minutes," the Mate replied.

"Thank you Sir," I said, then I turned and went down the steps to the night kitchen.

Don and Carl were in the there, so I decided to join them.

"Top 'o Morning, Lass. You're looking like you're full of thunder this morning," Don observed.

"Do I?" I said smiling. "I'm sorry, I was just thinking of some family B.S."

"I work this job so I don't have to put with the bullpoop at home," Carl said.

"Whatever it is, Lass, it will pass like a shooting star. My mother, god bless her, would always say-'trouble that comes quick, passes quick'."

"I'm sure you're right, Don," I replied.

"The waves are supposed to be moderate by this afternoon. I'm eating at the first feast, how about you?" Carl asked.

"Yes, I have the first dinner, too. I'm hoping you're right about the waves," I said.

"Can you trust a face like that?" Don wisecracked.

We talked for a while, then Mister McCracken entered the room.

"I would like to see you for a minute, Miss Strickland," he said.

"Certainly, would you please excuse me gentlemen," I said as I got up.

"Okay Lass, we'll see you later," Don said.

I walked out of the room behind the Mate. We headed below deck and to the ratwalk. When we got to the passageway, he stopped and looked around to see if anyone was down there.

"I just got off the phone with Tommy. His live-in girlfriend walked out on him, so he's mad at the whole world. I told him he has no reason to be angry with you or me. He started giving me crap about his mother, so I told him, I wished Emma was here to slap the silly crap out of him. I think he'll be okay in a little while," the Mate said.

I thought about my messed up attitude toward the world when I had the trouble with Bill.

"Oh, poor guy, I hope you weren't too rough on him," I said.

"I don't think so. He was always a mama's boy. Not that there was anything wrong with his mother, but I probably should have been there more often," the Mate replied.

"Well, don't feel bad. I'm sure he'll get over the hurt soon enough. Not everybody is cut out to be a seadog," I said, adding—"I'm going to head for my quarters. Thanks, I'll see you later," I said.

"Okay Nick. I'll see you later," the Mate replied.

I went to my quarters, got undressed and laid down on my bunk, under a warm fleece blanket. I thought about Tommy and the time we were children. We had taken my grandmother's big quilt down to the beach to make a tent out of it. It took us an hour to find enough drift wood and cord to make a serviceable tent. Unfortunately, it also took my grandmother an hour to discover that her quilt was missing from her bed. I don't think I ever saw my grandmother so angry. It was difficult for a child to appreciate the virtues of a hand sewn quilt. I thought about the last time I was with my grandmother. She was working on a Mariner's Compass quilt top. She said, "I'll put this up. It will take two people to finish it." "I'll help you with it, Grandma," I said, anticipating a new quilt for Chanukah. "No, we'll put it up for now. You'll finish it later," she said. I thought about the unfinished quilt, still in the big cedar chest at the foot of the bed. I wondered if David would be willing to help me finish it. I set the alarm for one o'clock PM and laid down for a nap.

CHAPTER 7

Thanksgiving Dinner

When I woke up, it was twelve thirty. I turned off the alarm and went to my locker and got a clean pair of blue jeans and a pull over sweater. After I got dressed, I brushed my hair and put it in a pony tail. I put on my new leather coat then headed aft. When I got to the aft deckhouse, Brad informed me that the dining room was off-limits until John was finished in there. I decided to wait in the recreation room. I saw the Chief and Hank sitting at a table, so I went over to them.

"Is there room for another person?" I asked.

"Sure Nick, sit right down," Hank said, adding—"I like your coat, very fashionable."

"Thank you," I said as I settled into a chair.

"We're talking about Thanksgivings of the past. It was common to serve wine and beer at Thanksgiving dinners before 1974," he said.

"I don't think it was allowed on the Giovanni," I said.

"It was allowed on our ships until a crewman fell off a Cliffs ship and drowned. Greg can tell you about it," Hank said.

"We sent six men down in a lifeboat, but they couldn't find him. It was Christmas and the water was very cold, naturally. The wind and the waves were bad enough, that the lifeboat was having difficulty getting back, so another ship picked them up," the Chief said.

"I bet there was a lot of hell raised over that accident," I said.

"Yes, a great deal of trouble fell on the Captain and the crew over that incident," the Chief replied.

"I remember the wheelsman from that ship. He went into the William's Maneuver when he heard that a man was overboard, but they never saw the guy anywhere," Hank said.

"Yes, that was old Russell Tdarsky at the wheel. He was a good wheelsman. He took the wheel with him when he retired," the Chief said.

"Those were Wheels men back in those days," Hank said, adding— "The steering gear was mechanical on those old ships, chains and cables. It required a full turn on the wheel in either direction, just to take up the slack. They were impossible to steer effectively in real shallow water."

"Why were they impossible to steer in shallow water?" I asked.

"Those older ships weren't designed right in the stern. In shallow water, the flow would become turbulent at the stern, that would decrease the efficiency of the rudder to almost zero, sometimes," the Chief replied.

"That must have made navigation very difficult in the rivers, back in those days," I remarked.

"Yes it did with some ships. My first ship was the Harvey Birch. It was one of those wooden ships built during the first world war. It had two diesel engines and twin screws. With some coordination between the bridge and the engineering department, the screws could be used to turn her in difficult waters," the Chief explained.

"My father was a coal passer on the Schumacher. It was one of those old wooden lakers. It ran aground during the storm and cracked in half. Nine men died in the after section, but my father survived by a miracle. The after section pitched so violently, that it threw him onto the cliff face. He hung on and eventually climbed to the top and walked to a farm house," Hank said.

"It's a wonder you wanted a job on the lakes after hearing that," I remarked.

"That was the only ship my father had wreck on him. He figured his one chance at dying had passed him by, so he never worried about it after that," Hank replied.

"Remember that British sailor, I think his name was Newhouse," the Chief said.

"Yes, Leslie Newhouse, he was a friend of my father's," Hank said.

"His ship was torpedoed four times. He had enough of that and started working on the lakes, no U-boats," the Chief remarked.

"Yeah, those guys in the North Atlantic had it pretty rough. My uncle was on a destroyer during the Second World War. The storms were so bad that they were under water half the time. Cruising around with just the funnel sticking out," Hank said.

"All my relatives were lakers," the Chief remarked, adding—"My grandfather, father, three uncles, five in-laws and two brothers all ended up working on the lakes. My poor mother wasn't happy about that. She would say-'If your grandfather had been a sheepherder, you'd have all been sheepherders. Always following the leader like a bunch of stupid sheep.' It killed my poor mother, us being away all the time. When my two younger sisters got married and moved away, she didn't have no one to fuss over, it broke her heart. My father was already gone, so she would fret over her missing children until it weakened her heart," the Chief said.

"That's terrible, I'm sorry to hear that. My grandmother died in November, last year, but she never said anything about being lonely," I said.

"What did she think about you being in the merchant service?" Hank asked.

"She never objected to me being in the merchant service. She probably could have used some help around the house. She never was bed-ridden though. She would say that someday I would find out what I really wanted out of life."

"My kids don't know what they want out of life, except to waste my money," the Chief said.

"I never wasted anybody's money. My parents did not have any for me to waste. They did a good enough job of that themselves," I said.

"Ever since my kids became teenagers, they've gone brain dead. Which is amazing, considering the food they eat," the Chief said.

"Yes, you'll have to go back to working those turn-about trips, just to break even," Hank said jokingly.

"Remember those turn-about trips on the cement carriers?' the Chief asked.

"Oh Jeesh, that was being awake in a nightmare. Those old tubs would shake themselves to pieces above two-thirds steam. I used to be afraid to go out in a storm, anything could go wrong," Hank replied.

"My wife drove me down to Detroit to catch my ship. One of those riveted hull, coal burners. My wife had a fit when she saw the ship. The mate had her painted, but the cold weather caused all the paint to come off on the first trip. It looked like hell, I tell you," the Chief said.

"You got plenty of experience working on steam engines there, I bet!" I exclaimed.

"Old Captain Hamilton would never take her out if there was anything wrong. Everything had to be reported to him, no matter how minor. If there was any problems with the engine, he'd take it into port immediately. That old ship was a crank, the Captain never took any chances with her," the Chief replied.

"Yeah, old Hummy was a pretty nice guy. I didn't care much for that first mate, Mister Darling, though," Hank said.

"I've heard of Mister Darling. He wasn't well liked by most people, I take it," I said.

"No, he wasn't," the Chief said, adding—"He thought everyone in engineering was stupid and he would let you know about it, all the time."

"I heard the other guys talk about beating him up when they were off the ship," I said.

"He was a tough old bird. Big as a horse. It usually took several guys to do a good job on him. But it didn't do any good, he was still the same miserable son-of-a-bitch. He always got a berth, even though a lot of Captains were sour on him," he said.

"I never was on a ship with officers like that or crewmen either," I said.

"Yes, most of those types are gone, but not lamented," the Chief said.

"During the big war, there were a lot of those types. My father used to talk about them. Drunks, no-goods, they'd take anybody back in those days to crew a ship," Hank said.

"I suppose the laws and the union regulations put an end to a lot of that sort of thing," I said.

"Unfortunately, not all of it," the Chief said.

"I've seen a lot of people get away with things because the company was afraid to take on the union. I've seen some guys get the crap beat out of them because they were doing something to endanger the other crewmen," Hank said, adding—"Have you ever seen that, Nick?"

"Nah, the fights I've seen have all been over stupid things. The guys start drinking and blowing off steam about something. That does it every time," I said.

"Is that what happened at the Wheel & Anchor?" the Chief asked.

"Was there a fight at the Wheel & Anchor?" I asked.

"I heard you were the one throwing the punches," the Chief said.

"Some masher in a three-piece suit, wouldn't take his hands off of me, so I hit him with a beer glass," I said, adding—"I wouldn't even call it a fight."

"I wonder if the police would," Hank said jokingly.

"We had this bar fight in Detroit. Some guy from an American ship, made a vulgar comment about me and the chairs started flying. We got the heck out of there fast. Now that was a fight!" I exclaimed.

"What was a fight?" the Bosun asked, suddenly appearing in the door.

"How yah doing, Munny?" Hank asked.

"I'm doing as good as you look," the Bosun shot back.

"My Lord, you must be dead then," the Chief said jokingly.

"Come join us. We were talking about our past high jinxes."

"I was waiting for the steward to open the dining room," the Bosun said as he sat down.

"Yeah, John won't let anybody in there until he is ready. By the time he's ready, we'll be in Duluth," Hank wisecracked.

"Don't worry Munny, we'll save you some," he added.

"Where did the name Munny come from?" I asked.

"My initials are E.M., that was an old slang term for 'easy money'," the Bosun replied.

"It was always 'easy money' for him," Hank wisecracked.

"Don't let these guys fool you, Miss Strickland. I was a deckhand back in the days when it took a superman to do the job. We didn't have it easy like those guys in engineering," the Bosun replied.

"You always had it easy. Remember that time you didn't get arrested in Ashtabula?" Hank said.

"Yes, but I had to marry the policeman's daughter. I don't know if you could call that an easy way out," the Bosun replied.

"I never heard that story," I said.

"It was in Ashtabula in sixty two. The ship was brought in there for a refit at Great Lakes Engineering, in December. I was coming home from a party, in a shipmate's car, early in the morning. I got pulled over by a policeman, who thought I had a little too much to drink. They weren't nearly as huffy about that sort of thing back in those days. Anyway, I was sitting in the police car and the guy's daughter was in there. She started talking to me and I began to like her, right off. She thought it was a fine life to be a sailor and we were talking about this and that and before

I knew it, I was asking her out on a date. Well, her father came back and says he's going to have to arrest me and take me downtown. So his daughter says that's not possible, because it'll put off our plans for a date. So after a short discussion between father and daughter, he tears up the ticket and lets me go. Three months of dating and we got married, been married ever since," the Bosun finished his story.

"Have you ever heard anything so disgusting. How could she be happy being Mrs. Emerson Munson," Hank remarked.

"I think that's sweet. I'm happy to hear that there's still men who know how to treat women like human beings," I remarked.

"Has that been a problem for you?" the Chief asked.

"Not on ships. In college it was!" I replied.

"How's that?" Hank asked.

"There were some Frat guys that wanted me to do their grocery shopping and house cleaning for them. I told them I wasn't their mother and they better learn to take care of themselves. Crap like that went on all the time," I said.

"Some of those old time Captains wouldn't do their own grocery shopping," the Chief said.

"It's hard to say what some of those old captains would do. My father sailed with Screwdriver Anderson on the Mather. He'd do anything to get his ship through," Hank said.

"Anderson would carry his ship on his back, if he thought he could get it through," the Chief said.

"Where did he get a name like that?" I asked.

"He used to carry a screw driver with him. He was always tightening screws in the Wheelhouse, or anywhere on the ship," Hank replied.

"Oh, I thought perhaps that he liked to drink 'screwdrivers'. There was this guy on the Giovanni, called 'Martini McCray', because he like to drink martinis," I said.

"My father had a partner named 'Boilermaker Bob'. So called, because he had a predilection for that drink. Actually, he seemed to be fairly catholic when it came to alcohol," the Chief said.

"What kind of business was your father in?" I asked.

"He and his partners had two bum boats at Sault Ste. Marie, originally. They worked both sides of the locks. During the Depression, the ship traffic was almost nil, so they did some fishing, hauled people around, anything to make a few dollars. In the late 30s, things started to pick up a little bit. By '41 it was going great guns. Then in '42, the army started to get paranoid about the locks and the ore boats. There was some curtailing of the bum boats around the locks, even though they operated there for years. In '43, they bought an old wooden freighter for trade on the lakes. Every ship that could, was required to carry ore on the lakes, so there was plenty of cargo for fetch and carry runs. Furs, artillery shells, copper ingots, everything you can think of. The big thing was to keep that leaky, old hull afloat long enough to get there. The price per ton was good, even though most years they didn't get out until May," the Chief explained.

"Trying to run those old wooden ships was a real hassle according to my father," Hank said.

"If the engine and boilers were working okay, they could get about ten and a half knots out of her. They had to keep a sharp lookout for ice and objects in the water, of course," the Chief said.

"Those old hulls were likely to burn if anything hot got on the deck," Hank said.

"The boiler area was covered with iron plates to make it fire resistant to some extent," the Chief replied.

"What happened to the ship?" I asked.

"The ship was originally seized by Court Order, because of debts owed to a salt company. My father and his partners, sold their bum boat business and got enough capital to pay off the debts and take possession of the ship and operate it until after the war. The original owner took the case to a higher court and got a decision in his favor. He tried to take my father to the cleaners, but the judge wouldn't go for that, so he and his partners got away clean from the mess. Just as well, because the fetch and carry business was going downhill after the war ended," the Chief finished.

"Yeah, you can't get any money at all from a wooden hull at the scrap yards. Maybe you could get something from the engine," Hank said.

"Not in this case. It was one of those low pressure engines. Nobody wanted those," the Chief said, adding—"The original owner sailed it away to the lower lakes somewhere. We never heard anything about it after that. I have some pictures of the old ship. I'll get them for you."

The Chief got up and headed for his quarters.

After the Chief left, John came into the room.

"Okay people, into the executive suite with you," he said.

The Gentry has two dining areas. One for the crew, and a larger one for officers and passengers. On this trip, the passenger dining area hasn't been used because the crews dining area has been sufficiently large enough to serve everyone. John had the good China set out and the tablecloth damp, so that the dishes wouldn't slide around on the table. There was an additional steam table and refrigerator in the crews dining area, and John and Louie were busy moving things from there to the table.

"Where do we sit?" Hank asked.

"Don't sit there, that's the Captains chair, John replied.

"Just sit anywhere you want to. Everybody is getting the same thing except for Nick," Louie replied.

"What are we having for dessert?" Al asked.

"Pecan pie, The Captain's favorite," Louie replied.

"What are you worried about dessert for?" John asked.

"I want to make sure I have room for dessert," Al replied.

"He's always doing the last thing first. You should have to work with this guy," Brad wisecracked.

"Officer on deck!" John shouted, as the Captain entered the room.

"Good afternoon people," the Captain said as he sat down at the table.

"This steward has been in the Navy too long," DJ wisecracked.

"I remember in the Second World War, many of the officers joined the Coast Guard reserve to please the government. A lot of the Captains and Mates liked to wear their white uniforms while on ship and on shore. I recall that the tunics were pretty fancy with their black and gold shoulder piping. They looked like admirals in the Japanese Navy. Of course, not one of them knew anything about the military. They couldn't march or salute. Couldn't tell a commander from a seaman. It caused some embarrassment when they ran into a real Navy or Coast Guard officer," the Captain remarked.

"DJ here is an old Carrier sailor. He can tell yah how to identify an officer," John wisecracked.

"If it shines-salute it, was how we were taught," DJ said, adding "Of course, most of the time we avoided officers because they would find extra work for us to do."

Just then the first Mate and the Chief entered the dining area.

"Now that we're all here, maybe we can start," Hank joked.

"Okay John, go into your routine," DJ wisecracked.

"What do you have there, Greg?" the Captain asked.

"Some pictures of the 'Sturgeon Bay'. My father's old ship during the Second World War," the Chief replied.

"I've heard of that ship. It was a wooden vessel of the Hackett class, wasn't it?" the Captain asked.

"Very similar to the Hackett in size and tonnage, but about twenty years later, so it was somewhat more modern," the chief replied, as he handed me the pictures.

"That's my father on the left and his three partners. The guy on the right is the wheelsman. See that big wheel? In the wintertime, my little friends and I used to sneak up there and turn the ships wheel and pretend we were steering the ship. My father didn't think too much of that until we caught some teenagers smoking up there. They threatened to beat us up if we told, and they punched me in the nose. So I told my father and he and his partners tracked them down and beat the crap out of them. Then the punks were arrested. After that we would visit the ship everyday," the Chief finished.

"Jeesh, that was kinda' severe, don't yah think?" DJ said.

"Not really. Those idiots could have burned the ship. They were from the Lumber company, so they had no business on the ship. My mother's uncle was the Police Chief and her father was the judge, so the matter was handled rather fastidiously. Sault Ste. Marie was a smaller town back in those days," the Chief said, adding—"That picture of me at the wheel, was taken at that time."

"Did she carry ore?" the Captain asked.

"According to my father, the only time they tried to load her with ore, a big chunk slammed through the inner planking and stoved the outer planking, so that was the end of that," the Chief replied, adding—"That's a picture of the crew unloading airplane engines at Montreal. The engines were made at an Auto plant in Detroit. That was the most valuable cargo my father figured that they ever carried. The picture is in color, because an army guy took some pictures and gave one to my father."

"What does Brayleed Shipping stand for?" Al asked, looking at a picture of a Model-T truck with that name on the door.

"Brady, Ayers, Lee and Edwards. My father and his partners," the Chief replied.

"My father had a truck like that, when I was a kid in Alpena. I was playing with my friends one summer, I guess I was six years old. I got into the truck and was standing on the floorboards, turning the wheel left and right. My friends asked me if I could make it go, so I said sure. The driveway had enough of a downgrade toward the house to make it roll when I pushed the clutch. That damn thing shifted with foot pedals, so clutching it took it out of gear. I couldn't stop it or steer it, so I ran into a tree to stop it."

"Did you get hurt?" Hank asked.

"Not until my father got home. It didn't hurt the truck at all. They were pretty durable."

"He doesn't drive any better now," DJ wisecracked.

"It would help if he wasn't half in the bag," Hank said.

"Here comes John with the Bird," Buster announced.

"That's the appetizer," Louie said, adding—"We have Antipasto salad, Chicken consomme, Shrimp cocktail and for Miss Strickland, our famous Borscht and sour cream."

He sat the bowl in front of me.

"Oh, that's wonderful. Just like my grandmother's!" I exclaimed. "How did you get my grandmother's special recipe?"

"Trade secret, we never tell," Louie replied.

I remembered what the Mate had told me earlier.

"Mr. McCracken must be the one behind this. How did you get my grandmother's special Borscht recipe?"

"Emma got it from her apparently," the Mate replied.

"My grandmother brought this recipe from Russia when she left in 1912," I said.

"Did she come to America in that year?" the Captain asked.

"No, they went to Germany originally, then to England, because the family had some money in a bank there," I replied.

"Did they have enough money for passage to America?" the Captain asked.

"There was a fairly large sum of money, but the stupid British bank wouldn't let them have it. England had just passed the antisemitic Alien Laws, which made it almost impossible for Jewish immigrants to get into England. So the limey bastards said it wasn't possible for my grandmother's brother to withdraw the money because Jewish rights had been revoked. In fact, it wasn't until 1922, when they got a letter saying that their parents and grandparents were dead, that my great uncle was able to go to England and get the money," I explained.

"I remember your grandmother talking about that," the Mate said.

"Yes, she wrote about the Alien Laws extensively, while she was at Mount Union," I said.

"Not to change the subject, but I received a telegram from an old acquaintance of your grandmother's, one Mrs. Kefauver, inviting me to a dinner party," the Mate said.

I laughed—"Mrs. Haw Closs. You better grab that babe before somebody else gets her. Maybe she could buy you this ship for a wedding present," I said, semi-scornfully.

"Now, lets not get vicious," the Mate replied in a subdued tone.

"Ask her why her name hasn't changed after four husbands."

"You sound like Emma," the Mate said.

"Her, my grandmother and I, used to get a big laugh out of talking about Mrs. Kefauver," I said, adding—"Did you know her first husband, the sailor?"

"No, In fact I never met any of her husbands," the Mate replied.

"He was a real decent guy, I guess, but all he left her was the house in Marblehead. Husbands number two, three and four were real disappointments to her, she said. Number two owned mucho real estate in Cleveland. Number three was into oil and gas big time. Number four owned an electric power plant in Virginia. They all left her millions when they died," I said.

"They don't sound like they disappointed her too much," Hank said.

"Well, when you marry for money, that's all you better expect to get out of it," I said.

"Maybe this old widow woman wants your money, David," DJ remarked.

"She's not that old. Forty four or forty five. She knows how to marry men and get their money before they die, that's for sure," I said, adding—"It sounds like she wants another old seadog type."

"I was afraid of that. This last summer, she invited me to go to Niagara Falls with her," the Mate said.

"How romantic. Have you ever been to the Falls?" I asked.

"When I was a kid, my father took us there," the Mate replied.

"I went there a couple of years ago with my grandmother. We went to see the Welland Canal, but we didn't have the faintest idea where we were going. Everyone we asked didn't know where it was, or they didn't know anything about the locks. In Canada, when you get away from a populated area, you drop off the edge of the universe. We finally ended up in Port Colborne. There was a lock there with a ship in it. So we took some pictures and headed back to Buffalo," I said.

"You should cross the Peace bridge at Buffalo. Get on the QEW, it takes you right over the locks near St. Catherine," Al said.

"Where are these geniuses when you need them?" DJ said, adding— "The locals are just about useless up there. I've driven for miles and not even seen a farmhouse. Tried to follow the signs to Welland, never could find the damn town. Couldn't find the QEW either. We used to have a joke-You know what QEW stands for? Quick and easy way. Any other way, forget it."

"Next time, I think I'll take a canoe and paddle up the canal from Port Colborne," I said.

"Didn't you ever go up the canal in a ship?" The Captain asked.

"No, our ship was too big. The smaller ships would take the taconite to the steel plants in Mississagua and Hamilton," I replied.

"The land is so flat around there that you can't get a vantage point from anywhere. I was there a thousand times with my father before I learned the area," Smitty said, adding—" I bet the Chief here knows the canal better than his own wife."

"I've been there a few times," the Chief replied.

"You were navigating the canal before it was made part of the Seaway," Smitty said.

"Yes, the canal was smaller then and the traffic wasn't nearly as bad. The fun part was going through the narrows. The Long Rapids, the Cedar Rapids, and the Lachine Rapids. If you can imagine steering a two hundred and sixty feet ship through the rapids like it was a canoe. That old wooden ship would pitch and roll, usually at the same time, twenty degrees or more. My father got it through every time though," the Chief explained.

"My father only made that trip once, when he was drafted during the war. An old passenger steamer took them to Montreal via the rapids," Smitty said.

"Was your father exempt from the draft during the war?" the Captain asked the Chief.

"Most of the time he was given an automatic exemption as a lake sailor in '43.

In '44, they said no more automatic exemptions, so he had to go for his Physical, even though he had kids. He was eventually rejected because he was color blind. I don't know how color blind he was, he could follow range lights sure enough," the Chief said.

"I remember the sailors griping about the change in exemption status. Even though the Great Lakes were the most important waterway for the war effort. The lakers never got the guaranteed exemption like the 'salties' did," the Captain commented.

"How did your father get his ship back into the lakes?" DJ asked the Chief. "Through the Lousanges and Cornwall canals, which bypassed the rapids in those days," the Chief replied.

"If there were canals, then why didn't your father take them on the down bound trip?" DJ asked.

"The depth of the water over the sills, wasn't enough to allow the ship to transit when loaded, so it had to be brought back empty until they got to Lake Ontario," the Chief replied.

"What was her draft loaded?" DJ asked.

"Fourteen feet fully loaded, four feet minimum empty," the Chief said, adding—"It was a pretty good ship for river travel, even though it didn't have Bow Thrusters. It was short enough to handle the Cuyahoga River without bumping too much. Of course, the Cuyahoga was much more difficult in those days."

"Remember that old Captain, in the Cliffs line, that ran into that van down in the Flats?" Al said to no one in particular.

"Yeah, that was Captain Johnson. After that, every one called him 'Van Johnson'. It was a good thing he was retiring that year anyways," Hank replied gleefully.

"Is this one of those 'fish stories' you guys like to tell?" I asked.

The guys chuckled at my skepticism.

"No kidding, Nick," Hank replied, "I was there when it happened. It was after dark, just up from the Detroit-Superior bridge. What they call 'Collision Bend'. This parking lot came right out to the wall. This van was parked there. It's extended back end was hanging several feet over the river. Johnson couldn't get the ship turned fast enough because she was in ballast. So we scraped the wall and took the van out. Just smashed the hell out of the back end. Anyway, this guy gets out in his boxers and this woman gets out, just wearing this guys shirt. It was pretty obvious what they had been doing in there before the accident. Anyway, the Coast Guard and the Cleveland Police had to come. No telling what they put into their reports, but we got a good laugh out of it, for sure," Hank finished.

"If you guys are gonna' be working your jaws, you might as well have something to put in your mouth," John interrupted, as he and Louie entered, pushing the large carts ahead of them.

"Here's Johnny," the Bosun Wisecracked.

"We have young Turkey with Cranberry sauce," John said as he lifted the big top off the first platter. Over here is Duck ala Orange, Baked Virginia Ham and Beef Bourguignonne flambe."

"What do you have for side dishes?" Hank asked.

"Wild rice Mackinac, my traditional Bread Stuffing, Mashed Potatoes, Sweet Potatoes and Broccoli and Cheddar," John proclaimed, adding—"We have Spoon Bread, Corn Bread, Irish Brown Bread, Buttermilk Bread and Croissants. Plus, we have Mushrooms here and four kinds of Gravy."

John and Louie set the trays and bowls on the table and the Captain said a short grace. When John lifted the cover, the Flambe burst into flames.

"Hey John! Are you trying to set the ship on fire with that Flambe," Buster wisecracked.

"I think he put a little too much brandy on it," the Bosun said.

"It smells like the Chief's degreaser to me," Brad joked.

"I got a rat from the bilges that I cooked up for you, Wiseguy!" John retorted.

"That looks great, John. I haven't seen one like that since I was in Chicago!" I exclaimed.

"I made it better than you can get in Montreal," John replied, as he was putting it on the mashed potatoes and Louie was serving it to us.

"It sounds like Nick is trying to get herself a big piece," Buster remarked.

"It looks like there is plenty for everybody," the Chief said.

Louie handed me a plate with the Flambe, mashed potatoes and a Croissant. Then he set a gravy boat and a bowl of Mushrooms in front of me.

"If you want anything else, let me know," John said to me.

"Thanks guys. I'm afraid that I pigged out on that Borscht. I don't know if I'll be able to eat all of this," I replied.

"What restaurant were you talking about in Chicago, Miss Strickland?" the Captain asked.

"I think I had Flambe at the 'Custom House' and the 'Green Zebra', I replied.

"Those are both good places to eat. I've spent some time in Chicago. There's a lot of good eating places there," the Captain said.

"Are they better than Helrigel's?" the Chief asked.

"Price wise, they're all about the same. The Cuisine is somewhat more varied in the Big City places," the Captain replied.

"What would it cost in one of those fancy places for a meal like this?" Brad asked.

"If you have to ask. You can't afford it," the Chief said.

Since Brad was looking at me, I decided to answer.

"I think the Flambe with Mashed Potatoes would run around sixty dollars a person. Of course, the wine was twenty dollars a glass."

"Whew. The way you drink, Bozo. One meal in that place would take you all season to pay for," Buster said.

"What did you call this rice stuff, John," DJ asked.

"Wild Rice Mackinac," John replied.

"It tastes like this Rice Pilaf stuff my wife used to make," DJ said.

"It's an old Indian Recipe from Mackinac Island," John shot back.

"So the Indians are trying to take credit for it," Buster exclaimed.

"What's wrong with Indians?" Billy asked.

"You can't trust indians, they drink a lot," Buster said.

"You talk," Billy replied.

"Don't be badmouthing Indians. Some of my relatives are Indians," Brad snapped.

"We're not talking about illegitimate children here," Buster said.

"You guys know how to have an interesting conversation," Louie remarked.

"Just so they don't start with the war stories," I said.

"I've heard that you've told some interesting fight stories in your time," Ron, the new guy, stated. "I'm excluding those from the last trip to Cleveland, of course."

"Those kinda' things aren't fit for a decent person to hear," I snapped out.

"Come on. Just one little story," Billy pleaded.

"Okay, one story, then we talk rose petals and pussy cats for the rest of this dinner conversation. It was almost this late in the season, two years ago. The Giovanni had docked temporarily in Detroit for a couple of hours. Some of the guys managed to talk Captain McCullough into going ashore with a promise to behave themselves. Against my better judgement, I agreed to join them. We no sooner got to 'Chastity's Bar and Girls', when these guys from the Eugene W. Pargny show up. Now these guys had obviously been doing the Bar circuit all day, so they were ready to blow off some steam, big time. Some big guy, smelling of booze something awful, gets up in my face and starts saying some things I won't repeat. My old buddy, Guiddo, breaks a wine bottle on his head. Just lays him out stiffer than a Carp. The bar is quiet for about two seconds, then all hell breaks loose. This other guy comes at me, so I palm strike him under the chin. I swear I felt neck bones snapping. Anyway, he goes down too. Then I see this guy pull a knife, so I pick up a chair and go after him. I shove the legs of the chair at him and he begins backing up. I shoved him right over the bar and he's screaming that I broke his arm. Then I turn and see that this big guy has Guiddo on the floor. I grab the chair by the back and swing it down on this guy so the front edge hits him on the head. It's one of those heavy wooden chairs. The seats are two inches thick, so it must have hurt. This guy just puts his hands on the back of his head. Then I heard the Police whistle. We all start heading for the back door. I was in front and the guys were pushing me from behind. I thought I would fall over frontward. There was this wooden screen door. I went right through it. My head hit this guy right in the stomach. All I saw was black leather shoes. Probably a cop. That straightened me up though. I ran like hell back to the ship. Captain McCullough wasn't too happy with us, needless to say," I finished.

"That sounds like more action than I saw in eighteen months in Vietnam," Ron remarked.

"Never a dull bar fight with Nick around," Buster smirked.

"I don't know Captain McCullough, but I know the Captain of the Eugene W. Pargny. He's been her Captain for ten years, so I'm sure he was around then," the Captain said, smiling.

"Did he say anything about the Giovanni gang making a sore hash of his crew?" the Chief asked.

"No, he's a pretty laid back kinda' fellow. I can't imagine him getting worked up about anything. I do remember stories about feisty women crewmen on the Canadian side, but I never gave them much thought, until now," the Captain said jokingly.

"I worked with an Indian that claimed he was from Mackinac Island. I heard that he was riding a horse down the street, drunk as a skunk, when he tried to ride through the Tavern door. The horse made it but he didn't come out too good. Never was quite right in the head since then, I guess," Hank said.

"It sounds like he took riding lessons from Nick," Billy wisecracked.

"I'll have you know that I rode with the Genesee Valley Hunt. That's no fluff outfit. I was right up with the Field Master most of the time," I stated.

"You could go to Mackinac Island and work with the horses, since your so knowledgable," the Bosun said.

"Yeah, I could work at the Grand Hotel with all those West Indies types. 'How the Broule today, mon?'" I replied.

"Now, let's not get vicious here," the Mate suggested.

"I've been through the straits many times, but I've never been to the island," John said as he pushed the dessert cart to the table. "We have Pecan Pie, Key Lime Pie and the usual Apple and Pumpkin Pie. Chocolate and Tapioca pudding."

"John, you have exceeded our utmost expectations," the Captain remarked, as he took a piece of Pecan Pie.

When the pie came my way, I passed it on without taking any.

"What's wrong, Nick?" John asked.

"I'm afraid I can't eat another bite. I've really pigged out. Maybe by the end of next watch, I'll be able to eat some, if there's any left," I said.

"I'll be sure to save you some of the Key Lime Pie," John replied.

"Too bad there's no after dinner drinks here," Buster said.

"Wait until the end of the season, then you can drink all you want," Ed said.

"He drinks too much during the season as it is," Mark remarked, adding—"Oh, if looks could kill!"

"This time of the year, it's antifreeze. Keeps your pipes from freezing," Buster said.

"Back in Engineering, they don't get cold. When we were back there pulling the turbine, it didn't seem cold to me," Al said.

"Did you poor babies get overheated?" Brad wisecracked.

"I've worked engineering with Diesel engines. They got pretty warm and there wasn't any insulation to protect us," I shot back.

"Was there any insulation on the exhaust headers and stacks," Hank asked.

"No, just heat shields. Except where they passed through the decks. The deck was insulated around the stacks," I replied.

"Those diesels were pretty trouble free?" the Chief asked.

"Not always. There was many a time when we had to run on one while fixing the other. One time we made two trips on one engine," I said.

"Why was that?" the Captain asked.

"We had a Cylinder liner cracked. It was letting water into the crankcase. We noticed water in the oil. That was one of the things that we checked for all the time," I explained.

"My father was on a Diesel ship. They had to heat the engine with torches to get it started. How do you start big Diesel engines like that?" Hank asked.

"With Compressed air blown into the cylinders of a starter motor. Once you got the engine turning over fast enough, the heat of compression would be enough to start the cylinders firing. Of course, there was a lengthy starting procedure to go through," I replied.

"What kind things did you have to do to start the engines?" Hank asked.

"Open the cylinder inlet and outlet valves to the jacket and cylinder heads. Pressurize the lube system with the hand pump. Pressurize the fuel system and bleed the air out of the fuel lines. Open the blow-off valves to the cylinders. Set the governor to starting rpm. Open the starting air valve to crank the engine. Test the cylinders for water by checking the blow-off valves right after the engine kicks over. There's a few more things to do and check but you get the general idea," I explained.

"It's funny. Nick is checking for water in the oil and we were checking for oil in the water," DJ remarked.

"Different strokes for different folks," the Chief said.

"I've run those old three cylinder Lenz marine engines," Hank said, adding—"There was a couple of times when we had to disconnect a cylinder and run on two when we couldn't fix the problem."

"Those old type engines are just about gone now," the Captain said.

"Since this is the last run. We'll have to have our Christmas party early," Billy said.

"Technically, it's the 'End of the Season Party'. In the past, the season sometimes went past Christmas, so we had to take time off for the holidays," the Chief said.

"Maybe the union can find us something else for another month or two," Billy said hopefully.

"Yeah, you can shovel snow out of the Soo locks for a couple months," Buster wisecracked.

"Maybe you can find him something on one of those Kanook boats. How about it, Nick?"

"Do either of you have a Canadian Maritime Certificate?" I asked.

"No, I don't," Billy answered.

"Unfortunately your Maritime Merchant Document is not transferable to Canada. Which reminds me that I have to get my MMD renewed in a couple of months," I said.

"You were Canadian most of the time, weren't you? Billy asked.

"Yes, but five years is five years," I replied.

"Maybe we'll all be working on diesel boats in a couple years," Hank said dolefully.

"If we're working at all," the Chief replied.

"We're supposed to be thankful and cheerful here. Not crying in our beer," I said.

"I still want Santa rigged out by the time we get to Sault Ste. Marie," the Captain said.

"Since the waves aren't too bad. We should be able to get to it in a couple of hours," the Chief said.

In a couple hours, my four to eight (evening)watch would start. The Coast Guard report said that the wind wouldn't let up any and the temperature would steadily drop as we headed north. Some of the guys were excusing themselves and talking about heading aft to the Rec room. I wondered if somebody still had a bottle of 'cheer' stashed back there somewhere. I was thinking about going to my quarters to kick back and listen to some music for a while.

"I think I'll head back to my quarters. Thanks for a great meal, John," I said, getting up from my chair.

CHAPTER **8**

Alone In The Wheelhouse

As I headed forward, I saw Carl and Mark carrying some electrical wire on reels.

"Hi guys. At it already?" I asked.

"No, just getting ready for later," Carl replied.

The wind was still coming straight from the north and the ship was beginning to pitch a little, but no roll. Good, I thought. I won't have to tie myself into my bunk. When I got to my quarters, I changed out of my good clothes and put on my work clothes. I laid back on my seabag and put on the headphones for my radio. After flipping through stations, I settled for 'Take on Me'. The next song was 'St. Elmo's Fire', so I changed the station. Why would I want to hear a song that reminded me of that jerk, O'Blake. So I got 'Sea of Love' and 'Night Shift'. I wondered if those turkeys ever had to work night shift on a Lake Freighter. I started to write a letter to my friend Lukesia. I told her that I would try to make the wedding in Thunder Bay over winter break. I read some and dozed for a little while until the watch bell rang.

I slipped on my parka hurriedly and headed down the passageway. I passed the Mate on the stairway and mistakenly called him 'Dave'.

He smiled and said, "Good afternoon, Miss Strickland," and he winked.

At the bottom of the steps, I put on my tool belt. Smitty and the new guy, Ron, met up with me.

Handing me the Clipboard, Smitty said, "The engineering crew will be hanging the Christmas stuff real soon, so watch out that those fools don't drop something on you. Be careful out there."

"Will do!" I replied as I put the clipboard back in its holder.

Al came over from the other side of the ship.

"The Bosun has some other things for Earl to do so he won't be joining us until the morning watch," he said.

"Okay, I figured there'd be something like that," I said. I walked aft port side while Al took the starboard side. We met again aft, at the towing hawse.

"Well, it don't look like this sea is gonna' get any better," I said.

"No, the waves are definitely coming from the north now. Just like the wind," Al replied.

"You see anything astern?" I asked as I saw him taking out his binoculars.

"No, I think it's only whitecaps," Al replied, while putting the binoculars to his eyes.

There's supposed to be a couple ships behind us, but these waves are too big and the visibility is getting worse by the hour," he added.

"Let's see if our eight tiny reindeer hangers have showed up yet," I suggested.

We walked around the port side of the after deckhouse and headed forward. It wasn't until we got halfway to the pilot house that I noticed two men up on the conveyor.

"That must be Mark and Carl running wires up there," I said.

One by one, we saw DJ, Gary, Buster, Brad and Billy emerge from the door to the forward storage room. Each was carrying a piece of the plywood Christmas display, which they unceremoniously deposited under the conveyor.

"This sucks in this wind," Billy complained.

"It's only gonna' get worse, so you might as well stop complaining," Gary said.

"Yeah, you're getting overtime for this, Admiral," Brad wisecracked.

"Would you stop with that Admiral crap!" Billy snapped.

"I wasn't aware of any promotions on this ship," I said jokingly.

"That's his new name. From Admiral Shepherd, the guy that sank the Bismarck," Buster replied.

"An admiral Shepherd sank the Bismarck? Did he do this all by himself?" I asked.

"He actually sent the airplanes and battleships that sank the Bismarck, but he got all the credit," Buster answered.

"That's funny, I thought his name was Tubby," I said.

"Now, let's not get vicious here. We can't all be young and beautiful," Brad said.

"That's your problem, Nick. You're always reading those queer books instead of watching wholesome, educational television like we do," Buster said.

"Oh, I'll try to do better in the future. Maybe some cartoons," I said jokingly.

"Hey, do you guys remember that reindeer girl?" DJ asked.

"No, why don't you tell us," Billy sneered.

"It was last year. A couple of us were at the mall in Duluth. It was colder than hell. Anyway, there was this Santa there taking pictures with the kids. There were two young babes dressed up as elves and two dressed up as reindeer. So Joe, three sheets to the wind, goes up to one of the reindeer babes and says, "Hey, babe, you wanna' join me in some reindeer games?" So she punches him right in the face and knocks him down. It was hilarious!" DJ finished.

"Why don't you guys quit jawing and hoist those reindeer up to the conveyor and secure them with those J-bolts," the Chief ordered, rather than asked.

"Do we get a break here?" Billy asked.

"The break you been on since four o'clock or is it a different break you're talking about? It's only gonna' get colder, so we gotta' finish this real fast," the Chief stated.

Carl requested that the Chief come up on the conveyor to check out a wiring problem.

"Well Al, we better let these guys get back to their fun," I said as I turned and headed for the forward deckhouse.

I entered via the door to the Crews hall. I saw Pete pouring some water into a cup, then, without acknowledging me, he went down the passageway and up the steps toward the wheelhouse. I thought it odd that he didn't have something smart alack to say. I got a cup of coffee and waited for Earl to show up. Instead, the Mate showed up.

"Pete was here a few minutes ago, but he was strangely quiet," I said.

"He's not feeling real well, I guess," the Mate replied.

"That's strange. Alcohol related?" I asked.

"I hope it's not some kind of Flu," he replied as he poured a cup of coffee.

"Yeah, that would be a bummer," I said, adding—"The Chief is really cracking the whip on the reindeer detail."

"Yes, he wants it done by the end of this watch," the Mate replied.

"I wonder what Mr.O'Blake would have thought about Rudolph," I thought out loud.

"Fortunately, I don't think he'll be around much longer. He has no experience in this type of business. It all depends on the 'Powers That Be' of course," the Mate replied.

"They sound like fickle bastards, even in the best of times," I said.

"Yes, It's hard to know what to do sometimes," he said.

"Most of the guys think he's the one responsible for ending the season early. That,'I'm gonna' be a dirty bastard' attitude just seems to run clear through him. And those 'private meetings' in his quarters. Can you believe the nerve of that pompous jerk?" I asked.

"I have to be getting topside. I'll probably see you later," the Mate said.

"Okay, later then," I said,smiling.

I decided to head aft and check on Earl and the reindeer guys. I crossed over and came out the door on the port side of the conveyor pivot. As I headed aft, I was surprised to see that the last couple of plywood pieces were being hoisted up. They're definitely making some progress here, I thought. I was also surprised to see Earl and Hank helping them, when I got there.

"You two got sucked into this project, too?" I asked.

"Yeah, The Chief had to leave so he put me in charge," Hank said.

I saw Earl hanging on to the foot of a reindeer to steady it in the wind as it was being hoisted into the air.

"Good job, old buddy. This job will be done in a jiffy with this kinda' progress," I said, adding—"On the Giovanni, we just had a Christmas tree at the end of the conveyor. It's an old pagan custom when building a house or barn to put up a pine tree. You've probably seen that when a building is being built," I stated.

"Yes, they still do that sometimes," Hank said.

"I like this better, much more visible. It will really get these guys in the Christmas spirit!" I exclaimed.

"I got some Christmas spirit waiting for me in Detroit," Billy said.

"A six pack and a rent-a-Ho at the Circus in Cleveland, is all you got, goofy," Brad replied.

"Did they have exotic dancers at that Chastity's place you were talking about in Detroit," Billy asked.

"If you consider some local bleach blonde bimbo in thigh high boots and a g-string Teddy, trying to do a pole dance, to be exotic dancers,then I guess they do," I replied.

"Wasn't there a woman in Detroit that danced with a snake?" Buster asked.

"I saw that in Nassau. This place called the Tropical Breeze. This totally nude woman, danced with this really huge snake. Damndest thing I ever did see. I saw these belly dancers in Las Vegas. They must have been among the best in the world. Now, that is exotic dancing as a true art form," I finished.

"I think Billy's having a coronary," Buster joked.

"I thought you thoroughly corrupted him already," I said.

"He thinks snakes are a real turn-on. We knew that letting kids watch those nature programs would do more harm than good," Brad wisecracked.

"I can't imagine what you were watching on TV," Billy retorted.

"We used to watch CFPL-TV in Canada. I liked the 'Avengers'. Some good wholesome womanhood in Diana Rigg, no doubt about it," Brad said.

"You guys will be done here pretty soon," I said to Earl.

"Yeah, I'll probably have to go back and help the cooks though," Earl replied.

"Well, we got a library run in Sault Ste. Marie, so be sure and get the deckwatch," I said, and I turned and headed aft.

When I got to the after deckhouse, I went to the Galley to get some coffee.

"Ready for another feast?" I asked Louie.

"Yeah, they'll be getting here any minute," he said as he changed coffee pots for me. I poured myself a big paper cup and put a lid on it.

"Tell John that I'll be back later for the Key Lime pie," I said jokingly as I headed for the door.

I walked over to the starboard side and ran into the Bosun and Al.

"Everything shipshape?" I asked.

"No, In fact, I just got a call on the phone. The Mate wants to see you as soon as possible in the Wheelhouse," the Bosun said.

"Jeesh, what did I do now?" I replied, adding—"Well, you'll have to take it from here, Al."

"I'll walk forward with you, so I can check things up there," Al said.

As we walked forward on the starboard side, the wind gusts really kicked up.

"J-C Al, this damn wind nearly blew us overboard," I said, leaning into it and clutching my coffee.

"It would have blown the 'old java' overboard if you hadn't had a tight grip on it," Al noted.

"Just as well. It will probably be frozen by the time I get to the Wheelhouse," I said.

When we were nearly to the forward deckhouse, we saw Pete coming out of the port side door and head aft.

"He doesn't look too good," Al observed.

"Yeah, he looks worse than he did before," I agreed.

"That's probably why the Mate wants to see you," he said.

"Okay, old buddy. I'll see you later," I said as I headed up the starboard side steps to the Wheelhouse.

When I came through the Wheelhouse door, the Mate told me to turn off the lights and he turned on the red lights.

"Would you take the wheel, Miss Strickland?" he asked.

"Very good, Sir," I replied, secretly wondering when I would stop calling him 'Sir'. After I sat in the wheelsman's chair, I checked our heading, position, speed and revolutions, then I checked the Autopilot.

"This strong headwind is slowing us down by two and a half knots. I'm not going to ask engineering for any more speed. You shouldn't have any problem holding this course," the Mate said, looking at the chart.

"Yes sir," I replied, adding—"Is there anything up ahead on the radar screen?"

"Nothing close, but we'll keep a lookout for smaller craft forward," he replied.

"Very good, Sir," I answered.

He looked at me for a moment, then looked forward with his binoculars.

"I'm afraid that Flu you mentioned earlier may be here," I ventured to comment, adding—" Pete didn't look to good when we saw him heading aft."

"He wasn't able to continue up here. Hopefully this is a short-lived thing," the Mate said.

After a few minutes, the Mate turned and looked at me. I had not realized that I had been humming 'Walking on Sunshine'.

"You seem happy," he said.

"Sorry, Sir. Sometimes I do that without realizing it," I explained.

"That's quite alright, I do that sometimes myself. I guess it's a habit of being alone," he said, adding—"Hank should be giving us the okay for the Christmas Lights. They're hooked up to the circuit for the boom flood lights, so as soon as they bypass those, they should be ready."

"That'll make the Captain happy," I said.

"Yes, he's a man that likes a merry Christmas," the Mate agreed.

"I'm sure he likes to be home with his wife and children and grandchildren. Uhh . . . I'm assuming he has grandchildren," I said, when the Mate turned and looked at me.

"Yes, in fact he does," the Mate stated in a low voice.

"That's good. Always good to spend holidays with friends and family."

An uneasy quiet seemed to descend on us. The terri-phone started beeping.

"Wheelhouse, McCracken. Yes Chief . . . Roger that. Yes, . . . I'm sure. Carl and Mark have to finish. Very well, McCracken out."

"The Chief said he would turn on the lights for the reindeer," the Mate said.

"I don't mean to pry, but have you heard anything more from Tommy?" I asked.

"No, not since the last time I talked to you about it," he replied.

"I'd like to see him. Explain things to him. Apologize to him for the mean things I did to him years ago," I said.

"I don't think he'll be coming over for Christmas. He hasn't since he left home," he said, adding—"Do you have any plans?"

"No, with the season ending early, it kinda' leaves me with extra time on my hands. I keep thinking about going back to school or taking a tramp freighter around the world or something crazy like that. Sometimes, I think I'm having a midlife crisis," I said jokingly.

"You should try it at forty four," the Mate said.

"I looked into Sealift, but they didn't have any openings at that time. Were you in the Military?" I asked.

"No, I went into the Merchant Academy and got married. Vietnam was cranking up, but I got an exemption from Cleveland Cliffs when I got out of the Academy. I don't think I'd be much good in a war. I never used a firearm until Emma showed me how to shoot her revolver. I guess, I'm a lover, not a fighter," he said.

"A good thing for Emma," I said jokingly, adding—"If you do talk to Tommy. Please assure him that I'm not trying to push him out of your Will."

"Will do," the Mate replied.

"I was thinking about traveling to Mississippi. I have some old friends from school, who live down there in Vicksburg. It's been a while since I've seen them," I said.

"I was in Mississippi once. I was even thinking of living in Vicksburg myself. I had an offer to Captain a barge tug but I found Mississippi too Faulkner-like," the Mate said.

"I noticed that too, but you're the first person I ever heard say that. I guess great minds think alike," I agreed.

"Any other plans? Like marriage, for instance?" the Mate asked.

He cut to the chase, I thought.

"That's always a possibility. Something I'll have to think about when I get back to Marblehead."

"Don't you think about it now?" he asked.

"J-C Dave, that's all I can think about. You and me in Church. You and me shopping. You and me in be . . . Well,you get the picture, I'm sure," I blurted out.

"Well, that definitely gives us something to look forward to," the Mate said.

I started thinking about my grandmother. When she put that Quilt top away and said someone else would help me finish it. She seemed to know so many things that never occured to me, until after the fact. Did she know I would get married, give up the lakes, go back to school. I didn't know what I wanted to do.

She would say—"Like a flash of light in the night. Like the twinkling of an eye. It will come to you and change your life forever."

Was that it? Was that the secret of life? Stop trying to think and plan things and just let them happen? I wondered if my grandmother had known everything. Had she known that she would never see me again?

I always felt so guilty for not being there to help her out. Letting her die alone at home.

"You look a million miles away," the Mates voice snapped me out of my thoughts.

"I'm sorry. I was just thinking about my grandmother," I said.

"Anything in particular?" he asked.

"It just seems that a lot of people I love and respect are dead or dying," I replied.

"I felt that way when I was a senior in high school. My mother said that that is a sign to get on with your own life. So I decided to go to the Merchant Academy," he said, adding—"I still have to take you to see my mother. I think you'll like her. She's very much like your grandmother. She has always had a way of talking to me that calmed me down and made me feel better."

"I think I would like to meet her," I replied.

The Mate got up from the Captain's chair and walked behind me. I thought he was getting a chart or something, but he moved my ponytail aside and started kissing and nuzzling the back of my neck.

"It'll all work out, Nick. We'll be happy together," he whispered in my ear.

"Oh David . . ." was all I could say, completely taken aback by what he did.

He stopped and returned to the Captain's chair. I moved my ponytail back. The back of my neck felt warm and I knew my skin must be pink there so I didn't want anyone seeing it.

"You bad!" was all I could manage to say.

I knew the watch would end in a few minutes, so I tried to keep my mind on the job. Inevitably, it drifted back to the Mate. I could have my usual three day fling, then as things went along, we could become very friendly neighbors, I thought. The mate turned around and saw me smiling.

"Keep it professional until we're back in Marblehead," I said softly.

He gave me the OK sign and started writing in the log book. In a few minutes, Andy and Mike came into the wheelhouse.

"Right on time, guys! How was the feast?" I asked.

"Great, but we didn't get the Flambe," Andy said jokingly.

236

"It was great. Take my word for it," I said, adding—"Well, I gotta' get aft and get my Key Lime pie."

"We made sure we ate it all," Mike said, getting into the wheelsman's chair.

"Catch you later. I gotta' get my beauty sleep," I said as I headed out the wheelhouse door.

Darkness hadn't brought any change to the weather except make it colder, I observed as I descended the wheelhouse steps to the deck. I saw Al and Ed looking at the Clipboard.

"Everything shipshape, guys?" I asked.

"Yeah, everything is fine. Here, sign your life away," Al said, handing me the clipboard.

I signed it and handed it to Ed.

"She's all yours. I hope you don't have a belly ache," I said, smiling, then I headed aft.

I was hoping that I'd run into Earl somewhere aft. I met no one on my way aft. I entered the port side door to the after deckhouse and went down the passageway to the galley. I entered the door.

"Hi John! You done slopping the hogs?" I asked jokingly.

"Be right with ya', Nick," John said as he left the room. I noticed the galley was looking smart and orderly. They must be working Earl's tail off, I thought. After a couple of minutes, John returned through the swinging doors with some coffee cups and a whole pie.

"Who else wants pie?" I asked.

"Oh, that's for you," John replied.

"Great, if I run into the Minnesota Vikings on the way into the Rec room, I'll be ready," I said, adding—"Have you seen Earl?"

"Louie has him pot walloping in the back," John replied.

"Well, tell him that I want to see him in the Rec room about the next watch," I said.

"I'll tell Louie," John said, then he went through the swinging doors.

I made my way to the Rec room. When I entered I saw Billy and Buster playing cards and Carl watching television. I went over to Carl.

"Can I join you?" I asked.

"Sure, Nick. Sit right down here," he said.

"You guys did a great job on Rudolph," I said.

Rudolph was the generic term for the entire display.

"Yeah, it really lights the place up," Carl said.

"UFO sightings will triple by the time we get to Duluth," I said jokingly.

"Maybe other ships won't run into us," Carl said.

Mark entered the Rec room and came over to our table.

"May I join you two?" he asked.

"Yes, of course. Do you want some pie? There's enough here for the Trojan Army," I said.

"No, thanks anyway," Mark replied. "I need to see you up front, about some conduits below deck," he said to Carl.

"I hope this doesn't take too long. I wanted to get some sleep," Carl said, getting up. "See you later, Nick," and he left with Mark.

After another five minutes, the Mate came into the Rec room and came over to my table.

"May I join you?" he asked.

"Sure, people are just coming and going this evening," I remarked.

"I won't take up a lot of your time. I wondered what caused the fight between Earl, Joe and Billy?" he asked.

"Joe was repeating some story by Pete, about you, me and the Captain having a threesome in the Chart room during the Dixon incident review," I answered.

"We were only in there for a few minutes," the Mate said.

"Pete can't let the facts get in the way of a good story," I said, adding—"Earl told Joe and Billy to stop talking silly shit that they know isn't true. Joe mouthed him, so Earl slammed him into the bulkhead. Billy tried to grab him and Earl kicked him real hard in the stomach. Two hits and two men down, real simple," I finished.

"I thought it was something like that. I've got some business forward. I'll see you later."

"Okay. I gotta' get some sleep here soon myself," I said.

A few minutes after the Mate left, Earl came in.

"Hi Nick," he said as he came over to my table.

"Hi guy! Sit right down and have some pie. Hey, that rhymes. Sounds like a song, Doesn't it?"

"Did you need to talk to me about something?" Earl asked.

"No, I was just running interference for you, so these guys would leave you alone and let you rest," I said.

"That's good. I've been going for about fourteen hours now," Earl said.

"Don't forget to log the overtime. Depending on the weather, we should be in Sault Ste. Marie between 6:00 and 7:00. The Library run and cookie run will be a breeze, unless there's a blizzard up there. So, bright eyed and bushy tailed at 4:00 AM, old buddy," I said.

"No problem, Nick," Earl replied.

"I'm going forward to get some sleep," I said, adding—"I wouldn't sleep on the belt If I were you."

"No, it's too cold down there now. I'll go to my quarters," Earl said.

"Okay, catch you later," I said, getting up and heading back to the galley fridge with the rest of the pie.

On the way forward, the wind was just as bad and an ice ball snow was pelting me. I was thankful that my quarters had good heat. It's gonna' get worse before it get's better, I thought. As I entered the forward deckhouse from the starboard side door, I ran into the Mate in the passageway.

"Can't sleep, old buddy?" I teased.

"No, just taking the scenic route," he replied.

"Oh, I thought you were coming to tuck me in," I wisecracked, feeling ornery.

"You bad," he replied, adding—"Sweet dreams."

I entered my quarters and shut the door. I pulled out the book, "Bark and Skin boats of North America," by Edwin Tappan Adney. I paged through the book until I came to a picture of a young Cree woman with her three children in a twelve foot canoe. I thought about what it would be like to live a minimalist existence like that. Take a 30-30 rifle and kill a bear or moose and eat off it all winter. Run a trap line or fish so you could buy flour and salt for the year. I thought about Adney living among the Indians. Continually complaining to the provincial government about the acculturation of the natives. They must have regarded him as some backwoods Colonel Kurtz. As yogi bear ruefully said so many years ago—'The deeper in the woods you go, the more nuts you find'. I put the book with the others that had to go back to the Library. I decided to risk sleeping in my night shirt. Like an Arab Thwab, it went all the way down to my feet. I went to sleep thinking about getting a canoe. I woke up about 1:00 AM. The ship wasn't rolling or pitching badly but I could hear the wind moaning as it blew around the deckhouse. The wind had to be at 50 mph to sound like that. I put on my work clothes before I went back to bed. I noticed the porthole was partly frosted. I was glad I put on my extra thick long underwear. Those Canadian coolers could be a real bear. Sometimes the temperature could drop forty or fifty degrees in no time at all. Some nasty weather front had to be driving this hellacious wind. I fell asleep, hoping to dream of Hawaii. When I woke up, it was 3:30 and I could tell by the frost on the window that it was colder than heck. I went to the Observation room and dropped off my books, then got a cup of coffee and a bowl of cereal from the night kitchen. As I sat on the foldout bench eating my cereal, the Mate came in with Hal and the Chief. I saw the Mate look at me, like he wanted to say something.

"Well, gentlemen, did you sleep well?" I asked.

"Sleep! What the hell is that?" the Chief replied.

"Tolerable well, Miss Strickland. How about you?" the Mate asked.

"I'm afraid that the sound of the wind kept me awake part of the time. Terrible moaning and groaning," I replied.

"Yes, we're in more sheltered waters now, but the wind won't start diminishing for another hour at least," the Mate said.

"We had some minor damage aft. The wind and ice also played hell with the Christmas lights," the Chief said.

"I'm sure Cappy will give you some slack. It'll be light in four hours," I replied.

"He would like them on when we get to Sault Ste. Marie," the Chief said, adding—"I don't know if we can do that without endangering crewmen."

"No, we certainly don't want to do that," I agreed.

"I don't see the need to hurry. The ship won't be able to dock until 6:30. While the deck hands are ashore, it should start getting light. The Problem shouldn't take that long to fix," the Mate said.

"Famous last words. Getting Mark and Carl moving on a morning like this may be the hardest part," the Chief remarked.

A minute later, Al and Ron came in.

"Well, everyone's bright and early this morning!", I exclaimed.

"It's early. Nothing particularly bright and cheerful about it," Al replied.

"It can only get better, guy," I said.

I noticed the Chief wasn't smiling either, but the Mate seemed pleased about something.

"I'll see you guys outside in ten minutes," I said as I got up and put my dishes away and headed back to my quarters. when I got to my quarters, I put an extra pair of gloves and a Canadian army wooly-pully in the pockets of my parka. I picked up my Library books, in the observation room, and carried them to the Crew's hall and put them in the canvas bag with the other books. When I opened the back door of the Crew's hall, I got hit with a blast of freezing air. I guess this is what's got everybody in such a 'good' mood this morning, I thought, as I stepped out and closed the door. Rudolph was definitely out of commission as were half the deck lights. The wires were covered with ice in many places. Not that drippy icicle ice, but that hard coating driven onto the wires by the wind and the cold. It's strange that I forgot to find out the temperature before I came out. It felt like it was -20 degree at least. When I got over to the Starboard side again, I saw Al waving for me in the window. I opened the door and entered the Crew's hall.

"The ink in your pen, freeze again," I asked jokingly.

"There's enough lights for navigation. Nobody wants to be out there in the dark when it's like this," Al replied.

"What temperature is it, anyway?" I asked.

"Minus nine degrees. The wind is still 30 miles per hour. It won't let up for a couple hours yet," he replied as he picked up the clipboard from the table.

"Where did Ron and Hal get off to?" I asked.

"They headed aft via the ratwalk," Al replied.

"Ah, yes. Better coffee back there anyway," I noted, as Al handed me the Clipboard. I looked at all the items listed by the previous watch.

"Yup, It's gonna' be a pain for sure. Plus the shore duty along with it. Oh, you know, I better go aft and make sure Earl is up and moving," I said as I signed the clipboard and put it in the dispatch pouch hanging on the old, wooden roll top desk.

I took out my gloves and put them on. When I opened the door, I was surprised to see the Mate approaching.

"You're getting around this morning," I said.

"Some more problems aft," he replied.

"Hadn't you better get topside? The Captain may want to get some sleep," I said jokingly.

"Enroute," he replied, smiling as he passed me.

I headed aft on the starboard side. It was one of those times when you know that an iron ship is the coldest thing in creation. When I got to the after deckhouse, the door handle was sticking somewhat but the door opened easily enough. I passed the engineers quarters, then made a right turn into the passageway, then into the galley. When I got to the Galley, John was pouring coffee for the Chief and Fred.

"Keep it coming, old buddy," I said as he looked up.

"Everybody forward seems happy and everybody back here seems grumpy," John observed.

"Apparently you're working in the wrong end of the ship," I wisecracked.

The Chief and Fred gave me a funny look.

"Has anyone seen Earl this morning?" I asked.

"You might try in the Rec room. I haven't seen him this morning," the Chief said.

"Okay, have fun," I said as I picked up my cup and left. When I got to the Rec room, Hal, Ron, Buster and Gary were playing cards there.

"Hi, Nick," Buster said.

"Hi guys. What's going on?" I asked.

"Oh, we're having all kinds of fun. Any more fun and we'd have to pay them," Buster exclaimed.

"Yeah, I just left the Chief and Fred. They said the same thing," I said, adding—"Has anyone seen Earl?"

"I'll see if he's in his quarters," Gary replied, then he got up and left.

"We had a mast cable snap at the turnbuckle. Kenny had to machine the broken stud out and chase new threads so we can put the cable back up when it gets light," Buster explained.

"You guys need help?" I asked.

"I don't think so. The Chief will call you if he needs you," Buster replied.

"Well, he didn't say anything to me, so I guess he figures you got it handled," I said. I saw Hal reach over and change the station on the Radio.

"Nothing on TV yet?" I asked.

"No, the cheap bastards won't get us cable. Up here there's nothing until 6:00," he replied.

For a couple of minutes, I sat down and drank coffee and listened to music. Gary returned and told me that Earl was on his way. The four resumed their card game.

I started looking through the magazine rack. As usual, the magazines were totally disorganized so I started pulling them out to organize them.

Half way through the mess, I found an issue of Modern Bride, which I threw up on the table with the rest of the magazines to be sorted. Interesting reading for a cargo ship, I thought. A few minutes later, Earl came in.

"Hey guy, give me a hand over here. Did you get sucked into that cable job?" I asked.

"No, I don't know anything about it," he said.

"Good, they probably won't stop you from working the deck watch with me," I said, adding—"I've been organizing these. I put the sports ones together, Popular Mechanics and the science magazines here," I explained.

I looked up and saw Earl looking at the 'Modern Bride'.

"I don't know where to put that one," I said.

"Your quarters, perhaps," Earl wisecracked.

"Not mine, old buddy!" I shot back, taking the magazine and putting it behind the others.

"Now, we can find a magazine without tearing the whole thing apart," I commented.

"Do we have something to do outside?" Earl asked.

"Yes, there's some lights out and other little things like that, but the Captain doesn't want anybody outside until it gets light and the wind dies down a little bit," I said.

"Have you seen the weather report?" Earl asked.

"It's minus nine degrees with a thirty knot wind right now. In a couple of hours the wind should die down, but it'll get colder at Sault Ste. Marie and there's going to be some snow on the ground," I replied.

"I think I'll go get my warm hiking boots since we'll be walking through snow when we get to the Soo," Earl said, adding—"I'll be back in a few."

"Okay, I'll be here," I replied.

I got another cup of coffee and sat in the recliner and closed my eyes. I was thinking about the tropics. That Cancun vacation was looking better all the time. I started thinking about my grandmother in her wedding dress. I had looked at the picture on the dresser shortly before I left the house. Some devil got in me and I looked down at the magazine rack. I pulled out the Modern Bride and checked the date. It was two years old. Some crewman must have been looking for a wedding dress for his daughter or maybe a fiance, I thought. I started flipping the pages.

The dresses did not look bad, but the models obviously never worked on a cargo ship. I was checking out shoes and accessories when I heard someone clearing their throat. I looked up and saw Earl and the Bosun looking at me.

"Sorry to interrupt your reading. There's some things I want Earl to take forward on the four-wheeler. It will take him about an hour," the Bosun said.

"No problem, I'll give him a hand," I said, fumbling to put the magazine back in the rack.

"Okay, if you want to," the Bosun said, adding—"You can take the magazine forward with you. I doubt that any of the guys back here, will be reading it."

"Well some guy brought it on this ship, so I better leave it here," I shot back as I got up to leave.

I noticed the four card players were looking at us. Great, that's throwing gasoline on the fire. Those gossipy yahoos will have a field day with this, I thought.

"There's some stuff in the old laundry room, plus there's boxes in the Galley store room and the Engineers' storeroom. The boxes are tagged, so you'll know where they go," the Bosun explained as we walked down the passageway to the Engineers' storeroom.

Since the storeroom had a hatch coaming, we could not take the cart in there, we would use the passageway door. Earl went to get the cart. The Bosun showed me the boxes then left. I was moving the boxes to the doorway when Earl got there with the cart.

"This may be a little more than a load," I said as I passed a box to Earl through the doorway.

"Let's grab a couple of those bungee cords and secure this when we get it loaded," Earl said.

"Right-Oh!" I acknowledged, as I passed another box to Earl, adding—"One more should do it."

I grabbed several bungee cords off the wall and sat them on a box and passed the box to Earl. In a minute, Earl had the bungee cords around the boxes.

"That should hold it," he stated as we started down the passageway.

"There won't be any snow drifts on the deck, but I can't guarantee that in Sault Ste. Marie," I said as I zipped my parka, put up the hood and put my gloves on.

As I opened the starboard side door on the after deckhouse, a blast of frigid air hit us.

"You got it there, buddy?" I asked.

"No problem," he replied as we got out on the spar deck. The wind had not lessened any, but the snow had almost stopped and there seem to be a small break in the clouds.

"It probably isn't gonna' get any colder than this," I said as we went forward.

The door to the forward store room was on the after side of the forward deckhouse. I opened the door and stepped over the hatch coaming. Earl handed me a box through the door and I placed it on a shelf. Carl and Mark walked by.

I heard Carl say—"It looks like a deckhand delivery service."

"We could have used those hangers yesterday," Mark said.

"Our Motto is-'It's on time, or get it yourself," Earl wisecracked.

"You'll never work for 'Flying Tigers' with an attitude like that," I said jokingly.

After two more round trips with the cart, we returned the four wheeler to the engineers' supply room.

"Well, we killed that job, old buddy," I said, adding—"Let's get some coffee while we back here."

"Sounds good," Earl said as we headed for the Galley. When we got to the galley there were no coffee cups in the rack, so I started ringing the bell. John came out with a tray of cups.

"I knew it was you. You're the only one who rings that bell," John said as he slid the tray on the rails of the rack.

"No coffee cups, for shame," I said jokingly.

"You can't believe how many times I've made coffee this morning. I'd have Earl wash for me, but you got him this morning," John said.

"Everybody gets behind sometimes," I said as I pulled the cups off the tray.

John came over with the coffee pot.

"Just don't start using that Chinese coffee."

"I think I'll throw that junk over board," John said.

"Take it home and give it as Christmas presents to people you don't like," I suggested.

"Yeah, no use in poisoning a bunch of innocent fish, I guess," John replied and he turned and left.

We headed down the passageway to the Rec room.

"As soon as it gets light, we'll have to go out on deck again," I said.

"That's a pain," Earl complained.

"We should be at the Soo. We'll have to help dock, probably, then run our errands ashore, of course," I stated as we entered the Rec room.

Fred, Billy and Kenny were in there, playing cards.

"You guys are up and at it pretty early this morning. Are you on the Rudolph detail?" I asked.

"No, we're discussing details of a bachelor party for the Mate," Fred replied jokingly.

"Oh, the Mate's getting married? I haven't heard that," I said as nonchalantly as possible.

I was thinking that these gossipy bilge rats are working fast. They must be sending out wedding invitations already. In fact he had not even officially proposed yet.

"That's like a woman. Playing it coy to the end!" Billy wisecracked, as we sat down.

"You think so? You see any rings here?" I said, pulling off my gloves and holding up my hands, cool as a cucumber.

"That's okay, Nick. I don't think his father explained that part to him yet?" Fred replied jokingly.

"Well, Ken, I heard you've been busy this morning," I said.

"Some work on the lathe and drill press. The Chief wanted it right now. You know how he is, no last minute stuff," Kenny replied.

"The other guys didn't sound too enthusiastic about being up on a ladder," I said.

"Yeah, someone will have to climb the Mast. Real fun in this weather," Fred said, adding—"We got young Billy here picked for the job."

"He'll have the safety harness, that won't be too bad," I said.

"If he falls, he can hang there until we get to Duluth," Kenny wisecracked.

"I'm sure the Chief will keep everything in order."

I saw Billy messing with the television. We watched him for a minute, but he could not get anything to come in.

"I think it'll be another hour before anything comes in," Fred said.

"We need a decent antennae," Kenny remarked.

"We need one of those video recorders. They're affordable now. Five or six hundred bucks and these guys can watch cartoons to their heart's content," I said.

"Do you have one at home?" Earl asked.

"My grandmother had one, but I put it back in the box and put it in the closet. I don't watch TV hardly at all," I replied.

"You wouldn't mind making a charitable donation to this cause?" Billy asked.

"Uh, possibly. We'll see what's gonna happen in the spring," I replied.

"I'm surprised you don't use your VCR. All those sappy love stories they have out on tape, now days," Billy said.

"I don't do the 'chick flicks'," I shot back.

"I still have to see Top Gun, Full Metal Jacket and Name of the Rose," Fred said.

"You've been at sea too long, old buddy. 'Top Gun' is a waste. Mister Tom 'I'm so beautiful, I must be a fighter pilot'. Phony as a three dollar bill. Full Metal Jacket' is the Marine Corps version of the Deer Hunter. Wasted when they went in, wasted when they got out. The 'Name of the Rose' is the only one worth seeing," I concluded.

"To hell with those movies. If we get a video recorder, we'll be watching 'skin flicks' back here during the third watch," Billy said.

"It'll be a wonder if any work gets done back here if that's allowed to happen," Kenny remarked.

"He'll be allowed to watch PeeWee's Big Adventure. That'll be just about all. If you think you'll pull any crap like that on the Chief, you got another thing coming boy!" Earl said.

"Earl, you're always pissing on somebody's parade," Billy sneered.

"Just giving you a solid reality check!" Earl said.

"We had some guys on the Giovanni that had some pictures on those View master things like little kids use. I've no idea where they got them. They left the things lying around. Some guests on the ship got ahold of them. Some crap hit the fan then. Fortunately, nobody's name was on them," I said.

"They can get real nasty about porno in the workplace. I saw it when I worked for the Cliffs line," Earl said.

"They can overlook a 'PlayBoy' or a deck of cards under your mattress, but don't push it," Fred said, looking at me.

"Don't look at me! There's nothing under my bunk, except for 'dust bunnies'!" I exclaimed with a grin.

"Is that anything like 'PlayBoy Bunnies'?" Billy wisecracked.

I rolled my eyes at the remark.

"My mattress feels like it's full of taconite pellets," Earl said, adding—"I got to go back to my quarters to get my other gloves. I'll see you guys in a couple of minutes."

After Earl left, I reclined the chair and took a sip of coffee.

"Feel free to look at the magazines," Billy wisecracked.

I closed my eyes and thought about the end of the season. I thought about going back to Alliance and visiting some old friends. I must have dozed off for a few minutes. When I woke up, Earl was sitting beside me. "The Bosun said we're in the upper St. Mary's River now," he said.

"Oh, we better get out on deck," I said.

As we went down the passageway, I zipped my parka, put up my hood and put on my gloves. When I opened the door, it looked as dark as ever, but the wind seemed to have died down.

"No sun yet, old buddy," I said stepping out on deck. The wind was coming over the starboard side now. The ship was definitely headed west, but I could not see any lights on shore yet.

"Let's go forward. I gotta' get my tool belt and the plug-in tester," I said.

As we headed forward, I checked out the deck lights.

"Still three out on the port side and one out on the starboard side. We won't be able to see the railing until it's light."

"Rudolph is totally out," Earl observed.

"Fortunately, that's the Chief's problem," I said.

I checked for other ships, but I saw no lights at all.

"We're still in the wilderness," I said as I opened the door to the passageway. "I'll get my tool belt and meet you in the lounge."

"Okay," Earl replied.

On my way up the forward stairs, I ran into Andy and the Chief.

"My goodness, nobody is sleeping this morning," I remarked.

"Just having a little pow-wow with the Captain," the Chief replied.

"Is he in his quarters?" I asked.

"No, he's in the Wheelhouse," Andy replied.

"Okay, catch you guys later," I said, and continued up the steps.

The Captain must be talking with the Mate about locking through at Sault Ste. Marie, I thought as I entered my quarters. I grabbed my tool belt, then I saw the wheel and anchor pendant on my desk. I pulled off the hood and unzipped my parka. Placing the charm between my shirt and thermal undershirt, I fastened the chain behind my neck. Nice and secure, I thought. I left my quarters and started going down the forward stairway, where I ran into the Bosun.

"Mister McCracken would like to see you in the lounge," he said.

"Doesn't he have a ship to steer?" I asked jokingly.

"The Captain is in the Wheelhouse now. It shouldn't take too long," he said.

"Okay, I'll see what he wants," I said.

When I got to the forward lounge, I found the Mate there with Earl, Smitty, Ron and Hal.

"Hi, guys what's up?" I greeted them.

"Help us out here, Nick," Hal said. "This guy's treating us like a bunch of 'trippers',"

"They're called 'boomers' on the railroad," I said.

"We'll all be riding the rails like a bunch of bums, if this company has its way," Smitty said.

"What's going on here, Dave?" I asked.

"A new policy from the company. Non-classified work has to be documented by the employees involved," he replied.

"I thought you and the Chief had all this paperwork taken care of?" I asked.

"We didn't foresee this happening," he replied.

The ever changing company policy 'merry-go-round' at work, I thought.

"Well, the Chief has a detailed log of the work and who performed it. It shouldn't be too much trouble to type up some generic reports and have everyone here sign them. When do these have to be done?" I asked.

"By the time we get to Duluth," the Mate answered.

"You and Andy can have them done in no time. You guys have the word processor. Set up a format that will work for everybody. Since everybody worked the 4:00 am to 7:20 PM, it shouldn't be too hard to do," I said.

"I suppose something like that could be done," the Mate said.

"If you need any help, let me know," I said.

"I'll talk it over with Andy. He types a thousand words a minute, so he shouldn't have any problem with it," he said.

"Okay, old buddy. Don't you think you should get back to the Wheelhouse before this ship runs aground," I said jokingly.

The Mate gave em that quizzical little smile, pointed at me and clicked his tongue. He did not say, "You bad". He turned and left.

"Way to go, Nick!" Hal said.

"Yeah, you're Da' Man!" Ron said, adding—"Expecting us to write reports. Does that sound like our job? I don't think so."

"In the old days, I guess reading and writing weren't required of a deck hand," I said, while getting myself a cup of coffee.

"That must have been the 'good old days'," Mark said as he walked through the door.

"The good old days before what?" Smitty said.

"MMDs, aptitude tests, drug tests," Mark replied.

"Hold on Nick, he's getting to pregnancy tests," Hal wisecracked.

"I never had to take one, have you?" I shot back, taking a scalp for a scalp.

"The Mate said to grab you for the gas tests . . . that didn't come out right, did it?" Mark said, when the other guys laughed.

"I think, I got it," I said, grabbing my tool belt.

"Do you have the Gas Trac?" I asked.

"Yeah, it's right out here. Are you ready?" Mark asked.

"Yeah, might as well do it now. They'll have to have the readings before locking through," I said.

Coal dust and coal gas (methane) are both highly combustible gases. The dangerous concentration is between the Lower Explosive 1 Limit (LEL) and the Upper Explosive Limit (UEL). OSHA and DOT require a ship carrying coal to monitor the gas levels in the cargo holds. Since the Gentry has five cargo holds full of coal, all of them would have to be checked. Aside from removing the hatches, the only way to do this, is through the inspection doors in the passageway, right below the spar deck, portside. After the refit as a self-unloader, access to this passage had been restricted. When we went out the door and crossed over to the port side, I noticed it was somewhat lighter, but no sunrise yet. We went through the port side door and down the short steps to the former crew's passageway. There are three inspection doors right below the plates of the spar deck for every cargo hold. Opening any other door would get you coal instead of the airspace above it.

"Have you checked that thing?" I asked.

"I'll check it again," Mark said, exhaling hard on the round sensor. "Yeah, it's working."

The Gas Trace detects carbon. If it can detect the carbon dioxide in your breath, it is working as it should. Using my socket wrench, I quickly loosened the bolts and swung the little door open. Mark quickly inserted the sensor on its flexible sheathing.

After a minute, he said, "Less than one percent. We don't have to check this hold anymore. Button it up."

I closed the door and tightened the bolts. As I was reaching up to do this, I noticed Mark looking at me.

"Something on your mind?" I asked.

He seemed reluctant to speak.

"Go ahead guy. I've heard everything, believe me."

"Is it true about your, uh . . . relationship with the Mate?" he asked.

"Well, I don't know what you heard, but for right now, we are neighbors and co-workers. I inherited the house in Marblehead, when my grandmother died, so we're neighbors. I left the Giovanni and came here, as a career decision. It had nothing to do with love, or anything else. I didn't hardly know the Mate at all. As for the future, I don't know. I wish I did."

"I didn't mean it like the other guys. I lived in Erie, before. I guess I'm about your age. I was married for a couple of years, but nothing seemed to go right. When I got home last year, the house was completely empty, just a box in the living room with some of my clothes. I guess she wanted a divorce. I never really told the other guys the way it really was," he said.

"I know what you mean. I had a relationship go south on me when I was in college. I ended up kicking the hell out of him. Put him in the hospital. If it hadn't been for my grandmother, it would have been a lot worse, I'm sure," I said.

"You don't look like somebody who carries around a lot of pain. You look happy," Mark observed.

"So do you," I said.

"It's like that Roger Miller song about being happy if you want to. Sometimes I think it's a facade," Mark replied, as we walked to the next cargo hold door.

"Think of it like this; one smile in the right place can open the door for you," I said as I reached up and began loosening the bolts on the door of the number two cargo hold.

We heard a noise above us.

"That sounds like chains on the deck. I wonder who's moving chains around up there," Mark said.

"They wouldn't start the Rudolph job with you, would they?" I asked.

"That's an electrical job. There shouldn't be any hoisting. Maybe there's something aft. We'll see when we get back there," Mark replied.

It took us another half an hour to do the sampling.

"I'll take these readings to the Mate," Mark said.

"Okay, I think I'll head aft."

I turned and headed aft. I figured that Earl would be at his usual hangout aft. When I reached the top of the steps, I looked out the port side door and could see it was getting light outside and the sky was clear. Amen and halleluiah, I thought.

CHAPTER 9

Up the Street at Sault Ste. Marie

A s I headed down the passageway to the recreation room, I saw the Chief and Billy coming the other way.

"Have you guys seen Earl?" I asked.

"I think the Bosun has him out on deck doing something," the Chief said as they passed by me.

I turned and took the passageway heading forward. I came out the door on the starboard side, zipped my parka and put on my gloves. Even though the wind had died down further and the sun was starting to come out, it was cold as heck. About half way forward, I saw what appeared to be Earl, standing at the portside mooring winch, jumping up and down, slapping himself. I decided to tease him about his dancing technique, so I approached him from behind.

"A nice warm sunny morning!" I half shouted as I came over from the starboard side.

"It is damn cold!" Earl complained as he was trying hard to shake off the cold.

"Why, you old salt, you should be used to this weather after sailing the lakes for ten plus years. By the way, was that the Hokey Pokey you were doing?" I stated, trying to humor him while trying to keep warm myself.

"What I need is a nice woman to keep me warm," Earl remarked, as he checked out the mooring winch.

"How about a cup of coffee?" I suggested as I looked over the riggings.

253

The city of Sault Ste. Marie looked frozen and desolate. A winter wonderland for cross-country skiers and snowmobilers. A good time for the locals to hibernate, no doubt, I thought, as I looked at the power station and the Valley Camp on the port side. I could see the lower lock gate of the MacArthur Lock. My thoughts turned to summer, when the city was bustling with vacationers. I remember when we were downbound and someone from the observational deck, asked what the crane on the deck was for. The Bosun yelled back—"It's not a crane, it's an unloading conveyor." The unloading conveyor does resemble a crane. I chuckled to myself remembering the Bosun's answer when asked: "How's the ship loaded?" His answer was: "With buckets." By that time, I was laughing out loud.

My concentration was broken when Earl asked, "Are you going to get us a cup of coffee?"

He was standing before me with his arms folded across his chest.

"Yes, of course," I stated as I noticed the Bosun heading in our direction.

He stopped to talk to Earl, but motioned for me to go ahead.

"Would you like some coffee?" I inquired.

"No, I have some here," he answered, holding up a thermos.

When I got to the Galley, Louie had already sat the sugar and creamer on the counter. He was pouring coffee into two large cups.

"Something smells very good," I remarked as I poured the cream into the coffee.

I just hope it's not turkey-something or ham loaf, I thought as I stirred the sugar in Earl's coffee. One thing I had noticed during my tenure on the Gentry, both John and Louie had a knack for disguising left-overs.

"You may need these," Louie stated as he handed me two lids for the cups.

"Thank you, Louie," I responded, taking the lids from his hand and placing them on the cups.

As I was getting ready to leave, I was trying to decide how I should carry the cups. I paused for a moment. Louie, sensing my dilemma, suggested that I use a cup holder. Handing me one, he told me that I can return it later. When I got back out on deck, I noticed that the Bosun was still conversing with Earl, pointing to the unloading boom.

"Trouble with the unloading conveyor, again?" I asked as I handed Earl his coffee.

"No, we were discussing the decorations on the boom," Earl replied, then he sipped his coffee.

He sat the holder down on a nearby hatch cover.

"What about them?" I questioned, not really interested.

"The lights aren't working, they can't figure out why," Earl answered.

"Well, did someone try to tighten Rudolph's nose?" I suggested, trying hard not to laugh.

The electricians had rigged a red beacon light, similar to those found on radio towers, to the nose of the foremost wooden reindeer, which the crew named "Rudy". I was told that years ago, Captain Kompsii had a wooden sleigh with eight reindeer made by an artist in Michigan. The entire composition consists of eleven parts, which are brightly painted and run half the length of the unloading boom. When the boom is raised, it looks like jolly old Saint Nick's sleigh and reindeer had taken off in flight. The electricians had used different colored Christmas lights to outline it. When lit, it was a spectacular sight to see. It had been reported that people who live near the shore can see it at night. Old Santa, his sleigh and reindeer have become the Gentry's holiday trademark.

"I'll have someone take care of the problem later," the Bosun interjected in a more serious tone, with his attention focused on shipboard operations.

An announcement came over the ship's intercom, informing us that we will be docking in ten minutes. Smitty, Ed, and Ron were coming toward us.

"Stand by for docking instructions," a voice said over the Bosun's radio.

"That's odd," I said as I noticed that Andy had come out on deck.

"How so?" Earl asked.

"The Captain always takes over the helm when the ship goes through the locks, and the First Mate is at the railing when the ship docks," I replied.

"Usually that is the case, but since he's retiring, the Captain wants to be sure that the Mate can handle it," The Bosun stated.

"Of course, he can handle it. I'd bet my life on it," I said, smiling.

"We all bet our lives on it," the Bosun replied as he pulled out his radio.

"Once we tie up, we will have a lay-over. This will give us adequate time to get the mail and return those library books. Andy is standing in for me at the bow," the Mate's voice said over the radio.

"Copy that, Munson out," the Bosun stated.

"Roger, McCracken, out." came the reply.

There is a library located next to the Visitor's Center, where sailors can borrow books. Sault Ste. Marie is a mailing address for many Great Lake sailors as well. Due to Dixon's accident, we were unable to run any errands on the downbound run. Since this was our last trip on the upbound run, the Captain wanted to take care of any unfinished business.

"Nick, after we tie up, I want you and Earl to fetch the mail and return all library books. Also, I was informed that there is a package for the Captain," the Bosun instructed.

"A package for the Captain, isn't it a bit early for Chanukah?" I questioned under my breath.

"Every year Mrs. Kompsii sends Christmas cookies to the Captain. He shares them with the crew with an understanding that we leave him at least one chocolate chip cookie," the Bosun explained.

I thought of the times my grandmother would bake Christmas cookies and give them to people as gifts. There were several occassions when I gave them to the officers and crewmen on the Giovanni. Several years ago, we had to deliver stone to a remote area on the north shore of Lake Superior, the day before Christmas. I gave some of my grandmother's cookies to the construction crew, who were isolated in that area. I thought about all the times we docked at the notorious undeveloped piers, way out in no man's land and I had to ride in an aluminum fishing boat to get ashore. On many an occassion, we had to moor the ship to a tree trunk.

"Nick must have locked her brain into neutral," Smitty wisecracked as he approached us.

"Uh-h, sorry I was daydreaming," I responded with a start.

"Well, there's certainly no time for that, we have work to do," the Bosun stated, as he looked over the clipboard.

"Do you want us to rig the ladder?" I asked.

"No, you'll be using the bosun chair down and the ladder up. The pier is too icy to secure the ladder. By the time you return, the pier should be cleared, then we should be able to utilize the ladder," the Bosun explained, adding—"I'm sending Ed and Smitty down to secure the mooring lines. After this is taken care of, then you and Earl can run those errands. Meanwhile Ron, you and Ed go get the books from the Observation room, they should all be there."

As Ron and Ed turned to leave, Earl spoke up, "Some crew aft, still have books back there!"

"Great, you and Nick can collect those," the Bosun remarked as he made a notation on the clip board.

"I thought we were told to take all library books to the Observation room," I said, as Earl and I headed aft.

"We were, but we have some lazy crew members," Earl remarked, adding—"Not naming any names, like Billy, Buster and Doinker."

"I was unaware that they even knew how to read," I said jokingly.

"The joke is what they read," Earl countered. "Last time Doinker returned a book about working-out. A book one would be expecting Gary to be reading. Buster checked out a book about gardening. Billy and Pete, both wanted to read 'The Joy of Sex'. The only one that made any sense was Mark's book about carpentry."

"Why's that?" I asked, still trying not to laugh.

"From what I understand, Mark is remodeling his home. He has a two story cottage in Portage Lakes. The interior of the house resembles a cargo ship. He built a ladder that goes up to a second story loft. The windows on the first and second storeys, are wide picture windows like those on the pilothouse. They provide a nice view of the lake. The kitchen looks like a galley. He told me that he's considering building a spiral staircase during the winter lay-up," Earl stated as he opened the door for me.

"It sounds like Mark is trying to rebuild the Titanic," I said.

"He's a talented carpenter for sure. I was invited to his house last year for a party, it was impressive. He offered to help me to refurbish the barn, but I told him to wait until I get out from under the legal mess my brothers are causing me," Earl stated as we entered the Crew's mess. Wait here, I'll go and gather up those stray books," Earl said, then he left.

Louie came in the room and handed two cookbooks to me.

"I heard that you and Earl are returning books," he stated, as I took the books from him.

"Don't worry, your secret's safe with me," I joked as I glanced at the titles.

"I'm just seeing what everyone else is doing wrong," Louie said.

"Yeah, right!" I replied with a wink.

Gary came into the room and handed me a book about scuba diving.

"Thanks, Gary," I said, as I sat the books down on the counter.

"I heard Earl coming through the passageway, griping about 'lazy people who can't follow orders to save themselves'," Gary stated with a grin, adding—"I'll bet that Old Earl will be glad to shed himself of porter duties come next season. I know that he's tired of being everyone's gofer. Go for this, go for that. I Don't really blame him though. We forgot about the books back here with all the confusion and everything going on during this hectic trip," Gary said apologetically.

"It's understandable. Sometimes the littlest thing are overlooked, hopefully it will be smooth sailing from now on," I said, trying to remember if I returned all the books I had checked out from the library.

Earl came back into the room with an arm load of books.

"I see that you were given books, too," Earl stated, as he sat the pile of books down on the table.

"Well, let's haul these out on deck." he stated as he picked up both stacks of books.

"Need help with those?" I asked as I got up from the chair.

"No, I got it," Earl replied, as we headed toward the door.

When we got out on deck, we placed the books in the sack.

"We'll lower this down to you, after we moor the ship," The Bosun said as he tied a line to the sack. Fortunately, there were only twenty books to return, making only one sack necessary. Needless to say, Earl and I were happy about that.

"We found two books in the Observation room, Casey Jones: Epic of the American Railroad and Clear the Tracks. They aren't library books. Any idea who they belong to?" Smitty asked.

"They belong to me. I'll take them back to my quarters later," I answered.

"We didn't know that you were interested in the railroad!" Ed said, giving me a puzzled look.

"I have many different interests," I stated as I watched the ship approach the pier.

"Let's get ready to move out," the Bosun said as he looked over the bosun chair to make sure that it was safe to use.

"Ron, I need you to take the lookout aft. Brad will take the watch at the bow. Nick, I have explained to Earl the docking procedure, but I want you to be with him in case he doesn't understand the routine. Meanwhile, Smitty and I will take our usual stations," the Bosun said, then we all left for our stations.

"As you probably already know, we stay in contact with the Wheelhouse by radio. Our job is to report the distance between the ship and the wall. If the ship bangs against the wall, it could damage the hull. Sometimes the ship does bump up against the side, this is unavoidable sometimes, especially for the thousand footers. The Giovanni would bump the wall of the Poe lock, no matter how careful the Captain would take it during transit. Fortunately, the only damage was scraped paint."

"Dixon told me that he used to work on a barge in the Mississippi river before signing on with lake boats. He told me that his barge had run aground on a sand bar in the middle of the river. The Captain ordered reverse of the engines. This caused the barge to dig itself even deeper in the muck. He told me that the Captain was inexperienced and unfamiliar with the river, otherwise he would never have reversed those engines. The crew joked about becoming 'gator bait'," Earl explained as he leaned over the railing to get a better view.

"I heard that a lake freighter got hung-up in the Cuyahoga river on the way to LTV steel," I countered.

"This was in Collision Bend, I take it?" Earl said, while looking down over the side.

"I don't know. How's Dixon doing anyways?" I asked.

"He went home to Jackson, Mississippi. He may fly up here to be at the party, if he's able," Earl answered.

"I bet he's enjoying the warm weather," I said as I adjusted the scarf around my neck.

"He told me that every time it snows down south, the whole town shuts down. The populous is not used to weather extremes like we are up north. One year there was a terrible ice storm and the entire region near Jackson was without power for about three days. It took that long to get the power plant back on line. Dixon told me that it did not phase him, because he was used to the 'Damn Yankee Cold'. During the summer months, he would complain about the weather, saying 'it is hotter than a delta summer'," Earl concluded.

"I've traveled below the Mason-Dixon line and know for a fact that it can get extremely hot down south during the summer and the 'critters' are larger!" I added.

"Critters?" questioned Earl.

"You know, pest, bugs, snakes, lake rats," I replied, rattling off the list.

"Nick, for your information I have not seen any rats down below. Now, the horse flies can be pesky, 'cause those sneaky suckers bite you hard before you even know it," Earl said.

I decided not to elaborate further.

"Two feet clearance," came a voice over the radio.

Earl keyed my radio, "We have two feet clearance amidship," he reported.

"Two feet clearance aft," reported a third voice.

"We have it now," I said, looking at Earl, adding—"An excellent parallel parking job."

He handed my radio to me. The sunshine disappeared and it began to snow. One of those intermittent squalls was moving through the area.

"Come on, light a fire under it!" the Bosun shouted at the guys at the bosun's chair.

Earl and I headed that way, since we weren't mooring from amidships. Ron was already down on the dock. Smitty had mounted the chair, secured the safety line and gave the signal to let him down. Earl climbed into the device after they brought it up. He gave the Okay to lower, and landed on the pier without incident.

"Okay, Nick your turn," the Bosun said.

"Child's play," I stated as I climbed onto the device.

I quickly glanced over the equipment. I looked at the pulley and cable. It seemed tight, so I tugged on it slightly. Since there was hardly any play, I decided it was safe. After all three men used it before me and I am not as heavy as they are.

"Ready, Nick?" the Bosun asked.

I motioned that I was ready. Once I was over the side, I had to push off the side of the ship with my feet. I was lowered fifteen feet . . . suddenly, I swung against the side of the ship and fell. Before I knew what had happened, I found myself lying in the snow.

"G-D, J-C, mother f—er! Those sorry ass bastards did that on purpose!" I cursed as I was trying to get up.

"Young Lady, that's not the way I learned the holy trinity!" Earl exclaimed as he helped me get up.

"Whoever said I was exempt from sailor vernacular?" I said as I shook my foot from the stirrup.

I heard someone ask—"Is she hurt?"

"No, I am not hurt," I answered as I brushed the snow off my backside.

"Boy Nick, That certainly was a near miss. We don't need another accident, for sure," Earl said as he brushed the snow off my back.

"The real accident happened when those jokers were born," I stated, trying to sound mad.

Earl and I both chuckled at the remark. I looked up and saw that the Bosun was checking the equipment. Evidently, during my descent, the cable came out of the sheave and I dropped about four feet to the wall.

Smitty and Ron finished tying the mooring lines and headed in our direction.

"Look out," Smitty called out, pointing upward.

Ed waited until we gave him the clearance to lower the books. All I need is for those to be dropped on my head, I thought to myself as I backed away from the ship. Earl waved that it was safe to lower the sack. After the sack was lowered, Earl untied it from the line.

"I'm beginning to wonder if those two have been drinking," Earl commented under his breath,loud enough only for me to hear.

"Could be," I said.

"In truth, I could use one myself," Earl stated as he slung the sack of books over his shoulder.

"No can do, buddy! We're still on company time," I said as I watched Ron and Smitty start shoveling snow.

"Let's go, Nick. I want to unload these books. The sooner, the better," Earl said as we walked over to the stairs.

As we climbed the concrete stairs, we had to push the snow off the steps with our boots.

"Wonderful," Earl commented.

"It's too early for the townies to be out here shoveling snow. Half of them hibernate and the other half are skiers and snowmobilers who think it's an affront to clear snow," I said.

Once we got to the top, it was a straight shot to the library. Taking the books from the sack, we dropped them into the book return a couple at a time. Earl folded up the sack and put it into his coat pocket. We crossed the snow covered lawn and the main street.

"I guess they won't mind some footprints in their nice blanket of snow," I said as we headed down the unshoveled sidewalk.

We passed the Lock Keeper restaurant and the Cast Off bar.

"Sorry, old buddy. I'm afraid they're not open," I said jokingly.

"Too bad. I was looking forward to the happy hour," he shot back.

"Just so the Post Office is open, we'll be okay," I remarked as we approached the door.

The post office has a lobby area where mail and packages can be picked up after hours, if the night watchman is awake to let you in. I rang the bell twice before a woman came to the door.

"Strickland and Franklin here to pick up packages and mail for the steamship Gentry," I said.

"Who are you again?" the woman asked.

"Nicolette Strickland and Earl Franklin," I replied.

"Well, the steamship Gentry is not on my list, but I think there's some stuff here. Do you have any identification?" she asked.

"Yes, I do. Could we come inside? I don't want to take off my gloves out here," I said.

"Yes, I suppose," she said.

I opened the door and Earl and I entered. I pulled off my gloves and put them in the pocket of my parka. Then I pulled out my wallet and showed her my drivers license and my company ID card.

"I have to check the date," she said, pulling out her glasses and putting them on.

"Yes, it looks real enough," she said, adding—"I never saw a woman crewman."

"Old Sam Houghton ran into me a couple of times," I said.

"Oh yes, he died last year, a sudden stroke," she stated.

"Oh, my goodness!" I replied.

"I think your stuff is over here," She said, walking toward the back.

She pulled out a flashlight to check the name.

"Did you bring a sled, or something?" she asked.

"No, we'll have to carry it," I said, signing the mail receipts.

There were three boxes and a bundle of mail. I stuck the mail in my parka and grabbed one of the larger boxes. Earl grabbed the other two boxes and we headed toward the door. The woman unlocked the door and held it for us.

"Thank you, have a nice day," I said.

"You, too," she replied, as she closed the door.

"We'll have to be careful when we get to those stairs," I said as we started down the sidewalk.

When we crossed the street, we sat the boxes on a bench and rested. Two kids pulling those Scandinavian style sleds came up to us.

"Where are you guys from?" one asked.

"From that ship over there," I said pointing.

"Wow! You need help with those boxes?" he asked.

"We could use your sleds," I answered.

"Sure," he replied, pulling his sled up.

Earl and I put the boxes on the sleds and the boys pulled the sleds for us. They hesitated when they got to the hill by the steps.

"Can we go down there?" they asked.

"Sure, you're with us, you can go anywhere," I said.

We walked down the hill, steadying the boxes, as they boys pulled the sleds through the snow. When we got to the wall, Al and the Bosun were lowering a small platform, called the basket. When it got down to the ground, we loaded the boxes on it.

The Bosun tossed down an instamatic camera and I took a picture of the two boys next to the ship. They were thrilled to have a picture of them next to a ship. I took them back up the hill and thanked them for helping us. When I got back to the ship, I noticed a small crowd forward but I did not see anybody aft as I started up the boarding ladder. When I got up to the deck, Al came running up.

"Good, I thought I was gonna' have to raise this ladder by myself," I said jokingly.

"The Chief's on the Warpath, big time! They want you forward."

"Well, that's appropriate. Chief-Warpath, Get it? Har har," I said, but he did not find anything amusing, so I headed forward.

Everybody seem to be examining the Bosun's chair, so I figured that someone saw my little fall and someone got screwed into the ceiling for it. I was going to keep my cool and my nerve.

When I got there, I said, "What's up guys?"

The Bosun, the Mate and the Chief were watching Brad and Ron take the pulley off the end of the boom for the bosun's chair.

"We're trying to find out what caused the accident," the Chief said.

"Accident . . . ?" I said, looking quizzical at the Mate.

"It was reported that you were thrown into the side of the ship and fell approximately four feet to the wall. Are you okay?" the Mate asked.

"Oh well, by the grace of God and soft Michigan snow. It's all in a days work," I replied.

"This is an OSHA recordable. At the very least, a near miss," the Chief was livid.

"The keeper, that holds the cable from coming out of the pulley at the end of the boom, was knocked out of position. The cable came out of the pulley, dropping you about four feet. Are you sure you're not hurt?" the Mate asked.

"Right as rain," I said.

"I checked the boom, the cable, pulley, everything," the Bosun insisted.

"It looked like the eye came up too far and knocked the keeper out like that," the Chief said.

"Excuse me, Chief. I looked over the equipment before I got on it, including the keeper, and it seemed fine to me," I said.

At this time, Brad and Ron were removing the pulley and keeper with its spring. It was clear that the spring had broken.

"It looks like the spring was definitely broken," the Chief said.

"It's probably been there since 1943. Forty-three years of fatigue and this cold, it just snapped," I said.

"That could be, I'd like to examine it," the Chief said.

"Sure, old buddy," I said.

"What about the incident?" the Mate asked.

"Kay surah, surah," I said.

"It's not going to be that simple," he shot back. "If it had happened up here, then you would have hit the side of the ship and maybe fallen fifteen feet into the water or the wall. You could have been killed."

"If I keep smoking, I could die too. I'm not about to write a first person incident report. I suggest you lock-out the equipment and put in a maintenance work order," I said.

They both knew I was "stonewalling" them. The Mate seem to like it less than the Chief, so I smiled at him.

"I better check with the Captain," he said.

"Sure, he's a reasonable man and he got his cookies," I wisecracked.

He pointed his finger and clicked his tongue, saying, "You Bad."

The Mate and the Chief headed toward the Wheelhouse with the broken spring.

"Way to go, Nick! You sweet talked them," Brad chortled.

"No, I 'stonewalled' them. If the Captain's in a good mood, maybe this will be the end of it. There's been enough trouble come to this ship," I said, then I walked toward the Crew's hall to get a cup of coffee.

When I got to the Crew's hall, I did not see any cookies in there, but there was a full pot of coffee, so I poured a cup and held on to it to warm my hands. A minute later, the Bosun came in.

"The cookies haven't made it down here yet?" I asked.

"No, that stuff was taken to the Captain," he replied.

"Oh, I got some mail here," I said, reaching into the pocket of my parka and pulling out the bundle of letters.

"Okay, I'll sort this mail later," he said.

"Are we gonna' be ready to shove off, here?" I asked.

"I don't think so. There's another ship, a salty, I think it's Russian. Those foreigners take all day, they don't know anything about transitting the locks," he stated.

"Well, they better get a move on it. The locks will freeze and they'll be stuck in an evil capitalist empire all winter," I said jokingly.

"Yeah, no telling," the Bosun said.

"Have you seen Earl?" I asked.

"He was taking boxes up to the Captain's quarters. I haven't seen him since," he replied, then he left.

I knew the watch bell would be sounding in a few minutes. It was gonna' be a bright, sunny day, but cold as hell.

I went back outside to look for Earl. I saw Don heading forward.

"Hi, guy. What's going on?" I asked.

"The John G. Munson is supposed to be locking through down bound. There's a thousand footer waiting up there and a Russian ship coming up behind us, that will lock through first." he said.

"That sounds interesting. I think I'll check out the Russian ship," I said.

"Aye, you might as well. You'll be off the clock in a few minutes," he said and he continued forward.

I started walking aft, checking cables and hatches. The lights were off so I could not do much about them. I returned forward on the starboard side and ran into Al, Hal, Ed, Smitty and Ron.

"Hail, hail the gang's all here," I said.

"Just hanging out, waiting for Captain Kompsii to keel haul your buddy," Hal wisecracked.

"Nobody's gonna get the Yardarm for anything," I remarked, adding—"Who's got the clipboard?"

"Earl went to get it," Al replied.

"There's suppose to be a Russian ship locking through before us," I said.

Just then the Chief came out on deck, with Earl.

"Nick the Captain would like to see you in his quarters."

When the Captain wants to see you, he means right now!

"Sure Chief, on my way," I said, handing the clipboard to Smitty.

"It looks like your 'last supper' is going to be in Duluth," Hal wisecracked as I turned and headed toward the top side.

The Captain's quarters has two rooms, one a living quarters and the other an office. Coming down the passageway, I tried to be brave, like I was earlier. I saw the Mate come out of the door and wait a moment for me to get there.

"Good morning, Mister McCracken."

"Right this way, Miss Strickland," he said, holding the door for me.

"Thank you so much, Sir," I said, before walking through the door.

"Come in, Miss Strickland," I heard the Captain say.

"You wanted to see me, Sir?" I asked.

"Yes, sit down there at the table."

"Very well, Sir," I said.

"Now, you're aware of OSHA and DOT regulations and the policies of this company, I take it," he said.

"Yes Sir," I replied.

"Mister McCracken says that you do not wish to consider this business as a Near Miss incident."

"No Sir," I replied.

"Very well. The only thing I don't understand is why Mister Munson did not report it when it happened. Make an entry of the incident in the log book and sign it," he said, handing me the log book.

I took the log book and wrote:

> ***While temporarily docked in Sault Ste. Marie; at approximately 6:48 AM, I was being lowered in the bosun chair when a mechanical failure occurred in that equipment. As I was very near to the ground, I did not consider myself in any significant danger and was not injured in any way. I therefore waive the right to a safety incident review-signed, Nicolette Strickland 11/86***

The Captain looked at it, signed and dated it as well.

"You like double chocolate cookies?" the Captain asked.

"Yes Sir," I replied.

He reached into a box, pulled out a packet and handed it to me.

"Too bad your little helpers don't get any," he said.

"I think they were thrilled to get a picture next to the ship," I said.

"Yes, I think so," the Captain said with a twinkle in his eye. "That is all, Miss Strickland."

"Very good, Sir," I said and I turned and left.

When I got back on deck the guys were still there.

"Did the Old Man blow his stack?" Smitty asked.

"No, he gave me some cookies," I said, pulling the packet out of my pocket, then dropping it back into my pocket.

"Oh Man! I knew you and the Mate would come outta' this smelling like a rose," Hal said.

We laughed at the comment. We heard a whistle as the John G. Munson passed by us starboard to starboard.

"What's the G-D hold up?!" Smitty yelled at them.

"What's your hurry? You scurvy rats are laid up this trip!" their bosun shouted.

"Eat Sh-t and snow in Ashtabula, for all I care!" Smitty shot back.

"We're never gonna' get any candy or cookies from them, talking like that," I said, referring to the old custom of throwing goodies to other ships or people on the shore.

"Those cheap ass bilge rats couldn't even spare a thin mint," Hal said.

A few minutes later, the Russian ship appeared aft and to the starboard. Their Captain must have seen the Burns Harbor. He stopped his ship next to ours, less than a hundred feet away.

"That ship hasn't been painted in a while," Al said.

"I've seen better looking guys in a police line-up," Brad said.

"Now, now, they're just like us, they just don't use deordorant," Ron wisecracked.

"They look friendly enough," I said, pulling back my hood so they could see I was a woman.

"Whoa, Nick! Show 'em some leg if you want to hitch a ride," Brad wisecracked.

Russian sailor: "ZDRAHST-voo y-tyeh, kahk VAH-sheh EE-myah? mah-YAW EE-myah dzhawn, kahk-vih puh-zhee-VAW-yeh-tyeh?" (Hello, what is your name? My name is John, how are you?)

Nick: "mah-YAW EE-myah NEEK-o-leTTah. "AW-chen pree-YAW-tnuh. Aw-chen khuh-rah-SHAW, spah-SEE-buh, ah kahk vih?" (My name is Nicoletta. I am pleased to meet you. I am very well, thanks and you?)

Russian sailor: "Shtaw vih DYEH-lah-yeh-tyeh syeh-VAW-dynah VYEH-cheh-rum? vahsh NAW-myehr tyeh-lyeh-FAW-nah?" (What are you doing tonight? Your telephone number?)

Nick: "Eh-tah neh-vahs-MOHZH-nah." (It's not possible.)

The Russian sailor smiled and nodded in acknowledgment. I noticed the guys were looking at me.

"What's he saying?" Brad asked.

"He's trying to ask me out."

"Damn Russky!" Brad shouted.

"No, Russky here!" the sailor shouted back in English.

An officer on the Russian ship shouted, "Stop looking at the American girl and get to work!"

The sailor smiled, waved and then walked away. We saw another sailor taking pictures of us.

"Don't they have to ask our permission to do that?" Brad asked.

"It's a free country, guy. Let him waste his film if he wants to," I replied.

Earl came up behind us, holding a box the size of a shoe box with a cord tied around it.

"It's time to practice a little Detente with these commies," he said.

"Where's your M-16?" Brad said jokingly.

"Not this time. There's enough pecan clusters in here to give the whole lot diabetes," Earl said as he swung the box over his head and heaved it at the Russians.

His aim was impeccable, hitting a Russian sailor right on the numbers. For a minute they seemed puzzled, then they carefully opened the box. They started shouting (Zok-ah-lot) chocolate in Russian. The officer shouted at them again and one of the sailors took the box away.

"Like little kids, we wouldn't want to spoil their dinner," Smitty remarked. the Burns Harbor had locked through and started passing the Russian ship starboard to starboard. The sailors started heading for the other side of their ship to check out any goodies from the Burns Harbor.

"How do ya' like that? A bunch of mooching beggars, looking for a handout," Ed remarked.

"Russian merchant sailors don't get much in the way of sweets, but they'll never beg," I explained.

The sailor that first waved at me, reappeared with a box in his hands. He tied a cord around it and heaved it over to us the same way Earl had done.

"For Nikoletta," he said.

Brad handed me the box. Since he had secured it with duct tape, I had to use my pocket knife to open to open the box. I pulled back the newspaper and saw a very finely painted nested doll set.

"Eh-tah el-leh-gahnt-nah, spah-see-bah vahm," (It's beautiful, Thank you.) I shouted to the Russian sailor.

"See you again, soon," he shouted back in english and waved.

The Russian ship started moving toward the lock.

"That sucker can speak english," Ron said.

"Just what he learned from Sesame Street," Brad said.

"The level should be down in both locks. We should be able to lock through pretty soon," I said.

The Bosun came over and told Ron and Smitty to get down on the wall and standby to release the mooring lines. He told Earl and I to standby forward and Al to standby aft. We would be going through the Mac Arthur lock. In a few minutes, the bell rang once and the order came to castoff and take in the mooring lines. After Ron released the forward mooring line, he ran toward the boarding ladder. Earl and I pulled the line in and coiled it in the tub. After five minutes, the whistle blew and the ship began moving forward slowly.

"There won't be any supply ship to worry about," the Bosun said.

"Once we get through, it's pedal to the metal," Al said.

The MacArthur lock is not nearly as big as the Poe lock, that the Russian ship was heading into. The Mate was taking it slow and easy. No showing off here, save the speed for the open water where it does some good. The lock doors were fully open before we got close. The level difference is twenty one feet. The depth over sills is thirty two feet. Those lock walls are massive and they look it when you're coming in upbound. The Mate was constantly receiving reports of Distance Off from the Bosun. The Mate had the ship centered perfectly in the lock when the lock doors closed. I looked down and saw the water slowly swirling between the hull and the lock wall. I walked over to the port side and saw our little friends with their sleds. They waved frantically at me until I waved at them.

"You want some of the Captain's cookies?" I asked.

"Yeah,Yeah!" they shouted.

I took the packet of cookies out of my parka and threw it over the fence. They scrambled in the snow to get it. They gleefully jumped up and down as they tore into the packet.

"What's your name?" one of the boys asked.

"My name is Nick," I answered.

"I'm Rusty, his name is Ricky," he said, adding—"What's that big white thing up there?"

"That's the boom conveyor to unload the ship," I said.

"What's in the ship?" he asked.

"Fourteen thousand tons of coal," I replied.

"Wow! How did you get it in the ship?" he asked. "We take the hatches off, then chutes are lowered into the open hatchways and coal slides down into the ship. Just like sliding down a slide," I answered.

"Where does the coal come from?" he asked.

"Railroad train cars," I replied, adding—"This ship can hold two whole trains full of coal."

"Here comes my mom. You can talk to my mom," he said.

"She probably wants you to go home. It's very cold," I said.

"Mom, the lady that took our picture, gave us some cookies," he shouted.

She called for them to come.

"See you next summer," I said and waved at them.

I went over to the starboard side.

"How are our Russian friends doing?" I asked no one in particular.

"They're dawdling as usual," Brad replied.

"We'll be ready to go here in another minute," I said.

The level of the water was nearly to the mark on the wall. I remembered the nested doll. I had put it in the crew's hall and decided to retrieve it and put it in my quarters. When I entered the crew's hall, Pete, Joe and Billy were there.

"How's the cable repair coming along?" I asked.

"The Chief's got Carl and Mark up there," Billy replied.

"I wouldn't want to be up there in this cold either," I said as I picked up the box and left.

I heard Pete and Joe laughing as I started down the passageway. Those two smart asses are going to get theirs sooner than they think, I thought. When I got to my quarters, I took the nested dolls out of the box. I took them apart and found a small piece of paper rolled up in the smallest one. Written on it was the sailor's name and address in Kiev. I'll have to write him and thank him, I thought. I put the doll away and went back out on deck. Looking aft, I saw one guy on a ladder and one guy on the Mast. Better to do it now before the ship is rolling and pitching, I thought.

I went over to the group of guys at the starboard rail.

"There's some problem with the Russian ship. They're being held for some reason," Al said.

271

"Maybe they're all a bunch of spies. Especially that sneaky bastard with the camera," Brad said.

"Oh yes, openly taking pictures of locks and ships that have been photographed and publicized for years. That's one clever spy," I said sarcastically.

"You can never trust a commie, like in Vietnam. Ain't that right, Ron?" Brad asked.

"You could never justify that war to me. They didn't have one flushing toilet in that whole country!" Ron replied.

"We should have air-lifted in a million port-a-potties for these guys," Al joked.

The whistle blew three short blasts.

"Bon Voyage, you commie pigs," Brad said.

The lock gates had already opened and the ship slowly began to move ahead.

"I can't see anything else up there," Smitty said.

"The Bosun said there's another ship, a Norwegian. I guess he's still a couple of miles away," Hal said.

I looked aft.

"I hope Carl and Mark get that job done. There might be some nasty waves out there," I remarked.

Hal waved for the Bosun. I heard him on the radio. "What's the wave forecast in Superior?"

"At this end, from the north, four to six feet, choppy," the Bosun replied.

"Copy that, Ostrander, out," and Hal put his radio in his pocket.

We watched silently as the ship cleared the lock gates and the gates closed. I knew they were thinking that this may be the last time they would be taking this ship through the lock. The clear cold air and the snow on the land, made for a distinct boundary between Lake Superior and Terra Firma.

"Looks kinda' pretty," I heard Billy say from behind me.

"Unusual, no cold fog, snow or spray to obstruct the view," I replied.

"The shoreline is so pretty in the summertime. Nice sandy beaches, sail boats. My parents used to bring me up here for a week or two. They'd rent the same cottage every year. I made a lot of friends," he said.

"I remember when my grandmother would rent a cottage in Marblehead. She always rented at the same place every year, too. I guess people figure they'll have the same good experience they had the year before."

"We use to rent a cottage on Grand Island in the summer time. Of course, I was just a kid then. In 1951, when Mather died, they raped that place. Killed all the animals, cut down all the trees. Ruined one of the last pristine wilderness left," Hal said.

"I remember Mather," Smitty said, adding—"Didn't he marry a young woman when he was seventy years old?"

"Yeah, he was quite a character. He took her on a honeymoon cruise on one of his ore ships."

"All his money and he took her on an ore ship?! Call the Guinness people, I think we found the world's biggest cheap ass," I declared.

"He was proud of his ships. He wanted to show them to her," Hal explained.

"I would have shown him a whup upside his head if he tried that with me!" I exclaimed.

The other guys laughed.

"Hey Nick, when you and the Mate get hitched, maybe the company can arrange a working honeymoon, touring the Great Lakes," Ron wisecracked.

All the guys were looking at me, so I decided to play it coy.

"I never heard about any plans for marriage, but I do know that my honeymoon cruise will be in the Mediterranean. The Italian Riviera and the Greek Islands, no G-D Allouez Express!" I stated emphatically.

"Sure Nick, we'll start a honeymoon fund for you," Al said jokingly.

"You sound like you already sent out the wedding invitations. I hope you aren't disappointed," I said.

I was wondering how all this banter would get back to the Mate. I knew men like to kid the younger guys, the same way they were teasing me, so I played along.

"Where do you live Nick?" Billy asked.

"Never you mind, boy! She's spoken for," Hal said.

The other guys laughed.

"I live on the Gentry. Oh, you mean my permanent address. I live in Marblehead, just west of Sandusky," I replied.

"The Mate lives there too?" he asked.

"Yes, about a quarter a mile away from my cottage," I answered.

"Oh, how cozy," Brad wisecracked.

"It was my grandmother's house. I inherited it a little over a year ago, when she died," I explained.

"Is it a good place to live?" Billy asked.

"It's windy, cold, no beach, solid limestone rock. I spent a lot of time in Alliance, where I attended college. I still have a lot of friends down there. I met Earl there originally," I explained.

"I may go to college. Maybe this winter," Billy said.

I heard the Bosun calling John on the radio.

"What's that about?" I asked.

"While you and Earl were having a gay old time in town. The Bosun and I were getting us some supper. Fresh Superior Whitefish," Ed said.

"Great, we haven't had that in awhile," I said.

Earlier in the summer, on a down bound run, we had to tie up in Sault Ste. Marie and wait for the supply boat and some relief crew. At the Visitor's Center, they told us that the Volunteer Fire department was having a fish fry at the football field. Half of us went over there and paid four dollars per person to get Whitefish. It seemed so warm then. I was feeling cold, so I decided to head back to my quarters.

"Catch you guys later," I said and I headed toward the forward deckhouse.

CHAPTER 10

The 24 Hour Bug

When I got to the passageway, instead of going up the steps to my quarters, I turned left and went into the lounge. I went into the adjoining night kitchen to get some hot water. I felt cold and started shaking. I knew I had the chills and that probably meant I was getting the flu. Instead of coffee, I poured some hot water into a cup and got a couple of bouillon cubes. I left a note for the Bosun, since I would not be able to stand my next watch. I knew it would hit me in the stomach real soon, so I headed for my quarters. When I got to my quarters, I realized I still had my tool belt. I took it off and laid it in the corner. I hung up my parka and took off my work boots. The chills hit me again, so I sat on my bunk and wrapped my blanket around me. This is a fine kettle of fish, I thought. Then I thought about the Whitefish I would not be able to eat. This has definitely been a lousy day for me, I thought. I looked at the clock, it was almost 0900 (9:00 AM). I tried to lay down for a few minutes, but my stomach began hurting. I propped myself up on my seabag and a couple of pillows. After about half an hour, I started nodding off, when I heard a knock on the door. I heard the Mate calling me. I got up and opened the door, still wrapped in my blanket.

"You look pale. I didn't know you were sick," he said

"Can you take my tool belt?" I asked.

"Sure, I brought the forms that you have to sign. I'll see if I can get you something for your stomach," he said.

I went back to my bunk. The Mate came in and picked up my tool belt.

"Let the Bosun know that I won't make the next watch," I said.

"Sure, I'll be back in a few minutes," he said, then he left.

As I laid propped up in my bunk, I thought about past flu outbreaks during the four seasons that I was on the Giovanni. There were three. The crew gave them the romantic names—the Creeping Crud flu, the Stinking flu and the Orange Piss flu. I had the Stinking flu, so called, because you smelled like rotten eggs during the four days you had it. I hoped that this was only going to be a one day thing. The ship was starting to roll. Not a bad roll, but much more noticeable in my condition. I heard a knock on the door.

"Come in," I said. The Mate entered with Earl.

"Hi guys," I said.

"Hi Nick, what seems to be the problem here?" Earl asked.

"Any excuse to get out of work, you know how it is," I replied jokingly.

"I brought some Tylenol Flu," The Mate said, taking out the bottle and setting it on the dresser.

"Thanks," I said, adding—"I don't know if I can drink any more water."

"How about some good old fashioned Cotton Club?" Earl asked, pulling the bottle out of his coat pocket.

"Oh Earl, that's a life saver. I didn't think there was another bottle of ginger ale on this ship," I said.

"My secret stash. The other guys waste it,but I always keep some around for medicinal purposes," he proudly stated.

"Just like your beer," I said jokingly.

"One likes to be prepared," he shot back.

He also had a thermometer and took my temperature.

"Is there anything else we can get you?" the Mate asked.

"Yes, tell your driver to stop rocking the cradle," I said jokingly.

"Would it help if we turned your bed the other way?" the Mate asked.

"I'll feel like I'm on a hobby horse," I said,adding—"I'll be okay, thanks guys."

Earl left, then the Mate quickly kissed me on the forehead as I drifted off . . . I was back at school, walking down an unfamiliar hallway. I couldn't remember where my classes were or what I was supposed to be doing. A Dean walked up to me and told me that I was supposed to be teaching professor Rogers' class. I said okay, but I didn't know professor Rogers or what class he taught. When I woke up, my hair was wet, my clothes were wet, the sheet was wet. I took a drink of ginger ale even though my stomach didn't feel like it. I took my clothes off and just covered with a sheet. A wonderful disease, I thought, maybe I would sweat it out of me. I thought of the time when we loaded coal in Conneaut. We loaded to twenty six feet of draft and it was hot as hell. All the way to Sault Ste. Marie, the Deck watch was continuously hosing the deck to try to keep it cool. Not one of our more pleasant trips to be sure. Someone blasted the music just outside my door for a half a minute, then hurried away. I put on my flannel nightgown and laid down again and drifted off. I was on the supply boat, coming alongside the Giovanni. The long gangway had been lowered from the spar deck. The supply boat kept rising and sinking violently, with the waves. I kept hollering that I couldn't get on. The first mate, Franky Pierce, was hollering at me, but I could not understand him. I woke up and heard the Bosun outside, calling for me. I got up and opened the door.

"Sorry if I woke you. John has some soup made up for you, if you feel like eating," he said.

"I didn't know it was almost eight o'clock," I said.

"Earl filled in for you," he said.

"Can you clear the rascals out of the night kitchen?" I asked.

"No problem," the Bosun said.

"I'll be down in a few minutes," I said.

"Okay, John should be on his way forward," he said, then he left.

I put on a sweater over my night gown and put on some house slippers. I wrapped myself in a blanket and headed down the passageway and down the stairs to the night kitchen. On my way, I heard the watch bell ring. When I got there, I saw Earl.

"Why don't you sit over here, the rolling won't be as bad," he said.

In fact, the rolling wasn't bothering me as much as it had before.

"Thanks, old buddy. How did things go on the watch?" I asked.

"Not too bad. All the navigational lights are fixed, Rudolph is working, all the problems aft have been fixed. It looks like everybody is happy again," he replied.

"Everybody else is doing well?" I asked.

"It looks like Joe and Andy have got it too. I heard the Mate say that he's got to work a double watch and the Captain's gonna' work one too, he said," Earl answered.

"How's the weather up ahead?" I asked.

"I don't know. It's not too bad now, really," he said. I saw John enter, carrying a pot with a lid.

"Hey, roughneck, how yah feeling?" he asked.

"Well, I'm still among the living," I said.

"This soup will fix you right up. It'll take some of the green outta' your face," he said while grabbing a bowl and spoon from the shelf.

He ladled some in the bowl and set it on the table in front of me.

"Thanks John," I said.

"Now, take it slow. Most guys were able to eat after ten hours. You gotta' get some water in you," he said.

"I'm sorry I missed your Whitefish," I said.

"No you didn't, Whitefish is tomorrow. Supper was steak and cream gravy," he said.

"Darn! The only time this month you have my favorite and I gotta' be sick."

"Yeah, that was good timing. It's all gone too. I'll try to rustle something up when we get to Duluth," John said.

"I owe Nick a dinner at 'The Wharf', when we get to Duluth," Earl said.

"That's right, we're gonna' be off this ship like rats on fire," I said.

"Aren't you going to port services? There's bound to be lay-up chores. Weeks more of employment," John asked.

"No, I never have in the past, unless I was drafted. I have some things to take care of at home. They may need a dozen men to handle things. I'm sure they can find them on this ship," I concluded.

"Yeah, it'll be great to be back home," Earl said.

"So you can flip burgers at Mc Donalds. It's gonna' take you a couple years to get that dairy farm going again. If everything goes right, it will be a 24/7 job," John said, adding—"I have to get back. Let me know if you need anything else.", then he turned and left.

"If those guys stay here, they'll have to bust their tails to get back to Cleveland in time for the party," Earl said.

"Yeah, it's gonna' be a bear for them. I sure in the hell won't work Port Services in Duluth. This soup is pretty good, I feel better," I said.

"Don't overdo it. I got some more ginger ale for you here," Earl said as he pulled a bottle out of his coat pocket.

"Great, that really does the trick," I said.

"Good evening to you two," I heard the Mate say.

"Good evening, Mr. McCracken," I replied.

"How are you feeling?" he asked, coming over to me.

"Somewhat better, John brought me some soup."

"He had to bring my dinner to the Wheelhouse," the Mate said.

"I heard about Andy. I hope it's not too much trouble for you and the Captain," I said.

"The weather isn't too bad, and there's not a lot of ships nearby. We shouldn't have any problems," he said.

"I'll be up at 4:00 AM to keep you company," I said jokingly.

"No you won't," the Mate shot back.

"Sure, another eight hours and I'll be rearing to go," I stated.

"I don't think so. Union rules and company policy both say that for an illness, you are required to be off for a minimum of twenty four hours. I have it in writing, so you're not going to buffalo me and the Captain this time," the Mate said.

What administrative sewer has he been swimming in,I thought.

"More observed in the breach," I shot back.

"You better behave, I'll tie you in your bunk if I have to. The rules are for your own good. You'll catch pneumonia in that cold," the Mate said.

I'll come up to the wheelhouse and tell you what I think of your rules for the next four hours, I thought. He gave me that smile like I had used on him.

"Very well, Mr. McCracken," I conceded.

"Earl is doing a good job on deck. Billy is doing porter duties."

I was surprised to hear him say that about Earl.

"I have to be getting back to the wheelhouse. I'll catch you later," the Mate said, touching my hand, then he turned and left.

"The nerve of some people," I huffed.

"Now Nick, you know he's right," Earl said.

"I hate it when a man is right. And he knows he's right and I just have to stand here and take it," I said.

"You remind me of the women that my uncle used to talk about. He owned a motel. He was the only man in the family that wasn't divorced. He used to say that you only apologize to a man once, but you apologize to a woman three hundred times. They never believe that you're actually sorry. They just want to see you throw away any shred of dignity that you may have left," Earl said.

I thought about Earl and the Mate. Are they getting along better now? There is an old sailors adage—"A few years, a few thousand beers, things get forgotten." I hoped something good like that would happen.

"I'll smooth things over later. You and him seem to be getting along better," I said.

"Yeah, he seems to be getting friendlier with me," Earl said.

I wondered if it had anything to do with what I told him about the fight.

"Well, keep doing a good job," I said.

"Sure, Al's an easy guy to work with," Earl said.

"I don't know what I'm gonna' do for the next eleven hours," I said.

"You want to play some five card?" Earl asked.

"Sure, why not?" I replied.

"You know how to play cribbage?" Earl asked as he dealt the cards.

"That's some fricking old mans game, isn't it?" I asked.

Earl laughed at my comment.

"Back in the days of the Cliffs line, it was quite a phenomena. The Mate and another fellow on the Champlain, were always neck and neck in the championships. Hell, we used to bet on the outcome of the games, just like a football game. More interesting than some football games I've seen. We used to call him "Money Making McCracken". I never lost any money betting on him," Earl said.

"Oh, Mr. High Roller, a side of him I haven't seen before!" I exclaimed.

"He was always pretty straight laced, except for that six months when his wife died, of course," Earl said.

"That must have been very difficult for him," I said.

"Yeah, things going to hell at work, things going to hell at home. A lot of us in the sewer. I've seen Steve have to carry him out, passed out colder than hell," Earl said.

"He never mentioned any of that to me. He never said anything about the cribbage either," I said.

"There's a cribbage board stashed around here somewhere," Earl replied.

After playing cards for half an hour, I told Earl to get some sleep and to set his alarm for 3:30 AM. My body was hurting from sitting down. I got up and got a cup for my ginger ale and then I headed for my quarters. When I got to my quarters, I decided to read for a while. I laid on my bunk and I started reading the short stories of Chekhov, which are in Russian. The way my grandmother spoke Russian was so beautiful. The writings of Tolstoy, Pushkin and Gorky, all sounded so wonderful when she read them to me. Such brilliant and sublime depictions of life, expressed in such simple language. I read for several hours before I stopped to get some more ginger ale. I heard someone outside my door, so I went to see who it was. When I opened the door, I saw the Mate.

"Are you off now? I didn't hear the bell," I said.

"The Captain relieved me a couple minutes early," he said.

"That's good. You had a very busy and difficult day. I bet you're ready for a rest. Oh, I have those overtime reports signed, do you want them now?" I asked.

"Yes, if you will," he replied.

"No problem," I said, fetching the paperwork from my dresser and handing it to him.

We looked at each other for a few moments.

"You were absolutely right, earlier. This illness must have messed with my head. If I spoke to you out of line . . ."

I stopped speaking when he gently held my hand.

"Well, I don't want you to get sick," I said.

"How are you feeling?" he asked.

"A little achy and tired, but I think I can eat in a couple more hours," I replied.

"John put some food in the night kitchen. Macaroni and cheese, Chicken and stuffing and there's some Mush and Toaster waffles. If you can keep that down, you're doing pretty good," the Mate remarked.

"Thanks for telling me. I'll check it out here in a little while," I said.

"Did anyone say anything to you about . . . uh, us?" he asked.

"The usual crap that they would give any young deckhand they thought was getting married. They were trying to help plan a honeymoon. I told them that they sound like they had already sent out the wedding invitations. I told them that I hope they're not disappointed," I replied.

"That's to be expected, I suppose. I overheard Pete tell Joe and Buster that your illness was due to pregnancy," the Mate said.

"That's ridiculous! When everybody else has been getting sick. Who would believe that horse sh-t?" I asked.

"Not many, I'm sure," he replied.

"I'm going to set that son-of-a-bitch straight. As soon as we're off this ship, I'll stomp his lying self into the ground, first opportunity," I declared.

"Try to make it after the season's over," the Mate said.

"Good, I'll do it after the party. He'll be drinking his meals through a straw!" I said.

"Well, I did not mean to get you upset. Try to calm down," the Mate suggested.

"Don't worry, when the time comes, you and the Captain won't see it," I assured him.

"Okay. I'll see you later," he said.

"Get some rest, bye-bye," I said, releasing his hand. After he left, I heard the watch bell for midnight. I laid down and listened to music until I fell asleep. I woke up at 3:30 AM and got dressed in my work clothes, even though I was not working the morning watch. I went to the morning kitchen without running into anybody on the way. The ship was rolling moderately, so the waves were not that bad. We were half way across Lake Superior, so my next watch, would be my last one on the water.

CHAPTER 11

Final Port of Call

I f everything went according to plan we would be arriving in Duluth between 1:00 and 2:00 AM tomorrow morning. It would take about eight hours to dock and unload if we do not have to wait on another ship. The usual delays to get to the layup location. Pack my stuff and have it shipped back home. The wait to catch the puddle jumper back to Sandusky. All that would take at least a full day. Earl and I had saved our vacation so we would avoid the lay-up chores and still get paid. Let Billy and all those other guys who were complaining about the season ending, get down in the conveyor tunnels and break their backs. I had done enough of that job to know that I did not want to do it. I checked out the frozen dinners and decided on the Macaroni and Cheese. I put it in the microwave and sat down for a few minutes in the lounge. I saw Fred come into the night kitchen, unplug the dorm refrigerator and pick it up.

"Stop thief!" I said jokingly.

"Hi, Nick. I didn't know you were there," Fred replied.

"Stealing refrigerators, now?" I asked. "I stoled it from my daughter last year. She didn't need it anymore. I'm thawing it out, so I can have it sent home," he explained.

"Are you staying around after we tie up?" I asked.

"For about two weeks. The Bunkers have to emptied and cleaned. Fire boxes and Boilers cleaned and inspected. Boiler water drained and pumped out," he said.

"My that sounds like a lot of work," I said.

"The Chief's got all the paperwork to do, he volunteered."

"It sounds like he volunteered with some persuasion," I remarked.

283

"He can take most of it home and still get paid for it," Hank said.

"Oh, how does he do that?" I asked.

"He catches another boat back to Sault Ste. Marie and brings the paperwork with him," Hank replied.

"When I get away from Duluth, I don't want to see it for at least another four months," I said.

"It's a little cold, but it's not a bad town," Hank said.

"The people are nice and friendly, but it's no Italian Riviera," I said.

"You like Marblehead in the winter?" he asked.

"There is always something to do or some place to go. I have friends all over the country, I can visit," I said.

"The only time I've been to Marblehead was when we used to run those old cement carriers in there to get limestone. It seems like people have to turn to the lakes. The Quarries don't offer much to young people," Fred observed.

"That keeps the town small, the way I like it," I said.

"Catch you later," He said picking up his refrigerator.

"Okay, Fred," I replied.

I was thinking about Marblehead. The blizzard we had in upper Lake Huron had moved across Lake Erie, dumping snow all over Ashtabula and Erie. West of Cleveland, we were fortunate enough to miss a major snow from that storm.

Marblehead would be so quiet at 4:00 AM, this time of year. I have laid in bed and heard the Grandfather clock ticking in the living room. In Alliance, living in a close proximity to a train yard, I would be awaken by the bumping of the train cars, or by the sounding of the air horn when a train would approach a grade crossing at four in the morning. Out on a cargo ship, one becomes accustomed to the constant noise to a point where sleep is no longer disturbed by it. You can always hear something on a ship when it is moving. "Ship noises" became legendary on some ore boats.

I went to the microwave and took out the dinner, since it looked slightly better than it did when frozen, I decided to eat it. The only drink I had to go with the macaroni and cheese, was some warm ginger ale. I am definitely having lunch aft, I thought, as I was eating the macaroni. I heard the 0400 (4:00 AM) watch bell. I saw Pete walking by the doorway, headed forward. A few minutes later, I saw the Bosun walk by, headed aft. I was hoping Earl would show up sooner or later. I was reading the Soo Evening News, the local newspaper in Sault Ste. Marie for about half an hour when Earl showed up with a broom and dust pan.

"Hi, Guy. What's going on?" I asked.

"Captain's orders. They're pulling one deckhand every watch to do the sweeping and mopping. Guess who got elected on this watch?" he said rather than asked.

"That's wonderful. When we start unloading this coal the dust is gonna' go everywhere," I said.

"The rumor is that some 'Big Wigs' will be coming on board before we off-load or while we off-load, something . . ." Earl said.

"Our Mister O'Blake, perhaps?" I ventured to guess.

"Nobody seems to know. The Owners, the Mayor, a congressman, Elvis, somebody. John is having a 'meltdown'. He's got to rewrite his grocery acquisitions and menus. There may be guests for four to five days. He has to plan a different menu for these people."

"Yeah, that kind of thing used to happen on the Giovanni. The first couple of days of lay-up, the shore birds think it's a party boat. They want to see the wine list. Guiddo would threaten to put saltpeter, or something in the food. The Captain would keep it under control after the first day," I said.

"Yeah, I'm glad we're gonna' be outta here early. That 'sucking up to' the shore birds really stinks," Earl said.

"I've met a few good people of that ilk, most were jerks like that lawyer in Cleveland," I said.

"They get the same treatment?" Earl asked.

"One guy did. 'Scoring Skorenski', they called him. Nice looking blonde fellow, spoke Russian. He tried to be real slick when we were alone together in the store room. He got a 'quicky' alright, one right upside the head. He even tried it again, groped me in the library. He was ready for my right hook that time, so I maced him then showed him my left hook."

"He took that as a 'No'?" Earl said jokingly.

"Some guys are pompous jerks, who think that they are entitled to grope a woman anytime they want. I say 'No' once, if they don't want to hear, then there is no use in saying it anymore," I said.

"Punching guys like that, we'll never get you married off," Earl said.

"You're not going to start that marriage crap like the other guys?" I asked.

"Just kidding, Nick. I use to tell my youngest sister Jenny that. She's been punching guys out since kindergarden," Earl said.

"I didn't know you had a sister," I said.

"Yeah, she lives in Beloit. She's married and has two children. She won't have anything to do with the rest of us," Earl said.

I helped Earl clean up the lounge area and night kitchen. It took about an hour to sweep and mop. Fortunately, nobody came in and saw me working. Earl left to do the Crew's hall and the Observation room. I went back to my quarters and decided to start packing some of my non-essential stuff.

The first thing I always pack is my custom made snow globe with a music box. It has the Round Island light house on the gravel beach. It was a present from my grandmother. It has a key in a hidden drawer. It plays the 'Rhapsody on a Theme of Paganini, Op. 43'. A theme nobody had heard of until the movie-Somewhere in Time. I went to my dresser to get my jewelry box. I pulled open the top drawer and reached down to get it but it was not there. I momentarily panicked and started pulling out my clothes, then I saw it in the back of the drawer. I pulled it out and opened it. I was relieved to see that nothing was missing. The rolling of the ship must have caused it to slide back there. The next thing to go was my soft makeup case. It is only as big as half of a loaf of bread. I do not know why I bring it every year. I am not gonna' go up the street for a hot date so there is no need for any cosmetics. I folded my good leather coat and my non-working clothes and summer clothes and put them in the box. I closed the box and duct taped it. I laid on my bunk and listened to classical music on my walkman. I took a short nap until the 8:00 watch bell rang. I had arranged to meet Earl in the lounge when he got off watch. I washed my face and brushed my hair then I put on my parka and headed out the door. I heard the Mate and Andy talking in the stairway that goes up to the wheelhouse. I waited a minute, hoping to run into the Mate in the passageway or the lounge. Apparently Andy was taking his usual watch and the Mate would work a double to get things back to normal watch rotation. I turned right and went down the passageway to the stairs that go down to the lounge. I realized that I had been acting like a school girl, waiting in the hallway for her boyfriend to pass by. When I got to the bottom of the steps, I turned to go into the lounge when I heard the Mate's voice.

"Good morning, Miss Strickland."

"Good morning, Mr. McCracken. Did you get some rest?" I asked.

"Yes, how about you?" he asked.

"Oh, yes. Plenty of rest but I'm afraid that my sleep pattern is thrown off," I said, adding—"Are you gonna' pull another double watch in the wheelhouse?"

"No, Andy will pull a double watch and then we'll be back to normal up there," he replied as he came down the steps.

"Very good," I said, trying to sound cool as I entered the lounge.

I did not see anyone in there or in the night kitchen. I wanted to embrace him and hug him.

"I was gonna' wait for Earl here so we could go aft and harass John," I stated, pulling out a chair.

"You must be fully recovered if you can eat those greasy eggs and Canadian bacon," the Mate said as he sat down.

"I feel like eating some real food. Ginger ale and frozen macaroni is terrible. It sounds like something they feed you in prison," I remarked.

"It doesn't sound very good," he agreed.

"I've been dreaming of that Beef Bourguinonne Flambe," I said.

"It's strange that you should say that," he said and he was quiet again.

"That sounds like an incomplete sentence," I remarked.

"I was at the 'Angry Bull' with Mrs. Kefauver. She was commenting that they didn't have her favorite Beef Bourguignonne flambe," the Mate replied.

"Marry her and you could have it every day," I wisecracked.

"I don't think that would work," the Mate said.

"Really? Maybe you're a little too-er,uh vigorous for her," I said, adding— "She's accustomed to those elderly men that lay in bed and wheeze."

"You're ornery! You're definitely feeling better," he remarked.

"That's what everybody keeps telling me," I said, giving him a cute little smile.

"We'll put all that energy to some good use. We'll be docking early in the morning," he said.

"Yes, I figured it will be between one and two o'clock. If we don't have to wait for another boat at the slip. It's gonna' be cold as hell so no one is gonna' feel like busting their humps out there," I said.

"You may have another think coming. There will be no goofing off when the top brass is watching," he said.

"We'll be at the Duluth Mesabi Iron Range dock, most likely. If there's not much wind at all, that coal dust is gonna' go all over hell's half acre. Those shorebirds don't show up until 8 o'clock in the morning. Coal dust and Pierre Cardin just don't go together," I said.

"Everybody has to be standing by on all bells, the Captain's orders," he said.

"Oh, no problem. I'm young and strong," I said.

"I'm still pretty 'vigorous' myself," the Mate wisecracked.

"You must be talking about playing Cribbage," I said laughingly.

The Mate cocked his head and looked at me for a few moments.

"A side of you that I haven't seen before, Mr. High Roller. I heard that you played a mean Cribbage game," I said.

The Mate was silent for a minute.

"That seems like a thousand years ago," he said.

I touched his hand.

"I heard the other guys talk about it. I didn't mean to upset you," I said quietly.

"It's okay. Just something I used to do," he said.

"I'm not much of a card player. I can't sit still long enough for that sort of thing," I said, adding—"It looks like Earl isn't gonna' make it. Do you wanna' go aft with me and get some breakfast?" I asked.

"Let me get my coat," he said.

"Can I walk with you?" I asked.

"Sure, but the other guys will talk," he said.

"They're talking already," I said as we both got up and headed for the door.

The Mate's quarters are on the port side, on the spar deck. It can be accessed from the passageway or the door at the rear of the forward deckhouse.

When we got to the Mate's passageway door, I said "Catch you at the back door."

"Be there in a moment," he said.

I went down the passageway while zipping my parka and putting the hood up. I felt the cold air when I opened the passageway door. I stepped out into the early morning sunshine and looked around but I did not see anybody on deck. A minute later the Mate came out of his back door.

"It doesn't look like anybody is out and about this morning," I observed.

"I'll have some trash to burn later. The Captain wants it all burned by the end of your watch," he said.

"All those nudy magazines and love letters from your girlfriend," I said jokingly.

"No, I'm keeping the love letters. The closest thing to a nudy magazine is this," he said, pulling a photograph out of his pocket and showing it to me.

It was a picture of me in the summertime, standing by the railing. I had my tool belt on my shoulder and I was flicking away a cigarette.

"You took that picture of me?" I asked.

"It was the only picture I could take without you or anybody else seeing me," he said.

"Well, it's not a very good picture. I look like a bimbo. I have pictures where I'm much more photogenic. I'll give you one when we go forward again," I said, handing the photograph back to him.

He seemed happy so we walked side by side in silence. I was resisting the temptation to hold his hand. I thought he was feeling the same because he was holding his hand behind his back. When we got to the after deckhouse, he opened the door for me.

"After you, Miss Strickland."

"That's very gentlemanly of you, Mr. McCracken," I replied, smiling.

I pulled my hood down and unzipped my parka as we walked down the passageway to the galley. We ran into Earl and Billy with the four wheeler.

"Hi, old buddy. I didn't see you forward so I came back here to look for you," I said.

"Yeah, these assholes won't do their own work so they figure they're gonna' work me around the clock," Earl complained.

"Why don't you take a break and have breakfast with us," I invited.

"I used my breakfast break an hour ago," Earl said.

"We'll be doing some trash burning on the evening watch. It should be loads of fun," I said.

"Okay, I'll try to make it," Earl said, then he and Billy continued down the pasageway.

"Everybody is getting antsy, this close to lay-up," the Mate said.

"Me and Earl are gonna' be down that ladder like this ship's on fire," I said as we went through the galley door.

"Hi Louie," I said.

"Good morning, people. Are you feeling better, Nick?" Louie asked.

"Good enough to try John's left over Goulash," I said jokingly.

"The very thought is disgusting. How about a western omelette with biscuits and gravy?" Louie asked.

"That sounds good," I replied.

"I'll have three minute eggs and Canadian bacon with toast," the Mate requested.

"It'll be a few minutes. The juice and coffee are in the officers' mess," he said and he went through the swinging doors.

"Oh, I get to eat in the officers' mess. How wonderful," I sighed.

"If you don't behave, we'll throw you out," the Mate said, smiling.

"I liked tying me in my bunk, better," I teased.

When we got to the officers' mess, the Captain and the Chief were there.

"Well, Miss Strickland, are you feeling better?" the Captain asked as he and the Chief stood up.

Manners are observed in the officers' mess.

"Much better, thank you," I replied.

"I heard that you lost your double chocolate cookies," he said.

"Our little friends with the sleds came by the fence when we were in the lock. So I threw the cookies to them," I said.

"That was very kind of you. I'll have the Bosun bring you down some more," he said.

"Very kind of you, Sir," I replied.

"I heard that you got a gift from the Russian ship," the Chief said.

"Yes, a set of nested dolls. A very nicely painted set," I replied.

"Gracey has collected a number of those over the years," the Captain said.

"Were you ever in the Soviet Union?" I asked.

"Yes, we were there a couple of years ago. Gracey is a big collector of folk art. She also has Ukranian eggs and all kinds of Celtic folk art, of course."

"That sounds very interesting. She has been collecting folk art for quite some time then?" I asked.

"Since she was a little girl. She has a couple items that her great grandmother brought from Ireland. I believe that was in 1854," he said.

"That sounds very impressive. I still have some of my grandmother's collection. Her second husband left her bag pipes and ceremonial daggers. Eichann had some marble busts and gold coins from all over the world but his daughter got that stuff," I said.

"When you meet Grainne, be prepared to talk about it. That's her favorite subject, after the grandchildren," the Captain said, smiling.

"Well, you definitely have me there," I conceded.

"Greg and I have some administrative matters to attend to in my quarters. Enjoy your breakfast," he said as he and the Chief got up from the table.

The Mate and I stood up as well.

"Everybody seems to be in a good mood, this morning," I observed when we sat down again.

"The weather forecast has been revised. The high tomorrow is predicted to be forty degrees," the Mate said.

"All that snow is gonna' melt. Whatta' mess," I said as Louie came in with our food.

"What's a mess?" he asked.

"This weather," I replied.

"People have been complaining about it since I can remember but it's still crazy," Louie said while handing us our food from his cart.

"Thanks, Louie," I said.

"Let me know if you want anything else," he said.

"Will do," I answered, then Louie left.

After a few minutes of attacking my omelette and biscuits, the Mate asked me what I was thinking about.

"How do you know that I'm thinking about something?" I asked.

"If a man has any brains, he learns to do that when he's been married a while," he replied.

"Is that right? A kind of meshing gears thing?" I asked.

"Something like that, I suppose," he answered.

"How perceptive of you. I was watching a segment on the news, probably ten years ago. This British fellow was talking about how the summer was a week shorter and the water in the English Channel is one degree colder. So he goes on for a while, then he says-'What's the government going to do about it'? Well, I remember watching the

'Avengers' when I was a kid. In that show the scientific community is portrayed as being absurdly eccentric. So I thought that this fellow must have just stepped off the set of the 'Avengers'. Then they're talking to all these other people and they're saying the same thing about the government. What do they want the government to do? Warm the water in the English Channel?" I finished.

"Maybe they forgot to talk to the people that have a more reasonable approach to climatic fluctuations," the Mate suggested.

"Early Americans believed that the government provided a police force and an army. Security from within and security from without. Now they have to control the economy and provide social security. Heavens knows, they do a bad enough job at that. What kind of lunatic would think that they should control the weather as well? How do these people get dressed in the morning?"

"Does this worry you?" the Mate asked in response to the political rhetoric.

"Only when I think about people like that having a vote that counts as much as mine. There are people who think that soap opera characters are real people rather than stage actors playing a fictional character. In other words, people who can't discern reality from fantasy-land. Can you imagine if you were on trial and people like that were on the jury?" I concluded my harangue.

I let the Mate open his soft boiled egg while I finished my Omelet.

"Louie does a good three minute egg," the Mate said.

"I've always had trouble getting it a hundred percent. Sometimes they come out alright, sometimes they're half raw," I said.

"I've learned to do them pretty good since Emma has been gone," he said.

"You may be a better cook than I am," I said.

"Didn't you learn to cook in college?" he asked.

"Peanut butter and Bologna sandwiches. I was on a tight budget sometimes. I didn't work as a student assistant, or anything. I spent most of my time at studies. That took enough of my time, believe me," I said.

"Darn, I could get a research paper, but no Flambe," the Mate said jokingly.

"You'll have to go back to Mrs. Kefauver. Did you ever find out if she can cook?" I asked.

"No, I'm afraid I didn't hang around long enough to find out about that."

"Oh, I see. The old hello, good-bye. Another side of you, I haven't seen before," I said jokingly.

"Does this put you off?" he asked.

"Quite the contrary. I find all this mystery to be rather alluring," I said trying to be serious.

"Are you serious?" he asked.

"Sure! Discovering things about a person you're attracted to can be very surprising and enjoyable," I said as I got up to get a glass of orange juice.

The Mate got up and came over next to me and got some coffee.

"Does that include sex also?" he asked softly.

"Of course it does. Sex is a part of every normal healthy persons' life. It's not the only thing in life. May be not even the most important thing in life, but it's definitely a part of my life that I don't want to do without," I said.

The Mate smiled at me and held my hand.

"You look awful happy," I observed.

"I just discovered something about you," He said.

"Oh pray tell, what pleasing discovery did you make?" I asked.

"I just observed that you have a way of giving a straight answer to a question. I don't recall ever seeing you sidestep, or avoid a question in any way," he said.

"Within reason, of course. You wouldn't believe some of the outrageous things men have asked me," I said.

"You didn't find anything I've asked you to be improper?" he asked.

"No, you follow the proper rules of dating," I replied, adding— "Emma must have taught you well."

"It keeps the beer glasses off my head," he replied jokingly.

"A good looking pig in a good looking suit is still a pig. There have been several guys that would have gotten the piece they were after, if they would have stifled the jerk in themselves," I stated.

"Like your professor friend you were telling me about?" he asked.

"He got his piece, then he totally changed for the worse. 'Why don't you wear makeup? Change the color of your hair! Stop wasting time sewing quilts', on and on. I didn't tolerate that for long, I'll tell yah," I said.

"I'll never try to change you," he said.

"You already have," I said.

"I'm sure that you have discovered that life changes all of us. Sometimes for the better, sometimes for the worse. I believe that I can always make myself a better person," the Mate explained.

"Did your parents teach you that philosophy?" I asked.

"Yes, I am sure that's were I learned it," he replied.

"Most of my philosophy about life, I learned very early and on my own, sometimes with help from my grandmother," I said.

We put our dirty dishes in the plastic tub.

"It feels so good to be able to eat a normal meal again," I said as we left the officers' mess and headed down the passageway.

"Let's stop by my quarters and I'll get a picture," I said.

"Okay. I hope nobody waylays us on the way forward," he said.

"We'll just walk together like two old shipmates talking about sea gulls," I said jokingly.

When we stepped through the door the sun was shining brightly even though it was still very cold. I put my hand up in front of my eyes.

"What's that bright light up in the sky?" I asked.

"That's the sun," the Mate said.

"Oh Yeah, it's been so long that I plum forgot," I said jokingly.

"It's supposed to be clear for the next couple of days," the Mate said.

"Good! The first chance we get, Earl and I will be heading back to Ohio via Polar airways," I said.

"You're going to leave me here, all alone?" the Mate asked.

"We'll meet again in Cleveland for the party," I said.

"You're going to Alliance?" he asked.

"I was thinking about dropping by and seeing some old friends," I said.

"It might be awfully cold up here in Duluth during those ten days," the Mate said.

"When the Chief shuts off the steam, it could be a problem. You have a girl in every port to keep you warm?" I asked jokingly.

"I've only got you!" he shot back.

"Such a monkish existence! Well if you can't do any better than Kefauver and Kinsey then it's probably just as well you wait for me," I suggested with a smile.

"That was my plan," the Mate said.

"Good, we wouldn't want you to bring back any strange diseases."

As we approached the forward deckhouse, I saw the passageway door open, and Ed and Carl emerged carrying a box and a trash bag.

"Hi guys. Whatcha' got there?" I asked.

"Some trash going aft to be burned later," Ed said, as they both stared at us.

"Okay, me and Earl will get it later," I said as we passed by.

"You think they were talking about us?" I asked.

"Well, we weren't holding hands. You're looking so happy, I would not be surprised."

"I am always happy when there's a shore leave," I said as I walked through the door, adding—"Are you ready for the party, did you bring your clothes?"

"I think that I will buy a new suit in Duluth," he said.

"Yeah, the Miller Hill Mall isn't too far away," I said as we started up the steps.

"I think I will look for a new dress. Probably go to the Carnation Mall in Alliance. I have trouble with formal wear. I don't think I'd be caught dead in some of these cocktail dresses I've seen."

"You may want to dress a little more conservatively. The Captain's wife will be there," he said.

"Should I wear an 'old lady' dress?" I asked when we got to my quarters and opened the door.

"Tasteful and fashionable are the correct terms here, I think," the Mate said.

I took pictures out of my dresser and selected the best one. I was sitting on the bridge at Mount Union, wearing a halter top and shorts. I went over to the Mate standing in the door way.

"This is a picture of me at college trying to look 'sexy'," I said, handing the picture to him.

He looked at it for a moment.

"Holy cow, you're looking good!" he exclaimed.

I looked down the passageway to see if anybody was coming.

"It won't keep you warm, but maybe this will help," I said putting my arms around his neck and kissing him for half a minute.

"That's returning the favor for when we were alone in the Wheelhouse," I said.

"I'll keep that in mind when you're gone," he said as we released our embrace.

He winked and whispered "bye-bye" in my ear, then he turned and left. I closed the door and laid on my bunk for a few minutes. I decided to pack all my clothes except for a couple sets of work clothes. I cleaned out the dresser, putting the clothes I would need in the closet. I swept and mopped the room and washed the walls. I returned the broom and mop back to the night kitchen forward. When I got back to my quarters, I gathered up the clothes I had been wearing when I was sick and put them in a laundry bag. Since we still had room in our pump-out tanks, everyone was permitted to do one load of laundry. Since it was already 1100, I figured I would head aft and do my laundry then try to meet up with Earl for lunch. I heard a couple of guys pass by my door, then a minute later I heard a knock on the door. When I opened the door the Bosun was there.

"Mister McCracken wants everyone not on watch to go to the Captain's quarters and sign articles," he said.

"Oh dear, that totally slipped my mind, I'll be right there," I said.

I knew the Mate would be there. I brushed my hair quickly and put it in a ponytail, then I headed down the passageway. When I got to the Captain's quarters there were three guys waiting in the passageway, Hank, Joe and Ron.

"Hi, guys what's going on," I said as a greeting.

"Same old horse sh-t," Joe said.

"They're signing articles and going over the draw list and any other last minute thing they can think of," Hank said.

"Who's in there now?" I asked.

"Earl, and he's taking frickin' forever. His draw list is probably a hundred feet long," Ron said as he shifted his lean against the wall.

The ships' articles is a contract between the company and the crewman that says that you serve voluntarily, in other words you were not shang-haied or something. You agree not to use drugs or alcohol while on the ship. Agree to abide by the workplace violence policy, yada, yada, yada. I am sure that most of the crew have never read it in its entirety. The draw list is a pay advance for expenditures made by crewmen during the season. It is usually taken out of the end-of-the-month pay.

"What's the hold up in there?" Joe said.

The Mate stuck his head out the door.

"Do you have anything better to do than get paid this month, Jenkins?" he snapped out, then went back inside.

"I guess that tactic isn't gonna' work," I said jokingly.

"Hey Nick, you got a cigarette?" Joe asked.

"I'm afraid not," I replied.

"You can't smoke up here. All this nice wood paneling. The Captain will skin you alive!" Hank said, adding—"They're gonna' make tobacco a drug, so you can't smoke on a boat anymore."

"Elephants will fly, before that happens," Ron said.

"They'll come up with some pill that will make you quit in one day," Hank said.

"My father quit in one day. It took him five years to get pass the urge for tobacco. He used to chew cigars. He wanted to go out in a blizzard to get more cigars when my mother told him that he was addicted to tobacco. He said he was not, and that he could quit anytime, so he did. If he had not been the stubbornness man in all creation, he would have never made it. Five years later, he would tell people that he had been addicted to tobacco." Ron finished.

After hearing that story, I figured I had better quit cigarettes.

Earl emerged from the door.

"What were you doing in there? Shining their shoes?" Joe wisecracked.

Earl gave a look that said, 'You're not worthy of the time of day'.

"Hi, guy. I was going to start a load of laundry, then meet you for some lunch," I said.

"Okay, I'll be aft. I'll see you later," he said.

"Okay, Buddy," I replied.

Earl continued down the passageway and the Mate called for Joe.

"Well, otherwise happy people don't seem to be coming out of there in a good mood," I said.

It only took a few minutes for Joe to emerge. Ron had just got on the boat so he had not accumulated any debts. He emerged in a few minutes also. Hank allowed me to go before him.

"Please, sit down there at the table, Miss Strickland," the Mate said.

"Very good, Sir," I said, smiling as sweetly and innocently as possible.

"You can sign the articles first, while I check the draw list," he said.

"Can I read it first?" I wisecracked.

"Certainly, if you want to keep us here until Christmas," he replied.

I initialed the provisions and signed and dated the bottom. The Mate signed as a witness.

"I see that you had an advance of fifty dollars," the Mate said.

"When was this?" I asked surprised.

"Back in August, the twenty second. Apparently from the supply boat," he said.

I hesitated for a few moments. About ten of us had jumped from the forward gangway door on to the deck of supply boat. I had picked up some stamps, stationary, envelopes, cigarettes, shampoo, a hair brush, tooth brushes and tooth paste. On a boat like ours, if you do not have your necessary personal items, you will do without until you have the chance to 'go up the street'.

"Oh yes, I picked up some stamps and envelopes so I can write to a 'secret admirer'," I said.

"At thirteen cents a piece, that is a lot of stamps," he said.

"Hope he's worth it," I said as I signed the deduction agreement.

"You'll find out soon enough, sweetie," he said, adding—"Now where were we? You're still planning on taking your vacation before we get to the lay-up yard?"

"Yes, Sir," I replied.

"You'll have to go up to the office in Duluth. I believe the payroll is handled by Mister Hunt," he said.

"No problem," I replied.

"You'll sign the paper work there, of course. I think we're done here, Miss Strickland,"

"Very good, Sir," I said.

We looked at each other for a few moments. I let him put his hand on mine, then I got up and left the office. I went back to my quarters, put on my parka, gloves, and grabbed my laundry sack. I was glad I booked some standby tickets for December. Old Broken Wing airlines was accustomed to dealing with lake sailors. I had always thought that they must be part of the same company that chartered buses for sailors. In fact I would not be surprised if everything in Duluth was owned by the same guy. He is probably sitting in Barbados, raking in the money and laughing his ass off.

I headed aft with my laundry. When I got out on deck, the sun was still shining brightly, and it seemed much warmer than it was at breakfast. I ran into Billy and Kenny heading forward.

"Don't go up there. The wolf is at the door," I said jokingly.

"Might as well get it over with," Kenny said.

I entered the port side door and went down the passageway to the steps before the galley. The stairs are steep and narrow. The laundry room is on the left, right before the engine room. I opened the door, saw nobody in there and the washing machine was empty. Great, I thought got here before the stampede. I put my clothes in the washer. Fortunately, I got it all in one load.

I started the washer and put the empty laundry sack on top of the dryer. Pete appeared in the doorway with a laundry sack.

"What are you doing?" he asked.

"I'm doing a load of laundry," I replied.

"You should be doing my laundry. It's a rule on this boat. The newest deckhand has to do laundry," he said.

"I never heard of any such rule, and I'm not doing anybody's laundry but my own," I said moving the detergent out of my way.

"I'm serious Nick!" he said.

"Yeah, so am I and I'm not your mother. If you want to take it up with the Captain, be my guest!" I snapped.

He threw the laundry sack down, gave me a dirty look then walked away. Just keep trying to mess with me ass hole, I thought. I sat in the laundry room and was reading my Casey Jones biography, when Louie came by with the officers' linen.

"Are those your clothes?" he asked pointing at Pete's sack.

"No, those belong to Pete," I answered, adding—"My load is in the washer."

"Well, he's gonna' have to wait. I've got Earl coming back here to do the officers' stuff," he said.

"Okay Louie," I said.

The two bundles of sheets and galley linen looked like four or five loads, easily. When my clothes were done, I took them out of the washer and put in a load of linen, since Earl had not shown up yet. Pete came by a few minutes later.

"Earl is doing the officers' linen," I said before going back to my book.

I heard Pete cussing as he was going down the passageway. After my clothes were dry, I took them out and put the linen in the dryer and put another load in the washer. I folded my clothes and placed them carefully in the laundry sack. I shook out and folded the linen from the dryer and put another load on. I will do this to help out Earl. Anybody else is going to fend for themselves, I thought. It was almost noon when Earl showed up.

"Hi guy! The laundry elves came by and did all the linen for you. The last load is still in the dryer," I said.

"Thanks Nick! I forgot all about it until I heard Pete cussing about it in the Rec room. I fell asleep back there," Earl said, sounding relieved.

"You'll have to sort this stuff out. I washed it as it was stacked in the bundles," I said.

"Good, the way it came in is the way that Louie wants it back," he said as he began taking the piles that I had stacked on the bench and tying them into bundles.

In another half an hour, we were done. I grabbed my laundry sack and Earl had quite a handful with the linen bundles.

"You need a hand there?" I asked.

"Oh, no. I got it," he said.

"I'll get the doors for you. Where you headed?" I asked.

"The Steward's quarters," he said.

"Okay, Watch your step," I said as we headed up the steep steps.

The Steward's quarters are aft of the engineers' quarters. They claim that there is no air conditioning or ventilation back there, so they keep the port holes open in the summertime. Since it is now December, I doubt if that is necessary. The cooks doing the laundry is an old tradition that goes back to the days of sail. The cooks were the only ones who had a stove to heat water. It is a job that our second cook could probably do without. I thought for a moment on how lucky we are to have two decent cooks on this vessel. The company ballyhoo is that the Stewards and the food on the great lakes are of the four star variety. This is absolutely true-in their dreams! The plain, simple truth is that everyone on a lake boat, on both sides of the border, is in some sort of union. Advancement and assignment to a boat is usually based on seniority. In the case of stewards, they are usually required to attend a school where they learn to make spaghetti from a jar and soup from a can. Whether they like to cook or want to learn anymore cooking skills is entirely coincidental. After Captains, they are the most talked about people on a boat. I have heard sailors say-'The Captain's an ass hole. The boat is a rat infested tub, but I stayed on because the cook was good'.

Guiddo is the best cook anywhere. Absolutely great in the kitchen. Top notch at meal planning and ordering the food. He likes what he does and is a sweetheart. We had four really bad stewards while Guiddo was on the Giovanni. Captain McCullough strangely forgot to pick up replacement cooks that had more time than Guiddo.

When we got to the Steward's quarters, the door was locked. Earl had the key and opened the door. The room was as large as the Captain's quarters but John and Louie had to share it. Earl placed the bundles on Louie's bunk and we left, locking the door behind us.

"I've gotta' take this forward," I said, indicating the laundry sack.

"No you don't. I'll take that for you. It's the least that I can do," Earl said.

"Okay, if you want to carry it," I said, handing him the sack.

As we walked past the after deckhouse, on the starboard side, I noticed that the north wind had died.

"It's supposed to be forty degrees by tomorrow," I said.

"Yeah, in a day or two, it will be that warm in Ohio," Earl said.

"We'll be back there to enjoy all the sun and fun," I said happily.

"It'll be nice to be back home, no matter what the weather is," Earl said.

I thought about how much I missed my friends at school and my former classmates that had graduated and moved on to marriage and families. We walked to the forward deckhouse in silence. I opened the passageway door and followed Earl as he carried my sack down the passageway and up the stairs to my quarters. I opened the door to my quarters and took the sack from Earl and placed it on my bunk. I went out and closed the door to my quarters.

"Let's see if we can rustle up some lunch," I suggested.

"Sounds good to me," Earl said as we headed down the passageway.

As we started walking aft on the spar deck, I looked to the right and saw another ship. A thousand footer on a parallel and opposite course. I wondered for a moment if it was my old boat, the Giovanni. I heard the whistle and the reply from us. I could see now that it was the American Voyageur.

"She's loaded to about twenty six feet of draft. Must be doing about fourteen or fifteen knots," I said when they were abeam of us.

"Yeah, they're hauling," Earl said.

"Full of taconite, I'll bet. As long as the weather is good, they'll make good time," I said.

We could see a few crewmen on deck but they were too far away to make out anybody without binoculars.

"I don't know anybody on there. Do you?" I asked Earl. Before he could answer, a voice came over the intercom.

"Nick, Captain Tommasson sends his greetings."

I looked at the bridge and saw him at the port wing, waving at me. I waved at him. I gave him the pirate sign then I saluted him. He saluted and blew me a kiss. That was very thoughtful of him to be looking out for me like that, I thought. After a minute, he went back inside.

"You old Icelandic pirate. Just can't give up the sea," I said in a low voice.

Earl and I continued aft.

"It's a great day," I said.

"My father always said-'Never judge a day until it's over," Earl said.

"Yeah, I guess there's some wisdom in that," I said.

We entered the after deckhouse and made our way to the galley. We waited at the counter for a minute before John came out.

"Hi Nick! Who was that hailing you from that thousand footer? An old Flame?" he asked.

That's a good guess on his part, I thought.

"No, that was old Captain Tommasson. He was the Captain on the Giovanni, back in '82 and '83. He was like a father to us younger crewmen," I said, adding—"I think I'll have a grilled cheese and a small bowl of that beef stew."

"I think I'll have a Reuben and a big bowl of stew," Earl said.

"Coming right up," John said.

The sandwiches were already made. All he had to do was ladle the stew into bowls and set the food onto trays. We picked up our trays and headed for the Rec room. When we got to the Rec room, we saw Andy sitting at a table by himself, so we went over to him.

"Hi guy. You mind if we join you?" I asked.

"Sure, plenty of room," he said, adding—"I see that you're also fully recovered."

"Yes,indeed. It's great to be eating normal meals again," I said.

I saw Andy pick up some pictures.

"What do you have there?" I asked.

"These are pictures of one of my old ships. Translated, the name means 'Star of the East'," he said, handing the pictures to me.

I looked at them for a minute.

"It looks like an old tramp steamer," I said.

"Yes, the shipping company was Indian. The Officers were British, American and Australian. Not too many like that anymore," Andy replied.

"No, I suppose not. Where was this taken?" I asked.

It was a picture of three African women, wearing grass skirts and naked from the waist up.

"Mombassa, in Kenya," Andy answered.

"Instead of being called 'The Land that Time Forgot', It should have been called The Land the Push-up Bra Forgot," Earl wisecracked.

"Those particular people were very friendly, but you never know in a place like Africa. You might have to cut your cables and run at anytime," Andy said.

"Is that where you became afraid of spiders and gave up the salties?" Earl asked.

"No, I'm not afraid of spiders. That was on our last down bound trip. We picked up some cheap sneakers in Cyprus then went to Egypt and picked up some bales of cotton. Lastly, we went to Israel and picked up a bulk cargo of Lentils. We went through the Suez canal and the Red sea, down the coast of Africa to Mombassa. We unloaded the sneakers and picked up some Ebony logs. We went down to Mozambique and unloaded the cotton and picked up some straw baskets. We went to St. Edwards, on the northern tip of Madagascar and shoveled the Lentils out of the cargo hold with the aid of buckets. There was this load of freshly picked bananas that had been left there earlier that day by another ship. So we loaded the bananas and got outta' there. Sitting out in the open like that, the bananas picked up these spiders. The spiders didn't find the climate of the cargo hold to be very appealing, so they started to migrate to other parts of the ship. The crews quarters in the fo'c'sle seemed to be a favorite area. The little buggers became active at night while the guys down there were sleeping. I heard the word for tarantula, screamed in five different languages while on the midnight watch," Andy said.

"Did they bother you?" I asked.

"No, there were fly screens over the port holes and vents in the officers' quarters. I would put kerosene on the threshold of my door. The little pests won't step over kerosene."

"So why did you leave the Salties?" Earl asked.

"I married Eileen and she was staying with her parents. About the time that she got pregnant, I was told that I had to be away for eighteen months. I told them to stick that job and I came to the Lakes of Amer-i-key."

"That tramp freighter doesn't sound very good, anyway," I commented.

"Africa is a very strange place. There's twelve inches to a foot, one day. On the next day it's ten feet to an inch. It's like your ruler is a rubber band. There's a lot of gun runners, stuff like that. I've seen times when you could buy an AK-47 or HK G-3 automatic rifle for a couple pounds of corn meal," he said.

"Wow! Me and Quaker Oats could do some business there," Earl said.

"I don't think I'll ever go back there again," Andy said.

"Are you afraid that you'll get seasick?" Earl said jokingly.

"The waves can be bad on the ocean, just like they can be bad here on the lakes. If you're the kind of person that goes running to their quarters in a little squall, then you don't belong on a ship any place," Andy answered.

"Did you ever go running to your quarters during a storm?" I asked.

"No, I never did," Andy answered.

"I did once. It was my second season on the Giovanni, back in November '83. We were half way across Superior, heading southwest for Two Harbors when this storm hit. It was a lot worse than anybody had thought. The lake was black and foamy. These waves dwarfed our thousand footer, I swear. I couldn't eat. The fear had everybody, but Captain Tommasson, crapping their pants. I went to my quarters, I prayed. I wrote a letter to my grandmother and put it in one of those clear plastic tubes for a big thermocouple. Captain Tommasson knocks on my door, calm as can be. He asks me 'What's wrong?' so I tell him that the storm has me feeling very apprehensive. He says 'Don't worry Nick, you'll live to be an old woman.' His Icelandic way of telling me that I wasn't going to die within the next few minutes. That was the most hellacious thing I ever saw and old Tommassan is the gutsiest, savviest captain on any body of water," I declared.

"Yes, a lot of sailors from Iceland don't seem to mind the big waves. I guess they see that a lot around Iceland. The sailors from the Azores were the same way," Andy said.

"Were you ever in the Azores? I asked.

"Yes, we stopped there several times for cargo and crew," he said.

"I heard that it's a very beautiful place," I said.

"In my opinion, it is. Most of the islands are still forested. The people don't have much money, but they seem happy. It hasn't been ruined like most of the Caribbean," he said.

"The fishing must be good around there," I said.

"Yes, it is. It is really impressive to see the dolphins and porpoises on their feeding migrations. I've seen thousands at once. Pods of different species, all around the ship. Giant yellow fin tuna, and killer whales also congregate around there. You would have to see it to believe it," Andy said.

"Any bad storms out there?" Earl asked.

"They get the hurricane season like the rest of the Atlantic. Most of the time it is just little rain squalls that keep the islands watered," Andy replied.

"I don't mind the squalls, it's the big ones I don't like," I said.

"Didn't your captain convince you?" Andy asked.

"All I could think about was the Edmund Fitzgerald. Look how quick the end came for that ship and crew. The waves drove her under and it couldn't come back up. Those giant waves were coming over our port side and completely covering our spar deck. One thing you don't take lightly is the power of waves like that. I don't have any problem with Gordon Lightfoot, but I don't want him writing a song about me being on the bottom of this lake," I said with a grin.

"I have some paperwork to do. I'll see you guys later," Andy said as he got up.

"Bring all that paperwork to the poop deck and we'll burn it," Earl said jokingly as Andy left.

I was finishing my stew when Earl said "I'm glad there's no big spiders on this boat."

"Yeah, I am no fan of spiders either. As long as they stay out of my way, they'll live," I said, adding—"There was this guy at college that was a prison guard in Arizona or New Mexico. I can't remember which state. Anyway, the younger guys had to work the night shift, so it was pretty quiet since the prisoners were locked up. Some of the locals would catch the tarantulas at night and put them in the cells. I guess it livened things up a little bit," I finished.

"Sounds like some real nice guys." Earl said, adding—"Gary was telling me about the scuba diving he did in the Florida Keys and the Bahamas. That Azores place sounds like it would be right up his alley."

"Yep, that sounds very interesting," I agreed.

"You wanna' play that dice game?" Earl asked.

"Sure we can for awhile," I replied.

The dice table was on the other side of the recreation room. Smitty and Al were over there watching the news program on the television.

"Hi, guys. Do you have the problems in the world solved yet?" I asked jokingly.

"Of course, it all has to do with drugs. Now, we take all the drug users and tell them that they got one week to quit. Meanwhile, we take some big useless island like Guam and turn it into a living quarters for these drug addicts. Everyday we send an airplane over to drop drugs to these people. When they overdose themselves to death, throw their bodies to the sharks. Drug use in this country will drop to nil, really fast," Smitty finished.

"Yeah, it probably would. I don't know about the constitutional rights violation, though," I countered.

"It would be less than going to prison," Smitty said.

"I think we're on a legal slippery slope here. Once the government sees how well this idea works, they'll do it with cigarette smokers. They'll put all you guys on an island and drop you unfiltered Camels everyday," Al said jokingly, then added—"We should send all these people with crazy ideas to Ashtabula, like Hamlet being sent to England."

"I don't think that the bosun on the Munson wants Smitty hanging around Ashtabula after his little tirade in Sault Ste. Marie," I said.

"He doesn't worry me none. He's my unworthy brother-in-law," Smitty said.

"Why is he your unworthy brother-in-law?" Earl questioned.

"Because he is married to my sister," Smitty replied.

It sounded like a family matter so I did not ask any more questions.

"I knew a girl in Ashtabula once. I guess it was ten years ago. A cute little thing with dark hair. She had been married for a year. I guess she had been divorced a year before I met her. She was full of fire. Always going on about Women's Liberation, that sort of thing. I was really attracted to her. If I could have calmed her down a bit we might have been able to stay together. I heard she went to Kent State," Earl finished.

"As Dixon use to say, 'A bastion of Yankee ignorance'," Smitty said jokingly.

We played the dice game for about a half hour before I started getting tired. I quit the game and told Earl that I had some things I still had to pack. I saw Kenny and the Chief working on the hatch crane as I walked forward. It was not unusual for them to be checking out the hatch crane. Most Captains are real stiff necks about the hatch crane. It better be working properly when it is needed. I entered the passageway door and went down the passageway and up the steps to my quarters without meeting anybody. I laid on my bunk and looked at the clock, it was a quarter til two. I closed my eyes and tried to think about the near future. I was not able to see things as clearly as I thought. I thought about the phrase-'looking through a glass darkly'. It took me a moment to remember where I had heard that one. It was at an inter-faith service at the college. The Methodist pastor was reading from First Corinthians Chapter 13:

> ***When I was a child, I spake like a child, I thought as a child, I felt like a child. Now that I am a man, I have put away childish things. What we see now is looking through the glass darkly; then we shall see face to face. What I know is only partial: then it will be complete-as complete as God's knowledge of me. Meanwhile these three remain: faith, hope and love; and the greatest of these is love.***

I had checked the passage in Eichann's Bible and it read: "faith, hope and charity". The next passage goes on about the attributes of charity while the revised standard edition has substituted love for charity in that passage. Since love and charity are no way synonymous, I sought clarification. No one seemed to know why love was correct and charity was not, or visa-versa. I eventually concluded that Christians were not the sticklers for translation that our Rabbi(s) are. I set the alarm for three-thirty, then read until I fell asleep.

I woke at three-twenty and shut off the alarm. I put on my work boots, parka and headed aft to find Earl and to tell John to save me some Whitefish. John usually does a good Whitefish so I figured that the entire crew would be back there hogging it all. I headed aft via the passageway door. When I got out on deck I ran into Smitty and Ron.

"Hi guys. What's new?" I asked.

"There's a whole bunch of trash up on the roof and there's still more coming," Smitty said.

"The Bosun said that Earl was going to help me with it, so it shouldn't be too bad," I said, adding—"Is engineering done with the hatch crane?"

"They had it started up and were running it back and forth, then they moved it back there and left it," Smitty said.

"Okay, I'll check with the Chief when I see him," I said, then I continued aft.

The hatches on the Gentry are ten feet wide and forty-four feet long. The hatch covers are one piece of plate steel with stiffeners welded on the bottom side. The hatch covers weigh six tons a piece. The entire crew probably could not lift one of the hatch covers. The crane travels fore and aft on rails that run fore and aft on the port and starboard side of the hatches. The hatch crane has a gasoline engine that drives a generator that powers the electric motors that drive the hatch crane and raise and lower the traveling beam that attaches to the hatches. I had operated a hatch crane on the Giovanni. The hatches were much larger and heavier on the thousand footers.

I entered the port side door on the after deckhouse and went down the passageway to the galley. When I entered the galley, I saw that John had a fresh pot of coffee and some bagels on the counter. I poured some coffee, and put a sliced bagel in the toaster, then I rang the bell furiously. John came through the swinging doors.

"Like a little child with a new toy. My daughter had this toy train and she use to bang the bell like that."

"I never had a toy with a bell so I am getting my bell ringing now," I said jokingly.

"I bet I know what you want. You want me to save you some Whitefish," he said.

"John you must be psychic. I bet you even knew that I would be back here checking out the side dishes and the dessert," I said.

"Of course, you do the same thing every day," he said.

"John it's such a delight to have you for a steward. Do you have any cream cheese?" I asked.

He felt under the counter.

"I'll have to go to the fridge. Be right back," he said, going through the swinging doors.

A moment later, Carl and the Chief came in.

"Hi, guys. Everything's shipshape with the hatch crane?" I asked.

"Yes, it's working fine. It will probably be pulled in lay-up and warehoused," the Chief said.

"That's good. Keep it out of the weather," I said.

John came back with the cream cheese.

"It's too hard! What am I going to do with this!" I exclaimed holding the package.

John and Carl began to laugh.

"That didn't come out right, did it?" I said.

"It's a rare complaint for a woman," John wisecracked.

"I'm sure I wouldn't know," I shot back as I was trying to cut the foil open with my knife.

"Oh by the way, Chief. The Bosun wants us to burn some trash in the tin man, up on the roof. I was going to use the basket to haul it up there," I said.

"Yes, that should be fine. The fire bricks are there also. Just be careful that nothing falls out while you're hoisting it," the Chief stated as a polite warning.

"Will do," I replied.

I finally got the cream cheese sliced thin enough to spread on my bagel.

"If you guys see Earl, tell him I'll be in the recreation room," I said.

"Sure, no problem," Carl answered.

When I got to the recreation room, Al, Buster and Billy were in there watching TV.

"What's on the tube, guys?" I questioned.

"A Canadian movie about some Indians torturing some Jesuit priests," Al said.

All I saw was some Indian couple getting it on while everyone else was supposedly sleeping. Not a lot of privacy in the old wigwam, I figured.

"Unusual style of torture," I observed.

"It's night time. They like to take a break," Billy said.

"Some lighter entertainment, no doubt. Fun times on the Canadian frontier," I wisecracked.

The movie turned out not to be too bad, but we could only see about twenty minutes of it before the watch bell rang. Since Earl had not showed up, I went forward with Al to relieve Ron and Hal.

When we got to the forward deckhouse, Ron and Hal were there with the clipboard.

"It looks like the Bosun has you and Earl burning trash this watch," Hal said.

"Where are the Bosun and Earl?" I asked.

"They should be along fairly soon," Hal replied.

"Okay, it looks good guys," I said as Hal and Ron signed the clipboard, then handed it to me.

I put the clipboard in the dispatch bag hanging on the roll top desk in the Crew's hall. When I came out on deck again, I saw the Bosun and Earl leaving the after deckhouse.

"Better late than never," I remarked.

"Okay, I'll check out all the rigging. I'll catch you guys later," Al said.

"Okay, check out Rudolph while you're at it," I said jokingly.

Al crossed over to the port side and I decided to meet Earl and the Bosun halfway.

"You have us on the trash burning detail this watch?" I asked the Bosun.

"Yes, unfortunately I'll need Earl forward," the Bosun said.

"The Mate said that the Captain wants it done by the end of this watch," I said.

"You should be able to handle it," he said.

"I don't think so. I don't think that the Captain wants anybody doing this by themself," I said.

He hesitated for a moment.

"Very well, Earl. You're burning trash," he said then walked away.

"Okay, I gotcha' out of any horse sh-t tasks forward. This is a two man job anyway," I said as we headed aft.

The tin man is a portable incinerator made from an open top drum which has a top that tapers to a vertical stack. The locking band is tightened with a bolt. Thus holding the drum and the top section securely together when assembled. The drum section has a crude makeshift door for loading the trash and to provide air for the burning. When assembled the device sits on fire bricks and is temporarily banded to an I-beam on the poop deck. We went aft to fetch the drum which had the top section and fire bricks stored inside it. Earl rolled the drum on its chine, to the starboard side where the boom and basket is. We went up the steps and I showed Earl how one crank extended the telescoping boom, and how the other one wound the cable in or out, thus raising or lowering the basket. I had Earl lower the basket to the spar deck, then I went down and put the drum in the basket and secured it with a small rope. Earl started cranking it up while I went back up the steps to the poop deck. I helped Earl retract the boom and remove the drum from the basket. Earl rolled the drum to the I-beam and started removing the top while I went to get the bander. When I returned, Earl had the top off, the stack and the fire bricks removed. We sat the stack on top and tightened the locking band to hold it together. We sat the tin man on the fire bricks, then banded it to the I-beam to secure it.

"Okay, we're ready to go here," I said adding—"Bring on the nudy magazines, back tax notices, demands for payment, love letters from secret girl friends that the wives don't know about."

"Coming right up," Earl said, as he brought two boxes over.

I threw some paper in, then threw some short pieces of lumber in to get those burning. I like some wood on the bottom to keep the papers from getting packed down in the bottom and not burning.

"Yes sir, we got it burning now," I said as I threw some more trash in.

The smoke was being blown astern by the slipstream of the boat.

"Gravy job, old buddy," I said as I sat on the spare life raft.

"Yeah, it's not a bad job when it's not too cold or too hot, and there's somebody to help," Earl said.

I lit a cigarette then laid back on the life raft and watched the tin man smoke while I blew smoke.

"Watch out for anybody coming," I said hoping that they could not see me from the Wheelhouse.

I was mesmerized by the smoke moving against the blue sky.

"You ever think about the future? If your life has some intended purpose?" I asked.

"No, I never bother thinking about those things. I guess I didn't go crazy in Nam because I never thought about the great life I was missing if I got killed," he said. "A man without a plan is not a man. That's Nietzsche." I said.

"Never heard of him. Did he work on the lakes?" Earl asked.

"I don't think he ever left Germany. Probably never left college either," I said.

"One of those guys that have been wearing a suit all their life, eh?" Earl asked.

"I suppose. He wrote a lot of books, and things," I said.

"Did he say anything else smart?" Earl asked.

"If a man doesn't know the cause he will die for, then he isn't fit to live. It is the normal and the usual to preserve the status quo. Therefore, progress can only be made through the abnormal and the unusual," I quoted.

"He must have been in Nam. It sounds like some of those poor shell-shocked souls I had to deal with," Earl said.

"Not to change this interesting subject, but how did you make out on the draw list?" I asked.

"I got hammered for 160 bucks," Earl answered.

"I got hit for 50 bucks, that I spent on the supply boat way back in August," I said.

"I don't know if I'll be able to take the plane with you," he said.

"Don't worry about it, old buddy. I booked the flight as a stand-by in December. That was last month. The plane won't even be half full. It's cheaper than the bus. I'll pick up the tab if you provide transportation from Alliance to Cleveland, for the party," I said.

"That sounds like a deal to me," Earl said.

"Put 'er there, shipmate," I said, holding up my hand. Earl hooked his thumb on mine and we shook hands. Earl tore up some of the empty boxes and threw them into the tin man.

"Somebody might miss those boxes," I said.

"They're supposed to put their name on them if they wanted them saved," Earl said. I looked forward and saw that the sun was setting directly in front of the ship.

"It will be getting dark soon," I said.

"Yeah, how long do you think this will take?" Earl asked.

"Another hour. We'll take the tin man down to the deck in pieces and hose the ash off. It won't take long to dry, then we'll secure it," I said sitting up.

"What do you think of the last election?" Earl asked.

"Same old, same old. Half of them are corrupt, the other half stupid," I replied.

"My, my such cynicism," Earl said, adding—"What does your friend Nietzsche say about it?"

"The state is a lie. Also we should be preparing the world for the superman. Something like your John the Baptist," I said.

"What are we supposed to do when this superman comes? Elect him for president?" Earl asked.

"I don't know. I guess I didn't read far enough. No group of people seems to be better than the other. We're all just a bunch of lying, cheating, whoring, boozing fallible human beings," I concluded flicking away the cigarette.

"That certainly covers a lot of sins," Earl said while dumping another box of papers in the tin man.

"All we can hope for is a good season next year. Or maybe I should say-Any season at all next year," I said.

"Hopefully I'll have the farm going by next year. You could come to Alliance and be a milk maid for me," Earl offered.

"Thanks. I'll keep that in mind," I said, adding—"How many cows do you figure you'll need?"

"Around forty. That should keep enough milking and enough in calves," he said.

"That would mean about eighty acres in corn and twice that in hay," I said.

"Yeah, that's about what I figured too," Earl said.

"That will take two men full time and at least a third man for half the year," I said.

313

"Yeah, I shouldn't have too much trouble getting some farm help," Earl said, adding—"I still have two tractors, a mower, hay rake and bailer. I also have that old two row planter and the single row picker. The plow and disc are still there. When my father had his stroke, my brothers sold the livestock but they didn't get anything else," he said.

"The cows will be hard enough to replace," I said.

I remembered Grandpa Eichann telling me about growing up on a farm in the Hebrides, in Scotland. All they could raise were cows and sheep. Sheep require less time and effort to raise and can stay outdoors most of the time.

"Maybe sheep would be better to start out with," I suggested.

"I figure I'll go to Kidron and get a dozen Heifers I can freshen. As soon as they have their calves, I'll be on the way," Earl said.

"That sounds good. You can sell your corn and hay to get enough money to keep things going," I said.

I took over for Earl and let him take a break. I had quite a roaring fire going. By the time it was completely dark, I was putting in the last box of trash.

"I'll go get us some coffee and let this fire burn itself out," I said.

"Okay, Nick," Earl said as he was laying on the raft.

When I got to the galley, John was in his usual jovial mood.

"Are you two going to come and get your supper?" he asked.

"Eight o'clock, just like always," I replied as I picked up the coffee pot.

"I don't know if I can hold it that long," John said.

"Well, if it's gonna' swim away, cook it some more," I wisecracked.

"I would like to get outta' here, so I can clean my quarters."

"Don't bother guy, When we unload the coal, all the coal dust is gonna' come back here. Old Cappy does it that way, so it doesn't get in his quarters," I said as I put the coffee pot back.

"I want to finish here, then turn in. I got a berth lined up as a relief cook on another boat. I should be able to pick it up by tomorrow afternoon," he said.

"That's gonna' piss of some people. Starting with the Captain," I said.

"The 'cruise ship' atmosphere never appealed to me. Let the shore birds eat at the greasy spoon. Louie will fill in until another cook is found," he said.

"We'll try to finish a little early. I guess they can't fuss under these conditions," I said, adding—"Catch you later," as I turned and left.

I grabbed another flashlight on my way to the poop deck. When I got back to the tin man, Earl appeared to have fallen asleep on the raft. I stirred up the ashes but they looked burned out. I woke up Earl and handed him the coffee.

"As soon as we get this secured, we'll go get some supper," I said sitting down on the raft.

"John is jumping ship."

"Yeah, he told me a couple days ago. I guess it will cause three other cooks to bump for their jobs. That's life," Earl said.

"I never been bumped from a job. Have you?" I asked.

"Oh yeah, when things get bad or a big outfit like the Cliffs line goes down the tubes. Even the lowest of the low like us have to start looking out," he said.

"Yeah, I suppose it will happen again," I said.

"Everybody says so," Earl replied.

When we finished our coffee, I set the cups on fire with my lighter and threw them in the tin man. I began taking it apart. Earl and I carried everything to the basket. Earl lowered the basket while I waited below on the spar deck. I took everything out of the basket, then Earl raised the basket and secured it on the poop deck. I rolled the drum and carried the stack to the fantail while Earl brought the hose around and began washing the ashes into the lake. After letting everything dry for a few minutes, we put the fire bricks and stack back into the drum, put the top on and secured it with the locking ring. We secured the drum to the railing with the straps and we were done.

Earl had more soot on him than I had on me.

"Well, if we take our coats off, maybe John will let us in the galley," I said as we started through the rear, port side door.

We could hear the noise of the engine room as we walked forward. When we got to the galley, John was cleaning up. Louie came out with our whitefish, chips and southern style Cole slaw.

"Oh, that looks great. Thanks so much, guys!" I said. We headed for the crews mess, just forward of the galley. There was nobody there, so we could eat in peace.

"Everyone must have ate and ran," I said as we sat down at the table.

"Yeah, a lot of people figured that this will be the last supper on this boat," Earl said.

"I hope there isn't too many more for you and me. I figured to be back in Ohio by the day after tomorrow," I said as I was putting lemon juice on the whitefish.

"Brad, Buster and some of the other guys were talking about going to the Mall and the Indian Casino," Earl said.

"If they go to the casino they better be planning on eating here because they won't have any money to eat anywhere else. Don't those guys ever learn?"

"They have a van that picks people up every hour by the Port Authority Visitor center," Earl said.

"They make it so easy to take your money," I commented, adding—"This whitefish is great. John really did a masterpiece of cooking here."

"He knows good food when he cooks it. That's what he always says," Earl said.

"I bet the cook they get here during lay-up won't be as good," I said.

"There is probably a lot of stewards going off now. Nobody will be too happy to work a week in Duluth unless they live there," Earl said.

"Poor Louie will have to stay here and do it all, without a porter to help him," I said.

"Young Billy wants the time. Let him put in the time like the rest of us had to," Earl said.

"Oh, this Cole slaw really kicks butt!" I exclaimed.

"Dixon always claimed that he brought the recipe with him from Mississippi. He said it's made with cider vinegar and sugar. He never liked mayonnaise," Earl said, adding—"An infernal Yankee concoction."

"Actually it's French. A French king introduced it after annexing the Island of Mayonne," I explained.

"I guess Dixon would have called him a French Yankee," Earl said jokingly.

"The last time we had this Cole slaw was back in the summer. Remember when Andy's wife was on board for a week?" I asked.

"Yeah, her and the Chief's wife Cynthia both had ridership the same week. We had to watch our swearing that week. It was hell, I tell yah," Earl said.

"The way you guys were gawking at Mrs. Botzum. You all seemed to enjoy her presence," I said.

"Built like a fashion model, with the waist-long, natural blonde hair. She definitely got our attention," Earl commented.

"She's a nurse practitioner. Smart as a whip. I talked with Eileen and Cynthia quite a bit during their ridership this past summer," I said.

"DJ's wife is a cute, feisty little redhead. You would like her, Nick."

"You shouldn't be looking at other men's wives. That kind of thing will get you into trouble," I said.

I remembered when I had to get Guiddo out of some crap in Conneaut. A red haired woman started flirting with him in a bar and her husband or boyfriend took exception to this. He pulled a knife and I had to break his arm. We were nearly finished when the Chief came in with a cup of coffee.

"Hi guy, is everything shipshape?" I asked.

"It depends on your point of view, I guess," he answered.

"No electrical failures, no conveyor failures, no turbine failures. No hatch crane failures," I said.

"I think we got all those handled," he said.

"That's good. We want to get unloaded and get out of here. Duluth in December, isn't my idea of a fun place," I said.

"Have you been corrupting Earl?" he asked.

"She's been teaching me about Nietzsche," Earl said.

"I've been on the lakes for thirty-two years and I never heard him mentioned until you came on board," the Chief stated.

"Blame it on academia. They put you in a class with a professor everybody absolutely hates. Ninety-Nine percent of the students are Pre-Med majors that see absolutely no reason to be taking this class. It's just a bum rap for the poor guy," I explained.

"You'll just have to reform academia. I'd love to help but I have to trim the dog's toe nails when I get home," the Chief said jokingly.

"Okay, I'll handle academia and you can set President Reagan straight," I said, adding—"This recent stock market crash really put the scare into everybody."

"It seemed to bounce back after a couple of weeks. Except for my pension, I don't have any stock, do you?" he asked.

317

"No, in fact, I don't. My grandpa Strickland always said that the stock market is a game for really rich people and half of them will go broke playing it," I said.

"My father said the same thing. The Great Depression turned a lot of people against the stock market. My grandfather had lost sixty thousand dollars in a bank collapse. That was like a million dollars back then. All in one bank. My father had a safe, I have it now. I only keep a couple of thousand in the bank. I keep gold, bonds and cash. No matter which way the economy goes I won't lose my shirt," the Chief finished.

"That sounds good. Some people I know have the YUPPIE mentality. They think that they can have it all as soon as they leave college. I don't want to have a debt like that," I said.

"My children don't know the value of money. In fact, I don't think they know what money is. They think that everything just falls from heaven," he said.

"Put those little urchins to work. They'll learn soon enough," Earl said.

"I'm sure they would if their mother didn't Molly coddle them."

"Send them to Earl's farm. He'll put them to work. No mama to go crying to. Right, old buddy?"

"You better believe it," Earl said, adding—"I'll feed them mush and fat back, three meals a day. That's what I had to eat when I was a kid."

"I had whitefish when I was living at home. The fishermen couldn't hardly sell it in the thirties. We traded for a lot of things. I'm probably the only one on this boat that's not a big fan of whitefish. Tomorrow, John is supposed to be having Honey and Orange Glazed Chicken," the Chief said.

"I've heard that he was jumping ship," I said.

"He'll be here at least until tomorrow night," he said.

"I wonder if we get anything else, except fried bologna sandwiches from him," I said jokingly.

"Fortunately we have two good stewards. Louie is a talented cook, so John always has to stay ahead of him," the Chief replied.

It sounded like sports and academics in college.

"I hope the relief cook isn't a real dog," I remarked.

"I heard it's gonna' be Jumbo Eggers," the Chief replied.

"You gotta' be kidding? That's not his real name?" I asked.

"The only name that I have ever known him by," he replied.

"He sounds like a real winner," I said sarcastically.

"He's barely mediocre as a cook. Doesn't get along with very many people. He thinks that he's a real intellect because he reads a lot of books about things like Atlantis and crop circles," he said.

"It's a good thing that me and Nick are gonna' be leaving," Earl said.

"Maybe this joker can come out to your farm and look for crop circles," I said jokingly.

"It's just the 'fun city' thing to do in England. Over here, you get shot or thrown in jail for trampling somebody's wheat," Earl said.

"This guy has probably been abducted by aliens," I wisecracked.

"They didn't show him how to cook," the Chief shot back.

"There was this guy in college, a real wierd Harold, his name was Tom. He thought he was a vampire. They called him Tom Collins. He would try to bite women on the neck. Honest to god. I don't know why they didn't do anything about it. He tried to bite me one night. I stomped the living sh-t out of him. He needed a dentist before he could bite anyone else," I said.

"Wow, sailors, lawyers, vampires, nobody is safe from you," the Chief wisecracked.

"This hillbilly burger flipper might be next on the list," Earl said.

"No way, guys. I'll be outta' here. All you lay-up guys can eat at burger barn. Earl and me get a steak at the Wharf and then it's Aloha big Kahuna. The dugout is all yours."

"You'll miss all the fun. The bus ride is always a kick. I'm taking a boat back home, myself," the Chief said.

"We're catching a plane to Sandusky. We'll wave at you when we fly over," I said.

"Wonderful. Well, it's been nice talking but I have to go forward," the Chief said.

"So do I. Gotta' get some sleep before we get to Duluth," I said.

"I'll see you guys later," Earl said as we got up.

Earl grabbed our trays.

"I'll take these to the Galley," he said.

"Thanks, old buddy. See you at docking," I said.

"Are you walking forward with me?" I asked the Chief.

"Why not. It will keep you out of trouble," he said.

"Are you one of those old fashioned sailors that think a woman is trouble on a ship?" I asked.

"No, in fact I have been on a boat with a female crewman on several occassions. There was a woman deckhand for a couple seasons. Usually it was a steward. The last one was five years ago. She was on for most of the season. Not all that young and attractive though."

"So Cynthia had nothing to worry about?" I asked as we came out on deck.

"No, she didn't worry about me. Of course, Elsa didn't inspire half the rumors that you do."

"My goodness! Maybe you shouldn't be taking this walk," I said jokingly.

"The only thing I have to worry about is Dave," he said.

"When he and I were coming this way, this morning, we got some strange looks. I feel like Madonna or something," I said.

"I guess people just like to talk," he said.

"There's no help for that, I suppose," I said, adding—"You're catching another boat back to Sault Ste. Marie instead of staying in Duluth during the lay-up?"

"Yes, I have a computer at home. I can do reports and orders from there," he said.

"A computer sounds expensive," I said.

"I didn't have to pay for it or program it. The company gave them to a couple people as an experiment. I had signed up so I got one."

"The Giovanni was gonna' be fully automated last winter. Everything could be checked on a computer screen. Some of the valves were already air actuated and the control valves could be set for a percentage," I said as we got to the forward deckhouse.

"This boat will either be automated or mothballed," the Chief said as we started down the passageway.

"I have to see Dave," he said.

"I had better pass. Send my regards," I said and I continued down the passageway. When I got to my quarters, I took off my parka and my boots.

CHAPTER 12

Happy Holidays, Duluth!

I took a shower and changed my clothes, then I laid on my bunk for a few minutes and read before I fell asleep.

I dreamed I took a work boat(a twelve foot aluminum fishing boat) with a mooring line, to tie off at one of the undeveloped docks around Lake Superior. I soon got lost in a fog. I have seen Superior completely enshrouded in fog. I could not hear our ship's fog horn and I could not see the sun, I had completely lost my bearings. A current seemed to take hold of the work boat and propelled it in some direction that I could not ascertain in the fog. I shut off the outboard motor to save the gasoline. After drifting for what seemed like hours, I started to hear and feel the wake of larger boats around me. Eventually the fog cleared and I appeared to be on the Neva River in St. Petersburg. I started the motor and made for the marble bridge with the lions, a familiar landmark in the city. I tied the bow painter to the bollard on the wall and killed the motor. I stepped out of the boat and on to the wall, then crossed over to the cobblestone walkway. I planned on crossing the bridge to the other side of the city, where the foreign consulates are. I did not know what I would do if someone asked me what I was doing there. I was thinking about what I would say-'Excuse me, I am an American sailor. I got lost in a fog, in that little boat and drifted eight thousand miles in a couple of hours'. It did not seem to be a very plausible explanation for my being there. I just hoped to get to the American consulate before somebody saw me. Far off I heard a church bell ring. I woke with a start. A small craft, probably a fishing boat, was ringing a bell. I got some water and went back to sleep. It was five minutes after midnight.

I slept soundly until I heard a knocking at my door. When I opened the door, the Bosun was there.

"Five minutes until the Aerial Bridge. We'll be off-loading five thousand tons at the D.M.&I.R. dock to reduce draft, then we'll proceed to the C. Reiss Terminal."

"Okay, I'll be there in a minute," I said.

The Bosun left and I got my boots and parka on, then went to look for a cup of coffee. I heard someone going up the steps to the Wheelhouse. I figured that it was probably the Mate. I went down the steps and headed for the night kitchen. When I got to the night kitchen, Hank and Al were there.

"You guys saved me some coffee?" I said.

"Got a new pot, ready to go," Hank said.

"Wonderful, give yourself a gold star," I wisecracked.

"Please, no verbal accolades. Write something out in check form," he shot back.

"Sure, I'll get the owners right on it," I said as I poured the coffee.

"Anybody heard what the traffic is like up ahead?" I asked.

"We're clear to enter. I heard the Captain tell the Bosun that there is another ship at the C. Reiss coal dock, but there is going to be plenty of room," Hank said.

"Good, I hate it when people dawdle," I said.

"You sound a little anxious," Hank remarked.

"Yes siree! I got a vacation coming and I'm taking it as soon as this ship is unloaded. Earl and I are taking the big white bird back to Sandusky," I said.

"I have a feeling that some people are going to be changing their minds and get off with you," Al said.

"It takes a dozen crew to move this boat. You'll be handling mooring lines and rowing this tub to Fraser," I said.

"I think we're going to LaFarge," Hank said.

"I'll be sure to be there to wish you bon voyage," I promised, adding—"Well, it's show time," I said as I headed for the door.

I went down the passageway and turned left into the Crew's hall. I grabbed my tool belt, put it on, then put my radio in its pouch and put on my hard hat. Before I went out on deck, I checked my watch, it was 01:28 AM Central time. When I stepped out on deck, it was not as cold as I thought it would be. All the deck lights and navigational lights were on. I went around the deckhouse to the fore peak. I could see the red and green lights of the north and south piers of the harbor entrance, beyond that, the lights of the Aerial bridge and beyond that, the lights of Duluth and the City of Superior. The air was clear and it was an impressive sight . A giant crescent of lights rising up into the hills that run right down to the lake. One of those places that looked a lot better at night than in the daytime. The City of Duluth is actually on the north side of the bay, while Superior is on the south. It's more of an estuary than a bay. It is protected by a natural barrier island that makes an ideal anchorage for vessels of the seaway size. The Aerial bridge is at the north end of the barrier island. After clearing the Aerial bridge and the headland, we would make a turn to port and head south then make a starboard turn and round another headland and pass under the route 535 bridge. The Duluth Mesabi and Iron Range dock will be on our starboard side. We will dock at slip seven to discharge some coal until our draft is only twenty-three feet, then we will back out and go further west to the C. Reiss Terminal and discharge the rest of the coal. We should be able to discharge at D.M.&I.R. in less than an hour and a half if their hoppers are empty. Four or five hours at the C. Reiss Terminal should be enough to finish unloading. The Captain should be kind enough to let us off there before heading to the lay-up dock at LaFarge.

I went back to the starboard side of the deckhouse. I heard one long and two short blasts of the whistle as we started into the harbor entrance way. The boat was slowing as we proceeded through the piers. As usual the Mate was practicing impeccable seamanship and keeping the boat right in the middle of the channel. In spite of all the lights, the city looked deserted. Not a city with a lot of night life, I thought. I hoped that somebody would be awake over at the loading terminal. The boat began to swing slowly to port, past the closed museum and the convention center. It took ten minutes to cover the two miles going south, then we made the starboard turn and passed under the highway bridge. There were navigational lights to guide us in the darkness. I saw the Bosun approaching with Al and Earl.

"Hi guys. I see they left the lights on for us," I said.

"We're unloading the 'Metallurgic coal' from number three hold. We'll have to self load to fill number three and put us back in trim.

323

Nick, you can drive the crane. We'll pull seven, eight, nine and ten," the Bosun said.

"Okay, as soon as they lift the boom, we'll be able to start," I said.

"Yes, we should get it done as soon as possible," the Bosun said then he left.

We would have to moor the boat when we get to the slip. Someone should be there to take the mooring lines. The coal hoppers are like grain elevators. When the boom is raised, the chute, which is tucked under the end of the boom, is swung down hydraulically and held at any angle that is desired. The boom is swung over the hatch of the hopper to be filled and the conveyor is started. All this handling of coal will certainly generate great amounts of coal dust.

"When we get to the hatches, it looks like you two will be using the hammers," I said, adding—"Have you ever removed hatch covers, old buddy?"

"No, I'm afraid not," Earl said.

"It's not that hard. As soon as I get the traveling beam down on the hatch cover, hammer in the pin, then get out by the railing where I can see you. As soon as I get the hatch cover down on the deck, knock the pin out then get away. Do you have a flashlight?" I asked.

"No, I don't," Earl said.

"There's extra ones in the Crew's hall. Make sure you get one that works," I said.

I was feeling a little apprehensive. A lot of accidents occur when handling hatch covers. Having somebody who is unfamiliar with the job and doing it in the dark, just made it even more dangerous. I heard the Bosun on the radio. I heard the Mate repeat his request for berthing at slip seven. He sounded a little irritated.

"It sounds like somebody is a little cranky, this morning," I commented.

"They better wake up over there. We can't dock until we get clearance," Al said.

Behind us, I heard DJ hollering for Gary. The Bosun gave the order to unshackle the boom. The shackles had been changed to a different type that could now be removed with an inch and a half socket on an air wrench.

"Well, old buddy, It's time to work," I said.

Al went with us to the Crew's hall and we got a couple of air wrenches out of the job box.

"Now, anytime it's near freezing, you should oil the hell out of these things or they'll freeze inside," I said as I picked up the oil can and squirted oil into the air quick disconnect.

I handed the oil can to Al.

"The geniuses also made the bolts the same size as the hatch cover clamps, so we don't have to change sockets out there," I said as I handed the air wrench to Earl.

I grabbed a short air hose and we headed out the door. Two stanchions and two cable stays held the boom when it was in the locked down position. One stanchion had to be lowered later when we remove the hatch covers. We headed toward the port side, Al would get the starboard side.

"You can work the air wrench, I'll hold the shackle. There are quick disconnects for the air by every hatch. Sometimes we have to beat the ice off them. Do you have gloves?" I asked.

"Just the cloth ones, but I don't have them with me," he replied.

"Those are useless anyway," I said as I pulled an extra pair of leather gloves out of my parka and handed them to him. "Those are extra large so they should fit you," I said.

When we got to the inboard stanchion, Earl sat the wrench on the hatch cover and put the gloves on.

"Plug it in here," I said, pointing at the air connection.

Earl plugged into the air line and into the air wrench.

"Check to make sure that it's turning the right direction," I said.

I knew it was not. He hit the trigger then looked for the reverse lever.

"This is the plunger type. When the plunger is sticking out on the left side then it will turn left," I explained.

Earl pushed the plunger and it turned left when he hit the trigger.

"Good, we can get it from here. You take off the bolts and hand them to me. I'll hold onto the shackle."

He began loosening the first bolt while we stood on the hatch cover. He handed the first bolt to me. I held onto the shackle while he loosened the second bolt. When the second bolt was off, I lifted off the shackle.

"These new suckers weigh twenty pounds." I said as I rested it on my leg and screwed the bolts back in.

"You need a hand with that?" Earl asked.

"No, I got it," I said.

I walked over to the railing and set it down. I saw Al and Ed working on the starboard side.

"They got it over there. Let's get the outboard shackle," I said.

The outboard stanchion was out near the end of the boom, between hatches seven and eight. Earl unplugged the air hose and headed aft. Earl plugged into the compressed air line by number eight hatch and we removed the outboard shackle and cablestay, the same way we had done before. The Bosun informed us over the radio, to remove the clamps on seven, eight, nine and ten. I showed Earl how to loosen the clamps and swing them down. I went forward to the Crew's hall to get hearing protectors, dust masks and another air wrench and air hose. I heard two short blasts of the whistle. I knew that the Mate was beginning a starboard turn to line up the boat with the D.M.&I.R. dock. When I got back out on deck, I saw Andy talking with the Bosun. He was taking the Mate's usual position when docking the boat. I heard the Chief talking to DJ on the radio. Al and Ed had started on number ten hatch. Earl was still working on number eight hatch so I plugged in the air hose and started on number eight also. I saw someone run by, but I did not see who it was. In a couple minutes, we had the clamps off number eight, so Earl and I moved to number seven. The Gentry had slowed to a crawl. Up ahead on the starboard, I could now see the huge D.M.&I.R. dock. Earl was doing well with the air wrench. Frequently, someone who is inexperienced with an air wrench will quickly get cramping and fatigue in their arms from holding the wrench too tightly. In no time at all, we had the clamps off of number seven. I double checked to make sure that we had not missed any in the darkness. We unplugged the air hoses and headed back to number nine, but Al waved us off.

"They're just about done, I guess. Let's take these back to the jobox," I said.

Earl nodded and we headed forward to the Crew's hall. As we entered the Crew's hall, I noticed that the Wheelhouse was even with the end of the dock, although we were about a hundred feet off. We put the air wrenches and the air hoses in the jobox, then went back out on deck. The Bosun was standing next to Andy. He waved at us to come over.

"Hi guys, what's up?" I asked.

"We're unloading into the trough. We'll need a mooring cable forward at number twelve bollard and one aft at number thirty two. Can you and Earl take the work boat and get that for us?" Andy asked.

"Sure, have someone up here to throw us the rope and there should be no problem," I said.

"Okay, we'll have someone standing by fore and aft," Andy said.

Earl and I headed back to the Crew's hall to get some rope.

"The fun never ends, guy. Have you ever moored with a work boat?" I asked.

"No, in fact, I've never seen the work boat used," he replied.

The work boat is a twelve foot aluminum fishing boat that you could buy anywhere. There are several two stroke motors kept in the engineers' storeroom.

"We'll use the polypropylene rope. We'll try to keep the mooring cables out of the water," I said as I removed two coils of rope from the wall pegs and handed them to Earl.

"Tie those good and tight to the loops of the mooring cables fore and aft.

"Right Oh!" Earl replied.

We went to the forward mooring winch and Earl tied the rope to the loop in the end of the mooring cable.

"Leave the coil of rope by the railing. They'll throw it down to us when we're in the boat," I explained.

We went aft and did the same thing at the after mooring winch.

"Good, now let's check out the boat," I said.

The boat was secured upside down, up on the poop deck.

"We'll have to carry it down," I said as we walked up the steps. When we got to the top of the steps, I turned on my flashlight. The work boat was just forward of the stack. It only took us a minute to untie the ropes and turn it over. I checked to make sure that the bow painter and oars were in the boat.

"Okay, old buddy," I said, rolling the boat on its gunwhale. "We'll carry it up side down. I'll get the bow, you get the stern."

"Okay," Earl replied as he moved to the back.

"Up she goes," I said as we picked the boat up over our heads and turned it over.

"Got 'er there, guy?" I asked.

"Yep, no problem," he replied.

"Okay, watch the turn when we get to the stairs," I said.

I felt Earl lift the stern and shift the boat, when I started down the steps. We got down to the spar deck with no problem, then headed over to the long gangway on the starboard side. We set the boat down and leaned it against the railing.

"You wanna' go back to the storeroom and get a motor? Make sure it has gas and carry it upright," I said as I handed him my flashlight.

"Gotcha'," Earl said, then he turned and left.

I rigged out the long gangway and lowered it. The lower steps went beneath the water. This did not hurt anything, since the boat was moving at a slow speed. We were moving past the taconite hoppers and would be nearly to the wall before we stopped. Earl returned with the outboard motor.

"Hang it on the railing there," I said, adding—"We'll get this boat in the water first, then come back up for the motor."

The stern began to swing to the right.

"Oh, Clever Chappy. If he gets it in there too tight, we'll need a tug to get out," I remarked.

"They got the money to pay for a tug," Earl said.

I had never seen the trough conveyor here. We could swing the boom ninety degrees to reach the trough. Let the Mate worry about driving the Gentry, I have my own boat to worry about, I thought. The Bosun came over the radio, telling us to get the work boat in the water.

"Okay, stern first, port side handles, down the gangway," I said, grabbing the handle toward the bow and swinging around so Earl could go first.

When Earl got to the last step before the water, he stopped. I took out the bow painter and held it in my left hand.

"Okay, real gently into the water," I said.

Earl lifted the boat and turned it right side up and let it slide past him. When it was in the water, I tied the bow painter to the gangway railing with a mooring hitch, to hold the bow at the bottom step.

"Okay, old buddy, grab the motor," I said.

Earl went up the steps to get the motor. I got in the boat and moved to the stern seat. I turned on my flashlight and checked the transom and the bottom for any leaks. Earl came down the steps.

"Step real easy. Only one person can stand up in the boat or it might tip."

Earl brought the motor back while I turned sideways on the stern seat.

"Let's tip it this way," I said as I pulled the propeller upward and allowed the lower end to slide over the transom.

I got ahold of the motor and Earl let go. The motor slid right into place, the mounting bracket centered on the transom. I tightened the clamps onto the transom.

"Alright, let's see if she starts," I said.

I flipped the switch to "On", set the choke, pushed the plunger twice, twisted the throttle halfway and pulled the starting cord. It did not kick over, so I pulled it again and it started. I gunned the throttle a couple of times to clear the cylinders.

"Pull the rope there and shove off," I told Earl.

Earl pulled the bow painter and the mooring hitch came undone, then he shoved against the railing and the gunnel scraped past the railing as the boat suddenly moved forward.

"Okay, we're underway now," I said as I moved the tiller a little to the left to get away from the ship.

As we headed forward, I brought the boat in closer so we could catch the coil of rope from above. Up on deck, the flood lights were turned down toward the water. The coil of rope was thrown down and Earl caught it. The Bosun was on the radio, telling us to moor at the number six bollard.

"Okay, guy. Just let the rope uncoil over the side. There should be enough to get there," I said as I turned up the throttle and moved the tiller, so we were heading to number six, which was almost in front of the boat.

It was less than a hundred feet away, so it did not take long to get there. I told Earl to grab the painter, while I grabbed the line. When we bumped the wall, Earl stepped up on the wall, went to the bollard and tied off the painter. I killed the motor and stepped up on the wall, bringing the rope with me. I handed the rope to Earl and we pulled it taut. We could hear the forward winch begin to let out cable, a foot at a time, 'Ker-chunk, ker-chunk'. Earl and I kept pulling the rope to keep the mooring cable from going into the water. In a few minutes, the big loop of the mooring cable was over the bollard, so we let it down on the bollard and I told the Bosun over the radio that the mooring cable was secured. We heard the winch again. It sounds the same, no matter which direction it is pulling. I went down to the wall and got into the work boat and started the motor. Earl released the painter and got into the boat and shoved off. I circled the boat around and came back to the starboard side. The Bosun told me over the radio to go to the towing hawse at the fantail.

When we got around to the stern, Ron threw us a coil of rope and we headed for bollard thirty two and secured the mooring cable as we had done previously. When we got back to the long gangway on the starboard side, I ran the bow right up to the steps. Earl got out and secured the work boat with the painter, while I killed the engine. The flood lights were not reaching over to us, so I used my flashlight to illuminate the steps as we ascended.

"This is what we get paid the big money for, old buddy," I said.

"I'm glad you reminded me," Earl shot back as we got to the deck.

The order came to clear the deck.

"Let's head aft and check the hatch crane," I said.

The hatch crane was just forward of the after deck house. When we got there, Fred and Al were looking at it.

"Is it ready for a test drive?" I asked.

"As soon as the boom is moved," Fred said.

The Chief was talking to DJ and Carl on the radio. From the dock a hollow booming noise began.

"They have started their conveyor," Fred said.

From forward, came a humming sound, then some metallic clanking and the boom lifted off the stanchions. A rattling sound, like anchor chains, started, as the boom slowly swung over the starboard side. It was almost Ninety degrees before it stopped. The conveyor screeched as the belt began to move. Within a minute it was up to full speed. From within the ship, we could hear more clanking as the cargo gates under number three were opened. I reached into my parka and pulled out a set of ear protectors, and a dusk mask and handed them to Earl.

"You may need these," I said.

A continuous roar began and grew in magnitude as the loop belt and cargo belts filled up with coal. There was not much wind, but it was blowing onshore. I was hoping that they would get the lions' share of the coal dust. Even with the light at the end of the boom, we could not see the coal fall in the trough.

"Doing this in the dark really sucks," Earl said.

"Hang around guy, the fun has just begun," I said.

For ten minutes the radio was silent, then the Bosun gave the order to remove the hatch covers.

"Okay guys, you got your flashlights?" I asked. Al pulled out his flashlight, but Earl did not have his.

"You must have left it in the boat," I said as I handed him mine.

We crossed over to the port side. I showed Earl how to hook up the air line and start up the engine. I showed him where the hammer is hanging on the side. I climbed up on the hatch crane and set the throttle at ninety percent and engaged the generator. Levers control the electric motors that move the hatch crane and raise and lower the traveling beam. Foot pedals provide a brake and a pedal that must be depressed constantly or the hatch crane won't operate. I checked left and right to make sure that Al and Earl were out of the way. I moved the hatch crane forward to number ten hatch. Marks on the hatch showed where to stop the hatch crane. I lowered the traveling beam over the ears on the hatch cover. The ears have holes through which the pins are driven. When the traveling beam was down on the hatch cover, I waved for Earl to come in. He turned on the flashlight, then hit the pin two blows with the hammer. I gave him the okay sign and he moved away. I saw that Al had the pin driven in on the starboard side. I pressed the lever forward to raise the traveling beam and the hatch cover. The hatch cover came up and cleared the hatchway. I moved the hatch crane forward and lowered the hatch cover between ten and nine. I motioned for Earl to come in. He shined his flashlight on the pin and hit it two blows on the forward end to knock it out of engagement with the lifting ear. I looked to the right and saw that Al was doing the same thing. When they were both clear of the hatch crane, I lifted the traveling beam and moved to number nine hatch. We repeated the procedure, except this time I moved the hatch crane aft and set the number nine hatch on the number ten hatch. The stanchion between seven and eight had been lowered, but that space could not be used to stack hatch covers. I put hatch covers seven and eight between hatches eight and nine. When we had the hatch covers off, I moved the hatch crane all the way aft and disengaged the generator and shut off the engine. Earl and Al joined me aft. I removed my hearing protectors, neither of them had put those on.

"Everybody still have all their fingers?" I said jokingly.

Earl held up his hands. It's not really a joke, earlier this year a deckhand lost four fingers when he got a hand caught between the mooring cable and the fairlead. Several people had been killed when they fell into open hatches.

"The coal dust isn't too bad yet," Earl said. I had noticed that the onshore breeze had gotten stronger.

"At least the wind is in our favor this morning. I've eaten enough coal dust," I remarked.

"My former father-in-law was a coal miner in West Virginia. He had all kinds of stories about that," Al said.

"Those get as obnoxious as the war stories," I said.

"You're right about it being unhealthy. By the time he retired at fifty-five, he weighed a hundred and twenty pounds. He had these big blue vein sticking out all over his chest and back. Just skin and bones," Al said.

"Did he get better after he retired?" I asked.

"He might have. He only lived about two years after leaving the mines."

"I heard guys talk about the coke ovens. The gas from them will kill the guys by the time they were fifty. They can keep that job, no thanks!" I said.

"How long is this going to take?" Earl asked.

"An hour now, maybe a little more," I said.

"You guys take a break, I'll stay out here. If they need us, I'll let you know," Al said.

"Thanks., we'll get a cup of coffee. Do you want one?" I asked.

"No, I'm fine," he answered.

Earl and I went through the port side door and headed down the passageway to the galley.

"You think anybody will be awake back here?" Earl asked.

"Not likely. I hope Louie put something out for us. All that running around in the work boat has made me hungry," I said.

When we got to the galley, there were two coffee pots going and a large tray of warm cinnamon rolls.

"How thoughtful! They must have known that we were coming."

Louie came through the swinging door.

"You're a little early. We weren't told to expect anybody for another hour yet," he said.

"Who were you expecting?" I asked.

"Who knows? Probably the night club crowd at this hour."

"Would they mind, if we took a couple of cinnamon rolls?" I asked.

"I don't see anybody around to complain," he said as he poured some coffee for us.

"Thanks, Louie," I said as I took a cinnamon roll from the tray, then picked up the coffee.

We went to the Crew's mess, forward of the galley. Even in there, we could hear conveyors.

"Vacation is so close, I can taste it," I said.

"I think that's a cinnamon roll," Earl said jokingly.

"Sweeter than this, old buddy," I said, adding—"What are you gonna' to do when you get back to the farm?"

"I'll have to get ready for next spring," he replied.

"Are you going to do any plowing this month?"

"I'll probably wait until the spring," he answered.

"All the farmers I know would do it before winter sets in. They claim that it's good for the ground and keeps the weeds down," I said.

"I still got some corn in the cribs and some hay in the barn. I could get a few animals now," he said.

"Do you still have that nasty goose Konker?" I asked.

"No, the coyotes moved in last year and all the geese disappeared. They didn't have enough sense to come into the barn at night," he said.

"That was a nasty goose. She would try to bite me whenever I was near her," I said.

"Yeah, the only one she would tolerate was me," Earl said, adding— "She was a good goose. Made a hell of a racket if someone came around the barn at night. There were some barns that burned last summer. I shot at some kids on motorcycles," he said.

"Did you hit anybody?" I asked.

"I don't think so, but I never heard about any more fires."

"You still have a job at Schaffers? I asked.

"I can always get a job there. I was in Nam with the owners son."

"I think about being there and all the other places I knew when I was in school. Sometimes I wish I was back there," I said.

"When I came back from overseas, it didn't seem like I belonged on the farm. Like that old song-A Stranger in a Strange land. So I eventually ended up on the Lakes. My father told me that the farm was mine when he died, so I got connected to my place on the farm."

"That's good. If it wasn't for my grandmother, I wouldn't have any place to call home. My lousy parents never learned financial responsibility. Even my grandmother gave up trying to help them with money, after awhile," I explained.

"They sound like my brothers. They blew all their money and are now trying to get their hands on my inheritance."

Buster and Joe came into the Mess hall.

"I thought you guys were suppose to be working out on the deck," Buster said.

"I thought you were," I shot back.

"Typical of the deck department," Joe sneered.

"Are you guys going to the casino after we dock?" Buster asked.

"No, we have to go to the office, then the Wharf, then the airport," I said.

"It'll be more fun at the casino," Buster said.

"I don't feel like giving my money away, even to the Indians," I said. "There's other things up there."

"Save your money and go to one of the titty bars," Earl suggested.

"Why don't you go with us, Earl?" Buster asked.

"No way, he'll get wasted and then we'll get thrown out right when the fun starts!" Joe exclaimed.

"Hey, that reminds me, cough up a twenty," Buster said to Joe.

"The only thing I'm coughing up right now, is phlegm," Joe said.

"Hey! We're trying to eat over here!" I snapped.

"Fricking Pete changed my bet on the trifecta and cost me four hundred and eighty one dollars! You should go and beat the twenty outta' him," Joe said.

"You're throwing away a great opportunity here," Buster said as Earl and I got up.

"Whatever you say, guy. We'll be sure to wave at you as we fly over," I said.

We returned the coffee cups to the galley. Louie was changing out trays.

"I think I'll steal this cup, since it has the ship's name on it," I said.

"The Captain is planning on handing them out to the crew at the party," he said.

"Darn, you'll have to wash them," I said jokingly.

"I pity your poor husband. I hope he doesn't have to take such abuse," Louie said.

"Sorry to disappoint you, no plans for marriage. All the stories about the Mate aren't true," I said.

"Oh, thank goodness, I like the guy. I wouldn't wish anything like that on him," Louie said jokingly.

"Not funny, but original, I'll give you a B plus," I said, adding—"I'll catch you later."

"Okay, be careful out there," Louie said and he went through the swinging doors.

"Well, let's go eat some coal dust," I said as we left the galley and headed down the passageway.

When we got out on deck, Al was sitting on the number sixteen hatch cover. The conveyor was not as loud as I thought it would be.

"Everything going okay out here?" I asked.

"Carl and the Chief went in and out, but everything seems to be working alright," Al replied.

"Good, let's go check number three," I told Earl.

As we walked forward the sound of the conveyor got louder. We stopped between number nine and ten hatches and looked in. The cargo hold had been filled right up to the hatches with coal. The level had not gone down more than a foot and a half.

"This is gonna' take a while, old buddy," I said as I turned my flashlight off.

Kick it in gear up there. Open up those cargo doors, I thought as I returned aft. After fifteen minutes, I was seriously thinking about finding a place to take a nap when the Bosun came back and told me that the Mate wanted to see me in the wheelhouse.

"I hope he doesn't think that I'm backing this son-of-a-bitch outta' here," I said as I stood up.

"Sure, you and Earl can do anything in that little work boat," Al said.

I crossed over to the port side and stayed close to the railing as I walked forward. About half way forward, I put on my hearing protectors. There is a portside door next to the bulwark, somewhat forward of the rear of the deckhouse. I seldom use that door, because it is too far out of the way. Just inside the door is a stairway that goes up to the Observation room. From there, another stairway takes you up to the wheelhouse. I arrived in the Wheelhouse still wearing my hearing protectors. The Mate was writing something on the clipboard then he handed it to Andy and

Andy left. The Mate turned and looked at me. We were alone in there. I took the hearing protectors off, folded them up and stuck them back in my parka.

"Good morning, sir. You wanted to see me?" I asked.

"Yes, we just received a communication from the office here in Duluth. Later on, probably at the C. Reiss Terminal, we will be receiving visitors. One of them is a Mister Larsen in Marketing and Public Relations. He claims that he knows you and is real interested in what you do on this ship."

"I run a work boat and secure mooring cables. I run a hatch crane and remove hatch covers in the cold and dark while he's safe and warm in his bed. I don't recall ever meeting any Larsen. Doesn't he have somebody there in the office that can tell him what a deckhand does?" I asked.

"You can tell him anything you want, I suppose. I'm sure that there will be somebody there taking pictures. You and him shaking hands, smiling, that sort of thing."

"Oh my goodness, do you think he'll die if I get coal dust on him," I wisecracked.

"You might want to wash up, put on clean clothes, brush your hair . . ."

"Too bad, I didn't bring my evening dress. Look, you tell the son-of-a-bitch that I've been up since 01:00 unloading coal. If he doesn't like the way I look, that's too damn bad," I said.

"I guess you can tell him yourself. I don't know what I'll tell the Captain," he said.

"He expects us to do our work. This is horse sh-t. He'll understand," I said.

"Okay, now that I thoroughly upset you, I want to tell you that I saw you handle the work boat and the mooring cables. Some people had to eat crow when you kept the cables out of the water. Great job!" the Mate said smiling.

"Earl did a great job, he deserves the credit," I said.

"I'll tell him, when I see him later. The Bosun has Ron and Billy to unhook," he said.

"Put your money on them to screw up and drop the mooring cables in the water. Both of them," I said.

"I'll take your advice," he said.

"What's taking so long? That conveyor is not running at more than fifty percent capacity," I remarked.

"The Captain is down there at the control console with the Chief and DJ. I don't know what their conveyor capacity is ashore," he said.

"Well, tell them to get it moving. Maybe I'll get outta' here before the shore birds wake up," I said.

"If we're lucky, we'll be unloaded by 10:30," he said.

"That would be great. I'll be able to get everything done and get back to Sandusky by tomorrow morning," I said.

The Mate put out his hand and I held on to it. Our eyes were locked together in the dim light for a few moments.

"You should keep your eyes on the boom," I said as he reached for my other hand.

I let him take it.

"Old Cappy won't like this in the Wheelhouse," I said.

After a few moments, he let go of my hands.

"When we get home, I won't be able to let go," he said.

"I won't want you to," I said, hoping that my words were true. We heard someone coming up the steps. I turned and started moving toward the steps, when the Bosun opened the door and came in.

"I'm sorry, sir. The Captain wants you to have a tug standing by in two hours," he said as a stepped aside to let me past.

"Very well, Mister Munson. I'll call them now," I heard him say as I started down the steps.

That was a close one, I thought as I went down the steps. I turned and went into the Observation room, then took the steps, port side, that I had come up. Before I got out on deck, I put my hearing protectors on, then opened the door and came out on deck. I walked aft very quickly along the port side.

When I got aft, Al and Earl were joined by Hank.

"Just the man to get this operation in high gear," I said.

"Your face is red," Hank said.

"Oh, I was holding my breath for a minute to avoid breathing in coal dust," I said, untruthfully.

"What did the Mate want?" Al asked.

"Later on, there are supposed to be some shore birds coming on board. This guy Larsen in Marketing and Public Relations says that he knows me. I never heard of the guy. They want to take some pictures and talk to me. Big Whoop Dee Do! I should give the pissheads a real earful, then they would probably leave me alone."

"That's our little Nick, dignified as always," Hank said jokingly.

"Eloquence and coal dust just don't exist together," I said, adding—"I'd like to get away before they even show up."

"Maybe they'll take you to lunch," Al said.

"No can do. Earl and I have a gift certificate for The Wharf, then it's Adios Muchachos. We're heading back to Ohio via the 'friendly skies'."

"Ah yes, my little chickadee," Hank said.

"I like the movie where he's sitting on a bench in a hallway and this tall skinny woman dressed in black, goes-'Young man, that cigar is slow death'. And W.C. Fields says-'What! Do I look like I'm in a hurry?!' Funniest thing I ever heard," Al declared.

"I saw George Carlin at the Palace Theater. I never laughed so much. I thought they were gonna' have to carry me outta' there," I said.

We sat on the hatch cover for another twenty minutes, when the Bosun came aft and told us that we could take a break until the unloading was finished. Ron and Billy would take our place.

"I think I'll get some more coffee and go to the Rec room," I said as I stood up and turned to go.

I knew the Rec room would be one of the quieter places on the boat.

"I've got some things I have to do in my quarters. I'll catch you later," Earl said.

"Okay guy, don't miss the fun," I said as I headed for the port side door.

Earl must have forgotten to pack his stuff, I thought as I made my way to the galley. Then again, I never knew Earl to be too fastidious about that. I have seen him throw his clothes into a heavy duty trash bag and get on the bus. I wondered what they would think of him at the airline baggage counter.

When I got to the galley, no one was out front. I helped myself to another cinnamon roll and a cup of coffee and headed for the Rec room. Ed and Al were there already.

"What's on the tube, guys?" I asked.

"KDLH Channel 3, in Duluth. The only thing on right now, except for the public TV station in Minneapolis," Al said.

"It looks like a soap opera or something," I remarked.

"A play. One of those Hallmark things," Ed said.

"Hal and Smitty are able to sleep with all this noise?" I asked.

"They're the bright boys that got quarters aft. I wish I had," Ed replied.

"Too late now, there's no more loading or unloading. You can paint the stack or scrape barnacles till you heart's content," I joked.

"What are you going to do for fun?" Ed asked.

"I've got to complete two more classes and I'll get my Bachelor of Science. I'll be in school until the end of May, it looks like," I answered.

"That should keep you out of trouble," Al said.

"Me! I never stay out of trouble," I said.

"Maybe the Mate can help you," Ed wisecracked.

"I don't think he has any plans to further his education. I haven't talked to him that much. In fact, I was on this boat for two months before I realized that we were neighbors," I explained.

"What a coincidence. It sounds like the alcoholic that ran into the whiskey wagon," Ed remarked.

"Jeesh! Don't you guys give it a rest. I just rode to Marblehead with him. I stayed at my own house. I assume that he was at his house, I don't know, I wasn't over there except for a short time on Friday," I said, trying to sound cool.

"A romantic, little tryst, eh?" Ed asked.

"No, in fact, I gave him a picture of his now deceased wife with my grandmother. He showed me some pictures of his son, Tommy. We had played together when we were kids. My grandmother rented a cottage at Lakeside during the summer. I only saw the Mate a couple of times back in those days. In fact, I had forgotten what he looked like," I said, secure in the fact that everything I said was true.

"Don't let these guys worry you, Nick. It ain't none of their business," Al said.

"When it comes to starting a rumor factory, they put the guys on the Giovanni to shame," I said as I reclined the chair. "I'll think I'll rest."

"Sure Nick. We'll wake you if anything happens," Al said.

I closed my eyes and tried to think of something pleasant. I though about the unicorn that my friend Mary-Beth has. It is Dresden Porcelain. I wanted to buy it from her. The unicorn is a Roman legend. When the

Roman army could not bring one back to Rome, they made up the story, that only a young girl, who never had a thought about a man, could even see one in the forest. I remember thinking about a man for the first time when I was ten years old. That man was David McCracken. I dozed off.

When I woke up, the television was off and I was alone in the Rec room. I checked the clock, it was 03:50. We were still off loading number three cargo hold. According to the Bosun's estimate, it would take another half hour. Unless they had opened the cargo gates further, it would take longer than that. I had never seen a boat self load while being pulled by a tug. Self loading might take an hour anyway. I decided to read a magazine for half an hour then go back out on deck. I found a National Geographic with a piece about a tomb found in Greece, which was believed to be a tomb of Phillip, the father of Alexander the Great. The tomb was intact after more than 2,300 years. Shaped stones stacked in a corbell arch, then covered with gravel and clay. The result was water proof and air tight. Very clever, I mused. The pyramids at Giza have sex appeal. No matter how you look at them, the angles formed by the corners, look the same. A deviation of less than two inches in length on the sides. Less than one minute of arc from true square at the corners. Less than half an inch deviation in true level from corner to corner. A real masterpiece, but it does not do a very good job of hiding the fact that a lot of gold and other goodies are contained within. At twenty after four, I put the magazine away and made my way back outside. The conveyor was still off loading into the trough. Ron, Bill and Buster were sitting on the number sixteen hatch now.

"You have a cigarette?" Billy asked as I approached.

I had never known him to ask for a cigarette.

"I didn't know you smoked," I said as I reached into my parka and pulled out a pack with four cigaretts and handed it to him.

He pulled out a cigarette and handed it back to me.

"So you guys have the sh-t job this time," I said.

"Yeah, maybe it will be getting light by then," Billy said.

"It won't start getting light until seven," Buster said.

"How long is this self loading gonna' take?" Billy asked.

"An hour to an hour and a half," I said, adding—"I heard the Captain tell the Mate to call for a tug to be standing by. That will be in another hour from now."

I pulled out my flashlight and headed forward to check number three cargo hold. It is twenty six feet from the deck to the cargo gates. The hold tapers for part of that distance. The top of the coal looked to be about ten feet down. I turned off the flashlight and headed back. I sat down on number sixteen with the other guys.

"They gotta' get moving or we'll be here until Christmas," Billy complained.

"If you're here until Christmas, you'll be paid for it. Probably get a bonus for working the whole season too," Ron said.

"These youngsters got nooky on the brain," Buster wisecracked.

"Who do you think you are, some old dude?" Ron asked

"I sure in the hell want to get off this boat. I got better things to do than talk to some big shot shorebird who normally wouldn't give me the time of day," I said.

"Who is this guy?" Buster asked.

"Some clown named Larsen, the Manager of Marketing and Public Relations. Claims he knows me, I never heard of him. Apparently he doesn't know what a deckhand does," I said.

"I'd tell him to stuff himself," Ron said.

"By that time, I'll be covered in coal dust and in a rotten mood anyway, so I just might!" I exclaimed.

"I wonder if he'll want to talk to me?" Billy asked.

"No, but he'll let you wash his car," Buster wisecracked.

"I'll get the short end of the stick no matter what happens," Billy complained.

"Cheer up, I'm sure he'll have some knee pads for you," Buster said.

"Oh, you're so clever!" Billy sneered. "By the pricking of my thumbs, something wicked this way comes . . ." Ron quoted from MacBeth.

"Yeah, it looks like the Bosun. He probably wants you to paint something or mop the floors," Buster said.

"Hi Munny, what's the good word?" Ron asked.

"The Captain wants safety tape around the open hatches. Nick and Billy can do that. You and Buster join me aft at the towing hawse. The Chief thinks there's a problem back there."

"We'll tie them off as a group or the chute will tear it off," I said.

"Yes, triple it and make it very visible. Also, before we start self loading, the Captain wants you in the forward deckhouse."

"For what?" I asked.

"I don't know, just be there," he said.

"When are we gonna' start self loading?" I asked.

"After the tug tows us outta' here, we'll anchor in the main channel and start self loading," he explained.

"Okay Boss," I said.

We all got up and started heading aft. We also had safety tape forward in the Crew's hall, but the Engineers' storeroom aft was much closer. It would take about two hundred and fifty feet of safety tape to go around once. We had to go around three times. A big roll has a thousand feet so one would be enough.

"Have you ever done this?" I asked as I handed him the tape.

"Sure," Billy replied.

"Okay, do you have a flashlight?" I asked.

"No, I'm afraid not," he replied.

"Okay, we'll go three times around then tie them together," I said as we left the store room and started forward.

"Is it true that you're going back to college?" Billy asked.

"Yes, a couple more classes and I'll have a BS. That should be in May," I said.

"I think I'll start this winter," Billy said.

"What college?" I asked.

"I was thinking about Southern Michigan," he replied, adding—"It's pretty close to where I live, so getting there shouldn't be any problem."

"If they offer your major, then it shouldn't be any problem," I said.

"My major is girls and parties," he joked.

"That major has a high drop out rate," I said.

"I was thinking about Architecture," he said.

"That might work."

"Is the first year really hard?" he asked.

"No, it's the third and forth years that are really difficult. The first year winnows out those who aren't serious about learning. The Party Majors, we used to call them," I answered.

We had arrived at the number ten hatch.

"Now, if the pipe stands haven't been mashed to hell, we'll be able to get the standing pipes in and get this tape on," I said.

The standing pipes were stored by being attached to the hatch coamings by spring steel holders. A couple were missing, so we had to take them from adjacent hatches.

"We'll tie the tape at the corners and wrap it one turn around at the rest." I told Billy.

Billy had no problem getting the tape on the pipes. When he had gone around the third time, I showed him how to tie the tapes together with the vertical strips of safety tape. I was sure that it would be an impressive sight when it was light enough to see it.

"Well, it looks like we killed this job. Let's take the tape back and check out the towing hawse job," I said.

"Some of the guys are not the assholes that you think. They're a little standoffish towards people who aren't from the area they live or that they haven't known for a long time," Billy explained.

"I've encountered that ignorant arrogance on lake boats for years. It may fly on the Lakes, but college is just like the military. You will encounter all kinds of people from different cultures and countries. You had better accept them and integrate or you just aren't going to make it," I remarked.

Billy was silent then, as we walked aft. He went into the storeroom and I walked around to the fantail. I saw Ron and Al back there.

"What's going on, guys?" I asked.

"Just a minor steam problem. The Bosun went to get the Chief," Ron said.

"Have you guys, seen Earl?" I asked.

"Not in the last hour," Al said.

There is a steam winch with a spool of cable for mooring and a spool of cable for towing. Ron and Al were pulling out some cable on the towing spool.

"Okay, catch you later," I said.

I walked around to the front side of the after deckhouse and I saw Earl sitting on hatch sixteen.

"Hi, guy, where you been?" I asked.

"I got swangled into moving some junk out of the pantry," he said.

"Some unwanted food that's going to the food bank? Remember that second steward on the Spirit Independent that found a hundred pound of T-bone and prime rib? Poor fellow claimed that he had to take it home because the food bank couldn't take it," I said.

343

"Yeah, I've seen captains, mates, porters, all kinds of people stealing food. According to John and Louie, this Jumbo Eggers is a thief. He's not even very clever about it according to them."

"He better get clever or the Captain will put him off, pronto!" I said. I checked my watch, it was ten after five.

"Let's check number three, it must be getting there by now," I said. Earl got up and we headed forward.

"Did you guys do this?" Earl asked when we got to the taped off hatches.

"Yeah, Captain's orders. I guess he figures that those shorebirds are so stupid that they will fall into an open hatch and get killed," I remarked.

"I remember a deckhand named Schmidt that came on drunk as hell and fell into an open hatch. It was a good thing that the cargo hold was half full of taconite. He got banged up pretty bad, but no broken bones," Earl said.

"Remember when we had to load wheat from that ship in Two Harbors, back in June? All of us in the deck gang, had to get down in the hold with those hoses. That was a frickin' mess. All we had were those little dust masks. We had to keep on top of the wheat by lifting our feet all the time. Hot as hell down there. I don't want to have to go down there again," I said, adding—"It looks like we may be finished here pretty soon."

I turned on my flashlight. The top of the coal was only a couple feet above the cargo gates.

"Let's get aft before the fun starts."

We turned and headed aft.

"We won't have to handle mooring cables, I don't know about the towing cable though," I said.

"That job was kind of a pain," Earl remarked.

"I've done it in a blizzard, with the water pretty rough. Except for the darkness and it being a little cold, this is about as good as it gets," I said, adding—"The Bosun should start screeching over the radio, pretty soon."

After a few minutes, Ed and Smitty walked by, both wearing hearing protectors.

"They're awake now, things should start jumping here, pretty soon."

Five minutes later, the Bosun walked by with the Chief. I lit a cigarette since Earl didn't seem very talkative. I wondered what I was supposed to be doing in the forward deckhouse, while we were shifting cargo to number three. I was wondering if I would get a talk from the Captain. I realized how strange it was now. It was hardly a couple weeks ago, when I became aware that the Mate was my neighbor. That his deceased wife and my grandmother had been friends. That his son and I were playmates when we were children. That he and I were subject to the natural attraction between male and female. If it meant doing something for the Mate, then I would do it. I would smile at the lowlife, groveling pig in a suit and tell him that I love working for the frickin' company. By the time I had finished with the cigarette, the conveyor suddenly came to a stop.

"It won't be long now, old buddy," I said as I walked over to the railing and flicked away the butt.

A horn sounded on the shore and the Gentry responded with one long blast of the whistle. I heard DJ and Mike over the radio. We could hear the clanking as the cargo doors slammed shut. In another minute, we could hear the humming and rattling sound as the conveyor boom began to swing back on board.

There were no orders to raise the stanchion. The boom would support itself.

"No stanchions, no cable stays and shackles this time," I said.

When the boom was centered back on board again, the Bosun came back to number eight and radioed instructions to the conveyorman, DJ for positioning the chute. When he was satisfied with the chute, he gave the go ahead to lower the boom.

"They'll have it ready to go," I said. "The wind is from the west. If we anchor out in the channel then it will blow the coal dust back here," Earl observed.

"Yeah, the captains do it that way so coal dust doesn't get in their quarters. John and Louie will be screaming when they have to clean up the galley again."

"They'll want me to do it," Earl said.

"No way, old buddy, you're getting off with me. Don't get paid for working when you can get paid for vacation," I said.

We saw Ron and Billy walk by, headed for the long gangway and the work boat.

"We might as well find a better place to watch," I said.

Earl stood up and we started walking forward on the starboard side. When we got to the long gangway, I looked down and saw Ron and Billy in the work boat. It took them a couple of minutes to get the motor going.

"Those turkeys are gonna' f-k it up," Earl said softly as Billy pulled the bow painter into a knot instead of releasing it properly.

"Big time, but let us be generous here," I said as we resumed walking forward.

When we got forward, Smitty was at the winch and Brad and Ed were at the railing.

"You have your gloves, old buddy? We might have to help these old men with the mooring cable," I wisecracked.

"Got 'em right here," Earl said, patting his coat pocket.

"Oh yeah, five dollars says that this cable doesn't go into the water," Brad declared.

"Ten bucks says that both cables go into the water. I'll put another five on both of them getting their asses chewed out for not wearing their life jackets," I countered.

"I'll take that money," Ed said.

"Hadn't you better wait a moment, Brad might want to give his money to the Indians instead," I chided. Brad stuck out his hand and I shook hands with both of them.

"I really hate to take your money. It looks like drinks along with our steak, old buddy," I said.

"Can't beat that," Earl replied.

The work boat had reached the wall, and Billy got out with the bow painter. Ron killed the motor before Billy tied off. Mistake number one, I thought. Smitty slacked off the cable slightly, so they could lift the loop off the bollard. They were unprepared for the tension on the cable and did not have a good grip on the polypropylene line either. They were pulled down to their knees and had to make a desperate grab for the line as it went shooting past them. The cable went into the drink with a splash.

"You might want to be standing by on the life boat," I called to Andy and the Bosun as they approached.

"Where's their G-D life jackets?" the Bosun demanded.

"They must have forgotten," Brad said.

"We're gonna' catch hell for this!" the Bosun snapped.

Since they seemed to be back on their feet, Andy told Smitty to pull in the cable. The winch started its usual routine. With every "Ker-Chunk" of the mooring winch, the cable was pulled in approximately a foot. On shore, Billy and Ron did not seem to have it coordinated with the rhythm of the winch. Being nearly pulled off the edge of the wall, they had to relinquish their hold on the rope, which went into the water with the cable.

"What in the hell are they doing?!" the Bosun yelled.

"A not very good job of unhooking," I said coolly.

The Bosun keyed his radio. "Get the boat back here. Forget the after cable," he snapped.

Billy untied before Ron was all the way in the boat, forcing Ron to jump for it.

"Nick, you and Franklin unhook aft," the Bosun snapped.

"Very good, Boss," I said.

"He'll have to start while the boat's adrift. Well, gentlemen, I think our bet is concluded here," I said.

"Wait, the after mooring cable hasn't gone into the water yet," Brad countered.

"Oh, you're gonna' try to weasel out of it now?" I accused.

"Pay her, you son-of-the-bitch," Ed snapped as he handed me a five and a ten dollar bill.

Brad pulled a twenty out of his wallet and handed it to me, so I gave him the five from Ed.

"Got your flashlight, Earl?" I asked.

"Right here," Earl said. I knew that Earl had left the life jackets at the railing.

"You want to run back and get the little red plastic gas can, old buddy?"

"No problem," Earl said.

"Wait a minute," Brad called out as I was leaving. "What if you drop the mooring cable?"

"To save you from another disastrous bet. If we drop the cable, I'll give you your money back," I said.

He frowned at my apparent confidence. As I proceeded to the gangway, I saw that Ron was turning the boat around and bringing it in. He bumped the steps with the bow and Billy tied off at the railing. Ron killed the engine and they both got out and headed up the gangway. I was putting on my life jacket and Earl was coming over with the gas can, when they got up on deck.

"I thought the show was after dinner," Earl wisecracked.

"Fuck off!" Billy shouted as he and Ron headed forward.

"He doesn't sound happy," I remarked, adding—"I can't imagine why, he got me thirty bucks. It's not his money, he should be happy about that."

I took the gas can from Earl and proceeded down the gangway while Earl put his life jacket on. I stepped into the boat and went back to the motor. I took the gas cap off the motor and poured some gasoline into the tank with one hand while holding the flashlight with my other hand. I replaced the gas cap and sat the gas can under the transom seat. Earl was coming down the steps while I started the motor. When Earl got settled in the bow, I told him to cast off. As soon as he got the bow painter in and shoved us off, I gunned the throttle and brought us around in a clockwise circle to number thirty-two bollard. I nosed gently into the wall and Earl climbed out and tied off at the bollard. I killed the engine and climbed out myself. I showed Earl how to hold the rope with your hands behind you and let the winch pull your hands in front of you.

"We've got a lot more cable out than they had forward, so it's gonna' take both of us to hold it. You stand behind me and do like I do," I instructed.

I told them on the radio that we were ready. The Bosun slacked the cable and we unhooked. I put my left foot up on the bollard to brace myself and held the rope back while Earl did the same. As the winch started pulling, I slid my hands and pulled in unison with the winch. Earl was having trouble getting it, so I moved around to the front side of the bollard to help hold the tension on the cable.

"You have to get with the rhythm of the winch. You can't hold it with brute force. That's what messed them up," I said.

"I got it now, Nick," Earl said as he pulled the cable behind me.

"Okay, old budy, we'll move back around slowly," I said.

Earl was handling the rope properly by the time we got back behind the bollard. It took less than two minutes to get the cable in and the winch stopped. We dropped the rope and they pulled it in. The Bosun told us to come back on board. I told him that I wanted to clear the motor on the way in. I climbed into the boat and started the motor, then I waved to Earl to untie. Earl got in at the bow and I told him to shove us off and to take my flashlight as I handed it to him. I gunned the motor and went around the stern to the port side and opened it up all the way, while going forward along the port side. After clearing the bow, I made a quick turn to the right and came around the bow and down the starboard side. When I got past the gangway. I cut the throttle somewhat and made another right turn and came real close to the hull on the starboard side and nosed it gently into the gangway steps. Earl tied off and I cut the motor. The Bosun told us over the radio to bring the boat up on deck. I loosened the motor and picked it up off the transom. Earl grabbed it and stepped out of boat and started up the gangway. I grabbed the gas can and followed him. When we got up on deck, Al and Ed said they would get the boat as they walked by us.

"Well, let's take this stuff aft," I said to Earl.

We headed aft to the engineers' storeroom. We ran into Buster and Joe at the after deckhouse.

"What was that little maneuver?" Joe sneered.

"What you talking about, Willis?" I replied.

"That little run around the boat. Was that some kinda' victory lap?"

"For your information, I was clearing the crap out of the outboard. But since you're nobody's boss, I guess you don't have to know that," I snapped.

They went on their way without saying anything else.

"Some people are gonna' be real assholes," Earl said.

"He still remembers how hard hard you can hit," I remarked.

We heard the air horn of a tug. "I wonder who they got to do that?" Earl asked.

"Probably Great Lakes Towing. That's the outfit they usually call," I said.

"I meant, who is handling the cable aft," Earl said.

"Oh, anybody can do that. They come right under the stern. Somebody has to throw the rope to them and they pull the cable out and hook it right to their cleat. From then on it's up to the tug captain and the Wheelhouse," I replied.

We secured the outboat motor and the gas can in the storeroom. "Let's go back there and see what's happening," I suggested.

When we got to the fantail, the Bosun, Hal and Smitty were there.

"Everything shipshape guys?" I asked.

"Yes, so far," the Bosun replied.

"The doodle bug is here, right on time," I observed.

"The Captain would like to see you in the Wheelhouse as soon as possible," the Bosun said.

"Jeesh, what did I do now?" I said, adding—"I better get up there before somebody blows a gasket. See you later," I said to Earl.

I went forward on the starboard side and saw nobody but Al and Ed. They were tying the work boat to the railing. I went up the steps on the starboard side and took the forward door into the Wheelhouse. When I entered, the Mate was on the radio to the tug boat. The Captain motioned for me to sit down in the vinyl chair. I sat down and listened to the Mate talking to the Bosun as the tug boat hooked up. After the Mate explained what he wanted done to the tug boat captain, there did not seem to be a lot of talking between them. The tug captain was an old hand at this and it did not take more than ten minutes to get us out of there and facing west in the main channel at a dead stop. From the radio communications, I could tell that the tug had backed up to us and unhooked. I heard the horn blow once and an answering blast on the whistle from us. When the tug boat passed by the Wheelhouse, I looked at my watch, it was 06:15. The Bosun called on the phone and said that they were ready to start the self loading of number three. The Mate instructed him to proceed. We could hear DJ and Mike talking. The screech, as the conveyor started moving, and the muffled roar building as the coal filled up the conveyor belts. I looked astern and could see coal dust coming out of the open hatches after a minute. The Mate instructed the Bosun to report every five minutes, then he sat down the phone.

They both turned and looked at me.

"Miss Strickland, how are you this morning?" the Captain asked.

"Very well, Sir. Thank you," I replied.

"Unfortunately, I had Mister Munson, Mister Karan and Mister Curtis in here a while ago. I had to reprimand them for not following procedures," he said.

"That's very understandable, sir. There were some very scary moments out there. I believe the lack of experience was evident," I replied.

"I quite agree. In contrast, you and Mister Franklin did a very good job. I was very impressed."

"Thank you sir, that is very kind," I said.

"Now, I believe that Mister McCracken told you earlier that we would be having visitors from the office here in Duluth," he said.

"Yes, Sir, he did indeed," I replied in a pleasant tone.

"You have some objective to meeting these people and being photographed?" he asked.

"Whatever objections I had at two o'clock this morning, I don't have now," I stated.

"Mister McCracken seemed to think that you were adamant in your objections," he said.

"Entirely my fault, Sir. I was messing with his head, in a friendly sort of way," I said.

They both were looking at me now.

"Now, there are no union regulations or company policy that requires you to participate in any public relations activities," the Captain stated.

"Yes, Sir. As long as it doesn't prevent me from taking my vacation on time, I have no objections," I stated.

"Very good. You're fine the way you are now. I wouldn't want you to get any coal dust on you and put you through the additional trouble of getting cleaned up hastily. After we get to the C. Reiss Terminal, they could show up anytime. I have already instructed the Bosun to have another deckhand available, if need be," he said.

"As you wish, Sir," I said.

"Good, I believe that Mister McCracken has some administrative matters to discuss with you. You can use my office," the Captain offered.

"Very good, Sir," I said.

The Mate and the Captain got up, so I stood up.

"This way, Miss Strickland," the Mate said as we headed for the 'little stairs' that lead down to the passageway where we were waiting yesterday, to sign articles. The Mate was silent when we entered the Captain's office, he closed the door.

"You did a hundred and eighty on me!"

"Did that surprise you?" I asked.

"Somewhat," he replied.

"Really, after being married for all those years, you didn't realize that a woman will do something just because a man wants her to?" I asked.

"I didn't think you would give in that easy."

"Oh, anything for the Captain. He's such a charming fellow, don't you think?" I asked.

"Speaking of Captains. Who is this Captain Tommasson?"

"He was the Captain of the Giovanni, back in 1983. He was like a father to us younger crewmen," I said.

"Just a father figure, eh?" he asked.

"Well, there was an occasion back in July, but I won't go into any details. I wouldn't want to get you aroused while you're trying to attend to this administrative matter," I said.

He went over to the Captain's roll top desk and looked through some papers.

"You got something on your mind?" I asked.

"In July, we were waiting up here for twenty two hours to load. I had a dinner date will Mrs. Marlowe in Personnel. She's probably about ten years younger than me, a bit overweight, very nice to deal with. She kept me out of some trouble in the past. She hadn't had a man in the five years, since her divorce."

"Oh, the old sympathy sex," I said.

"Something like that, I suppose," he said as he brought some papers over to me.

"A tall, handsome fellow like you, I'm sure she couldn't resist," I said as I took the papers from him.

He grabbed me and pulled me against him. I let him hold me for a few moments.

"Really, Dave! A quicky in the Captain's quarters is not an administrative matter," I managed to say, adding—"Somebody needs a hug this morning. Do you have any of those inter-office mail envelopes?"

He let go and reached up for an envelope in the mailbox by the door and handed one to me. As I slipped the papers into it, I noticed that last thing written on it was-C. Hunt, Personnel.

"Already addressed, how convenient," I said.

"All you have to do is sign those. Since you won't be working over the winter, the discharge will be mailed when your vacation is used up," he said.

"Is my face red?" I asked.

"Your cheek is on this side," he said.

"Oh, your whiskers got me. My face has always been sensitive to that! I'll have to go hide myself, you booger."

"You think the other guys will notice?" he asked.

"They noticed this morning. I had to say that I was holding my breath to avoid breathing coal dust," I said.

"That sounds plausible," he said.

"I can go to my quarters. The Captain is done now?" I asked.

"Yes, that is all. Try not to get dirty," he said.

"That sounds fine, coming from you," I shot back, smiling.

"By the way, the Captain says that you may come up to the Wheelhouse anytime and observe," he said as he opened the door.

"I don't know about that. Some of the guys up there, just can't keep their hands off of me," I said jokingly, then I headed down the passageway.

I got to my quarters without being seen by anyone. The sound of the conveyor was not any louder there than it was in the Wheelhouse. I changed my clothes and put on my last set of clean work clothes. I washed up and brushed my hair. I laid on my bunk and wondered if I could get aft later to get breakfast. If self loading in number three was done, maybe I could get aft without being ankle deep in coal dust. I was sure that Louie would have something decent for us. I closed my eyes and tried to to remember when I had met a guy named Larsen. Grandpa Eichann had a Larsen motor boat that he kept in Marblehead. His relatives got it when he died. In a few moments, I dozed off. I was woke up about a half an hour later by the ship's whistle. Another ship must have been passing us. I tried to sleep for fifteen minutes, but I could not. When I looked out the porthole, I saw it was getting light. I was reading Newsweek for about ten minutes when the conveyor stopped. Amen and hallelujah, I thought. Someone must have looked over the side to check the Plimsoll lines.

In a minute, I heard one blast of the whistle and the boat began to move. I had not heard us weigh anchor, they must have done that while I slept. The C. Reiss Terminal is about two miles west of our location. By the time we got there, it would be nearly full light. The sky was clear so there would not be any problems with fog. I decided to go to the Wheelhouse and watch the docking from up there. I passed the Chief and DJ in the passageway.

"How's it going guys?" I asked.

"Not too bad, nothing overheating yet," the Chief replied.

"Melt it down if you have to. Get us outta' here by noon," I said.

"Sure, no problem. Is there anything else, your highness?" DJ asked.

"Keep the coal dust down, it clashes with my mascara," I said as I passed them.

When I got to the Wheelhouse, the Mate and the Captain were there, Pete was at the wheel, Mike at the chadburn. The Captain motioned for me to take the watchman's chair. The Mate was on the radio talking to someone at the terminal. After a few minutes, he put the receiver down.

"It looks like fortune smiles upon you today, Miss Strickland," the Captain said.

"How's that, Sir?" I asked.

"Our visitors will be here earlier than we thought. Also, the MV Giovanni will be next to us when we dock," he said.

"That is a happy coincidence," I said, smiling.

"The weather is good and the hoppers are empty. No moves will be required once we dock," he said.

"It sounds like a fast unloading," I ventured.

"Yes, we've dropped five thousand tons already, so we can get it in there and run at full capacity on the conveyor," he said, adding—"Are you getting off right away?"

"Yes, I have some business with the office. Earl and I are having a steak dinner at 'The Wharf' and then we'll catch a plane back to Sandusky," I said.

"I'm sure I can get one of our visitors to take you to the office," he said.

"Very good of you, sir," I said.

"Not at all," he said

The Mate gave the order for a starboard turn. The boat slowly swung to the right. I could see the stern of the Giovanni ahead. We would be docking at the slip to the right of her.

"We're taking the boat straight in this time," the Captain said.

"Back one third," the Mate ordered.

"Back one third," Mike repeated, as he moved the lever on the Chadburn.

"There is a train there to take the coal right from the hopper," the Captain said, adding—"With the boom up high like that, we should miss most of the coal dust."

I turned and looked aft. I could see my Compadres in the deck gang, hosing down the deck.

"Some of our guests want to see the cargo hold," the Captain said.

"We got it taped up pretty good," I said.

We passed just to the left of the red flashing buoy. We had slowed considerably and were lined up perfectly for the next buoy.

"Back slow," the Mate said, adding—"Stand by to the raise the boom," over the intercom.

We could hear Andy talking to the Bosun on the radio. In a few minutes, we were at a full stop next to the giant hoppers. Ron and Al went down to the dock via the boarding ladder. In no time at all, we were moored to Andy's satifiaction. The boom was lifted up and swung over to the nearest hopper. From up here in the Wheelhouse, we could hardly hear the clanking and the rattling that I knew they could hear down on deck. The chute was lowered into the top of the hopper. DJ was talking to the Chief over the radio, then a few seconds later, the conveyor started. When I looked at the conveyor, I saw that the Christmas lights were on. It looked like Santa and his reindeers had taken off in flight.

"Merry Christmas, Duluth," I said softly.

The Captain handed me the receiver for the intercom. I keyed the microphone and said "Happy Holidays, Duluth!" The Captain smiled in approval and winked at me.

"A load of coal for Duluth's Christmas stockings," he said. We all chuckled, knowing that it was stated in good humor.

Nick's Interview

The muffled roar began as the conveyor filled up with coal. From up here in the Wheelhouse, we could see the coal on the conveyor belt as it ascended to the top of the hopper. The Mate was writing something in the ship's manifest.

"Are you going aft for breakfast, Miss Strickland?" The captain asked.

"The coal dust doesn't look too bad. I was thinking about going aft in a little while," I said.

"Mr. McCracken should be done in a few minutes. Perhaps he could escort you," he said.

I was beginning to feel like a guest on this ship instead of a deckhand.

"That would be fine with me, Sir," I said.

When the Mate was done writing, he took the papers off the clipboard and put them in a binder.

"Let's go aft and see what Louie has cooked up," he said.

"I'll bet it's fried bologna, breakfast, lunch and dinner," I joked as we went out the door.

"I'll have to get my coat," he said.

"So do I. Shall we meet in the Observation room?" I asked.

"Yes, I shouldn't be long," he said as we were going down the steps.

When we got to the bottom of the steps, I headed for my quarters and he went the other way. I put on my parka, but I did not zip it. I looked in the mirror, before I realized that I was doing it. I checked my face to make sure I was not turning red. I left my quarters and went to the Observation room. No one was in the Observation room when I arrived, so I sat down on the bench and waited. It took the Mate a few minutes to get there.

"Hi guy, you look a little tired," I said.

"The Captain's giving me a couple hours off." I got up from the bench and we headed for the port side door.

"Let's take the scenic route along the port side railing," I suggested.

"That sounds good," he said. We went through the door and turned left and headed down the steps.

"It has been a very rough morning for you," I said.

"Also for you," he answered.

"Oh no, I had a much smaller boat to steer. Handling a big ship like this must be a tremendous load on your mind," I said as we went through the door onto the deck.

"I remember when I was in college. Sometimes I'd come home at six thirty and just flop down on the bed and sleep until two or three in the morning. I never thought that using your head could tire you out like that," I said, loud enough to be heard over the noise of the conveyor.

"I guess our studies at the Academy weren't that rigorous," he said.

"Everybody hits the wall sometime. Not to change the subject, but Rudolf is making a lot of noise up there," I said.

"I'm surprised the vibration doesn't shake all those lights to pieces," he said.

"It would be really impressive if it was dark. I bet the Captain takes it home and puts it in his front yard," I said.

Halfway aft, I noticed that the Chief and DJ following us. I turned around and said, "Hi, guys."

"You two taking a stroll?" DJ remarked.

"No, we're getting some chow. The Mate here says he had to row this boat since the Aerial bridge and he's hungry as hell," I said jokingly.

"We're going to the tunnel aft," the Chief said.

"Well, don't get dirty. We'll have some visitors later," I said.

"Yes, I heard that they only want to talk to you," the Chief said.

"Yes, I don't know what the distinction is. I've been in more bar fights, perhaps," I ventured to guess.

"God only knows," the Chief replied.

"As long as they don't hold me up, they can ask anything they want," I said.

"They can ask her to work the rest of the season here in Duluth," the Mate said.

"You're scaring me here, Dave," I said jokingly. We entered the port side door of the after deckhouse.

"I bet it's fried bologna for breakfast, lunch and dinner," I said.

"Do you think the Captain will tolerate that?" the Mate asked.

"Sure, he can get the big shots to take him to breakfast," I said. When we entered the galley, Louie and John were both there.

"Hi guys, surprise us this morning," I said.

"Fried bologna sandwiches are all we have today," John said jokingly.

"That joke got around fast," I said.

"Anyone who makes jokes about my cooking shouldn't expect pancakes and sausage," John said, smiling.

"I've done nothing but praise your cooking. Haven't I, Sir?" I asked the Mate.

"Oh yes, I can vouch for that," the Mate replied.

"If your cooking was bad, I'd have thrown it back at you," I said, trying to sound incredulous.

"Oh yes, I can vouch for that also," the Mate said.

"Give me a couple of pancakes and some orange juice, Maestro, if you please."

"We have some turkey sausage guaranteed to be kosher by some Rabbi, somewhere," John said.

"Okay, a couple of those too," I said as I picked up the coffee pot.

"I'll have the pancakes with the link sausages," the Mate said.

"Okay, we'll have those to you in a couple of minutes," John said.

"Oh, we're going back to the Officers' Mess?" I asked.

"Sure, why not," the Mate answered. We grabbed our coffee and headed for the Officers' Mess.

"Clear weather for the whole day?" I asked.

"Yes, into tomorrow," the Mate replied.

"Good, there won't be any delays in the flights," I said.

When we entered the Officers' Mess, no one was in there.

"We have it all to ourselves," I said, as the Mate pulled out a chair for me.

"Very kind of you," I said as I sat down.

"What were we talking about today?" the Mate asked.

"Well, we've covered religion and politics, so I guess that leaves sex. We've always managed to turn the conversation to that topic anyway," I said.

"That Soiree with Mrs. Marlowe, back in July, shouldn't have happened," he said.

"Why not? She offered and you accepted. That happens all the time. It's not like you were married," I said.

"I had started writing to you prior to that," he said.

"You asked about Captain Tommasson. I had just gotten off the Steamer Spirit Independent in Gary. I took my seabag and travel case and went to the Moorea Lounge. I hadn't been there very long when somebody puts his hands on my shoulder. I heard that Islandic accent-'Have we met somewhere, New York perhaps?'. I turned around and said-'How are you doing, you old Pirate.' He told me that his ship was delayed in loading for twenty two hours and most of his crew had left the ship. He had a car and he took me to see his boat. It was a cabin aft former 'salty'. We went below and he showed me the engine room and I met the Chief and a few other crew. He showed me his quarters. He said if I didn't have a place to stay overnight, I could stay in one of the guest quarters. I told him that his quarters were big enough to accomodate both of us, so I spent the night there."

"Wow, did you get caught?" the Mate asked.

"The door to the office was ajar. The Chief and another guy came in and saw us, but Tommasson didn't see them. They left right away," I said.

"Why didn't he see them?" the Mate asked.

"He was chowing down," I said.

"J-C, you like the old guys, eh? It sounds like Mrs. Kefauver has a younger sister!" the Mate exclaimed.

"Hey! I do it for fun, not to get their money," I said, adding—"I do it on my own terms. Tommasson and Guiddo asked about marriage. Maybe they expected me to ask, but I wasn't interested in a long term commitment like that," I said.

"They had good judgement. They know a good woman," the Mate said.

"You say the most charming things," I said. We heard Louie coming with our breakfast.

"Are you having a good morning folks?" he asked as he came into the room.

"Are you kidding? We've been up since one thirty. I've been out in the dark and cold. Out in the work boat. Unshackling the boom, taking off hatch covers, eating a ton of coal dust," I said.

"My, my, all that overtime is gonna' kill ya'," Louie said as he put our breakfast on the table.

"It's going to be alot harder on you when John jumps ship," I said.

"It's only gonna' be for ten days. I've worked with some real strange brew. I never worked with Eggers, but we had this crazy Vet that would get up in the middle of the night and start searching for drugs that he was sure were stashed all around the boat. Had this other fellow that would be up all night mumbling to himself while he sharpened knives," Louie said.

"My Lord! If I had shipmates like that, I would have stomped the hell out of them and run them off the ship, first opportunity," I said.

"You'll run into those types, sooner or later," Louie said, adding—"If you need anything else, let me know," and he turned and left.

"John and Louie are so thoughtful. They always include toast," I said.

"Yes, you could be having oatmeal and you would get the toast," he said.

"I've never been on a ship with any 'Weird Harolds' like Louie was describing. Earlier this year, there were some guys on the Mariner Enterprise and the Spirit Independent that you couldn't exactly trust, but I don't think that they were violent," I said.

"About ten years ago, the Chief was stabbed on an ore boat. Apparently the Second Engineer was angry about some silly B.S. on a performance evaluation. He got drunk and used a little pen knife. He didn't do a very good job. They found him passed out in his quarters. He claimed that he didn't remember anything. It never got in the papers, I guess the company hushed it up," he explained.

"Yeah, I guess nobody wants publicity like that," I said.

"I've been wondering if you're going to visit your former shipmates on the Giovanni?" the Mate asked.

"I would have been there by now if it wasn't for our visitors. Maybe I'll go there for lunch. I've heard that Max Blackwell is the steward and Erma Fraunhofer is the second steward. I bet the struedel flies in that galley," I said jokingly as I continued to attack the pancakes.

We ate in silence for a few minutes. I thought about the Pegasus carved by Joe Westly, now securely packed away. His little note-'To my friend, Nicolette, a wild spirit as always.' I wondered how many times a man rides a horse before the horse becomes saddle broke. I was thinking about school as I finished my pancakes.

"You look far away," the Mate said.

"Oh, I was thinking about my friends at college," I said as I started on my sausage.

"What's their names?" the Mate asked.

"Mary-Beth and Tammy," I said, adding—"They have invited me to stay with them in Alliance. Earl will drive us up to Cleveland in that aging Jeep of his."

"That sounds like a workable plan," the Mate said.

"I'm sure that I'll have to help someone with their school work."

"The time will probably drag by up here," the Mate said.

"Are you taking a plane?" I asked.

"I think so. Probably directly into Cleveland, the day of the party."

"Book it now or you'll pay through the nose," I said. I finished my orange juice. "That was good. I don't know how I'll survive without John and Louie's cooking," I said.

"When we get back to Marblehead, you can come over to my house, I'll cook for you," he offered.

"That sounds like a ploy to get me to come over to your house," I said.

"My bad," he said.

"An offer I can't refuse," I said smiling. We both got up and put our dishes in the plastic bin.

"You look like you need to get some sleep," I said.

"I'll get some when we get forward. Are you going forward?"

"Yes, I'll probably go to my quarters and wait for our visitors," I said.

When we got out on deck, Hank and Al were standing by the hatch crane. I looked up at the conveyor.

"So far, we've been spared the coal dust," I said.

"Yes, the wind and the hopper have kept it away from us," the Mate said.

Over the noise of the conveyor, I could hear the horn of a diesel locomotive.

"My Grandpa Strickland used to say that the railroads aren't worth a damn since they gave up on steam."

"You will be telling your children that about lake freighters," the Mate said.

I was taken aback by his comment about children. "Yes, I suppose so," I said.

We kept to the port side as we went forward. I could see the Giovanni, off to the left. Its stern was more than a hundred feet ahead of our bow, but it still looked big. Three conveyors were dumping taconite into its massive hull.

"They'll be there until early this evening, at least," I said.

"Yes, we'll be gone before then," the Mate said.

When we got to the obsevation room, we parted company. I went to my quarters and took off my parka and boots and laid down on my bunk. I read Newsweek for about half an hour. I had just about finished reading everything that I wanted to read, when I heard a knocking on the door. When I opened the door, Don the wheelsman was there.

"Beg pardon, lass. The Captain would like to see you in his quarters."

"I'll be right there," I said.

I sat on my bunk and put my boots on. I checked my hair in the mirror then headed out the door, closing it behind me. For some reason, I felt awful alone as I went down the passageway and turned into the passageway leading to the Captain's quarters. When I got there, the door was closed. I knocked on the door. The Captain opened the door after a few moments.

"Come in Miss Strickland. I would like you to meet Nigel Larsen from Marketing and Public Relations. Brian Banner from Operations Management and George Fox, Logistics Comptroller," he said, as we shook hands all around.

"I'll be taking Mister Banner and Mister Fox on a tour. Mister Larsen here, would like to interview you for a segment in the 'Spotlight' page of this month's newsletter."

"Very good, Sir," I said.

"Miss Strickland will show you to the Wheelhouse when you are finished here," the Captain said.

"Very good, Captain," Larsen said, then they left.

"Good morning, Miss Strickland. You can have a seat there, if you will," he said, closing the door.

He came over and sat down opposite of me, opened his brief case and took out a tape recorder. This turkey is going to conduct a job interview. It's probably the only thing he knows how to do, I thought.

"I usually conduct an interview and write the article from that. You don't mind the tape recorder, do you?" he asked.

"No, not at all," I said, thinking that this fool could not write short-hand to save himself.

Larsen: Are you familiar with the 'Spotlight' page of our newsletter?

Strickland: Yes, I read the newsletter.

Larsen: This month, we feature Herbert Miller. He was a P.O.W. in the Korean War. Jean Marlowe in Personnel. She is an artist. Her father was one of the last of the Schooner captains on the lakes. And, Of course, you. Do you know those two people?

Strickland: I know of Mrs. Marlowe, but I never met her. I don't know Herbert Miller.

Larsen: You are twenty-six. Do you mind if we print that?

Strickland: No, not at all.

Larsen: How long have you worked on lake freighters?

Strickland: Five years now.

Larsen: Can you tell me what boats you were on?

Strickland: Certainly, I served on the MV Giovanni from 1982 all the way through last year, 1985. Earlier this year, I was on the Mariner Enterprise and the Spirit Independent, before coming aboard the Gentry.

Larsen: The MV Giovanni is Canadian?

Strickland: Yes, in fact, it's docked at the next slip.

Larsen: That large vessel over there?

Strickland: Yes.

Larsen: Do you know her Captain?

Strickland: Yes, her Captain is Bert McCullough. I've also served under Thorvold Tommasson, Pierre LeMand and Arnie Drewyan while on the Giovanni.

Larsen: Were there other women aboard the Giovanni?

Strickland: Yes, Lukesia Sims, a Wheelsman and Erma Fraunhofer, the Second Steward.

Larsen: Have you served with any other women this year?

Strickland: No.

Larsen: Have you always been a deckhand.

Strickland: No, I was a QMED and Conveyorman on the Giovanni.

Larsen: Of the three boats that you've been on this year, which one is the best in your opinion?

Strickland: This one is definitely the better one of the three.

Larsen: Better maintained, better officers and crew?

Strickland: Yes, much more professional here. The departments all get along.

Larsen: Captain Kompsii says that you're a top-notch crewman.

Strickland: Captain Kompsii is fair, honest and practices impeccable seamanship. You can't ask for more than that.

Larsen: Captain Kompsii says that you moored the ship from the work boat, unshackled the boom and removed hatch covers, then cast off from the work boat. All that in the darkness, early this morning?

Strickland: Yes, it's been a busy morning.

Larsen: Is this typical for the boats you've been on?

Strickland: The Mariner Enterprise and the Spirit Independent carried grain. They weren't self unloaders, so loading and unloading usually required more work by the deck department. Grain also has to be dry, so we had to put canvasses on the hatch covers.

Larsen: Self unloading makes it easier on the deck hands.

Strickland: Generally, but not always. On our last trip to Cleveland, we unloaded into barges. I had to handle mooring lines and spent a couple of hours on the end of the boom. Fortunately, it was inside the break wall and the rain held off.

Larsen: Are you planning to make this a career?

Strickland: That's difficult to say. I'll finish my degree this winter. After that, I don't know what I will happen.

Mister Larsen turned off the tape recorder. "Very good, I have enough to write the segment."

"I don't know why anyone would want to read about me," I said.

"You happen to be the only woman working on one of our boats. I think we have a mutual acquaintance, Mister Skorenski from Canadian Mining."

"Yes, I know Mister Skorenski," I said.

"I was going to ask you if you wanted to join me for dinner this evening. Mister Skorenski says that you date."

I hesitated for a moment. It occurred to me that he was after a piece. The term 'She dates' is a tactful way of saying that a woman puts out for any guy that takes her to dinner. The back of my neck got hot.

"I'm afraid that Mister Skorenski is pulling your leg. I never dated him. I'm getting off this boat as soon as we unload and I'm catching a plane back to Sandusky," I said.

"Okay, it was nice meeting you," he said as he held out his hand.

"I'll take you to the Wheelhouse," I said as I turned and headed to the door.

I waited, while he put his tape recorder away. We crossed the passageway and took the little stairs to the Wheelhouse. When we got to the Wheelhouse, the Captain was there with the other guys. A photographer was there and he took a picture of me shaking hands with Mister Larsen. I kept smiling throughout, like I was actually happy to meet the jerk. In a few minutes, they left with the Captain.

Andy had remained on deck, so Don was the only one in the wheelhouse with me.

"I expected your buddy O'Blake to show up," I said.

"Cleveland is cold enough for the little darling," he said.

"Maybe he won't like the climate and he'll go back to England."

"Tush, tush, such a pity," he said.

"Everybody says he won't be around long. Probably on his way back to Northern Ireland."

"If you don't see the little Brit at the Ceilidh, then he's departed the Company for certain," Don said.

"You're leaving after we unload also?" I asked.

"Yes, my Ellen and I must prepare for our return to Dublin," he said.

"There was a guy named O'Murphy, on the Giovanni. He came from Ireland when he was fourteen. He went back to Ireland when he retired. He came back to Canada, because the people were too laid back for him in Ireland," I said.

"Faith and begorrah. It seems a poor enough reason to leave Ireland," Don said.

"I think I'll go to Ireland. The tours seem very reasonable," I said.

"Ach, no Lass, you look me up in Dublin. We'll find you folk all over Ireland, that will put you up."

"Thanks, that's very kind of you," I said.

"Not at all," he said.

"My grandpa Eichann could speak Gaelic, but I'm afraid I never learned."

"A fair, young Lass, such as yourself, will have no problem. Leaving Ireland will be more the problem," he said.

The Bosun came into the Wheelhouse, and began to looking for something.

"Whatcha' looking for Boss?" I asked.

"The Captain wants to see the cargo manifests," he said.

"I saw the Mate put something in the white binder, over here," I said. The Bosun came over and removed the binder from the pouch.

"Yes, these are it," he said and he left with the binder.

"Everyone is in such a hurry," Don said.

"That's just not in the Gaelic nature. I'm gonna' mosey on down to my quarters. Let me know if the ship is sinking," I said.

"Will do," Don said.

I went through the back door and headed down the steps. The conveyor was still going full throttle. I went to my quarters without running into anyone. It was almost nine thirty. I signed the papers that the Mate had given me and I put them in the interoffice envelope. I wrapped the string around the button and set on the dresser.

I put on my parka and headed aft to look for Earl. I took the long way around and came out on the port side. As I headed aft, I heard a horn of a train. I looked off the port side and saw a train crossing the Grassy Point Bridge. I decided to check the number three hold on my way aft. There was not much coal dust in the air or on the deck. I did not have my flashlight, but in the daylight, I could see that it was a third full. I saw Hal, Ed, Brad and the Bosun standing by the hatch crane.

"Hey guys, It looks like we might be done here in another hour," I said when I got back there.

"Where's your buddy?" Brad asked.

"The Nefarious Mister Larsen? He went ashore with the others, I think," I replied.

"I was talking about the Mate," Brad said.

"I think he's getting some sleep. It's been a rough morning for him," I said.

"He looked pretty cozy with you earlier," Brad chided.

"He had to make sure I didn't get dirty, Captains' orders. Pierre Cardin and coal dust don't go together," I said.

"How did the interview go?" the Bosun asked.

"I thought it was a job interview. He didn't know what to ask. He seemed happy with it, though," I said.

"The other guys came out here and looked in the cargo hold, then went back to the Wheelhouse," the Bosun said.

"I've heard this Larsen guy had been divorced three times," Ed said.

"That doesn't surprise me. He seems to be a jerk," I said.

"When we're done unloading, we're be going to the other side of the point to let you guys off," the Bosun said.

"That's good. We'll avoid all those trains," I said, adding—"Has anyone seen Earl?"

"The Chief has him mopping the floors," the Bosun said.

"Okay, I'll catch you guys later," I said.

I entered the after deckhouse and took the passageway to the living quarters. I figured that would be the place that the Chief would want mopped. I found Earl mopping the passageway through the living quarters.

"Hi guy, what you up to?" I asked.

"The Chief wanted me to mop back here. I forgot to do it earlier, so I'm trying to get it done before I leave."

"Okay, I'll help you," I said.

"You gotta' be kidding," he said.

"No, if it has to be done, I'll help you do it," I said.

I went to the storeroom and got another mop and bucket. I filled the bucket at the hot water spigot outside of the storeroom. I carried the bucket into the passageway and began mopping from the after end. After about ten minutes of mopping passageways, we had almost met up in the quarters passageway. The Chief and DJ came through.

"Hi, guys. How are things in the tunnel?" I asked.

"Good, as far as I can tell. What are you guys doing?" the Chief asked.

"I'm helping Earl mop the passageways," I said

"There's no need to do that now. The visitors didn't come back here," he said.

"Now, you tell us!" I said as I was wringing out the mop.

"Little chores like that can wait until the lay-up," the Chief said, then he and DJ continued down the passageway.

"Let's empty the buckets in the wash tub and go take a break," I said.

There is an enameled trough in the firehose room that is called the wash tub. We left the mops leaning against the outside bulkhead and took the buckets in there and emptied them.

"Another fine job," I said as we collected the mops and headed for the store room. "After we unload, they're taking the ship to the other side of the point," I said.

"How long do we have?" Earl asked.

"Less than an hour now," I said. After we secured the mops and the buckets, we headed for the Rec room.

"You got all your stuff packed?' I asked.

"All ready to go," Earl replied.

"That's good. You can carry my steamer trunk," I said jokingly, as we entered the recreation room.

Joe, Buster and Billy were in there watching cartoons.

"There goes the neighborhood!" Joe sneered.

"Oh no, we have a celebrity here. May I have your autograph?" Buster said jokingly.

"Don't cheer, just throw money," I shot back as I was getting water from the cooler.

"You're gonna' be in the 'Spotlight' page this month?" Billy asked.

"That's what they tell me. Between the Korean war POW and the landscape painting secretary from the office here in Duluth," I said.

"What makes you so special?" Joe asked.

"I asked the same thing. Mister Larsen said that I was the only woman serving on a company boat this season. Big deal," I replied.

"Did he asked about the rest of us?" Billy asked.

"Yes, he asked which of the boats I served on was the better boat, so I lied and told him that it was this one," I said jokingly.

"How many boats were you on this year?" Billy asked.

"Three," I replied.

"I wish they would have talked to me," Billy said.

"Let me tell you, you aren't missing anything," I said.

"I wanted to ask you about college," Billy said.

"Sure, ask away," I said.

"How do you get into college?"

"You go to the admissions office. They usually have a packet for prospective students. You should get a college catalog, an application for new students and a release form for high school records. Did you take the ACT or the SAT?" I asked.

"No, I didn't," he said.

"You will probably be required to take one or the other. Find out about it as soon as possible. I would have someone back home start doing the leg work if you're gonna' stay up here for the lay-up," I said.

"Do you have to go through this rigamarole once you're in?" Billy asked.

"No, once you're a student in good standing, you register for classes every quarter, or semester, that's about all," I said.

"Hey Nick, you wanna' play some poker? Nickel and dime anty?" Buster asked.

"No can do, Captain's orders, no cards for money," I said.

"He won't mind. You're off this boat anyway," he said.

"Save it for the indians. They like to take your money," I said.

"You don't like indian casinos?" Buster asked.

"History condemns us for introducing native americans to alcohol. Someday we may be condemned for introducing them to gambling," I said.

"It's their way of making a living and getting a lick of revenge on us white men," he said.

"It certainly does nothing to preserve their culture," I countered.

"Are you and Earl gonna' roll the bones, russian style?" Buster asked.

"Are you ready for another dice game, old buddy?" I asked.

"Yeah, I guess we can play until the conveyor stops," he replied.

I went to the wall cupboard and got the cup and dice. Earl cleared the table and got a notepad to keep score. I let him roll the dice first.

"I don't know why I play this game. You always beat the ass off of me," Earl said.

"Keep your mind on the game and you'll do alright," I said as I wrote down the score. "You can pass or play," I said.

"I'll pass."

"Can three people play?" Billy asked.

"Sure, there's no limit on players," I said.

Billy brought a chair over.

"Tired of watching cartoons?" I asked jokingly.

"Hey, there's nothing else on," Buster shot back.

"The 'Today show' should be on. I think it's channel six," I said.

"Who cares about what's going on in New York," Joe remarked.

"Hey, did the Russians really play russian roullette?" Buster asked.

"As I understand it, it started out as a parlor game," I answered.

"That's crazy! Taking a chance on getting your head blown off!" he said.

"You've been watching too much TV. They use an empty cartridge case with just the primer," I said.

I explained the fundementals of the dice game to Billy. After a couple of rounds, he seemed to pick it up.

"Are your parents Russian?" Billy asked.

"No, my grandmother was," I replied.

"We used to live by this old guy and his wife. They were from some place over there. Their friends would come over and they would be talking loudly in Russian or something. They would smoke this awful smelling stuff in pipes," Billy said.

"Yes, that was probably Machorka. It was used in rural places where tobacco was not available," I said.

"We would call the police and tell them that someone was smoking dope over there. It was hilarious to see the police trying to deal with these people who couldn't even speak english," he said.

"Hilarious! I hope you don't find yourself trying to speak to the police in a foreign country where you don't know the language," I said.

"Were any of your family sailors?" Billy asked.

"No, no sailors," I replied.

"What did they do?" Billy asked.

"My grandpa Strickland's family were teachers and civil servants. My grandmother's family were land owners and merchants. On my mother's side they were poor Irish peasants. A few of them worked on the railroad," I replied.

"The way you handle mooring lines, I thought all your family were sailors!" Billy exclaimed.

"I learned about mooring lines the hard way. Back in '82, three of us were let off on the wall in the Rouge river. The Captain was holding the Giovanni against the current with the propellors. We were supposed to dock two hundred yards upriver. The starboard propellor started in reverse pitch, which threw the ship out of control. Engineering shutdown the propellors. Captain Tommasson managed to hold it straight with the bow and stern thrusters, but the boat was drifting downriver, faster all the time. Up on deck, they threw us the loops of the three mooring cables. Jean Sparrow put the forward one over a bollard. Whiskers threw the amidships cable over a bollard. I put the after cable over a bollard, then we ran like hell. The after cable let go first. Ten feet of cable, an inch and a half thick, disintegrated into shards. It cracked like lightning. The cable amidships went next. The end whipped back so violently, that it penetrated the hull, right below the railing. The forward cable held. I don't know how. It took the Chief a couple minutes to find out what the problem was and disengage the pitch control on the starboard propeller. We docked with the port side propeller that time," I finished.

"What caused the problem?" Billy asked.

"A two dollar O-ring failed in the hydraulic pitch control of the propeller," I said.

"Those mooring cables were a gamble," Buster said.

"The crew called it the two dollar trifecta. The hero was the Captain. He saved the ship and god only knows who and what else. He should have gotten the congressional medal of honor. The Coast Guard commander thought so."

"Did he put him in for it?" Buster asked jokingly.

"No, he's an Icelander. He was exonerated by the company. He saved a thirty four million dollar ship, just to be told that a mechanical failure wasn't his fault," I stated.

"Maybe they thought that the crew should pay for the broken cables and the hole in the boat," Buster said.

"Had it been our Mr. O'Blake, I'm sure that would have been the case," I said.

"I heard that he don't know nothing about boats. The Chief said that he worked for a British company, at a refinery," Earl said.

"I heard that he wanted a big bonus for riding down from Sault Ste. Marie. I heard that the company won't give it to him. They think that it's part of his job as Maritime Operations Manager to ride on a boat once in a while," Buster said.

"Typical jerk in a suit. The less experience they have, the more money they want," I commented.

"I heard that he was sweet on you," Joe said.

"He requested a private meeting in his quarters, to discuss shipboard operations. I told him that any questions he had about shipboard operations, he could ask the Captain or the officers," I said as I threw the dice.

"Damn, thirty two points on six dice. How did you manage that!" Billy exclaimed.

"When you see a chance, you take it," I replied, as I wrote it down.

We heard the order to raise the outboard stanchion. Twenty minutes later, the conveyor stopped.

"Well, old buddy, it's time to shove off," I said as I dropped the dice in the can.

"Wait a minute. I'm only forty five point down," Billy protested.

"If you're ever in Marblehead, come over to my house and we'll finish the game. I'm on Bayshore road."

I took the dice back to the cupboard. I put on my hard hat and my parka.

"Let's go see what mischief we can get ourselves into," I said.

When we got out on deck, I saw that the outboard stanchion had been raised. I heard the Bosun talking to the Mate on the radio.

"Are we gonna' shackle the cable stays to the boom?" Earl asked.

"Not us, old buddy."

With the conveyor stopped, we could hear the humming sound. The rattling sound began as the boom was swung onboard, still in the raised position. The boom was lowered onto the stanchions with a clanking sound. One blast of the whistle and the Gentry began to back away from the dock. I could feel a little warmth in the sunshine.

"These other guys will hit the town, while we're hitting the road," I said.

"I wonder if the bus will be there?" Earl said.

"If not, It probably will be soon," I said, adding—"The Captain said that he would have a car waiting for us.

After we finish at the office, I was thinking about coming back here and scrounging a lunch on the Giovanni."

"You think they'll let us?" Earl asked.

"I'm sure the guys will insist, once we get on board," I said.

"When is the airplane?" Earl asked.

"Seven ten this evening. They're running one in the morning and one in the evening. We should have plenty of time to get to 'The Wharf' and eat, then catch a taxi courtesty of Brad and Ed."

"Such great guys," Earl joked.

We saw some guys moving around forward. Andy and the Bosun must have those guys preparing the lower gangway forward. Doubtless, the Chief was opening the door for the engineroom gangway, I thought. In ten minutes, we had backed up and turned around and were heading for the other side of the Reiss Terminal. Small puffs of coal dust came from the conveyor belt as we headed into the wind. We heard the airhorn of another locomotive as we passed the rail yard. Three long blasts on his airhorn, he seemed to be blowing us a farewell. Nothing seemed to be permanent. Institutions of man, ship decks, all could be gone next year. The Mate brought the ship around in a broad starboard turn and lined up to dock at the wall. Ron and Billy came aft, on the starboard side and pulled out some cable on the mooring winch.

"They'll use the engineroom gangway to get someone on the wall," I said.

The Bosun was starting to talk to the Mate on the radio. More people were coming out on deck to watch the docking.

"It looks like the gang's all here. Where was everybody at two o'clock this morning?" I said softly.

"Safe and warm in their beds," Earl replied.

I did not see any cars or buses on the wall up ahead.

"Remember to meet me by the forward gangway," I said, adding— "I'm going forward to get my luggage."

I went forward along the starboard side. I ran into Smitty and Al at the forward winch.

"The Bosun wants to see you," Al said.

"Okay, I'm heading that way," I said.

Andy and the Bosun were at the Bulwark, starboard side of the forward deckhouse.

"Hi, guys," I said when I got up there.

"The Mate wanted to see you in the Wheelhouse," the Bosun said.

"Okay, I'll head that way," I said.

I took the outside steps and entered the wheelhouse from the forward door. The Mate and Don were the only people in the wheelhouse. The Mate was communicating directly with the Chief rather than using the chadburn. I took off my parka and sat down in the Watchman's chair and observed the docking. It occurred to me that this was the first time I ever saw a ship being docked without the Captain being in the wheelhouse. I refrained from speaking to the Mate while he brought the boat in to the dock. The Bosun was giving 'distance off' reports continually. Apparently, the Mate wanted to get within two feet of the wall. It was not long before the Mate gave the order for *All Stop*. I could hear the Bosun give orders to rig out the forward gangway and tie off with the hawsers, fore and aft. I saw the Mate write something in the log book. After he was finished writing in the log book, he sat it on the shelf by the helm.

"Okay, Don. Thank you and good luck!" the Mate said as he shook his hand.

"The Lass and yourself will look me up, when you're in Dublin," he said.

"Certainly, we'll have a gay old time," I said, and I shook hands with him as well.

I knew that he was taking a taxi directly to the airport. The flight to Erie was leaving within the hour. When Don left the wheelhouse, the Mate looked at me.

"You wanted to see me aboout something?" I asked.

"Yes, I have something I want you to take back to Marblehead, if you will."

"Pray tell what is it?" I asked, smiling sweetly.

"Some photographs in a frame," he said.

"If it's not too big, I suppose I can," I replied.

"When Andy gets up here, we'll go to my quarters and I'll get it for you," he said.

"Sure, as long as nobody sees me in your quarters," I said jokingly.

"In my quarters and receiving personal items, for shame," he said slyly.

"Secure the boom, there sailor. This is no time to be thinking about discharging cargo!" I said. I saw Andy pass by the windows. "It looks like your relief is here," I said.

A moment later, Andy entered the wheelhouse.

"Well, Nick it looks like your ride is here," he said.

"Where?" I asked.

"That sidewalk truck down there," he said as he pointed to a green, three-wheeled maintenance truck.

"Old Cappy said they would send a car," I said.

"It's only two miles to the office. I guess they didn't feel like sending the limo," he said.

"I guess, I'm only a minor celebrity," I shot back.

"I have to go to my quarters and get some items that Miss Strickland has agreed to take back to Marblehead with her," the Mate said.

"Oh Dave, you sly dog!" Andy said jokingly.

"Big time," I said as I got up and headed toward the back door.

"I hope you don't have too many things. That matchbox car they sent, can't handle much payload," I said as I went through the door. The Mate followed me through the door and down the steps. "When I get back to Marblehead, I'm going to buy a quilt for my friends Lukesia and Dante. I think I'll get a handmade one at the craft show. I have a quilt top at home, but I won't have time to finish it before their wedding," I explained.

"What are you planning to do with the quilt top?" he asked.

"It's a large mariner's Compass. I may need a hand to complete it," I said, adding—"Do you know anyone who is handy at sewing quilts?"

"No, I'm afraid not," he replied as we arrived at his quarters.

"I heard that Mrs. Marlowe is quite a painter," I said as the Mate opened the door and entered his quarters.

"Yes, she showed me some of her work."

I laughed at that statement.

"Was that funny?" he asked.

"My mind was in the gutter. I was thinking that that's not the only thing she showed you," I said, smiling sweetly.

"If you want to talk dirty, then come in and close the door," he said as he took the picture off the wall. I entered, but I left the door slightly ajar.

"The last time I was in here, you caught me down on my hands and knees. Subsequent events seem to indicate that that could be very risky," I said.

"You looked very charming," he said as he approached me, holding the picture frame.

I put my hand out and took the picture, still looking at his face. He grabbed me again. This time, there was only our shirts between us. He pushed his lips against mine. I did not resist, when I felt his tongue during our breathless kiss. After a minute, I broke off.

"You bad!" was all I could say for a minute as we stood there, looking at each other. "What do we have here?" I said as I looked at the picture frame I was holding.

It was a collage of snapshots from Marblehead. I recognized the photo of Tommy and me, waving from the observation deck of the lighthouse.

"I remember when this picture was taken. I wondered what happened to it," I said. I saw that that these pictures meant a great deal to the Mate. "I'll stick this in my travel case, it will be safe there," I said.

I thought for a moment about my plan to carry my hard hat.

"Here, you can take this back to Marblehead for me," I said, as I handed it to him. "Take care of that. That's my trusty old hard hat," I said.

"Something Old," the Mate mused.

"Yeah, whatever. I have to grab my stuff. I left my parka in the Wheelhouse," I said.

"I'll get it and meet you at the forward gangway," the Mate offered.

"Okay, I'll be there in a few minutes," I said.

I opened the door and started down the passageway toward my quarters. I could hear somebody shouting out on deck. When I got to my quarters, I put my travel case on my bunk and opened it. I slipped the picture frame and the interoffice envelope between my clothes and made sure that they were secure before closing my travel case. I put my seabag over my shoulder and grabbed my travel case and headed out the door. I went down the passageway and down the steps, then took the lower steps to the area forward of the number one cargo hold. John and Gary were standing in the gangway door. When I got to the gangway door, I heard Pete's big mouth.

"What's going on, guys?" I asked.

"Pete's got enough luggage to sink the Queen Mary," Gary said.

"So what's he bitchin' about?" I asked.

"He doesn't want his Beatles record collection to be put in the luggage compartment of the bus," John said.

"It looks like he's got more luggage than the frickin' President takes on a trip," I remarked. I saw Earl standing by the bus. "I'll be right there, guy," I shouted at him.

Gary and John were looking at me.

"Someone is supposed to be bringing my parka," I said. After a few seconds, I turned and headed for the steps. When I got to the steps, I saw the Mate coming down with my parka.

"Okay, Thanks guy," I said as I took my parka from him. I put it on, but didn't zip it up. "I'm shoving off now. See you in ten days," I said, putting my right hand out.

He took my hand, but he just held it. "The next time a ship comes between us, we'll be married," he said softly.

"That won't make it any easier," I said.

He winked, then he let go of my hand and turned and started up the steps. I headed for the gangway door.

"Nice blush there, Nick," John said, smiling.

"I must be getting sick or something," I said.

"Yeah, love sick," he shot back.

"If you're ever in Marblehead, feel free to come over and cook for me," I wisecracked as we shook hands.

"I'll send some pretty shells from Florida," Gary said.

"Send us some warm weather, while your at it," I said, as I shook hands with him.

I grabbed my seabag and travel case and went down the gangway. I walked by Joe, Brad, Pete and the mountain of luggage and headed toward Earl.

"Our ride is the green monster over here," I said, pointing at the sidewalk truck.

Earl grabbed a carpet bag and a trash bag and started heading that way.

"A nice, sunny day. A good day to be heading back to Ohio," I said. "Hello driver," I said to the young man in the driver's seat.

"Are you Miss Strickland?" he asked.

"That's right," I said as Earl and I threw our bags in the back.

"I've only got one seat up here," he said.

"That's okay, we'll ride the rumble seat," I said, as I threw my seabag on the front seat.

"I'm only authorized to pick up Miss Strickland," he said.

"I see, and who authorized you?" I asked.

"My boss," he said.

"Well, I'll take it up with him, when we get there, if you like," I said as I got in the back with Earl. "The Office, cabbie and don't spare the horses."

As the sidewalk truck pulled away from the ship, I saw the basket being lowered to the dock. I knew that it was the stuff, like Fred's refrigerator, that was being sent package freight. A few fortunate crewmen had family members arriving in cars to pick them up. The ship grew smaller as we drove away from it. The driver turned right after we got past some rail cars and the ship was lost from view.

CHAPTER 13

Farewell to the Gentry

he streets of Duluth did not appear to be very congested as the sidewalk truck sped along at its maximum speed of twenty-five miles an hour. In less than fifteen minutes, speed racer had us in the underground parking lot.

"If you would be so kind as to direct us to the Personnel department, my good man," I said.

"I was told to carry your baggage and escort you up there," he said.

"That's very good of you. What's your name?" I asked.

"Al Stanley, Mam," he said.

"One thing, Al, never call me Mam. That sounds like some old lady. Please, call me Nick," I said.

"Very good," he replied.

"I've got the travel case, if you get my seabag, we'll be ready to go," I said.

Earl already had his bags, so we headed for the fire doors. Once inside the doors, the elevators were on the right. Young Al pressed the up button and we waited for the elevators.

"Have you got all your Christmas shopping done, Al?" I asked.

"No, I still live at home," he said.

"You don't have a girlfriend to buy gifts for?" I asked.

"No, I'm afraid not," he replied.

"I'm always buying Earl something for Christmas," I said.

"Yeah, but I never get what I really want, a fifth of Jack Daniels," Earl said jokingly.

"I've gotten you that. It's not like you need it," I said as the elevator door opened and we got in.

Young Al pressed the button for the fifth floor.

"How long have you been doing this, Al?" I asked.

"Since June. I wanted a job I could work while I finished school," he said.

"Are you going to college?" I asked.

"I might, I haven't thought about it," he said.

"Well, think about it and go to college," I said.

"Nick is always telling people to go to college," Earl said as the door opened.

Earl and Al picked up the bags and we headed toward the Personnel counter. Young Al set my sea bag next to the counter and took his leave of us. A woman approached.

"Hello, I'm Jean Marlowe. How can I help you?" she asked very politely.

"Hi, it's nice to meet a fellow celebrity. I'm Nicolette Strickland and this is Earl Franklin," I said as I shook hands with her, and Earl did likewise. "We just got off the Steamship Gentry and we have to deliver some papers to Mister Hunt,"

"You can leave your baggage there and bring the paperwork to my office," she said.

"Give us a moment to dig it out," I said.

"Certainly, take your time," she replied.

I had the inter-office envelope out of my travel case in a few seconds. Earl took a little longer to produce the paperwork from his carpetbag. We followed Mrs. Marlowe to her little office. We sat down and she began tapping keys on her computer for a minute, then she went to the filing cabinet and looked throught the files until she pulled out two of them and returned to her desk. I noticed an exquisite painting of the Marblehead Lighthouse behind her desk.

"You painted that?" I asked.

"Yes, earlier this summer," she said.

"That's beautiful! Your talent was understated. How long were you in Marblehead?" I asked.

"I was never there. I painted it from photos," she said, adding—"Do you know David McCracken?"

"Certainly, he's the First Mate on the Gentry and also my neighbor in Marblehead," I said non-chalantly.

She hesitated for a few moments, but kept looking at her computer screen.

"It sounds like a beautiful place," she said, adding—"We'll start with Mister Franklin, if you don't mind."

"Not at all, we've got plenty of time," I replied.

Earl had not put his papers in an envelope, so they were not in pristine condition. After a few moments, Mrs. Marlowe got things sorted out and had some papers for Earl to sign. As we expected, the discharge notice would be mailed when we used up our vacation. After Earl was finished, I handed her the paperwork from the inter-office envelope. She seemed please that it was in good order. It did not take long for her to produce some paperwork for me to sign.

"When Mister Larsen interviewed me this morning, he said that your father was one of the last schooner captains on the lakes," I said, as I was signing papers.

"Yes, he sailed all his life. He was born on a sailing ship, in fact," she said.

"That's really interesting. Did you have any other family on the lakes?" I asked.

"No, I was born to him late in life. My older brother and sisters died from war and disease. None of them were over twenty years old," she answered.

"Oh, My Goodness. I'm afraid that your segment will be much more interesting than mine," I said as I handed her the papers I had signed.

"Do you and Mister Franklin need a ride anywhere?" she asked.

"We're headed back to my old boat, the MV Giovanni, which is tied up opposite of the Gentry at Reiss number five," I said.

"I'm going to lunch now, I can drop you two over there if you like," she offered.

"That's very kind of you," I replied.

Mrs. Marlowe got her coat and we followed her to the elevator. We got down to the lower level and into her car without saying much. I sat in the passenger seat, while Earl sat in the back.

"This is a much nicer vehicle than we rode in on," I said jokingly. Mrs. Marlowe did not get the joke, apparently. "The weather is great today. Last year, it was cold and snowy this time of year," I said.

"Yes, the last three winters have been severe," she said as we pulled out of the underground parking lot and onto the street.

It seemed to be a much shorter ride than it was earlier.

"When does the newsletter come out?" I asked.

"It should be in a couple days," Mrs. Marlowe replied.

"I'm anxious to see what they wrote about me. What does your husband think about it?" I asked.

"I've been divorced for a while. I still wear the ring out of habit," she said.

"When the newsletter comes out, you'll have to take that ring off. Men will be beating a path to your door," I said.

"You think so?" she asked.

"Sure, I'll bet money on it," I said.

"How about your door?" she asked.

"I'm heading back to college. You can't believe the guys coming on to me," I said.

"Is that it?" she asked, pointing to the Giovanni.

"Yes, straight ahead. The Gentry is over there to the right," I said.

"Where is the Gentry going?" she asked.

"To LaFarge, to lay-up for the winter," I said, thinking that she was thinking about visiting David McCracken.

"Is this close enough?" she asked, stopping the car before the railroad tracks.

"Yes, this will be fine," I said. I opened the door. "Thank you and it was nice meeting you," I said as I put out my hand.

We shook hands and I got out of the car. Earl got out and I helped him get the baggage out of the trunk.

"Bye-bye, see you next season," I said as I waved good-bye. The car slowly pulled away.

"There's a woman for you, old buddy. Take her down to the farm. She can milk cows and keep you warm at night," I said.

"No, she's a city girl, she wouldn't get near the barn," Earl remarked as we started walking toward the Giovanni.

The conveyors were not that loud and the dust from the taconite was minimal. We passed the bow and the bulwark forward. I looked up and saw the First mate, Franky Pierce, standing at the railing with another guy that I did not know.

"What's the G-D hold up!" I shouted.

"What's your G-D hurry!" the other guy shouted.

"Erma owes me a lunch!" I shouted back.

"You come up here and kick all our asses, you can have a free lunch!" he shouted.

"With me and Earl, that will take all of a half a minute," I said as I headed for the gangway.

Earl was right behind me, when I got up to the spar deck and set my sea bag and travel case against the railing. Franky Pierce was headed our way. I looked around. On a thousand footer, it takes three times as long to survey the deck because it is three times as large as the deck on the Gentry. I saw only one other crewman on the deck.

"Was that your boat over there?" he pointed astern as he approached.

"Yeah, we just finished unloading. We passed Tommasson outbound, yesterday," I said as we shook hands. "This is my shipmate, Earl Franklin," I said and they shook hands.

"You're in time for lunch. Max Blackwell is the cook now," he said.

"A week ago, I was in Toledo visiting Guiddo. He has trouble walking, but his head is okay," I said.

"It was real sudden. He sat down on the floor and began babbling incoherent nonsense. It's a good thing we were about to dock in Escanaba," Franky explained.

"He's waiting for the season to end, so his old buddies can come over to visit him," I said.

"It will be another month before I can make it over there, unless we dock in Toledo unexpectedly," he said as we were walking aft.

"Most of the guys go 'up the street'?" I asked.

"Half of them. Because of scheduling difficulties, we won't be able to get over to Hallet number six until tomorrow, so there's no use in being in a hurry," he explained.

"Is that Shorty over there?" I asked.

"Yes, they're working eight hour days while in port. Another eight hours and they'll all be falling on their faces."

"What does Captain McCullough think about that?" I asked.

"He's been off for two weeks. We might pick him up at the Soo. PeePee Laramie is in command now," he said.

"Hiding in the closet as usual?" I asked.

"We don't see too much of him even up on the bridge," he replied.

"This dude Laramie is squirrelly as hell. He must have invented the 'brain dead stare'. When he did talk, it was always about his wife that left him years ago. No big wonder about that," I said to Earl.

"He sounds like another weird Harold. Maybe he was abducted by aliens too," Earl wisecracked.

"They should have done us a favor and kept him," Franky said as we entered the cabin.

The cabin is a five storey building sitting on the stern of the ship. I knew it was a straight shot aft into the galley. The galley is huge compared to the galley on the Gentry. It is buffet style. You push your tray along the rail and take what you want. Earl and I were nearly to the end, when Max turned away from the meat slicer and looked at us.

"Are we feeding the homeless people now?" he wisecracked.

"We're editors from Fine Dining. This looks more like something they would feed the hogs in the Farm Journal," I shot back.

"Take it up with your buddy, Erma," he said.

"Where is she?" I asked.

"Who knows? Probably sleeping. Do you know that I have to share quarters with her?"

"Oh my lord. I can't imagine what kind of offspring that unholy union will produce," I said.

"Oh, that's hysterical, first PeePee and now you."

"Do you like cooking for old looney tunes?" I asked jokingly.

"I don't like living on the same planet as that miscreant," he said.

"Tell him that Erma would rather bunk with him. He'll stay away then," I said as I poured some coffee.

Franky had only gotten a sandwich and some coffee. We entered the adjoining Crew's mess. Barton, the second engineer, and Gabby (Gabriel), the QMED, were the only crewmen there.

"Come back here and we'll show you how to do an honest days work," Bart said.

"I haven't seen anybody working since I came on board," I said, adding—"This is Earl Franklin." We sat down at the next table.

"Nick has been in Toledo to see Guiddo," Franky said.

"How's he doing?" Bart asked.

"He seems to have lost the use of his right leg. Other than that, he's feisty as ever," I said.

"Was he still cooking?" Bart asked.

"He was talking with our mate, David McCracken, so I made lunch and supper," I said.

"That will kill him for sure," Gabby wisecracked.

"Get over to Toledo and see him. He misses his shipmates," I said.

"I heard you married some Russian guy and produced a whole litter of little commies," Gabby wisecracked.

"In your dreams!" I shot back, adding—"Luke and Dante have left already?"

"Yeah, they shoved off as soon as we docked. In a few weeks they'll be living in married bliss. Did you finish school?" Bart asked.

"Two more classes this winter and I'll graduate," I said.

"You can get yourself a real job," he said.

"These guys are going up to the casino later. Are you going up there?" Franky asked.

"No, we're taking a plane back to Ohio this evening. You may run into some of our shipmates there," I said.

"The Chief won't let more than one engineer off, so I have to wait for Chet to come back," Bart said.

"I'm surprised that Art wasn't the first guy off," I said.

"Art has been off nearly a month. Bill Lawrence took over for him," Bart said.

I remembered meeting Bill Lawrence in Gary, when I was on Tommasson's boat. I hoped I would not see him this soon.

"Old Mackey is having heart problems. They say he gets weaker all the time," Frank said.

"With all the drinking and smoking he did, it's a wonder that he lasted this long," I said.

"He's only forty-eight," Bart said.

"He always talked about this job he had in New York. Selling insurance, or something. They rode a train to work and played cards and drank for an hour, then they went out and drank at lunch. After work, they went out and drank at supper. He always said that he would have been retired by now if he stayed in insurance," Gabby said.

"He'd be dead! What difference would it make if he was retired?!" I exclaimed.

"The booze was always better on the other side of the tracks," Bart said.

"At least he was off the booze while he was on the boat. All those cigarettes weren't doing him any good either," I remarked.

"Supposedly he cut back to three packs a day," Bart said.

"Oh, that helped a lot," I said sarcastically.

"I'm sensing some hypocrisy here," Gabby said.

"I go through a pack in three or four days. I'm about to quit anyway," I said.

"Old Jacques had a divorce and some bad luck on his farm. I guess he lost it. He hit the skids, they say," Franky said.

"Why didn't he come back here? I'm sure Captain McCullough could get him a job."

"He was sixty, can you believe that? I never thought he was over fifty," Franky said.

"He did his job well enough. I don't think I ever saw him get angry with anybody," I said.

"Yeah, he was a pretty level headed guy," he said.

"Where do you live Nick?" Bart asked.

"In Marblehead, just west of Sandusky," I replied.

"Hell's Bells! We're going to Conneaut. You could ride with us," he said.

"That's a hundred and fifty miles away!" I said.

"You and your friend here could take the work boat. We need a new one anyway," Bart said.

"We have already been out in a work boat twice this morning," I said.

"You live in Marblehead, too? Uh, Earl right?"

"Yes, I'm Earl. No, I live in Alliance, Ohio, which is not far from Canton," he replied.

"Earl has a good sized farm there," I replied.

"You might as well make a living from your farm, this business is going to hell," Bart said.

"I grew up on a farm. It's work, all day, every day. There's no vacations like we get here," Gabby said.

"I saw this story about these giant birds called Emus that people are raising," Franky said.

"Yeah, I saw that. The meat is supposed to be better than chicken. They can graze like a cow. The price is suppose to be good. What do you think about that, Earl?" Bart asked.

"In a few years everybody will have them and the price will drop through the floor," Earl said.

"Earl is sticking with dairy cows," I said.

"My father had cows. He sold them, eventually. He went into raising chickens and turkeys. My mother and him could handle that by themselves. Cows are a lot of work," Gabby said.

"Maybe PeePee should raise cows. That might keep him out of trouble," Franky said jokingly.

"It sounds like the bovines would out smart him," Earl said.

"He got into trouble at this titty bar in Windsor. He went beyond the 'touchy-feely' point with this mexican lap dancer. The bouncer and him had a difference of opinion concerning service requirements. The police were called," Bart said.

"In Windsor! I can't believe that. All a guy has to do is keep paying her and he can go as far as he wants," I said.

"That idiot will f—k up everything he touches, literally and figuratively," Franky said.

"I'm surprised that somebody hasn't put him over the side," I said.

"It's a wonder that the Chief hasn't already. Bill is a pretty easy going guy, but he's all business when it comes to running his department. Dumb nuts didn't request that the supply boat meet us at Sault Ste. Marie. Chiefy didn't get his parts. Fortunately, he got the parts delivered here."

"Speak of the Devil," Gabby said as the Chief entered the Crew's mess.

"Hail, Hail, the loafers are all here," the Chief said.

"Now, is that any way to speak to our guests?" Barton remarked.

The Chief looked at me for a moment. "We met in Gary. Nick, isn't it?" he asked as he approached us.

"Yes," I replied as I stood up and shook hands. "Nick Strickland. This is Earl Franklin." The Chief shook hands with Earl.

"Are you a guest of Captain Laramie?"

"God forbid. I was on this boat for four seasons. I just stopped by to see some old shipmates. Our boat is docked at the next slip," I said.

"The steamship Gentry. Weren't you on the Spirit Independent?"

"Yes, Earl and I were both on the Independent. After we came back from vacation, we signed on the Gentry as deckhands," I explained.

"You were a QMED here. Why did you leave, to be a deck monkey on American boats?"

I should have known that that question would come back to haunt me.

"My grandmother was ill, so I had to be on a boat where I could be closer to home," I answered untruthfully.

"I thought you wanted to serve under Thor Tommasson," The Chief winked at me.

"Captain Tommasson was our captain here for two years. He's a great guy. Captain McCullough is a top notch captain also," I said.

"Nick is a restless spirit. I was like that before I got the farm," Earl said. "How long have you been on the lakes?" the Chief asked Earl.

"Ten years, farming is my calling now."

"Earl and half of the other crewmen were from the old Cliffs line," I said.

"So was I. Who's your Chief on the Gentry?"

"Greg Brady," I said.

"Oh yeah, I was third engineer with him back in the old grey fleet."

"Do you know Hank Andersen and Fred Westfall?" I asked.

"Sure, I've known both those guys for years. Who are the deck officers?" he asked.

"William Kompsii, David McCracken, Andy Botzum and Emerson Munson."

"I don't know Andy Botzum," he said.

"He came from the ocean. I think he'll go back pretty soon," I said, adding—"Greg is gonna' need a ride back to Sault Ste. Marie."

"How about you two?" the Chief asked.

"We're getting a steak dinner at 'The Wharf' and then we'll take the friendly skies back to Sandusky this evening," I said.

"Aren't you going to any of the fun activities? The Casino or the numerous bars around here?"

"We don't have time for any fun stuff until we get back to Sandusky," I said.

"Nick has been to see Guiddo," Franky said.

"How's he doing?" the Chief asked.

"His right leg isn't working very well. Otherwise, he's as feisty as ever. He misses his shipmates," I said.

"I'll go see him as soon as I'm able." He hesitated for a moment, then reached into the pocket of his dungarees and pulled out something. "These are Cab passes, I won't be needing them," he said, handing them to me.

"Thank you, that's very kind of you," I said.

"Not at all. It was nice meeting you, Mr. Franklin. You two have a happy holiday," the chief said as he got up.

"Same here, Merry Christmas!" Earl said.

"Nice meeting you again. Take care," I said.

After the Chief left, the other guys were silent.

"He looks tired. It must have been a hard season for him," I said.

"Back in August, his wife found out that she had cancer. He's been off quite a bit since then," Bart said. I thought about the Mate losing his wife to Leukemia.

"I hope there's something they can do for her," I said.

"He won't talk about it, naturally. I called his daughter when he first came on. She said it's Pancreatic cancer. There's nothing that they can do for it. She's got two months at the most."

I said a prayer softly, in Hebrew. "Blessed is the Lord God, ruler of the universe. The righteous judge. Be mindful of us in our hour of need." We were silent for a minute.

"Cal Chukowski isn't doing too good either. He had to leave the boat three times this year. The last time, they sent the Medevac chopper. I don't think that the company will let him back on," Franky said.

"He couldn't have been that old," I said.

"He's forty six, two years younger than Mackey. Of course, you would never think he would have problems. He never smoked and very seldom ever drank, unlike Mackey," he said.

"It was that medication that he was taking for high blood pressure or Cholesterol. I can't remember what it is. If he hadn't taken that, he would be fine. Damn doctors and drug companies kill more people than anything else," Gabby said.

"Yes, I suppose that sort of thing can happen sometimes," I said.

"Priminister Mulroney and the National Health Service people don't care. You can't sue the bastards when they mess you up," Gabby complained.

"Not to change the subject, but when is the season ending for you guys?" I asked.

"They have us going through to the end of this month. I wouldn't be surprised if they have us out in January," Franky said.

"This is our last trip. They're going to LaFarge to lay-up," I said.

"You wouldn't be going to Port Services since you're going back to school," he observed.

"No, I never have worked Port Services. Some of the guys are gonna' try to. I sure in the hell won't work up here. Even in Cleveland or Toledo, it would be a pain to work eight hour days and commute," I said.

"I always have a winter job working on the railroad. I'm a switchman part time. Those older guys, who have seniority, do everything they can to stay indoors in the winter," Gabby said.

"It sounds like a rough job," I said.

"I work at the power plant in Lewiston. Those wussies on the railroad don't know anything about ice and snow. I've worked waist deep in freezing water, all day, keeping the penstocks clear," Barton said.

"We would like to stay and hear all your stories but Earl and I have to be shoving off pretty soon," I said.

"Pulling the old eat and run, eh?" Gabby asked.

"I wouldn't want Max to think that we enjoy his cooking that much," I joked.

"Sure! Stay around for supper and take the abuse that the rest of us get," Franky said.

"We'll have to get a cab and head downtown," I said.

"I'll call one for you and meet you forward," Franky said as he got up.

"Well guys, it's been nice seeing you again," I said.

"We'll walk you forward," Bart said.

We headed out the door and down the passageway, forward. When we got out on deck, Shorty was still the only one out there. I waved to him as we walked forward on deck.

"Hopefully this weather holds and all of us can get outta' here before the sh-t hits the fan," Gabby said.

Earl and I both looked over the port side and astern. The Gentry was still there. It would be there until five or six o'clock this evening. When we got to the port gangway, I saw Franky coming forward. Before he got there, the cab pulled up to the gangway.

"That was fast," I said as I waved to the taxi.

We shook hands and agreed to meet over at Guiddo's house. It took Franky a few minutes to get there.

"Take care, old buddy and lay off the Linguini," I said as we shook hands.

Bart and Gabby grabbed our bags and followed us down the gangway. They put our bags in the trunk of the taxi and waved, then headed up the gangway. Earl got in the cab. I stood by the door and looked at the Giovanni for a moment. I wished that I had a camera with me. I got in and told the driver to take us to the library. The taxi pulled away from the pier.

"Do you have any Christmas shopping to do, old buddy?" I asked.

"No, I'm afraid not," Earl replied.

"I was gonna' hang out at the library for a while. Maybe catch a nap, then walk down to the Wharf about four. We should get outta' there in plenty of time to catch a cab to the airport."

"That sounds good," Earl said.

The taxi got on route 35 and took the land route parallel to the water route that we took early this morning. In a few minutes, the cab turned left at North Lake street and stopped at the corner of West second street. I handed the driver the cab pass. He released the trunk as Earl and I were getting out. We took our bags from the trunk and closed the lid. It was a short walk to the library entrance.

"The city is wearing it's usual holiday decorations," I said.

"They're not as impressive as those in Cleveland," Earl said.

The lights and displays are impressive in Cleveland. The stores and commercial buildings change themes every year.

"It's early yet, I'm sure there will be more later," I said, knowing that we wouldn't be here to see them.

We went through the outer and inner doors and headed for the checkout desk. I knew the librarian, Mrs. Ferguson.

"Hello Mrs. Ferguson. How are you today?" I greeted her.

"Hello Nick, the reading room is open. Would you like to leave your bags behind the checkout here?" she asked.

"Thank you, that's very kind of you," I said as Earl and I set our bags behind the checkout desk.

"Not at all. I know that you come here either to read or to sleep," she said.

Earl and I went through the door of the reading room which was just to the left of the checkout desk. Nobody else was in the reading room, so

I could stretch out on the couch and sleep. I took off my parka and folded it up to make a pillow. I laid down on the couch after I took my boots off. Earl sat down on the next couch.

"There's a book over here: Fear and Trembling by Soren Kierkegaard," he said.

"He was an exitentialist philosopher from Denmark. He died of Pneumonia in a gutter in Copenhagen," I said.

"He sounds like a real happy character," Earl said.

"He claimed that he couldn't get married because he was too melancholy," I said as I closed my eyes.

In a few minutes I was asleep. When I woke up, I instinctively looked at the clock, it was just past two thirty. I went to get a drink of water, then I came back and laid down again. I dreamed that I was in the middle of a vast prairie. I had no idea in which direction to walk. There was no road or path to walk along. I couldn't tell anything from the position of the sun in the sky. I wanted to start hollering. I figured that someone would be out there to hear me. I heard my grandmother talking, she was telling me that the steppes were endless. She said that she had told me how to navigate the mighty steppes when I was a child. I told her that I couldn't remember. My grandmother disappeared, and my mother was there. She started shaking me, like she did when I was a child. I reached out and grabbed her around the neck . . . When I woke up, I was grasping Earl's arm.

"Sorry to startle you, Nick. It's ten till four, I thought I should wake you," he said.

"Yes, very good," I said as I took my hands off his arm.

"You must have been dreaming," he said.

"Yes, how was Kierkegaard?" I asked.

"A little hard to understand," he said.

"Life can only be understood backwards, but it must be lived forward."

"Yeah, stuff like that," Earl said.

"Men demanded freedom of speech to compensate for the freedom of thought, which they hardly ever used," I quoted.

"Pretty deep stuff," Earl stated.

"Enough to drive anybody to drink," I wisecracked.

"Just two, I was a good boy," he said.

"You can sleep on the airplane, I guess," I said as we headed for the door. We collected our bags and said good-bye to Mrs. Ferguson.

"Down this way. It's a little walk, but we'll get there in plenty of time," I said as we turned and headed down the sidewalk. "The lights will look better after dark. It doesn't look like they got them all up yet," I added.

"I never noticed the Christmas lights up here, that much," Earl said.

"When I was a kid, they had these lights and displays at O'Neils and Polsky's in downtown Akron. I used to check out the lights and peruse the old bookstore and get something to eat at Woolworths. Anything, so I wouldn't have to go home and listen to my parents' nonsense," I said.

"Keeping with the spirit of Christmas, let us not badmouth our parents," Earl said jokingly.

"Are you kidding, they were at their most vicious at this time of year!" I exclaimed.

"Talk about a vicious joke. When I was six years old, and still believing in Santa Claus, my father put coal in our christmas stockings and hid our presents up in the attic," Earl said.

"I bet it was a very tearful Christmas morning," I said.

"I hope that he enjoyed his little joke, because none of us thought it was funny. It took a couple of years for us to trust our parents after that," he stated.

I thought about the time that my maternal grandmother had brought over a Christmas tree and I decorated it. My father came home drunk, late at night and threw it out the door, decorations and all. A jewish person does nothing to stop other people from celebrating and enjoying their holidays.

"My grandparents, on my mother's side were christian, if you could call it that. They were wasted most of the time," I said.

"You're through with all those dysfunctional people now, aren't you," he asked.

"Yep, I got my own house and those idiots can all stay away. I can have all the friends over that I want and none of the dysfunctional relatives that I don't want," I chortled, triumphantly.

"How about some Shipmates?" he asked.

"Sure, old buddy, you can stop by during the holidays or any time you want," I said.

"I was thinking about the Mate," Earl said.

"Uh . . . He never mentioned anything about it. I don't think I said anything either. His mother lives in Grand River and he's got a grown son. Maybe he has other plans," I suggested.

"I wouldn't be surprised," Earl said.

That comment seemed rather vague, so I let it go. I looked in the window of a Men's store. The mannekin was wearing a nice looking, dark blue suit.

"That's a very attractive looking suit. I think it would look nice on you, old buddy." I said. Earl rolled his eyes.

"I think I'll wear my work clothes, that way everybody will recognize me," he joked, adding—"My father used to say that he had only one suit. The one he stole off his father before they buried him."

"That is terrible! Did you ever think about your naked relatives coming back to haunt you?" I asked jokingly.

"Nah, All my kin folks died quietly at home, except for cousin Pooh."

"What happened to cousin Pooh?" I asked.

"I guess you'd call him a second cousin. It happened when I was at Jacksonville, Florida. My father and his brother Ed, both owned a half of the farm then. My uncle Ed had bought Pooh this cowboy outfit for his birthday. Boots, pistols, everything. Later on, Ed went out to brush hog this field that had overgrown with briars and things. I guess Pooh decided to ambush his grandpa from behind a wild rose bush. Unfortunately he was right in front of the tractor and uncle Ed didn't see him until the brush hog cut him to pieces," Earl finished.

"Thanks for telling me this right before we eat," I said half seriously.

"He was a spoiled little bastard. He probably would have grown up to be no good. I've seen some good guys get hit in 'Nam. It's funny how you learn to eat and sleep in the bush after seeing all this stuff-as gross as you can think of," Earl said.

"Very strange, I'm sure," I said.

I thought of a famous line in a letter from the Civil War—'Mother, thank God that you will never see the things that I have seen.'

"We'll cross the street at the light, then it's only a couple hundred feet."

"I've never eaten at this place," Earl said.

"I had steak there last year at this time. It was cold as hell then," I said.

"Yeah, we've had three cold winters. This winter and the next four should be normal or warmer than usual," Earl said as we got to the corner and waited for the light to change.

At the other corner was a bellringer for the Salvation Army. The Salvation Army had given some gum and cigarettes to my grandfather when he was wounded in the First World War.

"I have a few bucks for the Salvation Army," I said.

"That's very generous of you," Earl said as the light changed and we began to cross the street.

I reached into my parka to make sure that the money was still there. When we got to the corner, I set down my travel case.

"Hi, how are you doing?" I asked.

"I'm fine. How are you?" the bellringer asked. I put two dollars and some change in the bucket. "Thank you, merry Christmas," she said.

"Merry Christmas, stay warm," I said as I picked up my travel case.

Even though it was four o'clock in the afternoon, the sidewalks were almost deserted.

"Not much pedestrian traffic," I observed, as we headed toward The wharf.

"The snow is off the sidewalk, that's good," Earl said.

"Why didn't you wear your boots, instead of those deck shoes," I asked.

"I packed those away, to be sent in the package freight. I'm saving those for the barn," he said.

"Shame on you, making the company pay for your farm boots," I said jokingly.

"For what they pay me, I wish I could get a free tractor out of them," Earl said.

"I'm sure that our Mr. O'Blake will get a bonus that big," I said, adding—"Here we are, old buddy."

The doors were heavy tongue and groove pine with spar finish. Brass bound portholes and schooner door handles were the only fittings. I switched my travel bag to the other hand and pulled the door open. The floor of the entranceway was boards while the walls were painted murals of lakeshore scenes. Fishermens' nets, life rings and other sailing paraphenalia, decorated the walls. The coatroom looked like a chandler's shop. We checked in our coats and bags there. The Maitre de greeted us and took us to a table. Fortunately we didn't have to wait. I hate to wait in line for anything and I almost always will walk out of a restaurant, rather than wait to be served.

The hostess set menus on the table and said that Melanie would be our server then she left.

"We don't get prompt and pretty babes like this on the lakes," Earl said.

"We don't have to pay the galley gang either. I guess it's a trade off." I paused as I was looking around. "Even the bar looks deserted."

"It's probably a bit early for the supper crowd," Earl said.

"The old place looks like it's been redecorated. There's a lot more paintings and nautical gear," I said. In fact, there were a lot more things, like the whaleboat suspended from the ceiling.

"I hope nothing falls on us while were trying to eat," Earl said.

"It kinda' reminds me of your barn," I joked.

A young lady in an apron came to our table. "Hello, I'm Melanie, I'll be your server this evening," she said as she set down two glasses of water. "Are you ready to order or do you need more time?" she asked.

"I think we're ready. I'll take the eight ounce Filet Mignone, medium, baked potato with sour cream, sauteed mushrooms and the garden salad."

"What dressing would you like?" she asked me.

"House," I replied.

"Very good, and you sir?" she asked Earl.

"I'll have the eighteen ounce Porterhouse, well done, steak fries and hominy."

"There's a roll with that," she said, adding—"Would you like an appetizer?"

"Yes, the mozzarela sticks with marinarra sauce," I replied.

"Anything to drink?" she asked.

"I'll take a Bahama Mama from the bar," I said.

"I'll have a Whiskey Manhattan," Earl said.

"Very good, I'll be back in a minute," she said and we handed her the menus.

I looked at the painting on the wall next to us. I was surprised that it was a painting of the Cliffs Victory, inbound, between the north and south piers. I looked at the name, the painter was Marianne Marlowe. I had learned to assess the characteristics of paintings in my Art History classes. I could see that the style was similar to the painting of the

Marblehead light that I had seen in Jean Marlowe's office. I saw that Earl was looking at the picture also.

"There's an old friend," I said.

"A ghost. It ended up in the Philipines to be scrapped," he said.

I had seen ship after ship, being towed to the Maritime Salvage yard in Port Colbourne at the eastern end of Lake Erie. A lot of the ships that were built in the first half of this century, had already made their last voyage to the breaker yards on the Canadian side. Economics and environmental regulations sometimes made it possible to sail the doomed vessels to breaker yards overseas.

"Half the Cliffs fleet has been torched already. It's only gonna' get worse," Earl said.

"I wonder who painted the picture?" I asked.

"It looks like that lady we seen this morning. Wasn't her name Marlowe?" Earl asked.

"Jean Marlowe, this artist is named Marianne Marlowe," I said.

Earl shrugged as though the name didn't make a difference. In college, they teach you to figure it out or find the answer.

"I wonder if there are any more paintings of ships." I said, looking around. I saw Melanie and another guy coming our way.

"They'll be here in a minute," I told Earl.

"Good, a drink before dinner always helps the appetite," Earl said.

Melanie set the bowl of mozzarella sticks and the cup of marinarra sauce on the table.

"Hi, I'm Bob, the manager. You wanted the Bahama Mama?" he asked.

"Yes, that's for me," I said. He set it in front of me and the whiskey manhattan in front of Earl. "Do you know who painted this?" I asked, pointing to the painting.

"Yes, that was my old art teacher, Mrs. Marlowe. she painted a lot of ships and lake scenes. Her husband was a captain, a real old guy. They're both gone now," he said.

"We saw Jean Marlowe this morning. She's a talented painter also," I said.

"Yes, Jean is her daughter. She taught her to paint. When her mother died, she sold many of her paintings to us. We have a couple paintings by Jean on the other side of the bar."

"They're both very accomplished painters, I recognized the subjects instantly," I said.

"Unfortunately, Mrs. Marlowe couldn't teach me to paint. If you need anything else from the bar, let Melanie know," he said.

"Thank you, we will," I said, and he left.

I made a mental note to subtlely find out from the Mate if he had any artwork from Mrs. Marlowe.

"Well, that answers that question," I said, noticing that Earl was downing his drink like it was ice water in hell.

"You had two already," I said.

"Those were just beer, this is to thin the blood," he said.

"Your blood might start to boil when we get up in that airplane," I said.

"Really?" he asked.

"You'll be crawling on your hands and knees by the time we land," I said, trying to sound serious.

"I never thought about the effects of alcohol and altitude. I've always taken the bus or a ship back to Cleveland," Earl said.

I knew that altitude can magnify the effects of alcohol. "Yes, I've heard some stories about the bus rides. I'm glad that I always took the airplane," I said.

"One time, a person, who shall remain nameless, fell asleep in the back of the bus and woke up in the bus garage in the middle of the night."

"I hope he learned his lesson. I thought alcohol wasn't allowed on the bus," I said.

"The guys always managed to carry on a large quantity. The drivers never checked the carry on bags and the coffee thermoses," he said.

"They x-ray and open bags at the airport, so nobody is gonna' get away with tricks like that. These puddle jumpers don't even serve water because the flights are short," I said.

I wondered if we would run into anybody we knew at the airport. I have been surprised to see all kinds of people that I knew at the airport. The last time I flew, I ran into Delia, a flight attendant. Miss forty four D chest and former fiance of my friend Jeff. Delia had it all figured out: a husband in Ohio and a guy in every city where she could layover(or lay under). She gave a new meaning to flying the friendly skies. Fortunately, Jeff also figured it out before he married the tramp. I'm happy to say that she was the only flight attendant I ever met that was that way, I thought, smiling to myself.

"You look happy with yourself," Earl said.

"Oh, I was thinking about some adventures I've had while flying," I said.

"Oh my goodness, couldn't you wait?" he asked.

"Nothing like that, but I've seen people do that on those late night business flights," I said.

"I see, old fast and easy airlines. Live performances, instead of an inflight movie," he wisecracked.

"I guess some people don't mind where they do it," I said, adding—"I was thinking that I usually meet someone I know at the airport or on the plane."

"I haven't flown since I came home from 'Nam," he said.

"You can't beat it. We'll be home in a couple hours instead of the twenty hours by bus."

The hostess came up to us. "Excuse me, are you Nick Strickland?" she asked.

"Yes, I am," I answered.

"A mesage for you," she said, handing me a piece of paper, then she turned and left. I read the message then handed it to Earl.

"Well, I'll be dipped. I guess your friend, Captain Laramie, is a little upset that we took his cab," Earl said.

"I was wondering how it got there so fast. Old screwball should have been a little faster off the line. They should be rid of him by the time they get to Sault Ste. Marie," I said.

"Maybe he's another one of those people that have been abducted by Aliens. He'll have one of his UFO friends harass our airplane all the way to Sandusky. Have you ever seen these people on TV?" Earl asked.

"Yes, they appear to be morons in most cases," I said.

"I had a relative that claimed to have had several close encounters with Aliens. What makes people do that?" he asked.

"A psychology professor told us that people who claimed to have had contact with Aliens, ghosts or Elvis were self-mythologizing. A process where people invented untrue events to make something extraordinary about their own lives. That way they avoid dealing with their own emptiness and disappointments," I said.

"Yeah, this guy sounds a lot like this Captain Laramie. Nobody wanted to talk to him because he either talked about Aliens or his ex-wife," Earl said.

Melanie came by with the serving cart. "You had the filet," she said, setting the plate in front of me. She set the other plate in front of Earl. "Would you like anything else?" she asked.

"No, we're fine, thank you," I said, and she left.

Earl attacked his steak with the same ferocity that he went after his manhattan.

"Did they get it done right?" I asked as I was putting steak sauce on mine. Earl nodded.

I figured that he wanted to eat his steak in peace so I ate without talking. I wondered if the Mate thought that I talked too much. When I wasn't talking, he was asking me what I was thinking, so I figured he liked it when I talked. Maybe he was the kind of guy that liked his woman to do most of the talking. I would have time enough to find out about the mate over the winter. For a while, I was thinking about some other things I wanted to find out about the Mate. It's a good thing that Earl couldn't read my mind, he would have reached over and slapped me.

As I was finishing my Filet, Earl was finishing his steak fries. He looked at me and I smiled at him.

"You must have been hungry," I said.

"Yeah, a little bit of whiskey gives me the munchies," he said.

"That's what you told me earlier," I said.

"Are you done with your Christmas shopping?" he asked.

"Funny you should mention that. It used to be that except for a few shipmates and my grandmother, I didn't have much shopping to do. Now it looks like there may be a few last minute additions," I said.

"In Alliance or in Marblehead?" he asked.

"I'm sure that I'll have to get a few gifts for the little sisters in Tri Sigma. Maybe a few for some folks in Marblehead," I replied.

Earl cocked his head in puppydog fashion.

"Don't worry old buddy, I had you covered months ago," I said.

Earl smiled, then he tossed down the rest of his drink. "I can always count on you for Christmas."

"That's a hell of a thing to say to a wicked jew like me," I said jokingly. After I finished my garden salad, I drank the rest of my Bahama

Mama. "That filled me up. I don't think I need dessert, how about you?" I asked Earl.

"No, I'm fine," he said.

Melanie returned in a few minutes. "Would you like anything for dessert?"

"No, the steak was very good. Can you bring us the check?" I asked.

"Certainly, I'll be right back," she said.

I fished out my gift certificate and Earl took his out of his coat pocket. I took a twenty dollar bill out of my billfold to pay for the drinks. I knew that the other cab pass was in my parka.

"I'll have Melanie get someone to call a cab for us," I said.

"Are we going right to the airport?" Earl asked.

"I think we'll take a little detour and see if the boat has left," I said.

"Did you forget something?" Earl asked.

"Yeah, my frickin' camera. I would have liked to take a few pictures before the boat leaves," I said.

"They have some of those disposable cameras up front. I think they take twelve pictures," Earl said.

"That might work. I'll have to check it out before we leave," I said.

Melanie came back and handed me the check. I handed her the gift cards and the money.

"Keep the change for yourself," I said.

"I've never seen these before," she said.

"You haven't worked here very long. We got them back in July," I said.

"I'll have to ask Bob," she said.

"Would you have someone call us a cab?" I asked.

"Certainly," she said, then she left.

Earl was looking stressed. "If they hassle us about this, take your tip back," he said.

"Don't worry, Bob's a reasonable guy. If he doesn't want to take the gift cards, we'll have a four letter word with him," I said.

Melanie came back in a few minutes with Bob. Bob said that they would honor the gift cards and apologized for any trouble. He said we could have anything we wanted at the bar while we waited for the taxi. I knew that Earl could not resist that offer.

"Thanks so much," I said.

"You folks have a good day," he said, then he left with Melanie.

"I'm gonna' go look at those cameras, then I'll join you at the bar," I said.

"Okay, I'll see you in a minute," Earl said.

I headed for the front of the restaurant, where the hostess is. Behind the counter they have postcards, after dinner mints, newspapers and other things. I asked the hostess if they had any cameras. She took a little white and green box off the shelf and handed it to me. I thought the camera was inside the box, so I was trying to figure out how to open the box, when she told me that the box was part of the camera. She showed me the simple four step instructions on the bottom.

"Darndest thing I've ever seen," I said, and I gave her the four dollars and fifty one cents. I told her that we would be at the bar and that a cab would be coming for us shortly. It was only a couple of steps to the bar. Since the bar was well lit, I spotted Earl immediately.

"Hello sailor, new in town?" I joked.

"Sure Nick, sit right down here. These guys won't mind moving," he said. The guy sitting next to him, looked at me and got up and moved down two places.

"Thank you," I said.

"Whatcha' drinking there, old buddy," I asked.

"A whiskey sour," Earl replied.

"You told them that this one was on the house?" I asked.

"Oh yeah, I wouldn't forget to do that," he replied.

The bartender came over and looked at me.

"I'll have a Vin Rose'," I said.

"Coming up," the bar tender said, as he reached overhead for a glass. He poured the wine into a champagne glass. I wondered if he even knew the difference.

"Thanks," I said when he set the glass in front of me.

"Aren't you about at your limit," Earl said, smirking.

"Don't worry guy, I'm in a good mood this afternoon," I said in reply to his obvious reference to that incident at the Wheel and Anchor in Cleveland. "This is the darndest camera I've ever seen, It's a box," I said as I pulled the camera out and showed it to him.

"It doesn't come out of the box?" he asked as I handed the camera to him.

"No, it takes pictures as it is," I said.

Earl turned the camera over and looked at the lens. "Oh, there's the lens and the view finder," he said as he unintentionally hit the shutter release.

"I think you got a picture of the ceiling," I said.

Earl handed the camera to me and I advanced it to the next picture and set it on the bar. I noticed someone at the other side of the bar was looking at me. When I looked at him, he raised his hand off the bar and waved at me. I thought I recognized him as one of the guys who was on the Gentry this morning, but I couldn't remember his name. He got up from the bar and started heading in our direction.

"He's one of the guys that was on the ship this morning," I said to Earl.

I turned on the bar stool and faced him as he was coming toward us. I smiled at him and he smiled at me.

"Hi, I know I met you this morning in the wheelhouse, but I can't remember your name," I said as I held out my hand.

"George Fox," he said, adding—"You're Nicolette Strickland?"

"Yes, just call me Nick. This is Earl Franklin," I said and he shook hands with Earl.

"Can I buy you two a drink?" he asked.

"I'm afraid we won't be able to finish this one. We'll have a cab coming here pretty soon," I said.

"Where are you going? I might be able to take you two and you won't have to pay for a cab," he said.

"We're gonna' take a detour and take a few pictures of the Gentry before it leaves, then head for the airport," I said.

"I have to be back at the office at seven, so I can drive you anywhere. The Gentry will be leaving soon here, so we better get going, if you want to see her," he said.

"What do you think, old buddy?" I asked Earl.

He tossed down his drink and said—"Let's roll."

"We have to stop at the Coatroom," I said.

"Me too," Mr. Fox said, and we headed for the door.

It only took a minute at the coatroom, to get our stuff and get our coats on and we were out the door. Mr. Fox had a Mercedes Sedan and he was parked close to the door. We put our bags in the trunk and I got in the front while Earl got in the back. Mr. Fox knew his way around Duluth and the car was handling well.

"How did the interview with Nigel go?" he asked.

"Not too bad. I tried to steer him, he was trying to do a job interview," I said.

"What did you think of him?" he asked.

"I was told that he was a jerk that had been divorced three times, so I suppose that I was prejudiced before I met him," I said.

"Unfortunately, he is not very popular in the office," he agreed.

"I'm looking forward to reading the segment about me in the monthly newsletter," I said.

"I know the editor, so I'm sure that you'll get a good write up. I'll make sure that a copy is mailed to you." he said.

"That's very good of you." I said.

I saw him looking down. I figured he was looking for a ring. I smiled at him.

"I was surprised that you weren't married," he said.

"If I was married, I probably wouldn't be working on the lakes." I said, adding—"Are you married?"

"I got divorced this spring, after being married for five years," he said.

"Oh, that's too bad." I said.

"It was the darndest thing. She was a Louisiana girl. I worked in the New Orleans office for four years then we came here in the summer of eighty five. Everything was fine until the winter came. She hated the cold and snow. In February, she said that she was going back to New Orleans with or without me, so she did," he explained.

As Dixon used to say—"Just like the kudzu, can't stand the cold", I thought.

"Unfortunately, it's no Italian Riviera. I've lived in Ohio all my life, but I don't think I would want to live up here. Marblehead is windy and cold enough for my blood," I said.

We turned left at the stop sign and went past the railyard and came to a stop by the wall where the Gentry was. The mooring cables were already taken in. I could see the lay-up cables in coils on the deck. The spare tires were out. Spare tires are used Earthmover tires that are hung over the side to act as fenders. I heard the whistle blow. I got out and took the camera out of my parka. I saw Billy on the starboard side, we waved at each other. He was probably wondering how we left in a three wheeled sidewalk truck and came back in a Mercedes sedan. I took a couple pictures and the whistle blew again as the Gentry began backing

404

away. I knew the Mate and the Captain were in the wheelhouse. I got a couple three quarter shots along the port side as the Gentry turned until it was beam on to us. I got a couple more distance shots, until it passed the point and was lost from view.

"Is there any other place you would like to go?" George asked.

"I like the view from Spirit Mountain. Could you stop by there on the way to the airport?" I asked.

"Sure, it's just a little detour," he said.

We got into the car and headed out of the dock area. Instead of taking route fifty three, which goes right by the airport, George turned left at route two and headed west for Spirit mountain. There is a good scenic overlook by the ski area. Also a good late night make out spot for teenagers and sailors. The railroad tracks run right by there so you can see the trains up close as they crawl up the mountain side. It's quite a grade for a car as well, but the Mercedes negotiated the steep road easily. There was no one at the overlook, so we could park where we wanted. Since there were no leaves on the trees, we could see the ships. I spotted the Gentry, still heading east. It would make a starboard turn and head south to the lay-up dock in a minute or two. I took a couple pictures. I regretted having this mamby-pamby camera. With my Pentax, I could have gotten some real kickin' pictures from up here. We heard the horn of a diesel locomotive. We were at the top of the grade, the tracks came around in a right hand curve. Four red and yellow locomotives were pulling hard to get the consist up this final grade. As they passed, I took a couple pictures.

"They don't look like they're doing more than fifteen miles per hour," George said.

"Yeah and that's pulling empty cars," I said.

Sometimes the trains would be hauling coal and limestone to the Iron Range taconite plants. We crossed the road and got into George's car.

"Is it far to the airport?" Earl asked.

"Four or five miles. We'll take some back roads that will get us back on fifty three. Did you buy your tickets in advance?" George asked.

"I booked two standbys on the local to Sandusky," I said.

"Oh, bad news! Ever since the deregulation, those locals are just about useless. I'll help you check it out when we get there," he said.

"Thanks," I said as I saw two hundred and fifty of my dollars blowing away in the wind.

"The realestate looks a little better in the summertime," George said.

"Yes, Marblehead is the same way. If you're ever there, look me up and I'll show you around the place," I said, handing him a company card with my name and address on it. He looked at it for a moment.

"Where is Marblehead?" he asked.

"Just west of Sandusky, at the end of the peninsula," I replied.

"Okay, I've been to Toledo, so I should be able to find it," he said.

The smoothness of the ride and the Bahama Mamas were causing me to drift. I must have been in that state for several minutes, when the sound of a jet taking off, snapped me back into reality.

"Oh, we're here already," I said.

It was starting to get dark. We were on a road running parallel to the runway. George turned right at the entrance and took us to a parking lot right next to the terminal building. There didn't seem to be a lot of cars in the parking lot, so I hoped that things would go smoothly in the airport. We got out of the car and took our bags from the trunk. George asked to see the Standby tickets, so I took them out of the pocket of my parka and handed them to him. As we were walking toward the door, he took out a pen and began writing something on the cover of one of the tickets. When we got to the doors, they opened automatically and we entered the building, turning to the right,which was the direction everybody was going. George was still writing a mile a minute. For the first time in my life, I was glad to have a Logistics Comptroller with me. Normally sailors think of bean counters as the lowest form of life. After a short walk, George indicated the aisleway to the right. I saw that this was where the ticket counters were located. He went right up to a ticket counter. I don't know how he knew which counter to go to. I had bought the tickets almost two months ago at the Sky Harbor ticket counter, way out on the island. George was succinct and to the point as he laid the tickets on the counter in front of the young lady at the computer. She got up from the chair and stood stiffly as George questioned her. She tapped on a few keys and looked sideways at the screen.

"I'm araid that it will be at least twenty four hours," she said.

"That's not good enough, I want these people on a plane by no later than seven o'clock this evening," George said.

"Nobody has anything to Sandusky. United or NorthWest might have something to Cleveland tonight," she said.

"Can I use your phone?" he asked.

"We're not supposed . . . okay, go ahead," she said.

It must have been a phone for employees only. George hit a button instead of dialling.

"Hello Shirley, this is George Fox . . . . That's right. They screwed up on us over here. They're two prepaid Standbys for Sandusky, on the local. What can you get us, around seven this evening?" "They're usually pretty good. We've been dealing with them for years," he said to Earl and I, adding—"We'll have to settle for Cleveland or Akron-Canton." George paused for a few moments. "Yes Shirley . . . NorthWest, six twenty five at gate three. Yes, Business class. Hold on a minute. We want to transfer the ticket money to NorthWest," he said to the young lady at the ticket counter.

"That will take one business day," she said.

"No it won't. Just give Shirley the TR number over the phone and void it off your account on the next business day, as a ticket refund."

"I guess I can do that," she said, tapping on some more keys, then she took the phone from George and talked to Shirley directly. It took a few more minutes to get the transfer done, then she hung up the phone.

"Your tickets are at the NorthWest baggage counter," she said.

"Very good," George said and we headed for the baggage counter.

"How did the tickets get to the baggage counter?" I asked George.

"They'll have someone take them over there. The flight leaves at six twenty five, so there isn't a lot of time to get the bags checked," he said.

It was a hundred yard walk to the baggage counter. Fortunately, the only guy in front of us was just finishing. George told the man at the conveyor, that our tickets were brought over here. He went over to the podium and picked up the envelope and pulled out the tickets.

"Nicolette Strickland and Earl Franklin?" he asked.

"Yes," George replied.

He handed the tickets to George. "Let's see your carryon bags," he said.

I set my overnight bag on the rollers, then Earl set his carpet bag there also. The baggage man tied a tag on both. We took them off and set my seabag and Earl's trash bag on the rollers. The baggage man rolled his

407

eyes at Earl's trash bag, but he tagged both of them and set them on the conveyor belt. "Enjoy your flight," he said.

"Thank You," I said.

"Gate three is this way," George said, pointing to the left and we started walking that way.

"I can't believe that we didn't pay any more for the tickets," I said.

"It was forty two dollars more, but I put it on my travel account," George said.

"You really saved the day. If you come to Marblehead, you're more than welcome to stay at my cottage," I said.

"My pleasure and thank you for your kind offer, Miss Strickland," he said.

"Please, Nick," I said.

George handed an airline ticket to me and two to Earl. "I managed to get a connecting flight to Akron-Canton for free. Give the red one to the flight attendant here and give the blue one to the flight attendant at Cleveland-Hopkins," he said to Earl, adding—"The Shuttle bus to Alliance will cost you about twenty dollars."

When we got to gate three, we checked in with the flight attendant at the podium. I noticed that Andy and Mark were sitting next to each other in the gate area. they both looked over at us.

"There goes the neighborhood," Mark wisecracked.

"Is this the plane to partytown?" I asked, adding—"You guys must be lost."

"I know one thing, it doesn't go to Toledo," Andy said.

"You guys have met George Fox?" I asked.

"Yes," Andy said as he and Mark stood up.

"Nice seeing you again," George said as he shook hands with both of them.

"George got this ticket foul-up all straightened out for us," I said.

"Well, he's good at doing that sort of thing. You should have been here earlier to help us," Andy said.

"You were going to Toledo?" he asked.

"Yeah, but they cancelled the flight before I got here, not enough passengers," he said.

"Thank President Reagan for deregulating airlines," I said.

"I have to be going. You folks should be boarding soon," George said. We shook hands with him and he turned and left.

"I never thought I'd be happy to meet a bean counter. He really went out of his way for us," I said.

"Where did you run into him at?" Andy asked.

"At the Wharf. He took us down to the Gentry then up to Spirit Mountain," I said.

"The Gentry was still at the Terminal?" Andy asked.

"Just backing away when we got there," I said.

It took about ten minutes for the first call to board the plane for Cleveland. Minors and first class, board first. That didn't take long, so the call came for everyone to board. Earl ducked out for the restroom, so I waited for him at the back of the line. Andy and Mark seemed to be in a hurry to board. I don't know why, you're already given a seat, so why be in a hurry. I just tell the idiots who take forever to stow their carryon bag, to get the hell outta' my way. I looked at my seat number and hoped that Earl would be sitting next to me. Earl came back and I looked at his ticket. He would be sitting across the aisle from me. We handed our tickets to the flight attndant. She took the boarding pass and handed the rest of it back to us.

"Have a nice flight," she said.

We went through the bare metal tunnel and onto the airplane. The pilot or co-pilot was standing inside the door and said hello to us as we passed by. There was a short line behind a yuppie type, who was taking forever to stow his carryon bag in the overhead compartment. I saw Mark on the left and Andy on the right. My seat was right behind Mark and Earl was to sit behind Andy. We were in the Cheap seats, close to the trailing edge of the wing and over the landing gear.

"What's with the hat, guy?" I asked Andy.

"He's trying to impress the flight crew," Mark said.

"I'll put Earl behind him, that'll keep him in line," I said, as I pointed out the seat to Earl.

At the window, next to my seat, was a young man about seventeen, six feet two inches tall, blonde hair to his shoulders. I got the impression that he was trying to emulate Julian Lennon and wanted us to believe that he was in a rock and roll outfit. He looked at me as I put my travel case in the overhead compartment and sat down.

"You got it there, old buddy?" I asked as Earl was stuffing his carpetbag into the overhead compartment.

"Yeah, no problem," he said as he closed the door, then sat down. Andy turned and looked at me.

"How are you gonna' get back to Toledo?" I asked.

"I called the airline and told them to get a message to Eileen when she gets to the gate. She's not gonna' be happy about it, but I couldn't reach her at home or at her office," he said.

"I hope she get's the message. I'll probably rent a car," I said.

"Did you get the connecting flight to Akron-Canton?" Mark asked Earl.

Earl nodded.

"You guys will be going together," I said.

"I didn't know you two were going together," Andy wisecracked.

"You must be jealous," Mark shot back.

"Did you make it over to the Giovanni?" Andy asked.

"Yes, in fact Earl and I had lunch over there. Max Blackwell is the Steward and Bill Lawrence is the Chief. Do you know Bill Lawrence?" I asked.

"Oh yeah, I know him from the Cliffs line," Mark replied.

"He seems nice enough. The rest of the guys are Canadian," I said.

"Did you see anybody on the Gentry?" Mark asked.

"Billy was the only one we saw on deck. I'm sure the Captain and the Mate were in the wheelhouse," I said.

"There should be ten or eleven guys still onboard. I don't know if they can get a relief watch gang together at LaFarge," Andy said.

"Poor babies, they'll have to stay onboard instead of going to the casino and giving their money to the indians," I remarked.

"If there's any way in hell to get off the ship, they'll do it," Mark said.

"They'll be walking home if they do it too much. Those are the tightest slot machines anywhere. Those dice and card games are a ripoff," I said.

"Buster said that while you sit at the card table, they bring you free drinks," Earl said.

"The first one is free, the rest are watered down," Mark said.

I saw the flight attendant close the door and the tunnel pulled away.

"It won't be long now, buddy," I said to Earl.

I saw the tractor with the baggage trailer pull away from the plane. The tractor that pushes the plane by the nose gear, must have hooked up already, because we started moving backwards, away from the terminal building. After backing for about a hundred yards, the tail end started swinging to the left. After turning the plane ninety degrees, the tractor stopped pushing and unhooked from the nose gear. We heard the whine as the pilot started the engines. The co-pilot started talking over the intercom. He said to fasten our seat belts. The flight attendant stood in the aisle and demonstrated how to fasten and unfasten a seat belt. Then she showed us how to access the emergency oxygen mask while the co-pilot explained it's use. The no smoking light came on and the plane started taxiing toward the runway.

"It's a little bit like a roller coaster, but don't worry guy," I said.

"Yeah, don't worry, just pray," Mark wisecracked.

"That flight attendant is gonna' come back here and slap the hell outta' you," I said.

Earl was looking a little pale. He was probably wishing he'd had more to drink.

"It'll be a lot better than taking the bus," Andy said.

"I wonder what Pete did with his record collection," I said.

"Those are all original Beatles albums. He's got to be an idiot, hauling those around with him," Mark said, adding—"It smells like somebody is barbequeing." Another airplane came in and landed.

"We'll have to wait a minute or two. If he gets the clearance, the pilot will turn us onto the runway," I explained to Earl. After about half a minute, the pilot turned left then turned left again onto the runway. We could hear the engines whine as they revved up.

"It sounds like our turbines on the Gentry, doesn't it," I said to Earl. The airplane lurched ahead and began to pick up speed rapidly.

"Flap your wings, you big ass bird," Earl said, adding—"That's what we used to say."

"That's the spirit," I said.

The engines were really roaring now. The nose of the airliner lifted up and we felt the main gear lifting off the runway beneath us. The plane was really climbing as the nose lifted even higher.

"When we get a little altitude, you'll feel the wheels come up," I said.

Earl looked a little stiff and his eyes were wide open. It took less than a minute for us to feel the bump as the wheels came up.

"Okay, old buddy, we're on our way," I said. The plane banked while still climbing. "There's Superior, we should fly right across Lake

Michigan. It'll take less than two hours to do what it took five days to do in the Gentry," I said.

"This airplane isn't carrying nineteen thousand tons of taconite either," Andy said.

"Good point," I agreed.

"Excuse me, do you guys work on a cargo ship?" the rocker asked.

"Earl and I work on ships, these other two guys just provide comic relief," I said.

"Are you going one way?" he asked.

"Some of the crew go both ways," Mark wisecracked.

"You should have stayed with Buster and Billy," I said.

"I wouldn't pick those guys up if I was gay," Mark said.

"Now he's getting personal. Unusual for a guy who was on an aircraft carrier," Earl observed.

"There was this guy that would pee the bed. Unfortunately, he was in the bunk right above me," Mark said.

"He never complained about Brad," Andy wisecracked.

"He only loses control of his bladder when he's drinking," Mark said.

"That should be amusing for the indians," I joked.

"You think there's gay indians?" Earl asked.

"Sure, what straight guy would be wearing all those beads and feathers," Mark said.

"How long have you been working on cargo ships?" the rocker asked me.

"Five years now," I said.

"That's very interesting. I'm a drummer in a rock band," he said.

"What band?" I asked.

"Rough beat," he said.

"Let me guess: Heavy metal or punk rock," I said.

"Punk rock, we're gonna' have an album out this month," he said, adding—"I'm Dan."

"I'm Nick."

"Is that Nicole?" he asked.

"Nicolette," I answered.

"I've never heard that name," he said, adding—"Do you live with your parents?"

"No, I have my own house," I said, thinking that I must look younger to him than I really am.

"Whatcha' doing over there, Nick?" Andy asked.

"Robbing the cradle," Mark wisecracked.

"Oh my goodness. What's the Mate gonna' think?" Andy joked.

"When punk rockers start washing up on the shore in Marblehead, we'll know he found out," Mark said.

"Are these guys your older brothers?" Dan asked.

"They just like to clown around. They're just like that on ship. Don't mind them," I said.

Apparently the punk rocker didn't like my shipmates. He began looking at a magazine.

"When does this plane quit climbing? My ears have popped three times already," Earl complained.

"Because you've never flown before. The next time you'll hardly notice it," I said.

"Don't worry Earl, we'll stop at the lounge in Hopkins and grab a quick one. You won't be feeling no pain when you get to Akron-Canton," Mark said.

"I got news for you, it'll cost you three times as much at the airport. You won't have that much time anyway. If you miss that plane, you'll walk home from Hopkins," I said.

I could tell that the plane was leveling out. In a minute, the pilot came over the intercom and said that we were at thirty five thousand feet and cruising at five hundred and forty miles an hour. He informed us that when the seat belt light went out, we could get up from our seats. We all took off our seat belts.

"Duck soup, old buddy, and it's clear weather ahead. One time we were flying out west and we ran into a couple of storms on the way. The plane was bobbing up and down like a boat. I could see the tip of the wing bending up and down about two feet," I said.

"I've seen them bend six feet. Helicopters are really scary. We had some rotor blades come off in a storm. We found ourselves in the ocean that time," Mark said.

"Aren't you supposed to say-'This is no shit, man," I said.

"No, that really happened, in the South China sea. If we hadn't been in the middle of the task force, we all would've drowned," Mark said.

The flight attendant came by, pushing a little cart, offering soft drinks and selling little bottles of beer and mixed drinks.

"You got anything bigger than that, young lady?" Mark asked, when she showed him the mixed drinks.

We laughed at his question.

"He's always been hungup on size," Andy said.

"You have to work with these guys?" the flight attendant asked me.

"This is their best behavior, believe me," I said.

I could see that the rocker would have liked one. A few minutes later, the co-pilot came down the aisle and looked us over.

"What do we have here, the four stooges?"

"Good guess, we're actually the cast from the Love Boat," Mark replied.

"What's the name of your boat?" he asked.

"The steamship Gentry," Andy replied.

"Since I started these daily flights to Duluth, I've run into some Lake Sailors," he said.

"You must be talking about the bars," Mark said.

"Now that you mention it, I could get you some lounge passes," he said.

"That would work for me and Earl. Andy's wife is taking him home straight away and you don't want Nick drinking alcohol," Mark said.

"Is that right?" the co-pilot asked, looking over at me.

"Yeah, she goes crazy and starts fighting," Mark said.

"Wild exaggeration," I shot back.

"She put four guys in the hospital in Detroit. One was a cop!" Mark exclaimed.

"I was trying to get out the door in a hurry. The collision was unavoidable," I said.

"On our last trip to Cleveland, she cold cocked this lawyer. Then for good measure, she jumps over this table and knocks Earl here, down to the floor and stomps the hell outta' him," Mark continued.

"Now, is that true, Earl?" I asked.

"Well, your foot was on my neck," Earl said.

"In the friendliest possible manner," I said.

The co-pilot laughed at that. "Please wait until you're on the ground. I hate doing those FAA reports," he said, smiling at me.

"I'm sure that there will be no trouble like that," I said. I certainly didn't intend to cause any trouble, but I wasn't too sure about Mark and that flight attendant. The co-pilot went forward again.

A little girl who was sitting with her mother, in the seat behind Earl, began to cry. I saw that she had dropped her Barbie doll. I got up from my seat and picked up her doll and handed it to her.

"That's a nice Barbie Doll. I have some Barbies too. Is that a Rock star Barbie?" I asked.

The little girl nodded.

"My name is Nick. What's your name?"

"Me Chrissy," she said.

"That's a pretty name. Is that your Barbie book?" I asked.

She nodded.

"Can I read the book with you?"

"Ask my mommy," she said.

"Sure, if you want to sit here," her mother said.

"That's good, you can sit on my lap then," I said. Chrissy nodded and moved over toward her mommy and I sat down. Chrissy climbed up on my lap.

"There we go. Now what's the name of this book? Oh, it's called Barbie takes a Cruise."

I read the title and showed her the cruise ship. The other guys were making some snide comments, but I ignored them. I read each page and talked with her about the pictures. I was showing her the sea creatures and telling her their names.

"Don't get too technical back there, Nick," Earl joked.

I got her a juice cup from the flight attendant. When we finished the book, I told her some Russian children's stories that my grandmother had told me. She started to fall asleep and her mother took her from me.

"I think she likes you. She usually doesn't take to strangers," her mother said.

I went back to my seat.

"Will Aunt Nicky tell me a story?" Mark wisecracked.

"You've already heard all I wanna' tell ya'."

"Nick, you managed to put Earl to sleep," Andy said.

"Excuse me, Nick." the rocker said.

"Yes." I said.

"Is that stuff true, about kickin' butts when you drink?" he asked.

"Hmm, Well shipmates like to talk, but in truth, it's four or five times what they said, and I usually wasn't drinking," I replied.

"Awesome, man!" he said.

"I think I'm a woman," I said jokingly.

"I wish you could meet my band buddies," he said. He wants to treat me like I'm his trophy. Maybe he's too young to realize that all women aren't brain dead groupies, that want to bed a rock star.

"I may run into you guys sometime," I said.

"If you give me your address, I'll send you an autographed album," he offered.

I took a company business card and wrote an address on the back. "There you are. I'm looking forward to getting your album," I said.

The pilot came over the intercom—"We will begin descending into the upper traffic pattern. Please take your seats and fasten your seat belts. Thank you."

Earl was awaken by the intercom. The two flight attendants passed us, as they walked forward, checking seat belts. The airplane circled for about ten minutes before it descended then turned on the final leg before landing.

"You'll feel the thrust reversers. It really puts the brakes on," I told Earl as we felt the wheels come down.

I could see the houses flashing by and the flaps coming down. The ground was much closer now and I could see the taxiway. We felt a small bump as the main landing gear touched down.

"We're on the ground, safe and sound," I said.

"Okay, what a ride!" he exclaimed. We heard the roar as the thrust reversers kicked in.

"We needed those on the Gentry," Andy said as we lost speed rapidly.

The airplane taxied to the terminal building and stopped. Earl said that he could see the tunnel extending. I looked out the window and saw the tractor with the luggage trailer, pull up next to the plane. It took a few minutes for the pilot to speak on the intercom.

"Good evening. It is now nine thirty two eastern standard time. It is forty two degrees and partly cloudy. We hope you enjoyed your flight. Please fly with us again."

The flight attendant opened the door and walked backwards, letting the people in front get off first.

"Let's try to stay together," Mark suggested.

"Don't worry, the co-pilot will recognize you," I said.

"Let's make it easy for airport security to round us up," Mark joked.

The line moved pretty fast. As the flight attendant passed us, we stood up and opened the overhead compartment and removed our carry on bags.

"Well old buddy, by midnight, you could be home," I said to Earl as he got into line behind me.

"Those other guys on the bus, are probably still in Minnesota," Earl said.

"Now you've spoiled him. He'll never get on that bus again," Andy said.

"Buses are for idiots like Pete, that take three tons of personal property with them. The rest of us know how to travel 'lean and mean'," Mark claimed.

"Like Nick's cosmetics, which she never uses," Earl said.

"Hush Earl. It's not as big as your two hundred pound toolbox," I said.

"Are you the fearsome foursome?" the pilot asked, when we reached the front.

"Andy Botzum, Third Mate," Andy said as he shook hands with the pilot.

"Eric Adkins," the pilot said.

"Mark Cauley, Radar/Radio technician," Mark said as he shook hands.

"Nicolette Strickland, Deckhand," I said.

"Are there many women on the lakes?" he asked as he shook my hand.

"A few, most are Stewards," I said.

"Earl Franklin, Porter," Earl said.

"Hi Earl, I'm Eric Adkins," he said as he shook hands with Earl.

The tunnel at Cleveland-Hopkins was bigger than the one at Duluth and it was painted. When we came out of the tunnel, the co-pilot was there. He handed a lounge pass to Mark.

"No, thank you anyway, I'll be driving," I said and I shook hands with him.

He handed one to Earl.

"My name is Skip Wells. I hope I can fly with you again," he said.

"There's always next season," I said and waved at him. The four of us walked together through the gate area and into the main concourse. We heard a small child shouting gleefully, "Daddy, Daddy!"

"Somebody found you," I said to Andy, but I doubt if he heard me.

He dropped his brief case and threw his arms around Eileen and they kissed. It's gonna' take a while to get them separated, I thought. The two little girls were jumping up and down, trying to get their daddy's attention. After a minute, Eileen looked toward me and Earl and let go of Andy.

"Hi Nick, you're looking well," she said.

"Hi, it's nice seeing you again. I hope the drive over here wasn't too bad," I said.

"Horrendous! I had to go home from the airport and pick up the girls. Thank goodness the traffic wasn't too bad on the turnpike," she said.

"Who are these pretty little ones?" I asked.

"Kaleigh and Desiree, come over here and meet Nick. She works on daddy's ship," Eileen said.

"The girl on daddy's ship!" the older one said and they came running over to me. The younger one always follows her sister.

"Hi, Hi, Hi, you work with my daddy?" Kaleigh asked.

"Yes, I do. Earl and Mark here, also work with your daddy," I said, pointing to them. They frowned at Earl and Mark.

"Don't worry, they're friendly. Just big old Teddy bears," I said. The girls waved at them, tentatively.

"We had better go downstairs and get our bags," Andy said.

"Come on girls," Eileen said.

"Can Nick be my aunt?" Kaleigh asked her mother.

"Ask her yourself," Eileen said.

"Sure, I'll be an aunt to both of you," I replied. Kaleigh grabbed my hand as we headed toward the escalator.

"Aunt Nick, was there a bad storm?" she asked.

"Coming through Lake Huron, we had a storm. When we got into Lake Superior, Your daddy and I were both sick," I said.

"Andy, you didn't tell me that you were sick!" Eileen exclaimed.

"Just a case of the twenty four hour flu that was going around he ship," he explained.

"Aunt Nick, are you coming with us?" Kaleigh asked.

"I'm afraid it might be a little out of your way," I said.

"You still live in Marblehead?" Eileen asked.

"Yes," I replied.

"No problem, we'll get off the turnpike and drop you off, then we'll take route two home," Eileen said.

"That's very kind of you," I said.

"Aunt Nick, can I stay at your house?" Kaleigh asked.

"I think mommy and daddy would rather have you at home. Maybe after the party, you could come over or I'll come over and see you," I replied.

We got on the escalator and went down to the lower level, where the baggage claim is. Halfway down the aisle, we found the conveyor belt with our flight number.

"I wonder if your trash bag made it through, intact," I said to Earl.

"Those are heavy duty lawn bags," Earl said.

"Don't get mad, get Glad," Mark joked.

"I hope the tag stayed on or those people will throw it out with their trash," I said.

Kaleigh and Desiree invented a game where one would set a little ball on the moving belt and the other one would pick it up on the other side. Soon they invented variations to the game, bouncing and rolling the little ball on the belt. It didn't take long for the ball to go through the rubber curtains.

"You'll have to wait for it to come out the other side," Andy said.

"There's too many people, put your ball away," Eileen said.

In a few minutes, we were cheek to jowl at the luggage belt. I told Earl to hang back, I would get his trash bag for him. We heard a thumping noise. I knew the luggage would start coming through. The rubber curtains parted as Earl's trash bag came through.

"It looks like you're in luck, old buddy," I said.

"Fortune favors the foolish," Mark wisecracked.

I picked up Earl's trash bag and saw the little yellow ball, so I picked that up as well and turned around. I handed the ball to Kaleigh and the trash bag to Earl.

"As always, Auntie Nick comes through in a pinch," Earl joked.

"Take all that money you saved on luggage and get that jeep running," I shot back.

My seabag came by and I grabbed it and stepped back, so Mark could take my place at the conveyor belt. It took about ten minutes for Mark and Andy to get all their bags.

"I'll be in Alliance in a day or two. I'll call you before I leave Marblehead," I said to Earl.

"Don't worry, I'll take care of Earl," Mark said.

"You've got less than an hour so re-check your luggage and drink quick," I said.

Earl waved, then he and Mark headed back to the escalator. We started down the long corridor to another corridor which would take us to the parking lot.

"Aunt Nick, I'll help you," Kaleigh said.

"I think it's a little heavy for you," I said.

"Kay, you hold Mommy's hand until we get to the car," Andy said.

"Aunt Nick, have you seen Santa Claus?" Kaleigh asked.

"Yes, in fact, Captain Kompsii had him on the boom of the conveyor," I said smiling.

"Wow, he was on your boat!" Kaleigh exclaimed.

"Yes, with his sleigh, reindeer and everything," I said.

"Do you have a sister?" Kaleigh asked.

"No, I'm afraid not. I have no brothers or sisters," I said.

"Where's your mommy and daddy?" she asked.

"They're in Akron now," I said. Kaleigh paused for a moment.

"Aunt Nick, do you have a grandma?"

"I did, I'm afraid she died about a year ago," I said. Kaleigh paused again. I was wondering if she had ran out of questions.

"Aunt Nick, how old are you?" she asked.

"I'm twenty-six. How old are you?" I asked.

"Me four, Dez three, Mommy, daddy twenty-nine," she said.

"My goodness, you know everybody's age. You must be very smart. Do you take care of your little sister?" I asked.

She nodded. We turned right and got onto the people mover. I sat down my seabag and travel case.

"We don't walk here. The ground moves for us," Kaleigh said.

"That's great, I was getting tired carrying all this stuff," I said, smiling at her.

"We'll get off at door C2," Eileen said.

"Our car is blue and white," Kaleigh said.

"I hope it can carry all of us, I hate to ride in the trunk," I joked.

"It's a Jeep Wagoneer, there's plenty of room," Eileen said.

"The PR guy did an interview with Nick this morning. They said that they would send a car for her. Instead they sent one of those three wheeled sidewalk trucks. Nick and Earl had to ride in the back," Andy explained.

"Ghastly, why did they do that?" Eileen asked.

"Mister Larsen was under the impression that I was an easy date. I'm afraid I had to disappoint him," I replied.

"I would have ran him over with that sidewalk truck," Eileen said.

I saw the sign for the door C2. I picked up my seabag and travel case. Andy picked up his luggage as well. We stepped off the side of the belt and the door opened automatically. A cold drizzle was falling when we got outside, but the parking lot was well lit and the jeep was parked nearby.

Eileen opened the doors while Andy and I went around back. He opened the tail gate, we slid our luggage in and he closed the tail gate. I went to the right side. Kaleigh and Desiree were having a little fight about who would sit next to me and who would sit next to the window. I elected to sit in the middle, so they both could sit next to me and a window. Andy helped to secure Desiree in her car seat, then he got in and started the Jeep.

"Aunt Nick, do you know where we live?" Desiree asked.

"Yes, I do," I said.

"Will you come and see us tomorrow?" she asked.

"I have to go to school for about a week. I'll come to see you after the party. I'll bring your daddy's other friend with me," I said.

They seemed happy with the prospect of meeting another shipmate of their father.

"Aunt Nick, can you tell us a story?" Kaleigh asked.

"Not one of your true stories," Andy said jokingly.

"How about a story my grandmother would tell me? It's called, *The Princess and the Bear*."

"Yeah, we want to hear that story!" they both exclaimed.

I started telling the story while Kaleigh and Desiree listened with rapt interest. It is a long story, so they both were asleep before I finished.

"You're very good with children. You'll have your own children before long," Eileen said.

"I really hadn't planned anything like that," I said.

"Sometimes you don't plan it, you just feel compelled to do it," Eileen said.

That is what my grandmother was trying to tell me. I thought about my grandmother and her view of God and the world. Eichann had a different view of God. He believed that a person was evil because God had made them that way. He believed that a person died before their time, because God preordained it that way. Eichann would say that God took Emma because I was to be with the Mate now. A person does not question God, or rather, there is no point where you can stop questioning God's Will, because there is no point where you can begin to question God's Will. Eichann would point to the pyramids and Greek temples and say that there were governments and supreme courts that told us all about how to deal with God, but those civilizations have come and gone and God is still here. I felt Kaleigh slump sideways, her head coming to rest against my arm. I slouched in the seat, so I could rest my head and I closed my eyes. I thought about when I was a kid. We lived next to a big farm. The farmer had a reddish-brown shetland pony named Penny. They would let me ride her when they were in the barn. When the pony was out in the pasture, she would run from me. I learned to trap her between the hog fence and the garden fence. Once I had the lead rope on her, she gave up playing games and was a good saddle pony. Most of the time, I rode her bareback. I drifted off to sleep after a few minutes.

I woke up when the car came to a stop. Andy was paying the woman at the toll booth. We headed north on route 250. After several miles, we turned left and headed west on route two. There were not many lights in the bay when we crossed the bridge. I could see the distant green flashing light of the Marblehead lighthouse. After crossing the Thomas Edison bridge, I told Andy to make a right at the first road.

"You know you have to make a right, then a left turn when coming back on Bayshore," I said.

"Yes, Dave showed me that the last time I was up here," Andy said.

The road was very dark because there were no street lights here and it was cloudy. We did not see any cars on the road, up ahead I could see the lights on the limestone conveyor over the road. I saw the name D. McCracken on a mail box.

"There's the Mate's house, make a left at the next road," I said, adding—"My house is the second one on the left. You'll see the wagon wheels at the end of the driveway."

Andy turned left on the gravel road. He saw the wagon wheels before I did and turned into the driveway and pulled up to the house. I carefully moved Kaleigh to the other side of me, as I got out of the jeep. Kaleigh woke up for a moment, then went back to sleep. I closed the door as gently as possible. Andy got out and opened the tailgate.

"I'll help you carry your stuff in and check your house," Andy Said.

"Okay, that's very kind of you," I said.

Andy carried my seabag and travel case, while I dug out my keys. I opened the door and turned on the outside light and livingroom light. I went into the kitchen and bathroom, Andy went upstairs to check the bathroom and the bedroom.

"I didn't see any bats," Andy said, when he came downstairs.

"Okay, thanks alot. I'll see you at the party," I said, shaking hands with Andy.

"You're welcome, have a good night," he said.

"Tell Eileen and the girls, I said good-bye," I said.

"Sure, will do," Andy said as he left. I waved at them and closed the door.

I locked the door, checked the back door and the windows. I went into the kitchen and put on some water for macaroni and cheese. I went to Grandma's bedroom and opened the top drawer. I opened the travel case and removed the picture frame and set it on the dresser. I took out my jewelry box and put it in the top drawer. I hung up my coats in the closet. Setting my seabag aside, I put the makeup case on the dresser. I picked up the picture frame and took it downstairs with me. I looked at the pictures in the frame. I saw a picture of the Mate and Emma holding a baby; the Mate in his academy uniform ; the Mate when he was about ten years old, with his parents and brother; a photograph of the crew on the Victory; a picture of Tommy and I at the lighthouse when we were kids; a picture of my grandmother and me at sixteen, dancing in Russian costumes; a picture of my grandmother and Emma, sitting down on the shore. I remembered seeing the picture of me and Tommy in the lighthouse. Apparently my grandmother had given it to Emma.

When I started eating my macaroni, I heard a knock on the door, so I got up and went to the door. When I opened the door, I saw that it was my neighbor.

"Good evening, you're up late," I said.

"I have some mail for you," he said, handing me a large handful of envelopes.

"Oh, thank you, you didn't have to bring it over tonight. I was going to stop by tomorrow," I said.

"I was checking to make sure that everything was okay," he said.

"Thank you so much and thank Betty for me," I said.

"Okay, good night," he said and he turned and left.

I was thinking that it is such comfort to have neighbors that look out for me like that. I went back to eating macaroni and looking at the pictures in the frame. I thought it a rather strange coincidence that there were some pictures that had some significance to me. Before I could finish my macaroni, the phone rang. Who could this be, I wondered as I picked up the phone.

"Hello," I said.

"Hello Nick, this is Dave. I hope I didn't wake you."

"Well hello sailor, couldn't wait?" I joked.

"I just wanted to make sure that you made it home okay," he said. There are seventeen other guys, I wonder if he called any of them, I thought.

"Yes, in fact, we ran into George Fox at the Wharf. He gave us a ride to the airport and got us another flight. We flew to Cleveland with Andy and Mark. Andy and Eileen drove me home," I said.

"That's great, I'm glad that everything went well for you," he said.

"We were up on Spirit Mountain, we could see the Gentry still heading for Lafarge," I said.

"The popular makeout spot!" the Mate exclaimed.

"Don't worry, it wasn't dark yet and Earl was there," I said.

"How was the steak at the Wharf?" he asked.

"Very tasty, a nice ambience at that place. Did you have Jumbo Egger's cooking?" I asked.

"No, Eggers got here too late. We actually called out for pizza and subs," he said.

"Was that on a purchase order?" I asked.

"No, we had to chip in for that," he said.

"Try to stay away from that fast food, it will give you ulcers," I said.

"Okay . . . I really wish I was home."

"I was kinda' wishing the same thing when we drove past your house," I said.

"Holding you this morning seems like a year ago," he said.

"After the party, we'll hold each other quite a bit," I said.

"Is that a promise?" he asked.

"You can take it as fact," I said.

"Can I call you tomorrow?" he asked.

"Sure," I said and I gave him the phone number for Mary-Beth at the soroity house. He promised to give me the number when they got a phone line hooked up to the wheelhouse.

"I have to get off now. Bye-bye sweetie, I love you." The moment of truth had come.

"I love you too, Dave, Bye," I said and I hung up the phone.

When I got back to the kitchen, the macaroni was cold, so I threw it out. I went to the bedroom and opened the top drawer. I checked grandpa's pistol and my jewelry box. I got ready for bed and turned off the lights. As I lay in bed, I thought about being in Mount Union again. If I go to graduate school, some things would have to change. I was determined to get my bachelor's degree before I got married or went back on the lakes.

As I closed my eyes I could hear the wind sighing continuously outside. I figured it would be sleet or snow by tomorrow morning. I was wondering what the mate was thinking up in Duluth, when I fell asleep. When I woke up, I saw daylight in the window. I sat up with a start, thinking that I had missed my four to eight watch. I remembered that the season was over and I was back home. It was a little past nine in the morning. I put on my house coat and went in the kitchen to make coffee. I turned on the radio to catch the weather. The oldies station was playing Itchycoo Park. I was sitting at the kitchen table drinking coffee and feeling real disappointed that John or Louie wasn't here to make breakfast for me. I put some frozen waffles in the toaster oven and made a mental note of the few things I wanted to get at the grocers before I went to Alliance. The phone rang, when I answered it, it was Mary-Beth. She said that she would be in Marblehead around four o'clock to pick me up. I went back to the kitchen to finish my breakfast. As I ate, I thought about the ten days I would be with the little sisters of Tri Sigma, Mary-Beth,

Tamara and Shelly. I knew them, but I had never lived with them before. I hoped that they would behave like shipmates. In other words, I hoped that they wouldn't act like giddy, brain dead teenagers. After Breakfast, I cleaned up the dishes, then went to the bedroom to unpack my clothes. My cottage has a washer and dryer on one side of the closed off back porch, behind the kitchen. I washed my work clothes and blankets. While my clothes were drying, I put on my parka and went out to the garage and started my truck. I checked on the motorcycles, while the truck was warming up. I backed the truck out and closed the garage door. I drove east, under the quarry conveyor belt and into town. I stopped at the little IGA store and got some milk and cereal. I ran into the mayor's wife at the checkout, she asked me about David McCracken. I told her that since August, I had been a deckhand on the Gentry and that David was staying up in Duluth for about a week to complete the lay-up. I told her that I would be in Alliance for about a week, with some college friends. She said for me and David to come over and visit her and Adam when we got back. That was very kind of her. She had been a good friend of my grandmother for years. I drove down by the lighthouse and saw a ship at anchor on the lake. It must have been waiting to load limestone. It was too cold to go to the cemetery, so I went home. I saw the ferry boat was still running, when I went past the Neumann dock. Some deer hunters and fuel oil trucks, were the only vehicles going to Kelleys Island. I parked the truck in the garage, then locked the doors and activated the alarm system. After putting the groceries away, I called Guiddo and left a message on his answering machine. I called my lawyer and talked to him and the legal secretary. He informed me that my parents were still threatening to sue me, but neither one of us was worried. He was my grandmother's lawyer and had done an excellent job in probating her will. I told him that I would send him a check to cover the additional taxes. After I got off the phone, I put on my parka and went outside to pick up some small branches that had fallen in my backyard. I began talking to my neighbor, Chuck. He was always interested in lake freighters, but had never been on one. His wife, Betty, invited me in for lunch. While we ate, I told them of the storm while upbound in Lake Huron. Bud was amazed that the ship lost three or four knots of forward speed, due to the wind and waves. I told them that I would be in Alliance for about a week and that I would be coming home after the end of the season party. As usual, they promised to watch my house and get my mail for me while

I was gone. I gave them a packet of the Captain's cookies, before I left. It was one o'clock when I got home. I looked through my mail. It was the usual stuff, letters from my employer and letters from the union. It's always the same deal, it's gonna' cost me more money for less benefits. I got an invitation to a Wiccan Yule celebration in a barn in the Cuyahoga Valley. I don't know how these people got my name and address. A couple Hanukah cards and two letters from people I never heard of. I put those in the pocket of my coat, to read later. I packed some casual clothes and college clothes, in my big suit case, along with some makeup and toiletries. I put some stuff in my grandmother's safe and took out some money. What are friends for, if not to borrow money. It seemed like I was barely finished securing the house when Mary-Beth pulled in the driveway in a silver-gray Renault Alliance. When she came to the door, I handed her a grocery bag with milk, bread and cheese. I grabbed my big suitcase and locked the front door. When we got to the car, I put my suitcase on the back seat. I told her that I would drive. I wanted to save the engine and the clutch from further anguish.

Mary-Beth slept while, I took the turnpike east and route seventy seven south to route sixty two, and sixty east to Alliance. We were there in a little over two hours. The Tri Sigma house is a small house off campus, but only a block away. The Greek letters on the mailbox and above the front door, are the only thing that distinguish it from an ordinary residence. When we arrived, Tammy held the front door for us, while we brought my stuff in. Tammy and Shelly gave me a hug and said that they were glad to see me. Shelly said that two men had just called. One said that he would call back every hour and the other said that he would be over around seven. I told her that the guy coming over was Earl and the guy calling back every hour was our First Mate, David McCracken. One of the other girls had left, so I got a room to myself. I gave them a hundred dollars for rent and told them that I would bring home some groceries later. They accepted the donations with a great deal of enthusiasm.

At seven o'clock sharp, the phone rang, I knew who it was. Tammy said it was for me, as I came down the stairs.

"Hello," I said, answering the phone.

"Nick, it's me, Dave," he said.

"Hello sailor, are you laid-up yet?" I asked jokingly.

"No, but I'm looking forward to it," he replied.

"Have you gotten a good meal out of Eggers yet?" I asked.

"No, I'm afraid that it was Burger Barn today," he replied.

"If you don't lay off that junk food, you'll be a broken down old man when I see you next," I said.

"A sick, old man sweetie, if I have to eat Eggers cooking," he said, adding—"So, what do you think?"

"Two things, actually. If you're a sick old man, I'll have to send you back to Mrs. Kefauver. Umm . . . never mind the other thing."

"You bad, Nicki," he said.

"Only my grandmother would call me that, but you can call me Nicki," I said.

"How are things going down there?" he asked.

"Pretty good, Earl should be stopping by soon and we'll go grocery shopping," I said.

"I hope he doesn't take you out drinking," he said.

"You must have me confused with somebody else," I said jokingly.

"All I can think about is holding you," he said.

"That was the thing I didn't want to mention. You had better think about how you're going to get back to Cleveland in time for the party," I said.

"I'm definitely taking an airplane," he said.

"Well, you'd better check it out. Those airlines are all screwed up, up there," I said.

"Will do," he said.

"I have to be going, Dave. Do you have a phone in the wheelhouse?" I asked.

"No, not yet, probably by tomorrow," he said.

"Okay, call me tomorrow. I love you, bye, bye," I said.

"I love you, sweetie, bye, bye," he said and I hung up the phone.

A few minutes later, Earl came by in his jeep. Tammy let him in, while I was upstairs.

"Hey, old buddy, I'm surprised to see you up this early," I said jokingly, as I came down the stairs.

"The damn rooster woke me up at five this morning and I thought I was still on the boat," he said.

"Yeah, that old cock reminds me of the Bosun," I said.

"I've been fixing the fences," he said.

"That sounds like a wonderful job in this weather," I said.

"I couldn't get the tractor started," he said.

"I'll help you with that while I'm down here," I said, as we went out the door.

While we were at the store, I stopped at the cooler to get some rootbeer. Earl picked up a twelve pack of beer and put it in the cart.

"This is for later," he said. How much later, I wondered. I saw him looking at some money in his hand.

"I got it this time, old buddy," I said.

When we got to the checkout, I had to show my drivers license. When we got home, Earl helped me carry in the six bags of groceries. We played cards for about half an hour, then Earl left. For a couple hours, I helped Tammy translate a Russian text for a research paper that she was writing for a class in International Studies. Mary-Beth was in Premed, going into Veterinary school. Shelly was an Education major. For the next nine days, I knew that I would be occupied in arranging to get my own classwork finished, while helping my room mates, who were going after-term in their research papers.

Everything went smoothly, until a week later, when Shelly decided that she had to have the house to herself that night, so she could entertain her musician boyfriend. Earl was kind enough to come over and pick me up. I spent the evening cleaning Earl's house, while Earl worked on his tractor. I didn't notice Earl coming in before I went to bed. Earl was right about one thing, that crazy rooster starts at five in the morning and goes every five minutes. By six thirty, I decided to get up anyway. I got dressed and went into the kitchen to make breakfast. All Earl had for breakfast was mush and eggs, so I fried both. Earl wasn't in the house, so I put on my boots and my parka and went out to the barn. Going to the lower level, where the cows are kept, I saw a foam cooler full of empty beer cans. I saw the rooster perched on the hay manger. When I approached, he grudgingly stepped aside and I saw Earl, lying in the manger, covered with a horse blanket, while a cow looked on forlornly. I tapped him gently on his arm.

"Wake up, old buddy," I said.

"Okay Munny, I'm coming," Earl said, half asleep.

"I've killed men for less than that," I said jokingly.

"Is it watch time already?" he asked.

"No, I think it's cow time, already. Feed these animals and come in and get some breakfast," I said.

Earl threw the blanket off and slowly raised himself up and sat up in the manger. He rubbed his head and blinked a couple times.

"Hey there, Nick," he said, trying to smile at me.

"Throw some hay in there and come in and get some breakfast," I said.

"I guess I'd better feed the old girls," he said, grabbing a hay fork.

I waited until he had filled the manger with hay, then we walked to the house. I put breakfast on the table, while Earl washed up.

"You wouldn't be so stiff and sore if you slept in your own bed," I said.

"Yeah, I fell asleep trying to figure out what's wrong with that damn tractor," Earl said, as he sat down at the table.

"All I could find is Mush and Eggs," I said, putting the plate in front of him.

"Thanks, that's what I usually have," he said. I sat down at the table.

"So, what's wrong with that tractor?" I asked.

"I don't know. I can't get the engine to kick over," he said.

"I'll help you look at it later," I said, adding—"That little Ford still runs, doesn't it?" He nodded.

"What kinda' tractor is that?" I asked.

"A McCormick-Farmall M, forty nine or fifty, I can't remember the year," he said.

"It's gasoline?" I asked.

He nodded.

"It shouldn't be too hard. Those old tractors are pretty durable and simple," I said.

"I gotta' get it running. That's my tractor for plowing and disking," he said.

"Is there any gas in that LandMark tank?" I asked.

"No, I'll drain some outta' my jeep, if I have to," he said. He showed me some letters and documents from his lawyer. "These papers say that I own the farm, free and clear. I just have to pay insurance and taxes," he said.

I read the documents and explained to him that his grandfather had set it up so that Earl's father and uncle could only sell their halves of the farm to each other. Since his father had acquired the entire farm, then he could pass it on to Earl in it's entirety. I understood that his brothers had received a substantial cash settlement from insurance policies.

"Yeah, It's yours now. You just gotta' make it go, old buddy," I said, carefully putting the documents in the envelopes. "Get yourself a safe to put these in," I said.

After breakfast, Earl went back to the barn, while I did dishes and cleaned up the kitchen. After I finished, I headed out to the barn. I heard the tractor cough and backfire. That didn't sound anymore encouraging than Earl's cussing and damning.

"What's the problem, old buddy?" I asked.

"I think the battery is down," he said.

I climbed up on the drawbar, while he lifted up the battery box cover. I saw that there were two six volt batteries in series, to make twelve volts.

"Let's put the charger on here, set for twelve volts. Then we'll see what else we can find," I said.

Walking around to the other side, I could see that the fuel bowl was half full of dirt and water.

"This fuel bowl needs help," I said.

We took it off and cleaned it and put it back on. As soon as Earl turned on the gas, it filled up with crap again. We drained the gas tank into glass jugs and found that all the gasoline had been contaminated. After cleaning the gas tank and the fuel bowl again, we removed the carburetor and cleaned out the float chamber and jets, then reassembled everything. Those old tractors were simple and relatively easy to work on. After draining a couple gallons of gas out of his jeep and putting it in his tractor, we took the battery charger off. Earl got up on the tractor and pulled out the choke, set the throttle and pressed the starting pedal. It started right up. We took the gasoline that we drained out, behind the barn and burned it. I told Earl that his brothers may have put sugar in it. Earl put some five gallon cans in his jeep, so he could get gas later. I helped him clean some stalls and change out the water buckets. He told me that I was a good farmhand and could have a job on his farm. Since we are shipmates, I told him that I would help him out anytime. I really enjoyed doing some manual work, instead of writing research papers. Later that afternoon, Mary-Beth came by to pick me up. We asked Earl if he wanted to come to the mall with us. He said that he had learned not to go shopping with women. While we were going back to the sorority house, Mary-Beth said that I smelled like the barn. I thought this was an unusual comment coming from someone going into Veterinary medicine. After showering and putting on some clean clothes, we headed for the Carnation mall.

We stopped at the hairdresser, so I could make an appointment for two days hence. The hairdresser was very professional and suggested a half updo, which was a popular prom style. After seeing the other styles that were possible with my hair, I agreed to the half updo. We must have visited a half dozen dress shops before I found a lace scarf dress that looked like something that Carole Lombard had worn in 1940. Although it was sleeveless, the hem went down to the floor. The scarf hung down a couple feet in the back. I had a ruby brooch that would go good with the ivory color of the dress. Next, I picked out some Tracy strap pumps in metallic pewter. Mary-Beth said that I would be the best dressed woman at the party. I told her that I may be the only woman at the party. Only the Big Wheels can bring their wives and girlfriends. Captain Kompsii would bring his wife, of course. When we got home, Shelly's boyfriend was visiting and had brought another guy with him. He was trying to talk Tammy into going out with him. Tammy already had a hot date with Eddy. Like a soldier going overseas, Tammy was trying to get all she could before her two month trip to the Soviet Union. This other guy, Kyle, started talking to me. He was amazed that I work on lake freighters. He was a nice looking, athletic type, but he had nooky on the brain. When he started talking that 'guy in every port' crap, I excused myself. Shortly after the jerks left, the Mate called. I told him that I helped Earl get his tractor running and went to the mall to get a dress. He told me that he hadn't bought a suit yet. I told him that I saw a nice suit in a men's store by the library. He told me that it had taken a couple days to get the airlines straightened out. I fervently hoped that he would get to Cleveland on time. He told me that he and the Captain and the Chief went to The Wharf. I told him that I had fried mush and eggs at Earl's house. At least he was getting a good breakfast and lunch from Louie. Apparently Louie wouldn't work in the galley when Eggers was there. One more day of ship food and then those guys would be heading back to Cleveland. I spent the rest of the evening, finishing a rough draft for Tammy. I spent part of the next day talking to the Dean and some professors that had been good friends of my grandmother. They had been very helpful in arranging it so that I would be able to take my classes as independent study. later, I went to the library with Mary-Beth. She was having difficulty finding some journal references. I had to teach her to use the Citation Indexes. I can't believe the number of students who can't use the reference indexes. When I first started college, a professor told us that you don't need to know anything, you only need to know how to find it. I spent the rest of the afternoon and evening, helping her write her research paper. The next morning, it was snowing heavily in Alliance. A travel ban was in effect for Stark county, but Summit and Cuyahoga counties were okay to travel. I spent the morning revising Mary-Beth's research paper, until we had an acceptable rough draft. At noon, Earl came by and took me to get my hair done. I expressed some concern about the weather. Earl wasn't worried at all, he had complete confidence in that old jeep of his. One thing it lacked was adequate interior heating. Fortunately the snow stopped about this time, giving us hope that the travel ban would be lifted. Earl dropped me off at the sorority house and said that he'd be back at five o'clock. After a quick lunch, I packed my stuff, except for the clothes that I would be wearing and my boots. I took a walk with Mary-Beth to pick up some stuff to decorate the place for Christmas. Somehow, I got volunteered into helping those three put up Christmas decorations. At four o'clock, I took a shower and put on my new dress, but I wore my work boots. When I came downstairs, Tammy whistled.

"When he sees you in that dress, you're gonna' find a new meaning for the word-Mate!" she exclaimed.

I put on my leather maxi coat and my scarf. I put my little clutch purse in the coat pocket. I put my new pumps in a plastic bag and set it next to the front door with my big suitcase. Tammy was dressed in travel clothes. Warm travel clothes, since she was going to the Soviet Union via Canada and England. A few minutes later, Earl pulled in the driveway in his jeep. He and Mary-Beth helped us carry our luggage out to the jeep. Tammy got in the back seat and I got in the front, while Earl put our baggage in the back of the jeep. Earl had taken my suggestion and put two blankets in the jeep. We were covering ourselves when Earl got in.

"Are you cold already?" he asked.

"No, and hopefully we won't be when we get to Cleveland," I said.

"Those freeways are all crappy up there. I know some backroads through the Cuyahoga Valley," he said as he backed the jeep out of the driveway.

Earl is proud of his four wheel drive jeep and shows it by challenging, rather than avoiding, every snow drift he can. Earl assured us that he had plenty of gas, even though his gas guage was broken. The lack of mats and carpeting on the floor, meant that our feet were on the steel of the floor pans. It was a quarter to seven, when Earl turned onto East Ninth street. We went almost down to the pier then turned right on Marginal road and headed for Burk Lakefront airport. It didn't take long to get there. Earl stopped in front of the terminal and I helped Tammy with her bags. We went to the Air Canada baggage check-in. We hugged before parting.

"Write me and stay out of trouble over there," I said.

"I will and if I meet any good looking MIG pilots, I'll send them your way," she said.

When I got outside, the jeep was still in front of the terminal. When I got in, Earl was trying to tie his tie.

"We'll get that later, guy. Let's roll," I said.

Earl got back out on the shoreway and I showed him how to get to the Erieview building. The parking deck was only half filled and we parked fairly close to the entrance. After entering the building, we walked down a hallway to the elevators. The Top Of The Town restaurant is on the top floor and I had just enough time to tie Earl's tie before we got there.

CHAPTER 14

End of the Season Party

When the elevator door opened, we stepped out and into the grand lobby. We headed for the coatroom on the right. I took off my work boots and put them in the plastic bag. I put on my heels and buckled the tiny buckles on the straps. It always takes a few minutes for me to feel steady on heels. After checking in our coats and boots, we headed for the ornate wooden doors of the banquet room. The sign declared a welcome to the officers and crew of the Steamship John L. Gentry.

"All these months living together and I never knew his first name," I wisecracked.

On a table to the right of the doors was an ice sculpture of a straight deck cargo ship with a wire unloading boom. It was a few hatches short of the Gentry, but it was a good job, nonetheless. I could have kicked myself for forgetting my camera again. Earl opened the door for me and we entered the banquet room.

"These are some fancy digs," Earl said, obviously impressed by all the chandeliers and candles.

The banquet room had a wide aisle between five tables on each side. By the left wall, there were tables for appetizers. By the right wall, there was a bar, which was where everybody was at, so we headed that way. Earl was clearly enthusiastic about the prospect of free alcohol.

As we approached, somebody whistled, then everybody took up the chorus.

"I haven't seen such enthusiasm from this crew since we docked next to Hooters," I declared.

"It looks like the princess and the pauper," Ron wisecracked.

"Nick looks like she just stepped out on the red carpet," Smitty said.

"I think she's a movie star. It can't be our Nick," Al said.

I held up my hand, "Autographs later," I said jokingly. Andy moved to the left and Mark moved to the right, when we got to the bar.

"Didn't I meet you gentlemen on an airplane. Was it in Paris or Rome?" I asked.

"Put this pretty young lady's drinks on my tab," Mark said jokingly.

"Thank you, my good man," I said, adding—"I'll have a rootbeer for now."

"I'll have the same without the root," Earl said.

"I saw that Earl got home okay, but I never heard anything about you," I said to Mark.

"After getting Earl on the van, I went out on a date with that stewardess," he said, grinning.

"You must have bombed out or we'd be reading about it in the Plain Dealer by now," Ed wisecracked.

"Let's just say that we parted as friends," Mark said.

"You found yourselves mutually incompatible?" I asked.

"That's putting it tactfully," Andy said.

I was looking up and down the bar to see who all was there.

"She's looking for the Mate, now," John wisecracked. Some of the guys laughed.

"Actually, I was looking for Dixon. I thought I heard him," I said. Dixon has a distinctive bass voice and a Southern accent that you can hear over other people talking.

"He's down at the end," John said.

"I thought you'd still be out," I said.

"I got off to come here. I'll catch my boat in the Rouge river," John answered.

"Up the ladder from the Westcott. Like Earl and I had to do this past summer, when we boarded the Gentry?" I asked.

"No, the boat will be docked for a couple of days," he said.

"The first morning that I was home, I was disappointed that Louie wasn't there to cook my breakfast for me. For the last nine days, I've been living on sorority sisters' cooking," I said.

"My god, you're still alive!" Gary exclaimed.

"Don't feel sorry for her, she didn't have to eat Eggars cooking," Ron groaned.

"Nobody ate space boy's cooking. They threw it over the fence then ordered out," Ed informed us.

"The delivery boys must have been working over time up there," I joked.

Earl said that Kenny and Billy were coming. As they approached the bar, I saw Kenny had his sizable bulk in a Tuxedo and Billy was wearing a church suit.

"A little over dressed, aren't ya' guy?" Brad shouted.

"Don't listen to him, he's jealous," Billy said, adding—"Hey Nick, you're looking good this evening!"

"Thanks, Billy. How did things go?" I asked.

"It couldn't be better. Southern Michigan waived the entrance exams because I was on the lakes. I'm applying for state and federal grants. I got a scholarship for spring semester, that will pay for books and tuition. I'll stay with my parents for the first year, at least," he said.

"Have you registered for your classes yet?" I asked.

"No, when I get home, I'll meet with somebody in the Dean's office and see my whatcha' callit guy," he said.

"You mean, your academic advisor?" I asked.

"Yeah, my academic advisor. They'll tell me the courses I need and how to register," Billy said.

"Yes, they probably have an open registration. You'll have to go down there and wait in line. You probably won't get locked out of any courses at the freshmen level," I explained.

"I'm really excited about it!" he exclaimed.

"Well, stay focused on your classes, forget about parties and you should do alright," I said.

"I think I owe you a hard hat," I heard Dixon say. I turned around and saw Dixon wearing a neck brace.

"My goodness, I didn't know if you were gonna' make it or not," I said, while shaking hands with him.

"Six more months and I should be back out on the lakes," he said.

"That's great! I was thinking about visiting some friends in Vicksburg. If I do, I'll stop by and see you." I said.

"Not in that dress, I hope. Women in Mississippi don't wear dresses like that," he said.

"This is a California dress, like you see on TV," I said.

"I'll catch ya' later, I have to see some guys at the other end."

"Okay, you be careful over there," I said.

The waiters were doing something on the VIP tables at the front of the room. I figured that this was a prelude to the Big Wheels making their entrance. I know the Captain isn't real keen on that sort of thing. I saw Earl talking with John. Earl looked over at me.

"You guys seem to be enjoying your beer," I observed.

"Some of these guys are making fun of my suit," Earl complained.

"I think it's a Jim Dandy suit. It looks like you got a new shirt and tie, very fashionable," I remarked.

Earl looked embarassed. "I was telling Kenny that you helped me get my tractor running. I said that you spent the night over at my house. Joe said that he'd be sure and let the Mate know about it."

"Don't let a little thing like that, worry you. I'll explain things to the Mate, if need be and some people like Joe, may be getting knocked on their ass before this party is over," I said, gently slapping Earl on the back. Earl smiled at me.

"You're like my mother. She would make me feel better about things by talking to me like that," Earl said.

"Shipmates," I said.

"Shipmates," Earl replied as we hooked thumbs and shook hands. "I don't understand what all these dishes are for," Earl said.

"This is a place setting for a formal dinner. They always go all-out here. Starting on the right, we have the soup spoon, teaspoon and knife. Above those, we have the white wine glass, the red wine glass and water goblet. In the middle is the Dinner plate. They always fold up the napkin and set it on the dinner plate. Above, we have the dessert fork and the dessert spoon. On the left, the dinner fork and salad fork and above those, the bread and salad plate with the butter knife," I explained.

I saw that the seating was by division. Everyone had a name plate indicating where they were supposed to sit.

"That's a lot of dishes. I'm glad I'm not a porter in this outfit," Earl remarked.

"Food is usually served from the left and drinks are served from the right," I said, adding—"Someone will be around later to ask you what you want for dinner."

438

"I hope they're not talking French. I don't understand any French," Earl said.

I heard the door open and I looked over and saw the Mate entering with the Chief and the Bosun. I knew the Mate could hardly fail to notice me, especially since I was the only one in the room wearing an evening dress and heels. The Mate announced that the engineering guys would go with the chief. The deck gang would go with the Bosun. The Wheelsmen and stewards would go with him. We were to be photographed by departments and as a group, while standing behind the ice sculpture. Us in the deck gang headed toward the Bosun. I was all smiles as I passed the Mate.

"Good evening, Mr. McCracken," I greeted him.

"J-C, you're looking good," he said softly.

"Let's not get religious here," I said, jokingly.

After the photographer took pictures of the four departments, Captain Kompsii came into the lobby, accompanied by Kenny Ring and a guy I didn't know. With them were three women. For the group picture, the Captain stood amidships, next to the port side of the ice sculpture, while the officers and crew flanked him on both sides, according to rating. I noticed that two of the three women, seemed to have their eyes on me. After the picture taking was over, the Mate told us to be seated at the table with our name plate.

I had just about made it through the door, when I heard the Mate say—"Miss Strickland, one moment, please." I stopped and turned around. Waiting a moment for the engineering gang to get clear, I walked toward the Mate, who had joined the group the Captain was with. I felt rather awkward. I wished that I could have saluted or something.

"Miss Strickland, this is Aldrich Bruenstein, the new Maritime Operations Manager."

"It's a pleasure to meet you, Mr. Bruenstein," I said as I shook his hand.

"This is his wife, Ethel."

"It's a pleasure to meet you, Miss Strickland," she said.

"Please call me Nick," I said as I shook hands with her.

She was wearing a Sarong style pants set. Large flowers on a black background, with Leopard borders. A very unusual dress to see in Cleveland.

"You know Kenny Ring, of course," the Mate said.

"Of course, nice seeing you again," I said as I shook hands with Mr. Sourpuss.

"And this is his friend, Meredith James."

"Hello, nice meeting you, Meredith," I said as I shook hands with her.

"You can call me Mary," she said.

I could call her a 'rent a Ho', I thought. Her black velour top with the plunging V-neck and sheer, see thru sleeves, along with the raggedy hem, black velvet skirt said paid escort.

"Miss Strickland, please meet Grainne Kompsii," the Mate said.

"I'm so happy to meet you, Mrs. Kompsii."

"I've heard quite a lot about you, Miss Strickland. Please call me Grace," she said, shaking my hand.

"You can call me Nick," I said.

"I love your dress, Nick," she said.

"Thank you, your dress is very lovely also," I said.

Mrs. Kompsii is a tall woman. At least five feet, nine inches, without her heels. She was wearing a beaded and embroidered Bolero and a halter dress in iced mocha satin. I wouldn't have guessed her age at over fifty, if I hadn't known that she was sixty two, like the Captain.

"Shall we go in?" Mr. Bruenstein asked.

"After you," the Captain said.

Mister and Misses Bruenstein went through the door first, followed by Kenny Ring and his date, then Captain Kompsii and Grace. The Mate and I, brought up the rear. I intentionally lagged a little bit.

"Too bad you couldn't bring a paid escort to the festivities," I said, smirking as we parted company and I took my seat next to Al.

"What was that all about?" Ron asked.

"The other women wanted to check out my dress, apparently," I said.

"What were you telling the Mate?" Al asked.

"I was telling him that I'll bet Mister Ring's date is a paid escort," I replied.

"You clowns knock it off. Act like human beings, for once," the Bosun requested.

I saw Andy take my place next to the Mate.

"You looked better there," Ed wisecracked.

The other guys laughed. When the "couples" got to the front, they turned and went behind the table, so they would be facing us when they sat down. Mr. Bruenstein sat in the middle with his wife at his right side. Kenny Ring sat at her right side with Meredith to his right and Andy at the right of Meredith. The Captain sat at Bruenstein's left and Grace to the left of him. Grace indicated that the Mate should sit at the end, leaving an empty seat between them.

"That's odd. There must be another guest coming," The Bosun said.

"Maybe it's for Nick," Smitty said.

"Maybe it's for Elijah," I said, referring to the custom at the Passover table, but nobody got the joke. A man in a red jacket, came to our table without being seen by anyone.

"Miss Strickland, Misses Kompsii requests your presence at the head table," he said after bowing. I rose from my chair and curtsied. The man accompanied me to the head table and announced my name, causing everyone to rise as I stepped to the empty place at the table. I had to bite my tongue to keep from laughing. I thought of that old jump rope song-'salute to the Captain, curtsey to the Queen'. We all sat down when Mister Bruenstein did. I was still biting my tongue. This was causing me to use more self control than I had planned on using this night. The guys in the red jackets came by with the dinner cocktails. I really wanted a drink of some kind, right then, but I acted cool and said please and thank you when the young man set one on the table in front of me.

"Gin and Vermouth cocktails are a little too dry for me," Mrs. Kompsii said.

"Umm . . . this one certainly is," I said.

"I hope I didn't take you from your friends," Grace said.

"They'll manage without me, I'm sure," I replied.

"Bill tells me that you live in Marblehead, not far from David."

"Yes, Marblehead is small, so you can't live far from anyone else who lives there," I said.

"Yes, Fairport is like that," she said, adding—"You go to school in Alliance?"

"Yes, I'll finish this semester. I'm not going back on the lakes or anything else until I get my degree," I explained.

"Mount Union is a lovely school. I went to Lake Erie College. I got a degree in Education," Grace said.

The Captain began talking to Grace, so the Mate rather eagerly struck up a conversation.

"I noticed you right away in that dress," he said.

"Since none of the other twenty seven guys were wearing one, I figured you would," I said jokingly. I noticed he had a dark blue suit like the one I saw in the men's store in Duluth.

"So how was life with the little sisters?"

"Pretty boring actually. Most of the time, I was buying them things or writing their research papers. The only interesting part was the night I spent over at Earl's," I said. That put a flap in his sail.

"Say what?!" he exclaimed without raising his voice.

"Shelly wanted the house to herself, two nights ago, so she could entertain her musician boyfriend. Earl came over and picked me up. I cleaned his house, while he was out in the barn working on his tractor. I didn't see him come in before I went to bed. The next morning, I made breakfast and went out to the barn and found him sleeping in the hay manger," I explained.

"You expect me to believe that?" he asked.

"Knowing Earl like you do, could you believe anything else?" I asked.

"No, that sounds plausible in Earl's case," he said.

"After I got him in for breakfast, we went out to the barn and I helped him get his tractor running," I said.

"What was wrong with his tractor?" the Mate asked.

"It looked like muddy water and sugar had been put into the gas tank. I noticed it in the fuel bowl. We drained it out and cleaned the gas tank, fuel bowl, carburetor, and recharged the battery. Earl drained some gas out of his jeep and put it in the tractor. It started right up. We burned the old gasoline behind the barn," I explained.

"I didn't know that you were so talented with engines," the Mate said.

"Those old tractors are pretty simple and durable. I was a QMED for two years, so I know a little bit," I replied.

"I see. Was there any other interesting events involving other men?" he asked.

"No, the usual crap, 'Hello sailor, new in town?' 'You got a guy in every port?' Shelly's boyfriend brought this other guy over. He tried to get a date with Tammy, then he tried to talk me into it," I explained.

The waitress came by with a large variety of hors d'oeuvres on carts. The Mate took the antipasto, while I took the zakuski. Mrs. Kompsii took the canapes.

"These are great!" I said.

Zakuski is seasoned beef and lamb with cheese and pickled vegetables. Not too much different than the antipasto salad that the Mate had.

"The Hors d'oeuvres tell the tale. Any place that has good hors d'oeuvres will have good food and drink all around," Grace said, adding—"What did you order for dinner?"

That question put a major flap in my sail.

"I took the liberty of ordering the Presidential Beef Bourgignone Flambe for her," the Mate replied.

"That's a good choice for a hard working young lady like you," Grace said.

After hors d'oeuvres are served, there is a stand up cocktail hour before dinner is served. This gives everybody a chance to duck out to the bathroom or do anything else that they might want to do before dinner.

A harpist was playing Celtic tunes. A pretty young lady, who looked to be eighteen, with red hair and a white gown. There was also a large grand piano, but no piano player. After finishing the hors d'oeuvres, I went over to the cocktail bar and got a Pink Lady. I saw the Mate talking to the Bosun on the other side of the room.

"You like Pink Ladies?" Grace asked.

"Yes, I don't get them often," I said. I was thinking that I would have liked a rye whiskey right then.

"I always felt an attachment to David. Did you know that he is from Grand River?" Grace asked.

"Yes, he mentioned that a couple times in our conversations. I guess his mother still lives there," I replied.

"Back in nineteen forty, his father piloted the diesel launch at Mentor Lagoons Yacht Club. He was a real handsome fellow, just like David. I would sneak out during the Commodores dinners and Calvin and I would go for rides in the launch. The lake was pretty calm, so he would really open it up out there. Gosh, that was a lot of fun. My parents pretended that they didn't know anything about it, as long as remained just launch rides, my brother told me at the time. It really wasn't acceptable behavior for a sixteen year old girl, but it's nothing like the ghastly behavior you see nowadays," Grace explained.

I got the feeling that she was telling me that David could have been her son.

"That must have been a very happy time for you," I said.

"Yes, fortunately my parents were very good about things. I went to Lake Catholic school and was doing well and planned on going to college," she said.

"You met the Captain in college?" I asked.

"No, it was at a football game in high school. Lake Catholic was playing Fairport, back in October of nineteen forty one. Of course, we stomped their pathetic little school into the dirt. As the players were leaving the field, we went down by the exit to wave at our guys. I saw this Fairport running back take his helmet off and walk toward the exit. I just kept looking at him, then he looked at me. I waved and and he waved back at me. I was in a panic, I had to find someone who knew him and could introduce us. Fortunately, I ran into Calvin and he said that he knew him. So he went into the locker room and arranged to take Bill home. Irene sat in the front with Calvin and I sat in the back with Bill," she said.

"Did your parents have any problem with a finnish guy from Fairport," I asked, not really serious.

"You know how it is. When love has you in it's grip, you don't worry about things like that, you must obey," she said.

"I have always found him to be a very straight forward and charming fellow," I said.

"Yes, most Finns are like that," she said.

"I'm sure that he'll be missed in the wheelhouse," I said.

"I need him at home to help me raise these grandchildren," Grace said. She must have noticed my quizzical expression. "Our son and daughter are too busy trying to make their way in the world. We have to help them out by taking care of their children."

"That's very good of you," I said, figuring that it was some finnish custom.

I saw the Mate approaching with the Captain, they both looked pleased about something. The Captain and Grace went over to talk to Mister Bruenstein and Ethel. Mister Ring and Meredith weren't doing a very good job of entertaining them.

"So, what have you gentlemen been up to?" I asked the Mate.

"Oh, I've been listening to some darn good stories about you. Apparently you were causing all kinds of trouble on the Giovanni. You were coming onto some punk rock kid on the airplane. They said that you gave him your address and phone number. And, of course, you spent the last ten days and nights at Earl's house," he finished.

"I went over to the Giovanni, to tell the guys over there, how Guiddo was doing. This kid on the airplane, thought that every young woman is a brain dead groupie, so I tried to be polite to him. By the way, I gave him your address, so if you get an autographed album, it's mine," I said.

"I'll be sure you get it," he said.

"You know that I was at the Sorority house, because you must have called me there at least twenty times," I concluded.

"I heard a rumor that you stole the Captain's cab."

"That was totally unintentional. The Mate said that he would call a cab for us, so when we saw the cab, we got in," I explained.

"Everybody says that Captain Laramie will wildly exaggerate things," the Mate said.

"Did the rumor mongers happen to mention that I spent most of the flight, reading stories to a little girl," I asked.

"Yes, Andy had mentioned that and he also said that his daughters had taken to you very well, Aunt Nick."

"So, I guess you know what's horseshit," I said.

"Of course, I never doubted your character for a moment," he said.

We saw Meredith over by the piano, so we decided to go over there and check it out. The harpist had taken a break, so Meredith sat down at the piano and began playing the Can-Can. It didn't seem a very fitting tune for the occassion. She got up and the Mate at down and began playing Funicula'. He got through the verse and stopped.

"That's Funiculi-Funicula', an old Italian love song. It needs some vocals. Play it again, Sam, second verse, same as the first."

The Mate began playing Con Spirito while I Sang:

> Aissera, Nannine', me ne sagliette,
> Tu saie addo?
> Addo stu core ngrato chiu dispiette
> Forme non po
> Addo Ilo fuoco coce, ma si fuie,

Te lassa sta'
E non te corre appriesso, non te struje
sulo a guarda'
Jammo ncoppa, Jammo, Ja'
funiculi', funicula'

Ne . . . jammo: de la terra a la montagna
No passo ne'e;
Se vede Francia, Proceta, la Spagna . . .
E io veco a te.
Tirate co lli fune nnitto, nfatto
Ncielo se va;
Se va comm'a llo viento, a l'antrasatto,
Gue, saglie, sa.
Jammo ncoppa, jammo, ja . . .
Funiculi,-funicula!

Ne n'e sagliuta, oie Ne, se n'e sagliuta,
La capa gia;
E ghuita, po e tornata, e po e venuta . . .
Sta sempe cca!
La capa vota vota attuorno, attuorno,
Attuorno a te,
Llo core canta sempe no taluorno:
Sposmmo, oie Ne!
Jammo ncoppa, jammo, ja . . .
Funiculi, funicula!

Everyone at the head table, except Andy, had come over to the piano.
"Slide over, Maestro. I'll hammer those keys for a while," I said.

I was glad that I took a little time to practice while I was at the Sorority house. I sat on the piano bench, next to the mate and flexed my fingers. I began playing Moonlight Sonata without sheet music. I didn't know if I could do it, so I figured that I would play as much as I could remember. I relaxed and blocked out everything, but the piano keys as I played. I surprised myself when I made it to the end.

I noticed then, that the Mate had his arm around my waist, while the others were politely clapping. When I got up from the bench, the harpist was standing beside the piano, smiling at me. She asked me where I studied music. I told her that my grandmother had taught me to play the piano. We went back to the table because the waiters were bringing the food in.

"Your *Moonlight Sonata* was simply charming!" Grace complimented.

"Thank you," I said, thinking that she was the only one other than my grandmother or shipmates, to compliment my piano playing.

"It looks like the food is almost on the table," the Mate said.

"Did you take the liberty of ordering Flambe for Andy?" I asked jokingly.

"Perhaps for all the guys on third watch," he replied.

"There's an idea, get a doggy bag for Mrs. Kefauver," I wisecracked.

"You must be feeling the alcohol already. I think John is too," he said.

"He always says he knows good food when he cooks it. I'll bet he's thoroughly shlocked by the time he gets to Detroit," I said, adding—"Too bad our Mister O'Blake isn't here to enjoy this little celebration."

"Mister O'Blake left the company to pursue other interests. Mister Bruenstein is Operations Manager now," Grace said.

"Is that right? He and Mister Ring seemed to enjoy their little cruise, down from Sault Ste. Marie," I said.

"He apparently did not like it all that much. He told the Board of Directors that he would never do it again," Grace said.

The Mate goosed me in the ribs, apparently communicating that Mrs. Kompsii did not wish to talk about Mister O'Blake.

The waiters came in with the food. A young man stopped in front of me, with a cart bearing a large, covered silver bowl. He lifted the lid and tried to light the Flambe. His brandy was not quite as flammable as the type John had used. He poured on some more brandy and finally got a rather weak fire going.

"John woulda' got it burning," I wisecracked.

"He'll never let us live this down," The Mate said.

I saw that the Captain and Grace were having lobster. When the flame died, the waiter served my Flambe on mashed potatoes, while the

Mate had his over noodles. We both got buttered asparagus and dinner rolls. I said the grace silently before eating.

"Maybe that joke about the Chief's degreaser, wasn't a joke," I commented.

"John didn't appreciate it," The Mate replied.

I heard the Captain explain the little joke to Grace.

"Your steward is a good cook?" Grace asked me.

"Yes, he's probably in the top five on the lakes. On the American side, anyway," I replied.

"Bill said that the relief cook was a real dog."

"Yes, I heard that about him. Poor Louie wouldn't work in the galley with him," I said.

"Bill usually won't tolerate a lousy cook on his boat," Grace stated.

I was thinking that Captain Kompsii doesn't like any half ass on his boat.

"So, how did you manage, Dave?" I asked.

"Burger Barn most of the time," he replied.

"By the way, Mister Hunt wasn't in the office, so Jean Marlowe took care of our paperwork," I said.

"She's a very pleasant person," the Mate said.

"Very talented also. Behind her desk, she had an exquisite painting of the Marblehead light. I'm afraid that her segment in the newsletter will be much more interesting than mine," I said.

"Excuse me, Nick. Did you say that you are featured in the Spotlight page?" Grace asked.

"I'm supposed to be. I haven't seen the newsletter yet," I said.

"I haven't either, but I'll send someone out to get one," Grace said.

I saw mister Bruenstein talking to mister Ring, then mister Ring got up and left. A pathetic yes man, if there ever was one, I thought.

"When was your interview?" Grace asked.

"When we were unloading at the Reiss terminal in Duluth. It was in the Captain's office, in fact," I said.

"Who did the interview?" she asked.

"Nigel Larsen from Marketing and Public Relations," I replied. Grace began talking to the Captain.

"My goodness, I didn't realize that this interview would make me into a celebrity," I said to the Mate.

"Did Jean say anything about me?" the Mate asked.

"When I mentioned that Earl and I had just come off the Gentry, she asked if we knew you. I said, of course we did. I told her that you were the mate on the Gentry and my neighbor in Marblehead. That put a flap in her sail, but thanks to my nonchalant manner, she recovered rather quickly."

"I didn't take the opportunity to visit her while I was up there," he said.

"There was this Poindexter type guy that kept eyeing her while we were there. I'll bet he's put the moves on her already," I said.

"You think so?" he asked.

"Oh yeah, he's ready to spring. He's probably been reading doctor Ruth for a year, in preparation for the big move," I said jokingly.

"I hope she finds happiness," he said.

"I tried to get her and Earl together. Earl said that she's a city girl and wouldn't get near the barn."

"She probably wouldn't know a lot about tractors," the Mate remarked.

"Oh well, nobody's perfect," I said.

"I don't know a lot about tractors, either," the Mate said.

"Nothing to it, they got a throttle and a clutch and a gear shift. You haven't forgotten how to drive a stick shift, have you?" I asked.

"No, I still remember. I bought the van in automatic because Emma and Tommy couldn't drive a stick," he said.

"Are you renting a car to get us home?" I asked.

"No, didn't I tell you? Tommy and his new girlfriend, brought the van earlier this evening and parked it in the parking deck. I saw it there when we came in," he said.

"That was very nice of them," I said.

"Yes, I talked to his girlfriend on the phone for a few minutes. she seems to be a very pleasant and upbeat person," he remarked.

"Did Tommy tell her anything about us?" I asked.

"In fact, she said that she was looking forward to meeting both of us. She's from Oregon, so she never met a lake sailor. She didn't even know about lake freighters," he said.

"I've been surprised by the number of people I've met who didn't know lake freighters existed," I said.

"Tommy said that they might stop by sometime this weekend."

I was thinking that since today is friday, I hoped they would give us some time to sleep it off. The waiters came by with the wine and asked us what we wanted for dessert. I requested cheesecake with strawberries. I had finished the Flambe and was working on the asparagus.

"How was your Flambe?" Grace asked.

"Tasty," I answered.

"You mean, you've had better?" Grace asked.

"Yes, I'm afraid that our Steward, John, made a better Flambe for thanksgiving," I replied.

"Bill told me that you got a set of nested dolls from a Russian ship," Grace said.

"Yes, the Russian ship stopped, just off our starboard side while we were waiting to lock through. I began talking to the sailors in Russian. After Earl threw over a box of pecan clusters, one of the Russian sailors threw over a box with the nested dolls," I said.

"I got a couple of those and some Ukranian eggs, when we were in the Crimea, a couple years ago. Have you been to the Soviet Union?" Grace asked.

"Yes, I was there for two months, back in nineteen eighty one," I replied.

"What cities did you visit?" she asked.

"Leningrad, Moscow and Kiev. I saw a lot of the surrounding countryside. They still had steam locomotives, so I liked riding the trains," I said.

"Did you bring back any folk art?" she asked.

"Yes, a couple Ukranian eggs, a couple lacquer miniatures and a small wooden box which is relief carved and painted. I was told that if you tried to mail a package, it would be stolen, so I was limited to what I could carry out," I said.

"Yes, it can become quite a chore, sometimes," she said.

"Of course, I've bought some nested dolls and other items. I have my grandmother's collection of folk art."

"What did your grandmother have for folk art?" Grace asked.

"She had some ceramic and brass household items, like candleholders and samovars. A sword that belonged to her father and some regional clothing. Her second husband, Eichann, had marble busts and gold coins from all over, but his daughter got those. Grandmother got a couple ceremonial daggers and bag pipes, which I have now," I said.

"It sounds like quite a collection," Grace said.

"I keep some of it in Grandpa's safe. I've never had any break-ins, but you never know," I said.

The waiters came by with the dessert cart. They made the strawberry shortcake for the Mate and they put strawberries on the cheesecake, for me. Grace and the Captain had those flaming brandy apples on ice cream.

"Dave, if I manage to eat this, you'll have to carry me outta' here," I said jokingly.

"I thought we'd be carrying Earl out of here by now, but he's holding up pretty good," the Mate said.

"I told him that he'll be driving home, alone. I hope he doesn't get too sloshed," I said.

"I heard him talking about not missing any school when he was a kid. Something about that," the Mate said.

"That sounds like Weany-Beany. Earl used to ride him all the time on the Spirit Independent. He was this queer porter that used to get on everyone's nerves. He claimed that he never missed a day of school. Earl would tell him that he was in Vietnam, getting hundreds of wounded men off the battlefield while this worthless fool was filling space in a school chair," I explained.

"He claimed that he was more scholarly than Earl?" the Mate asked.

"There was no way that he could claim that. I don't know if he could tie his shoes," I said.

"What was his real name?"

"Bill Bean," I answered.

"His name sounds like some comedian," the Mate commented.

"This is the honest to God truth. when I started my second semester at college, I had this Institutions of Government class. On the first day, when the professor was calling off names, we had a mister Bill, a Bill Murray and a Rosanna Santana in the class. The old prof couldn't believe it," I said.

"What do they say in college, in place of—'this is no sh . . . man'," the Mate asked.

"Do you really think I could make that up?" I asked.

"Greg was telling me about the Vampire you encountered at college," the Mate said jokingly.

"This idiot was always pretending to be a vampire. He bit me on the neck. I stomped the living hell outta' him. Broke his jaw and displaced some teeth. I had to go before the Student Review Board. My grandmother gave them hell that time," I said.

"That I can believe," the mate said, adding—"Perhaps this semester will be less eventful."

"I wouldn't count on that, not at all," I said.

I saw kenny Ring approaching. He handed an interoffice envelope to Misses Kompsii. She pulled out the company Newsletter and turned to the last page, where the Spotlight segments are.

"Oh, here's a picture of you shaking hands with Nigel," she said.

"Yes, that was taken in the Wheelhouse," I said.

She began reading out loud-

"Also in the spotlight this month is twenty six year old, Nicolette Strickland. Nicolette is a deckhand and is the only woman working on a company boat this season. A resident of Marblehead, Ohio, this is Nick's fifth season on the great lakes. She attends Mount Union college in the off season and will graduate this spring. Nick spent the previous four seasons on the Canadian MV Giovanni, as a conveyorman and QMED. Serving under Captains Thorvold Tommasson, Pierre LeMand, Arnie O'Boyle and Burt McCullough. Earlier this season, Nick was a deckhand on the grain carriers, Mariner Enterprise and the Spirit Independent. She came to the steamship Gentry in August, in the Detroit river. Captain Kompsii said that Miss Strickland is a topnotch crewman. He explained that she had moored the ship from the work boat, unshackled the unloading conveyor and removed hatch covers, then cast off from the work boat. All this in the darkness of the early morning. "Yes, it's been a busy morning," Miss Strickland said casually. Nick stated that the steamship Gentry was definitely the better of the three boats that she has worked on this season. We hope to see Nicolette Strickland on our boats in future seasons."

Grace finished, adding—"You made only one mistake, dear. You told them your real age. You never want to do that with these media vultures."

"That is an impressive resume, young lady. I certainly would like to have you working on one of our boats next season," Mister Bruenstein said.

"Thank you, sir. That's very kind of you," I said.

"There's a Herbert Miller in the Spotlight page. He's a Korean war veteran and a POW. He may get the Chairman's award this year," Grace said.

"What's the Chairman's award?" I asked.

"It's an award of one thousand dollars, given for service outside the company. Veterans are frequently recognized for their service in the military," she explained.

"Too bad they didn't ask me," I commented. The Mate goosed me in the ribs.

"Would you like to nominate someone else?" Grace asked.

"The bravest man I ever knew is Earl Franklin. He was a Navy Corpsman. He spent two years in Vietnam. He has twenty two combat citations. Probably two hundred men are alive today because he picked them up on the battlefield, while under enemy fire and got them on a helicopter. I don't know how anybody could do better than he did," I stated.

I heard Mister Bruenstein ask Captain Kompsii if he knew Earl Franklin. Captain Kompsii said that he did indeed know Earl Franklin. Mister Bruenstein asked the Captain if he agreed with what I had said about Earl. Captain Kompsii said that in his opinion, Earl is deserving of the Chairman's award. Mister Bruenstein asked if Earl Franklin was present. The Mate rose from his chair and headed for the other side of the room.

"If Aldrich and I back Earl Franklin, he'll be sure to get the award," Grace said quietly.

"He doesn't look like much but he's a real ball of fire," I remarked.

"Well, it's a service award, not a beauty pageant," Grace said.

"I'm really happy to have someone else nominated for this award. All I've been hearing is vice presidents nominating each other," Mister Bruenstein said as the Mate approached with a perplexed looking Earl.

We rose to our feet and the Mate introduced Earl to Mister Bruenstein.

"Congratulations Mister Franklin, you have been nominated for the Chairman's award," Mister Bruenstein announced.

"Thank you, sir. This is quite a surprise. I'm honored to be nominated for this award," Earl said, still looking puzzled.

"Congratulations, You're the first crewman I've had, to be nominated for this award," Captain Kompsii said as he shook hands with Earl.

"Thank you, sir," Earl replied.

"Congratulations, Mister Franklin. It's a pleasure to finally meet you," Grace said as she shook hands with Earl.

"Thank you, I'm pleased to meet you, also," Earl said.

I smiled at Earl and leaned over and whispered—"It's in the bag, old buddy," as I shook hands with him.

"Congratulations, Earl. Good job," the Mate said.

"Thank you, Sir," Earl replied as he shook hands with the Mate.

Earl turned and headed back to the other side of the room. Everyone at the head table, sat down,except for Mister Bruenstein. He congratulated the officers and crew for a successful season, summarizing the trips and the tonnage hauled. He gave a short presentation of Captain Kompsii's forty three year career on the lakes. I thought it was odd that a new comer like Bruenstein was telling this crowd of lake veterans about Captain Kompsii. The Captain was presented with several gifts, including a gift from the crew. A large silver tray with a line drawing of the Gentry and the names of the officers and crew engraved on it. The Captain had a gift for us, the coffee cups with the boat's name embossed on them. The Captain gave a short speech, telling us that he had never wanted to do anything else but sail on the Great Lakes. He wished us good luck and safe sailing. Everyone stood up and applauded. There was an after dinner cocktail hour where people could talk to each other and leave whenever they liked. I ducked out for a short break, then came back and got a glass of Champagne from the waiter. The Mate was talking to the Chief and Hank. The Captain was talking to Andy. I didn't want to look like I was hanging on anyone in particular, so I just hung around in front and admired the style of the Harpist.

"Are you enjoying yourself, Nick?" Grace asked, coming up behind me.

"Oh yes, very much," I said, turning around.

"Bill told me that you're only the second woman that he's sailed with. The other one was a steward named Elsa."

"Oh yes, I've heard her name mentioned," I said.

"Excluding Bill, who was the best Captain in your opinion?" Grace asked.

"Almost all the Captains I've known, have been good captains. There's a lot of close seconds, but the best would be Thorvold Tommasson. He's the gutsiest, savviest Captain I've ever seen. Back in Eighty three, we had this god awful storm on Lake Superior. Those nonharmonic waves were coming clear over our spar deck. Everybody was scared, except Tommasson. He kept the rest of us from freaking out," I explained.

"Which direction were the waves coming from?" Grace asked.

"The port quarter," I replied.

"They say that nonharmonic waves sank the Edmund Fitzgerald," Grace said.

"I believe that the Captain of the Arthur M. Anderson did report nonharmonic waves from astern. Waves like that could hold a vessel under water and pound the hell out of it. Whatever happened, happened fast," I answered.

"Bill knew Captain McSorley and a lot of the crew. I'll have to ask him if he knows Captain Tommasson," Grace said, adding—"Catch you in a minute."

She turned and headed in the direction of the Captain.

Someone tapped me on the back and I turned around and saw Earl there.

"You're not getting too schlocked, are you?" I asked.

"I was gonna' ask you that. If I don't feel like driving home, I'll sleep in the jeep until morning," he said.

"Well, use the blankets so you don't freeze to death."

"What's this award they're gonna' give me?"

"It's the Chairman's award for being a war hero. It's a thousand bucks. You use it for the farm. Buy a couple cows or something. Mrs. Kompsii says she'll back you, so you're a shoe-in," I explained.

"That would be a nice chunk of change," Earl said.

"It looks like it'll be more than the end of season bonus," I said.

"You should have got a bonus for taking all the abuse that you did," Earl remarked.

"The only thing for that is to give it back, tit for tat," I said.

"Hello again, Mister Franklin," Grace said.

"Hello, Misses Kompsii," Earl replied.

"Bill said that he has talked to Captain Tommasson on the radio, but he has never met him," Grace said, adding—"Nick says that you're quite a war hero."

"I don't know about that . . ." Earl paused.

"You know the old saying-The Marines are looking for a few good men, Navy Corpsmen," I said lightheartedly.

"Do you have a silver star?" Grace asked.

"Yes, I think I do," Earl replied.

"He's got three silver stars and two bronze stars. I've read his combat citations," I said.

"That sounds very impressive," Grace said.

"Yes, for a corpsman that doesn't normally even carry a gun, that sounds really impressive," I said.

"Can you tell me how you got your first silver star?" Grace asked.

"Nick probably remembers it better than I do," Earl said. Misses Kompsii looked at me.

"It was when you were on the Rockpile, at the start of the Tet offensive. Remember, you guys had taken heavy mortar and artillery fire. When the Hueys came in, you loaded eighteen wounded men into the helicopters. NVA regulars began to assault your position, while you were putting some wounded guys in a Huey. You took a forty five off one of the wounded guys and killed seven of them. You went through the helicopter and killed one with your k-bar knife. Two more were coming at you with bayonets, so you killed them by knocking their heads together," I finished.

"Is that the way it was, Earl?" Grace asked.

"I got my K-bar stuck in the Dink, I couldn't get it out. I remembered that our principal used to knock our heads together when we were fighting at school. I guess I did it too hard, the gyrenes said I killed them," Earl said.

"He's one crazy son of a sea cook," I said.

"My father was a marine in the First World War. He laid on the battlefield for twenty four hours when he was wounded. A French outfit picked him up, but they didn't take care of him very well," Grace said.

"My grandfather would tell me about the First World War. He was in the Argonne forest. It's very rough terrain in that area. The French were happy to let us have it. It sounds like Vietnam. I wouldn't want to be in a war without Earl. I've always been able to count on him in a clutch," I stated.

"How long have you known Earl?" Grace asked.

"It's been eight years now," I answered.

"Did he serve with you on the MV Giovanni?" she asked.

"No, he's a veteran of the Cliffs line. I've been on boats with him since the beginning of this season. I've known him since my college days. Earl worked at Schaffer's when he was off the boats," I explained.

"You can certainly count on my vote," Grace said to Earl.

"Thank you, I appreciate that," Earl said.

"I've got to get back to Bill. Be sure to catch me before you leave," Grace said.

"Will do," I replied.

I looked in the direction that Grace was going. I saw the Captain talking with the Mate and Andy. I saw the Mate glance my way for a moment. I flashed him a smile.

"It looks like Dave hasn't forgotten about you," Earl remarked. I think that's the first time I heard Earl call him by his first name.

"He's got thirty other people that he can talk to. We've got all winter to talk. What do you think of Mister Ring's date?" I asked.

"I've never seen a woman dressed like that," Earl replied.

"She's a paid escort, a rent-a-ho. Her name is Meredith James. I can't believe that jerk would show up here with a woman like that. It just goes to show ya' that he's a pathetic yes man that doesn't have any real friends in the world," I said scornfully.

"She doesn't look like a farm girl," Earl said.

"For a hundred dollars an evening, she'll be anything you want her to be," I joked.

"Maybe you should take it easy with the drink," Earl suggested.

"I got it under control, old buddy."

"Some people might try to start some sh-t with you, later," Earl said.

"Would their names be Joe and Pete, by any chance?" I asked.

"Yep," he replied.

"Those assholes have been looking for trouble ever since we got on in August. It'll be my pleasure to give them some hurt," I said.

"That doesn't sound like a good jewish girl," Earl said.

"Sure it does. It says right in the Torah—"Smite the Amalakite. Hurt that son of a bitch real good."

"Your hebrew translation might be a little lacking," Earl joked.

"Any dialogue between me and those two, will be in plain english, no bones about it," I declared. I saw the Mate approach with the Chief.

"Hi guys! I hope I didn't take you away from anything important," I said.

"Such as?" the Chief asked.

"Listening to fictitious stories about people," I replied.

"It's the stuff that legends are made of," the Chief shot back.

"I ran into an old friend, Bill Lawrence, on the Giovanni," I said.

"Oh yes, we go back quite a few years. The old US Steel fleet and the Cliffs line," he said.

"Who did you get a ride with?" I asked.

"Rayborn, on the Spirit Independent," he replied. I laughed at that.

"You laugh!" the Chief exclaimed indignantly.

"That old Lentz Triple Expansion engine was about to shake that old boat to pieces. I don't think we ever went over nine knots," I said.

"That would be pushing it. I found Laddy Landon a turbine engine for cheap. It would pay for itself in half a season, at the rate they were going," he said.

"How about those boilers? Did you bring your bubblegum?" I joked.

"Three could be rebuilt, the other one could sit there empty. I don't think she'll be around for another ten years," he said.

"Did you have to shovel clinkers," I asked jokingly.

"Let's not get silly here, now," the Chief said.

"Did you?" the Mate asked.

"Are you kidding? I had enough to do in the deck department," I replied.

The Chief excused himself and Earl, to get a drink.

"I hope Earl doesn't drink any more," I said.

"I'm sorry that I've been ignoring you," the Mate apologized.

"Nonsense, I've got all winter to talk to you," I said.

"I like your hair," he said.

"It's a half-up do, a popular prom style," I said.

"I've never seen a dress like that."

"The Oscars, nineteen forty. Too bad neither of us was there," I said jokingly.

"Very tasteful, very fashionable. HELLO SEXY!" he exclaimed.

"That's what they told me in the dress shop.

Your suit is very nice looking as well," I said.

"I took your advice and went to the men's store downtown."

"I hope it wasn't too expensive," I said.

"I was going to ask you the same thing about your dress."

"It comes with a guarantee," I joked.

"A guarantee?" he asked, puzzled.

"Yes, I'm guaranteed to learn a new meaning for the word—Mate," I said softly.

"That's a definite possibility," the Mate said.

"Have you got a berth lined up for next year?" I asked.

"All bets are off, right now. According to the Captain, it will be another lean season," he said.

I tried not to think about all the sailors I knew, who were waiting for a job to come along.

"Earl says that I can have a job milking cows. You could be plowing and planting corn by next spring," I said jokingly.

"I shudder to think," he said. I saw Andy and Mark approaching.

"I hope we're not interrupting anything," Mark said.

"Such as what, filthy rumor mongering?" I asked.

"IT WAS HIM!" they both said, pointing at each other.

"I've heard three different versions of the punk rocker story. It reminds of that song-'the tales keep getting taller on down the line'. Have you come back for more material?" I asked jokingly.

"We come in peace, paleface," Mark wisecracked, adding—"I heard that you were a real hit with the big shots. I was hoping to catch some of the stardom."

"Follow behind Earl's cows with a basket and catch something more useful," I said.

"I was talking with Dave about this ocean charter in Florida. The owner is an old friend so we wouldn't have to pay," Andy said.

"Oh yes, Those are fun. Of course, there's transportation and hotel rooms. Fuel costs and booze for the boat. You wouldn't mind cleaning fish for a couple hours at the end of the day. You would leave Eileen and those charming little girls and live on a boat with some foul mouthed drinkers who can't wash themselves. Don't you get enough of that at work?" I asked.

They laughed at my harangue.

"Fishing the Keys sounds like some great memories," Mark said.

"I was just kicking the idea around with Dave and some of the other guys. Of course, if it interferes with any plans you've made . . ." Andy said.

"What makes you think that Dave would need to ask my permission for something like that. By the by, I made a promise to your girls and I wanted to visit Guiddo next week sometime," I said.

"Sure, just give me a call next week to make sure that I'll be home," Andy said.

"Will do," I said.

"We have to see the Captain before he leaves," the Mate informed me.

"Sure, go ahead. I'll talk to some of the guys while you're gone," I said.

All three of them headed in the direction of the Captain.

I looked around the room, but did not see the Bosun or Dixon anywhere. I saw Smitty, Brad, Ron, Hal and Ed standing together by the door, so I headed their way. They all turned and looked at me as I approached.

"Hi guys, how was your dinner?"

"Probably not as good as yours," Brad grumbled.

"Mine wasn't that great. I was expecting better. John certainly did better," I said, adding—"Where is John?"

"We carried him outta' here about half an hour ago," Ron said.

"I hope you laid him somewhere soft. Where's Munson, Dixon and Al?" I asked.

"They left a few minutes ago," Ron said.

"I didn't know it was that late," I said, looking at my watch.

"You must have been having a lot of fun," Brad sneered.

"Not really. I had to exercise a lot of self control up there,"

"The conversation must have been interesting, then," Brad shot back.

"Most of the time, we were talking about the shipping season next year," I said.

"So, what's the good word?" Ed asked.

"They're being cautious and saying that it won't be any better than this year," I replied.

"I don't see how it could be worse," Ed griped.

"They're not through with all the sales and mergers yet. That stuff could go on for another five or six years," I stated.

No one seemed happy with my news, but I was not going to sugar coat it for them.

"The Chief has cleaned all the engineers outta' here?" I asked.

"Those old geezers can't stay up this late," Brad quipped.

"What did he do with Earl?" I asked.

"I think he hit the head," Ed said, pointing to the doors.

I thought it was strange that Earl would be looking for a bathroom in the lobby, when he knew that there was one in here.

"He must be lost. I'd better go check on him," I said.

"I'll get the door for you," Brad offered.

"That's very gentlemanly of you," I said as he opened the door.

I went through the door and heard voices on my left. When I looked to the left, I saw Billy, Kenny, Joe and Pete standing on the other side of the ice sculpture. I looked to the right, to see if Earl was there, then I scanned the room from right to left. I saw Pete come around the ice sculpture.

"Hey Nick," he shouted.

I looked directly at him.

"I see that you can suck dicks at any level of this company. Since you don't mind being the crew's pass around, whad'ya say you come home with me tonight," he sneered.

"You foul mouth son of a bitch. What part of 'f-ck off' did you fail to understand the first time? I'm gonna' beat you until you die," I said, trying to keep a normal voice, while I kicked off my left shoe. The right one wouldn't come off, so I reached down to pull the straps off while keeping my eyes on Pete.

"Hold there, Nick," I heard the Mate say.

"Stay out of this, McCracken. This is a fight between crewmen," I said.

I saw the smirk leave Pete's face.

"It's my fight now," the Mate said, putting his hand on my shoulder as he went past me.

I was flabbergasted. I could not believe that he was going to do the fighting for me. I saw Pete put his fists up.

"I've bit my tongue and put up with your nonsense long enough," the Mate said.

Pete threw a straight right punch and the Mate blocked it with his left. The Mate threw a low, right punch into Pete's stomach, which doubled him up. I saw Joe start running toward them. The Mate threw a fierce uppercut to Pete's face and sent him backward onto the table and the ice sculpture. Pete and the ice sculpture slid off the table and onto the floor. The ice sculpture broke in half, while Pete lay still on the floor. Meanwhile, Earl appeared out of nowhere and threw a roundhouse left into Joe's face, hurling him backward and onto the floor. The lobby was totally silent for half a minute. I came up behind the Mate and looked at Pete and the broken Ice sculpture on the floor.

"If I'd hit him, he wouldn't have broken the ice boat," I said, then I picked up my shoe and put my left foot on the table and put my shoe back on.

Everybody started gathering around to view the aftermath of the fight. It took a minute before the Captain and Grace came into the lobby.

"What's going on here?" Grace asked.

"It looks like a fight between crewmen," I said.

"Those two men?" Grace asked, pointing at Pete and Joe.

"It sure looks like it," I said.

"Bill, they've broken your boat," Grace said, indignantly.

"Well, it was my last season on her, anyway," the Captain said philosophically, then he and Grace walked toward the elevators.

"He took that rather well," I observed.

Earl came over to us. "Are you alright?" he asked.

"Of course, I wasn't the one fighting. How's your hand?" I asked Earl.

"Just like hitting a home run," he said, smiling.

"Are you two, shipmates?" I asked.

"Shipmates," the Mate said.

"Shipmates," Earl said.

They hooked thumbs and shook hands. I looked over and saw Billy and Kenny trying to revive Joe. I saw the Chief come through the doors. He came over to us and looked at Joe and Pete, still laying on the floor.

"It looks like there's been a fight," he observed.

"What did you see?" I asked.

"I didn't see anything," he stated.

"That's funny, that's exactly what I saw," I said.

"Let's see, there was a fight and Nick was there. Where have I heard this before?" The Chief asked himself outloud.

It looked like Joe was starting to regain consciousness over there.

"As soon as he feels up to it, he can revive his buddy, Pete," I said.

"Man, that was the damndest thing I ever saw. I'm signing on with you guys next year," Gary said.

"What did you see?" the Chief asked.

"Three punches and two guys out cold. It musta' took a whole five seconds," Gary said, while imitating the punches in the air.

"Go see if you can get some comments from the losers," I invited.

Gary left, still punching at the air. Pete moaned and rolled over, holding his hands on his face. I saw that Joe had sat up and Billy was wiping his face with a wet towel.

"Why didn't you jump in with me?" Joe asked.

"Oh no, I learned the last time. This is your mix, I'm gonna' stay out of it," Billy replied.

"Is it time to get going. I'm feeling a little tired," I said.

"I'm not surprised," the Chief said, smiling.

"Yes, we can go now. How's the weather out west?" the Mate asked the Chief.

"Smooth sailing. Everything west of here, missed the snow," the Chief said. He must have driven in from that way, I thought.

"Thanks Greg, I'll get back to you in about a week or so," the Mate said.

"Sure, I'll be in touch. We should be hearing something soon," he said as he shook hands with the Mate. He turned toward me and stuck out his hand.

"It certainly has been interesting, having you onboard," he said.

"Sure, the next time you need to pull a turbine, give me a call," I quipped, shaking his hand.

"Will do," he said.

"Say hello to Cynthia for me," I said.

"Okay, see you next season," he said.

We headed toward the coatroom. I saw Buster and Brad helping Pete to sit up on the floor. The Mate and Earl were also looking that way.

"Catch you next season, guys," I said to Ed, Hal, Ron and DJ.

"Yeah, take it easy, Nick," DJ said, the other guys waved.

"They must be disappointed," I said softly.

"You can only take so much abuse. Those assholes have been mouthing all night. They had it coming, no doubt about it. Don't you think, Dave?" Earl asked.

"Yes, Mr. Hall was definitely trying to provoke you," the Mate said, adding—"You didn't hit anybody, so they can blow it out the hawse pipe."

"My, that's pretty strong language coming from you," I said, putting my hand on his shoulder.

"I'll try to control myself," the Mate said as we arrived at the coatroom.

I took off my heels as we waited for the young woman to get our coats and bags. The Mate held my coat while I put on my work boots and put my heels in the plastic bag. We put on our coats and headed toward the elevator.

"Are you okay to drive, old buddy?" I asked Earl.

"Oh yeah, I'm feeling fine," Earl replied.

"Hopefully the roads are a little better to the south," I said.

"I'll take route eight," he said as I pressed the down button and the elevator door opened.

"Those neighborhoods are frightful, especially at night," I stated, as we entered the elevator.

The door closed and I pressed the button for the second level parking.

"What level are you on?" I asked the Mate.

"I'm on the second level also," he said.

"That's good, we can see Earl off," I said, adding—"I have a confession to make. I tried to get Tamara to teach me to play cribbage, but I'm afraid that I'm totally ignorant of the game."

"You apparently have quite a bit of confidence in your fighting ability. You were going after Mister Hall like a house on fire." the Mate declared.

"I did some practice on the heavy bag. I practice my punch and kick combinations," I said.

"Do you believe that, Earl?" the Mate asked.

"Sure, and don't let her sucker you into that Russian dice game. She always beats the ass off me," he replied as the elevator door opened.

I remembered the aisle that Earl parked in.

"This way," I said, indicating that we should bear to the right as we left the elevator.

It was a short walk to Earl's jeep. Earl walked around back and removed my large suitcase and handed it to the mate. Earl got in and started the engine.

"Don't forget to take Tammy's bag and the blanket back to the sorority house," I said.

"I'll do it tomorrow," Earl said. I hugged him.

"Thanks, old buddy. I'll see you soon," I said.

"Bye, bye guys, stay warm," Earl said.

He waved as he backed out, then headed for the exit.

"My van is over here," the Mate said.

His van was only two aisles over. He opened the door for me and closed it when I got in.

"You wanna' take the scenic route?" he asked when he got in the van.

"We might as well. The Christmas lights are impressive," I replied.

After leaving the parking deck, he took us east to Nineth street and turned again on Superior avenue and headed west through the business district. The stores were decorated in a multitude of Christmas themes and the traffic was nil at that time of night, so we could take our time and enjoy the holiday lights.

CHAPTER 15

Toward a New Horizon

Crossing over the Detroit-Superior bridge, we could see the Christmas lights down in the flats. On the west side were residential districts. The Mate took some side streets and got us onto route ninety, westbound.

"Are you getting on the turnpike or taking route two?" I asked.

"I was thinking about staying on route two," he said.

"Do you have enough gas?" I asked.

"Yes, nearly a full tank," he answered.

"Do you mind if I rest?" I asked.

"No, go ahead. I got plenty of rest earlier," he said. The van was very warm, so I unbuttoned my coat. I reclined the seat somewhat and closed my eyes. I felt his hand touch my hand as I started drifting off.

"I hope you don't need that hand for driving," I murmured.

"Don't worry, Sweetie. I have everything under control," he said softly.

We'll see about that when we get to my house, I thought as I drifted off to sleep. I woke up briefly and shifted myself around in the seat. The Mate's hand was on my leg, so I put my hand on his and went back to sleep. I woke up again when I felt the Mate put on the brakes momentarily. I sat up and saw that we were approaching the Bay bridge. The sky was clear and the moon looked big and bright.

"The driver in front of us, put on his brakes after making a sudden lane change," the Mate said.

"I hate these road idiots," I remarked.

"Out of state plates. They probably have no idea where they are going," he said as we started across the bridge.

The bay didn't look too bad in the moonlight. I thought of that song-'I only have eyes for you'.

"It's a good night to be coming home," I said.

"Yes, it certainly is," the Mate agreed.

After crossing the bridge, we got off on the first exit on the right, which took us to Bayshore road. I looked at my watch, it was almost eleven thirty.

"Do you have to stop at home for anything?" I asked.

"No, I have clothes in my bags," he said.

"Good, you can help me check the house for bats," I said.

"Do you have a fear of bats?" he asked.

"No, bats used to be a real problem when the house was unoccupied and the weather turned cold," I replied.

"I've had problems with field mice," he said.

"I left the heat at seventy two, so the house shouldn't be cold," I said. I pulled the clutch purse out of my coat pocket and opened it.

"There's a map reading light here," the Mate said, reaching over and pressing the little button to turn it on.

"That's handy," I said as I pulled out my keys and closed the purse again.

It didn't take long before we could see the lights on the conveyor. In a minute, we passed the Mate's house.

"It looks like Tommy didn't make it over yet," he said. He turned left on the gravel road and signaled for a left turn.

"I'm afraid that you won't be able to park in my garage tonight," I said.

The Mate chuckled as he turned into my driveway.

"I forgot about that old colloquialism," I said.

"I'll get the door for you," he said as he turned off the lights and shut off the engine.

"Such a gentleman," I said. He picked up my large suitcase and came over and opened the door or me.

"Thank you, Mister McCracken," I said.

"You're welcome, Miss Strickland," he said.

I went to the front door and opened it. The Mate was right behind me. I turned on the lights to the living room and the stairs.

"Would you check the upsatairs for me?" I asked.

"Sure," he said, sitting down my suitcase and heading for the stairs.

I went to the kitchen and turned on the lights. I took off my work boots and my coat. I put my Gentry coffee cup on the kitchen table and I looked at the newsletter. I heard the Mate come up behind me.

"Damn, I look like a train wreck in this picure."

"You look sexy in coal dust," he said, gently putting his arms around my waist and kissing and nuzzling the back of my neck.

"I see you remember where you left off at," I said.

"Just like in the Wheelhouse," he said.

I turned around and he pulled me tight against him, while we kissed. After a minute, I pulled my mouth away from his.

"Give me some room here," I said softly as I moved my hand between us and started to unbutton his suit jacket.

He moved his hands a little lower than I expected.

"Really, Mister McCracken! What are your intentions, sir?" I asked in the proper Victorian manner.

"Wild sex, give you babies and marry you," he said, as I removed his jacket and tie.

"I'm shocked, sir," I said in mocked seriousness as I started unbuttoning his shirt.

"Is that too forward for you?" he asked.

"No, I'm shocked that you don't have the order right after all these years," I said, kissing him while I continued to remove his shirt.

"I think that order will suit you fine," he said as I undid his belt.

"Oh, David . . ." I gasped.

He grabbed on to me tightly and took over. In a few minutes, he had us both undressed. His hands and mouth were all over me. I could not say much, except to cry out in pleasure. He picked me up and carried me to my grandmother's bedroom and set me on the bed. He was all over me, completely in control, while I held on tight and forgot about everything, except loving him. After exhausting ourselves, we lay together, limply. After a few minutes, I began kissing the side of his neck and rubbing his back with my hands.

"You booger!" I said softly in his ear.

"Hmm . . . ," he replied.

"The first night is for fun, the second night is to get acquainted and the third night is for love. You were going for love," I said.

"Hmm . . . you noticed," he said as he rolled off me, his eyes still closed.

"Good night, baby love," I said softly. The sun will catch us in bed together, I thought as I drifted off to sleep.

The sun was not the only one to catch us in bed together. I was awakened by a knocking at the front door. I hastily put on my pajamas, house coat and slippers and went to answer the door. When I opened the door, I saw my neighbor, Chuck, holding a box.

"Good morning. This box came for you about a week ago," he said. I recognized it instantly as the box I sent from the Gentry.

"Oh, thank you so much. I forgot all about it," I said.

"It's heavy, I'll bring it in for you," he said.

"That's very kind of you," I said, adding—"You can sit it on the kitchen table, if you like."

"Sure, no problem," he said

He handed me the mail when he came in, then took the box into the kitchen. I looked at the mail for a few moments, then I heard Chuck in the kitchen.

"Well, hello there Dave. Are you back from the sea?" he asked.

"Yes, the shipping season is over for us," the Mate said.

We are straight up busted, I thought.

"That's good. Stop over and see me and Betty when you get a chance," he invited.

"Sure, I'll be happy to," The Mate said. Chuck emerged from the hallway entrance.

"Thank you again," I said.

"No trouble at all," he said, adding—"See you later."

"Bye-bye," I said and I closed the door. I turned around and saw the mate standing in the hallway entrance, wearing his trousers and t-shirt.

"Would you like to put it in the Sandusky Register?" I asked.

"It may end up there anyway. My van in your driveway, kinda' gave it away," he said, grinning.

"Oh my goodness, my reputation is shot. What's gonna' happen when this gets back to Misses Kefauver?" I asked in mocked seriousness as we embraced and kissed.

"She'll be outraged, I tell you, outraged," I quipped, adding—"She'll have you kicked out of the yacht club."

"I'm not in the yacht club," he said.

"See there, you blew it before you even had it, Mister McCracken."

"I like what I have now," he stated, holding me tightly.

"They say that love won't pay the rent," I said.

"Love will keep us together," he countered.

"Well, it's not going to cook us any breakfast," I said, adding—"I'm going to take a quick shower and get dressed."

"Okay, I'll make some coffee," he said.

"All I have is coffee creamer in the cupboard," I said as I went into the bathroom.

I took the pins out of my hair and took out the braid. I shook my head to bring my hair down. The warm shower felt great. I washed the mousse out of my hair. I dried my hair with a towel and wrapped a big towel around me and went into the bedroom. The Mate was in the bedroom getting dressed. I took my hair dryer and comb and stood in front of the dresser mirror, while I combed and dried my hair. The Mate sat on the bed and quietly watched me.

"Your hair looks really pretty when it's down like that," he remarked.

"You like it like this?" I asked. He nodded and smiled.

"I look like Veronica Lake. Would you please hand me that barrette on the night stand?" I requested.

He handed it to me. I fastened it in my hair and gave my hair a final brushing. I opened up my large suitcase, pulled out a pair of blue jeans and a plaid flannel workshirt. I took some long underwear out of my dresser and began putting my clothes on. The Mate watched me silently.

"You seem to be watching with rapt interest," I remarked.

"I learned to wait patiently while Emma got dressed," he said.

"I'm not on the Gentry and there ain't no watch bell, so I'll take my time," I said. I put on my work boots and bent over to tie them.

"Sure baby, take your time," he said, playfully smacking me on the rear end.

"If you knew how many men got punched for that," I said jokingly.

We both started laughing at that statement. Apparently we were both thinking about the fight last night. We went into the kitchen and I got my parka.

"Where are we going, Mister McCracken?" I asked.

"Please call me Dave. Can I call you Nicki?" he asked.

"I haven't used that name in a long time, but you can call me Nicki," I said.

"How about the Ship's Bell?" he asked.

"It's always a winner," I said as I zipped up my parka.

After going out the front door, I locked the door and checked the mail box. The Mate opened the door of the van for me.

"I'm gonna' expect this all the time." I joked, as I got in the van. He got in and started up the van.

"I'll have to stop at the grocery store later," I said.

"Okay, we'll stop there after breakfast," he said.

He backed the van out of the driveway and drove up the gravel road to Bayshore road. The sky was still clear and the sun was shining brightly.

"This frost won't last long," I said.

"It's supposed to be in the forties today. We'll be fine if it doesn't rain," he said.

It's a short drive to the Ship's Bell. The lake looked rough and gray. The gulls were gathered together in a large group in the Coast Guard parking lot. I didn't see any freighters on the lake.

"Just the ferry boat out today," I observed.

There were only a couple cars in the parking lot when we arrived at the diner. The Mate parked the van and I opened the door and got out.

"I wonder if we'll meet anybody we know in here," I said.

"Such as?" he asked.

"Hopefully, none of your old girl friends," I answered.

"I don't think they frequent this place," he said, as he opened the door and we entered.

We sat down at a table by a window. The other window tables were occupied. After a few minutes, the waitress came over with the coffee pot.

"Would you like some coffee?" she asked.

"Yes," the Mate answered.

After she poured the coffee, she asked us if we were ready to order.

"Yes, I'll have the stuffed waffles with strawberries and whipped cream," I said

"I'll have the same thing," The Mate said.

"Very good, that'll be right up," she said, and she left.

"I ran into the mayor's wife before I went to Alliance," I said.

"What did she have to say?" The Mate asked.

"The same old thing. She asked if the season was over and said for you and me to stop over when we got back," I said.

"Oh, I see. Did any thing interesting happen on the Giovanni?"

"They offered me and Earl a working cruise to Conneaut," I said.

"You didn't take them up on it?" he asked in mock seriousness.

"No, part of the trip would have been with Pee Pee Laramie. I don't know anybody in Conneaut to give me a ride," I said.

"I've never met Captain Laramie, but I've heard some stories about him," he said.

"The latest story is a real hoot. He had some problem with this lap dancer in Windsor. I guess the police were called," I said.

"Buster and Billy ran into some of the Giovanni guys at the Indian Casino and they brought back that story," The Mate said.

"When Burt McCullough gets on at Sault Ste. Marie, it will be a happy ship again," I remarked.

"Is it their last trip?" The Mate asked.

"According to the mate, Franky Pierce, they'll be out at least to the end of this month or maybe into January," I replied.

"I don't dig winter navigation. I tried that in my younger days," he said.

"I've never been out much past New Year's Day," I said, looking out the window at the limestone dock. I saw someone in a cherry picker, working on the lights in the Coast Guard parking lot.

"I was thinking about what I'm going to do today," I said.

"Anything special?" The Mate asked.

"No, just do a little grocery shopping and put my stuff away. Maybe read or watch a movie."

"That doesn't sound like your usual energetic self," he observed.

"Sometimes those boyfriend's just wear you out," I said smiling.

"Do tell," he quipped.

"I'm sure you know all about it," I replied.

"I noticed the picture in the stairway. I don't know art, but it seemed to have a sexual theme," he opined.

"That painting is by Salvador Dali. It's called—'A bee buzzing around a pomegranate a moment before wakening'. It is supposed to show how a dream becomes all confused and crazy when you get woke up while dreaming. I also have 'Atomic Leda'. That is the painting of the nude woman with the swan. You probably saw it in my bedroom, upstairs. I believe that painting is sexual," I explained.

"That style of painting is surrealistic, isn't it?" the Mate asked.

"Yes, Dali is definitely a surrealist. I'm more fond of the impressionist style. I tried to paint like that, years ago. Unfortunately, I wasn't nearly as good as Jean or Marianne Marlowe."

"I didn't know that you painted," the Mate said.

"My grandmother used to have one of my paintings hanging in the living room. I used to take my sketch book and pastels with me, on the boat. I haven't done that for a couple years, now," I said, adding—"It looks like the food is coming."

The waitress was coming our way, carrying a plate. A man, who I recognized as the cook, followed behind her, also carrying a plate.

"That cook looks pissed. Maybe there's something wrong with our order," I whispered, as the pair approached our table.

The Waitress set the plate in front of me and took the plate from the cook and set it in front of the Mate. She refilled our Coffee cups.

"May I get you folks anything else?" she asked.

"No, we're good to go," the Mate said, and I nodded in agreement. She turned and left.

"Dave, I'm sorry I missed you last time," the cook said as he held out his hand.

We both stood up and the Mate shook hands with him.

"Ernie, have you met Nicolette Strickland?"

"I've seen her around," he said, turning toward me.

"Nick, this is Ernie McLaughlin."

"Hello, Ernie," I said, shaking hands with him.

"You couldn't be that hell raising young woman that's been terrorizing sailors on both sides of the border?" he asked.

"Ernie has been a steward for just about forever," the Mate said as Ernie pulled up a chair and we sat down.

"What's the good news?" the Mate asked.

I got the impression that Ernie keeps in contact with a lot of people.

"Your buddy Steve got a berth on Captain Dietzmann's boat, a cement carrier," he said.

"That's great, Captain D is fair and honest. He's old fashioned enough to understand a guy like Steve," the Mate said.

"He had better be. He's driving an old fashion boat. He's not the kind to go see the judge and get a sailor out of jail, though," Ernie stated.

I remembered when I beat up my old boyfriend, Bill. My grandmother's lawyer got a continuance until Bill got out of the hospital. He threatened Bill with all kinds of counter charges, until Bill dropped the assault charges against me. I had heard of Captains doing similar legal maneuvering to get sailors out of jail in the old days.

"You and Steve are getting along better?" the Mate asked.

"Sure, no one can be mad at Steve for long, except maybe a few ex-wives. I wasn't gonna' call the Bulls the last time you were here. I was gonna' just tell him to get out. Since he was with you, I let him go. I refused to take his money when he was in here last week. I mean, what was I gonna' do, we were shipmates," Ernie concluded.

"That's great. I'm glad that everything has worked out for the both of you," the Mate said.

"I have to get back to the kitchen. It was nice meeting you, Miss Strickland, and you watch out for this guy," Ernie said as he got up from the chair.

"It was nice meeting you, and I'll do that," I said.

The Mate remained quiet while Ernie went back to the kitchen.

"You guys seem to know a lot of the same people. I never heard of this Captain Dietzmann," I said as I attacked my waffles.

"He's a veteran of many years on the lakes. Even the hardships of winter navigation, doesn't stop that man from taking the boat out," the Mate said.

"I'm beginning to feel lucky that I don't know this guy," I remarked.

"I assume that he's still married to that beautiful, but ill-tempered Greek wife, Sophia. They have been married for about thirty years now. He's been working the winter navigation runs for that long, so rumor has it," the Mate explained.

"She doesn't sound like Grainne Kompsii at all," I said.

"Steve always liked working with Captain D, but he hated the times when Sophia came aboard for ridership. She was called the 'Gypsy Queen Bitch' by those sailors that had the dubious honor of meeting her in person," he concluded.

We ate in silence for a minute.

"You say this woman was called the 'Gypsy Queen B—' ?" I asked.

He nodded.

"Do these people live in Harrisonville, on Mackinac island?" I questioned. He nodded again.

"They have two bratty twins that you would want to smack the sh-t out of?" I asked.

"You know them?" he asked.

"Fortunately, no. Guiddo had several run-ins with her and the kids. Sicilians and Greeks are like bears and dogs. There's no way that they can come together without fighting. The kids pulled some crap and Guiddo tracked down their mother to redress grievances. Needless to say, he wasn't very successful. People over there have this evil eye thing," I finished.

"When Emma, Tommy and I were up there, those kids knocked down some bats on top of us. Tommy chased them up the hill and past the fort. We had to go looking for Tommy," he said.

"The little bastards must be grown up now. I wonder where they're living, the county jail perhaps?"

"I heard that one was on the lakes and the other in school. They were always well behaved around their father," the Mate said.

"Those are the ones I hate the most, the actors that play sweet and innocent. Just like my old boyfriend, Bill. I really love to stomp the shit out of them," I declared.

"Like Pete?" he asked.

"Exactly! By the way, I'll give you a 9 point 5. Not much for style or degree of difficulty, but simple and effective. No wasted motion in those hands," I remarked.

"How about last night?" he asked quietly.

"Oh, you scored much higher. As you said before, you're a lover, not a fighter," I said.

The Mate looked very pleased and we ate in silence for a few minutes.

"Oh, this is too big. I can't finish this," I said as I moved the plate and picked up the coffee cup. The Mate was laughing to himself.

"What's so funny?" I asked.

"That's what Misses Kefauver said. In another context, of course," he answered.

"Mind in the gutter McCracken. Talking about that in a public place, shame on you," I said in gentle reproof, adding—"I haven't seen enthusiasm like that since we got off in Duluth."

He reached over and held my hand. I had become accustomed to being alone, setting my own pace and daily routines. Yet something kept telling me that that was about to change.

"What are you thinking about?" he asked.

"I was thinking that the sunlight has some warmth in it today. It's gonna' bring us some adventure," I said.

"Holy cow, I love your attitude. You're so much fun to be with," he said.

"Most people say it's my attitude that they don't like," I said.

"Your animal energy is tremendous. I felt that on the Gentry. Last night, it just blew me away."

"You seemed to handle it pretty good from what I saw," I said, smiling at him.

He took my other hand and held it tight. I let him enjoy it for a minute.

"The waitress is coming. Are we done here?" I asked.

He let go of my hands and whistled at the waitress. He took out his wallet as she approached.

"The check, please," he said.

"Ernie says it's on the house," she said.

"Then take this," he said, handing her two five dollar bills.

"Thank you, have a nice day," she said, smiling. We put on our coats and headed for the door.

"The IGA next?" I asked as he held the door for me.

"Yes, I need to get some groceries too," he said.

It was a short drive to the grocery store.

"The red boat is out today," I observed.

"He looks like he's going to Middle Bass island," he said.

"I haven't been there in a couple of years."

"I was there back in nineteen seventy," The Mate said.

"That was back in the lawless days," I joked.

"There was a lot of stuff going on back in those days. There was only one policeman. A lot of hippie types thought it was some free drug island between America and Canada. They kept it out on the boats most of the time. It wasn't like the Bahamas," he said as he turned into the parking lot.

I thought about grandpa Eichann's seventeen foot Larsen boat and the islands we visited. He parked the van and we got out. He grabbed a shopping cart and we went through the automatic doors.

"Remember those stories about sailors who wouldn't push a shopping cart?" I asked.

"John Wayne Types," he said.

I still had food in my freezer and cupboards, so I only needed bread, milk, cheese and fresh fruit. The Mate on the other hand, selected some frozen entrees along with meat, fish and cupcakes.

"Are you expecting an army to come over for dinner?" I asked.

"Tommy and his girlfriend will be over. I wanted to have some food in the house," he explained.

Far be it from me to question his grocery shopping, I thought. He let the cashier ring it up as a single grocery order and he paid for it.

"I had plenty of money,Dave," I said as we were leaving the store.

"I know, I just wanted to make it simple," he said, smiling at me.

Without really understanding why, I put my hand on his arm as he pushed the cart out to his van. I helped him put the groceries in the van, then he opened the door for me and I got in.

"Too bad the farm market isn't open," I said, when he got in.

"I'm afraid it will be several months," he said as he started up the van.

"Is there anywhere else you want to go?" he asked when we got out to Bayshore road.

"No, I guess not," I replied.

When we got home, the frost was gone. A few sparrows and starlings were hopping around in the driveway, reluctant to yield the right of way. I unlocked the front door and the Mate opened the back of the van and took out my groceries. I held the front door for him as he brought my stuff in. He asked to use the phone and I started to put the groceries away. About the time I finished, he came into the kitchen.

"That was quick," I said.

"Uh . . . Tommy and his girlfriend are over at my house. I told him that I was out with you," he said. That was the first time I ever remember seeing him look nervous.

"You should have told him that you were in with me," I joked, as I embraced him and kissed him.

"You don't mind going over there and meeting them?" he asked.

"Not at all," I replied. I was putting up a brave front and acting calm.

"Are you ready now?" he asked.

"How does my face look?" I asked.

"Red on this side," he said.

"You booger,you didn't shave this morning. Well, there's no help for it now. Let's roll." I didn't bother locking the front door.

"Any man that can steer a ship through locks like you can, shouldn't have any problem with meeting a girlfriend," I stated, as he parked the van next to his house.

"I'll help you with the groceries," I said.

As we approached the front door, it opened and I saw a much older Tommy then I remembered. He stood at the doorway, looking dumbfounded. The Mate wasn't talking either.

"Tommy, long time, no see. You're looking well," I said as he stepped aside and I entered the house carrying a grocery bag.

I barely had time to remember that the kitchen was through the arched doorway and to the right.

"I got your newspaper," Tommy said to his father.

"Thanks, Tom," the Mate said as he followed me into the kitchen, carrying two grocery bags.

"I have no idea where you put your groceries," I said as I put the soda in the refrigerator, adding—" The frozen foods go in the freezer, correct?"

We both chuckled at my silly question. The Mate put the other food in the overhead cupboard.

"We should make some coffee," the Mate suggested when we were done. Tommy had not come into the kitchen yet, so I went into the living room.

"How have you been doing?" I asked Tommy.

"I'm doing well," he said.

"Your father tells me that you're living in Dearborn now," I said.

"Yes, I've been there for a year now," he said.

"Tommy, I didn't know you had company," a woman's voice came from behind me.

I turned and saw a young woman coming down the stairs. She had long, wavy, strawberry blond hair, a cherub-like face and was medium height. She was wearing a dark brown autumn sweater, a long tan skirt and dark brown leather boots. She had a likeable smile as she looked at me.

"Hello, I'm Madison Lindsey Nolan the Third," she said as she held out her hand.

"Hi, I'm Nicolette Strickland. My parents couldn't afford a middle name," I said as I shook hands with her.

"You can call me Maddy," she said, still smiling.

"You can call me Nick," I said.

"Tommy calls you Nicki," she said.

"You can call me Nicki. I haven't used that name in a while. You know how boys are in high school," I said, adding—"They're just as bad on lake freighters."

"Absolutely fascinating, I never met a Lake sailor. You'll have to tell me all about it," Maddy said.

"Have you met David McCracken, Tommy's father and our First Mate?" I asked.

"I've talked to him on the phone," she said, Adding—"It's a pleasure meeting you."

"Hello, I'm happy to meet you," The Mate said as they shook hands.

"I'm afraid that I misspoke, Tommy and I are the guests here," she said.

"That's quite alright, please make yourself at home," the Mate said in a very congenial manner.

"Tommy and I went up to Bay City last week and we saw a lake freighter. I was hoping that it was yours, but Tommy said that you were in Duluth," Maddy explained.

"Yes, we were getting our boat ready for winter," the Mate said.

"Tommy said that the freighters are frozen in the ice all winter," she said.

"Yes, it's fresh water, so it doesn't hurt the hulls," the mate said.

"I'm from Oregon, the water never freezes there. None of my family ever worked on ships. My parents took a cruise to Alaska a couple years ago, but they didn't learn anything about ships," she said.

"Nothing to it, port is left and starboard is right. Red right returning. One toot, passing left. Two toots, passing right," I explained.

"Is that why they blow the horn? I thought it meant hello and good-bye," Maddy said.

"It used to, we have radios for that now," I said.

"Are there any ships around here?" she asked.

"Just down the road, at the limestone dock, ships come in sometimes. Of course, you can see ships frequently out on the lake," I replied.

"Can you go on the ships?" she asked.

"We can go up to the ship. If we know the captain, he'll let us on," I replied.

"Really?" she said excitedly.

"Oh yeah, we'll show them the old Z card, that's a free pass for everywhere," I said.

"Wow, isn't that fantastic, Tommy? I'll bring my camera and get some great pictures. My family back in Oregon won't believe it."

"Where are you from in Oregon?" I asked. "Coos Bay, it's about sixty miles north of California."

"That's a very scenic coast, isn't it?" I asked.

"Yes, there are all kinds of bays and inlets. This time of year is very nice, because seals and sealions come down from the arctic and there are all kinds of birds," she said.

"I'm afraid that you'll find this coast to be rather disappointing, especially this time of year," I stated.

"In Coos Bay, all we see is the big ships as they go sailing by, ten miles out."

"Well, if you can stand our winter, it will look a little better in the summer," I said.

"Dearborn is too far from the water and too many people for me. You seem to have a much better location here," she said. She still had that infectious excitement in her voice.

"Check out Sleeping Bear dunes in the summertime. It's about one hundred and fifty miles from you. Just fantastic in the summer," I suggested.

"Really, Tommy never told me about that," Maddy said.

"We've been too busy at work to be able to plan any trips," Tommy said.

"What are you doing now?" I asked.

Tommy didn't answer right away.

"I'm an Automotive Design Engineer. Tommy is a design draftsman," Maddy stated with pride.

"Those sound like very good jobs, very challenging," I said.

"The biggest challenge is the people we have to work with," Maddy commented.

If they're anything like Tommy, I feel for you, I thought.

"What do you do on a ship?" Maddy asked.

"This season, I was a deckhand. The previous four seasons, I was a Conveyorman and QMED on a thousand footer," I replied.

"Is that how long the ships are, a thousand feet?" she asked, amazed.

"Yes, the newer ones are that big. They are motor vessels," I said.

"The largest aircraft carriers are a thousand feet. I've seen those in Oregon."

"Lake freighters can't be more than one hundred and five feet wide, so they can fit in the locks at Sault Ste. Marie," I said.

"I was shown some taconite pellets. How much can a big ship like that carry?" she asked.

"Sixty eight thousand tons at current draft requirements, which is twenty six and a half feet. Of course, a large boat like that takes much longer to load and unload," I explained.

"I'd like to see that." she said.

"Dave, why don't you call down to the terminal and see if anything is coming in," I suggested.

Tommy and he had been staring at each other silently.

"Sure, that sounds good," he said. He picked up the phone and dialed it. "Yes Zeke, this is David McCracken." He paused for a minute. "Yes, it's over for us now . . . . No, I'm not looking for a job, not yet anyway. I was wondering if you have anything coming in?"

"Zeke is a real character. He messes with all the sailors and won't even talk to anybody else," I said.

"Me and Nick just passed that way . . . , he paused. "Okay, I know the captain, so there shouldn't be any problem. See you in a little bit, bye.", then he hung up the phone.

"He said that the North Bay has been loading for the last two hours."

"That lying sack of sh-t, we were just by there," I said.

"Allowing for the Zeke factor, we'll go there in about an hour," the Mate said.

Tommy didn't look too enthusiastic about visiting a ship.

"Did Tommy get you a winter coat?" I asked.

"I have my skiing clothes," she answered.

"It's supposed to be in the low forties, so your skirt will probably be okay," I said.

"Does it get cold when you're out on a lake freighter?" she asked.

"Yes, it gets very cold and the wind and waves can be hellacious out there," I said.

"I have some pictures of ships," the Mate said, getting up out of his chair and going to the china closet.

"In Oregon, the ocean keeps it from getting below freezing on the land," she said.

"It doesn't help too much here. Fresh water freezes much faster than salt water," I said.

The Mate returned with a couple photo albums. Opening one album, he showed her some pictures of ships covered with ice.

"You took those pictures?" Maddy asked.

"Most of these pictures, I took myself," he said.

"How do you load the ship when it's covered with ice like that?" she asked.

"We get Nick and her buddies out there to knock the ice off," he said.

"You gotta' be kidding!" she exclaimed.

"I'm afraid he's not kidding," I declared.

"The deck gang worked thirty six hours straight to get the hatches off that time," he said. The Mate was showing her pictures for nearly an hour.

"I think it's about time to go," I said.

"Is it far?" she asked.

"Oh no, I can see it from my house," I said.

"I didn't know you lived that close!" Maddy exclaimed.

"Just on the other side of the woods. I've walked over here many times," I said.

"That is so cool," Maddy said as Tommy handed her her coat and camera bag.

"I can see the lighthouse from my bedroom window," I said.

The Mate handed me my coat and I put it on. The sun was shining brightly as we got in the van. The Mate turned the van around and got out on Bayshore road.

"The lake looks a little better than it did earlier," I commented.

"The wind has moved around to off shore," the Mate said.

"Out on the island, the sheltered side is on the north. I've been on some rough rides on the ferry," I said to Maddy.

"Do people live out there all year?" she asked.

"There are about twenty families out there year round. It's a pleasant enough place in the summertime, except for the fact that there's a lot more people," I said.

The Mate turned left at the Coast guard station and parked in the gravel parking lot next to the gate in the fence. We got out and walked toward the gate. I saw Zeke in the little guard shack, as we got to the window.

"Hi Zeke, can you open the gate?" the Mate asked.

"Come through the door," he said.

He's gonna' mess with us. I'd love to cuss him out, I thought, as we entered.

"This old troll will need to see some Z cards," he said.

The mate pulled out his wallet and showed him his mates license. I pulled out my billfold and dropped the clear plastic holders.

"I don't know if I can accept that. What is that, french or something?" he wisecracked.

"Your interpretation is as good as mine," I said, putting my billfold away.

"The captain left as soon as they docked. I hope they don't give you any trouble," Zeke said as he unlocked the back door.

"I'm sure we'll be fine," the Mate said as we headed for the back door.

When we got outside, I could see that the ship had just docked. If the captain had left, he beat his ass off that boat, for sure. Maddy had her camera out and stopped to take some pictures. I saw their first mate on deck, forward, and the Bosun and deckhands aft at the hatch crane. We headed for the portside boarding ladder, which was the only way to get on the boat, the way it was docked.

"It doesn't look like the hatches are off yet," I said. The conveyor was not running, either. I heard someone on the intercom. When we got to the boarding ladder, the first mate called down to Dave.

"That's Joel Gallagher. I've known him since our academy days," The Mate said as he indicated that we should go up the boarding ladder. I went up first, followed by Maddy, Tommy and the Mate.

"Well Maddy, here is your first lesson about lake freighters, getting up the boarding ladder without getting blown off or falling off," I joked as we climbed the ladder.

Maddy was staying right behind me and was having little difficulty negotiating the climb. The guys followed behind us silently. When I reached the top, I swung one leg over the railing and pushed off, landing firmly on the deck. The first mate held out his hand as Maddy tucked her skirt and swung her leg over the railing as I had done. Tommy put up both his hands as Maddy went over the railing like an old hand.

"Relax Tom, she's got it," Dave said as Maddy landed without incident.

A few moments later, Tommy and his father were on board. I looked at the first mate, Mister Gallagher.

"McCracken, long time, no see. How the hell are you?" he said as he held out his hand.

"Great! I want to introduce a shipmate, Nicolette Strickland."

"I've met Miss Strickland at Buehler's in Buffalo," he said, while shaking my hand. I remembered that I broke some guys arm in Buehler's bar and I haven't been back there since.

"This is my son's girlfriend, Maddy Nolan, and my son Tom. This is Joel Gallagher, first mate and a former classmate from way back," he said.

Maddy and Tommy shook hands with Joel.

"Is the skipper on board?" McCracken asked. Joel laughed.

"That's a good name for him. He ordered the ladder down before we even tied up. I don't know where he was going in such a hurry. I never saw Captain D move that fast," he joked.

Dave was acting cool, like he knew it was Captain Dietzmann all along.

"Yes, that sure doesn't sound like him," Dave agreed, adding—"I heard that Monk was on board."

"Oh yeah, the gang's all here. We even picked up Shaughnessy, early this morning in Cleveland," he said.

"You hear that Nick?" Dave asked.

"Was he conscious?" I asked.

"He might be by now," Joel said.

"Maddy is a west coaster, she has never seen a lake freighter. Do you mind if she takes some pictures?" Dave asked.

"If they don't get that hatch crane going, there won't be much to take pictures of," he said, adding—"Let's get you folks some hard hats."

They had a crew's hall on the starboard side, similar to the Gentry. We would wear the blue visitors' hard hats. Tommy had to help Maddy with her hair as she put on a hardhat. We had to wait in the crew's hall for a minute, while Joel went out on deck and directed the unloading conveyor as it was swung over the starboard side. Maddy went to the doorway and took some pictures of the operation. When the boom stopped, Joel waved for us to come out.

"This is a good day for taking some pictures on a boat. It's unusual for December," I said to Maddy. She still had both hands on the camera, poised and ready for action.

"Those deck hands are taking the clamps off the hatch covers. The bosun and the other two are removing the hatch covers with a hatch crane. The hatch covers probably weigh around six tons, like on the Gentry," I added.

"Awesome! I've never seen how bulk cargo is loaded on a ship," Maddy eclaimed as we walked aft.

There was a loud bang that made Tommy and Maddy hesitate for a moment.

"The Bosun is a little heavy handed with those hatch covers," I observed.

"Bill Kompsii wouldn't like that," Dave commented.

"Captain D runs a tight ship. They're getting sloppy with him gone," Joel said.

We stopped for a few minutes to allow Maddy a chance to get more pictures of the hatches being removed.

"When they get enough hatches uncovered, Joel here, will give them the go ahead to start the conveyor on shore," Dave said.

Maddy took the opportunity to take a sequence of pictures with her camera on auto advance.

"Nikon cameras are nice. You need a movie comera to get this action," I said.

"What are those men doing?" Maddy asked.

"They're hammering in the pins that will lift the hatch cover," I said.

Joel led us aft, past the hatch crane, to the seven hatches that were uncovered.

"The bottom of the cargo holds are slanted, so the limestone will slide down onto the conveyor belt when the cargo doors are opened," I explained.

"That's fantastic!" Maddy said excitedly, as she approached the hatch. Tommy grabbed her on the shoulder, pulling her to a stop.

"Hatches are dangerous, get back a couple of feet!" he demanded.

"She's safe where she is," I said.

"I'd believe that if it came from my father," Tommy snapped.

I could not believe that he said that to me. I wanted to tell him off, right then and there. I have been on the lakes for five years, and I have never fallen through an open hatch into a cargo hold, I thought as I glared at him. Dave put his hand on my shoulder.

"Tommy, we'll talk about this later," Maddy said.

Tommy let her go and she proceded to take some pictures of the cargo hold. She turned left and took a picture of the open hatches, looking aft. I noticed a short guy, half hiding behind the after mooring winch. Maddy noticed him, also and let her camera down.

"Do the workers mind, if I take pictures of them, while they work?" she asked.

"No, they usually don't mind as long as you don't get in their way while they're working," he said.

The little guy waved shyly, then stepped out of sight behind the winch.

"Don't mind Charlie, he's got a complex about his height. He's kind of a social outcast," Joel said.

"Maddy, call them sailors," I said quitetly.

"Oh, my goodness, I'm sorry," she said.

"Let's go aft and see if your buddy is still alive," Joel said jokingly.

We headed aft. When we got to the after deckhouse, we turned left. The galley must be similar to the galley on the Gentry, I thought as we entered through the portside door. A guy, I did not know, was walking down the passageway in front of us. We went through the swinging door on the right. The galley had the familiar long wooden counter with the cabinet doors. A large woman in her mid-forties with natural blonde hair, came through the half doors.

"Elsa, you know David McCracken?" Joel asked.

"From the Cliffs line," she answered, nodding in his direction.

"This is Nick Strickland, also on the lakes," Joel said.

"That Canadian girl from the Giovanni. By reputation of course," she said, coming over and shaking my hand.

"This is Tommy, Dave's son," Joel said.

"My goodness, you were just a kid," she said.

"And this is Maddy Nolan from Oregon," he said.

"Hello, Maddy," she said, shaking hands.

"It looks like you got some dinner for us," Joel said.

"Yes, but we'll need to stop in Toledo to provision for four extra sailors," she said.

Joel laughed. "They're just visiting. They won't be going out with us."

"Well, I'll be! We're short a mate, two deck hands and an oiler. You sure you don't need a job?" she asked.

Just then, John came through the half doors carrying trays, and froze. I could not help but to laugh.

"I must have died and went to hell," he said, staring at us in disbelief.

"You only got as far as Marblehead," I shot back.

Elsa and Joel laughed at that remark.

"I heard there was a fight after the party," John said.

"Pete and Joe slipped on a bar of soap," I said.

"That's what they all say," John shot back.

"Soap is very dangerous when wet," I said.

"We got pork Reubens and cornbeef," John said as he set trays in front of us.

"What are those french fries cooked in?" I asked.

"I didn't cook them," he said.

"You should have cooked the flambe last night," I said as we pushed our trays along and took our food.

"We have to get outta' here before I have to cook you supper," John wisecracked.

"I can't believe how much I miss your sense of humor," I said as I poured a cup of coffee.

"I really can't stand the Captain's wife," Elsa said, adding—"I don't cook Greek and I don't cook for Greeks. The Queen can stay in Harrisonville."

"The Queen may be on Mackinac Island, but the Princess must be in Marblehead," I said quietly as I picked up the tray and headed for the crew's mess. The others followed me into the crew's mess.

The crew's mess was even more spartan than the one on the Gentry. Instead of formica tables and vinyl covered chairs and stools, vintage nineteen fifties, this mess hall was furnished with wooden picnic tables. I recognized Lief the Chief and there was some other guy, I did not know.

"Looks like we got us some fresh fish here," Lief wisecracked.

"Don't get your hopes up, Lief, we're just passing through," I shot back.

"You could introduce yourselves, Miss Smarty Pants," he said.

"You know Dave. This is Tommy and Maddy," I said.

"This is Marty, short for Martin Banks," Lief said.

"Lief's name is Garrison. We use to call them the Garrison's Guerillas on the Spirit Independent. I thought you were gonna ride that old tea kettle to the bottom."

"Sorry to disappoint you, I jumped ship back in October," he said.

"You left old hairy Larry Laramie for greener pastures?" I asked.

"Larry's not a bad guy. Nothing like his brother Pee Pee," he said, adding—"What's Franklin up to?"

"He went back to Alliance. His father left him the farm," I answered.

"He hit the glass ceiling like the rest of us. Like that old song about 'he left the lakes to become a priest'," Leif said.

"Your name is McCracken, isn't it?" Marty asked.

"Yes, it is," Dave said.

"My father was the captain on the Harvey Birch, Henry Banks," he said.

"Sampson was the captain when I was there, back in sixty two," Dave said.

"My father was captain before him. Your brother was a school teacher?" he asked.

"Yes, he still is," Dave replied.

"My younger half brother had him in eighth grade. I remember my father saying that his teacher's brother was a mate on his old boat," Marty said.

"I heard Monk was on board," Dave said.

"He should be here any minute, since the engines are down," Lief said.

"Good, he can give us the nickel tour of the engine room," Dave said.

"I can't imagine that Miss Sunshine here wants to see another engine room," Lief wisecracked.

"She helped pull a turbine a couple weeks ago and kept Greg and the boys in line while she was at it," Dave said.

"Do tell! All we've been able to get is a bunch of stupid hillbillies," Lief complained.

"Two of the oilers volunteered to help the machinist. I asked one, how many thirty seconds were in an inch, so he said thirty. I asked the other guy, and he said he didn't know," Joel said.

"Which one did you pick?" I asked.

"The one that didn't know," Joel replied.

I looked up and saw a greasy looking Steve Monk come through the doorway with a cup of coffee. He hesitated for a moment when he saw us.

"Lord God in heaven! How did four normal people get on this boat!" he exclaimed.

"How you doing rough neck?" Dave greeted him, adding—"You remember Nick."

"Yes, of course, you're looking well," he said as I rose and shook his hand.

"You're looking kinda' greasy," I said jokingly.

"Sorry about the dungarees. I have to go back down there in a few minutes," he said.

"Steve, this is my son Tom and his friend Maddy. This is Steve Monk."

"It's nice meeting you," Steve said as he shook hands with them.

Even though he was covered with grease and dirt, he was wearing an attractive smile, that he didn't have the last time I saw him. He sat down at the end of the picnic table.

"Steve, I was wondering if you could give us a walk through tour of the engine room?" Dave asked.

"Sure, maybe we'll get to run the engine for you," he said.

"Maddy and Tom would like that," Dave said.

"I take it that you're in for the year," Steve asked.

"Yes, we laid-up in Duluth," Dave said.

"This boat is better than some I've been on. She might make it through the winter."

I didn't know if Steve believed that or he was saying it because the First Mate and Chief were there.

"I have to get topside. You guys stay out of trouble," Joel said, as he got up from the table.

"Okay, we'll meet up with you later," Dave said.

"They should start loading pretty soon," Lief said.

Maddy was looking anxious.

"Don't worry, they have a single conveyor. It takes hours," I told her.

"How do you have power if the engines are stopped?" Maddy asked.

"We have two auxillary turbines that run generators constantly and we also have a back up diesel engine," Lief explained.

"Running the conveyor takes more power than anything," I said.

"That's right," Lief said, adding—"The engineers have to run both generators at full capacity when we're unloading."

"If you folks are done here, we can head on back to the engine room and check things out," Steve said.

We got up from the picnic table and returned to the galley.

"Where are you folks going in such a hurry?" John asked.

"Engineering," I informed him.

"Abandon hope, all ye who enter there," he said.

We left the galley and started down the passageway, heading aft. I saw Tommy open the camera bag and hand Maddy her camera and some film.

"I'm glad I ran into you guys. We might be away for a while," Steve said.

"Are you going up the street?" Dave asked.

"Dietzmann won't let nobody off until he comes back. It'll probably be too late by then anyway," he said.

"You had some time in Cleveland?" Dave asked.

"Yeah, we had a whole twenty four hours. That's where we picked up your friend, Shaughnessy," Steve replied.

If Steve had got plastered, he sure didn't look like it. He was standing by on all bells. We made a right, then down a steep stairway and came to the Throttle deck. Most of the cylinders are visible from here. Only the very top of the cylinders come through the deck above. Steve began explaining some fundamental things about triple expansion engines. Maddy appeared to be faster with her camera than he was with his explanation of the engine. I asked a few questions to give Steve a break. We went down another steep stairway to the Crank deck. In contrast to the throttle deck, the machinery in the Crank deck is dirty and oily. The smell of oil and solvents is ever present. Our view from the after end, looking forward, revealed a forest of connecting rods, valve rods and Stephenson linkages.

"That's incredible!" Maddy exclaimed.

"You should see it when it's moving," I said, adding—"That crankshaft is coupled directly to the propeller shaft. There are no gears or electric motors to transfer power, like there are for turbines and diesel engines. What you get for steam is what you get for propeller shaft RPM," I finished.

"How often do you have to stop this engine to oil everything?" Maddy asked.

Steve started to laugh at that question.

"The Oilers do it once every hour, while the engine is running," I said.

"You must be joking!" Maddy exclaimed.

"Oh no, the job of an Oiler isn't easy on a ship like this," I said, adding—"That guy over there is an Oiler. You see that his shirt has no sleeves and he wears no watch or rings. They do what they call 'feeling around'. As they're oiling, they touch the machinery to feel for anything getting hot," I said. Maddy was incredulous.

"Old Juell has got one lick of sense to his name. He won't oil when he's been drinking," Steve said.

Mister Juell came over to see what we were doing. "Vern, tell the Chief, I would like to uncouple and run the engine slow for our guests," Steve said.

Mister Juell went over to the phone while Steve continued to explain things.

"Where did you learn about steam engines?" he asked.

"I was on the Mariner Enterprise and the Spirit Independent earlier this year," I said.

"You know Lief and Rayborn then?" he asked.

"And Stinky and Skids, Martin and Robinson," I said.

"Robinson is on third watch," he said, adding—"Dave, you weren't joking about Nick being an old hand."

"I told you that she had five years on the lakes. She doesn't miss a trick when she's on boats," Dave said.

"Don't let Dietzmann know that. He won't let either of you off the ship."

Mister Juell came over and we turned toward him.

"The Chief will be right down," he said.

"We have one generator going full tilt. I'm sure that will be enough, but Lief will want the other one kicked in to pump ballast water or something," Steve said.

"Those are DeLaval turbines?" I asked.

"Yes, about six hundred horsepower apiece," Steve replied.

"Where are the turbines?" Maddy asked me quietly.

"Over here," I answered, Adding—"They are coupled directly to the generators, here on the starboard side. The diesel engine over there on the port side is a backup, with its own generator."

The turbines are completely covered with insulation, while the generators look like electric motors. Maddy went closer to take some pictures.

There is a simple spline coupling between the crankshaft and the propeller shaft. They can be uncoupled in a few minutes using hydraulic pumps. Another man came over to us.

"This is Lloyd Christiansen, the first engineer," Steve said. He shook hands all around.

"Nice seeing you again, Dave," he said, smiling.

"I thought you would return to teaching science," Dave said.

"The only job available was in junior high school. I didn't want to deal with mental coworkers or prepubescent hoodlums," he remarked.

"And you can work on the lakes?" Steve asked jokingly.

"I can always ignore the son of a bitches here," he replied.

"We're uncoupling and running for a few minutes, when the Chief gets here," Steve said.

"I wouldn't do that for my own mother. Since we're old shipmates, I'll do it for Dave," he declared.

"I'm sure Lief will want to check things out while it's running without a load," Steve said.

"Not many people have seen what you're about to see," I said to Maddy and Tommy.

"If they can hold it at twenty RPM. I can set the auto advance to take pictures at fifteen degree intervals and have the lab make it into a movie film. I've done this before," she explained.

"You'll have to steady the camera," I said.

Steve and Dave were looking at us.

"We have to have twenty RPM for about ten revolutions," I requested.

"Sure, we'll get it for you," Lloyd assured us.

The propeller shaft was covered with a cage. Lloyd began pulling up the toggle levers that latched the cage. When all the latches were disengaged, Steve and Lloyd lifted the cage and set it aside. They attached the manual hydraulic pumps and began working the levers like a grease gun to supply pressure to the hydraulic cylinders that retracted the spline coupling. The Chief showed up while they were in the process of uncoupling.

"Have you got these guys all straightened out, Nick?" he asked.

"I don't think they need my help," I said.

It took only a few minute to get the uncoupling done. Steve and Lloyd disconnected the hydraulic pumps and went up the steps to the Throttle deck. Maddy took a few pictures then got herself in position to photograph the machinery in motion. The Chief picked up the terri phone and was talking to one of the engineers. He told us to stand clear. In a minute, we heard the hiss and rumble of steam as it entered the high pressure cylinder. The machinery began moving immediately, as the engineers rocked the pistons up and down to remove the water. After a minute, the engine started turning slowly in the forward direction. The noise increased with the rotation. I showed Maddy the indicated RPM gauge.

"Good, I can see the RPM from here," she said eagerly.

"I've never served on a ship with a steam engine," Dave said.

"I'm sure Captain D will love to have you aboard," I said jokingly. The RPM held steady for a minute. "It looks like you can start," I said to Maddy.

She started the auto advance and held the camera still while the connecting rods and valve gear moved up and down in their eccentric paths. Meanwhile, the chief took a piece of brass tubing and placed one end on the journal bearing and the other end to his ear.

"What's he doing?" Maddy asked.

"Listening to the bearing," I answered.

"It's singing sweetly," the Chief stated as he got up, adding—"Did you get your pictures?"

"Yes, thank you," she replied.

"They're starting to load topside," he said.

"Oh my goodness!" Maddy exclaimed.

"You can take the back stairs if you like," he said as he pointed toward the after stairway.

"Take care Chief," I said as I held out my hand.

"See you next season," he said as we shook hands.

Maddy, Tommy and Dave also shook hands with him and we headed topside via the after stairs. When we got out on the fantail, we could hear someone on the intercom. As we started heading forward, past the after deckhouse on the starboard side, we heard a screeching as the conveyor started.

"The loading is starting," I said. I saw Maddy putting more film in her camera.

When we got past the after deckhouse, I pointed out how the long belt from the quarry discharged onto the transfer belt, which discharged into the cargo hold of the ship. It took only a minute for the belt to be going at full capacity.

"Even at sixty tons a minute, it takes a while to load a twelve thousand ton ship," I said.

Maddy was taking pictures while Tommy crossed his arms on his chest and looked disgusted and bored. Maddy went up to the hatch and took pictures of the limestone going into the cargo hold. Joel came back to where we were standing.

"You folks wanna' see the control cabin for the conveyor? There's a decent view from up there," he invited.

"Sure!" Maddy replied.

We started walking forward. The control cabin for the unloading conveyor of the North Bay was added on to the after side of the wheelhouse. It is much larger than the diminutive one on the Gentry, which is above the pivot of the conveyor. Dave was in front, talking to Joel. Tommy was walking next to Maddy, neither of them looked happy at the moment. We took the outside stairs as though we were going to the wheelhouse. Tommy and Maddy both seemed leery of these stairs.

"Try running up during a gale, when the ship is rolling like crazy," I said.

Maddy turned her head momentarily and smiled at me. Joel opened the small steel door and we entered. There was plenty of room for the five of us in there. Maddy began taking pictures immediately, as Joel explained the instruments and control levers. Maddy asked about the catwalk that ran along side of the unloading conveyor. She was amazed when Dave told her that I had been out on the end of the boom many times.

"There must be a great view with the boom swung out over the water like that," she said.

"Usually I am too busy working or the weather was too crappy, to enjoy anything out there," I said.

I showed Maddy that the deckhands were removing the hatch cover in front of and below us.

"This is a great angle," she said as she took some pictures of the hatch covers being removed.

After spending about twenty minutes in there, we went out the "back door" and into the wheelhouse. It was a 'modernized' old style wheelhouse, somewhat like the Gentry. The old binnacle compass was still in front of the wheel and the auto gyro was off to the left. Old style rudder indicator and RPM indicator were over the window in front. The GPS and radar looked as modern as any I have seen. Like a lot of vessels, this one had a strange admixture of old and new machinery. Joel showed Maddy how to tell if the ship was on an even keel by looking at the lights that were arranged vertically on the stack aft. After a quick tour of the forward end, Joel led us out on deck on the port side. He informed us that Captain D's daughter had just had a baby and that the captain sends his regrets that he was not here to meet us. He had a card from the crew and wanted to know if we wanted to sign it.

"Sure," Dave said and he signed it and passed it to me. I wrote the usual congratulatory message and passed the card to Maddy. I felt a bit foolish that I had jumped to conclusions about the reason for Captain Dietzmann's quick departure from the boat. I would have done the same thing. It was obvious that Joel had other things on his mind, so we started heading toward the boarding ladder. When we got there, I shook hands with Joel and started over the railing.

"You look us up if you change your mind about working this winter or next year," he said.

"Will do," I replied, then I started down the ladder.

I was almost to the bottom, when I saw Maddy start coming down the ladder. It took another minute for Tommy and Dave to come down the ladder.

"Are you ready to sign on for next season?" I asked Maddy when she got down on the dock.

"That was very interesting and exciting, but I don't think I could work on a ship like that. I like to be home and in my bed every night," she replied.

"That's a noisy ship. It would probably keep me awake at night. All the same, it's nice to know that there could be a job waiting for us next season," I remarked as we walked toward the guard shack.

"I don't understand the turnover in personnel on that ship. The first mate seems friendly and you say the captain is fair," Maddy commented.

"Sailors are in a union. We normally work two months and take one month off. Some guys like to be out in the winter or need the extra money. The guys with seniority will bump other guys if they want on a particular boat," Dave explained as we got to the door.

"Hey, you guys and gals jumped ship already?" Zeke wisecracked as we entered through the back door.

"Some of us know when to leave before we wear out our welcome, Zekiel," I shot back.

"Charming as always, Miss Strickland," he countered, as he opened the front door for us.

"Oh how cute," Maddy said as she led the way out the front door.

Two seagulls were right in front of the door, playing tug-of-war with a bread stick. There was quite a flock of gulls attacking the bread that Zeke had just threw out there before we came.

"Nasty, disgusting, filthy critters," I said as I shooed them away from us. "Watch out for their droppings. That twit is always pulling sh-t like this," I said as Dave and Tommy were trying to get them away from the van.

"We'll just run the goddamn things over," I snapped as I opened the door of the van.

When we were all in the van, Dave asked Maddy if she wanted to drop off the film. Maddy said that she would use the lab at work.

"To the lighthouse, Dave," I said as we got to Bayshore road.

It was a short drive to the lighthouse. On the way, Tommy was griping about his ears ringing from the noise on the ship.

"The noise on the production floor is several decibels louder than on that ship. You're in the design loft or your cubicle all day while I'm out on the floor doing quality control inspections. You don't hear me complain, now do you?" she stated in a dignified voice.

I felt much satisfaction in the fact that Tommy got put in his place without Maddy having to hit him.

"That looks like a nice little cemetery over there," Maddy said as we past it.

"The realestate looks much better in this sunshine," I said.

Tommy and Dave did not say anything. We pulled into the parking lot next to the keepers house.

"Oh, that's wonderful. A lighthouse keepers house with a white picket fence around it," Maddy said.

"Unfortunately, you can't take pictures from over there. The house is owned by a crotchety old man that won't let anybody over there to take pictures," I said.

"If I could get into that little woods, I could get a picture with my long lens," Maddy said as she was happily taking pictures of the lighthouse.

"Yes, you could do that," Dave agreed.

"The picture frame that Dave gave me, has a picture of me and Tommy up there on the observation deck when we were kids," I said.

"Really, I would like see that!" Maddy exclaimed.

"Sure, come over with me later and I'll show you," I said.

We walked down to the rocks and looked over the water.

"What's that, over there?" Maddy asked.

"The roller coasters at Cedar Point," Tommy answered.

Maddy took a few more pictures of the landscape.

"What is this Lighthouse made of?" she asked.

"Bricks. The walls are four feet thick," I replied.

"Wow, it must have been here quite a while," she said.

"Since eighteen twenty two. People say that during the nineteen sixty nine storm, the top of the waves reached the observation deck," I said.

"That must be fifty feet up to there. Our lighthouse is just a steel frame with a big light on top," Maddy informed us.

"It's just a rotating green light up there now. It was a constant green light years ago. The Confederate prisoners on Johnson's island wrote about it," I said.

"There was a prison camp here?!" Maddy asked, still amazed.

"Yes, just down the road and across the causeway, at Johnson's island," I said.

"Can we see it?" Maddy asked.

"The only thing left to see is the cemetery," I said.

"If you're done here, we can head down there," Dave said. We headed back to the van.

"Tommy, this is great. In the summer, we can tour the lighthouse and see the islands. That will be so cool," she said.

"This place doesn't hold many attractions for me. I guess it's because I was born here," Tommy remarked as we got to the van.

It was only a short drive to Cadotte road, which goes to Johnson's island.

"I wonder if the toll gate is working. The property owners are fighting with the state, so they want people to pay to come across. Some enterprising soul usually breaks the gate. My grandmother brought me here years ago and we had to wait eight hours for the waves to subside enough to get back across the causeway," I explained.

"Is it a big cemetery?" Maddy asked.

"Over two hundred people are buried there." I replied.

"It must have been a big prison," Maddy said as we drove across the causeway.

"One of the smaller ones. Officers and a few important civilians were kept there," I said.

We parked next to the cemetery fence. The lock was on the gate, but it was unlocked.

"The Confederate Prison was over there in the woods. Most of the guards compound was quarried away years ago," I explained.

Maddy took some pictures of the headstones and the statue of the Confederate soldier. There was a small plaque which read:

"Farewell thou lake, Farewell thou inhospitable land.
Thou hast the curses of this patriotic band.
All, save the place, the holy, sacred bed.
Where rest in peace, our southern warriors dead."

"Awesome! We don't have any Civil War sites out in Oregon," Maddy said.

"Most of the action here was in the war of 1812. Out on Middle Bass island is the Perry monument. It's huge, but you need a clear day to see it from the boat dock or the light house," I said.

"There was a battle here?" Maddy asked.

"Yes, a big naval battle out on the lake. West of here, in Perrysburg, there was a big land battle," I explained.

"Incredible! This seems like such a peaceful place!" Maddy exclaimed.

"It has been for a long time," I said. With Tommy and his father back together, it might not be so peaceful, I thought.

"In the summertime, we're gonna' have a blast," Maddy said as we were walking back to the van.

"In the summer, my father and Nicki won't be here," Tommy said tersely.

"I'm sure we'll have some time off in the summer," Dave said.

Tommy is cruisin' for a bruisin' here, I thought as we got into the van. In a few minutes, we were back out on Bayshore road.

"Would you guys like to stop at the Anchor Bar?" Tommy asked.

"No, we should probably get home and start supper," Dave said, adding—"I do a pretty good spaghetti and meatballs."

"Really Dave, I think the Edmund Fitzgerald stew is a better choice for a day like today," I chimed in.

"Well, if you want to. How long does it take to make it?" he asked.

"If two of us work on it, we'll have it done by six o'clock," I said.

"That's great! I'll help you and these guys can watch football or something," Maddy said.

When we got to the Mate's house, Tommy did not look too happy about the arrangements, but he did not say anything to us. When we got in the kitchen, I explained the cooking procedure to Maddy. She understood the sauteeing of the vegetables and the frying of the steak. We made a quick trip over to my house via the road, to get the Beef consomme and diced tomatoes.

"You have a darling little house, it's so cozy," Maddy said as I showed her around.

"Yes, it's solid rock beneath us, so I don't have to worry about beach erosion. The view is great and my neighbors are very friendly," I said, adding—"You could spend the night here, if Tommy doesn't mind."

"That would be great. I'd like that," Maddy said.

I put the stuff for the stew into two plastic bags and we headed out the back door. "I call this my secret path. I'm the only one who uses it," I said. We went down into the gully and I crossed the creek on the log.

"Look, you have stones here," Maddy pointed out, and she proceeded to cross the creek on the stones.

"My grandmother would use the stones. Her second husband, Eichann, put them there," I said.

"This is so cool. In Oregon we have pine forests," she said.

When we came out of the gully, we were in the Mate's backyard. We entered the side door and went directly into the kitchen. Tommy came to the kitchen doorway.

"Nicki has a little path through the woods that comes right to the backyard. There is a creek with a log across it," she said.

"Yes, I remember the path," Tommy replied.

After adding the tomatoes and the beef broth, we let the stew cook for an hour.

"I'm gonna' go over to Nicki's house later and look at pictures and things," Maddy said to Tommy as we went into the living room.

"I'm afraid we won't have time, dear. We have to find a Motel for the night," Tommy said.

"Nonsense!" I blurted out.

"We have two houses here and you're family. We wouldn't think of having you stay at a Motel," Dave said. Obviously he was trying to steer clear of a confrontation.

"Great, Maddy can bunk with me. We'll have a blast," I said, smiling at Maddy.

Tommy was looking real unhappy and the Mate wasn't looking too good either.

"Is there any problem with that, Dave?" I asked.

"No, Tommy can sleep in his old room," he said.

"In that old bunk bed!" Tommy exclaimed angrily.

"You can use the rollaway bed," Dave said.

"That's very kind of you two," Maddy said.

"Tcch, think nothing of it," I said.

Maddy asked some questions about steam engines and lake freighters. Since I had been on a thousand footer, she wanted to know about those. She had a good knowledge of diesel engines and nearly reached the limit of my knowledge by the time the stew was ready. We went into the kitchen and got the food ready to serve while Tommy and the Mate set the table in the dining room.

"Nicki said that this is the real stew that was served on the Edmund Fitzgerald," Maddy said as she started to ladle the stew into the bowls.

I laid out the bread and the grilled cheese sandwiches.

"How would Nicki know about that?" Tommy asked.

"I got the recipe from the First Steward on the Fitz. Naturally, he wasn't on the ship when it was lost," I said.

"I didn't even know about the sinking," Maddy said, adding—"I have an old National Geographic from nineteen sixty that has the Edmund Fitzgerald featured in it."

"Yes, it was a well known boat. She was launched in nineteen fifty eight," the Mate explained.

"Sailors always refer to the boats as 'she'," I said in response to Maddy's quizzical look.

"This is authenic sailors stew. You can't find it anywhere nowadays," Dave declared.

"I wonder what John is making for supper," I said.

"The cook didn't seem very friendly," Maddy observed.

"Because he was plastered at the party. Every trip he finds someone to pick on. Elsa won't put up with that for very long," I said.

"Wow, there's a lot of different people on lake freighters. It sounds like the office where I work," Maddy said.

"It takes a different breed of person. Sometimes it seems like a very solitary existence," I said.

"It must seem like a solitary existence when you're the only woman on the ship," Maddy said.

The Mate and Tommy were being strangely quiet.

"We had a Wheelsman and a Steward that were women, on the Giovanni," I said.

I thought for a moment about all the things that I had missed while I was out on the lakes. I should have asked Grace Kompsii what she thought about being the wife of a sailor. I made a mental note to ask Eileen about it.

"We're having chocolate cream pie for dessert," Maddy said.

"Is that from the lake freighters too?" Tommy wisecracked.

"No, it's from the grocery store," Maddy snapped as she got up from the table to get the pie.

"That was wonderful stew. I don't think John could have done any better," Dave said.

"Maddy is a great cook. You're very lucky, Tommy," I stated.

"I never noticed," Tommy said as he poured the coffee.

"How are things going in the auto industry," The Mate asked.

"We didn't make any money this year. Probably some more plant closings next year," Tommy said as Maddy came in with the pie.

"We hear that every year. Honda, Toyota and Volkswagen have plants in this country. There's always something new coming up," Maddy said as she cut the pie.

"I'm sure that people will keep buying cars," I said.

"Made in Mexico or Japan," Tommy sneered.

"It's gonna' be a blast at Christmas time. We're going back to Oregon. All of my brothers and sisters will be there. Tommy will get to meet them."

Tommy did not look too happy about that, either.

"How big is your family?" I asked.

"I'm the second oldest of six. Three boys and three girls," she replied.

"That sounds like quite a family," Dave said.

"Yes, we've always gotten along and been happy together," Maddy said.

It felt like an icicle had been jabbed into my heart.

"Maddy, we've got to talk," Tommy said as we were gathering up the dishes.

"Sure, I'll be right out," she said.

We took the dishes into the kitchen and set them in the sink. If Maddy was in 'lock and load' mode, she did a good job of hiding it.

"I'll give you a copy of that recipe, if you like," I said as we went back into the dining room.

"Maddy, we have to talk about all these plans. Going here—"

"We'll talk about this in the other room," Maddy snapped.

They both headed for the downstairs bathroom. The Mate had a real painful look on his face.

"The fur's gonna' fly now," I said quietly as we heard the door close. Inspite of the door, we could hear Maddy telling Tommy that Sybil was history and that he could stop being mad at the world. Tommy told her that I was always a mean little witch and that I should stay out of his father's pants. I didn't know whether to laugh or get angry. The Mate looked like he was in shock. We heard somebody get slapped on the face, three times.

"That was crude and out of line. Stay out of your father's life if you can't act like a man," Maddy shouted.

After a moment, Maddy came out of the bathroom, looking as fresh as a daisy. I couldn't believe that her face wasn't red or anything.

"Tommy will wash the dishes, Dave. Are you ready to go?" Maddy asked.

"I'll just grab my coat," I said.

"Thank you ladies, for cooking that lovely dinner," the Mate complimented.

"You're very welcome. See you tomorrow," Maddy said.

"Catch you later, shipmate," I said and he winked at me.

As we left the house via the side door, I noticed that the wind had shifted around to the northwest.

"The weather is gonna' turn crappy now," I predicted.

"The weather is so changeable here," Maddy observed.

"We have spring, winter, summer and fall. Sometimes in the same week," I told her.

"Tommy said that he also used this path," Maddy said as we went down into the gully.

"Yes, when we were kids, we used to sneak down to the lake this way."

"That's so cool," Maddy said.

"We used to make little boats and launch them here in the creek and try to retrieve them before they were lost in the lake," I said.

Maddy used the log when we crossed the creek. I showed her the way down to the shore.

"The North Bay is still loading," Maddy observed.

"It will be a wet and cold night for those guys," I said. We watched for a few minutes, then went back up the path toward my house.

"This was your grandmother's house?" Maddy asked.

"Yes, she used to rent one of the cottages just over there, in the summertime. When my grandpa Strickland died, she bought this place," I explained.

"Do your parents visit you up here?"

"No, my parents aren't any good. I told them to stay away," I said.

I figured that Maddy wouldn't understand that, from what she said earlier. I checked the mail, then opened the front door and we entered.

"It will be dark soon," I said as I turned on the lights. We went into the kitchen and I put on some water for tea.

"I'll show you some pictures in a minute," I said as I went into my grandmother's bedroom. I hurriedly changed the bed clothes and got out my grandmother's photo albums.

"This one has the pictures from here in Marblehead, when we were kids. All except for the picture of Tommy and I up in the lighthouse," I said as I sat down in a chair and opened the album.

She looked at the pictures of Tommy and rest of us for a few minutes before she pointed to Tommy's mother.

"Is this Tommy's mother?" she asked.

"Yes, it is," I answered.

"What's her name?"

"Emma Louise," I replied.

"Tommy really favors his father," Maddy said.

"If only it were true," I said quietly.

"Tommy refuses to even talk about his mother. What happened to her?" she asked.

"She died two years ago, from Leukemia," I replied.

"Oh my goodness, that must have been terrible for him," she said.

"Terrible for both of them. She's buried in that little cemetery down the road. I don't think Tommy has ever been there since."

"I know that Tommy can't accept it, but I don't know why," Maddy said.

"Tommy always accused his father of running away and abandoning a sick and dying wife. The truth is that Emma found out in the summer while Dave was away. She kept it hid from him until he got home in October. The Cliffs line was shutting down and those guys didn't have a job and were gonna' lose benefits, like health insurance. Emma hung on until February. Dave was with her for every minute, during those last four months," I explained.

"She must have been very brave," Maddy said.

"Surprisingly, she was very much like you," I said.

"You really think so?" she asked.

"I thought that when I first saw you," I said.

We spent the rest of the evening looking at pictures. I explained about my grandmother dying and how my worthless parents were trying to take everything from me.

"You will be happy with Tommy's father. It will be great. Our children will be related," Maddy said as I showed her the pictures in the Mate's picture frame.

I tried to hide the fact that I was somewhat taken aback by her statement about me having children with David. Maddy had a cup of herbal tea and I had sassafras tea before going to bed. I told her that she could sleep in my grandmother's room. I gave her a night gown and house coat from my grandmother's closet. I went upstairs and got ready for bed. I was reading a sci-fi novel that Tammy had given me. It was so boring, it actually kept me awake. I put it down and started to think about things. I thought it was gonna' be an easy, lay around day. It seemed that I had to think twice about a lot of things. Far away, I heard a ship's whistle blow. The North Bay was leaving. A miserable, wet snow had been falling since shortly after nightfall. Putting those hatches covers on in the snowy darkness, was not going to be much fun for those guys, I thought. After a while, I closed my eyes and started to drift off to sleep. I was awaken shortly thereafter by a thud on the balcony door. I put on my housecoat and grabbed my big railroad flashlight. I saw another snowball hit the door. I pointed the flashlight toward the ground and turned it on. I was surprised to see Tommy in my back yard. I opened the back door.

"I was looking for Maddy," Tommy said sheepishly.

"We have a front door, Romeo," I snapped.

I turned off the flashlight and closed the door. When I got to the front door, Tommy was waiting there.

"Maddy is in the downstairs bedroom," I said when Tommy entered.

Tommy went to the bedroom door, which was ajar, and softly called her name. Tommy went into grandmother's bedroom and closed the door. I waited a few minutes to make sure that Maddy was receiving him, then I went to the phone and dialled the Mate's number.

"Uh . . . McCracken," he answered.

"Hello love, I'm sorry that I woke you. I just wanted you to know that Tommy came down here. The front door is unlocked and I'm in the upstairs bedroom," I said.

"Uh . . . okay, sure," he replied.

"Okay, bye-bye," I said and hung up the phone.

I sat in the living room and waited. I figured that my double bed would be big enough for us. I heard him coming in the snow and I went to the front door.

"Not ideal weather to be calling on a young woman," I said as he came in and took off his coat.

I put my arms around him and we kissed tenderly. I let go and we started for the stairs.

"It's a good thing that our shipmates don't know about this," I said quietly as we went up the stairs.

We went into my bedroom and the Mate closed the door. I had definitely developed a distaste for sleeping alone. Oblivious to the weather outside, we slept comfortably together. I got up and got some water from the pitcher. I laid down and thought about us sleeping together on a ship, before I went back to sleep. When I woke up, it was already light outside. I could see the gray sky between the curtains. I rolled over and got on top of David. He opened his eyes and smiled at me.

"I'm not getting up this morning, Mr. McCracken. I'm just gonna' lay here and make love to you all day. What do you think of that?" I asked, then we kissed.

"I thought the second night was to get acquainted, not for love," he said.

"I wouldn't have you any other way, now," I answered.

"I'll have to install a watch bell, so you won't get lazy," he wisecracked.

"You think I'm Pavlov's dog?" I asked jokingly.

I closed my eyes and lay on him for a while, then Tommy knocked on the door.

"When you two are done in there, Maddy and I are making breakfast."

I remembered telling Maddy that I like my eggs over easy and Dave likes three minute eggs.

"Well, hells bells, I get served breakfast in my own house. You can't beat that," I said as I rolled off of the Mate and sat up in bed.

I grabbed my clothes and headed for the bathroom, downstairs. I washed up quickly and dressed and put my hair in a ponytail. When I came out of the bathroom, I saw the Mate coming down the stairs. I went into the kitchen and saw Maddy and Tommy fixing breakfast.

"We took the liberty of making breakfast. I hope you don't mind," she said.

"Not at all, that's very kind of you."

"You mentioned that you came off the four to eight watch and would go to the galley and get breakfast," Maddy said.

"Yes, that's the way it was unless we were loading or unloading," I said.

"What did you do if you loading or unloading?" she asked.

"Put down the overtime," I said as I poured a cup of coffee.

I pulled out a chair and sat down. After a minute, the Mate came into the kitchen.

"Maddy does some good three minute eggs," Tommy said as Maddy was taking the pan off the stove.

I didn't know that he also liked his eggs that way. In a few minutes, they had breakfast on the table and they sat down as well. In opening a three minute egg, Tommy was as good as his father.

"Maddy would help her mother cook, when she was living at home," Tommy said.

"She does a good three minute egg," the Mate said, smiling.

"Dave will cry when you leave," I said jokingly. We ate in silence for a few minutes.

"I was thinking about going to see mother, after breakfast," Tommy said.

On a cold, miserable, snowy day like today. Yesterday would have been much better, I thought.

"Your mother would like that," the Mate said.

Everyone else seemed happy this morning. Apparently I was the only one who didn't look forward to going out in the snow and cold. A few minutes later the phone rang.

The Mate picked up the phone, "Hello, Strickland residence," he said.

"One moment," he said and he handed the phone to me.

"This is Nicolette Strickland," I said into the phone.

"My name is Francesca DeLorenzo. I am the wife of Adolfo Grimaldi," a woman's voice on the phone, said. Obviously, this woman had not been speaking english for very long.

"I'm afraid that I don't recognize either of those names," I said.

"Adolfo is the younger brother of Guiddo Scarapitti. Guiddo is taken ill. You may expect a phone call from him within the hour," she said.

"Uh, okay. Tell Guiddo that I'll be here," I said.

"Very good, Ciao bella," she said and she hung up the phone. I was silent for a moment after I hung up the phone.

"Is there something wrong, Nick?" the Mate asked.

"Guiddo has taken a turn for the worse, apparently," I said.

"I'm sorry to hear that," the Mate said.

"Dave, I have to wait here for a phone call. You guys go ahead and go to the cemetery," I said as I sat down at the kitchen table.

Maddy and Tommy were looking at me.

"Guiddo is a shipmate from the Giovanni. I've known him for years," I said.

"You showed me some pictures last night. You said he had a stroke," Maddy said.

"Yes, Dave and I went to see him a couple weeks ago, in Toledo. He had lost the use of his right leg. This Francesca is married to his brother," I explained.

"His brother is there with him?" Maddy asked.

"I doubt that. He always said his brothers were criminals and he would sink them in the lake if they ever came around," I said.

"My goodness, that doesn't sound very friendly," she said.

"Guiddo is a great guy. If he hates his brothers, I'm sure that he has very compelling reasons for doing so," I said.

"We'll go over there later if you want," The Mate said.

"I'm sure that Guiddo would like that," I said.

In a few minutes, we had finished breakfast and put the dishes in the sink. The three of them, put on their coats and Maddy grabbed her camera bag. The Mate kissed me.

"Don't get wet out there," I said as they went out the door.

I thought about Guiddo as I started washing the breakfast dishes. This strange Italian woman calling me like that, didn't seem too good for Guiddo. after wiping down the kitchen, I picked up the phone and dialled Guiddo's number. A woman with a plain midwestern accent, answered the phone.

"Hello, my name is Nick Strickland. I received a phone call from Guiddo's sister-in-law, a little while ago. Is Guiddo there?" I asked.

"No, he was sent to the hospital, a couple of hours ago," she said.

"Are you his nurse?" I asked.

"No, I'm a nurses aide. I'm removing all this equipment, per his doctor's orders," she said.

"He is in the Toledo Hospital?" I asked.

"Yes, he is," she said.

"Okay, thank you very much," I said and I hung up the phone.

I knew that Eileen worked at Toledo Hospital. I had kept the business card that she had given me. I took it out of my wallet and wrote her work and home phone numbers in my address book. After waiting a few more minutes, I picked up the phone and called Andy's house.

"Botzum residence," Andy said.

"Hi Andy, this is Nick Strickland. Is Eileen there?" I asked.

"No, I'm afraid that she's at work," he said.

"I just found out that my old shipmate, Guiddo Scarapitti, was taken to the hospital a couple hours ago. Could you have Eileen get a message to him?" I asked.

"Sure," he said.

"Have her tell him that I'll be there in a couple hours. Do you think she can do that?" I asked.

"Oh yeah, I'm sure that will be no problem for her," he said.

"Okay, thanks so much. I may be seeing you guys later," I said.

"I hope so. The girls are going nuts here," he said.

"Alright, tell them that I'll be over later this afternoon. Bye-bye."

"Okay, bye," he said and I hung up the phone.

I wanted to start up my truck and head up there immediately, but I decided to wait until the Mate came back. I went out to the garage and started up my truck, to warm it up for later. I came back in the house and sat by the phone. I started thinking about things. David, Earl and Guiddo were my three best friends and the three important men in my life. It took another half hour for Dave, Tommy and Maddy to return. I informed them that Guiddo was in the hospital and that Eileen was getting a message to him. The Mate said that he would gladly come with me. I apologized to Tommy and Maddy for leaving them suddenly. Tommy said that he would lock up his father's house when they left. When we got outside, they took the gully path while Dave and I got in his van. Taking route two, it's about forty miles to Toledo. We parked in the parking deck and went to the information and visitors desk. I told the woman at the desk that I was Nicolette Strickland and that I should have a message from Eileen Botzum. She didn't have any message from Eileen, so she called her. After talking on the phone for a minute, she hung up the phone and told us that Eileen would meet us in the third floor surgical waiting area. It only took us a few minutes to get there. As we left the elevator, I saw Eileen talking to a young woman with long, dark hair and olive skin. As we approached, she looked our way.

"Nick, David, Hello. Have you met Francesca DeLorenzo?" she asked.

"We talked to her on the phone," I said.

This woman wears only the best clothes, I thought as I shook hands with her.

"Doctor Monroe has called in Doctor Weissenfeld. The procedure is experimental. It involves removing the skull on the right side. The section of skull will be temporarily placed in his abdomen. Guiddo can't talk, but with hand signals, he has indicated that he refuses this surgery," Eileen said.

"Absolutely, They will kill him with this experimental thing," Francesca retorted.

It sure didn't sound like something Guiddo would agree to.

"Can we see him?" I asked.

"As soon as the doctors come out," Eileen said.

We talked for nearly twenty minutes before the doctors came out. Doctor Monroe talked to us for a few minutes, then he left. Guiddo was half sitting up in the bed when we entered. He waved at us weakly with his left hand. I fought back wanting to cry and I took his hand and smiled at him.

"You've got a few tubes in you, guy," I remarked.

He tried to reach over and grab the pen and pad on the little table. I swung it over the bed for him.

"I was on the Giovanni. All the guys were asking about you, Franky, Gabby, Bart, Shorty."

He picked up the pencil with his left hand and wrote-'shipmate remember'.

"Sure, old buddy, everything is just as you said," I replied.

He waved at Francesca.

"I will leave you now. Ciao paisan'," she said and she left.

"Is she a spy for your brother?" I asked quietly. Guiddo nodded weakly.

"We didn't tell her anything," I said.

Guiddo wrote-'Doggett'.

"You mean Doggett, your lawyer?" I asked.

He tapped my hand lightly.

"I'll call him early tomorrow morning," I said.

'Always good girl' he wrote.

I kissed him on the cheek and tried to embrace him, but the tubes got in the way. "It'll be okay, old buddy. Just like in Detroit and Conneaut, I'll get you outta' this jam," I said softly.

Just then a nurse and an orderly came in.

"We have to take mister Scarapitti to the fifth floor for some tests. It will take a couple hours at least," the nurse said.

"Okay, old buddy. We gotta' leave now," I said. Dave and I shook his hand. "We'll see you again, real soon," I assured him, then we left.

When we got back to the surgical waiting room, Francesca said that Eileen said that she would see us at home. We thanked her and asked if she needed a ride anywhere. She said that she had a car and accomodations in Toledo. She didn't seem too anxious to leave the hospital.

"We might as well head over to Andy's," the Mate said, and we headed toward the elevator.

"She looks awfully young to be a sister-in-law to Guiddo," the Mate said after we got into the elevator.

"Guiddo said that his youngest brother got rid of his first wife and married her a couple years ago. She's from Sardinia. They look different and speak different than Sicilians."

"She's very beautiful," Dave said.

"She doesn't make pizza worth a damn, according to Guiddo. She's from a good family, so Guiddo will talk to her, for now," I said as the elevator door opened.

It was a short walk to the van.

"Are you gonna' be okay?" the Mate asked when he opened the door for me.

"Yes Dave, thanks for asking," I said as I got in.

He got in and started up the van. It was only a ten minute drive to Andy's house. Kaleigh and Desiree were riding their bikes in the garage when we pulled in the driveway. When the van stopped, they came running out to greet me.

"Aunt Nick, Aunt Nick," they shouted.

"Well, hello there. You're both looking well," I said as I stepped out of the van.

"We missed you!" Kaleigh exclaimed.

"Give me a hug," I said as I squatted down. I hugged them both at once.

"Oh, you girls are so precious. Let's go give Uncle Dave a hug."

They went around to the driver's side and the Mate picked up both of them at once.

"Well, you girls are getting bigger every day."

"Uncle Dave, do you live with Aunt Nick?" Kaleigh asked.

"Uncle Dave is my neighbor. There is a nice little path through the woods to Uncle Dave's house. Would you like to see it?" I asked.

They both nodded their heads.

"Let's go in the house. Eileen should be rolling in around one o'clock," Andy said.

The Mate set the girls down and they came running over to me and took my hands in their little hands as we headed into the garage.

"You have a nice house here," I said.

"I would like a little bigger house with some land," Andy said.

We passed through a kitchen and a dining room, into a living room. Andy talked with the Mate while the girls showed me all the cartoons that were on TV. Andy cooked some hotdogs for lunch and I read to the girls until Eileen came home. Eileen thought that the girls were too young to spend a night away from home, but they insisted on sleeping with Aunt Nick. Andy put a car seat in the Mate's van while Eileen got the clothes they would need. I told Eileen that the girls would call her as soon as we got to my house. Kaleigh and Desiree were looking forward to the trip, but Andy and Eileen were looking a little traumatized as they waved good-bye to us as the van pulled out of their driveway. All the way to Marblehead, the girls asked questions about everything under the sun. I promised to show Kaleigh the nested dolls that the Russian sailor had given me. I realized that to children their age, going to another house is like entering a strange new world. When we got to my house, they couldn't wait to see the snow, which was still on the ground. We let them play in the snow for a few minutes, then I called them in to talk to their mother on the phone. After I showed them around the house, they asked where the toys were. I took them upstairs to my room and showed them the storage cubbyhole. They looked at the toys and pulled out an old game called Mousetrap. This game kept them amused for an hour or so, then they wanted to play with my old Barbie house. I gave them some dolls to play with as well. Unlike the Mousetrap game, they didn't require any assistance to play with Barbie dolls for a couple hours. Before nightfall, we drove the girls around and showed them the lighthouse and some ships out on the lake. We took them to a Buffet restaurant. They really enjoyed the fact that they could get anything they wanted to eat. After supper, we took them to one of the few gift shops that was still open. They picked out some stuffed toys and I got them each a suncatcher and had their names engraved on them. It was fully dark by the time we got back to my house. The girls wanted to watch TV, so I played some christmas video tapes for them and helped them get into their pajamas. Eileen talked to them on the phone and told them that it was time to go to bed. I took them to my grandmother's bedroom.

"Aunt Nick, will you sleep with us?" Kaleigh asked when they got under the quilt.

"Let me say good-bye to Uncle Dave and I'll come in and tell you a story," I said.

I went into the kitchen and talked to the Mate for a few minutes. We kissed and I walked him to the door. I watched until he backed out of the driveway and headed up the road. The girls were still awake when I came into grandmother's bedroom. I got ready for bed and laid down next to them. Kaleigh asked about my grandmother. I told her about some places that my grandmother had taken me when I was a child. It took a half hour to talk them to sleep. I thought about Guiddo for a while, then I went to sleep. I dreamed that I was on a lake freighter. I could hear familiar voices but when I looked toward where I thought the voices were coming from, I couldn't see anybody. I woke to find the girls were trying to sleep on me. I turned them around right and went into the kitchen to get a drink of water. It was almost one o'clock. It was so quiet in the house, not even the sound of the wind blowing. I laid crosswise at the foot of the bed to get away from the restless Kaleigh and Desiree. I was woke up by the sound of the phone. I checked the clock, it was seven thirty. As I suspected, Eileen was calling. I told her that the girls were still sleeping and to meet us over at the Mate's house in a couple hours. I got dressed and called the Mate and told him to have breakfast for us in an hour. I read the newspaper until the girls got up. I told them that we were going over to have breakfast at Uncle Dave's house. I could see that they weren't morning people. They're like their father in that. I helped them get dressed and put the stuff I bought them and the mousetrap game, in a big plastic bag. I locked the door and I took them on the path through the gully. Kaleigh said it reminded her of Hansel and Gretel. I told her that there were no witches around here. The Mate opened the side door for us as we approached. He seemed his usual happy self and helped me get the coats and boots off the girls. I helped cook breakfast while the girls watched TV. The Mate called the girls in while I served the oatmeal and grits.

"You like oatmeal?" the mate asked Kaleigh. She nodded.

"Uncle Dave, are you married to Aunt Nick?" she asked.

"No, not yet," he replied.

"My mom and dad are married," she said.

"That's what they tell me," the Mate said.

"Aunt Nick says she likes you," Kaleigh declared.

"The Courtship of David McCracken," I joked.

"I've known Aunt Nick for a long time. I'm sure that we'll always like each other," he said.

We talked about little girl things like Barbie dolls for the rest of the breakfast conversation. After breakfast, the girls watched TV some more, while Dave and I cleaned up the dishes. At nine thirty, Eileen and Andy pulled in the driveway. Dave opened the door and let them in.

"Mommy! Daddy!" both girls shouted, when they saw them.

"Now, you don't yell in other people's houses, remember," Eileen scolded them.

"That's okay. They were very well behaved," I said.

"Aunt Nick gave us this game," Kaleigh said, showing her the bag.

"I hope you thanked Aunt Nick," she said.

"They are such charming girls. I can't believe it," I said.

"You'll be having your own before too long," Eileen predicted.

"Kaleigh was suggesting the same thing," I said.

"She very perceptive," Eileen said.

"She speaks her mind, for sure," I replied.

Dave talked with Andy for a few minutes while Eileen got the girls dressed. We did hugs all around and I promised to visit them again, soon. Eileen wrote down a phone number for the hospital and then they left.

"I have some things to do. I have to call this lawyer, Doggett," I said.

"You can do it here, if you like," the Mate said.

"Where's your Toledo phone book?" I asked.

"Over here, in the bottom of the coffee table," he said as he bent down and pulled it out.

I thought about what Kaleigh had told me earlier when we were walking over here and I smiled at the Mate.

"You're looking happy," he said as he handed it to me.

"Kaleigh told me earlier, that if we were married, I could live over here with you," I said as I set the phone book down and and put my arms around him.

"Is that how it works?" he asked as he put his arms around me.

"I was wondering how it works on a boat," I said.

"We'll make it work," he said as he locked his lips onto mine.

"Somebody was lonely last night," I said after a minute.

"Let me make this phone call."

He let go of me. I looked in the Yellow Pages and found Edward Doggett-Attorney. I called the number and talked to Mr. Doggett. I told him that I was a former shipmate and good friend of Guiddo. He told me that he did not know that Guiddo was in the hospital. He told me that he had written instructions from the client. He took my address and phone number. I felt better knowing that his attorney was handling it now.

With arranging my schooling and seeing my attorney and Guiddo's attorney, it seemed like I hardly had a free moment for the next two weeks. The Mate had arranged for a couple day fishing trip with Andy in the Florida keys. I found myself at Mount Union, buying my text books and picking up assignments. I went over to Earl's farm. I saw him out by the barn, when I pulled in with my pickup truck.

"Hi guy, What's the good news?" I asked as I walked toward the barn.

"I got a plaque and a thousand dollars from the company," he said as I approached.

"Great, you can buy some cows," I said, adding—"Have you seen anything of a bonus or the pictures taken at the party?" I asked as I stuck out my hand.

"No, I haven't seen either," he said as we shook hands.

"You're looking well," I said.

"Things are going pretty good. Sarah is a big help around here," he said.

"Oh, do tell," I said.

"She's a mennonite girl. I met her at the sale in Kidron. She's a hard worker, like you."

"I'm pleased to hear that. You can always use some help around here."

"She'll be over later this evening. Can you stay until then?" he asked.

"No, I'm afraid that I'll have to be going here before long. I wanted to get back home before the dark and the snow gets here. I'll be back in a week or two," I said.

We went in the house and he showed me the Chairman's award. I was impressed with the plaque. I helped him hang it on the wall. I made some coffee and we talked for an hour. I told him about Guiddo. I told him that the Mate was with Andy, on a fishing trip. He seemed to accept that there was a relationship between Dave and me. We went out to the barn and he showed me a couple hiefers he had bought. He showed me where he had been plowing earlier. I was impressed with the way the farm was looking and I told him so. We walked to my truck and I hugged him before I left. I took seventy seven north to the turnpike and made it home in two and a half hours. There was a phone call from the Mate on my answering machine. As usual, he would call me back in an hour. When he called, I got so excited. He told me that he had a pleasant flight and the weather was great down there. He told me that he wanted to go to his mother's for Christmas. I told him that I went to college and to see Earl. I told him that his Christmas plans were fine with me. We talked silly nonsense for a few minutes, then he had to go. The next three days were snowy and miserable. I went to visit Guiddo and ran into a couple former shipmates. I went to the synagogue on friday night, after I went grocery shopping. On saturday, I waited around the house for the Mate to return. Andy dropped him him off at his house at two o'clock in the afternoon and he called me. He had left the side door unlocked for me. He called to me from upstairs, when I came in. When I saw him, he was sitting on his bed in his boxer shorts and t-shirt.

"Did you catch any fish?" I asked.

"No, I only caught sunburn."

"So I noticed, a nice shade of red there. You should have wore a straw hat," I said.

He removed his t-shirt and he looked terrible. I went to his medicine cabinet and got solarcaine cream and carefully rubbed it on him.

"I see that all you were wearing was shorts and dark glasses," I said.

"It was very warm there and no clouds."

"Is this all you caught?" I said, referring to the sunburn.

"A few striped bass in the freezer," he said.

"Well, no lovey dovey for you until this heals," I said.

"I may need more doctoring. Are you gonna' stay with me tonight?" he asked.

"Sure, I'll go over to the pharmacy and get you that spray for the pain. They'll think I'm crazy buying it this time of year."

"You take such good care of me," he said.

"We have a wedding to go to in a couple days," I reminded him.

"Really Nick! I didn't know you were in such a hurry," he joked.

"Ha, Ha, I bet you were telling the guys all about it," I said.

"No, Gary was still going on about the fight," he said.

"I'm famous for a fight where I didn't hit anybody," I remarked.

After two days of nursing the Mate, he was looking and feeling much better.

The next day, he drove us to the airport and we caught the Air Canada commuter to Thunder bay. Lukesia picked us up at the airport and drove us to the hotel where they had reserved rooms for guests and the reception. She showed me the list of guests. I recognized a few old shipmates and acquaintances. The Mate didn't know too many people on the list. Early the next morning, I drove with Lukesia in a van while the Mate went with some guys in a car. We drove to a large Presbyterian church which was made of stone. Lukesia insisted that I be there, while she got dressed. I was beginning to think that I would be sucked into being a bridesmaid. A photographer took some pictures outside the dressing room, then we went into the sanctuary and took our places. I was very happy to find the Mate there. Lukesia looked great coming down the aisle. Everything went splendidly. People applauded as the bride and groom walked down the Aisle. Since it was too cold to wait outside to throw rice, Lukesia and Dante got right into a car and the rest of us followed. When we got back to the hotel, we went to the banquet room and were subjected to more picture taking. Jean Sparrow insisted on introducing Dave and I to all the sailors there, that we didn't know.

After meeting all Lukesia's family and friends, I was afraid that I didn't remember anybody's name. Several of the younger guys noticed that I didn't have a ring. In fact, there were more men than women there and all the unmarried women were getting a lot of attention. I spent a lot of time telling the old shipmates about Guiddo. Our old Chief, Art, got plastered and started telling some stories that would have been better left untold. A video camera had been running the whole time. While dancing, a few guys passed out on the floor. A good time was had by all. By four o'clock, Lukesia and Dante left for their honeymoon and the party started breaking up. Sam Hammond, a fellow QMED, waited for us to go upstairs and get changed and get our luggage, then he drove us to the airport. We waited an hour to catch the plane back to Cleveland Hopkins. It was after eight o'clock and a miserable wet snow was falling when we left the airport. It took us an hour and a half to drive home.

The next day the Mate took me to the mall and I quite unexpectedly ended up in the jewelry store, looking at diamond rings.

"I wouldn't want you to have the problems that you had yesterday," he explained as I put on a nice looking diamond ring.

"Sure Buddy, I bet you tell all the women that," I said as I admired the ring.

I liked the way it looked on my finger and I decided that I wouldn't mind wearing it. It coincidently came with a matching wedding ring. He paid for the ring with cash, which surprised me.

"Something new," he said. I kissed him and told him he was a booger. Later on we ran into Misses Kefauver and another woman at the Brown Derby.

"Dave, long time, no see!" she exclaimed.

"Have you met my fiance, Nicolette Strickland?" he said.

"I've seen her around," she said, only glancing my way.

"Must dash, give me a call later," she said, and they left.

"Can you believe that wench," I said, adding—"With her money, you'd think she could afford some common decency."

"She wasn't born into money," he said.

"You can take the girl out of the trailer park, but you can't take the trailer park out of that girl," I sneered.

"When are we gonna' get the sailor out of you?" he asked jokingly.

"Come on now, I didn't hit her," I rebutted.

On Christmas day, we left early in the morning, taking route two east through Cleveland and into Lake county. It was only a short drive from route two to his mother's house. When we got there, his brother was there to greet us. He explained that their mother had went to church with some other women and would be back around noon. His brother's wife, Melodie, was cooking the holiday dinner. I asked if I could help. She thanked me and she said that she had everything under control. The Mate's brother, Calvin, seemed a very personable guy. I guess it was from teaching junior high school all those years. I told him that when I finished with my education, the only teaching I would do, would be in college. They showed me some pictures when they were younger. Except for Calvin junior being an inch shorter than Dave, they resembled each other strongly. They both looked like their father. Right on time, their mother came home. The Mate introduced her as his mother and she told me to call her Irene. Although she looked older than Grace Kompsii, she didn't lack for energy. Apparently she knew quite a lot about me already. I felt that I should be honest and straight forward with her. Irene said that her grown children handle their own affairs and she had always gotten along with Emma. I told her that eventhough I was wearing a ring, Dave and I hadn't really planned a wedding or set a date. Dave explained that Tommy and Maddy were out in Oregon, visiting Maddy's family. Irene had seven brothers and sisters, so there were a lot of relatives to talk about at dinner. She was surprised that I knew Grace Kompsii. She was also surprised that I didn't have any living relatives that I cared to associate with. We had a very pleasant afternoon and I really felt like they were family. On the way home, I was thinking about the Mate and his family and Maddy and her family. We talked about his family. I began to think that I was the only one in the world with dysfunctional asshole parents. I told him that I wished my grandmother was here. He held my hand and I laid my head on his shoulder for awhile. I asked him what he was holding in his hand. He showed me a shipswheel stickpin that his brother lent him. It had belonged to his father and his father had lent it to him when he married Emma. "Something borrowed," he said.

The winter turned out to be not as miserably cold as the three previous winters had been. Two months after Christmas, we drove to Rochester, New York for Guiddo's funeral. After the funeral, Attorney Doggett handed me an envelope. I didn't open the envelope until I got back to Marblehead. I had Dave open the envelope for me. He said that twenty five thousand dollars had been put into a trust fund for me. I wanted to cry again. March was such a busy month for me that I didn't have time to feel sad about anything. I went down to Mount Union to turn in some class work and see my academic advisor about my thesis. I stayed overnight with the little sisters. Shelly had the temerity to suggest that I looked pregnant. When I got home, the Mate came over and gave me my mail. Aside from the letter from my lawyer and some bills, there was a letter from Captain Dietzmann, which was to inform me that there would be a position for wheelsman on his boat. I asked the Mate about him. He said that Captain D was an old fashioned sort and that it was an honor for him to send me a letter like that.

"Hmm, that's interesting," I said,setting the letter down "I have to check something in the bathroom."

"Sure baby," he said.

I went in the bathroom and nearly choked when I looked at the indicator.

"Oh, hell no, we didn't. I should have sent you out on the cement carrier," I shouted.

"Something Blue. How sweet it is," the Mate said.

WB-6213 OUT

Crew Roster-Twenty Years Later . . .

Captain Kompsii

Retired in 1986. He and his wife, Grace traveled extensively for a while. They still live in Fairport and continue to enjoy their great-grand-children.

Andy Botzum

Worked on the Great Lakes for a few more years, then accepted a position on an ocean freighter. He moved to the west coast with Eileen and the girls. Kaleigh entered the medical profession, Desiree works as an officer on a cruise ship.

Don MacDonough

He and his wife had moved back to Ireland at the end of the 1986 season.

Peter Hall

After his difference of opinions with the first mate, thought it best to work for another shipping company.

Mike Ely

Continues to work as a wheelsman and a conveyormen on the Great Lakes.

Bosun, Emerson Munson retired in 1996. He lives in St. Ignace, Michigan.

Jim Dixon

Returned to Mississippi and worked for a while on a barge on the Mississippi river before suddenly dying from a stroke.

Smitty (Jonothan Smith)

Became a bosun on a Canadian ship where he worked for years before retiring to his home in Port Stanley, Ontario.

Ron Karan

Left the lake service after a couple of years to take over his father's electrical parts company when his father died.

Hal (Harold Ostander)

Worked for shore services another several years before retiring with a disability.

Ed (Edward Stephenson)

Took a land job with the railroad, becoming a locomotive engineer.

Al (Allen Saunderson)

Still an "ol' sea dog" on the lakes.

Chief, Gregory Brady

Retired in 1999.

Hank Andersen

Became cheif engineer on a freighter. When the freighter was laid up he took a job at the power plant in Sault Ste. Marie, MI.

Fred Westfall

Took a position on a diesel superlaker in 1987 and eventually was promoted to Chief. Retired in 2002.

Kenny Fern

Continued to work as a machinist on steamships until a fatal heart attack in 2002.

Billy Curtis

Continued to work on and off lake freighters for ten years, until he received his masters degree in Architecture.

Bradley O'Connell

Went to work for a Canadian line and lost contact with his fellow shipmates.

Buster (Albert Jones) and Joseph Jenkins

Both got jobs on diesel boats in 1987.

DJ (Duane Jackson)

Continued to work as a conveyorman usually on the same boat as Mike Ely.

Carl Bromley

Left the Lakes after 1987 and took a job with the Niagara power company.

Gary Tycon

Never returned to the lakes, after the 1986 season. He became a scuba diver instructor and a water skier at a resort in Florida.

Markus Cauley

Left the lakes in 1991 and took a job with the Corps of Engineers on a dredger in the lower Missisppi.

John Shaughnessy

Left the lakes after getting a divorce in 1994 and married a woman who had a ranch in Montana, raising Black Angus cattle.

Louie Franz

Also left the lakes in 1994. Becoming the head chef at several upscale restaurants before coming back to Cleveland.

Earl Franklin

Left the lakes at the end of 1986, to run his dairy farm outside of Alliance, Ohio. Six months later he married Sarah, a mennonite woman. He is godfather to Nick and Dave's children.

Tommy and Maddy

After being dumped by his spoiled bitch girlfriend, Cybil, Tommy Married Maddy Nolan, a sensible woman who values family and slaps him upside his head when he needs it. They have two children, Eric and Dakota. Eric has started working on the lakes. They both enjoy hanging out with their aunts and uncle.

Nicolette Strickland & David McCracken

Nicolette married David McCracken in March of 1987. Eight months later, they had their first child, Natalie Emma. In 1989, they had a son, David Isaiah. In 1991, they had their third and last child, Nicole "Baby" Rose. David McCracken is a Captain, looking at his last season on the Great Lakes. Nick is a professor of Geography at a college in Sandusky. Natalie Emma is in her first year at Kent State. She is becoming more involved with a man than her parents would like. David Isaiah has finished his first summer on the lakes and is starting his senior year in high school. Nicole Rose (Baby) can't wait until she is sixteen and can get an MMD and work on a lake freighter. This plan does not thrill her mother as much as you would think, although Captain McCracken thinks it may work out alright. Nick knows that the older two have the level-headed good sense of their father, but little Nikki is just like her.

THE LAST WORD

"These kids are driving me nuts. Now that you're gonna' retire, I'm getting my MMD and you can stay home and deal with this crap," I said.

"Sure Sweetie, anything you want," he said.

"You're being awful agreeable," I said suspiciously.

"The lakes are in her blood. She was conceived when you had ridership. Baby can bunk with you when you go back out, Doctor McCracken," Captain McCracken said.